Agent of the Wild

ALSO BY CHRIS TULLBANE

THE MURDER OF CROWS
See These Bones
Red Right Hand
One Tin Soldier

STORIES FROM A POST-BREAK WORLD
The Stars That Sing
The Storm in Her Smile
A Sure Thing

THE STORM WHO RIDES
The Queen of Smiles
The Queen of the Road

THE MANY TRAVAILS OF JOHN SMITH
Investigation, Mediation, Vindication
Blood is Thicker Than Lots of Stuff
Ghost of a Chance
The Italian Screwjob
A Dead Man's Favor
Godswar *
John Smith Doesn't Work Here Anymore *

THE (SECOND) LIFE OF BRIAN
Speaker of Tongues
Agent of the Wild

*Forthcoming

AGENT OF THE WILD

CHRIS TULLBANE

GHOST FALLS PRESS

NEVADA

First published by Ghost Falls Press 2025
Agent of the Wild. Copyright © 2025 by Chris Tullbane.

GHOST FALLS PRESS

Publisher's Cataloging-in-Publication Data
provided by Five Rainbows Cataloging Services

Names: Tullbane, Chris, author.
Title: Agent of the wild / Chris Tullbane.
Description: Henderson, NV : Ghost Falls Press, 2025. | Series: (Second) life of Brian, bk. 2.
Identifiers: ISBN 978-1-955081-20-7 (paperback) | ISBN 978-1-955081-16-0 (ebook)
Subjects: LCSH: LitRPG (Fiction) | Fantasy games. | Animals, Mythical--Fiction. | Fantasy fiction. | Novels. | BISAC: FICTION / LitRPG (Literary Role-Playing Game) | FICTION / Fantasy / Action & Adventure. | FICTION / Fantasy / Dragons & Mythical Creatures. | FICTION / Fantasy / Dark Fantasy. | GSAFD: Fantasy fiction.
Classification: LCC PS3620.U45 A44 2025 (print) | LCC PS3620.U45 (ebook) | DDC 813/.6--dc23.

Book cover design by Jake @ jcalebdesign.com

This novel is entirely a work of fiction. The names, characters, places, and incidents portrayed in it are either the product of the author's imagination or are used fictitiously, and any resemblance to actual persons, living or dead, events or locales is entirely coincidental.

FIRST EDITION

For Nami,
the reason for everything,

and for Lynn,
met too late and gone too soon

Acknowledgments

I'd like to thank *all* the usual suspects:

My angel-wife, Nami.

Johanna, who's *really* just waiting for another John book.

Jamie, possible ninja and one-time defender of the free world.

Claudia, Denise, Kerri D., Mark E., Sam, Sarah, and Scotty B.
Go read their fabulous books!

Cory, Mitch, Montie, Tom, and Ziggy, beta readers and friends.

Aaron, Anthony, Charity, Deanna, Joe, Kerri K., Kevin, Lara, Mike, Nicholas, and Reid, for all the support they've given over the years.

Keith and Shawn, still and forever trapped in a chat-channel hellscape of their own making.

And always last but never least, my parents.

The Story So Far

Former barista Brian Fieldings was summoned from our world to the war-torn, magic-infused reality of Eos for one reason: to save the synossian species in a war against a vastly superior foe. He failed.

Rescued from certain death by Shan, one of the gods who had brought him there in the first place, Brian was teleported to the opposite ends of Eos along with Miko Naseri, a synossian shrine maiden, and the spear that had nearly killed him, a weapon baptized in the blood of both a hero and a monster.

The duo found a small village called Harborton, nearly bringing death to everyone within it by virtue of the Titan snake chasing them, and then were forced to work as indentured servants. Eventually, they joined a small party of adventurers fallen upon hard times and managed to retrieve the wild herbs necessary to cure Erlund, one of Harborton's founders, paying off their incurred debt.

Now officially members of a party that featured Lace, a blood-scorned amazon, Skaal, a sickly reaver from the southern steppes, and Mordecai, an Adept of the Crimson Needle, Brian and Miko left Harborton behind to journey to the larger town of Madea. There, they joined the Adventurer's Guild and began doing missions with the others.

Their short-term goal? Get stronger utilizing the gods-created Framework, a system that codifies levels and skills and progression into something tangible.

Their long-term goal? Get powerful enough *and* rich enough to build a new home for the remnants of Miko's people, some of whom had already left for this same continent on a seafaring journey that was certain to take multiple years.

A mission for the Adventurer's Guild took the party into the swamps southwest of Madea, to a set of unexplored ruins overrun by the Mage-created weapons of war called the blighted. There, they found the kidnapped daughter of a duke, imprisoned and experimented upon by a cult of a banished god called Khamani, the Ever-Hungry. They freed her at the cost of Mordecai's life and brought her back to Madea, only to find that neither the blighted nor Khamani's cultists were willing to give up their prize.

What followed was a days-long desperate defense of the town. Most of the defenders died, including the entire guard leadership and two-thirds of the available adventurers. In the final battle against the head cultist, one of Madea's strongest defenders, Arrius Vitellius, broke and fled, betraying Skaal and abandoning the reaver to his fate. Brian managed to kill the head cultist, but it was a dying Skaal who ultimately routed the remaining blighted, using his cursed artifact Tempest at the cost of what little life he had remaining.

In the dust that settled, only Lace, Miko and Brian were left to move forward. While the eventual security of Miko's incoming people remained their long-term priority, they added a new mission to the list:

They would find Arrius Vitellius, and they would kill him.

<u>KNOWN RANKS FOR ASPIRANTS:</u>

RANK	LEVEL
Unranked	1-10
Tin	10-20
Copper	20-30
Iron	30-40
Bronze	40-50
Silver	50-60
Gold	60-70

<u>CAST AND RANKS:</u>

Brian Fieldings	Unranked
Lace	Tin
Miko Naseri	Unranked

Book 5: Survivor

"In bloodstained alleys they gather,

robed in shadow
& moonlight

to whisper of weight,
the calamity of consequence."

-Excerpt from *The Lament of Lachesia*

1

The afternoon sun, red as blood, caught on the blade whistling toward my face. I twisted aside, let the knife sweep past, and struck back. Not at the body behind the blow, but at the arm holding the weapon instead as I'd been taught.

I'd been told, time and time again, that parrying was a devil's bargain until I'd drastically improved my Finesse stat and acquired a gauntlet to protect my fingers, but my opponent did just that, the most subtle of movements bringing her knife into contact with mine and redirecting it past her. A booted foot, barely seen and impossible to avoid, caught me in the chest, and despite the iron hauberk I wore and the quilted gambeson beneath it, the air was blasted from my lungs.

I gave in to gravity and fell backwards, tucking my chin down as I brought my knees up to my chest and turned the fall into my best attempt at a roll. As soon as my feet were back under me, I surged upward again, knife striking at where I knew my opponent would be.

Except she wasn't there, but several feet to the side, safely out of the path of my wild swing. One step brought her in close enough to lay her own blade, heavy and hot, against the unprotected skin of my throat.

"And stop," said Caleb, standing off to the right, the trainer's bald head gleaming like bronze.

I hadn't waited for his word to stop, because Lace didn't use blunted training weapons. The knife at my throat was one of her usual blades, and sharp enough to open me up with a flick of the wrist.

Thankfully, we were on the same side, training exercise notwithstanding. She tucked her blade away and gave me an unreadable look, her braids looking strangely naked without their usual red beads.

"You're getting better," said Caleb.

"How can you tell?" It was, by my count, the twenty-seventh time Lace had 'killed' me in the past few glasses of this extended training session.

"It's my job to know these things." The older man offered Lace a short bow. "Thank you for your assistance."

The Marauder nodded, turned on her heel, and left, slipping out of Madea's lone training hall like a wraith fleeing the light.

"Not big on words, is she? Or smiles?"

"There's not a lot to be happy about, I guess."

"We're all alive. That's something."

He was right, but Lace didn't see it that way, and there were times I struggled with it too. Especially with the burials of both Skaal and Mordecai so fresh in our memories. I shrugged and collected my spear from where I'd leaned it against the wall.

"Anyway, today's time is up," added Caleb, keeping to our schedule with uncanny precision despite the lack of watches or clocks in Eos. "You *are* improving though. We might improve your *Knife* skill yet."

He wasn't just talking about the numbers that displayed next to the skill, I knew. There was quantity and then there was quality, and while the former had seen some gains over the past few seven-days, the skill remained common-tiered.

I wasn't entirely sure how tiers worked with skills. Sometimes, rarity denoted just that… how hard it was to gain the skill at all. Other times, like with weapons, it seemed to indicate a better understanding of the weapon… but what that meant in reality remained unclear. Still, Caleb seemed to think it was important, and I was paying him hard-won copper and slightly less hard-won brewing advice for his expertise.

If he said it mattered, I was going to believe it.

"Maybe today will be the day," I said, though I hadn't seen anything to suggest that would be the case. "Or maybe, like so many other things, it will only happen when I'm fighting for my life."

"We do grow best under duress," he agreed. "I will see you tomorrow. And if you have the time, I should have a new batch of ale to test a few days from now too."

"What did you add this time?"

"Leaves from a scarlet thorn."

"The *carnivorous tree?*"

"That's the one. The leaves are sweet and can cause some numbness. I want to see how they interact with the brew."

I did my best to hide my reaction as I left, but I was pretty sure the answer was going to be *not well at all.* Still, it was far from the strangest thing Caleb had added to his ale since I'd started offering my help. And the closer it came to killing me, the more likely it was I'd get a point in *Brewing.*

Not that I *needed* another point in *Brewing,* especially when I didn't want the Brewer profession, but… seeing numbers go up was kind of addicting.

The smoke had cleared from Madea within days of the final battle, but as I walked the sparsely populated streets, it was clear a different kind of pall still hung over the town. We had survived, yeah, but we'd paid a price for that survival, and people were still coming to grips with that. A few families had even left once they knew the fighting was done… uprooting and heading west toward the safety offered by towns not quite so far out on the frontier.

Others had taken the town's near-destruction as a wake-up call. The guard, all but wiped out in Madea's defense, had seen more fresh new recruits than they were equipped to handle. Most were level one or two at best—people who had focused solely on their professions as Dedicated—but a handful were retired Aspirants and though *their* skills had decayed in the intervening time, they'd be invaluable to the town when back in fighting form.

In the meantime, Lace was one of only a half-dozen remaining Tins in the whole damn place, and the only one not dealing with injuries beyond the capabilities of the town's two Healers. It wouldn't take another army of blighted to roll over Madea… it wouldn't even take much of a breeze.

There was a reason it had been harder to find time and space to train with Caleb lately. There were a lot of people suddenly realizing that personal defense mattered out here.

I passed Mayor Aulson, walking the streets with his bodyguard and an aide. I didn't care for the man, and I *really* didn't like his views on non-humans, but I couldn't deny that he was working as hard as any of us to bring Madea back from the brink. The mayor pretended not to see me, eyes fixed on some future prize. His bodyguard, on the other hand, had been up on the wall with the rest of us in those final hours. We traded nods.

I didn't know his name, his class, or his level, but I was learning that that kind of experience bonded people, just a bit.

I'd been on Eos for just more than four moons, and I'd already lived more of a life than I'd managed in twenty-three years back in

Midton, Ohio. Then again, I'd also almost died more times than I could count. Some days, that tradeoff felt less fair than others.

The common room of the Adventurer's Guild was mostly empty, as usual. There'd been two other full-sized parties when the blighted arrived, but only four of their members had survived. Three were Tin, like Lace, and two of those had accepted an offer from Aulson to head up the new town guard. They'd taken the places of Guard Captain Pike and his primary lieutenant, Lissiana, who had both died in the attack.

Carlson was nowhere to be seen, but Melligula sat behind her desk. I waved to the horned turbinga and headed upstairs to the room I shared with Miko and her patient. When I entered, my nest-sister was busy attending to the sleeping body of Wilhemina Annerose Lakesia Willerton, the glow of another healing spell mixing prettily with the later afternoon sunlight streaming through the windows. I waited for her casting to finish and then headed for the bed at the far wall.

"Brian," said Miko, the slight sibilance in her words telling me she had once again accidentally lapsed into using her species' High Tongue instead of Trade. "How did your *Knife* training go?"

"Lace only killed me twenty-seven times today."

"You are improving then."

"So people keep telling me. I guess we'll find out. No change with Wilhemina?"

Instead of shaking her head, the former shrine keeper tapped the scales on her right arm in a gesture that meant much the same. "None, but at this point, I would not expect it. Thankfully, her father the duke will have access to healers far greater than me."

"Higher level, maybe. But greater? I can't imagine."

That won me the sharp-toothed synossian smile that would have been terrifying only a handful of moons earlier, back when the very idea of lizard-like people had seemed something out of a drug-infused nightmare.

Things had changed a lot since then.

"Commune with the Framework, nest-brother," said Miko. "I will have food and drink here for us both when you are done."

After a hard-spent few glasses in the training arena, food sounded *really* good, but it paled in comparison to the lure of advancement. I tugged off my hauberk and dropped it on the wooden floor. Rather than dirty my bed sheets, I took a seat on the floor next to it and closed my eyes.

Miko's clawed footsteps faded into the distance, leaving me alone with my thoughts. I'd spent my first weeks in Eos—my first few seven-days, by the local parlance—reeling from my father's slow death, caught in a fog of depression, grief, and uncertainty. In some ways, I *still* hadn't fully dealt with that death. In some ways, I suspected I probably never would, not in a manner that ever felt truly satisfactory. Since then, I'd seen and experienced even more tragedy, including the brutal killing of too many people that I genuinely liked and respected… but I wasn't going to fall back into that emotional morass again. Not if I could help it. There were too many things to do, and those things required action rather than inaction, growth rather than stagnation, steps taken forward rather than backwards.

I needed to get stronger. Every day was a one-time chance to move further down that road, and I couldn't afford to waste any opportunities.

I'd learned that different cultures had different ways of calling on the Framework. Different ways of utilizing the gods-created pipeline between spiritual and physical realms to internalize their experiences in a way that translated into raw progression of the soul and was then reformulated as physical and mental advancements. The synossians who had rescued me at the very beginning preferred to meditate, and since they'd been the ones to teach me, I did too.

I cleared my mind of its distractions, the soreness in my body, the pit in my stomach, the rank smell of my unwashed body, and focused instead on my actions from the day: the morning spent in Madea's small archives, searching for new knowledge in the few scrolls and tomes I was allowed to access; the afternoon at the training arena with Caleb and Lace; and all the time in between, pitching in when and where I could with the town's restoration. I let those activities wash over me and through me, like water slowly draining out of a tub, except here, instead of copper piping carrying dirty remnants out into the back alley, the Framework was transporting my relived experiences to the realm of the soul.

After an indeterminate amount of time, I opened my eyes to see the most recent fruits of that progress, rendered as always in a dialogue window of monochromatic grey and black that looked like nothing so much as a browser alert from the early days of the internet:

```
Congratulations, Warrior.

You have reached level 6!

You have one point to allocate to an attribute
of your choosing:

    Strength: 12 [+1] / Finesse: 11 [+1]
    Vitality: 16 [+3] / Intellect: 13
    Discernment: 10 / Will: 15
```

I gave myself a moment just to revel in the accomplishment. *Six whole levels* since I'd appeared on Eos. Six levels in less than half the eleven-moon year they called a cycle. That sort of pace wouldn't have been possible without the quests I'd completed as a Chosen or the sheer number of life-and-death situations I'd just barely survived. As Caleb had said, it was challenge that sparked growth, and I'd experienced little else since my arrival.

And yet I still had such a long way to go.

I focused back on my new level and the choice awaiting my input. My Strength attribute had reached twelve on its own a few days earlier, a reflection of the endless hours I'd been putting in with Caleb and the heavy lifting I'd been doing during reconstruction. Since coming to Eos, I'd earned similar increases in Vitality, Intellect, and Will, increases earned through study, effort, or simple pain. Those kinds of gains were different from the one awaiting my decision, reflections of purely mental or physical growth rather than something rooted in the soul itself. As a result, they weren't included in the bracketed numbers to the right of each attribute. Worse, they required work to maintain, much like skills themselves. An attribute's natural score could decrease as well as increase, either through a crippling injury, a head wound, or simple laziness. Only the numbers in the brackets, gains reached through leveling the soul, were permanent.

Still, whatever the source, numbers *were* going up, and in a reality defined by the Framework, that mattered.

Leveling was deceptively simple. Odd levels offered three technique choices, either entirely new abilities or upgrades to existing ones. Even levels like this one granted a default point in Vitality and a second point that could be freely distributed to any attribute. In each case, the onus was on the Aspirant to not just choose... but to also do sufficient research to make that choice. The Framework didn't come with help text or even simple descriptions.

Information was the currency upon which the whole system ran and nothing in Eos was free.

Six levels in, I at least understood what my attributes did, and that made this selection relatively straightforward. Vitality was increasing just fine on its own—and was already my highest stat besides—so that was out. As for the others? Intellect and Discernment each impacted technique reuse time, while improving my memory and social skills, respectively. Will, much like Vitality, increased my maximum pool of energy for technique usage. They were all useful.

Strength and Finesse were less esoteric, but every bit as important, especially to someone with the Warrior class and a need to stab opponents to death before they could do the same in return. The fact that those were also among my lowest attributes stuck out. Particularly because they impacted both my physical effectiveness *and* my techniques. The extra damage inherent in *Lunge* or *Deceptive Strike* would be further bolstered by more physical force behind the blow, or a slightly more accurate thrust. To say nothing of all the times in a battle where my techniques would be on cooldown, and I'd be fighting with nothing but my weapons and natural abilities.

Research and study had worked to increase Intellect, and that meant I'd be able to improve technique reuse speed naturally. At ten, Discernment was by far my lowest attribute, but it was also the least relevant for my continued survival. Social skills would have their place, no doubt, but for now?

Combat was king.

A part of me wanted to add the new point to Strength, because there were few purer expressions of *power* than being able to crush things with your bare hands. And I still held out hope that an increase to Strength would eventually add inches to my deeply unimpressive height. While I'd met one species on Eos that was shorter than I was, I was almost inevitably the shortest person in every room I wandered into.

But Finesse had proven every bit as useful in combat, and for now, I wanted to keep those two attributes balanced, if possible. Maybe I'd find a trainer one day who could help me improve Finesse naturally, or maybe I'd reach a point of diminishing rewards with one attribute and not the other… but until then, I was going to stick with my plan.

I allocated the available point to Finesse.

As usual, nothing overt occurred. No flashes of light. No dramatic reshaping of my physique. The Framework didn't work like that, but it *did* work, harnessing the improved quality of my soul and channeling it into attributes, skills, or techniques. Still, attribute increases were generally only noticeable through use.

A second window, also expected, took the place of the first:

```
You have increased the following skills:

Major skills:
Knife [+1]: 21/35
Tactics [+1]: 30/35

Minor skills:
Athleticism [+1]: 30/35

The following skills have decreased:
Scribing [-1]: 3/10
```

Okay… so, they weren't *all* steps forward. Save for the day I'd spent translating a single ritual before the blighted attack, it had been months—or moons, in the Eosian system—since I'd put any significant time toward writing-related work. That lack had finally shown in the point I'd just lost in *Scribing*.

I wasn't *too* upset about that. After all, I knew how to get the point back if I really wanted to.

Both the skill gains and my new level were fully expected. I'd been busting my ass training with Miko and Lace during our downtime, grinding away at those last few skills that had been all that stood between me and level six. If the changes hadn't come today, they would've come tomorrow or the next day, because while the Framework was largely unknowable, it *did* reward consistent effort.

So yeah, those first two pop-ups had been predictable.

The third one though?

That was a surprise.

You have gained access to an advanced class:

Spearman (Uncommon)

[Accept | Decline]

I hesitated.

I'd known about advanced classes for a long while. Riok and Berys had both had them, as had at least a handful of other members of the doomed synossian squad who had rescued Miko and me. And Lace and… the others… had long since progressed beyond the class they'd received in their Dreaming. Advanced classes were a known thing, and ultimately just another step on the road to power.

I just hadn't expected to get one offered to me so soon.

Despite the rarity listed next to it, Spearman was, to my understanding, a relatively common advanced class. One I had earned, no doubt, because of ranks in the relevant weapon skill. By all accounts, it was a perfectly fine upgrade from Warrior, taking me a little bit further down the path I was already traveling.

Still, I hesitated.

Information on the Framework remained one of the most valuable things on Eos, but that applied more to specifics, things like class descriptions, leveling guides, and especially the recipes of skills, achievements, or attributes necessary to unlock new paths. Basic, universal information was more freely available, and that was why much of my free time had been spent in Madea's small library, perusing the relevant tomes and scrolls I could find in its unrestricted sections.

Even though it was the Framework that supplied the terminology, *advanced class* was a bit of a misnomer. Really, these were class evolutions, and they in turn gave rise to further evolutions down the line. Lace, for example, had begun as a Rogue, advanced to Skirmisher, and then become a Marauder at some point after ranking to Tin. Spearman would just be the first step of many on my road.

The problem was that each evolution *was* a step, and like all steps, they worked to define your path. An ancient scroll I'd read suggested that classes in Eos were like trees. The basic class you were given in your Dreaming by the gods formed the trunk of that tree. The first advanced class you took was a large branch off of that trunk, and it then split further into a myriad of smaller branches, each representing subsequent evolutions. But if I took Spearman, any future advanced classes would be offshoots of its branch, just as Spearman was a subset of Warrior.

Taking the advanced class would unlock an entire host of further evolutions, but it would *also* permanently define my direction. I liked using a spear—both because my weapon was all that was left of the hero known as the Windwalker *and* because a spear still seemed a hell of a lot safer than something more up close and personal—but did I want it to be the entire basis of my future build? Or would there be some other advanced class available in the future that allowed me to keep using the spear but offered additional advantages as well?

I didn't know. I *couldn't* know, not with the limited information I had access to. And that made me leery about locking in my future path.

Before I could second-guess myself, I mentally tapped the *Decline* button and watched the dialogue window fade away. I'd stay a simple Warrior for now. I'd keep advancing my skills and my techniques, I'd do further research once we reached Grand Duke Willerton's capital city, and I'd see what, if any, alternative builds presented themselves.

And in the meantime, I'd hope I hadn't just screwed up royally.

For the first time in days, I summoned my full personal record:

```
Name: Brian Fieldings
Class: Warrior (Common) - 6
Profession: None
Deity: None
Ideal: Freedom

Attributes:
Strength: 12 [+1] / Finesse: 12 [+2]
Vitality: 16 [+2] / Intellect: 13
Discernment: 10 / Will: 15

Skills:
Major: Formations: 14/35, Knife: 21/35,
Light Armor: 25/35, Medium Armor: 18/35,
Spear (U): 30/35, Tactics: 30/35, Throwing: 1/35

Minor: Acrobatics: 1/35, Athleticism: 30/35,
Avoidance: 30/35, Focus: 24/35,
Leadership (U): 4/35, Pain Tolerance: 30/35

Professional: None

General: Animal Behaviorism: 10/10, Brewing: 2/10,
Caretaking: 7/10, Danger Sense (R): 10/10,
```

```
Deception: 10/10, Diplomacy: 1/10, Hunting: 1/10,
Meditation: 5/10, Mercantilism: 4/10, Riding: 2/10,
Scribing: 3/10, Stealth: 10/10, Tracking: 1/10

Techniques: Beast Skin (C), Deceptive Strike (U),
Lunge (C)


Achievements: None
Titles: Agent of the Wild
Traits: Speaker of Tongues, ???, ???

Quests:
  • Help Miko Naseri make contact with the
    synossian enclave in Trynfall.
  • Return Wilhemina Annerose Lakesia Willerton to
    her home.
  • Find the owner of the crest ring.
  • Deliver justice for a fallen brother.
```

My eyes wandered to the quests at the bottom. At some point, that second quest had silently updated, filling in Wilhemina's full name where she had once simply been called 'the girl'. I was pretty sure the quest would complete once the duke arrived to reclaim his daughter. The first quest, the one that required us to travel to Trynfall, would have to wait until we finished the fourth quest.

But the quest about the crest ring?

Hell if I knew what to do with that one. The ring in question had been found in the cult leader's possessions, along with the documents that had detailed their process to try and transform Wilhemina, but there'd been no indication of who or what had originally possessed it, and Madea's archives hadn't been any help. Maybe a larger library would have the information I needed or maybe there was some other avenue of research I was missing. As usual, the Framework wasn't giving me much to work with.

I let the window disappear. I had a long, long way to go to get where I needed to be to accomplish not just my gods-given quests but the larger reason I'd been summoned to Eos at all… but even so, I felt reassured, just a bit, by the visible reminder of the work we'd already put in.

Miko still hadn't returned with our dinner. It was just me and Wilhemina, the light from outside still bright enough to sketch the little girl's sleeping form. We didn't know how the Grand Duke's heir had wound up a prisoner of cultists of Khamani the Ever-Hungry, any more than we knew exactly what it was that afflicted her, keeping her comatose since her rescue. What we did know was that Miko had so far been the only one able to keep her stable, and that the duke, who had just conquered the small city-nation he'd blamed for her kidnapping, was on his way to retrieve his daughter.

We were stuck in a holding pattern until then. Miko had been spending her days training and healing the heir. I was training and studying. Lace was training and… well, I wasn't entirely sure what else she was doing, but at least some of it involved drinking and a lot more of it involved increasingly sadistic plots for revenge.

Somewhere out there was a Copper named Arrius who had bad things coming his way when we were finally free to hunt him down. The oversized warrior hadn't been foolish enough to return to Madea after the battle was won, but as Skaal had once told me, Lace had been made a hunter of men by her demon goddess.

Wherever Arrius went, she would find him. And we would be with her. How we'd fare against a Copper, when Lace was only Tin and Miko and I were both unranked was just one more problem for future-Brian to deal with.

The door cracked open; I rose to help Miko with the tray of food. We cleared a space on the floor closer to Wilhemina and the Priestess' white scales shined as she crouched down to eat.

"Were you successful?" she asked.

"Level six," I confirmed.

"The gods bless us." Miko grinned. "In only a half-dozen moons, you have caught me, nest-brother."

"It would be different if you'd been up on the wall with us."

"Perhaps. As it is, my skills, at least, are already halfway to level seven. Priest Berys said he received his advanced class at that level, and I am hopeful I will as well."

"You're hoping for Battle Medic?"

Clawed hands full of food, she nodded instead of tapping her left forearm. "That or something similar. *Flare* is my only offensive spell, and it deals no damage. In these dark times, a servant of the Dawn Maiden must be able to do more than heal."

The Dawn Maiden being Aurea, the goddess she worshipped and one-fourth of the Synossians' remaining pantheon.

"We'll get you there as soon as we can," I promised. "And then onward to Tin."

"And beyond," she reminded me. "To whatever rank it takes to make a place for us and my people."

"And beyond."

ooo

Power wasn't the end goal. Not really. It was all about what we could do *with* that power. We needed it to accomplish our goals: not just to help Lace kill Arrius, but to make a home on this continent for the remnants of Miko's people, even now sailing across the great ocean. Being stronger or faster or even having devastating new abilities would help with that first goal, but we needed a different kind of power for the second. The sort of power that came with political authority or wealth. And *that* wasn't something the Framework would provide, no matter how hard we trained.

That was where Wilhemina came in. We hadn't rescued her because of who she was—we hadn't known her identity at all at the time—but if there was anyone who could not only carve out some living space for a fleet of refugees but also create the infrastructure to find and support them upon their arrival, it was Wilhemina's father, Grand Duke Willerton.

The kingdom we'd found ourselves in, the kingdom of Elthor, was nominally ruled by a king, but it was the four grand dukes beneath him who had true power. Their duchies divided up the kingdom's lands save for the capital city itself, Elthoris. That made Wilhemina's dad one of the four most powerful people in the country, and as the people who had rescued his daughter, we were banking heavily on his gratitude paving the way for *both* our difficult tasks.

And so we'd come up with a plan:

Wait in Madea until the duke arrived to collect Wilhemina.
Cash in the favors he'd owe us for having saved his heir.
Hunt down Arrius.
Prepare for the arrival of Miko's people.

It was a simple plan, but simple was good. Simple *worked.*
Or so I wanted to believe.

2

T he first sign that our simple plan was already falling apart was when word reached me in the archives that the duke's troops had arrived. It was Julla who told me, carrying the message from Miko outside. My nest-sister hadn't paid the copper bits required for archive access and that meant she wasn't allowed indoors.

I thanked the elderly Scholar, but her attention had already moved on to the scroll I'd been reading. She inspected it for damage before she returned it to its appointed rack. As much as I liked to think Julla and I had built a bond of trust, the woman's children—the scrolls and tomes that populated her archives—would always come first. And given how jealously information was guarded on Eos, it was hard to blame her for that, even if the scroll I'd been reading came from the non-restricted section.

I said goodbye, dutifully ignored the lack of reply, and met Miko at the door. The Priestess' crimson and orange robes were stained with dirt, proof that her morning training had been eventful, but her orange, sclera-less eyes were wide in a way I now interpreted as excitement.

"They're here! Finally!"

"Don't forget to use Trade, nest-sister," I reminded her.

The tap on her left forearm was more impatient than normal, but she adjusted, mid-speech. "The mayor speaks—*is speaking*—with them now. Deputy Keeper asked me to bring you and Lace to guild hall."

"Do you know where Lace is?"

A tap on the right forearm this time. "One of new—*the new*—guards said she left town this morning."

"I guess it's just us then." Lace had been missing more often than not, but I wasn't going to press her on the issue. As hard as Miko and I had taken first Mordecai and then Skaal's deaths, Lace had known the reaver for years. They'd owed each other their lives, and I was pretty sure they'd been working their way towards something more than friendship.

Arrius had a lot to answer for.

In the meantime, our party leader was dealing with grief in her own way. And given that Lace was a worshipper of Hashoggath the Night Hag, a nine-breasted demon goddess who seemed to preach spite, poison, and vengeance?

I definitely didn't want to know the details.

Most of Madea had turned out to see the new arrivals—likely the only time any of them would lay eyes on their distant ruler—but that congestion was clustered around the western gate. We headed south instead, past the shop of the herbalist who had denied Miko training and then the warehouse where one of the town's three healers had died to an essoli attack. The street on which our favored tavern sat was mostly empty, and a few buildings down from there, we entered the guild hall again.

This time, Deputy Keeper Carlson was at his desk. And he wasn't alone. He was speaking with a stiff-backed, grey-haired human man in fine clothes and a traveling cloak streaked with dust from the road. Melligula was there too, a towering figure doing her best to be perfectly attentive and invisible at the same time.

The head of Madea's branch of the Adventurer's Guild looked up at our approach, the habitually sour expression on his face not lessening in the slightest.

"These are two of the adventuring party I mentioned," he said, words forever brisk.

The look the other man turned on us made Carlson seem almost warm and cuddly. I felt myself measured, judged, and discounted in a fraction of a second before that same gaze turned upon the significantly taller Miko at my side.

"A scaled, Deputy Keeper?"

"She's the Priestess who has kept the heir safe since her discovery," I said. "Your Grace."

Not knowing whether to salute or bow, I did neither.

"*This* is not the grand duke," Carlson told me in a voice so smooth and controlled I couldn't tell if he wanted to curse or laugh. "This is Lord Arbiter Hawthorne."

"His Grace remains occupied with the safe transfer of power in Zaris," Hawthorne said stiffly. "When word reached him of his daughter's presence on the frontier, I was dispatched to bring her home to Trynfall."

The news that Miko had brought to the archives suddenly took on an entirely new significance. The *duke's troops* were here, we'd been told… because the man himself was not.

"The duke's not coming?" I managed.

Judging by the expression that crossed the lord's face, that was the wrong thing to say.

"If you are concerned about a reward, you need not be. Grand Duke Willerton's reputation for fairness is well earned. You and the other members of your party will be paid before I depart with the heir."

That was a problem.

Money was good—great, even—but unless we were talking multiple golden crowns, it wasn't going to solve the problem of the coming synossians. Especially since the charter for Harborton, a village of a few dozen people, had cost eight silver towers on its own. We needed *political* power to help accommodate thousands of refugees, and that required either an ally who already had authority or sufficient money for us to buy ourselves one.

And something about the cold look on Hawthorne's severe face told me the promised reward would be more on the level of silver than gold. Again, that would be silver we badly needed, but it wouldn't do a thing to solve our larger issues.

"While we greatly appreciate the gesture," I said, trying to recover from whatever misstep I'd made, "we were hoping—"

"My Lord Arbiter?"

The words came from a young, almost cherubic man making his way down from the second floor. Like Hawthorne, his clothes were well made, if travel stained. A heavy medallion in a metal I didn't recognize rested atop his chest.

"What is it, Priest Humber?"

"The heir," said the apparent Priest. "I think we have a problem."

"Is still sick—" began Miko.

"Take me to her," said Hawthorne, ignoring my nest-sister. He swept an imperious gaze across the four of us, Melligula included. "You will all remain here until I return, or we will have more than words."

Grey haired or not, the lord arbiter crossed the common room to the stairs in a handful of swift strides. He was up and out of sight just as quickly.

Carlson gave me a look.

"What?"

"I'm not going to ask what your Discernment score is, both because it is unspeakably rude and because the answer was just made apparent from that conversation."

I shrugged self-consciously, still holding my spear in one hand. "I've been focused on other things."

"And that works out here on the frontier. Most of the time. But for future reference, nobles are *not* like us. Some are kind, some are less so, but they all play a game that the common people are rarely aware of until far too late. While Hawthorne might take a more hands-on approach with problems, there are nobles who will simply issue a quiet order from the comfort of their homes and then sleep the night away, secure in the knowledge that said problem will be resolved in a matter of days if not hours. Should your travels ever take you toward civilization, you would be well advised to prepare yourself accordingly."

The closest thing we'd had to nobility in Midton had been the Powell family, who'd owned both the town's only gas station and the steakhouse across the road. And while they had been treated by many of our town like their shit didn't stink and their eldest son wasn't a raging alcoholic with a bad habit of doing burnouts in the grocery store parking lot while naked, I didn't remember a ton of actual bowing and scraping going on.

Then again, they hadn't had literal armies backing them up.

"I'll work on it," I decided.

"See that you do. Lace and Miko will both be given some small allowances for social missteps given their respective people's unfortunate reputations, but the rulers of this kingdom are human and thus, more is expected of our kind." A scowl came and went. "Where *is* your party leader anyway? I requested all of you."

"Is out of town," said Miko, and though her scales were smooth and her back straight, her broken Trade told me the latest mention of her species' reputation bothered her. As difficult as it had been for me to adjust to this entirely new world, Miko might have had it even tougher. She was a native of Eos, but so much of the history she'd been taught was either wrong or woefully incomplete. And her proud people had a not-so-proud history on this continent. "Could not—*we* could not—find her."

"I see. Well, she will show, or she will not, I suppose. There are worse things than having a blood-scorned amazon absent during a discussion with a nobleman. Especially that one."

"Who is he? Lord Arbiter means… he's some kind of judge?"

Melligula's snort filled the common room with noise, but Carlson gave me a grudging nod.

"In a way. The arbiters are Grand Duke Willerton's peacekeepers, and the Hawthorne family have long held a hereditary position at the head of that force. This lord is the sixth of his line to fill that role. His Grace largely employs him as a problem solver, which makes him more dangerous than most nobles. Out here on the frontier, he speaks with the Grand Duke's voice, senior even to the baron who nominally rules our lands."

This was the first I'd heard of a baron, but I was more concerned with the nobleman currently under our roof. Maybe it was the conspiracy theorist in me, but when someone said *peacekeeper*, I had a hard time not thinking *secret police* instead. And if that was anywhere close to the mark, Lord Arbiter Hawthorne was someone we needed to avoid pissing off.

Unfortunately, as the man himself stormed back down the stairs, eyes burning above a face of cold iron, I was starting to think *that* ship had already sailed.

"What in the nine demon realms did you do to Lady Willerton?!" Hawthorne demanded, looking not at me, but at the synossian who loomed at my side.

"Kept her alive," said Miko simply. "Has sickness from time with cultists. Am able to heal but not cure."

"Are you speaking of the darkness that infests her?" asked Priest Humber, following his lord down the stairs. "You can actually influence it?"

"Not influence. Only push away. But always returns."

Carlson cut in smoothly. "There were three healers in Madea before the attack. Of them all, only Priestess Miko was able to help the heir. We are not sure why that is, but it is entirely through her efforts that Lady Willerton remains whole."

"Is Aurea's light," said Miko. "I am but vessel for her blessings."

"Well said," murmured the other Priest, eyeing Miko with renewed interest.

"If want," she told him, nodding to the stairs. "Can heal again while you watch. Maybe do better if heal together?"

"It is worth an attempt, yes. And at the least, I can see how your heal spell interacts with the infestation." The Priest rubbed his chin, as if searching for a beard that wasn't there, then looked to Hawthorne. "If you will permit us, my lord?"

The older man sent them both on their way with a flick of his fingers. Cold eyes turned back on Carlson and me.

"I will need *details*. Though Priest Humber is talented, he is merely Tin. The grand duke's personal healers will surely be able to cure this malady, but they will need to know what it is they are dealing with."

Carlson launched into the retelling of the story we'd shared with him upon our return to Madea: how we'd found Wilhemina held captive by cultists of the banished god, Khamani; how the Ever-Hungry's high priest had been conducting rituals to make the duke's heir into what he called a vessel; and how Miko had tirelessly worked for multiple seven-days to keep the young girl in some semblance of health.

"It would have been preferable if you had been able to take the cultist leader alive," mused Hawthorne.

I exchanged looks with the deputy keeper, my maxed-out *Deception* skill the only thing keeping my expression blank.

"He was a Copper," Carlson said simply.

"Ah." The nobleman shook his head. "Pity. There is much I would have liked to ask him about how the heir ended up out here and what connections his Zarisian kidnappers had with the Ever-Hungry."

I opened my mouth to ask why he thought Zaris had had anything to do with it at all, given that the freshly conquered city was on the far side of the duchy, but the door opening behind us saved me from yet another political misstep.

Lace slipped into the hall like a shadow escaping the morning sun. The woman's leathers were spattered with blood, Tempest was a wrapped presence on her back, and a sack in one hand dripped crimson across the hard-packed floor.

Carlson's sigh was plainly audible.

"Five irkonnen for the bounty," said the Marauder. She went to toss the dripping bag onto Carlson's spotless desk, but the deputy keeper got there first, taking it from her hand.

With a look of poorly concealed disgust, as much for the mess as the bag's apparent contents, he handed the sack over to Melligula.

"I will add it to the tally," said the turbinga, in a voice that was surprisingly melodic given her frame.

"Ears?" I asked Lace in Gorash, the language of the south.

"Tails. Easier to count." She looked the lord arbiter up and down. "It seems that the dirt farmer duke finally showed up?"

"That's not the duke."

"I didn't say it was. A duke wouldn't be standing alone and unguarded next to three armed adventurers. Is Willerton up with his daughter?"

"We speak *Trade* in this guild hall," said Carlson, interrupting our quick discussion.

"I was just telling my associate the same thing," lied Lace. She turned to Hawthorne. "I'm Lace."

"She is the third member of the party who rescued the heir," added the deputy keeper.

"The third *surviving* member," corrected Lace, voice as sharp as her blades. "There were five of us at the start."

"My condolences on your losses," said Hawthorne, his tone robbing the words of anything approaching sentiment. "The adventuring life is a risky one. Or so I'm told."

"All life is risky if you try hard enough."

I wasn't sure what Lace's Discernment attribute was like, but something told me it wasn't a hell of a lot higher than mine.

○○○

Thankfully, yet another conversation doomed to go to shit was interrupted by Miko and Humber's return. The nobleman gave the Priest a long look and received a careful nod in return.

"It is as the scaled woman said, my lord. Her healing spell helped in a way none of mine could."

"Do you believe that is because she is the one who cursed the heir in the first place?"

Miko's orange eyes flared wide, not in panic but outrage. "I would not—"

"Would not what?" snapped the lord. "Seize upon the opportunity to make yourself indispensable to the ducal family?"

"Yes!" snapped Miko. "That."

"Peace, Priestess Naseri," said Carlson, though his words were sharper than usual. "It is the lord arbiter's job to make certain of these things."

"Her magic appears to be the antithesis of the rot," confirmed Humber. "Light instead of dark. Warm life instead of cold emptiness. In my opinion, she is not responsible."

The nobleman turned his sharp-eyed stare back on Miko. "How often must you heal the heir?"

"Every few glasses," said the synossian, still trying to tamp down her outrage. "Can reduce to *maybe* four blessings a day but would not suggest fewer."

"Then there's nothing to be done for it. You will be coming with us to Trynfall."

Miko hesitated and then nodded. It wasn't in her nature to abandon a patient, let alone one who was a child and would die—or worse.

Hawthorne dismissed the rest of us with a glance that felt a lot like a glare. "The rest of you can be on your way."

"I go wherever Miko does," I said, and while I remained by far the smallest person in the room, there was a spear in my hand and steel in my voice.

"Miko and Brian are members of my party," agreed Lace. "The three of us travel as a unit."

"Yes," said Miko, her word carrying weight.

The lord's sigh was as harsh as the rest of him, but he waved a hand. "So be it. You will be responsible for your own supplies and transportation. The scaled is necessary. The two of you are not."

"Are necessary to me," said Miko.

"There's also still the matter of our reward," I added.

"By your own will, you are traveling to Trynfall with my soldiers," said Hawthorne. "Upon arrival, you will become someone else's problem. When His Grace hears the full story, he can choose the manner of your rewards."

It sounded almost ominous when he said it like that, but I wasn't going to complain. Our chances of getting more than a handful of silver had just gone up. *Significantly*, given Miko's continuing importance.

"Priest Humber," continued the lord, "how soon can the heir be made ready to depart?"

"A glass, my lord. Faster if you send her maid to help."

"Very well. I'll have the carriage waiting out front."

This time, it was Carlson who spoke up, and for all his earlier words about caution, the deputy keeper couldn't hide the anger in his words.

"*You're leaving? Already?*"

"I was sent to retrieve Lady Willerton, deputy keeper. That is what I am doing."

"And the blighted?"

"According to your tale, they were routed."

"There are still dozens remaining," said Lace, as if the bag of tails hadn't already made that clear. "Irkonnen, at the least."

"And the survivors will serve as a beacon for others of their kind," agreed Carlson. "To say nothing of how quickly they breed."

"Then I suggest your guild recruits additional adventurers to thin their numbers. I have neither the men nor the time to assist you. The heir *must* be back in Trynfall before the duke returns." For the first time since we'd met him, the lord arbiter softened his voice. "We will be stopping in Sakeld on our return trip. I will speak with the baron about sending troops to help."

Carlson gave a stiff nod. "Mayor Aulson and the Adventurer's Guild both would be grateful, my lord."

"A nobleman's duty is to his lands and the people upon them," said the lord, turning back to the rest of us. "One glass and no more. If you are coming with the scaled and Lady Willerton, you *will* be ready."

And just like that, he was out the door, headed… somewhere.

Priest Humber cleared his throat. "The lord arbiter does tend to be precise with his timelines." The younger man hurried upstairs.

In the ensuing silence, Carlson's cursing was quiet but heartfelt.

"Are you going to miss us that badly, Keeper?" asked Lace.

"You, not at all. Your blades? Yes."

"The baron—" I began.

"Has barely enough guardsmen to defend Sakeld most days, and from what I'm told, all but a tithe of those were sent to aid the grand duke in his invasion of Zaris. Madea doesn't even pay the baron taxes. In return, we are responsible for our own defense."

"Still, if the lord arbiter does speak with the duke's voice…"

"Yes. Perhaps." He shook his head.

"The irkonnen I found were scattered," said Lace. "You and I both know that will change, but without a greater force to organize them, you should have time. A few moons at least."

"We can pass on word at the next guild hall we reach," I suggested.

"I have messages out already, but an additional voice would be helpful. Thank you."

"Has been enough death," said Miko.

"Not yet," countered Lace, her voice hard. "There's at least one death still coming."

"On that note…" Carlson retrieved a piece of parchment from one of his desk's carefully organized drawers. It had already been folded in thirds and then sealed with wax and some sort of crest. "As you are now going to Trynfall anyway, you can deliver this in person to the Adventurer's Guild there."

"What is it?"

"My recommendation that Arrius be excommunicated from the guild. As deputy keeper, I have authority over only my hall. The keeper will be able to extend that to every hall in the duchy." He tapped the parchment against his other palm then held it out to Lace. "It's not much, but it is all that I can do to help."

I traded glances with Miko. None of us had shared our pact to hunt down the turncoat Copper, but Carlson wasn't dumb.

Lace made the parchment disappear and headed for the stairs.

"Will gather our packs," Miko told me. "Can speak with Seanna and Mrrl for me, nest-brother?"

"Of course. If you need help…"

"Melligula will assist her," said Carlson, nodding to the turbinga, who rose to follow Miko up the stairs.

"Then I guess I better get going."

○○○

Seanna and Mrrl lived on the far side of Madea, on the outer fringes of what passed for the town's slums. That was not by accident: the Smith and her husband were both kithrizal, and while Wilhemina's dad had a rare reputation of tolerance toward other species and religions, it was hard not to notice that many of Madea's poor came from the beastkin races: kithrizal, lupine, and corbins. There were even a handful of synossians like Miko, though these were remnants of her race who hadn't fled the continent centuries earlier. They called themselves scaled and their downtrodden attitude and lack of piety was a continuing source of frustration for my nest-sister.

As kithrizal, Seanna and Mrrl were bipedal cat people from the jungles south of the Waste. They were also the closest friends we had in this town. Seanna had crafted my iron hauberk—and then replaced its many, many broken links after the battle of Madea—as well as my new dagger and the bronze bands of Miko's short staff.

The grey-and-black-striped Mrrl was manning the front desk as always. I had my *Stealth* skill maxed out for a General skill, but the merchant's ears still twitched the moment I stepped inside. A moment later, he looked up with a wide, sharp-toothed smile.

"Brian! I didn't think we would see you today with the duke's men in town. They arrived altogether too late, as usual, but Chala teaches us patience, and I would be ungracious to ignore that lesson."

"I'm surprised you're not out there with the rest of Madea." The further west I'd gone, the busier the streets had been. It looked like the town's remaining merchants had all jumped on the opportunity to hawk their wares to the newcomers. For a few glasses at least, the recent tragedies were forgotten.

"Chala's lesson works with soldiers as well. It is often best to wait until well after the initial drinking and carousing is over. They will have less money on hand then but will have also exorcised some of their more violent impulses." The kithrizal fished out a familiar glass decanter and two cups. "And speaking of drinking… I just opened a fresh bottle. Would you care to greet the sun with me?"

The concoction the kithrizal favored was called sunlight. It tasted like alcoholic honey and good vibes and hit like an eighteen-wheeler doing eighty down a one-lane highway. I was genuinely surprised to realize just how disappointed I was to have to say no.

"Unfortunately, I can't. The duke's men are leaving in less than a glass and so are we."

"I see. Perhaps this was one time when patience was the unwise option." He shook his head. "By *we,* do you mean you and young Miko?"

"And Lace."

"Ah yes."

The blood-scorned amazons and the kithrizal shared borders down south, and while all three individuals had left their respective tribes or clans, the relationship between the three had never really progressed past cautiously polite.

"We always knew you would not stay forever, but the memory of your time with us will stay at least. Is there anything we can provide for your travels?"

"Whose travels?" Another kithrizal emerged through the door in the rear wall. Like her mate, Seanna wore only a loose vest over flowing pants. Her limp was all but unnoticeable now, thanks to the many healings Miko had given her since our arrival in Madea. "Ah, Brian! How is your repaired hauberk serving you?"

"So far, it's kept me whole despite Lace's best efforts."

Her toothy smile joined Mrrl's. "And the knife?"

I patted the bronze blade at my hip with my free hand. "Much better than the one I lost on the wall. And thank you again for the sheath."

"Every blade needs both a wielder and a home," she said, coming to stand next to her mate. "Besides, this town owes you and your fellow Aspirants that much and more. Now, what is this I hear about travels?"

"They are leaving us, dearest," said Mrrl.

"All the way to Trynfall," I added. Wilhemina's presence in town remained a secret, and while I trusted Mrrl and Seanna both, I'd found secrets were better off being kept.

"A pity, but Chala knows that adventurers come and go much like the birds in the skies." The Smith's tail, seemingly of its own volition, entwined with Mrrl's. "When is the day of departure? Provisions are lacking with the farms burned and abandoned, but we have enough to put together a small meal… and I see my heart already has brought out the sunlight."

"We have less than a glass until we leave," I admitted.

"So soon?"

"They're departing with the duke's men," added Mrrl. "And given the timetable, I suspect there are events at play that we are not privy to." He waved off the wince that not even my *Deception* skill could fully mask. "Nor would I expect otherwise. The games your nobility play are not for the likes of us to participate in."

"Are you and Miko in trouble, Brian?" asked Seanna. "We are close enough to the western wall that we could have you out of town in a quarter-glass or less. Say the word and nobody will know that you have disappeared or to where."

"It's not like that." I swallowed, feeling oddly touched. I couldn't help but hint at the truth. "We came across something of importance to the duke. His men are here to retrieve it, and we're going with them."

"*Something of importance…*" For a few seconds, I was graced with the look of a thoroughly confused kithrizal, which was as adorable as any expression a housecat back on earth might have made. Then, Seanna's features went slack. "*Oh.*"

Mrrl's ears twitched. "Dearest?"

"I will tell you later, in silence and moonlight."

Apparently, that was enough for her merchant mate. He leaned back on his stool and said nothing further, toying with the empty glass in his hand.

"Anyway," I added, "Miko's busy packing, but she sent me over to say goodbye for both of us."

"If you are saying goodbye for friend Miko, then you must pass on my hug to her!"

Seanna made her way around the table. I barely had time to set aside my spear before she picked me up and squeezed me like a girl would her favorite doll. Kithrizal were shorter than most humans, but then again, so was I, and my twelve Strength didn't give me anything like the Smith's physique.

"Be well, friends Brian and Miko," she murmured. "And know that we will not forget the kindness you have shown us… nor the sacrifices made upon Madea's wall."

I squeezed back and tried not to grunt as at least a few of my vertebrae spontaneously decided to rearrange themselves. *Pain Tolerance* let me ignore most of the discomfort, Seanna gave good hugs, and honestly? All that fur kind of made it feel like I was being wrapped in the world's most snuggly blanket.

It wasn't a glass of sunlight, but it didn't suck either.

3

I had yet to find any watches or clocks on Eos, but I was pretty sure we were packed and ready to go ahead of schedule. It helped that we didn't have much stuff, and that what we did have fit into the two backpacks we'd been given long ago in Harborton. In fact, Miko had spent most of the allotted time sorting and stowing the herbs and other ingredients she'd gathered over the past few moons. My nest-sister still hadn't found an Herbalist willing to train her in the final skills she'd need to take the profession as her own, but even the rudimentary poultices and tinctures she could make had proven useful.

When I'd first made it back to the guild hall, after saying goodbye to a handful of other people we called friends, I'd found Miko in the common room, speaking quietly with Priest Humber and Melligula. All three had been evicted from our room by Wilhemina's maid, who was changing the duke's heir into something suitable for travel that also better fit her station. Mayor Aulson's wife had donated a few old dresses to replace the soiled clothes we'd found Wilhemina in, but apparently, those didn't pass muster for the ducal court.

We had a small meal delivered from the tavern next door as we waited. Humber was about my age and already Tin-ranked, though by his own words, he'd never actually faced true combat. Instead, a combination of schooling, sparring, and healing—a *lot* of healing—had gotten him to tenth level, and almost four moons of intense reflection had helped him break through to Tin.

It put my current level back in perspective. Yeah, I'd progressed faster than anyone but Miko and Lace would ever truly know, thanks to both my quest rewards and the sheer level of near-fatal experiences we'd survived, but I was *still* behind the curve. And if Miko was any better off on that front than me, it was because she was two cycles younger. At only level six, we both had a lot of ground to make up.

Regardless, Humber seemed like a nice enough guy, and not *just* because he'd paid for our lunch. I didn't need a high Discernment stat to see he wasn't entirely comfortable with Miko yet, but when it came to a shared interest—healing—the two got on like a house on fire.

Which… was a weird saying, when I thought of it. Like a lot of Earth sayings, really. I'd done better about keeping colloquialisms from slipping into my everyday speech, but I had to wonder what Miko would make of that one.

We hadn't seen Lace again, which meant she was either still packing upstairs or had slipped back out of the hall and was doing something secret elsewhere. As our party leader and one of the only other Tins in town, she was more than capable of taking care of herself, but it was hard not to worry. The words she'd shared today were more than she'd spoken in the past seven-day, and I had no idea how she'd feel about our plan's sudden, if temporary, derailment.

Trynfall is somewhere we'd have had to go anyway, I reminded myself. *And traveling there now should both net us a better reward and improve the chances of Arrius getting kicked out of the guild. Those are all good things that will help with the hunt.*

I just… wasn't sure Lace would see it that way. Hashoggath, the demon goddess she worshipped, wasn't a nice entity in the slightest, and lately, the Marauder had seemed more like an avatar of her deity than the acerbic yet reliable woman we'd first met.

Another problem for future-Brian, I decided. *We're going to be on the road for a long while before we reach the capital. Plenty of time for us to talk things out.*

If all else failed, I'd call in the secret weapon that was Miko. Even puppies were less devastatingly effective.

I was polishing off the last of my mystery meat stew with a hunk of bread when Wilhemina's maid appeared at the top of the stairs. She was not what I expected—at least half again my age and stout enough to hold off a cavalry charge on her own. Wilhemina looked even smaller than normal in the woman's arms, more a collection of purple ruffles than a child.

"Priest Humber," she said, in a voice almost as pretty as Melligula's, "I have left her lady's bag upstairs. Please bring it to the carriage."

The speed with which Humber leapt to obey was impressive. I didn't think the maid was ranked—I didn't think she was an Aspirant at all, in fact—so it was another sign that there were types of power beyond what the Framework provided. And even a maid could order around a Tin-ranked Priest if they were in the service of someone influential.

It was one more thing to remember when we went to Trynfall.

ooo

Our departure from Madea was very different from our arrival, moons earlier, and not just because of the painful absence of both Mordecai and Skaal. Most of the town turned out to see us go, although I think that was more about the lord than the adventurers trailing in his wake. There were a few very satisfied merchants and a much larger number who clearly hadn't gotten a chance to make any sales at all. The latter group was at least smart enough not to make a fuss where the lord or his men could hear.

Mayor Aulson, his wife, and their newly appointed guard captain all waited at the western gate. A few words were exchanged, but the carriage didn't slow at all. Then we were through, our unexpected journey officially begun.

Wilhemina, her unnamed maid, and Lord Arbiter Hawthorne all rode together in the horse-drawn carriage, a sturdy thing clearly made for long journeys that was still fancier than anything Madea had had even before the attack. Our party joined a line of two dozen or so soldiers on foot. Thanks to Miko, we at least got to march next to the carriage with Priest Humber instead of behind it, a position that saved us from having to dodge any steaming gifts the two horses left behind.

Our presence drew more than a few looks from the still-dusty soldiers in file with us. I met those looks with a friendly nod but kept my spear in hand, a matter of necessity as much as security. The weapon was taller than I was, after all, and without any mounts of our own, it was impossible to carry it otherwise.

Besides, that had been the very first lesson I'd been taught on Eos: the spear went where I did.

Traveling in a column of soldiers, even a small one, was very different than traveling as a party. Whereas Lace might have once taken detours to show us things of note, the carriage and its scouts dictated the route. We were there only to follow. The lord's men had cleared this road on their way in, but the confirmed presence of irkonnen in the area made those first few glasses a tense affair.

After we'd left Madea and its surroundings far behind though?

It got boring fast.

According to Humber, it would take us nine days to reach Sakeld, though we'd pass at least one town along the way, and then another twenty days to reach the capital from there. That was a *lot* of walking and a lot of time not going to training.

I needed to figure out a way to multi-task. In the meantime, Miko and I talked quietly together, mostly in the High Tongue, while Lace kept to herself and Humber wandered up and down the column, speaking with the soldiers and spreading cheer. As a Tin, the man had Vitality to spare, but I tried not to hold it against him.

Instead, I focused on my own gains. I'd been in decent shape back in Ohio, but walking for hours while wearing armor and carrying a full pack and multiple weapons would have wrecked me. Six levels later, my improved Vitality was showing, as were the points in Strength that made my pack and armor mere impositions instead of crushing burdens. Hell, even my improved Finesse contributed; my steps were more certain, and I was pretty sure the chances of randomly turning my ankle were down to almost nothing.

Eos was a dangerous, scary place, but the Framework gave us the tools to survive it. I wasn't stuck in a dead-end job with a mountain of medical bills and credit card debt. I was growing, and I was changing. Sometimes *literally* changing, as the brownish patches of skin that marked past injuries made clear. With each wound I'd taken—and I'd taken a *lot* of wounds over the past few moons—my passive technique, *Beast Skin*, had replaced my normal pale skin with a tougher, if thankfully furless, version. Greater durability was always a good thing, as far as I was concerned, but the patchwork nature of it left me looking like a calico cat… minus any cuteness.

Of course, unless I eventually upgraded that technique to something more all-encompassing, the only fix to my appearance would be to progressively take even *more* wounds, targeting the currently unaffected areas. That didn't hold any appeal, as much as my *Pain Tolerance* skill would like it.

Despite Hawthorne's urgency, we'd left Madea in the early afternoon. It was still winter, and the days were almost as short on Eos as they'd been back on Earth, so we only had a half-dozen glasses to travel before Eos' sun was replaced with both moons. Shortly after that, we made camp, Miko and I erecting our shared tent inside the perimeter, close enough to the carriage that Miko could heal Wilhemina as needed.

Both my increased Vitality and my broken-in boots had proven their value: when I pulled the latter off, my feet were sweaty and smelly, but there were no blisters to heal, and the soles weren't even all that tender. Physically, it seemed I'd be fine with the weeks-long march ahead of us. Now, I just had to figure out some way to cope with the boredom.

A small fire was set to cook food for Hawthorne, Wilhemina, and her maid, but the rest of us made do with warm tea and cold rations. Despite Hawthorne's threats, Lace and I were fed with the soldiers. The Marauder disappeared shortly after, but I saw her later, talking with the two scouts on the far side of the fire. One of her techniques allowed her to see in the dark, so it was possible she was offering her services on watch.

Miko was spared that duty so that she'd always be available for healing, and by virtue of sharing a tent with my nest-sister, I was too. Before we went to sleep, I watched over her as she meditated, and then she did the same for me. Neither of us received any fresh gains. I'd been warned that skill improvement would slow as we leveled; now, I was starting to see it in action. Over the last couple days in Madea, I'd gained another two points in *Knife* and one in *Medium Armor*, but my other skills—particularly those that I'd maxed out at level five—hadn't budged.

I hated to even *think* it, but I probably needed some actual combat to hurry things along.

Oh hell. Was this how adrenaline junkies got started?

○○○

The next day was more of the same. *Literally* more, given that this time, we marched from sunrise to past sunset. Miko was allowed in the carriage every few glasses to continue her healing of Wilhemina, but otherwise, we walked side by side, her longer stride making it seem like she was out for a casual stroll. Lace wasn't with us at all; apparently, her talk the previous night had convinced the scouts to include her in their sweeps. She spent most of the day ranging either ahead of us or behind, and only the frustrated look on her face told me she hadn't found anything to kill.

The further we went, the less I liked traveling in a large group. The horses and carriage were loud; all the soldiers in armor were even louder. The horses were smelly, but the men and women around me were somehow even worse. And when that stench started to fade, I knew it was only because I had joined them in their rankness.

Baths weren't a thing on the road, and so far, streams hadn't been either. And while it *was* winter, the skies were clear, and the sun was strong and bright. So we marched, and we sweated, and we stank, and the leagues slowly passed beneath our boots. By the end of the third day, we were both desperate for something—anything—to do. Miko and I had already taken to helping set up and break camp each day. As the former shrine keeper went to offer to help with the maid's cooking, I left in search of my own opportunity for progression.

I found it on the far side of camp, where five of the soldiers were squaring off under the unsteady glow of a few torches. They all looked to be around my age. The largest, whose multiple days' growth of facial hair wasn't quite up to calling itself a beard, stared me down as I approached.

"Can we help you, *sir?*"

"I'm not a sir. Just an adventurer." I held out my hand. "Brian Fieldings."

"Jenkins." He didn't take my hand but gestured to the men around him. "These are Holloway, Nixon, Kitchens, and Samhill. What can we do for you?"

"It looked like you were going to get some training in. I was hoping I could join." I hefted my spear in case they needed further explanation.

The weapon got a derisive look from one of the other men— Kitchens, I thought—and Jenkins shook his head.

"An adventurer, you say? A likely tale. That old thing looks like it would snap at the very first parry. Regardless, we're not training weapons."

"Fists and feet," said Samhill, a head shorter than Jenkins but with shoulders like a linebacker. "As the Warbringer intends."

I'd spent enough time in Madea to know that the Warbringer was one more god from the expansive human pantheon. Why any god—especially one linked with war—would want his worshippers to go without weapons was beyond me, but training was training.

"I don't have any real skill in unarmed combat," I admitted, "but I'm here and happy to learn."

There was nothing friendly about Jenkins' smile. "You look like *you'd* snap just as easily as your spear. The duke doesn't pay us to train children." He gave me another look up and down. "Or... whatever you are."

"If you want a teacher, *adventurer*, go chat up Old Rawhide," said the man I thought was Kitchens, his comment sparking derisive chuckles.

"Yeah, he'll teach you anything you need to know," added one of the others, his grin even nastier than Jenkins.

I'd suffered through high school, so I recognized when someone was screwing with me. But I'd also survived multiple moons on Eos and knew better than to start something with five people, all of whom were bigger and possibly higher level than me.

Being Chosen wouldn't save me from getting beaten to death.

"I'll seek him out," I said, ignoring the fresh laughs that triggered. "Any idea where I can find him?"

"As close to the fire as he can get," said one.

"Just listen for the snores," said another.

With that, they went back to their training.

Cheeks burning, I left.

I had no plans on actually seeking out this *Old Rawhide* person. Judging from the assholes who had made the suggestion, the man would be useless at best and outright dangerous at worst, and I wasn't going to be the patsy in someone's idea of a practical joke. But I *did* have to pass by the fire to reach my tent.

Miko was there with the maid, although only the latter was preparing the food. My nest-sister was instead crouched a careful distance away, offering suggestions in her quiet, still-broken Trade, as the other woman either nodded or shook her head accordingly.

It seemed weird to not let the woman singlehandedly keeping Wilhemina healthy touch her food, but Hawthorne seemed the sort to indulge in paranoia. Skaal had let Miko pitch in on several of our meals out in the field and I knew the synossian had come a long way since the days of badly burned catosaur. Hopefully, she'd be able to improve her *Cooking* skill further by offering mentorship even if she didn't do the actual work.

I gave her a nod that she returned with an abbreviated form of the synossian salute. There were a few other people around the fire, but none of them were conspicuously snoring. One of the scouts had come in for tea, spelled by either Lace or the third member of their newfound trio, and two other soldiers were sitting next to each other, caught up in quiet conversation, but whoever this Old Rawhide was, he wasn't—

Oh. There *was* a sixth person near the fire, just inside the circle of illumination, but he wasn't sleeping or eating. Instead, he had a small book in his hand, head bent over it so that the shock of white hair on top pointed in my direction.

I didn't know about *rawhide*, but I recognized *old* when I saw it. He had at least a decade on Valestia back in Harborton. Seated, it was hard to truly gauge his height, but he looked tall. He was also gaunt, like someone who'd been left out in the sun too long and had most of his excess flesh simply melted away. I realized I'd seen him once or twice over the past few days, always in the distance, marching near the front of the column.

Old though he was, he wasn't unaware. I'd studied him for no more than a few moments when I found myself being studied in turn, dark eyes in a dark face under that white hair. The man tucked his book away into a coat pocket and rose to his feet, immediately demonstrating that he was exceedingly tall for a human. He stepped lightly but with clear purpose, approaching me directly.

"Is there something I can help you with, young man?"

It was almost exactly the same thing Jenkins had asked, minutes earlier, but the man's thin voice lacked any of the thinly veiled annoyance the younger soldier had had.

Unfortunately, the fire's light had been enough to tell me exactly why Kitchens had sent me to this old man for training.

Old Rawhide was missing his right arm from just above the elbow.

In a world of magic, crippling wounds weren't necessarily career enders, but if my experience in Harborton and Madea was anything to go by, healers were a prized rarity. Anyone high enough level to *regrow limbs* would be able to write their own ticket, likely working for the nobility and charging ungodly amounts for their services.

You could have said charging an arm and a leg, the voice in my head murmured. *The pun was* right *there.*

I ignored it. Disabilities weren't a laughing matter, any more than incurable diseases. Although my dad *had* had some great one-liners—meaning truly awful ones—until the disease had taken them from him along with everything else.

Unfortunately, even if this man could still serve, it was clear he wasn't going to be able to help me with the spear. And while there was a sheathed knife on his belt, I wasn't going to go there. Not until I knew that asking wouldn't just be me poking at an old hurt.

Which left me fumbling for a different reason to have been staring at him from across the fire. I called on my *Deception* skill and went with the obvious.

"I'm Brian," I said, "and I didn't mean to intrude. I was just surprised to see a book anywhere outside of the archives."

"There *are* a scant few of us who do still read," he said dryly, pulling that same book out of his coat pocket and flashing it in my direction. It was about the length of a comic book, its cover fashioned from some kind of leather. The title had been carefully picked out in contrasting thread that matched the binding used for the few dozen pages inside.

I frowned. "*Meditations on Mortality?*"

"I'd be happy to share, but as you can see, it's not—" He paused, and those dark eyes sharpened. "I'm sorry; what did you say?"

"Meditations on Mortality? That's the title… right?"

He stared at me for a long while. "You can not only read in general, but you also understand Old Imperial?"

The answer was apparently yes, thanks to my *Speaker of Tongues* trait. Not that I'd realized it was a new language—my thirteenth, if you counted the irkonnen and essoli languages. I did my best to hide both my surprise *and* my annoyance that *Deception* wasn't a class skill that could increase beyond the cap of ten on General skills. God knew I was getting way more use out of the skill than something like *Leadership* so far.

"Languages are a specialty of mine," I said, vastly underselling my Framework-given capabilities.

"That already makes you more interesting than most of these people." The book went away again, but he extended his only hand in my direction, fingers gnarled and knobby. "I am Kacellius Thryn, a knight of Sakeld."

The knight's grip was stronger than it looked, which told me he was probably decently high leveled.

"Sakeld? You serve the baron?"

"As I did his father before him, yes. When the lord arbiter stopped by on his way to Madea, he requested that someone accompany him and our duke's men to your town." The fire cast the lines of his face into deep shadow, but I thought I detected concern in his worn features. "With most of my baron's forces called to Zaris, there were only a handful of us to choose from. I volunteered."

"You were that eager to see Madea?"

"I preferred to leave my liege with as many able-bodied protectors as I could," said Kacellius, and if there was any bitterness in his words, he had buried them so deeply I couldn't find it. "Sakeld is peaceful enough, most days, and the baron's family has long been loved, but the new lord is fresh to his rule. His safety is paramount."

"That uh… makes sense," I said.

"I'll tell him you said so. He was quite put out when I left."

"Put out?"

"Ah." He studied me for another moment. "Not from these parts after all, I take it?"

"No. My party and I came from the east. Past Harborton."

"A town I *haven't* heard of."

"It's new. They bought their charter only a few cycles ago."

"I see. You're one of the adventurers the lord spoke of then? Along with yon scaled lass doing her best to keep Neesa from burning their supper?"

"Yeah." The maid's name being Neesa threw me off just a bit. Not that long ago, we'd rescued a bunch of farmers from bandits and one of their daughters had had the same name. I wondered if it was the John Smith equivalent here in the kingdom of Elthor. "Us and the amazon who's been helping out the scouts."

"A rare woman, that one. And dangerous."

"Definitely."

"Well, as a relative newcomer to both the duchy and my lord's barony, you are likely unaware that the previous baron passed away a few years ago. His heir has only just had his Dreaming and been inducted into the Framework and his inherited profession."

"Baron Sakeld is only ten cycles old?"

"Yes. But despite the tragic circumstances, I believe he will grow to be as well regarded as his father before him."

I was starting to understand why Carlson wasn't holding out hope for help from Sakeld. Most of their troops were off fighting the duke's war and the baron himself was barely a teenager.

Still, it wouldn't hurt to ask. Thankfully, Kacellius unwittingly beat me to the subject.

"Tell me, young Brian, is it true what the people of Madea were saying? That you all survived an army of blighted?"

"It's not really the sort of thing people make up."

"True, but I've found those unused to battle have a tendency to inflate the numbers involved. Not through any malice or even pride, mind you, though there are always miscreants who seek to profit somehow, but because it is difficult to judge such things fairly when the blood is flowing."

"I stood on the wall," I said. "We fought off at least a thousand irkonnen, at least two dozen essoli, and twenty or so cultists of Khamani the Ever-Hungry." After a second, I added. "And a shadeweaver."

The old man's grin was bright against his dark brown skin. "You had me until the last detail. There hasn't been a shadeweaver seen in a hundred cycles."

"It was so large it reached the top of the wall without even having to climb," I told him, voice flat. "First, it summoned a mass of smaller shadow spiders. Then, it breathed a darkness that sapped the energy from those it struck. Two Coppers stood against it, and the guard captain finally brought it down before losing his own life to the Khamani high priest."

For a brief while, the only sound was the crackle of fire nearby, and the low murmurs of Miko to Neesa. Eventually, Kacellius swallowed.

"By the anointed trinity, you are serious, aren't you?"

"As the grave." I held his gaze. The truth was, I had nightmares about our two-day war almost every night, and the shadeweaver was the very smallest part of all that. "We lost half our party and still came out ahead of most of the town's defenders."

A gaunt but deceptively strong hand gripped my shoulder. "Then I apologize for my ignorant words. Having faced true battle myself, I would never make light of such events. The fact that you three stood against such an array of forces and not only survived but helped to save that town…" He shook his head. "Baron Sakeld will want to hear the tale, if you are willing."

That was exactly what I'd told Carlson we'd do, so I nodded and buried my misgivings down deep, along with the grief I felt for all the people I'd lost since coming to Eos.

"I am. Willing, that is. And honestly, Madea could use the baron's help."

"When he hears, I have no doubt he will dispatch supplies…"

"*Military* help. We broke the irkonnen forces, but we didn't kill them all. There are still packs of them out in the woods southwest of Madea. The town is going to need its farmers back out in the fields if anything is going to be salvaged for the spring harvest, but…"

"But they do not have the forces to root out the threat. And will risk famine if they cannot do so."

"Yeah. To say nothing of what happens if the blighted return."

He blew out a long breath that was almost as creaky as he was.

"With Zaris taken, the baron's men will be on their way back to either Sakeld or their respective hometowns, but even if they all survived, that's a fist or two of soldiers, at most."

"Anything will help."

"Yes, well. I am but one old knight, but I give you my word that I will speak with my lord as well. And perhaps his council will have advice to offer. In the meantime," he said, once again pulling out his book, "I believe you could stand to read this more than me. It once offered some small comfort to a broken veteran of the Kingdom Wars. Perhaps it can do the same for you."

I took the slim book from him, feeling its warm leather cover between fingers that had gone cold.

"I *will* want it back," added Kacellius softly. "It was a gift from… someone who is no longer here. And as you noted, there are not so many books available outside of the archives. Especially on the eastern edge of the kingdom's smallest duchy."

With those words, he gave a strange sort of bow, head lowered with his left and only arm angled across his chest to tap his own shoulder. When he straightened again, he spun on one heel and left the fire behind.

"Who was that, nest-brother?" asked Miko, joining me as Neesa carried clay bowls of some kind of stew toward the carriage.

"Another survivor," I told her. "Like us."

4

Without any source of light, the tent I shared with Miko wasn't conducive to reading, but *Meditations on Mortality* stayed on my mind throughout the following day's march. And when the Priestess went off to help Neesa with dinner again, it was my turn to find a spot by the fire and page through.

I wasn't sure what I'd expected. What I got was… *poetry.*

I hadn't read a poem since Shakespeare in school. Or was it Whitman? One of the two, although honestly, all I remembered was that one was old, dead, and English, and the other was old, dead, and… American?

Even that much, I wasn't sure of.

Speaker of Tongues gave me the ability to understand damn near any language, including the telepathic horror show that was the essoli tongue, but it seemed even gods-given traits struggled with verse. Nothing rhymed, and I couldn't tell if that was due to the translation magic or if the originals had been that way too. Nothing followed a recognizable format either.

Maybe Eos didn't have limericks or sonnets or whatever?

I pushed through the thirty pages of hand-copied text at speed. Probably faster than I should have, honestly. A glass or so later, I was done, with absolutely nothing to show for it. The words and the individual poems had all kind of run together in my brain, leaving no impression. It was like listening to an album while focusing on something else entirely… you vaguely knew there'd been music playing, but hell if you could remember any of the words.

I closed the book and looked down at its worn leather cover. Then, I sighed, opened it back up, and started over again with the first poem.

After all, it was called *Meditations on Mortality*, not *Speedreading Mortality*.

This time, I puzzled over each line of verse, looking for meaning. Trying to divine the writer's intentions as well as their state of mind. I doubted I would ever figure out any secrets locked within the meter, if there even was meter, but the words themselves were a different story.

Maybe literally.

On my second readthrough, I made it through a grand total of three of the twenty poems before heading back to my tent. Even so, I felt like I'd found my footing. What had begun as a collection of random imagery and often simple words was starting to resolve into something different. Those three poems stood apart from each other in subject matter and style, but taken together, they started to paint a picture of a person—man or woman, I wasn't sure—facing down something insurmountable.

I felt like I was *still* missing a lot of the subtext of the individual pieces, but the meta story was engaging enough that it took longer than usual to sink into meditation that night.

Maybe that's why I got my first skill-up since we'd left Madea:

> **You have increased the following skills:**
>
> **General skills:**
> Meditation [+1]: 6/10

The unexpected gains made me focus back on the title of the poetry book. Did *Meditations on Mortality* have a secondary meaning? Was this some sort of primer for *Meditation* or was it coincidence that I'd just gained my first point in the skill in literal months?

Hell if I knew, but it gave me something to occupy my mind as we hiked along the road day four. In fact, it niggled at my brain enough that I soon found myself taking the book out and doing my best to read through a few more pages as we walked.

That went… about as well as could be expected at first. My twelve Finesse wasn't quite up to the challenge posed by an uneven dirt road and my own distraction. Still, after Miko saved me from a half-dozen near falls, I sank into a sort of rhythm. By the end of the day, I'd made it through an additional ten poems, and while I knew I was still missing finer details, the speaker's story was becoming clearer.

There had been a battle, the latest in a series of defeats, and as the poet retreated to the next in a long line of hastily made defensible positions, his or her mind was starting to find fresh significance in the mundane world around them. The azure birds whose songs greeted the sunrise. The stalks of grass that lined the path like a nation's borders and the impressions of footprints that blurred with each subsequent soldier's passage. Faces that changed with every battle, scars made by blade or time or loss.

The word *mortality* had yet to make an appearance anywhere except on the cover and decorative title page, yet its presence as a thought, as a looming threat and overriding concern, was unmistakable in each poem.

I didn't see any skill-ups that day, but I didn't let that slow me down. The next day, I stumbled a little bit less as I read while marching, not so much more *surefooted* as I was more *aware*. Part of my brain focused on navigation, on keeping an eye out, not just for obstacles but for new developments. The rest drilled down even more into the words on the page.

Seventeen poems done now out of twenty, and I was starting to think these had all been written over the span of several moons. The long fighting retreat was coming to an end. The poet's army had been driven back to a city where they found themselves surrounded, huddled behind walls only marginally higher than the fortifications they'd previously lost.

The poems turned strange in this final quarter of the book. Less physical, more abstract. Maybe even spiritual. The handful of names that had once made regular appearances—Grim Jaw and Achaestus, Cainos and Trella, Shaz Losar and the One-Eyed Crow—had faded out, one by one, giving the impression that the speaker was alone, left to defend an entire city by themself. The singing birds from the second poem had been replaced with winged scavengers, the grassy fields with smoke-filled skies and the ruddy glow of a hundred campfires in the night. Even the penmanship suffered, and though this was almost definitely a copy of a copy, the carefully reproduced difference between the precise arrangement of letters on the initial pages and the wide, wild loops toward the end spoke as much to the speaker's plight as the words themselves.

I wasn't sure what solace Kacellius thought I would get out of this read, outside of maybe that *my* situation could always be worse. Because this was pretty damn dark.

I read the last three poems under the light of our own camp's fire and found the mood changing yet again. There was no more talk of war, of battle, or even of the city they'd been trapped in. The poet's gaze had turned inward. A woman, unnamed and apparently distant, received her very first mention, and I couldn't tell if she was the speaker's lover or family member. The nineteenth poem was almost jovial, written as a letter to a friend waiting with a glass of something warm and alcoholic. And the twentieth poem barely even qualified as such:

> *the sky is torn*
> *fragments spill through golden light*
> *every piece an answer*
> *to questions never asked*

Huh. I closed first the book and then my eyes. The fire's warmth was tangible even through my dusty traveling clothes, the noise of the camp ever-present, as horses shifted, armor clanked, and soldiers murmured to each other in the darkness.

I wasn't sure what to make of *Meditations on Mortality*. There was a lot that I didn't understand, I knew, but the overarching story was a sad one. A survivor of a long campaign and dozens of battles staring down the unmistakable end. Who was the woman mentioned? Who was the friend? Had any of the names mentioned ever existed? And if the poet was the protagonist of his own story, if he or she had been there and presumably died, then how had their book ever seen the light of day?

In the absence of any great personal insight or epiphanies, I went looking for Kacellius instead. Thankfully, the old knight wasn't far away.

"I can tell by the look on your face that you've finished," he said, looking up from the same fire I'd been seated at.

"I don't know about *finished*," I said, "but I've read through it, at least. I'd like to read through it again, if you don't mind, but first… I have questions."

"Of course." The harsh lines of his face were only emphasized by the fire's light. One of these days, we were going to have a conversation in the daytime. "Ask and I will answer, if I can."

I held up the book. "Is this true? The story in it, I mean?"

Kacellius didn't respond at first. When he did, his voice was thoughtful. Reflective, even.

"I'm not sure anyone has the answer to that. What I can tell you is that the battles mentioned did happen. Not in the Kingdom Wars of my and my father's time, but in one of the many smaller campaigns after the fall of the Endless Empire. The city-state of Jewel was ultimately sacked, with all surviving defenders either put to the sword or sacrificed in the opposing army's victory fires."

"Then how did these poems make it into a book?"

"The legend goes that a collection of pages was found in the wreckage of Jewel by the city's conqueror, King Dicaeus. Despite widely being regarded as a bloody warlord, Dicaeus saw himself as something of a warrior poet. It was he who chose to make a book of the found poems, either as a warning to his enemies or as a tribute to the nameless fallen."

The knight shrugged gaunt shoulders, his tied-off right sleeve swaying with the motion. "Is the legend true? I don't know. The unnamed poet might not have been a soldier at all. They might have been a camp follower in the campaign. Or a family member of one of the veterans, distant enough to survive the slaughter. They might even have been a historian, born many cycles later, who simply chose that particular war as a fitting backdrop for their fictional epic."

History, I was starting to realize, was a bit of a mess.

"I suppose the greater question," continued Kacellius, "is this: does that matter?"

"You're asking me if it matters whether this whole thing was fiction or fact?" I didn't bother to call on *Deception* to hide my incredulity.

"All memory—all experience—has some element of fiction, young Brian. It is colored by our own beliefs and shaped by our own blind spots. That does not change the value of memory nor discredit the lessons that can be gleaned from it.

"What matters to me," he added, "is not whether the events in *Meditations on Mortality* happened as described or not. What matters is the truth the poet was seeking to convey through their words."

"What *truth*?"

Kacellius' smile was bone dry, any warmth stolen by his own lifetime of experiences. "That is for each of us to decide for ourselves."

It was a *supremely* unsatisfying answer.

"Think of it as training for when you break through to Tin," he said, not unkindly. "Even the Framework recognizes that truth is often a very personal thing."

I frowned, the fire's crackle a counterpoint to my thoughts. What did any of this have to do with ranking to Tin? I thought back to what I had learned of the process, first from Riok and then from the archives in Madea.

"Are you talking about Ideals?"

"In a way. I do not know if you have an Ideal yet, but you will never reach Tin until you not only find one but begin to grasp the shape that Ideal will take in your own growth. Every Ideal means something different to the individual who claims it, and a sizable part of ranking is the pursuit of self-knowledge."

I looked down again at the poetry book in my hands. I did have an Ideal—Freedom—and I felt like I'd already made progress on figuring out what it meant to me. But what sort of truth could I glean from a poet's possibly fictional account of his own slow demise? The undeniable existence of mortality? The persistence of the human spirit? The universality of grief? I wasn't sure. I'd gotten all those things and more from my reading, but none of them felt right.

Kacellius read me like I was just another book and patted my shoulder with his only hand. "Don't chase it. The woman who gifted me those poems believed everything is a journey. Life, growth, and even knowledge. And I have come to see her wisdom in that belief. The truths I knew when I was young have been replaced by the truths I know in my twilight years and will surely be replaced anew when my soul walks into the next life."

I didn't get what he was saying, not really, but nodded. The knight had said he'd found comfort in reading *Meditations on Mortality*, but so far, I'd only gotten this strange blend of questions and emotions. Still, we had four more days until we reached Sakeld, and I was going to read through the book again at least one more time to see if and how that changed.

An hour later, in our tent next to a sleeping Miko, I emerged from my own meditation to find something truly unexpected:

```
You have increased the following skills:

General skills:
Meditation -> Meditation (Uncommon)
Meditation (U) [+1]: 7/10
```

I didn't know much about *truth*, universal, personal, or media-created, but I was sure as hell seeing some growth.

ooo

As usual with the Framework, I was left to guess at what difference my new gains made. Certainly, it was easier to read the book as we marched, part of my mind falling into a sort of fugue state of reading and absorption, while the rest focused on traversing the dusty road. But was that *it*? And what did reading have to do with *Meditation*, the title of this particular book notwithstanding?

Once again, I didn't know. It was rude to ask someone about their personal record and outright impossible for them to display it for you, but Miko volunteered that she had a maxed-out *Meditation* skill. Her skill, however, remained only at the Common rank. Which meant she couldn't help me either.

That said, she did want to see if she could upgrade her *Meditation* skill the same way I had. Miko didn't read Old Imperial, of course, but I agreed to read the poems aloud as we marched. We could see if that worked... and if there was some sort of *Oratory* general skill I might pick up in the process.

Honestly, I doubted either would happen, but it was kind of cool to read through the poems with Miko and get her take on things. Coming from a militant nation, if one that had long held honor as one of its guiding principles, she had very different interpretations of many of the lines of verse, and I think that distinction helped solidify my own viewpoint.

Maybe the old knight from Sakeld was onto something with his whole *individual truth* thing.

It was somewhere around mid-afternoon that day when things changed in a hurry. I was halfway through reciting the seventh poem for Miko—and for Priest Humber who was making no secret of his fascination with our makeshift book club—when the column came to a halt. Lace was at the front with another of the scouts, speaking with Kacellius and the much younger lieutenant who commanded this platoon of the duke's troops. The officer called out orders that were passed down the line and our relatively ragtag force came to attention. Weapons weren't necessarily unsheathed, but they were held at the ready, twenty-plus individuals poised to spring into violent action.

My spear didn't have a sheath, and it was in my hand already, so I just focused on our surroundings.

It took a while to learn what had prompted the sudden alert. Several minutes passed in silence. Soon, some of the soldiers behind us—Jenkins and Kitchens among them—were starting to shift and mutter.

Then, the first stranger appeared on the road ahead of us.

He wasn't much to look at: hair and beard uncombed and clothes so heavily caked in road dust that the stains beneath were almost masked. He carried a pack over both shoulders, an old weapon on one hip, and what looked like an unsheathed knife in his opposite hand.

He looked like an axe murder who'd fled into the woods and somehow gone even *more* feral, but it was hard to imagine why the scouts would stop the column for just one man.

When another person emerged from the woods, equally filthy, if slightly stockier and bearing a shield that looked like it had been beaten to shit by someone with a Strength attribute three times my own, I started to understand the concern. Especially since she was followed by a third warrior, this one covered in dirt and long-dried blood, and he was followed by yet another. By the fifteenth such stranger, I could even hear noises from the surrounding forest, suggesting that additional troops were out of sight, marching along either side of the road.

It said something for the approaching army's stench that we could easily smell them over our own steadily worsening funk. The lead warrior passed by without comment, dark, shadowed eyes fixed on the eastern horizon. The woman at his back spared the ducal carriage a single glance on her way past. While no army of any size could move in *actual* silence, not a single one of the strangers spoke. Nor did their grim demeanors invite conversation from the rest of us. Instead, a column of the duke's soldiers stood witness to the steady passage of a small army.

"I can't believe it," said Humber.

"Believe what?"

"They are the Nameless Dead." It wasn't the Priest who answered me, but Kacellius, who had initially slipped back to the ducal carriage to report in and now found his way over to us.

"I didn't think I'd ever see them, let alone operating in our duchy," added the Priest.

"They go where they are needed." Kacellius watched the army pass by, something unknowable in his fixed gaze. "None in the kingdom would choose to block their path."

"Who are they?" I asked. I spoke in a near whisper, conscious of the warriors shuffling past us just a dozen feet away.

"Former farmers, merchants, and tradesmen. Beggars, orphans and fallen knights. Those who have forsaken their lives and their futures in pursuit of a single shared goal."

"The eradication of the blighted." Humber's voice was solemn.

"They must have heard the news out of Madea."

I traded looks with Miko. An army should have no problem cleaning up the remnants of the horde we'd faced… and long before they could reform into something more dangerous. If Kacellius was correct, the Nameless Dead drew their numbers from former Dedicated as much as Aspirants, but nothing I saw in the faces—and weapons—of those passing by our column suggested they'd be anything but brutally efficient.

When you dedicated your life to fighting the blighted, I had to assume you either saw rapid growth… or died early.

A new voice cut in, one I recognized as much from its mocking tone as anything else. *Jenkins.*

"Their stench alone could bring down a herd of phloxl… and probably their owners too," said the big soldier. "I'm sure they'll have no problem taking care of a handful of yapping irkonnen dogs."

Kacellius spun on the larger man, his voice going hard. "They have sacrificed *everything* for their mission. If your tongue cannot remain civil, sergeant, then it should not be wagging at all."

Any question I had about Jenkins' level was answered as an aura of violence sprang up around him, one that seemed to want to rip and rend the very air. It was weaker than Arrius' or Skaal's had been, making the man Tin but not Copper… which wasn't much comfort to someone unranked like me.

"No half-knight from a dirt-poor barony gets to speak to the men of the Third Company like that, does he, boys?"

The other four men I'd briefly met a few nights back crowded in, one of them—Kitchens again, I thought—also unleashing the aura of a Tin.

Even if Kacellius was similarly Tin, he was outnumbered, one-armed, and had only a knife. Meanwhile, his opponents all had weapons, Samhill's words about the Warbringer preferring fists and feet clearly forgotten.

None of this was my business, but *freedom* gave me the right to make bad decisions as well as good ones.

I stepped up beside the old knight, the spear of Riok Diocil in my hands. Miko, I couldn't help but notice, had already taken a step to the side. Most people would think she was separating herself from the coming conflict; the clawed grip on her short staff told me otherwise.

Humber, on the other hand, *was* trying to make himself scarce.

I tried not to hold it against the man.

"Looks like all the country rubes want to stand together," said Kitchens, reaching for the great axe on his back.

"No weapons," said Jenkins. "We're going to beat a little education into these simpletons and call it a day."

I did *not* set my spear aside. Hell if I was going to just take a beating, let alone stand by while Kacellius or Miko took one. But it was a single Tin against two, and three total combatants against five. If we were going to come out on top somehow, we needed to strike hard and fast before they could—

A dark shadow materialized behind the five soldiers, and I exhaled. *That* made this fight a lot more even. And a whole lot more deadly too.

"What *exactly* is going on here?" I didn't have to turn around to know that Lord Arbiter Hawthorne had emerged from his carriage and taken note of our standoff. His voice, equal parts sharp and ice cold, made that much clear.

Jenkins and the others stiffened, the two Tins even coming to attention and saluting.

"Just a friendly disagreement, my lord."

"Sergeant Jenkins, you have been warned of precisely this sort of behavior before. Report to Lieutenant Ender and tell him that I said there will *not* be another such occurrence."

"Yes, my lord. Right away." The brutish soldier swallowed, and if the look he sent me as he left was damn near malevolent, his voice was appropriately servile.

"As for the rest of you, you will return to your designated places. That includes you, Sir Kacellius."

"Of course, Lord Arbiter Hawthorne." The old knight, who had not even touched the knife on his belt, gave the other man a salute, and headed for the front of the column.

The rest of our opponents went the opposite way, one of them visibly flinching when he discovered that Lace had been behind them the whole time. While the amazon's blades were sheathed, her silver eyes were sharp enough to cut on their own. She stared all four of the soldiers down as they split apart to move around her, then followed Kacellius toward the front, brushing past us and the carriage without a word.

Miko and I were already where we were supposed to be, so we stayed put. We did turn around at least and found the cold-faced lord examining us both. Behind him was Priest Humber, answering the question of who and what had gotten the lord arbiter's attention.

I mentally apologized for any bad thoughts I'd had toward the Priest. I didn't think Hawthorne's intervention would be the end of things—not if Jenkins and his cohort followed in the footsteps of other bullies I'd known—but this would have been a bad place and a worse time for a showdown. *Especially* if it had somehow spilled out into the ranks of the Nameless Dead still trooping by us.

"As for you and your party," said the lord, his voice losing some of its edge, "I will remind you that the scaled Priestess—"

"Miko Naseri," said the woman in question.

"—is *necessary*. You and the amazon are not. And interfering with members of the duke's regiment while they are on official business is an infraction that carries with it minimum jail time."

"Like the sergeant said, it was just a friendly disagreement."

Hawthorne's sharp eyes drilled into me, but I held firm. I'd lost my first life on Earth. I'd lost friends on both worlds. I'd fought blighted and gyr beasts and horse-sized centipedes… and run from a titan snake and a bird that literally commanded the storm. I had grown since my arrival and only some of that growth was reflected in the Framework's mechanics.

Maybe Carlson was right and the nobility represented a whole new caliber of threat, but something told me the lord arbiter wouldn't think highly of a man who couldn't stand his ground.

Then again, Discernment *was* my lowest attribute.

After a moment, he sighed. "Very well. See that it does not happen again."

"Will not," said Miko.

"Yes… sir," I said at the same time.

And just like that, a potentially deadly encounter was over without even a drop of blood spilled.

That wouldn't make Lace happy.

As for the Nameless Dead, still marching toward their distant enemy? If they thought anything of the whole exchange, insults and barely averted violence included, they kept their thoughts to themselves.

It was a lesson we all could probably stand to learn.

○○○

By the time we went to bed, I was second-guessing everything about the encounter. One thing I'd come to recognize in the past few moons was just how much anger I carried inside of me; anger I'd brought with me from Earth; anger that had boiled over here on Eos a few times already. I had a pretty good handle on it, most days, but a blowup here had far greater potential consequences than it would have in my old life in Midton, Ohio.

And not just for me.

"Did we make a mistake in supporting Kacellius?" I asked Miko in the quiet of our shared tent.

My nest-sister was a barely seen shape in the darkness, so when she tapped an arm, I had no way of knowing which one it was. I think she realized that, eventually, because she spoke.

"From what you have told me, Kacellius is an honorable man, while the soldiers he confronted are not. I do not think it is a mistake to support good people when and where we can."

Even if I hadn't heard the sibilance in her voice that told me she was speaking the synossian High Tongue instead of Trade, the perfect grammar would have made it clear. Miko had once asked me to remind her to speak in Trade, but as a language nobody on this continent even knew, the High Tongue was perfect for conversations we didn't want overheard.

"But what about the larger picture?" I asked. "Sakeld is apparently a small, poor, and weak barony. Any help they might offer with your people will be limited. Meanwhile, the duke is our single biggest hope for an ally. Angering members of his personal guard…" I shook my head. "I could have tried to play the peacemaker instead. Or at least not dragged you into the whole thing."

"I make my own decisions, nest-brother, and a Priestess of Aurea is more than just a healer. We are tasked with bringing the Dawn Maiden's light wherever we go. Sometimes, that means standing with those who need support. Other times, it means standing for those who need protection."

"I just don't want to poison the well for your people before they even arrive."

She paused. "*Poison the well?* Is that a saying from your home? Because even though it is new to me, it actually makes sense."

"It's from Earth, but I guess it would; wells are a thing on Eos too, after all."

"Yes." She made a sort of clicking noise with her forked tongue against sharp teeth. "I don't have answers as to what we should do, when, or how, any more than you do, Brian Fieldings. I have only what I was taught. I believe we must operate according to our consciences, but you are also right in that we must be judicious with the choices that we make."

I waited, knowing she had more to say, and she proved me right moments later.

"However, if the well that you are speaking of is metaphorical?"

"It is."

"Then it was already poisoned by my own people's actions a thousand cycles ago. We unleashed the Swarm, after all. We created the Waste. You have witnessed how the remnants of my people are treated here and how they seem all too comfortable in their own misery. A quarrel with a handful of soldiers, one of whom apparently has a reputation for trouble? It is a single additional drop in a well already thoroughly poisoned."

"The duke's different though, if his reputation holds true. I don't want to wreck his attitude toward the synossians."

"Our party saved his eldest daughter and heir. That will surely outweigh anything we have said or done on this journey."

She was right. I *knew* she was right. But having an entire people's fate resting on my shoulders was a pressure beyond anything I'd felt before. I'd spent years as my father's caretaker, wondering if *this* was the day something would go horribly wrong, if I wouldn't be there when it mattered, or if something *I* did would lead to his death. But my dad had been one man and his disease—*our* disease—had made that death inevitable anyway.

This was so much bigger than that. So much heavier.

Miko's words made sense, as usual, but the truth was I wasn't a teenager anymore. I wasn't a small-town kid dealing with high school bullies. I needed to be smarter, needed to pick and choose my moments. I wouldn't betray my conscience or my nest-sister's ideals, but there had to be a middle ground between doing that and diving headfirst into trouble every time it appeared.

Stick to the plan, I told myself. *Focus on what matters. Once the synossians are safe again, there will still be time to live your life.*

There wasn't anything more to say to that. Miko meditated first this time, and I watched over her. When it was my turn, I slipped easily into my mental review of the day, letting the experiences, good and bad, wash through me and over me, letting the Framework do its thing. Long minutes later, I opened my eyes again and stared at the screen that had appeared in front of me, the only thing visible in the darkness.

```
You have increased the following skills:

Minor skills:
Leadership (U) [+1]: 5/35
```

The Framework didn't make moral judgments. You could advance your skills by killing innocents just as easily as protecting them, provided the dangers were equivalent. As a result, nothing about a given skill-up indicated conscious approval or support.

Still, it was hard not to think I was doing *something* right.

5

Sakeld didn't conform to my expectations for what the seat of a barony should look like. In fact, it seemed pretty similar to Madea from the outside: a wall ringing a bunch of one-to-two-story buildings, most of them made of wood. Maybe it was a little bit larger, but not by much. The biggest difference was simply that it, unlike Madea, had been built on a hill.

I imagined even the small incline would be hell on farmers bringing their goods to market, but it also helped add a foot or so to the town wall's height and would make defending it even easier. That seemed a worthy tradeoff to me.

The other obvious difference wasn't in Sakeld at all, but outside it. Whereas the geography and soil quality had dictated that Madea's farms were almost all to the southwest and a good distance away, Sakeld was surrounded by farmland. We had spent almost two glasses following the road through such fields, some of them fallow, others simply dormant for the season, and still others showing the first growth of winter crops.

None of it screamed *abundance*, but it did suggest they'd have enough of a surplus to send emergency supplies to Madea. Between that and the Nameless Dead's arrival, I thought Mayor Aulson's town—and our friends there, by extension—would be in decent shape until the spring. And that was a relief for a variety of reasons. I'd never been a boy scout, but my dad, before his decline, had always said we should leave places better than when we found them. On Eos, just maintaining the status quo was already sufficient challenge.

Like Madea, Sakeld had sufficient space to temporarily house our whole group, although this time, it wasn't because so many people had recently died. Lieutenant Ender led Priest Humber and the duke's soldiers off to one of the town's two inns, while Kacellius escorted the rest of us through the town's winding streets and up to the flat peak of the hill where the baron lived.

I'd expected a keep or a castle or *something* with a moat. Instead, we got a small stable and a two-story house whose main distinctions were its size and that its first floor was made of stone rather than wood. Word of our arrival had clearly preceded us: two stableboys were waiting in the empty space that passed as a courtyard. They had the horses unhitched in moments.

An unarmed man in rich clothes met Kacellius with that distinctive shoulder-slapping salute and then turned to the nobleman emerging from the carriage.

"Lord Arbiter Hawthorne, Sakeld welcomes you once again. The baron is currently holding court, but you are of course invited to dine at his table when the judgments are done. In the meantime, we have rooms set aside in the manor for you and the Lady Willerton both."

Hawthorne nodded and waved a hand in the direction of Miko, Lace and I still an apparent afterthought. "We will need a third room as well, Steward Matheson. One that is situated near Lady Willerton's suite."

If the steward had any questions about who we were or why we were getting a room in his lord's manor, he didn't let them show. "Of course," he said, a snap of his fingers sending the young woman in the doorway scurrying back into the manor. "While that room is being prepared, I will escort you, the lady, and your respective servants to your appointed spaces, that you might refresh yourselves after the long journey."

"Very well." Hawthorne stepped down from the carriage, making space for Neesa to emerge with her ruffle-clad burden. They were followed by the carriage driver, who took up a guard position behind them both. The lord turned to the three of us, though his words were meant only for Miko.

"Wait here until your room is ready. Once you are situated, have a servant show you where the duke's heir is staying. If her condition unexpectedly worsens, you will be called upon to heal her. Otherwise, remain in your room unless summoned. Strangers in the baron's halls make his few remaining guards nervous."

He didn't wait for replies or even acknowledgment but simply spun about and entered the manor with the steward. Neesa and the guard followed swiftly.

"I'm starting to think that man doesn't like us," muttered Lace.

"I can't imagine why. We're such pleasant people, all of us."

"I fear I must report to my lord," said Kacellius, drawing near. "I will speak with him about setting aside time to discuss Madea's plight with you. And should there be insufficient space at his table tonight, I will also make sure that food and refreshments are sent to your room."

"Thanks, Kacellius." I found it hard to relax as I watched the tall knight disappear into the house. Other than the stableboys, currently caring for the horses in individual stalls, we were alone. Still, I could feel eyes on us from inside the manor.

There were times I felt kind of awkward about being a short, patchwork man carrying an overly long spear that looked to be one blow away from falling apart… but at least I was both human and relatively average looking. That made me the least noteworthy of our party. Most of the unseen eyes were no doubt reserved for the scowling Lace, who came from a notoriously savage people rarely seen north of the Waste, and for Miko, the representative of a thoroughly reviled species who nevertheless held herself with uncommon dignity and poise.

"A bath would be very nice," sighed the former shrine keeper, sticking with her steadily improving Trade. "Do you think they will have right kind of oil?"

"We can ask." Synossian scales offered a lot of advantages, especially in battle, but they also required a little more upkeep than human skin. While Miko still carried the stiff-bristled brush she used to really scrub the larger and tougher scales on her torso and legs, she'd run out of the last of the accompanying oil shortly before our departure from Madea.

Having tried the brush route once myself, I'd be a lot happier with good old-fashioned soap, even though the stuff they had on Eos was a far cry from *zestfully clean*.

A good while later, the same young woman we'd seen before returned with a nervous bow to take us to our room. We entered through a foyer that was larger than my dad's trailer in Ohio, went down a hall, up a stairwell, and past a half-dozen doors on the second floor. She ushered us through the seventh such door into a room with a canopy bed, a large table to one side, a fireplace on the other, and windows along the far wall.

"L-l-lord Arbiter Hawthorne has a-a-a-asked me to tell you that the L-l-lady Willerton is…" Her stutter grew only more pronounced as she tried to decide which of us to address: the scaled, an amazon, or the small man with his strange skin condition. Apparently, I was the safest option, as she ended up focusing on me. "…is d-d-down the hall."

"Thank you," I told her. "We'll stay here then until we're summoned?"

"Y-y-y—" Cheeks flaming, she gave up. With a hasty curtsey, she turned and fled.

"I think she like you," said Miko. "Like barmaid in Madea and tailor daughter in Harborton."

"I think she's just not used to guests."

"That seems like it would be a fatal flaw in a baron's maid," said Lace. The Marauder was already prowling through the room we'd been assigned, checking each of the windows in turn. "It's an easy drop to the courtyard below." Seeing my look, she added, "The first rule of adventuring is to always check your exits."

"Sounds a little bit paranoid."

"That's what makes it such a good rule."

It was hard to argue with that after all that we'd been through. Frankly, I was just glad Lace was talking.

I took my own survey of the room. There were no doors other than the one we'd come through. A chamber pot was in one corner, thankfully empty. If this was anything like the guild hall in Madea, the bathtubs would be in a separate room somewhere, but something told me it would be a bad idea to go searching for it on our own.

Maybe Carlson's words about the nobility *were* sinking in?

And then there was the bed. The one and *only* bed. It was larger and nicer than anything I'd seen in Harborton or Madea, but it wasn't anywhere near big enough for three people, even if we'd been that kind of party. I tried not to sigh as I lowered my pack to the bare floor where it wouldn't dirty the nearby rug. "You two can take the—"

A knock at the door interrupted me.

Lace was there almost before I could turn around, a hand on the hilt of one of her many knives. Like me, she'd replaced her lost longer blade, but if my lessons with Caleb had taught me anything, it was that you used the appropriate weapon, not just for the situation, but also for the space. And close quarters were tailor-made for knives.

The Marauder tugged open the door, then stepped back to allow two new servants—both men—to laboriously carry a copper tub into our room. Without a word, they set it up in front of the fireplace and left. Minutes later, they were back again, large buckets of steaming water in each hand.

I didn't know if they were former Aspirants or if their unknown profession gave them boosts to manual labor, but lugging all that water around the manor would have definitely taxed my twelve Strength. I fished a couple of copper bits out of my coin purse and went to meet them as they finished filling the tub.

"Thank you," I said, handing over my hard-earned copper. I wasn't sure if tipping was a thing in a baron's household, but the speed with which the men made the money disappear told me it was at least appreciated. And since I'd worked in the service industry my whole life, that was enough for me.

"Of course, sir," said the older of the two, pale eyes bright within a heavily lined face. "Is there anything we can get you or your companions?"

"If you have any oil for Priestess Naseri's scales, I know she would appreciate it," I said, pointing to Miko. "As for me, is there somewhere I can go to train? Any large open space would do, although I'd prefer it to be out of the way of foot traffic. Since I'm already dirty, I'd like to get some work in before I bathe."

The older servant hesitated, but the younger one smoothly filled in the gap. "There is the circle near the rear garden," he said. "I can take you there."

"Supper occurs promptly at the fifth evening bell," added the older gentleman. "That gives you a little less than three bells to also wash and dress."

I wasn't sure what bells had to do with time but just nodded. Someone was almost definitely going to insist on guiding me back to my room anyway; I'd let them figure out the schedule. In the meantime, I could give Miko and Lace some privacy for their respective baths.

If we weren't sharing a bed, we *definitely* weren't sharing a tub.

The older servant approached Miko to ask her about the type of oil she required, and I followed the younger one out into the hallway we'd so recently come through. Training was something I'd already let slide too much on this trip, and while I was in no danger of my combat skills degrading yet, I was certainly *feeling* rusty.

ooo

If the servant felt paranoid about having an armed adventurer at his back, he did a fantastic job of hiding it. We saw a second maid on our way back downstairs, and then passed a bustling kitchen dominated by a very thin woman armed with a wooden spoon. She wasn't precisely *yelling* at the other cooks, but her voice had a way of piercing the hubbub and bringing people to heel at the same time.

"Head Cook Temperance," said my guide, hurrying me along before either of us could fall under the woman's baleful eye. "She is usually *somewhat* less sharp-tongued, but we only received word of your group's impending arrival this morning. And then seven of you arrived instead of four."

"If it helps, my party and I would be happy to eat in our room. Although… Kacellius did say we'd get a chance to speak with Baron Sakeld."

"What Sir Kacellius says is usually what happens," agreed the servant. We'd followed this latest hall all the way to the back of the manor where a wooden door led us back outside. The gardens the servant had mentioned were visible to my left, though winter's embrace meant nothing was in bloom. A stone path led into the gardens, but we followed its other fork to an open dirt space surrounded by grass.

It wasn't quite the circle they'd described, but it was close.

"It's okay for me to train here?"

"Yes, sir. The old baron's father was an accomplished duelist and had this circle built to official specifications. Most of the guards train down in Sakeld's hall, of course, but our new lord practices here thrice a week with Sir Marten."

I wasn't sure who Sir Marten was, or why dueling circles had official specifications, but just nodded again. One thing I'd learned as a barista was that people loved to talk and it was easier to just let them do so than to ask questions or invite attention.

"If you don't need me for anything else, sir, I should probably assist with the feast preparations." His words were proper, but the look on his face was halfway between professional and pleading. Given what I'd seen of and heard from the ironically named Temperance, I could understand his pain.

"I don't suppose you're trained in the *Knife* or *Spear* skills?" I asked, throwing him a lifeline.

"I am not, sir… but I *have* watched the guards training a time or two?" He blushed as he said that for some reason.

"It sounds like I'd be a fool not to make use of your wealth of experience and knowledge then." I grinned and after a moment, he answered with a smile of his own. "But if we are going to be training partners, you should call me Brian. I'm not a knight and I'm from a small town where *formal* meant shoes *and* shirt."

"Brian it is then. And I'm Jaesun… called Jaesun the Small, on account of there being a bigger Jaesun who works with the hunters."

Jaesun the Small topped me by a good five inches, which would have put him at perfectly average height back home and made him maybe a little bit shorter than average here on Eos.

"Okay, Jaesun the Small." I spun my spear slowly in both hands as I took the center of the ring. "I'm going to start with the basic forms I was taught. Let me know if anything seems off."

○○○

Sometime later, I had moved past weapon forms and on to more experiments with *Lunge* when I heard what could only be described as a loud squawk from Jaesun's general vicinity. It was followed very quickly by actual words.

"My lord baron! Welcome! We were uhm—"

Danger Sense hadn't triggered, so I probably wasn't about to die for co-opting the baron's private training space. Then again, the skill was notoriously flaky, even maxed out and at Rare rank. I planted the butt of my spear in the earth, point facing skyward to make sure it wouldn't appear threatening, and turned.

Two men stood in front of a bowing and sweating Jaesun. The first was almost as tall as Kacellius and significantly wider, built like a giant brick that had decided to grow its own arms and legs. He wore a tabard over dark mail, and his boots were well worn, but nicer than anything I'd owned on two planets.

I had become way more conscious of people's footwear ever since I'd been forced to flee in bare feet from the snake titan, Nikkaali. Honestly, it was starting to feel like a problem.

The man's orange and white tabard bore the image of a two-headed deer standing before a fiery sun… and his broad, unsmiling face bore a mustache bushier than any deer's tail; it seemed like a minor miracle that he could breathe through the thing.

The boy—young man—at his side could only be Baron Sakeld himself. His attempts at a beard and mustache were far less impressive, but according to Kacellius, he had only recently had his Dreaming. That made him somewhere in the vicinity of ten cycles old, which put him around thirteen Earth years. I hadn't had much luck with facial hair at that age either. The baron was slim and wore clothes fancy enough for a wedding or a funeral.

"Brian Fieldings, I presume?" he asked, in a voice that bore all the trademarks of having until recently been high-pitched and was only now starting to head towards a deeper range.

"'Ware, my lord," said the mobile mountain at his side. "Remember your lessons. He is armed and remains unidentified."

"Are you suggesting that someone snuck onto our estate unnoticed, Marten?" For all the seeming brattiness in the baron's words, his bright blue eyes twinkled mischievously. "Could guards trained by you and Kacellius ever be so lax?"

"All things are possible," said the presumed Sir Marten.

"Oh very well." Baron Sakeld turned to Jaesun the Small. "Jaesun, can you confirm the identity of this man who not only fits the image of the adventurer Kacellius described but appears to wield precisely the described spear as well?"

"Uh… my lord?"

"His name, son," growled Marten.

"Oh. This is Brian, my lord. He asked for a place to train, and I knew your lordship didn't want anyone going down to the town until you'd met them, and so I uh…" Jaesun came to a teetering halt and started edging toward the manor. "Well, here we are. But I should be helping Head Cook Temperance, now that my task here is done."

"That you should," said the young baron, shooing the older teenager on his way. "Oh and Jaesun?"

A few feet from sanctuary, my guide and training partner froze. "Yes, my lord?"

"If Temperance asks where you've been, let her know you were performing a service for me. I don't know that it will save you entirely, but at the least, it should shield you from her tongue."

Baron Sakeld, I was realizing, was nothing like the thirteen-year-olds I'd known back home. And not just because he spoke like a drama student who'd been taking voice lessons on the side.

With Jaesun gone, the baron turned back to my sweaty self. "Will you walk with me, Adventurer Fieldings?"

He was stopped by Sir Marten's rumble. "My lord…"

"Oh fine." The young man waved a hand. "Could you put aside your spear and dagger first? While *I* would not ever worry about being attacked by someone spoken highly of by Sir Kacellius, Sir Marten takes my safety quite seriously."

The first lesson of the spear was that it went where I did. But I could understand the knight's concern, especially if I was going to spend time in close contact with the baron rather than speaking to him from across a larger and more defensible space. And frankly, I doubted I'd be able to carry weapons with me to visit the duke either. This was one lesson I'd have to be okay with breaking from time to time.

I took a careful step away from the baron, rotated the spear and thrust it down again, driving its point into the dirt. The weapon's uncommon sharpness made up for my limited strength; as I left it behind, it remained upright in the earth, looking like a branchless tree that had been struck by lightning and afflicted with some sort of terrible rot.

Whatever else the Buried necromancer's blood might have done to Riok's old weapon, it had robbed it of all its aesthetic appeal. That had led to me being underestimated a few times, which was good. It had also led to quite a bit of quiet mockery, which was… less enjoyable.

I unbuckled the sheath that held my new knife and placed it in the dirt next to the still quivering spear, and held both of my hands up, spinning around slowly as I presented myself to Sir Marten.

The big man gave a grunt, which was apparently more than enough for his charge, as Baron Sakeld crossed the space between us in an instant. Despite his age, he was already taller than me. I tried not to take that personally.

"We will tour the gardens," he announced grandly.

I was having a hard time holding on to all the dire warnings Carlson had given me about the nobility. Whatever his rank, Sakeld seemed every inch a too-young teenager, one part relentlessly instilled courtesy and three parts irrepressible goofiness.

I fell in next to him as we retreated to the fork in the path and headed toward the stunted-looking garden. Behind us, Marten was a shadow, just far enough away to give the illusion of privacy but close enough to bring his abilities to bear if something went wrong or I decided to attack the baron with my bare hands instead.

"What can I do for you, my lord?" I asked after about thirty seconds and three turns through what would probably seem a maze when the plants all had their leaves.

"One moment, please."

Two turns later, we reached a wooden bench carefully placed under the outstretched branches of a tree. Both trunk and branches were a silvery grey instead of brown, and despite the season, fresh buds dotted the branches above us.

Baron Sakeld hopped down onto the bench, heedless of the stains his tunic and pants collected in the process and motioned for me to join him. When I did so, he turned to me and grinned, all formality falling away. "Kacellius tells me you fought at the battle of Madea? Against actual blighted?"

"Yes, my lord."

He waved a hand. "We are men of action, you and I. Call me Eustace when we're alone. Kacellius spoke a little about what he saw and what you told him, but I wanted to hear the story from someone who was there in the thick of things. It seems so exciting!"

If he'd really been a man of action, he would have known, much like Kacellius himself, that there was nothing exciting about blood and death and pain, but it was surprisingly easy not to snap at him. I'd been young once, after all. Before Dad's diagnosis and then mine. And it wasn't like he hadn't known loss either; there was a reason he was a baron long before his time. So, I simply nodded—for probably the twentieth time that day—and told the story of Madea's near-destruction.

There were things I *didn't* share, of course. My origin on Eos as a Chosen. Details about Wilhemina and my ability to understand the twisted tongues of the various enemy species. Anything about Tempest, the artifact a dying Skaal had used to rout the blighted's final charge, and which Lace had taken as her own, even though she wouldn't be able to use it safely for multiple ranks.

Enchanted items were a big deal on Eos, and artifacts were the biggest of them all. The fewer people who knew of Lace's inherited weapon, the better for our party. Even the handful of witnesses in Madea had been told the spectral reavers had come from Skaal's technique, overcharged with his own lifeforce.

Still, if I withheld a few pieces of information, relying on my *Deception* skill to mask those omissions, I otherwise gave Eustace the unvarnished truth. By the time I was done, his eager smile was gone, his eyes were wide, and his face looked a little bit green. He didn't speak at first, but simply sat there in silence, digesting my words.

"That is a sad story," he finally said, speech lapsing into that of a boy rather than that boy's somewhat strange impression of a man. He swallowed a few times. "It's not like in the bards' songs, is it?"

"I guess not."

"Steward Matheson says a lord should never apologize, but I *am* sorry for the loss of your friends. I'm told Madea barely even considers itself part of the barony, but if we were larger or more prosperous… if we fielded more than two fists of soldiers and most of those hadn't been sent to Zaris to fight in the Grand Duke's war…"

"What happened at Madea wasn't your fault," I told him.

"Still." He looked despondent, then straightened up again as some fresh idea struck him. "Kacellius said the Nameless Dead were on their way to Madea."

It wasn't a question, but I answered anyway. "That's right. We passed them on our way here."

"They'll do for whatever remains of the blighted horde, no doubt. But I would like to help somehow. Maybe my knights and I could join—"

"Actually, there's something else you could do," I said, gently interrupting before that idea could take seed in the young man's brain. There was no way in hell Kacellius *or* Marten would look kindly on me encouraging the baron to leave his hometown and head into danger. "Something that *only* you can do."

"Really?" Eustace perked up, then deflated again almost as quickly as realization set in. "You mean sending supplies, don't you?"

"It's not glamorous or exciting, I know. But it'll save a lot more lives than a few additional swords. No matter how strong those swords might be," I added, doing my best to protect the boy's ego. "Anybody can stab things, but that won't make crops magically appear on fields that were overrun, and it won't put food on the tables of hungry families."

A bell chimed in the distance, six times, and the baron straightened. With a cough, he cleared his throat; his words took on the oddly formal affect he'd dropped when we first reached the bench. "I have heard you, Adventurer Fieldings, and will speak with my council on how best we can assist the people of Madea. But we have only one bell until supper, and I suspect we both have things to do before that time comes. Thank you for your tale."

Before I could reply, he was off the bench and headed for the manor. I followed at a more sedate pace, joined soon after by the ever-looming Sir Marten.

"Was I *too* honest?" I asked the big man. I was pretty sure he was at least Tin-ranked, like Kacellius, and I had *Lunge* prepared as an escape measure if he attacked.

"He needed to hear it from someone other than Kacellius and me," rumbled the knight, easing my nerves considerably. "At his age, it probably still won't sink in, but every step forward is a step earned."

We reached the dueling circle, and I reclaimed my spear and the dagger in its sheath. Sir Marten cleared his throat.

"We do not have many soldiers in our barony, but we do have a Smith and a well-stocked armory. If you would like to trade in your spear for something sturdier, I can make that happen."

"Thank you, but this is an heirloom," I told him.

"So be it. Still, I would strongly suggest *not* stabbing it into the earth. Even the best-made bronze can bend or deform when poorly used, and your weapon appears to have suffered a significant amount of corrosion at some time."

"You're right," I agreed, even though both spearhead and shaft had proven to be damn near indestructible. Tempest wasn't the only item worth keeping secret. Riok's spear had been a thing of deadly beauty before the necromancer, but since that battle, it had shown signs of becoming something significantly better.

And hell if I was going to ever let *anyone* take it from me.

6-Interlude

Lace remained in the copper bathtub until long after the water had cooled, eyes closed but senses alert for any intruders. Little Miko had been summoned to heal the girl and that left their assigned bedroom feeling empty and still.

Empty was good.

Still, on the other hand… was difficult.

Skaal would have said—

She shook her head, braids swishing about. It didn't matter what the reaver would have said. It didn't even matter what they had both left *un*said. All that mattered was the blood that was owed. Since their flight from the Dusk Panthers, the son of the storm had been her clan and her home. Two Coppers had conspired to take that from her. One was now worm food in the fields outside Madea. The other… the other would bleed enough to flood the Waste.

And will that make you happy, daughter of dusk?

She shook her head a second time, trying to ignore that voice, the words of a foolish, shortsighted, maddening treasure of a man. He was dead. He'd given up his freedom for her, she'd given up her name for him, and then he'd had to go and ruin it all by dying while she was too weak to save him, too weak to even be up on the wall as an unranked did what she could not.

Brian Fieldings is a Chosen. The world will bend around him in a way it does not us.

More words that she didn't want to hear, not here and now when there was nothing to drown them out.

She sprang to her feet in the tub, splashing ice-cold water onto the floor, and stood there shivering, the winter sun tracing the many pale scars in her skin. Brian was the only Chosen she'd ever met, likely the only Chosen to walk Eos in the last five hundred cycles, but his circumstances didn't excuse her weakness.

Not then and not now.

Her clan had stripped her names from her when she fled with Skaal. Lace was the only name she'd earned since, and her failure in Madea threatened to cost her even that. Her people had little patience for the weak and her goddess had none at all.

The clothes she pulled on were as black as her mood, the cloth-wrapped weapon, Tempest, a weight across her back. Using *Stealth*, she slipped into the hallway and past a dirt farmer servant who never knew she was there, would never have seen the blade coming if Lace had chosen to strike. She traced the steps Brian Fieldings had taken, down to the first floor, past a kitchen filled with enough chaos to make the Night Hag smile, and out again into the tamed wilderness these soft northerners called gardens.

The Chosen was busy training, still slow, still awkward as any unranked would be, but leagues better than when they had first met. That was more than the four levels he had gained; it was the real-world experience of fighting for his life in a wide range of situations. She could see the intentionality in his movements, the awareness that true combat was a balancing act on the dagger's edge, that any misstep would end in death.

He was learning, and at a furious pace, but he remained far too weak. He and little Miko were both too weak. Still, at least *they* had the excuse of being unranked.

Like a wraith, she swept past her party member and the moon-eyed servant watching him train, slipped unnoticed to the far edge of the property, to the beginning of the downward slope that would lead to the town below. Beyond Sakeld's buildings was the town wall, and beyond that wall were farms and then the wilderness where challenges awaited, challenges that would do more than wet her blades and temporarily sate her anger.

Her skills were ready, but her soul needed strengthening.

She needed to level.

She needed to march on toward Copper.

To do either of those things, she needed to kill, but there was nothing to kill and no time to do it, not here in the baron's manor, in the midst of these soft dirt farmers.

There is a time for killing and a time for reflection.

It was easier to ignore the words of a dead man out here in the open, where the world was empty but not quite so still. To stop moving was to fall and she had already fallen once. A second time might be her last and she refused to meet her next life with vengeance unclaimed. A hunter was patient, yes, but she had buried that patience in Madea. What remained was purpose, and Brian Fieldings was not the only individual with a connection to the divine.

Lace lowered herself to the stiff grass and activated *Night Hag's Embrace*, the technique she'd been granted in her Dreaming.

If Hashoggath had stirred for another god's Chosen, the nine-breasted demon goddess could damn well listen to her sworn daughter's plight.

7

I returned to my shared room to find it empty. Miko was almost definitely away healing Wilhemina, but as for Lace? Hell if I knew. None of the windows looked to have been opened, so she'd at least left through the door like the rest of us.

Nobody in our party was particularly good at following Lord Arbiter Hawthorne's instructions.

The bath was still present in front of the fireplace but was now empty of water. Given how filthy even Miko had been, I was guessing someone had emptied and refilled the tub after each bath, but I didn't know where that well was or how the water had been heated before it was brought in.

So, I headed back out into the hall, leaving my spear behind but keeping my knife, and flagged down a harried-looking maid. It wasn't until she stopped that I realized she was the same young woman who'd initially led us to our room.

"Sorry to bother you," I told her, "but could you show me where to get water for my bath? I was busy training when they brought the water by earlier and I still need to clean up before supper."

Her eyes went wide, and she shook her head so furiously I thought her linen coif would fly off.

"N-n-no, sir!"

"You can't show me where to get water?"

"It w-w-wouldn't be p-p-p-"

I was pretty sure the word she was going for was *proper*, but jumping ahead might just make her feel worse. So, I waited.

"-proper, sir!"

Nailed it.

"I will s-s-s-end s-s-s—" She grimaced and wrinkled her nose in frustration. "*Someone* to help."

"Thank you. That would be—"

She was already on her way.

"—great," I finished, feeling dumb as I stood there alone in the hallway. After a moment, I gave up and retreated to my room.

Neither Lace nor Miko had returned by the time the water showed up. There were two men again, one of whom I recognized from earlier. Jaesun the Small, on the other hand, failed to make a second appearance and had almost definitely been put to work in the kitchens.

Once the tub was full and I was alone again, I stripped out of my dirty clothes. I didn't see a hamper or laundry chute, but I also didn't see any piles of cast-off clothing from Miko and Lace, so there was clearly *some* setup for getting our clothes cleaned. I dropped mine on the floor near the door, keeping them off the area rug that, though worn and a bit faded, was still probably ludicrously expensive to clean.

And then it was just me, the tub of water, and a somewhat lopsided chunk of soap. The groan I made slipping into the hot water would have no doubt scandalized Jaesun the Small, the stuttering maid, *and* Head Cook Temperance. Or maybe not. If my time in Madea had taught me anything, it was that at least some of the people of Eos were way less repressed than my neighbors back home.

Regardless, if there was a skill available for vegetating in a bath just a shade shy of too hot, I was going to dedicate a significant portion of my new life to earning it.

Sadly, there were things to do in the meantime. I stood, scrubbed the sweat from my body, dunked myself back in the bath, and then repeated the process a second and third time to tackle the underlying dirt. There was even soil under my fingernails, raising the possibility that the pretty maid had been terrified rather than attracted.

In retrospect, it was kind of amazing that Baron Sakeld had even opted to share a bench with me. Either he had a head cold and couldn't smell at all, or he was way more polite than I'd realized.

By the time I was done cleaning, the water in the copper tub looked like something from a horror film and the appeal of lounging in it had long since faded. I stepped out and onto the cold wooden floor. Towels on Eos were linen and flat but served their purpose well enough; within a few minutes, I was reasonably dry and pulling on fresh clothes from the bottom of my pack. Everything else got dumped out on the floor with the outfit I'd just taken off.

If there was laundry service, I'd leverage it to the hilt.

Of course… that meant the clothes-washer probably deserved a tip too. My lifetime of scrimping and saving back on Earth briefly warred with my better impulses. Money was easier to come by on Eos than it had been in Midton, Ohio, but that didn't mean I could be careless with it.

There had been no question about Skaal's share going to Lace, or that Mordecai's was earmarked for his lost love at the Crimson Needle. Even so, Miko and I had two plugs and seven bits remaining between us, with a bank notice for another nine plugs that we could withdraw at any location in the kingdom. With ten copper bits to a plug, ten plugs to a silver tower, and ten towers to a golden crown, we almost had a full tower to our names. And that was *without* counting whatever reward we received from Wilhemina's father. A copper bit here and there was certainly affordable.

Still, I made a mental note to find Jaesun and get some clarification on how all this stuff worked before we offended someone, or I ended up destitute again.

Dry and dressed, I settled into the room's only chair. Several days' worth of facial scruff meant I probably looked more beast than human, but without a mirror or fresh water, I wasn't going to put my shaky straight razor skills to the test. I still had Kacellius' copy of *Meditations on Mortality* but lacked the time to really get into any of its poems again. So instead, I closed my eyes and let the day's experiences cycle through me. It was extremely unlikely that my training session would have netted me any gains—even with the questionable assistance of Jaesun the Small—but if it had, I might as well lock them in now.

This was the first time I'd meditated during the day since leaving Madea and some changes immediately became clear. First, I was highly conscious of the world around me: the sounds and the smells especially. Normally, that would be a problem—half my difficulty in learning the practice had been figuring out how to let those other senses go—but this time, it didn't hamper my meditation in the slightest. Even as I parsed through what I'd done for the day, letting those actions drift up the Framework's metaphysical pipeline to the soul, a part of me remained aware.

Long minutes later, the door to our room opened, and the clicking of claws against wooden floors, accompanied by the scent of some kind of perfumed oil, told me Miko had returned. Footsteps marched up and down the hall as servants tackled the hundreds of things needed to keep a manor this size running every day. And outside, the stableboys laughed as they chased each other around the courtyard.

When I finally opened my eyes again, I wasn't even that bothered by the lack of any fresh skill gains. Because I was pretty sure I'd figured out what ranking up *Meditation* had gotten me.

And it didn't suck.

Miko was there waiting, as I'd known she would be. Her orange eyes widened as I told her what I'd discovered.

"Retaining awareness of the physical realm while communing with the Framework would be invaluable," she said. "Do you think you'll even be able to end the process early, if need be?"

"I can't imagine why not." That had been the single biggest risk with meditation and why one of us was always watching over the other. Once you entered the process, you were deaf and blind to the world around you, and that made you vulnerable. This... potentially changed all of that. "And if we can get the skill up to Rare, we might be able to do even more."

"Like meditate while doing other things?"

"Exactly." It would be one hell of a cheat code.

"I must tier up my *Meditation* skill," she decided. "Will you read the poems to me again?"

"Absolutely. We can—"

Our planning was interrupted by a knock on the door. The older servant who'd filled both of our baths stood there, looking harried.

"Supper will be served shortly," he told us. "I am here to take the three of you to the banquet hall."

"That sounds good. Only I'm not sure where—"

"Let's go," said Lace from the hallway, causing both the servant and me to jump. "I'm hungry."

The Marauder looked like a shadow given life, the black of her outfit matching the color of her skin, but I was certain she hadn't been there a second earlier.

Mostly certain.

○○○

The banquet hall wasn't large or ornate enough to really merit the name, but it did hold two tables, a rectangular one up on a raised platform, and a circular one down on the floor and closer to the door. Wilhemina and Neesa were absent, but Hawthorne was already seated at the rectangular table, along with Kacellius, Marten, and an apple-cheeked blonde in a green dress who looked to be the second knight's wife. Both of the baron's men had removed their armor and now wore simple tunics in Sakeld's colors, while the grey-haired lord arbiter stood out in a rich, fur-lined black coat, red silk tunic, black pants, and boots that shined in the torchlight.

It was a little showy for my taste—more 70's Harlem pimp than he'd ever know—but I couldn't deny that Hawthorne had style. And the money to support that style. Older women might even find him handsome if he ever remembered to smile.

There were four empty chairs at that table, but we were guided to the circular table below instead. It seemed class hierarchy was sometimes taken literally here on Eos. At the low table, we were seated next to a man whose oft-broken nose and sizable build suggested he was one of the guardsmen under Kacellius and Marten's command. The woman squeezing his enormous paw of a hand had her pale hair up in a bun and wore a dress that was both simple and threadbare in places. She was doing her best not to stare at the hall around her even as she whispered excitedly to her date.

The man's name was Isaac, and he was new to the baron's service, hired on in the past moon to help bolster Eustace's guard with so many men away in Zaris. His wife, Camilda, was the primary apprentice to Sakeld's lone midwife, and extremely concerned with not embarrassing her husband. Neither had ever been invited to eat with the baron's family before and while it seemed like they were only there to help fill the second table that had been added for our party, they were clearly thrilled to be included.

I liked them both immediately, and that feeling stayed when they welcomed the three of us—Miko included—without visible reservation.

At our guide's request, I'd left my spear in the bedroom, but I wasn't the only person with a knife on his belt. Lace had one in sight, with another half-dozen no doubt tucked out of sight. Miko, on the other hand, still had her staff, because she was Miko, and ten minutes of unbiased time with her was apparently enough for anyone to realize she meant no harm. Of us all, Kacellius and Marten were the only people with longer weapons, swords sheathed and hanging from the backs of their chairs.

The barony's continued lack of manpower was made evident by the absence of anyone standing guard in the room or even at the door. Still, there were enough weapons and Aspirants present that I felt confident we'd have a fighting chance if someone attacked. And a *Flare* from Miko and a careful usage of *Lunge* would get me back out into the hall if I needed to run to our room to retrieve my spear.

Exactly *why* someone would want to attack the teenage baron, and *how* they'd get into the manor unnoticed in the first place were both great questions I couldn't answer. It seemed Lace wasn't the only one feeling paranoid. Which reminded me … I scanned the chamber for additional exits, finding a wide door near the back of the hall. Unless our theoretical attackers managed to surround us, there'd be an available escape route at hand.

We'd barely finished the introductions at our table when Steward Matheson and his considerably younger and prettier wife made their appearance. Both climbed onto the dais, where the man seated his partner then turned to the room. His voice was grave and formal, pitched to carry across vastly larger spaces.

"The Lord Sakeld and his mother, the Lady Sakeld."

Everyone around us stood up, so we did too, just in time for Eustace to make his way into the room through the rear door, followed by a middle-aged woman with a thin face and sad eyes. The young baron had changed again and was now wearing his own surcoat in orange and white, while his mother wore a simple, if visibly well-made, black dress.

For all the quality of the tailoring, neither outfit held a candle to Hawthorne's. I didn't know if they adopted a simpler style out here on the frontier or if a noble from the capital was just that much better off than a provincial baron and his family.

It kind of felt like a bit of both.

Eustace helped his mother to her chair and then took his own seat at the head of the table. After a pause in which I could practically see him counting the seconds in his head, he nodded to the rest of us.

"Please, be seated."

○○○

Dinner stretched out over five full courses. While several members of the high table picked at their food—Hawthorne and Lady Sakeld among them—the two knights and Marten's wife all dug in with abandon and our table was quick to follow their example. After multiple days on the road with cold rations, I was ready for something more substantial, and what Temperance had produced on a few hours' notice was on par with anything we'd gotten from Madea's taverns.

While training, I'd come up with some wild ideas of what a meal with the noble class would be like, but the reality was relatively mundane. There was no entertainment, because Sakeld didn't have a bard in residence… although the addition of our second table meant there wouldn't have been sufficient room anyway. There was only a single toast, given by the steward at the start of the meal, and everyone at the low table had been served cups of warm fruit juice rather than alcohol.

For the most part, people just ate and talked, the conversations that took place at the high table far too quiet to hear over the sounds of our own supper.

As things began to wind down, the young baron rose to his feet. "Please," he said, in his somewhat stilted fashion, "eat until you are full and then rest well. I will escort the Lady Sakeld back to her room."

His mother hadn't, as far as I had been able to tell, uttered a single word through the entire meal, but as she took her son's arm, she gave him a small pat of encouragement. Standing, she was a head taller than Eustace but had a way of fading into the background even as they departed.

Despite the baron's words, the steward's pointed look toward our table made it clear that supper *would* be ending shortly. Camilda picked up on that subtext, even if Isaac didn't, and a few hushed words had the bigger man mopping up the last of his plate with a crust of bread.

"It was a privilege to meet actual adventurers," she told us brightly, her sweetest smile reserved for Miko, who sat on her left. "May the Seven Sons and Daughters watch over you all on your travels."

I waited until we had made it back to our room before I turned to Lace. "Seven Sons and Daughters?"

There were five gods in the synossian pantheon if you included lost Synos himself. Since coming to the Great Wilds, I'd heard Tantalas call out to the Twelve in Harborton, mention of an anointed trinity, and more than a few people had sworn by or against the Nine Demon Gods and Goddesses, but seven? Seven was a new number of deities.

She shook her head. "Human gods, I think. The immortal children of Corros who survived his banishment after the war."

"How many gods are there in total?"

"Hashoggath is the only one I concern myself with." After a moment, she relented. "Hundreds, I think. Maybe more."

"That's… a lot."

"There are dozens and dozens of pantheons, most with strict guidelines on how their faithful should live their lives. Meanwhile, the Night Hag has only a simple creed."

Remembering our monstrous encounter with the nightmarish nine-breasted demon goddess, I wasn't going to ask. Unfortunately, Miko was curious enough for both of us.

"What creed?"

"Do what you will and do it to them before they do it to you."

"Oh," said my nest-sister.

Lace's smile was savage. "You should know that Trynfall is sometimes referred to as the city of a thousand gods. Wilhemina's father is as open to other faiths as he is to other species. I hear it makes for an interesting experience for those who live there."

"In other words, keep on our toes," I extrapolated.

"With one hand on your purse and the other on a blade."

Lovely.

It had already been a very long day, but a sixteen Vitality meant it didn't wear on me nearly as heavily as it once might have. Lace was here and communicating, so it seemed like the ideal time to check in with her and see how she felt about our forced detour to the duchy's capital.

But first, I'd promised that I'd read Miko some more poems from *Meditation on Mortality*. After all, it was important to keep your word… and not *just* because it put off a delicate conversation with the Tin-ranked woman whose goddess' motto boiled down to 'get them first or else.'

The Marauder didn't seem interested in our book club, even after I'd told her about my Uncommon rank in *Meditation.* While I read the poems to Miko and the two of us shared our takes on what the speaker had meant, Lace pursued her own brand of self-education: juggling knives. Poisoned knives, if the green glow that came and went around some of the dancing blades meant what I thought it did.

She didn't drop any of the weapons, which was good. She didn't cut herself either, which was probably even better. Still, it was distracting.

After a long stretch of poetry study, I decided I couldn't put off the discussion any longer. I closed Kacellius' book and put it on the desk, then turned to our party leader.

She was still juggling. At some point, she'd added in a paper weight I hadn't even noticed her steal from the desk. There were six objects in the air now, and while only a couple were still glimmering green, they were all differently shaped or weighted. I didn't know how to juggle—Mike Pritchard of Pritchard's Coffee & Baked Goods would have said I couldn't multi-task at all and found it riotously funny—but I was pretty sure it got harder the more the items varied.

There didn't seem to be a perfect time to interrupt so I just went for it. "Do you think—"

A knock sounded at the door, so quiet and timid I almost couldn't hear it.

"If that's the maid who fancies you," said Lace, "remind her you're already sharing this room with two other people."

I didn't roll my eyes, but only because she'd have seen it and pissing her off when she wasn't in a great headspace seemed dumb. I did get up though and went to answer the door. Because even if my disease meant I wasn't looking for romantic attachments, the maid had been sweet in her own way, and I didn't want to leave her with a bad impression of adventurers.

Except… when I opened the door, it wasn't a young woman at all, but an even younger man, still dressed in his baron best.

"Eus—" I started to say, but he was already slipping past me into our room. He stopped dead at the sight of the still-juggling amazon, shook his head, and headed for the far corner.

I'd been informed recently that I wasn't a great judge of people or social niceties, but I was *pretty sure* he wanted me to join him over there. So I did.

"How can I—"

He waved with both hands as if trying to calm an irritated phloxl, and then, when I didn't get it, frowned and put a finger to his lips.

Fair enough. I tried again, this time speaking at a whisper. "How can I help you, Lord Sakeld?"

His voice was even quieter than mine and had lost its veneer of sophistication entirely. "Can I trust you, Brian? One man to another?"

I still remembered being thirteen, so I kept a straight face and gave it the consideration the question deserved.

"Yes," I said, when I figured enough time had passed. "I mean… we just met, and I've been told my Discernment attribute is not up to popular standards, but you seem like a good guy. And Kacellius speaks highly of you, which means a lot on its own. If you need something and it won't cause harm to anyone, I can try to make it happen."

"That's exactly what I need. And it won't. Cause harm, that is. At least I don't think so. It shouldn't!"

For the first time since she'd started, Lace almost dropped a knife. As she fell back into rhythm, I could see her shoulders shaking with silent laughter.

"Why don't you tell me what it is," I offered, "and I'll tell you if I can help?"

"You're headed to Trynfall, right? With the lord arbiter?"

"We are, yes. To see Lady Willerton safely home to her father."

"Good, good. What I need you to do is in Trynfall."

I waited. Eustace was only ten cycles old and gave every impression of being nice and polite, if slightly under-socialized. Even after all this build-up, how bad could his request be?

"There's a girl, you see," he finally said.

And just like that, I started to worry.

"A girl?"

"Yes. Elina. Elina d'Kay. She's the fifth daughter of a minor landed noble and currently serves as a handmaiden to Earl Marchon's eldest." He blew out a breath and finally met my gaze, as if that had answered everything.

It hadn't.

"And…?" I prompted.

"Oh. Uhm." He patted his bony chest in a momentary panic and then found and retrieved something from beneath his surcoat. Several sheets of parchment had been folded into thirds, then enclosed within another piece of parchment that was sealed with wax. Pressed into that seal was what I could only assume to be his official seal. He held the letter in both hands, took another deep breath, and held it out to me. "I need you to deliver this to Elina."

"Is it a declaration of war?"

"What? No!" For a moment, he forgot to keep his voice down.

"Some sort of black-market trade proposal then?"

This time, he just stared at me.

"I'm trying to figure out why you need an adventurer you just met to deliver it instead of giving it to Hawthorne or having it sent to the capital via a courier," I explained.

"Where do you hail from?" he asked.

"A very, very long way away."

"And do you have nobility there or some archaic and lesser form of government?"

I cleared my throat. "The nobility exists, sort of, but I haven't had much contact before now."

"That explains it then. Within our kingdom's nobility, there are... formal *rules* regarding what my mother would call the *fraternization of near equals*. Adults might encourage the occasional dalliance with commoners," he added, shaking his head with a mystified look on his face, "but if you should find someone of a noble line who is utterly brilliant and has the best ideas for parties, every word and action must suddenly be monitored, scrutinized, and controlled."

"You like this Elina."

"Yes. We met before. A few times, before my father..." He coughed and looked away. "I have been thinking about her a great deal these past few moons. I want to know if she feels the same way."

"And you can't tell your mother? Maybe she could arrange a match or something?" I was floundering, admittedly. I'd never seen *Downton Abbey* and only vaguely remembered reading Jane Austen's *Emma* for English class.

"You really don't understand at all. She's a *fifth daughter*. If Elina..." His frustration had him pacing back and forth in front of me. "It's all in the letter I wrote. She will understand. I am hoping to renew our friendship. If we do still have that connection—if she feels the way I think she must—then I swear I will broach the situation with my mother, social standing be damned. But I cannot risk bringing shame upon my house by making this a public concern. Not until I know for sure."

"I see."

"Will you help me then, Adventurer Brian? Please?"

I waited for the now-familiar quest window to appear, but there was nothing. Apparently, the gods, or the Framework, or whoever kept sending me tasks didn't care about some newly raised teenage baron on the kingdom's easternmost frontier.

That realization, more than anything, had me nodding.

"I'll see it delivered."

"You will?"

I nodded again before I could second-guess myself. "Yes."

"Elina d'Kay. Of House d'Kay."

"Got it." And I did, at least partly because the name was written in exceedingly careful calligraphy on the parchment that served as a makeshift envelope.

Eustace handed over the letter and sagged, all the tension fleeing his body. "Thank you. I know our barony is not the most impressive, but you will have an ally in House Sakeld. I promise you that. And if there comes a time when you should need our aid—"

"Actually, there *is* something you could help me with."

"Already?!" He colored. "I mean… of course. What is it that you need?"

"You're familiar with the noble families of this and other kingdoms, right?" I asked, examining the letter in my hands and the impression that had been made in the wax seal.

"The notable houses, yes. If I was not, Steward Matheson would have me studying even now instead of sleeping… like I'm supposed to be doing."

"Good." I retrieved my pack and dug through it to find the signet ring we'd stolen from the desk of the Ever-Hungry's High Priest. "Does this signet mean anything to you then?"

Eustace frowned and took the ring from me, turning it about in his hands. "Some sort of winged creature. And is that fire?"

"I think so."

After a few minutes, he shook his head, looking frustrated. "I do not know it. It might be from a smaller house or it might be from somewhere other than our kingdom and its neighbors."

"Do you think it could be from Zaris?"

"No."

"No?"

"Before its annexation, Zaris was a merchant nation. They did not have a noble class, and their merchant clans prefer geometric sigils to animal-based iconography."

"Huh." Maybe he *did* know his stuff. That made it even more pressing to find out who it belonged to. Carlson and I had assumed it had something to do with Wilhemina's kidnapping. If some nation other than Zaris was responsible, the duke would want to know.

Especially since he'd just conquered Zaris in retaliation.

"I am sorry I could not be of greater service," said Eustace.

"A lord is never supposed to apologize, remember?" That won me a grin that made him look every bit his age. "It's okay. Sometimes, learning what something isn't is the first step to finding out what it is."

"That is… both wise and confusing," he admitted. "I will have to try it out on Steward Matheson and see how he reacts. But I should return to my room now before my absence is noted." He didn't salute me—I wasn't sure that was allowed—but did offer a regal sort of nod. "If I am unable to speak with you before your departure tomorrow, please travel safely. Take with you my thanks and my assurance that I will do all I can for the people of Madea."

"By sending supplies," I prompted.

He scowled but quickly relented. "Yes, yes, with the supplies they need rather than the swords they do not."

"Thank you, Lord Sakeld."

Another slow nod. "Farewell, adventurers. If a bard visits Sakeld, I will commission a song of your deeds on the walls of Madea."

With that frankly ominous promise, he slipped out into the hall and was gone.

There was a moment of silence.

"If this love letter gets us all killed, I'm going to petition the Night Hag for governance of your eternal torment," announced Lace, making a show of tucking her blades back into various hiding spots on her body. "In the meantime, blow out the candles; I'm going to bed. Whichever of you will be sharing the bed with me tonight, remember this: I am always armed."

I traded glances with Miko.

It seemed like I wouldn't be having that talk with the Marauder after all.

8

Breakfast the next morning was cold bread and sliced fruit, served in our respective rooms. Soon after, we were on our way. Baron Sakeld met us in the courtyard, flanked by his two knights, and looking appropriately sleepy for someone whose Vitality hadn't been bolstered yet by multiple levels. While the horses were being hitched to the carriage, the baron and lord arbiter exchanged a few clearly ceremonial words of farewell. Then, Eustace retreated into his manor with Sir Morant, and Kacellius guided us down the hill into the town, then over to the western gate.

The duke's men were waiting outside the wall, even though the sun had yet to make its formal appearance in the eastern skies. At least a few of the soldiers—Jenkins and his crew included—looked positively green in a way I recognized from Mordecai's own late-night benders. Miko would *probably* have healed their hangovers, if they'd asked, but I doubted the thought would ever occur to them, and I sure as hell wasn't going to suggest it.

I returned *Meditations on Mortality* to Kacellius with a fair bit of reluctance and a promise to Miko to find a new copy when we made it to Trynfall. The knight made his farewells, and then our column was on its way.

Outside the wall, we found a flour mill, and beyond that, encountered only fields, farmers already out and working their land. Some of the larger properties had bits of land fenced off, phloxl and other domesticated beasts roaming about within. It was almost idyllic as long as we didn't get too close to the livestock. Harborton had been dominated by smells of the sea, especially fish. In the spring and summer, I could imagine that Sakeld would be all earth and growing things and… well, *manure*.

Farm life was farm life, both here and back on Earth.

The western road was half again as wide as the one between Sakeld and Madea and far more heavily trafficked. We passed some of those farmers driving their goods to market and at least one merchant and his wagon. Miko tried waving but didn't get any responses beyond the occasional suspicious look; she eventually settled into the march beside me.

It took a glass or two to move beyond the farmland. Trees started to show up again, small copses that eventually gave rise to full-on forest. By midday, we were deep in the woods. Instead of farmers, we now encountered the occasional hunter, either making the long hike into town to sell their game or disappearing off into the forest with hungry eyes and full quivers.

A glass or two later, and even that traffic had petered out. Living a long way from civilization was probably less attractive on Eos, given all the very many things that wanted to kill and eat us.

Even without the poetry book, I did my best to practice *Meditation* as we walked, but it seemed my Uncommon rank in the skill wasn't up to the task. I couldn't reach that perfect flow state I'd managed while stationary. My thoughts wandered and my feet did too and neither one seemed to bring me any closer to a connection with the Framework.

By evening, I'd given up. By the time we stopped for the night, I'd put together a different plan. Leaving Miko and Neesa by the fire, I went in search of Lace.

One of the scouts pointed me in the right direction, but even then, I almost missed her. The Marauder's tent had been pitched just off the road where it seamlessly blended into the undergrowth near a large, leafless tree. Of the woman herself, there was no sign… not until a low whistle had me craning my head to spot a shadow perched in one of that tree's larger branches.

"Always look up," she said, dropping soundlessly beside me. "There are plenty of creatures that climb, and even more that fly. And most of them want you dead."

"So far, that's been true for the ones who couldn't climb or fly too, but point taken. That's part of why I came looking for you."

"I'm listening."

I had to take her word for that, given how dark it was this far from camp.

"I uh… wanted to check in with you. How are you feeling about our detour to Trynfall? I know it's a delay we weren't expecting."

"We don't have much choice if we want to get paid. And we *need* to get paid if we're going to hunt down Arrius." I could feel her eyes on me even if I couldn't see them. "Which we're going to do."

"Of course we are."

"And after the Copper is dead, maybe this duke can help you and little Miko out with your other problem. Assuming there really are shiploads of scal—of *synossians* on the way."

I wanted to doublecheck our surroundings, just to make sure we were alone, but I still couldn't see a damn thing. And Lace knew better than to talk about such things where anyone could hear. We'd filled her in on our respective situations in one of the few conversations that had occurred following the defense of Madea, a conversation Lace had insisted on after learning that I was a Chosen. The amazon hadn't batted an eye when we'd explained the magnitude of the task ahead of us… but she hadn't dedicated her services to the cause either.

"That's the hope," I admitted. "That he'll be willing to help, I mean."

"And there you have it. But what does this have to do with—" She paused. "Were you worried that *I* was one of the creatures who wanted you dead?"

"What? No. Not unless my part-time courier gig gets us in trouble, anyway." I shook my head. "They're totally different topics. You're the party leader; I wanted to make sure you were good with how things were going."

"As long as it brings us closer to killing Arrius, I will be fine."

If ever a sentence could be both convincing *and* concerning, that was it.

"As for the other thing I wanted to talk about…" I shrugged. "I need to get stronger."

"Yes. You do." After a moment, she allowed. "We *all* do."

"Well, there are still multiple seven-days until we reach Trynfall. I don't want to waste those days. And since there doesn't seem to be a skill for walking, and we for once seem to be lacking in life-or-death situations, I figured I should try working on something else."

"Such as?"

"Scouting. Hunting. Even juggling, maybe? If anything is going to help me improve my Finesse naturally, that would do it."

"You came to me in the dead of night to learn how to juggle knives?"

I flushed. "I meant during the day sometime. And I wanted to ask you to take me with you when you go scouting. Miko's able to use her class abilities with Wilhemina and make some progress on the next level. I'm not that lucky, so I need to find something I can do. I'll improve my foundation if I can't add an attic."

"The clans have lived in the jungle for hundreds of cycles, Brian Fieldings. Our homes are tents not much larger than the one you're using. Save your strange construction metaphors for the longbeards and dirt farmers."

"If I can't level up, I need to broaden my knowledge base," I translated. "New skills. Physical or mental exercises to improve my attributes. But both things require opportunity and instruction."

"And you want me to provide them?"

"You *are* the party leader."

If she was grinding her teeth, she was doing it very quietly. And if she was preparing to stab me instead, *Danger Sense* was flaking out again, because I couldn't sense a thing.

"Fine. I'll speak to Quincy about you joining me tomorrow." I couldn't see her at all, but her ability to see in the dark let her read the confusion on my face. "He's Hawthorne's lead scout."

"Thank you."

"Don't thank me yet. You'll be traveling half again as much as the rest of the people in this unit and through the woods, not on a soft northerner's road. Even in those boots, your feet will hate you for it. As for juggling…" I heard a soft swish that almost had to be her braids. "We'll start with two knives and then proceed from there."

"I was thinking we could try something that wouldn't maim me. Like pinecones maybe?"

"If you wanted safety, little Miko's gods brought you to the wrong world."

ooo

That was how the next two days went. I woke up with the rest of the camp, but sometime during the day, Lace would come by, and I would leave Miko and Priest Humber behind to venture into the woods. Even before we'd reached Madea, I'd become familiar with the Marauder's teaching style. It had worked wonders in netting me the *Stealth* skill and had been completely unhelpful when I was trying to learn *Knife* instead.

I just had to hope this would be more like the first than the second.

At the end of those two days, my feet hurt, my head hurt, and I'd only narrowly avoided cutting both a hand and a leg with a spinning, airborne knife when I mistimed my grab. That convinced Lace to switch to pinecones for juggling, although she made it clear on multiple occasions that it was the *soft* way of doing things.

Soft or not, keeping my fingers seemed like a win.

I *still* hadn't seen any skill or attribute gains.

On our fourth morning back on the road, I woke up and ran through my self-examinations, the series of tests I'd designed to verify that I was still in control of both my extremities and my mind. And if my hands shook more than I remembered them doing in previous days, I was pretty sure that was from the juggling.

I was only twenty-four. It was too early for symptoms.

Miko caught me before I could leave our tent. Ever since she had reached level six, she'd been able to cast a few *Minor Healing* spells beyond what it took to keep Wilhemina stable. For the second morning in a row, she healed my feet and lingering headache.

"Thank you," I told her, surreptitiously wiggling fingers that seemed more controlled now that they were no longer aching. It remained amazing to me that one little spell could undo so much of the damage we inflicted on ourselves. Just like that, I was ready for my day.

Except Miko held on to my arm even after she had finished her spell. After all the time we'd spent together, I could read the determination clearly on her reptilian features.

"Nest-brother," she said in the High Tongue, "I am done with instructing friend Neesa in *Cooking*."

"Did you get any points out of it?"

"One, but it is time to focus on my lagging class skills instead."

"How can I help?"

"In the absence of a weapons master to continue training me in the short staff, I thought we might spar in the mornings. Staff against spear, while the others break their fast."

Ever since I'd sought out Lace, my days felt over-stuffed, but I nodded anyway. It was a good idea, and even if sparring wasn't true combat, it was closer to it than my weapon forms. Maybe that would help us both.

"And at night?" I asked. After all, if we were sparring in the morning, there was nothing preventing her from continuing to work with Neesa.

"I will join Priest Humber and help care for the soldiers. While I might not have the energy to cast many blessings, there are injuries that do not require magical healing, and *Field Dressings* is one of my Major skills. Also…"

"It's a good way to make them see you as a person?"

"Or at least acknowledge my value. And perhaps understand that my species is not responsible for the sins of the past but should be judged on our actions in the present."

Given the fact that racism was still very much a thing back on Earth despite us all being the same species, I had my doubts that even Miko could singlehandedly turn the tide on Eos. Then again, she didn't have to change *everyone's* minds, and this handful of soldiers was a decent place to start. Jenkins and his crew aside, my experience so far had taught me that the duke's men were a practical bunch. If something helped them, that something was good, and any orders to the contrary wouldn't change that.

Still…

"Be careful," I told her. "I know Humber is Tin, but given how he was leveled, I doubt he'll be able to protect you if something goes wrong."

"We are in the Great Wilds," she reminded me. "We must both *always* be careful."

Miko was two cycles younger than me—or a little under three years in Earth time—but it was easy to forget that sometimes.

"Good." I grabbed my spear from its place of honor next to my sleeping roll. "Shall we spar then?"

The synossian grin had long lost its fear-inducing qualities after I got to know first Miko and then Riok… but it remained alarmingly toothy. Miko held her short staff in one hand and banged the other against her scaled chest, the sound only slightly softened by the orange and crimson robes.

"It will be an honor to test my skills against you, Brian Fieldings."

From anyone else, that might have been ominous, especially when you added the predatory grin into the equation. But from Miko…

Okay; it was still kind of ominous. Despite my levels, the Priestess was just as strong as me, owing to her species' natural advantages in that attribute. And while my spear gave me reach, she was almost a foot taller, which nullified some of that range.

Regardless, I found myself grinning back at her. As a Warrior, I *should* have the edge, but there were so many other factors at work that I couldn't predict how things would play out. And that made it all kinds of fun.

Unfortunately, when we emerged from our tent, we found someone waiting for us.

Even *more* unfortunately, I recognized the man.

If possible, Jenkins looked even *more* hungover than he had the day we'd left Sakeld. In fact, the sergeant seemed like he'd spent his night on the worst tequila bender known to man, thrown all of it up, and then dragged himself on his belly through the camp to our tent.

Even if he *hadn't* reeked like death, I wouldn't have had time for this. I went to move past him.

"Wait. Please." His voice was hoarse, strongly supporting my theory on tequila's revenge.

"Do not want trouble," said Miko, her words calm even as she tightened her grip on the short staff Seanna had sold her. Hungover or not, the man *was* Tin.

"Me neither," grated Jenkins, swaying on his feet like we were aboard one of Harborton's fishing boats and not on firm earth in the middle of the woods. "The lieutenant made it… damn clear… your life is worth more than ours, Priestess."

"Then what *do* you want?" I asked. I tried to be a good person, but there were limits, and as far as I was concerned, Jenkins and the rest of his crew had blown past those limits before we reached Sakeld.

"To apologize. For me and the others—" He stopped as a fit of coughing wracked his body and he dry-heaved right there before us.

I waited, but the coughing continued, and the man dropped to one knee.

Miko's grip on her staff loosened. A long step took her to the afflicted man, and she pressed her other palm against the soldier's heaving chest. Light flared, golden like the first touch of sunlight on the ocean.

Touch of the Dawn.

She'd cleared a few of my hangovers in the past with the same spell, but even as the Tin drew his first deep breath since we'd found him, Miko was turning to me, orange, sclera-less eyes gone wide.

"He was poisoned!" she told me.

"I mean… *all* alcohol is poison, really."

"True poison, nest-brother. Not enough to kill, but…"

"That's the other reason I came," said Jenkins. His voice was still hoarse, but color was slowly returning to his drawn face. "To ask you to call her off."

"Her?" The question escaped before my mind had fully caught up. Because there was only one woman I knew who might want to bring harm to Jenkins and the others. The fact that she knew her way around poisons and worshipped a goddess that seemed to favor the same just made it that much clearer.

"The amazon," said Jenkins, stating the obvious. "I don't know how she's doing it. We thought it was just food poisoning that night in Sakeld, but it's been three nights on the road, we've eaten the same as the rest of you, and each time it's gotten worse. It's all the boys can do to even walk, or they'd be here with me."

"Why ask us and not Lace?"

The big man almost scowled but thought better of it. "We've heard the stories. People who talk to blood-scorned amazons end up dead or as chattel for their tent and clan. You two are partied with her, so I guess that wagon's already left the warehouse, but me and my boys? We have our oaths to the duke to think of."

I wasn't sure what he was talking about regarding wagons, but it was clear Jenkins didn't know Lace was a refugee from her own clan or that she wouldn't be taking anyone's name or freedom anytime soon. And *that* presented an opportunity for us.

I sent Miko a look that stopped her moments before she could agree to the soldier's request.

"I can talk to her," I said, "but you know how her kind are. She's going to want something in return."

"Kid, are you—" Once again, he bit down on whatever he was going to say. "We're soldiers. The others are privates and Samhill's so green he hasn't even gotten his first payday. We don't have much coin."

That sucked, but I hadn't expected otherwise. People with money rode on mounts or in carriages. They didn't march on their own two feet, sucking down road dust and navigating around the steaming deposits left by the four-legged beasts ahead of them. And I wasn't interested in coming away with a few copper bits.

Instead, I was thinking of that night I'd first met them.

"I was thinking about training instead," I said, smile just a little bit colder for being called *kid* by a man begging for our help. "Every evening. Fists and feet, as the Warbringer prefers."

○○○

Our conversation with Jenkins meant that the first morning of sparring between Miko and me had to be cut short, but I still managed to verify a few things. First, while she was tougher than I was, my Finesse stat was higher. And second, despite us both being level six, I had a clear edge when it came to wielding our chosen weapons.

Part of that was that *Spear* was an Uncommon-ranked skill for me, whereas *Staff* was still Common for her. Part of it was that my weapon skill was a few points higher. And the last part of it was that *all* weapon skills were only Minor skills for Priests.

That distinction mattered; a twenty-seven in a Minor skill was *not* the same as a twenty-seven in a Major skill, let alone the thirty I had. Presumably, the same rule held true when it came to General skills like *Stealth* versus when that same skill was a Minor or Major skill in someone's class. Although there, the Aspirant also had the benefit of the skill's cap being lifted from ten.

Advanced classes could elevate existing skills from General to Minor or even Major, and they could reduce others just as easily. That made class choice even more important, which made in-depth knowledge about those choices absolutely critical.

Regardless, I more than held my own against Miko, able to nullify her greater strength while using my reach advantage to decent effect. By the time we had to stop to break camp, we were both gasping for breath, but she gave me a second salute.

"I thank you for the instruction, nest-brother," she said in the High Tongue. "I have not fought against the spear since military camp."

"I learned a lot too," I told her. "You're a much different combatant than Lace or Caleb."

"If by different, you mean inferior, then I am sure you are correct." She grinned as she said it, not troubled in the slightest by her defeat. "But one must be aware of both the past and present to shape the future with intention. I will be better tomorrow. Every day, we *both* will be."

"No fate but what we make, huh?"

"Under the light of Aurea's star and with her fire in our hearts." She cast her eyes toward the light filtering through the trees from the east. "Yes."

After all that had happened to my dad, not to mention the ticking time bomb of Huntington's locked inside my own genetic code, I had long had a *difficult* relationship with even the idea of God. My experiences with Shan, one of the deities who had brought me here, hadn't fixed that. But damn if Miko wasn't doing her part to at least change my mind on *religion*.

I was slated to go scouting with Lace as soon as we'd finished with camp, but the Priestess caught me again as I left.

"No fate but what we make," she said, as if tasting the words. "That was well said."

I made sure I was still using the High Tongue when I responded. "It was from an old movie my dad loved." And then, because she wouldn't know what I was talking about: "Movies are a kind of play that can be recorded and seen again at will."

"Like a memory?"

"A memory mixed with Slanit's upgraded version of Farseeing so everyone can see it," I told her, referencing one of the scouts who had died at Whitehall so many moons ago.

"I would have liked to experience such a thing." She took my pack and slung it over her other shoulder, lessening my burden and increasing the possibility that I'd keep up with Lace for once. "Your world seems like it was a strange but magical place."

"If only." A little magic might have made Earth more bearable for the unwashed masses of the human population, myself included. Assuming it hadn't been hoarded or controlled by those in power. "Of all the things I miss, movies are pretty far down the list."

"I am always available to listen," said Miko, putting on her metaphorical counselor hat.

"It'll have to be some other time. If I'm late again, Lace might add knives back into the juggling rotation."

Much later, after a day guaranteed to leave both my body and brain aching until the following morning's healing, I came out of meditation to find a now-familiar screen waiting:

```
You have increased the following skills:

Major skills:
Medium Armor [+1]: 19/35
Spear (U) [+1]: 31/35
Unarmed Combat [+1]: 1/35

Minor skills:
Athleticism [+1]: 31/35
Avoidance [+1]: 31/35
Leadership (U) [+1]: 6/35
```

```
        Pain Tolerance [+1]: 31/35

        General skills:
        Juggling [+1]: 1/10
        Tracking [+1]: 2/10
```

The tent was pitch black, my glowing skill-up screen visible only to me, and I let myself celebrate for the first time in what felt like forever.

If fate *was* what we made it, the Framework was our key to making that fate a good one.

One step, one level, one skill at a time.

ooo

Three days later, and that initial flurry of skill-ups felt like ancient history. As ever, as soon as I found something that worked, it seemed like the Framework decided to make things harder in response. I *knew* that wasn't true—that the Framework was a mechanism and not some all-powerful, thinking being—but damn if it wouldn't have been nice to have a succession of easy wins for once.

Instead, I'd seen nine skill-ups and then… nothing. As days passed, I reminded myself that progress was almost definitely still happening somewhere beneath the surface. If each skill-up was a single point, who was to say progression didn't occur in smaller, fractional slivers, both the Framework and my soul acknowledging them only once they had accumulated enough to be measurable?

Leveraging the Framework required more thinking than I'd *ever* done working as a barista. More planning, more strategizing, and more effort too. It was almost as exhausting as the physical labor that was an unavoidable piece of the process, from the spars in the morning, to the expeditions with Lace, to the training that left me sore and winded despite my Vitality.

But when it was your life at stake rather than just a dead-end job—and not just your life but hundreds of thousands of others—well, motivation was a whole lot easier to come by.

And it helped the time go by, something I sorely needed now that I didn't have Kacellius' book to distract me.

A single, way-too-late warning from *Danger Sense* was all I got before a blade appeared at my throat. Sometimes, I thought the skill should be called *Hindsight* instead.

The only good news was that *this* knife wasn't poisoned.

"Distraction will get you dead," Lace murmured in my ear. "Especially when you're out in the wilds alone."

I *wasn't* alone, which was kind of the reason I'd let my mind drift, but I wasn't going to say that. Instead, I kept very still and pointed to a disturbance in the earth just beyond the shrub I'd stopped by to daydream.

"I was just trying to identify those tracks," I lied, once the knife had left my throat. *Deception* was increasingly feeling like my most valuable skill, which probably said terrible things about me or the people around me.

"Boar," said Lace, her tone almost matching the beast's name.

"Not deer?"

"No. Look at the shape of the hoof print. A deer tapers more to a point at the front, with *its* dewclaws keeping in line rather than flaring out." She paused and looked a little bit closer. "Huh."

"What?"

"There are four dewclaws for each print instead of two." She pointed out lighter indentations behind the deep prints of the hoof.

"What does that mean?"

"This particular boar has ascended and may even have gained itself an aspect." She shook her head, dark braids still absent of beads. "If we had the time, I'd suggest we hunt it down. It would make for a good fight, and the tusks and meat will sell in most markets. Since we *don't* have time and these tracks are both a day old and moving away from the road… we'll let it be." She shrugged and patted me on the back. "Still, you did well to notice those tracks."

"Imagine what I'll be able to do once my *Tracking* skill reaches three," I muttered. "The world will never be the same."

"Given what you are, that much is likely already true."

And just like that, any positive vibes were gone.

Maybe twenty minutes later, I dared to broach the silence, speaking in Gorash, the language of the south.

"I didn't ask for any of this, you know."

"Nobody does, Brian Fieldings. Do you think those blank-eyed killers now marching to Madea asked for their lot in life?"

"The Nameless Dead?"

She nodded. "It's a terrible thing, giving up your name. You become just a face, a phantom, or a memory, with nothing to bind you to the world. Nobody does that unless they're pushed to it."

"You did it."

"That's how I know what I'm talking about."

As far as I could tell, Lace's people took names more seriously than most, but her point stood.

"You gave up your name, they gave up their futures, I gave up my life," I said instead. "But we're all still here. That must mean something."

"Maybe, but we won't know exactly what until we're dead, and only then if the Night Hag's feeling chatty."

Lace was not always a nice person, and lately, she wasn't particularly fun either. I wasn't going to blame her for that, given what she'd lost, but part of me wanted to remind her that Mordecai and Skaal had been *my* party members too. And well on their way to being friends.

"We should head back," she said. "I have no idea what Quincy believed he saw to send us all the way out here, but it's long gone. If we're quick enough, you'll have time to get some juggling in before you volunteer to get thrown around again like a sack of grain."

"*Unarmed Combat* isn't a bad skill to have."

"No, it isn't. But the price was high."

"The price? You mean *not* poisoning them anymore?"

"Exactly."

And that was all there was to be said as that.

We'd traveled a long distance from the marching column and had to hurry if we were going to get back before dark. My *Stealth* skill had been capped out since well before we left Madea, but I still felt loud and clumsy following the Marauder back through the woods. There was nothing I could do about that though; unless I found an advanced class that incorporated the skill, it would always be the case.

I shortened the grip on my spear to bring it closer to my body and did my best to follow in Lace's footsteps exactly, eyes trained on the woman in front of me. It was the opposite of how she'd been teaching me to traverse the woods—eyes and senses open to the forest around us—but we'd just finished scouting the area; at this point, it was easier to keep her in view and simply follow behind.

Which meant, when *Danger Sense* alerted me to an attack coming from above and behind me, I knew that this time, it wasn't Lace who was responsible.

9

I'd learned on the walls of Madea that techniques were an Aspirant's trump card. They could make or break a fight. Use one at the right time and you were past your opponent's guard, ripping their throat out with a conveniently sharp rock. Use one at the wrong time and it wouldn't be available when the right time came around.

Choosing the moment mattered. Blowing through my techniques early meant, at my level and attributes, a minute or more of having nothing but base combat skills to rely on.

Still, when *Danger Sense* went off, I didn't stop to think; I just yelled a warning to Lace and triggered *Lunge.* The technique activated instantaneously, and I blurred from a place of imminent peril to temporary safety, roughly seven feet away and off to the left.

It wasn't enough—

—but it did save my life.

Something hit me midway through my movement, spinning me about even as I continued to flow forward. Agony followed, only slightly dulled by *Pain Tolerance*, but it wasn't until *Lunge* had ended that I saw the arrow sticking out of my right side. It had penetrated multiple layers—iron hauberk, padded gambeson, flesh, organs, and then gambeson and hauberk again—until its head protruded from my abdomen like the world's edgiest body piercing.

I didn't have time to care.

Pain Tolerance kept me lucid.

The rest was up to me.

Lunge was on cooldown, of course, but as I touched down, I spun back to the right and drove forward, back in the presumed direction of my attacker. Another arrow streaked past me, aiming for where I would have been if I'd kept fleeing instead, and I had the presence of mind to look to where it had come from. Whatever variant of *Stealth* they'd been using had dropped with their ambush and I could see a shape up in the trees about a hundred feet away. They had their bow raised and were already nocking a third arrow.

Behind me, Lace made a noise halfway between a laugh and a snarl, swiftly followed by someone else's lower-pitched grunt, but I didn't have time to check on her. I wove between trees as I charged my opponent, bark spraying my face as that third arrow came an inch or two from putting me down. The tree the archer had chosen was large enough to bear their weight, surrounded by a sizable root system that would make approach treacherous. Worse was the ten feet of open space that I'd have to cross to reach them.

Finding a tree of my own to hide behind and waiting things out had a certain appeal, but Lace was almost definitely still in the open, battling her own opponent. Going to ground would buy me time at the cost of her life… and then there'd be multiple attackers to flank me and run me down like I was one of the beasts the Marauder had been teaching me to track.

And it wasn't like hiding was particularly safe anyway, I realized, as another arrow ripped through a smaller tree's trunk as easily as it had my armor. Whoever I was facing clearly had techniques of their own, after all. Getting hit mid-*Lunge* told me that much.

It had been *maybe* ten seconds since I'd been shot, which meant *Lunge's* minute-long cooldown might as well have been an eternity. I was still running, still dodging, and almost definitely still bleeding. More importantly, I was running out of space as I approached the kill zone.

If they were Tin, they had to be in the lower levels of that tier, or I'd already be dead. I thought they'd shot five arrows so far, which meant they were unfathomably firing an arrow every three seconds. That would be enough time to cross the kill zone, but then what? I'd been *twelve* the last time I'd tried climbing a tree, and I couldn't leap twenty feet into the air like Lace or the now-dead Guard Captain Pike.

Or… could I? I'd improved both my Strength and my Finesse by two points since my arrival on Eos and that had to count for something. I didn't move like an Olympian and I sure as hell didn't feel like one, but… maybe?

I baited the archer into a sixth arrow that still came a hair's breadth from splitting my head open like a cantaloupe and sprinted across the open space. Two strides, then three. Without slowing, I threw myself up and forward, spear still in hand, aiming for the archer fifteen feet above ground.

Either Pike and Lace had been using techniques when they made their respective jumps, or their attributes were a hell of a lot higher than mine, because I didn't come close. In fact, it was all I could do to grab onto the lowest branch, one that I could have reached from the ground if I had run to the trunk rather than jumping from distance. Even then, I was forced to drop my spear as I wrapped both arms around the thick branch to pull myself up.

Either the arrow in my side snapped or a rib did. Given how much sensation made it past *Pain Tolerance*, it might have been both.

In a better world, the archer would have been too busy laughing to line up a shot. In a perfect world, they'd have laughed so hard they fell right off their perch, once again forcing gravity to accomplish what I could not.

But this was Eos, and by the time I was halfway stable on my branch, the archer had found an unobstructed vantage point; I looked up to see a man in mottled grey and green crouched a half-dozen branches above me, another arrow nocked and poised to fire.

My spear was down on the ground below, but even if I'd somehow held onto it, it was bigger than I was and awful for throwing. My knife wasn't balanced for throwing either and *it* was still in its sheath on my waist. So, I did the only thing I could think of. In the instant that the archer started to release his shot, I finally gave voice to my pain, screaming at him in the broken, awful, profane, damn-near telepathic language of the essoli.

I'd used the tactic at Madea to confuse the blighted we were fighting there. It had been *considerably* less useful against Khamani's high priest. And I had no idea if it would have any effect at all on the person currently poised to end my largely unsuccessful life.

Unless he, too, was one of the Ever-Hungry's cultists, the archer didn't understand a word I was saying—hell, even with my *Speaker of Tongues* trait, *I* didn't understand what I was saying—but the thick *wrongness* of the foul language had an impact that went beyond simple comprehension. As he released his arrow, he did something unexpected:

He flinched.

It wasn't enough to save me from yet another arrow making a mockery of my freshly repaired armor and the increasingly leaky flesh beneath, but I was still breathing and that had seemed impossible even a moment earlier.

I surged to my feet, my slightly augmented Finesse making the movement easier than it would have been, and jumped for the next branch up and over. That put the tree's trunk between me and the archer. I was bleeding all over the place, but that was a problem for later. Right now, all I had to do to keep him from getting off another shot was to circle the tree as I climbed.

That part went surprisingly well. Our attackers hadn't had a ton of time to pick their ambush spots, which meant this tree had been picked for its vantage point as well as how easy it was to get into position. That latter bit now worked for me.

Of course, the archer knew that too. Probably even figured it out first, since he hadn't just been shot… twice. I rounded the side of the trunk to find the other man waiting, crouched just above. He'd tossed his bow aside and the short blade now in one hand darted at my head and upper torso like an adder.

My knife was in my hand as well, but I didn't try to parry the blow. I didn't know how strong the man was, and I didn't want to find out, especially when he had the high ground. Instead, I ducked aside and lunged forward, the dagger in my hand flashing. He saw it coming, of course, and had both the time and the presence of mind to check his earlier swing and bring the sharp edge of his blade down across my outstretched wrist—

—which wasn't there.

As *Deceptive Strike* completed, I materialized a foot past the image of me he'd just attacked, positioned on the other side of the branch. The technique was meant to put me in the optimal spot to land a critical strike, but I was still standing below the other man. That meant my target couldn't be his chest or throat. Instead, I slashed the back of his ankle, ripping through the tendon and whatever else was down there. And as he roared in pain and teetered, I grabbed his other foot with my free hand and pulled.

At the end of the day, gravity remained an equalizer and my greatest ally. With one foot unresponsive and the other yanked out from under him, the man fell and crashed chest first into the branch he'd been standing on. And *that* put the rest of him in range.

I'd been training in *Knife* for several moons now. This bore no resemblance to the ground-based spars I'd had with Caleb or even Lace, but one principle remained the same: the pointy side goes in. And out and back in again.

Somewhere in all that stabbing, he died.

I sagged as the adrenaline drained out of me; only my grip on the branch that now held a corpse kept me upright. My chest was bleeding from a cut I couldn't remember taking, but the real problems were the two arrow hits. The remnants of the arrow still in my side kept that wound from gushing blood, but the second arrow had gone straight through the muscle of my left arm. It was a miracle I'd been able to use it at all.

As horrible as fighting on the wall had been, at least there I'd mostly been backed by allies whose strengths balanced my weaknesses. It was a whole different thing to fight solo, and I didn't like it at all. Any of those arrows could have killed me easily.

A man's roar of pain interrupted my bloody introspection. The continuing sounds of combat told me Lace was dealing with a lot more than my one archer. And that meant she could probably use some backup. I wiped my dagger clean on the dead man's pants and sheathed it so I'd have both hands free to climb back down the tree. Insofar as my left arm was working, anyway. I hurried as much as I could, but breaking my neck because of a misstep wouldn't help anyone either. I had to find a balance between speed and safety.

Which was appropriate, since *balance* was all that kept me from my own disastrous fall.

At the last branch, the one my not-so-heroic leap had taken me to, I considered using *Lunge* to get down. But *Deceptive Strike* wouldn't be available again for a while and that made *Lunge* my only remaining trump card. So, I went belly-down on the branch, wrapped my good arm around it, then lowered myself until I dangled above the ground. The resulting drop was only a few feet, and if my ankles twinged at all from landing on the uneven nest of roots, the pain from my *actual* wounds masked the sensation magnificently.

I scooped up my fallen spear and took off running.

It had taken me fifteen to twenty seconds to reach the archer's tree in the first place, but without the threat of arrows flying, I made it back to Lace in ten, wincing with every step. There were two bodies already down, one of them still twitching. The Marauder was dancing with a third who moved like smoke, but a fourth was rising out of a tree's shadow behind her, wielding a blade as long as my forearm that dripped crimson darkness.

Lunge.

My spear caught the fourth fighter a moment before they could strike Lace, my spear driving through boiled leather and flesh. I pulled back my weapon, swept the man's legs out from under him, and thrust a second time. And then a third. In a world with defensive techniques and crazy Vitality levels, it took more than even a *Lunge*-assisted spear strike to be sure.

When I was done, Lace was pressing the attack on her final opponent, whose aura felt almost as slippery as the man himself. The amazon was bleeding, but she was smiling as she fought, white teeth brilliant against the black of her skin.

I wasn't going to get between her and her Tin-ranked prey, but the last man standing didn't know that. I moved to flank him, my spear a threat he couldn't afford to ignore.

In the span of a single second, the other man took two hits, the second one spraying the nearest tree with his blood. In desperation, he activated a technique that sent darkness billowing out around him like some kind of smoke bomb from an old ninja movie.

Having seen Lace at night, I could have told him that that wouldn't work.

Another hit landed, and now it was like Lace was carving up a turkey. There was something savagely gleeful in the Marauder's smile, a kind of malevolent joy that would find itself at home in my nightmares about being up on the wall.

The other man took another hit, but this one seemed planned; it bought him the space to turn and flee with a speed that spoke to Tin-ranked Vitality and a Finesse attribute way beyond anything I'd managed to achieve.

Having seen Lace throw knives, and her technique that turned one knife into five, I could have told him that *that* wouldn't work either… but before the amazon could finish her kill, a shape materialized in front of the fleeing man, two blades extended.

The last of the assassins ran right onto those blades and died.

The new arrival let the body fall, bent to retrieve his weapons, and then moved to join us. As my heartrate dropped back to somewhat normal levels and the pain started to seep back into my awareness, I recognized Quincy, the lead scout from our column.

The man gave me a nod and headed over to Lace.

"I'm glad I got here in time. Are the two of you—"

He was three feet away when Lace spat in his face… not saliva, which would have been bad enough, but a stream of corrosive liquid that hissed as it spattered.

Quincy staggered and fell, screams dying somewhere in his chest and throat because the ruin of his face didn't allow for noise.

Before I could do more than make my own strangled gasp, the Marauder had finished the job, driving a knife up under the rubs of the collapsing man and into his heart.

I finally found my voice. "What did you just do?"

"What was necessary."

"*Necessary?!*" I gathered myself and tried again. "Lace, that was *Quincy*. The head scout for the duke's column of soldiers. *The duke we're trying to ally with.*"

"Take a breath and use your head instead of your tongue," said the Marauder, cleaning her blades as calmly as if we'd just finished a spar. "Why was he here, when he was supposed to be a full glass away from us on the other side of the column?"

"I…"

"Why did he not appear until the battle was already decided? And why send us out this far at all?"

"You said he'd seen sign of something out here," I pointed out.

"*Animal* sign, not indications that there was a fist of assassins lying in wait." She waved a hand at the bodies around us. "And while I'm *not* a Scout, as shown by their ability to ambush us, my *Tracking* skill is sufficient that I would have seen whatever animal threat he was talking about had it existed."

"So… what? You think he sent us out here to die?"

"And followed to make sure the job was done, yes. Only, we both lived and were still ready to fight." She gave me a once over and her silver eyes narrowed. "*Mostly* ready to fight. You need a bandage on that arm, and we need to get you back to Miko."

I wasn't going to argue on either front, because *Pain Tolerance* was a hell of a long way from *Pain Immunity*, but I was finding it hard to tear my eyes away from the rapidly decomposing body of our supposed ally. I couldn't answer Lace's questions, but that didn't mean there *weren't* answers other than betrayal, and she'd just brutally murdered the only person with those answers.

"What if you're wrong?" I finally asked.

"Then the Night Hag will laugh at our misfortune," she said, bending to tear off a long strip of mostly clean grey and black cloth from one of the assassin's shirts. "Either way, we should come up with a story the northern lord will believe. Maybe the assassins killed Quincy before they came for us? Regardless, that's not the question you should be asking."

Despite everything, I realized what she was getting at.

"Why try to kill us at all?"

"And why now?" she agreed.

I almost didn't want to say it, but…

"Hawthorne didn't want us to come along in the first place. All he cared about was Miko."

The Marauder frowned as she wrapped the cloth multiple times around my wounded arm. The makeshift bandage immediately began to darken as blood seeped through. "Assassinating a lord isn't something you should just casually propose, Brian Fieldings. Even to me."

I didn't know if she was messing with me or not, but by the time I had decided, based on the evidence lying a few feet away with his smoking wreckage of a face, that she probably wasn't, Lace had gone to check the bodies of those we'd killed.

Other than Quincy, who had a coin purse but no pack, they had nothing but weapons, clothing, and armor.

"There must be a camp somewhere," she said. "I'll come back and search for it once the carriage has stopped for the night. In the meantime, we'll say we got attacked but leave out any mention of Quincy."

"They're going to notice he's missing."

"Yes, they will." She came back and examined my other major wound. "We should leave the arrow in until we're back. I don't know how much more it'll bleed once we pull the arrow out."

Even saying that made me kind of woozy, but I wasn't going to let the whole Quincy thing drop.

"What about *him*?"

"He's already dead. I'm not concerned with his wounds." She shrugged. "There's only one other scout with the column, and Quincy was supposed to be checking the southern woods. When he doesn't return, they'll go looking for him there."

"And when they don't find him?"

"Hopefully, they'll assume he got ambushed like we did. And if not, we'll figure something out." She nodded to the arrow still protruding from my side. "Quincy didn't use a bow and neither of us has one either. That's evidence of our story."

Maybe it was the loss of blood, but that seemed halfway plausible. Either Lace had murdered an awful lot of people before and been forced to cover it up or she was quick on her feet in a way that had nothing to do with her inhuman Finesse stat.

"That's enough talking," she said. "We need to get you back to the column before all this blood attracts a real predator."

With that, she stalked off into the forest.

I tried to find a stride that *didn't* send pain shooting through me with every step and hurried after.

I'd finally gotten the combat I'd been practically praying for during the tedium of our early march from Madea… and was regretting every second of it.

ooo

The further we went, the more grateful I was for my enhanced Vitality; I don't think I would have made it another five feet without it, let alone five miles. But long minutes later, the wound in my arm was starting to clot, as was the more minor cut to my chest. It left only the wound in my side to worry about. And that gave me space to think about something more than just not bleeding to death.

Like the fact that we'd never actually answered the second of Lace's questions. Even if Hawthorne *was* behind our attempted assassinations—and I wasn't sure that was the case—why *now*? We'd been traveling together for days and days, after all. The only thing that had changed was that I was now joining Lace on these scouting missions. Had he seen us heading off together and decided that this was the perfect opportunity to rid himself of some unwanted baggage, while saving his duke a fair bit of reward money at the same time?

Given what I'd heard of Wilhemina's father, that didn't seem like the sort of ploy that would go over well… but Miko *was* the only one of us who was strictly necessary for the little girl's continued survival.

And if Hawthorne *hadn't* been behind the plot, then who was Quincy working with? And again, why had *today* been the day they'd decided to put their plot in motion? We were somewhere between Sakeld and our next destination, so maybe it was just a question of location and opportunity? Or maybe…

Lace tilted her head. "Do you hear that?"

"Hear what?"

"Battle." Silver eyes narrowed.

…or maybe they'd just wanted one of the column's few Tins out of the way so they could attack the soldiers transporting the duke's heir to Trynfall.

"The column is under attack?"

"Yes." She gave me a once-over. "Can you run?"

"Miko's in danger," I told her. "If I need to, I'll fly."

○○○

I *couldn't* fly, of course, but I *did* run, chasing Lace through the woods as fast as I could. Blood dripped down my arm and my side as one wound reopened while the other just kept doing its thing, but *Pain Tolerance* was active again and that let me push everything to the side. If the duke's men were under attack, it meant the assassins hadn't been working for Hawthorne after all and Quincy was some kind of double agent.

Or… totally innocent. That remained a real possibility, whatever Lace thought.

It *also* meant that our unknown enemy had sufficient resources to risk attacking a column of twenty soldiers and at least a few Tins.

That was bad enough.

When we burst back out onto the road, the reality was somehow even worse.

A defensive circle of soldiers had formed around Hawthorne's carriage, but they were being pressed on all sides by armed men and women in nondescript clothes and leather armor or bronze hauberks. Other clusters of resistance were scattered along the road. There were a dozen bodies lying still and at least half wore the duke's colors.

"Stay with me," said Lace, somehow only slightly winded by our sprint through the forest. Tempest remained shrouded on her back, an artifact too powerful for either of us to use. "Guard my left."

I'd finally reached the limits of *my* Vitality, so I didn't even have the breath to answer. Still, I fell in at her side, spear in hands. I was right-handed, so my wounded left arm was there more to control and guide the weapon as my right delivered the power.

Even so, said the part of my brain not overcome by exhaustion and pain, *your injury means you're not going to be as precise as you are in practice. And watch out for someone trying to strip you of your weapon.*

All good advice… and something I internalized and then otherwise ignored as I followed Lace into the melee.

If we survived the fight, I was sure I'd be able to look back on it and track the individual moves of that long sequence of combat: the adjustments, the strikes, the parries. But in the heat of the action, it all boiled down to a few simple things.

Step.

Thrust.

Disengage.

Step.

Lace's class was centered around mobility, but without Skaal, it was left to her to be our vanguard, and even in my battle delirium, I could tell that hampered her. She didn't leave me, didn't dance around or past her opponents, didn't use the techniques that seemed to let her fold space at will. Instead, she moved forward in lockstep with me, long blade in one hand, dagger in the other, cutting her way through a writhing wall of limbs, muscle, and bone.

She also spammed her other techniques, tearing into the enemy like a one-woman blender.

I moved with her, stabbing whatever target presented itself, using my spear to keep the enemy from pressing in on her left as they turned to face us and died. I kept both of my techniques in reserve and just focused on the weapon in my hands, the forms I'd been taught, and the person-shaped obstacles in our path.

Along the way, we gathered some help, a woman in the duke's colors who'd been about to die before we cut down her attackers. She took Lace's right, and though she only had a short, single-edged blade she used like a cleaver, our half-sized unit stabilized.

Techniques were triggered on both sides, some of them flashy, some of them not. More bodies fell. I didn't know how many attackers there had been to begin with, but it was a lot. The press was lessening, but defenders were dropping just as quickly.

Somewhere in there, the voice in my head started telling me how goddamn tired I was, but that had to be the blood loss speaking. I'd spent hours on Madea's walls; this was nothing by comparison.

I stomped down on the voice and kept fighting.

It felt like an hour—a glass—before we neared the carriage. More defenders had fallen, leaving seven people standing. I didn't see

Hawthorne, but a sweaty-faced Priest Humber was behind the soldiers, hands glowing as he cast some sort of group heal.

Miko, on the other hand, was up front with the others. Slashes in her orange and crimson robes suggested she'd been hit already, and more than once, but she stood tall and fought on. As we neared, she cast *Flare* in one attacker's face; when he flinched away, she followed with a blow from her short staff that folded the man over. A second enemy grabbed her free arm, but she broke his grip and struck back, clawed hand tearing through flesh as easily as any weapon.

Still, she'd been pulled out of the defensive circle, and a third attacker was approaching on her flank, spiked morning star in hand.

I was too far away for *Lunge* to matter, even if there hadn't been people blocking the path. I was too far for her to hear my warning cry over the grunts, the screams, and the clash of bronze on bronze or even iron. Still, I found another gear somehow, the weapon in my arms now a feather that danced its way past the guard of my opponents to find the gaps in their armor.

Miko couldn't hear me, but Lace did. She batted aside an attack with her left blade and then hurled the dagger in her right hand. It flickered and became three, then five, streaking toward the morning star wielder—

—only to embed themselves in a different enemy's back as the tides of battle shifted them into the way.

Miko turned and started to retreat, finally aware of the incoming threat, but the man was already there, spiked weapon arcing down with a force mere scales could never resist.

Instead of mortal flesh, it met a raised shield, glowing with some unnamed technique, as the soldier nearest Miko stepped out of position to defend the Priestess. The resulting impact shattered the shield and created a shockwave that sent several people on both sides to their knees, but before the morning-star wielder could recover, Miko had been pulled back into position, guarded again on both sides.

On the far side of the defensive circle, Lieutenant Ender unleashed another technique, and three people fell in bloody chunks. We were close enough now that Miko could see us; orange eyes widened as she fought to help clear a path.

And then we'd been folded into the defensive circle. The woman we'd brought with us took one step and collapsed at the feet of a sunken-eyed Priest Humber, but I turned and added my spear to the defense. Lace stood to my right, Miko to my left, and Samhill—

Wait. Samhill?

I took another look in the heartbeat between one attacker and the next. It was indeed Samhill on Miko's left. Samhill, the smallest of Sergeant Jenkins' cronies. Samhill, who had just saved my nest-sister, lost his shield, and likely broken his arm in the process.

Huh.

It was a good thing Lace had stopped poisoning them all.

10

Whoever had planned the attack had miscalculated the strength of the defense. Another ten or so troops—or hell, even one more Tin—might have let them roll right over the duke's men. Without those extra numbers, and with Miko's addition to the mix, the column had *still* been losing, but it was a closer thing.

Our arrival changed that.

To be more specific, *Lace's* arrival changed that. Maybe Quincy and the squad that had tried to kill us had originally been meant to serve as reinforcements to the assault, arriving as a second wave once they'd dealt with us. Instead, a pissed off, bloodhungry Marauder showed up with her spear-wielding sidekick in tow.

My addition to the ring around the carriage helped stabilize the defense in a way that had a lot less to do with my level and a lot more to do with pure numbers and the reach of my spear. Miko parried a sword strike, her ironwood short staff more than up to the task, and as the armored attacker reeled back, I pivoted and drove my spear into their unprotected armpit. On the other side of me, Lace danced forward, leaving the line just long enough for a lightning-quick attack that left a woman with a bloody stump instead of a hand, then danced back into position.

The Marauder, ironically, worked less well in the tight ranks of our defense. Still, her attributes made up for that, especially now that most of the combatants had blown through their techniques and were either waiting on cooldowns or out of energy entirely.

Most of the combatants.

Danger Sense had me ducking aside as something tore through the air. It was only when it struck the carriage above and behind us that I realized I'd never been the target. The vehicle *rocked* from the impact of what had to have been a Technique-aided arrow, a hole blasted clear through its wooden frame.

If Wilhemina—or Hawthorne—had been hit by that arrow...

I traded glances with Lace and just like that, the amazon had left our line again, a shadow slipping into the press of killers surrounding us. A second arrow streaked in, this one almost tipping the carriage over entirely, but Lace or another defender must have found the archer soon after because a third arrow never came.

In a way, the fact that they'd resorted to taking pot shots at the carriage was a strong indicator that the battle had turned. Even so, we fought on for long, bloody minutes. Next to Miko, a shield-less Samhill fell, only to be replaced by the soldier Lace and I had escorted over, her own wounds freshly healed. Behind us, Humber collapsed, not from injuries, but exhaustion.

Miko crushed someone's skull with her staff, parried another strike with the metal vambraces she'd claimed moons earlier and generally fought with the ferocity of someone who'd been forced to sit back and listen as the rest of us bled on Madea's wall.

Anyone who thought a so-called *scaled* would be the weak link in our defense was learning otherwise, and fast.

We fought on. With allies to either side, I was free to make full use of my spear's length. *Deceptive Strike* ended one life and then, minutes later, another. A few attacks made it past my guard, but this time, the armor did its job, reducing desperate strikes to glancing blows that left bruises but wouldn't add to my blood loss.

Which was… good, because at some point, cloudy darkness had started to creep in around the edges of my vision. Riok's spear had long since gone from a feather to a titanic weight, clutched desperately by numb fingers and hands slick with sweat and blood.

Still, I fought. We all fought.

By the end, my tunnel vision was such that I didn't even notice when the press around us lessened, didn't realize that the handful of attackers left were finally breaking and running, didn't even recognize Lace when she appeared out of the darkness. I just thrust, smooth and efficient, relying on hard-learned technique for both power and speed.

The Marauder swayed to one side, letting the spearhead dart past her, and then yanked the weapon out of my slack hands. Remembering the first rule of the spear, I reached for it, but for some reason my feet didn't travel with me. I was falling, falling not to the blood-soaked ground but into the darkness that pooled beneath it, fathoms deep and forever cold.

Miko shouted something, but not even *Speaker of Tongues* could tell me what she said.

And then I was gone.

○○○

I woke sometime later, my own pack beneath my head as a makeshift pillow. For the first time in years, I hesitated to start my forms, the wounds I'd taken in battle still fresh in my mind. Still, what had begun with my diagnosis ten years earlier as a way to reassure myself had turned into a habit and then grown beyond that into a compulsion; I began with my fingers, wiggling each and verifying I still had control, then raised my arms, wincing as I waited for the pain to come.

My left arm still hurt, but it was a deep ache instead of a sharp, bright flash of agony. My right arm felt completely fine, and my side… that looked to have been healed far beyond even multiple castings of *Minor Healing*.

Priest Humber must be back in action. How long was I down?

If my *Meditation* skill had been even higher tiered, maybe I would have woken to skill-up notifications but communing with the Framework while unconscious remained beyond my reach. *For now.* So, I went through the rest of my forms, making sure that the legs and feet that had failed me were back under my control, that it was blood loss that had taken them from me and not the disease Miko was so many levels and at *least* a few ranks from being able to cure. And then, when I was done, I finally sat up.

I was in a tent. *Our* tent, from the looks of it, with Miko's gear and bedroll just an arm's length away to the left. Light filtered through the fabric, telling me it was still daytime. Or… was daytime *again*, more likely. After all, both of our healers would have had to rest and recover their energy after the battle, and putting up tents would have been low on the priority list. I'd been stripped out of both armor and clothing, the former stacked on the far side of my pack, the latter either piled somewhere for washing or recycled into bandages if it had been beyond saving. My injured arm was tightly wrapped, but the only thing that showed I'd taken an arrow through my midsection was the discolored patch of tangibly tougher skin that had replaced pink flesh on either side. *Beast Skin* continued to do its thing.

I wasn't sure how I felt about that.

It was the noise outside our tent that had woken me as much as the light. The sounds of battle—the screams, the clash of metal—had been replaced by groans and complaints and at least one very persistent hammer. With my forms done and my body at least mostly healed, there was nothing keeping me in the tent; I laboriously changed into a fresh set of clothing, tugged on my socks and boots, and crawled to the entrance flap, blinking against the brightness as I emerged into sunlight.

We were maybe twenty feet down the road from where the column had been attacked, the tent in line with a half-dozen others. A bare handful of able-bodied soldiers manned the hastily erected defensive perimeter, and the ducal carriage sat at the center of that space, where it had been since the attack. Now that the battle was over, I could see why: one of its large wooden wheels had cracked all the way through, splinters all that remained of several of its spokes. I didn't know how or when that damage had happened, but the carriage wasn't going anywhere until it was fixed. Hawthorne was standing nearby, looking none the worse for wear, and discussing the damage with his carriage driver and the soldier wielding that incessant hammer.

In the space between us, bodies had been laid out carefully, as if arrayed into military ranks. They all wore the duke's colors. The attacker's dead hadn't been touched yet, strewn across the road and surrounding woods where they'd fallen. Of the twenty-some soldiers that had marched in our column, eleven had died, compared to more than thirty or forty of the enemy.

I was pretty sure we had Miko and Humber to thank for some of that disparity and my suspicions were confirmed when I spotted Samhill working with another of Jenkins' squad. The man's arm was in a sling, but he otherwise seemed hale and hearty. Yet again, I was seeing just how vital healers were in any prolonged conflict. Fatal blows would always be just that, but if someone could be stabilized until the healers got to them? A lot of people who might otherwise die of infection, organ failure, or yes, even blood loss, would instead live and potentially even flourish again.

Of course, as I'd seen with Khamani's High Priest, magic could also literally *eat people*… so there were downsides too.

If only *I'd* gotten the chance to explore those upsides and downsides personally.

Then again, I was still alive, all these moons later. Maybe Shan knew best after all when he'd made me a Warrior instead of the Mage I'd requested.

A haphazard medical station stood on the opposite side of the road, as far from the bodies as possible while remaining within the defensive perimeter. Humber and Miko were both there, the synossian watching her human counterpart as he healed an injured soldier. There were four bedrolls nearby. One held bandages, herbs, and other paraphernalia of the trade, while the other three held patients: two unconscious men and a woman missing both of her legs below the knees.

Magic was great and terrible, but it couldn't do everything.

Miko spotted me and patted Humber on the shoulder before coming over.

"Brian! How are you feeling?"

"Better than I was. My arm hurts, but—"

Synossians couldn't really wince, but I'd spent enough time with Miko to recognize the expression she made. "Is my fault. Heals are limited and we had—"

"—to prioritize life-threatening wounds. It's okay. I get it and I'm not complaining." Especially with the stark reminder of the dead behind me and the maimed still being treated by Humber. "I'm just glad I woke up at all."

"Yes. You scared me, nest-brother."

I looked away, the memory of her own close call returning.

"The feeling's mutual. And I think I owe Samhill a new shield. Or at least a drink when we reach the next town."

"That will not be soon. We must repair carriage and figure out transport for injured once healed. Until then, Lord Hawthorne says we stay."

I didn't know how I felt about that. It was hard to deny that some people *clearly* weren't in any condition to travel on their own. And without a carriage, the still-comatose Wilhemina would have to be carried instead, which was far from ideal. On the other hand, someone had just thrown several dozen men at us. If they had more troops in reserve, staying where we were—where they *knew* we were—seemed unwise.

"Did Hawthorne say anything else?"

"Did not say anything at all. Not to me at least. Am not part of leadership. I am not invite—*invited*—to such discussions." She sent me that synossian smile. "But if am nearby to overhear while tending to duke's daughter? There is no help for that, yes?"

"That seems reasonable to me." I matched her grin and switched to an even more important topic. "Wilhemina's okay?"

Miko nodded, looking to the damaged carriage. In addition to the broken wheel, there were gaping holes in the sides where those two empowered arrows had struck "Was dragged to floor by Neesa when attack began. Lord Hawthorne and his man were both struck with—" She paused and switched to the High Tongue. "What is the word for splinters?"

With an effort, I made sure I was speaking in Trade when I replied with what my brain was convinced was the exact same word. "Splinters."

Translation powers were *so* weird sometimes.

"Yes. Were struck with *splinters*, but both Neesa and Wilhemina were unharmed."

"That's a relief. It looked like they were gunning for her at the end." I caught myself. "Sorry. Gunning means—"

"Is okay. I can interpret from context."

"Still, I promised not to do that anymore." I scanned the road, looking for the one person I hadn't spotted yet. "What about Lace? Where is she?"

"Is away looking for bandit camp," said Miko. "Explained—*she* explained—that you were ambushed. With Quincy missing, we think he was also."

I nodded as casually as I could and switched back to the High Tongue. "Don't tell anyone—don't even react to this, if you can avoid it—but he might have been involved in this whole attack."

Miko lowered her voice and leaned in. "What? How? Why?"

Her rendition of *casual and non-suspicious* was a hell of a lot worse than mine. I wondered if that was the *Deception* skill at work again? Something told me hers would be at one or two, if she had it at all.

"The why is an open question still, but he showed up right after our ambush. Killed the last assassin just before Lace could finish the job herself." I was careful not to say Quincy's name again. Nobody in camp spoke the High Tongue, but names didn't need translation. And if someone overheard us, they might make wonder what exactly we were saying about the missing scout and why we were using a foreign tongue to say it. "And then…" I coughed. "Lace killed him."

Miko stared at me, sharp-toothed muzzle hanging wide open, forked tongue flickering in the air as if to taste the truth of my words. "She *killed* him?"

"That was my reaction too. At first, anyway. Once we saw that the whole column was under attack… well, I'm finding it a lot harder to argue with her reasoning. He should have been scouting to the south, not a glass-or-so's walk to the north, shadowing us."

"The *attackers* came from the south," said Miko, eyes distant. "If Lord Hawthorne's driver hadn't given warning, they might have overrun us with the initial assault."

"How did he know they were coming?"

She spread her clawed hands. "I am not certain. Maybe it was a skill like yours or a passive technique related to his Bodyguard class. It was because of him that we were not taken entirely by surprise."

I eyed the man next to Hawthorne with increased respect. *Bodyguard* seemed like an overly specialized class, but that didn't mean it wasn't powerful in its specific role. Hell, maybe it was more powerful *because* of its specialization. And it had helped keep the people that mattered most to me alive.

I switched back to Trade. "Is the lieutenant around? With Lace gone, I should see what I can do around here to help."

Miko tapped her right arm in swift negation. "Should rest instead, nest-brother. Unhealed wound will tear open if you use it too much. Will be able to heal tomorrow after Wilhemina. In meantime, can rewrap with fresh poultice."

"Take your time. I'll get some meditation in. See what this debacle gained me, if anything." To be honest, I didn't *want* to rest, but overdoing things and putting even more of a burden on our healers seemed like a remarkably ungrateful thing to do. And the lure of potential progress after a battle like that was hard to deny. So, I returned to our tent, took a few sips from the waterskin in my pack, and sat down to commune with the Framework.

If *Meditation* had still been Common ranked, I was pretty sure that damn hammer would have made things all but impossible. I'd never gotten migraines back on Earth, but I could feel one in the wings, creeping closer with every ringing blow. It wasn't quite as bad as trading words with an essoli. Then again, I could always just *kill* the blighted, so maybe it was even worse.

Still, I did my best to ignore the noise and the distractions. I focused on my breath, on opening myself up to the metaphysical pipeline between body and soul, and on letting the experiences of the last day flow through me.

The hammer was blessedly silent when I opened my eyes again:

```
You have increased the following skills:

Major skills:
Formations [+2]: 16/35
Knife [+4]: 27/35
Medium Armor [+6]: 25/35
Spear (U) [+2]: 33/35
Tactics [+2]: 32/35
Unarmed Combat [+1]: 2/35

Minor skills:
Acrobatics [+2]: 3/35
Athleticism [+2]: 33/35
Avoidance [+2]: 33/35
Focus [+2]: 26/35
Pain Tolerance [+4]: 35/35

General skills:
Hunting [+1]: 2/10
Meditation (U) [+1]: 8/10
Tracking [+1]: 3/10
```

Holy crap.

I hadn't seen skill-ups like that… ever. The closest I could remember was my near-death versus the Buried necromancer, back on another continent. *Spear* and *Tactics* were two and three points away, respectively, from the level cap, and *Medium Armor* had caught up to *Light Armor* in a fraction of the time the latter skill had cost me. With my Minor skills, *Athleticism* and *Avoidance* were only two points away and…

It took all my recently enhanced focus to *not* sigh.

Pain Tolerance was already maxed out for the level. Because of course it would be. Whatever weapon I used, whatever armor I wore, whatever tactics I adopted, the one consistent feature of my life as an adventurer or even a Chosen appeared to be pain.

On the other hand, if I were feeling positively inclined, I'd be grateful I'd at least been given a skill to help manage that inevitable pain. And given the boatload of improvements I'd just netted, I was feeling somewhat positive.

I don't love leveling Pain Tolerance*, but I do love having it.*

Unlike the actual games that the Framework sometimes represented, there was no granular display for tracking what those games would have called *experience points*. The method for determining how close you were to advancement was far more vague and generally less-than-helpful. Miko's people thought of it as *energy satiation*. My brain and my body interpreted it along more familiar levels of fullness. If it felt like I'd just had two Big Macs, an order of large fries, *and* two apple pies? Well, I was primed to level whenever my skills hit their requisite numbers. If I was famished, like the time I'd worked a double at Pritchard's while the owner's bastard son kept me from sneaking any baked goods that might have dropped below the nebulous and entirely subjective description of *fresh*? It meant I had a very, very long way to go to level.

In Earth terms, I was low on experience.

A part of me had hoped that my gains from the battle of Madea would take me all the way to level seven, but I'd learned otherwise soon after reaching level six. And even now, after two pitched battles against numerous opponents and at least one Tin, I was only about halfway to where I needed to go.

Or, to put it in a way that made sense to my brain: I'd had a few cookies but could still go for something fried and greasy. And maybe a milkshake afterwards.

Still. Level seven wasn't *that* far away. I just needed some opportunities. *Opportunities that won't end with me once again surrounded by death*, I hastily clarified, in case any of the world's many deities were somehow listening. Lace's people had legends about those who had been brought across the Veil to Eos, those who were called Chosen, and *all* of those legends were drenched in blood.

I was here to save a species, but in the meantime, everyone around me kept dying.

I blinked away those thoughts when the hammer started up again. How long had I just been sitting there, marinating in my own drama? The best way to save people—and not just the synossians, but everyone who mattered to me—was for Miko, Lace, and me to keep growing. The path forward *would* be bloody; that was my new life on Eos. All I could do was give everything I had to make sure that that blood was our enemies' instead of our allies'.

It was a weird thing for a twenty-four-year-old ex-barista from Midton, Ohio to think. But for an eighteen-cycle Chosen in the Great Wilds of Eos?

Somehow, it almost felt right.

If anything, that bothered me just as much as the deaths.

ooo

Lord Arbiter Hawthorne wasn't an Aspirant, but he *was* pretty good at ordering people around. Between him and the lieutenant, our impromptu camp was in top shape even before my arm was healed the next morning. With only ten healthy combatants, including our party *and* Hawthorne's carriage driver, I wasn't confident about our ability to defend that camp, but it was a hell of a lot better than nothing.

The carriage, on the other hand, remained a problem.

There had been a couple soldiers in the column with limited knowledge of woodworking or even carpentry, but both had died during the assault. The rest of us, if supplied with the proper tools, were fully capable of bringing down a tree and rendering it into firewood, but repairing a carriage's wheel? That was way beyond anyone's expertise, and a full day's effort hadn't netted anyone the starting-level skills.

Per Miko's continued eavesdropping, the lord had finally accepted that we'd have to leave the carriage behind. Both horses *had* survived, and the lord would take one, while Wilhemina and Neesa would take the other. It left the duke's heir uncomfortably exposed to future ambushes, but hopefully, Hawthorne's man would be able to keep her safe.

It was literally in his class name, after all.

Those plans were upended late on the second day after I'd woken up, when our new head scout came racing back to camp. His quick strides made it clear that, for all he wasn't Tin, he had emphasized Finesse in his training and progression. And had probably also started with a higher score in that attribute than me.

Those of us on guard duty went on alert and the hubbub behind us in camp suggested we weren't the only ones. Lace was off scouting the eastern road, but I traded worried looks with Miko. A second attack anywhere close to the size of the first would overrun us easily, dirt embankment notwithstanding.

After meeting with the scout, Lieutenant Ender went to brief Lord Hawthorne while Sergeant Jenkins made his way over.

"At ease, maggots." He hesitated and gave Miko a respectful nod. "And uh… guests. Carrioc spotted people headed our way but says it looks like a merchant caravan. Stay sharp in case they aren't who they appear to be, but don't start anything either."

What all of us had forgotten in the aftermath of the battle was that this *was* a road. It was honestly surprising it had stayed empty this long.

Samhill, a dozen or so feet away, raised an arm that had been broken until just that morning. "If they *are* merchants, what happens then?"

"Do I look like a boy fresh off his mother's apron strings to you, Samhill?"

"Uh… no?"

"Then why would you act like I'd just had my Dreaming and woke up some kind of demons-cursed oracle?"

"Is that a real class?" I whispered to Miko. "Oracle, I mean?"

"If so, it must be at least Bronze."

Either our conversation was quiet enough that Jenkins didn't hear it, or the big man was all too aware he *still* didn't know how Lace had managed to poison his squad… because he didn't call us out like he would have his own men.

"I was asking about the wall, Jenks," said Samhill, who'd turned out to be both ever cheerful and more than a little slow. "Didn't want you to predict the future or nothing. Just thought we might have to make a path for the wagons."

Someone groaned at the idea and Jenkins stared them down.

"If the lieutenant says we take down the wall, we take down the wall. If he wants it back up again a glass later, we'll do that too. And if he wants the latrine filled in and a new one dug, I know exactly the men to volunteer for the task!" He lowered his voice. "We're soldiers. This is what we *do.*"

I wasn't a soldier—and after that speech, I was pretty sure I never wanted to be—but both the grumbling and the ass-chewing seemed to help settle everyone's nerves.

It was a full glass before the slow-moving caravan reached us. During that time, Lace had come in from the east, heard the news, and promptly gone west to scout the newcomers herself. She returned only minutes before their arrival.

"They do look like merchants," she said. "One even has his children with him. Four wagons in total. Ten guards, but they're lightly armed and I don't think any are Tin. We can take them if we need to."

"Hope we will not need to." Miko's voice was grim.

"Hope is just a tool gods use to toy with us," said Lace.

"Should find better gods then."

Instead of igniting a holy war, Miko's comment drew a savage grin out of Lace. "I like it when you show your teeth, kitten."

Miko sent me a confused look, but before I could explain the phrasing, we all heard the caravan's approach, horses and wagon wheels and even the casual chatter of people talking.

"No outriders," pointed out Lace as they came into view. "Enough guards to be safe if they run into bandits, but without any real expectation of doing so. Meaning this road is generally safe, even for dirt farmers. Meanwhile, *we* were jumped by almost forty people, five of them Tin."

"As if we needed any more confirmation that they weren't bandits, whatever Ender is saying." I nodded as the wagons slowed and then stopped entirely at the sight of our camp. "Between the attackers targeting the carriage and…." I lowered my voice. "…*other* things, it's clear someone sent trained troops after Hawthorne or Wilhemina."

"The lord suspects they were Zarisians disguised as bandits," said Miko in the High Tongue, "but has ordered the lieutenant to maintain this bandit fiction for now."

Lace looked between us. "I understood *one* of those words."

"Zaris was just conquered," I reminded the synossian in Trade. "And it's a long way away."

She tapped her left arm in agreement. She didn't buy Hawthorne's theory either.

As a long-time member of the guard and citizen of the duchy, Quincy's role in the attack made the idea of another Zarisian plot even *less* likely. The logistics of the foreign country hearing about Wilhemina's rescue, putting together a force deep within the duchy's territory, *and* suborning a key element of the retrieval party made my head spin. All signs pointed instead to a domestic faction opposed to Wilhemina's return… maybe even a faction in the duke's court itself.

Unfortunately, we couldn't come out and *say* that. Because Lace had left the head scout out of the story she'd spun while I was unconscious, we remained the only ones who knew the part he'd played in the matter. And until we had more information, until we chose to get involved or not, it was better for everyone if Quincy was simply one of the many tragic casualties in the assault. Changing the established story would just open a whole new can of worms.

Can of worms. Another Earth phrase I can't use anymore. Not until I found out if they *had* cans on Eos. Worms were less problematic; I'd seen plenty so far, both the regular ones used as bait in Harborton and the oversized, glowing variety found on the cliffs to the village's east.

We watched the caravan as its members debated what to do. The longer they waited—just out of arrow range if we'd had any bows to speak of—the more obvious it became that both Lace and the other scout had been right. They *were* exactly who they seemed to be… a collection of merchants whose hired guards were clearly reticent to advance upon a well-guarded encampment in the middle of the road.

In the end, I think it was the sight of the soldiers' uniforms—torn and bloodied but still recognizably dyed in the duke's colors—that convinced the merchants we might not be bandits ourselves. After a fair bit of debate, an older, heavyset man came forward, a bearded man in boiled leather armor at his side. We didn't hear the short conversation they had with Ender, but soon after, he was leading them over our embankment and toward to the carriage and lord arbiter.

I traded glances with Miko.

"Should go check on Wilhemina," she murmured. "Might need healing again." She patted me on the shoulder and tailed the lieutenant and his guests to the carriage.

It had only been a glass or two since the last such healing, but to Hawthorne, she was all but invisible, and Neesa seemed to welcome her company. Who was going to stop her?

"It's a shame the Framework made her a Priestess," said Lace in Gorash, the language of the South. "Because she'd have made a damn good Rogue."

11

The merchant caravan ended up being a godsend. Not a *literal* godsend, with deities forbidden from interacting directly with Eos, but probably the closest thing we'd get without Shan finding a way to break those rules again. While the merchants didn't have anyone with the Carpenter profession, they did have several people who possessed some of the associated skills. It took two days, but by the end, the holes in the carriage's exterior had been patched, its broken wheel removed and repaired.

The help didn't stop there. Hawthorne hired two of the caravan's guards on the spot, and by the time we left, he was also the temporary owner of a moderately used wagon and the two-cycles-old horse that pulled it. According to Miko, the lord had shelled out an exorbitant sum to rent both from one of the three merchant families. Both vehicle and mount would be held until the merchant passed back through Trynfall to reclaim them.

We spent a glass helping to move wares from one wagon to the next, and then another glass moving the column's excess supplies— tents, packs, and personal belongings for the recently slain—into the newly empty wagon, followed by the soldiers that wouldn't be able to travel under their own power.

I wasn't entirely sure what to make of the lord arbiter, whose bedside manner could comfortably be described as arctic, but the steps he took to make sure the injured were cared for were a big, big mark in his favor.

As for the dead? The bodies themselves were burned in two separate piles. The soldiers' possessions would be returned to the capital and delivered to their next of kin. Hawthorne had had the enemy bodies searched too, first for evidence that they were from Zaris, and then to simply strip them of everything of value. Those items would be sold in Trynfall—either to city merchants or to the duke's guard—and a portion of the resulting proceeds would also be sent to the next of kin. The remainder would be shared among the survivors as hazard pay.

As adventurers, we were *not* employed by the grand duke, and that meant we wouldn't be seeing any pay, hazard or otherwise.

Which didn't mean we came away with nothing.

Lace had found the enemy camp—to the south, where Quincy would have practically tripped over it if he'd been searching for enemies instead of working for them. Although it had been empty of identifying markers that could prove where the band of attackers had come from, and who, if anyone, had hired them, there had been plenty of supplies. A long trip out and back made sure the column would have food. But she also returned to the scene of our smaller ambush and came back with a bulging pack.

"These were *our* kills," she'd told first Lieutenant Ender and then Lord Arbiter Hawthorne. "We will donate a share to the dead so that their names are not lost, but the rest goes to the party."

It wasn't too much to ask, and eventually even the lord realized that. The night before our departure, the Marauder had met Miko and me in our tent to divvy up the spoils. Four ways now instead of six, because Skaal and Mordecai were gone. Skaal had no family other than

Lace and while we still intended to deliver the mage's share along with his belongings to his estranged lover at the Crimson Needle, he'd stopped earning further coin with his death.

Miko and I both got daggers, plain and unmarked, but well made all the same. Since I already had a blade from Madea, I tucked the backup into my boot. Miko added hers to her belt as a secondary weapon to her short staff. I wasn't sure if *Knife* was a skill for the Priest class, but it would still be helpful for gathering herbs, if not. Lace claimed the archer's bow and its quiver of five remaining arrows, while the other weapons—daggers that were in considerably worse shape than the first two—went back into the pack to be sold in Trynfall.

Only a few of the assassins had worn armor at all, and it had all been leather and in terrible shape after the battle that left the wearers dead. Faced with the prospect of cleaning off all the various solids and fluids that had stained the armor, the Marauder had elected to simply leave it behind.

Coin, on the other hand, was something that retained its value no matter how filthy it got.

"Six plugs and four bits," she said, after pouring copper into a small pile on my bedroll. "That's a plug and six bits for each of us, and the same for the shared party fund."

Despite being a barbarian from a culture that seemed to take pride in that fact, Lace's math skills were always on point when it came to divvying up the loot.

Combined with what we already had, that meant Miko and I were sitting on four plugs and nineteen bits… five plugs and nine bits once I did the conversion. Add in whatever we'd get for selling the extra knives as well as the nine plugs we had a letter of credit for, and we likely would have well over two silver towers between us.

It wasn't a ton of money, but it was something. Wilhemina's safe return remained our ticket to real wealth or, even better, a noble patron who would take on the task of preparing for the synossian refugees.

Honestly, as someone who'd fought for every paycheck while trying to pay down bills that had only mounted as my dad's health worsened, I just liked the satisfying weight of a full coin purse. It felt… prosperous. *Successful*, even if none of the coins held within were silver, let alone gold.

I wasn't rich, but I'd come a long way from minimum wage.

○○○

When we finally got moving again, our column consisted of six soldiers and two hired guards on foot, our party of three, one wagon, and the carriage. Hawthorne's man drove the carriage again, while one of the injured soldiers, Jenkins' crony, Nixon, drove the wagon. The woman who'd lost her legs rode in back with Priest Humber, as comfortable as he could make her.

It wasn't long before Lieutenant Ender found me and asked if I could take on more scouting duties. With all the casualties, they needed a third scout, and I was the only one who had any experience at all at that point.

I wasn't going to turn down an opportunity to continue raising my skills… but I didn't have skill points in *Mercantilism* for nothing either. By the time I had agreed to pitch in, Lace, Miko, and I had *all* been added to the payroll for the remainder of our trip to Trynfall. Lace and I would be paid as the lowest tier of scouts at two bits per seven-day, while Miko would net the comparatively princely sum of four bits that went to entry-level healers.

Money for doing what we would already be doing. If *Caretaking* was my least favorite General skill, *Mercantilism* might just be my favorite.

With… apologies to *Deception*, of course. And it wasn't like the two skills didn't complement each other fantastically anyway.

As soon as Ender was gone, Lace took me aside to give me a refresher on all the very many ways Eos might try to kill me while I was out on my own. Barons were responsible for clearing out the more dangerous species of flora like scarlet thorn, false dawn, or whatever a *corpsewood* was, but those efforts focused on the area immediately around well-traveled roads. And beasts, both mundane and monstrous, tended to ignore things like borders on a map.

So, while the area we were in was nowhere near as dangerous as the deep woods south of Harborton or even the swamps in which we'd found the blighted, it could still easily kill me if I wasn't paying attention.

That was probably a good lesson for life on Eos in general.

Despite my paranoia, we reached our next stop without coming across anything even vaguely threatening. The animal tracks I found were mostly smaller beasts, and while I spotted the distinctive cylindrical nests for a species of bird that Lace said drank blood, those nests were old and empty, their former inhabitants gone for the winter.

Each morning on the road, I'd trained with Miko before heading out, then trained with Jenkins and Samhill on my return. Kitchens and Holloway had been among the dead, and Nixon was too injured to participate, but the quality of my training didn't change much. I didn't see any gains in *Spear* from my sparring with Miko, but I did pick up two more points in *Unarmed Combat*, to go along with a point in *Tracking*, and another in *Mercantilism* from my bargaining with Hawthorne.

Best of all? After I wandered off course one morning, Lace *and* Miko took it upon themselves to give me a crash course in wayfinding. And that added another new entry to my ever-growing list of General skills: *Orienteering*.

After three days, we reached the village of Land's End, a collection of houses that had sprung up around the inn of the same name. As I'd promised I would, I offered to buy Samhill an ale, but the man wasn't in the mood for celebration *or* commiseration. In fact, our whole stay was a subdued affair. Simple, hearty food, an innkeeper who spent most of his time in the private room where the lord arbiter and his man ate, and an early departure the next morning.

We'd been the only people in the common room. The inn's only barmaid, a teenager thoroughly bored with her job and our presence, said that much was normal at this time of year. As mild as the winters were this far north, most *thinking* people saved their travel for the spring and summer months.

The first time I saw her smile was when we left. Part of me wondered why she was working a job she clearly hated. She was well past the age when she would have had her Dreaming, which meant she had a class. Why not focus on leveling that instead?

"Part of it is the lack of training," volunteered Humber when I voiced the question our next night on the road. "But I assume a greater part is simple comfort. Not everyone wants the life of a soldier, a guardsman, or an adventurer. There are some for whom danger is a lure. For many others, it's a deterrent. Better to be safe and to progress as a Dedicated. Though," he admitted, "it would seem she has not yet found the profession that best suits her."

"Could also just be one bad day," suggested Miko. "Might— *she* might—love the inn most other times. Cannot judge from one moment."

It was hard to argue with that. Even working at Pritchards had had some good moments. The only job I could think of that I'd unreservedly hated was being Erlund's caretaker in Harborton, and that had mostly been because I had so many bad memories associated with those duties.

Caretaking, I couldn't help but notice every time I opened my personal record, was one skill that *hadn't* degraded, even though I hadn't used it since Harborton.

The day that skill disappeared from my sheet entirely would be the day I finally broke away entirely from the life I'd led back on Earth. It couldn't come soon enough for me.

Slowed by the addition of the wagon, it would be six days from the oddly named Land's End, situated on the boundary between two baronies, to our next stop, Leffing. Soon after that, we'd be in the heart of the duchy, towns separated by farmland or carefully cultivated forests rather than true wilderness.

Jenkins estimated we were at least eighteen days from Trynfall, and while we had ample supplies for the trip, given our reduced numbers, Hawthorne's careful mask was starting to show cracks, revealing the growing stress beneath. He'd made a big to-do about getting Wilhemina back to the capital before the duke's return, and the attack had made that prospect significantly less likely.

Still, there was only so fast we could travel. Better that we arrive late and with a live heir than that we blunder into another ambush. And in the meantime, our party would more than earn our salaries.

Hours by myself in the woods gave me a lot of time to think. A year earlier, that would have been a very bad thing; I'd have doom spiraled over thoughts of my dad, of our bills, of the repairs I couldn't afford to make to the trailer, of my ex-girlfriend, Kate, off living life in New York City. On Eos, not only were those concerns literally worlds away, there were far more interesting things to occupy my brain.

For starters, there was my class and what I wanted to evolve it into. To date, I'd been picking up skills almost at random, based on whatever felt useful or necessary at the time. Those skills, however, would factor into any advanced classes I was offered. Classes more specialized than *Spearman*, at least.

But what was it that I wanted?

Asking about someone's class was almost as frowned upon as asking about their skills, level, or rank, but I was betting that Jenkins had evolved his class from Warrior at least once on the way to Tin. And while Samhill was unranked, just like me, he was clearly orienting his skillset around fighting in rank and using a shield.

As an adventurer, that wouldn't be my path, and I spent a considerable amount of time over the next several days trying to figure out what that path should be. Shan had robbed me of the opportunity to wield magic, but *techniques* were honestly the next best thing anyway. And how I shaped my progression was entirely up to me.

Spear was a continued no-brainer. Riok's weapon had changed somehow with its baptism in the Buried necromancer's blood. It wasn't outright enchanted, as far as I could tell, but we had yet to find anything that could break it, and in a pre-steel world, that was worth its weight in literal gold. More importantly, I *liked* spears, and this one helped make up for my deficit in height and reach.

I wanted to stick with *Knife* too. Easy to carry and quick to draw, it was a pretty good complementary weapon for when the spear proved impractical. *Unarmed Combat* was more of a nice-to-have. Useful, but I never wanted to base my class around it when I could instead have a sharp pointy end and five feet of unbreakable metal between me and my opponent.

When it came to armor, I'd switched from *Light Armor* to *Medium Armor* back in Madea, and while the improvement in protection hadn't been quite as overwhelming as I'd hoped, I still didn't want to go back. Maybe I'd try for *Heavy Armor* once money was no object, but that might come with other tradeoffs like mobility. For now, I liked where I was at.

As for my other Major and Minor skills? I didn't see any reason *not* to level them if I could. Skills degraded over time and without use—again, with *Caretaking* so far being the aggravating exception—but outside of maybe *Throwing*, I thought the class-related skills I had all fit my needs. And the fact that they kept increasing with every fight only reinforced that belief.

Which left my General skills. *Deception* and maybe *Stealth* had clearly been part of why I was given *Deceptive Strike*, my best attack technique. I'd also maxed out *Animal Behaviorism* and *Danger Sense* and had to assume those might factor into the mix for future techniques or even class evolutions. But was there anything else I should be focusing on? Would *Mercantilism* or *Meditation* have a direct impact on my advancement as an Aspirant, or were those always going to be purely secondary skills?

Again, the lack of actual *knowledge* frustrated me. I needed to get my hands on an established advancement path. Really, I needed *multiple* advancement paths, both to improve my chances of finding one that worked and so I could compare and contrast between them to maybe get an idea of how all this worked. And I needed a list of what other skills were out there and how they all might fit together.

Get our reward from Wilhemina's dad.

Create a plan for settling potentially thousands of refugees.

Kill Arrius.

Somewhere in there, I'd need access to archives. And not just a town's entry-level tomes and scrolls, but the stuff hidden away for favored individuals or a noble family's heirs. If the duke didn't include that in his hopefully significant reward, I could try to leverage my gods-given translation ability. A translator of old texts, once professionally established, might be permitted access to information that was otherwise out of reach for anyone not in society's elite ranks.

But that was, at best, multiple seven-days in the future. In the absence of any knowledge, and with only Miko and occasionally Lace to bounce ideas off of, I was left to switch focus to myself instead of the Framework. Not *how* I would progress, but what it is I wanted.

And there I hit a bit of a mental wall. I wanted to keep wielding a spear, obviously. In terms of combat style, I preferred something closer to Lace than Samhill, because not getting hit at all seemed a lot better than the alternative. And *Lunge*, even in its current form, already lent itself to the concept of battlefield mobility. But what else?

Protect the people I can protect.

That should have gone without saying, but in my mind, it also circled back to fighting like Samhill. I couldn't carry a shield *and* wield my oversized spear, even if I'd wanted to.

Get them before they get you.

That was something Lace would say, but... maybe?

As a Warrior, I didn't know if I'd ever have the options she'd had as a Rogue. I didn't know if the branches of our respective trees would almost intertwine if we followed them far enough; her in the direction of dealing damage, me in the direction of mobility and speed. The bigger problem was that our party already *had* a Marauder. If the three of us were going to continue working together past killing Arrius—and I *thought* we probably would—I'd need to find and fill my own niche.

I spent four days going back and forth in my brain and not getting anywhere. I didn't want to *just* be a Spearman, but I wasn't sure what that left. Riok's unnamed advanced class? Something that mixed in the wide range of skills I was racking up points in? I had to imagine there were wilderness-based fighter class evolutions available, and those would seem like a great fit for an adventurer... but did I want to specialize so much?

This had all been a lot easier in the games my friend Bug had run back in Midton. Read the rules book, pick a direction, and min-max your way to success and profit. The lack of information, coupled with the massively raised stakes of actually being here, left me fumbling. It wasn't truly decision paralysis, because I didn't have any decisions to make yet, but it was maddening just the same.

So, on day five, I switched to an equally thorny topic: my Ideal.

Kacellius had said part of reaching Tin would be me figuring out how my Ideal could shape my development. And that to do so, I had to first figure out what that Ideal truly meant to me. *Freedom* should have been easy; it was a word that got a whole lot of play in the town and country I'd grown up in, after all. But what did it mean to me?

Facing down death outside the walls of Madea, I'd decided it simply meant the ability to choose. Which sounded simple, until I started digging into it. Was it *my* ability to choose, or everyone's? If it was the first, was that actually freedom? And if it was the second, where did it stop? What was the difference between freedom and chaos? How could you have the former without drifting into anarchy?

Rules, Shan had told me. *There are always rules.*

What did that mean for my Ideal?

What did it mean for the person I wanted to be?

More questions. More one-sided mental conversations that never reached a conclusion, no matter how many times they replayed in my brain. I didn't know enough about the Framework and I didn't know enough about myself either and that was a big problem if I was going to make it to Tin.

If I hadn't already capped out *Pain Tolerance*, I was pretty sure the headache of trying to gameplan my future would've gotten me there on its own.

Instead, by the time we reached Leffing, I'd gained a point each in *Tracking* and *Athleticism*, as well as a desperate need for something strongly alcoholic.

ooo

Leffing was the largest city in its barony, but the baron didn't make his home there. I wasn't entirely sure why, and Humber's attempted explanation went so far down a rabbit hole of family trees and ancestral lands that I was fairly certain he didn't know either. Regardless, the city was a relatively impressive sight, at least three times the size of Sakeld—which had itself been significantly larger than Madea—with multiple districts and a market square large enough to park all of Harborton in the middle.

Of all the places I'd seen since coming to Eos, only Whitehall, the doomed capital of Miko's people, had been larger, and that was like comparing Cincinnati to Midton.

The houses in Leffing were predominately made of wood, but multiple stories were the norm there, rather than the exception, and some of the people we saw walking about were, if not extravagantly dressed, more fashionable than in Madea or Sakeld, with brightly colored outfits made from fabrics other than wool. We'd arrived in the late afternoon and marched right in, the guards at the gate falling away and saluting when they saw the lord arbiter's carriage and soldiers in the duke's colors. The streets weren't packed, but the people who *were* present moved aside as swiftly as the guards; we had a straight shot up the road to a large inn about a block from the market.

Hawthorne and Priest Humber led the way inside upon our arrival, trailed by a Wilhemina-carrying Neesa and the lord's guard. Lieutenant Ender turned to the rest of us.

"Sergeant, get our wounded into the common room and then pick someone to help the stableboy with the horses. We'll need another two to keep an eye on the stables tonight. His lordship wants to head out again tomorrow."

As the lieutenant trailed Hawthorne into the inn, Samhill's curse was quiet but heartfelt. The original schedule had called for a full day's rest in Leffing, but our tardiness had ruined those plans. To now lose even this one night of comfort in the inn seemed more than the man was willing to bear.

"I can do both," I found myself volunteering.

It wasn't quite the drink I'd offered to buy Samhill. Then again, it was probably worth even more to him right then. And it wouldn't cost me any coin.

"What do you know about horses, adventurer?" growled Jenkins.

The answer was *not much*, but I *had* been taught how to care for dalysi, which were vaguely similar. A maxed-out *Animal Behaviorism* skill would hopefully handle the rest.

"Enough to make sure the stableboy doesn't do anything wrong," I told him. "And when it comes to standing watch, my eyes work as well as the rest of yours."

Not counting Lace, but I didn't expect the Marauder to volunteer, and from the look on her face, she couldn't even begin to guess why I had.

"Must see to Lady Willerton," said Miko, breaking the silence. "But will return to stand watch with Brian afterward."

Miko's role in the defense and her treatment of the injured afterward had evidently earned her a lot of new friends as three other soldiers suddenly were volunteering to take her place. The Priestess flashed her sharp-toothed smile—causing at least one of those volunteers to flinch—and shook her head.

"Thank you but no. Should—*you* should—enjoy the inn. Am happy to spend time out here."

"I'll bring you both food when it's served," said Ullra, one of the only women in the column.

"One is grateful," said Miko.

"*This* one," I murmured.

"This one, yes." The synossian patted my shoulder in thanks. "I will return soon, nest-brother."

I stood for a moment, watching them all head into the inn. Miko was a head taller than anyone but Jenkins, and the only non-human among them, but the soldiers had closed in protectively around her as they walked. They looked almost like an honor guard. If anyone in the inn had a problem with Miko's presence, I was pretty sure there'd be two or three veterans more than eager to settle the matter.

Anti-synossian sentiment—anti-*scaled* sentiment, in the local vernacular—was something we were going to deal with anywhere we went on this continent. And yet the Priestess herself remained the next best thing to a diplomatic cheat code. Another seven-day or so and the whole unit would probably consider her an adopted sister.

I needed a trait that did *that*.

A low cough broke my reverie, and I turned to find the stableboy waiting, half my age and at least three inches taller. Unlike some of the people we'd seen in the streets, he wore sensible, if slightly worn, wool. He also had some straw in his hair, but I wasn't going to mention that.

"Sorry about that," I told him. "I'm here to help with the horses." And then, seeing his face droop like I'd just threatened to steal his favorite puppy, I added, "It won't impact your tip."

Just like that, he was all smiles again.

"After we move the wagon and carriage inside and unhook the horses, I will show you where we keep the brushes, *sir*."

ooo

Much later, Miko and I finished off our dinner: some kind of stew, which seemed to be the default dish of every inn we'd stayed at so far, and bread that had almost definitely been baked that morning. In place of wine or ale, we got water, because we were going to be on watch, but I was okay with that. A hangover would just make the early departure worse and given that I'd be scouting again, I'd need to have my full faculties.

We didn't have access to the inn's baths—and I was pretty sure they cost more than I wanted to pay anyway—but there was a well out back and the stableboy, still flush with his copper bit tip, had been happy to lend me a clean bucket before he climbed up to his own bed in the stable's loft. Miko and I took turns pouring water over our heads until the worst of the road dust was gone. She pulled her robes back on while I changed into a fresh set of clothing and tugged my gambeson on over it.

The hauberk could wait until morning… we'd be resting in shifts, and I'd learned that sleeping in iron was all but impossible.

With my stench somewhat cleansed, the smells around us seeped in. Woodsmoke from the fireplace in the common room. A lingering scent of the stew we'd had for dinner and whatever higher-priced fare had been available. And the stable smelled like a stable, with two other horses housed inside in addition to our four.

Still, it was warm enough. We stowed our packs in the wagon and laid out our bedrolls there too, safely above the scratchy straw but close enough to react if someone decided this night, of all nights, was the time for horse thievery.

The lord arbiter's carriage was parked next to the wagon, but even though its doors didn't lock and the vehicle was almost definitely more comfortable than the wagon, we left it alone. As the head of the grand duke's police force, I could all too easily see Hawthorne having some way of knowing when someone intruded. And we didn't need to borrow trouble, especially when even this was a pretty sweet upgrade from our little tent.

"I saw Lace sneak back out of the inn when I returned the bowls," said Miko, speaking in the High Tongue. Her voice was pitched low so as to not disturb the horses.

I responded in kind. "Did she say where she was going?"

"She did not." Miko hesitated. "Should we be worried about her?"

"Yes. And no. And I'm not sure."

"I don't know which of those answers to trust, nest-brother."

"She's doing better. I think. She is talking more, at least. But until Skaal is avenged, I'm not sure she'll ever be entirely here." I looked over at where the synossian lay in the darkness. "You were trained in this sort of thing. What do you think we should do?"

"I do not know. When I raise my concerns, she changes the subject or stops speaking entirely. I think we just have to support her, but I was taught resilience can be best found in community. Instead, she seeks solitude."

"Different cultures, I think. I get the impression the amazons aren't quite as emotionally evolved as your people."

"Then we should simply make certain that she knows she is *not* alone. That we are here when and if she needs us." Miko's sigh filled the wagon. "It is not an answer that fills my need to do something, but I must remind myself that this is not about me."

We lay there in silence for a while, and when Miko shifted again, I knew the subject had been at least temporarily laid to rest.

"Speaking of the need to do something… why did you volunteer for this duty?" she asked.

I wasn't going to tell Miko it was payback for Samhill because then she'd want to know why and would probably make a thing about me not being responsible for paying back her debts. Luckily, I'd had other reasons too.

"I'm trying to make friends in low places." I shot her a grin that she couldn't see in the darkness. "Endear myself to more than just our party. After all, we don't all have special Miko diplomacy powers."

"I only try to do what is right."

"That's why it's so damn effective." I leaned back, using my pack as a pillow. The wagon's ceiling was significantly higher than our tent's and I couldn't make it out above us. "Also, I can't see Hawthorne paying for rooms for any of us, especially now that we're working for him. And the stables seemed better—if a bit smellier—than an over-full common room would be."

"I question if it is *actually* smellier out here." She paused. "I apologize. I should not have said that."

"What do you mean?" I waited. "Miko?"

"It's just that… your species—especially the men, and especially after they have eaten…"

"Oh. Well, yeah."

Gas was a problem, even here on Eos, and the duke's soldiers, even the women like Ullra, didn't seem overly concerned about that. I knew Miko didn't sweat, but it hadn't occurred to me that she might process food differently too.

Wait. "Do *I* smell?"

"Only sometimes," she was quick to say. "And my nose is often blinded by the scents of the road anyway. These horses defecate with far greater frequency and volume than the dalysi ever did."

I took advantage of the darkness to carefully sniff my own pits. Things weren't going great down there, but in lieu of a true bath and an inter-dimensional deodorant delivery, I thought I was doing okay.

"It was not you I was thinking of, nest-brother," said Miko, a touch of concern in her voice. "I just meant to say that staying out here was a wise choice, even if we will only get half the usual amount of sleep."

"On that note, why don't you get your meditation in? Then you can get a few hours of rest." Now that my *Meditation* skill was Uncommon rank and I'd gotten a little bit more used to what that meant, I didn't need her to watch over me unless we were outdoors.

Even with half my mind turned to communing with the Framework, I'd be able to hear any intruders sneaking into the stables.

"Yes. Of course. I will." For a moment, she sounded very, very young, a marked contrast to the trained counselor from a few minutes prior. "You are not upset with me, are you, Brian Fieldings?"

"I'm upset that we only got you two extra sets of robes in Madea and that Nixon's repair job looks like the work of a drunk," I said. "I'm upset that I couldn't get you a higher salary with Hawthorne, despite your outsized importance to his mission. And I'm *really* upset that I not only don't know what kind of meat was in our stew tonight but kind of *don't want* to know, just in case it was something gross. But upset with you? *Please.*"

A clawed hand carefully sought and found mine in the darkness, the pebbly skin of Miko's scales cool.

"It was tusker, nest-brother."

"I'm sorry?"

"In the stew. The meat was tusker."

"Oh. Well, that's alright then."

12

After Leffing, the landscape changed. The vast stretches of wilderness were gone, replaced by individual forests or large tracts of farmland. The road west remained packed dirt, but it was well-traveled and wide enough that wagons larger than ours could pass in opposite directions. We encountered a variety of other roads, big and small, leading north and south to distant locations in the duchy. And towns and villages grew far more numerous, now rarely more than a day or two away.

We stopped in some of those towns, but Leffing's inn was the last we visited. Instead, Hawthorne would speak with the local mayor or magistrate while the rest of us camped outside. On occasion, villagers would come out to us, setting up stalls to sell their wares, but they were the exception rather than the norm. For the most part, people seemed eager to let us be.

I blamed Jenkins for that. And maybe Lace. They were both Tins, after all, and seemed to unconsciously give off angry vibes.

As we traveled, I continued to serve as a scout, though I questioned the need. I came across more livestock than anything else. If that livestock hadn't been predominantly phloxl, it would have almost felt like I was back on Earth, if in a completely different time and era, traveling through the rural countryside in a largely peaceful agrarian society.

Thanks to both the lack of danger and the lack of challenge, neither *Tracking* nor *Orienteering* saw any additional gains. Neither did *Hunting* after the lord announced through Lieutenant Ender that we would make do with our existing supplies.

Athleticism, on the other hand, apparently found some small value in my traipsing all over the fields and through the small pockets of forests. Eight days after we left Leffing, I gained another point in the skill. Coupled with the one I'd earned on our way *to* Leffing, I had finally maxed *Athleticism* for my level:

```
You have increased the following skills:

Minor skills:
Athleticism [+1]: 35/35
```

Pain Tolerance was already at its cap, of course, so all I had left for my next level's skill requirements were *Spear* and one of either *Medium Armor, Tactics,* or *Knife*. Unfortunately, a quick internal survey told me I was still a long way from level seven when it came to my energy satiation. At best, I'd finally eked past the halfway point.

A big part of the problem was that I only earned progress towards my level—experience points, even if the Framework didn't call them that—when I did things that qualified as duties of my class, and *those* mostly seemed to involve real combat. Training had so far been the only other thing that sufficed, and without true instructors, the experience I'd earned from that on the road had been minimal. Growth came from overcoming challenges in the service of your class duties and outside of learning, repeatedly, how poorly matched I was barehanded against opponents a foot taller and at least fifty pounds heavier than me, this part of the trip wasn't providing much opportunity.

The sad truth was that the biggest gains I'd seen since leaving Madea had come from the battle that killed half the lord arbiter's soldiers. If that was the only efficient way for a full quarter of all Aspirants to level, it was no wonder that war was a near-constant thing on the continent. And that Miko's people had been so dramatically under-leveled after centuries of peace on their own continent.

My nest-sister had reached peak satiation soon after we departed Leffing. She spent a fair bit of time and virtually all her energy every day on activities that fit squarely into the duties of her class, after all, and while those gains remained small in the absence of life-or-death stakes, they were adding up a whole lot faster than mine. Now, she only needed to finish leveling two of her Minor skills.

Level seven would be a very big deal for both of us because it brought with it a new spell or technique, and I was as thrilled as she was about her impending advancement. I just wanted *my* share of that sweet leveling fun.

You only just reached level six a moon ago, I reminded myself. *By any standards, that's fast.*

And it was, but… I wanted *more*.

Complete your quests and you'll be leveling in no time.

That was more a guess than anything. The amount of experience I needed to progress almost definitely increased with each new level and I didn't know if the reward I was given for quest completions would do the same. But I had two, maybe three, quests that could be finished in Trynfall, and I had to believe those would put me over the edge.

So, I kept grinding, even as we left one road behind to take another one north, forest and farmland fading out to be replaced with rolling hills better suited for what could have been sheep if it weren't for the extra legs. Weapon spars in the morning, with Lace now sometimes joining in to torment us both. Unarmed training in the evening, where Miko's inclusion proved there was no such thing as an unarmed synossian. Scouting during the day, even though there was nothing to hunt, barely anything to track, and I hadn't managed to gain a single point in Vitality from all the extra leagues I'd hiked.

Over the course of the final twelve days, I eked out single improvements in *Spear, Knife,* and *Unarmed Combat,* but my energy levels? They were still stuck at *well, that was a great first course, but what's next on the menu?* levels.

I was busy obsessing over that stagnation when Trynfall finally came into sight.

ooo

It was strange to think but, in less than half a cycle on Eos, I'd already been to significantly more places than I had in twenty-three years on Earth. I'd seen tiny villages like Harborton and Land's End, towns like Ilya and Madea, and even cities like Leffing and Whitehall.

But I'd never seen anything quite like Trynfall.

Even at a distance, it loomed above us, and the road we were on stretched to meet it, rising toward a massive wall of dark and unlovely stone that masked many of the buildings behind it. Further up was another wall with more buildings behind it, and then a third wall even higher. Looming behind that last wall were three towers of differing heights.

I couldn't decide if it was a city that wanted to be a fortress or a fortress that had grown into a city. Either way, it was imposing as all hell.

It took all afternoon to climb the road toward the southern gates and while the incline wasn't steep, it felt never-ending. Even the horses seemed put out, littering the road behind them with steaming piles in silent protest. There was a steady stream of traffic in both directions, most of it pedestrians, with the occasional mounted rider or horse-drawn wagon. Hawthorne's carriage was the only one of its kind in sight, and drew as many looks as the tired, heavily armed soldiers—and three adventurers—marching in front and behind.

If Whitehall had been bright and widespread, sprawling out from the banks of the river it had been built around, Trynfall was the opposite: enormous but oddly compact, as foreboding as it was formidable.

"It's always a bit of a sight," Humber was admitting to Miko when I returned to the column. "His grace's ancestors believed in security above all. And given the times they lived in, who could blame them? Trust me, the view more than makes up for it once you reach the Upper City."

"View?" I asked, inserting myself neatly into the conversation as only someone with a ten *Discernment* stat could do.

"Ocean," replied Miko. "City is built into mountain overlooking water."

"Precisely." Humber beamed. "The city has three main districts—Lower, Middle, and Upper. Then there are the cliffside docks, practically the unofficial fourth district, both part of and separate from the Lower City. The ocean has always played its part in the city's prosperity, and we boast the kingdom's greatest fleet."

"We?"

"I was born here, Brian. Born and raised in the Lower City. It's hard not to take pride in Trynfall's accomplishments."

"Is only proper," said Miko.

"Maybe you could show us around once we've met with the duke?" I suggested.

"Absolutely! I'll have my duties at the church, of course, but it would be a pleasure."

I smiled my thanks and mentally moved another of my quests—*Help Miko Naseri make contact with the synossian enclave in Trynfall*—closer to completion.

Just inside the gate, we were met by ten city guards in the duke's colors and a handful of sharp-eyed individuals in black that Humber pointed out as arbiters. After a short conversation with Hawthorne, they formed up around the lord's carriage. Lieutenant Ender turned to address the rest of us.

"Sergeant Jenkins, choose two men and take the wagon and our casualties to the Lower barracks while I report to the captain in charge. Adventurers, Priest Humber, you'll be staying with the carriage until instructed otherwise. The rest of you are free to return to your homes in the city. Consider this a very temporary leave. You'll all be brought in for debriefing within the next day."

"That means no drinking yourselves into stupors, maggots," announced Jenkins. "And the angels of the streets will be deprived of your blessed company for a while longer yet. Especially yours, Emillia."

A heartfelt curse came from the woman in the wagon who'd lost both her legs but retained a sense of humor.

Ender made a face but said nothing.

After our last moon on the road, the remaining soldiers didn't have a whole lot of discipline left in them. Still, they managed to come to attention and salute the lieutenant before dispersing into the city. Jenkins, Samhill, Pierce, and the wagon stayed with us for a few blocks, then turned down a side street, breaking away from the procession.

Samhill, at least, offered a parting wave.

My first real impression of Trynfall was one of noise. There were people *everywhere*, half of them hurrying about like they were late for exams, and half seemingly content to just congregate on the streets. The guard's presence made space for our carriage's passage, but that space filled right up again behind us, a wall of sound as much as individuals.

If New York City was anything like this, maybe I shouldn't have been so envious of Kate all those years.

It wasn't just humans, of course, though they did seem to make up the majority of the population. I saw corbins and kithrizal, synossians and lupine. I even saw a handful of dunsmen and one heavily armored contingent of the vaguely elf-like species that Tantalas in Harborton and Lieutenant Lissiana in Madea had belonged to. A woman, blue-skinned, bald, and even taller than Miko, argued with a living refrigerator box on stilts, while someone whose shape seemed to flicker and shift watched them both with a smile, giant, sabretooth-like fangs on full display.

That was almost enough to forget the noise. Trynfall and its leader were both reputed to be welcoming to *all* species, and ten minutes within its walls, I'd seen ample evidence to reinforce that reputation. It also showed me that I needed to do more than just study the Framework; I needed to continue broadening my understanding of Eos itself. Starting with the people living on it.

The road we took through the Lower City seemed to be a primary thoroughfare, twice the size of the streets that spun off from it to forge their own routes through the chaos. We went forward multiple blocks and then circled about a feature that seemed ubiquitous in Eosian settlements: the market square.

From what I could see of it from the outside, Trynfall's market was in full swing. Semi-permanent stalls stood next to more temporary lean-tos, tarps providing some form of shade for the merchants who had laid out their wares on tables or brightly colored blankets. I couldn't make out what was being sold but promised myself I'd return to check it out when I could. When it came to flea markets, I had a half-full coin purse, five points in *Mercantilism*, and absolutely no conscience.

The crowds lessened as we left the market square behind and then lessened again when the road started up the hill to the distant second wall. The second half of the Lower City was tiered like an ancient Earth ziggurat, with multiple blocks occupying each tier. The houses on the second tier were no bigger than those below, but they weren't quite as squashed together. The houses on the third tier were almost all made from stone and the houses on the fourth tier had multiple levels and the occasional fenced-in courtyard.

It wasn't trailers versus country mansions, like back home, but I recognized gentrification when I saw it. A few more tiers and we'd no doubt come across wide open, carefully manicured parks and the Eosian equivalent of artisanal coffee houses.

After our long hike *to* the city, I wasn't loving the continued incline. Stairwells cut more direct paths up the hill, but our road curved back and forth, making it viable for vehicles like the lord's carriage. My sixteen Vitality meant I wasn't exactly *taxed*, but I could feel the burn in my quads.

That burning kept me distracted through the third, fourth, and fifth tiers. I didn't think I'd even *had* quads before coming to Eos.

The sixth tier held only the wall to the Upper City. A pair of guards manned each of the two gates I could see, and pedestrians were slowly trickling inside. I took the opportunity to look back over the parts of the city we'd just come through.

The market square was obvious from above, a huge space at the first tier and near the center of the Lower City. It seemed to serve as the hub of that region, with first shops and then housing developments flowing outwards like concentric rings in a semicircle. At either end of that semicircle, tunnels led into the rock of the mountain itself.

"Passageways to the stairs and lifts that connect the Lower City to the docks," said Humber, when I pointed those tunnels out to him. "The other districts have their own lifts, of course, but they're even more highly regulated."

The neighborhoods around those tunnels seemed well kept, but Trynfall was not without its blemishes. After my time in Madea, my eyes strayed almost unconsciously toward the Lower City's exterior wall, and there, far from the market square, the south gate, *and* the second tier, the houses were small and visibly shabby, crammed together off twisting alleyways instead of the well-kept streets.

Trailer parks weren't a thing on Eos, mainly because trailers didn't exist, but I recognized the local equivalent when I saw one. Slums by any other name. We were too far away for me to tell who lived there, if it was predominantly beastkin as had been the case with Madea, or if location in Trynfall was a question more of poverty than of species.

Given the duke's reputation, I figured it was the latter.

Which made it… *better*, but still not particularly great. Especially when you looked at the other tiers of the Lower City and realized the *social* hierarchy was almost a *literal* hierarchy in a city that had been built vertically.

Brian, chided the voice in my head, *get rewarded first. Kill Arrius second. Save Miko's people third.* Then *you can worry about social and economic changes that you're neither equipped to design nor in any position to implement.*

Yeah. That made sense.

It was a rare day when my inner voice gave good advice.

○○○

Once we passed through the inner gates, the Middle City spread out before us. In some ways, it was a repeat of what we'd already seen below, with multiple tiers gradually leading up to yet another wall.

From where we stood, I could barely see that wall, let alone the towers I knew were behind it. In the opposite direction, the wall we'd just passed through hid the Lower City from view entirely.

I wondered how much of that was by design.

In pretty much *every* other way, the Middle City was a revelation.

Kate's family back in Midton had been well off. Not *Powell family* rich, but there'd never been any concerns about student loans or scholarships when she went off to college. I'd been over to her house dozens of times while we were dating and every time, I'd had to squash that tiny feeling of envy as I walked up the long driveway, past a lawn so green it looked like it had been color corrected, to a house larger than five doublewides and *nicer* than the whole park put together.

The Middle City was like that. Wide streets, perfectly straight and surprisingly clean, led from the gate into what seemed to be curated communities. Many of the houses in sight had courtyards surrounded by their own walls, walls that were far nicer and more decorative than the ones segmenting each of Trynfall's three cities. I saw stained glass windows and gargoyles carved into alien shapes, bell towers, and more than a few decorative columns.

This was how Trynfall's rich lived, and I wanted a piece.

Directly ahead of us, the buildings were even larger, butting up against the street with only small side yards to separate them. Judging by their size and the number of people casually strolling in and out, they probably weren't homes. In fact, if I had to guess, they were shops or museums.

"Are those *temples?*" breathed Miko.

Or temples. Right.

"They are," said Humber, that same note of pride back in his voice. "You're in Trynfall, city of a thousand gods, and this… this is the Worshipper's Ascent." He pointed to a long, narrow staircase at the far end of the street. Unlike the individual flights of steps we'd passed in the Lower City, these reached all the way from our tier to the very top. "During the Feast of the Anointed Trinity, pilgrims from across the duchy make the climb after a full day of fasting."

"What about on Fell's Night?" asked Lace, materializing at my shoulder from out of nowhere.

Or… from right behind me. It was hard to know sometimes.

Humber swallowed. "I haven't participated in *those* revelries, but I'm told they have their place here too." He took a breath and his face cleared. "All religions are welcome in Trynfall, though not all are represented in the Middle City."

"If the Bright Lady has a temple here, I would like to see it," said Miko, for once remembering all her nouns and verbs when speaking in Trade.

"Your goddess?" Humber nodded. "I'll have to ask around. It might be off the beaten path up here or down in the Lower City. Perhaps near your people's enclave?"

Given that the *scaled* that Miko had met in Madea didn't even worship the synossian pantheon anymore, I wasn't going to hold my breath. Still, the mention of the enclave caught my attention.

"We'll want to visit the enclave, regardless," I said. Not only would doing so hopefully complete one of my quests, but it would put Miko in contact with more of her kind. And hopefully, *they'd* be more interested in the return of thousands of their long-lost cousins than the downtrodden family in Madea had been.

"Of course. When we're done, we can make it the first step of the tour. Although," mused the Priest, "the Temple of the Weeping Crone might make for a more impactful starting point. I get choked up whenever I so much as pass by."

If the whole *City of a Thousand Gods* title hadn't already made it abundantly clear, that just confirmed one thing for me: Eos had too damn many deities.

We marched right down that center street, passing between temples that were as numerous as they were varied. One building might be nothing but columns reaching for the sky, an altar at the center and no roof to speak of, where the next might look like a miniature fortress, plopped right down in the middle of a city block. Another temple was simply a leafless tree set in the middle of a barren plot of land. I'd have thought it the world's worst park if it hadn't been for the handful of people praying beneath the tree's spindly branches.

Much like in the Lower City, there was a hierarchy clearly at play. A temple's proximity to the center road and its vertical location on the Worshipper's Ascent combined to indicate how popular or powerful the given religion was. That didn't always align with the temple's actual architecture—the tree was located on the third tier while a temple with gold-leaf doors was down on the first—but so far, it was clear vertical elevation was an indicator of status in Trynfall.

As someone who was vertically challenged, I didn't love it.

The stairs that formed the Worshipper's Ascent were dangerously steep for pedestrians and entirely out of the question for anything with wheels. We followed the carriage up another series of switchbacks instead. On every tier, streets split off to the side, leading to a series of increasingly extravagant houses and properties, seemingly competing for attention with the temples that had been given pride of place in the Middle City. Armed men and women in differently colored tabards watched us go by from estate walls. Some exchanged words with the city guards, others maintained their vigilance in silence. None gave our party more than a passing glance.

On the fourth tier, halfway up to the next wall and the Upper City that would be found behind it, we took one of those side streets and left behind the road we'd followed so far. In lieu of houses, this street had shops, smaller than the walled mansions, but almost as fancy. Each had a single, immaculately dressed guard out front by the ornately carved doors. There were very few signs, for reasons I couldn't fathom, but large windows revealed some of the contents of each shop as we passed by, and the scents drifting through open doors made some others just as clear.

My stomach rumbled after we passed what was clearly a bakery. It had been a long time since we'd had our lunchtime rations, and whatever that bakery had just made smelled better than anything I'd had since coming to Eos.

We traveled for a couple of blocks and then came to a halt before a two-story building with guards out front and a low murmur of noise emanating from within. This shop did have a sign in dark wood featuring some sort of a carving of a star-filled sky.

Hawthorne's guard dismounted from the front of the carriage and then, for the first time since we'd reached Trynfall, the lord arbiter himself made an appearance. He walked over to us.

"We will be taking Lady Willerton to the duke's personal healers in the Upper City. Priestess Naseri and Priest Humber, you will both attend. I have no doubt the healers will want to question you before they attempt to break this curse or cure this infection. You two," he continued, spearing first Lace and then me with his gaze, "will stay here at the Night's Sky. Your companion will return by nightfall, and someone will come to escort you all to the palace in a day or two's time."

"You want us to wait here for a full day?" asked Lace.

"I go where Miko does," I said, at almost the same time.

"No, you don't. This is Trynfall, not Madea, adventurer. There are rules and regulations to be followed." Hawthorne turned to Lace. "One day at the *very* least. There are things to do and decisions to make before any assembly can be arranged." He paused. "Alternatively, I can pay out your salaries here and now and your reward will be whatever remains in my purse afterward. There would be nothing keeping you here at that point."

"We're not leaving the city without Miko," said Lace.

"Then I suggest you take advantage of the hospitality on offer and allow matters to proceed in the prescribed fashion."

"It will be fine," Humber told me. "I'll be with Miko."

"Am capable of taking care of myself," added the woman in question. "And want to speak to healers about the curse. I will come back afterward."

There wasn't much to say about that and there was even less to do. I didn't like being separated from Miko, and I didn't like being stashed in an inn and told not to go anywhere either, but nobody was giving us a choice. And we *had* to stick things out, with our future hopes pinned on whatever reward Duke Willerton would give us.

"Fine." That was all I'd been planning to say, but *Mercantilism* nudged me to follow up. "Who's paying for our stay here then?"

Hawthorne looked at me for a very long moment. Finally, he sighed. "I will see that it is taken care of."

"What about food?"

Another meaningful pause and indecipherable look. If I didn't get a skill gain out of this, then the Framework was deeply broken.

"Two meals a day, and only here at the Night's Sky. But this generosity ends with your audience. After that, you and your party will be responsible for your own needs." Something vaguely representing humor flickered in his eyes. "I suspect you'll want to find somewhere down in the Lower City should you opt to stay."

I was pretty sure he'd just called us poor. It was probably a savage cut among the nobility, but Lace had spent her life in a jungle, and I'd spent mine in a trailer home with a sick dad. *Poor* wasn't an insult. It was just reality.

Hawthorne disappeared back into his carriage and one of the black-clad arbiters approached in his place.

"I will take you inside and speak with Manager Tillis on the lord arbiter's behalf," he said.

The carriage was back in motion, horses and vehicle doing the medieval equivalent of a three-point turn as they reoriented back the way we had come. I ignored the arbiter and looked to Miko.

"Be careful," I told her in the High Tongue. "If we don't hear from you by tonight…"

"It will be fine, nest-brother. Hawthorne is right; there were protocols for this sort of thing even with my people. Security matters, on this continent as well as the last." She eyed the inn. "Save me something to eat, if you can."

"I'll see what kind of sweets they have. And if they have anything like kallnor here in the capital."

She flashed me her signature smile, but the carriage was already headed back for the main road; she hurried after and caught up with the waiting Humber.

"I will show you inside," repeated the waiting arbiter, one hand extended in the direction of the inn's front door. "Follow me, if you please."

ooo

The Night's Sky was the nicest inn I'd stayed in yet. In fact, it was hard to imagine even a 5-star hotel back on earth that would compare, not that I had any experience with those. Everything was spotless, beautiful, expensive, or some combination of the three, and the expansive suite I'd been given had a separate chamber with an honest-to-God enchanted chamber pot. Within moments of my business being completed, runes in the polished bronze receptacle flared to life and the contents disappeared.

Given the rolling heat that dissipated slowly afterwards, I was guessing the enchantment was somehow tied to fire, but beyond that, I didn't know how it worked, why, or what it might cost to get my own portable version. As it was, it was the closest thing to a toilet that could flush, and it didn't even require plumbing.

Magic was *cool*.

As nice as the room was—and Lace's room across the hall was every bit the equal of mine—the food might have been even better. The amazon griped about *fancy this* or *fancy that*, but when we sat down for dinner in the dining hall, she cleared her plates even faster than me. And when the waitress offered to bring out more, mine wasn't the only head nodding.

Even better, about a glass after Miko left with the carriage, I got a notification I'd been waiting for:

```
QUEST COMPLETED: Return Wilhemina Annerose Lakesia
Willerton to her home.
```

Apparently, Miko and the others had arrived at their destination. As usual, completing a quest didn't give me any physical rewards, but a quick internal check told me I'd just gone from about halfway to my level to somewhere around three-quarters. Another quest and I'd almost definitely reach level seven.

So, all of that was great… but there were two problems.

First, the arbiter assigned to us had taken up permanent residence just outside the inn's front door, and while he seemingly never looked up from the leatherbound journal in his hands, I could feel his eyes on me throughout dinner and then again as we climbed the stairs to turn in for the night. If he planned to sleep at all, he was hiding that intent masterfully.

When does a resort feel more like a prison?

When there's a warden at the door.

But the second problem was of even greater concern. It had me up again before the sun threatened to grace the sky, eyeing the darkened street below my room and trying to plot a safe route out the window and onward to the Upper City.

Because an afternoon, an evening, and a night had passed… and the second bed in my room remained undisturbed.

Miko hadn't come back.

13

It didn't take long to gather my things. I'd had a bath the previous night in a tub that heated the water all on its own; now, I pulled on a fresh set of clothes and put the laundered set in my pack with the rest of my worldly possessions. Knife on my hip, spear in my hand, and I was as ready as I was going to get.

Of course, if the arbiter downstairs *was* Tin, then wherever Miko was being kept would have guards of a similar rank. Maybe higher. I'd killed one Copper, but the chances of me doing so again without our full party's support were infinitesimally small. *Almost* as small as the chances of me defeating all of Trynfall's guards and secret police in some kind of insane frontal assault.

Getting to Miko would require sneakiness.

Getting her out would require even more.

Thankfully, I knew someone who specialized in sneakiness.

I crept across the hall to Lace's room. As far as I could tell, we were the only guests in this inn and the staff had been scaled down accordingly. Still, *someone* would be up and about, if just to clean or start the day's cooking, and I didn't want to alert them.

Having a maxed-out *Stealth* skill didn't mean too much when it was just a General skill that remained capped at ten… but I was as quiet as I could be as I made my way to Lace's door.

It was locked. Understandable, of course, but that presented another problem. I still hadn't gotten my promised lockpicking lessons from Lace, and trying to break down the door would alert everyone in the building. And probably get me stabbed by a sleepy Marauder. So, I tapped lightly on the door, like a cat bent on discovering what nefarious activities were occurring out of sight.

No response.

"Lace," I said, my voice barely over a whisper, "are you up?"

Given the Marauder's rampant paranoia and our uncertain situation, I'd expected her to be on a hair trigger, reacting to every hint of a noise, but even that failed to wake her. Which made me question what exactly I was doing.

Could I be overreacting? Yes, they'd said Miko would return by nightfall, and she hadn't, but there were plenty of reasonable explanations for that. Like magic being hard, for example, or Wilhemina's affliction needing more intensive study to cure than anticipated. And yet…

Hawthorne didn't even want us coming to Trynfall at all. Just Miko… and only after he realized she was necessary. And the moment we were in Trynfall, he found a way to separate us.

No, something was wrong, and I needed Lace's help to find out what. Instead of tapping, I gritted my teeth and knocked firmly on her door.

"Your companion's not in there," said a voice to my right.

I turned to find Darcie Tillis, the middle-aged woman who had been our waitress, receptionist, and laundress, looking at me curiously, greying curls spilling out from under her crisp white cap. She had a woven basket filled with linens in her hands and her voice was a perfect blend of professionalism and courtesy.

I'd assumed we would find ourselves instant friends given our shared history in the service industry. Sadly, Darcie had been in that industry way too long to fall for a friendly smile.

"Do you know where she is?" I asked.

"Downstairs, eating." She made a small face that was gone just as quickly. "And drinking too. She was up even before I was."

That made things easy, if not particularly stealthy.

"Are you checking out?" She tilted her head at whatever expression she saw on my face. "You have your pack on your back and are armed."

"No, I just… like to keep my things with me."

"I can assure you that your belongings are safe within these walls. We've had dignitaries from every duchy in the kingdom stay here and not a one had complaints when they left."

Unspoken—but kind of heard—was that *we* didn't rise to that level of importance and therefore couldn't possibly have reason to complain either.

"Of course," I said, relying on *Deception* since my Discernment wasn't trustworthy at all. "I'd expect nothing less from a place as highly regarded as the Night's Sky. You'll have to forgive an adventurer's old habits."

I couldn't tell if she was less impressed with the fact that I was an adventurer or that someone half her age was referring to *old* habits. Either way, I got a distinctly cooler, if still professional, look.

"Very well. If you wish to break your fast with your companion, my daughter will come by to take your order."

"I'll go do that."

She didn't show any indication of going on with her business until I got on with mine, so I gave her a half-hearted bow, waved with the hand that wasn't holding my spear, and smartly pivoted and walked away. I could feel her eyes on my back the whole way to the stairs and, though it should have been impossible, most of the way down those same stairs.

Maybe she has some sort of Innkeeper's Awareness *technique or something? Instead of eyes in the back of her head, she has eyes throughout her establishment.*

Or maybe *I* was the paranoid one in our party.

When I made it downstairs to the room too nice to be described as a common room, I found a little bit more evidence to support that second possibility.

"Brian!" said Miko, looking up from a wooden bowl of what appeared to be some sort of shredded fish. "You are awake!"

Next to her, Lace's bowl was empty, but the amazon cradled a mug of something dark and—by the smell of it—deeply alcoholic in her hands. She looked at my spear and then back at me. "I know your original weapon master told you to take that wherever you went, but I think your knife is probably enough indoors."

"Said by someone who probably has a dozen weapons on her right now."

"Sure, but none of them are quite as obvious as *that.*"

I rolled my eyes and joined the two of them at the table, resting the weapon in question against the back of the chair next to me.

"I didn't know Miko had returned," I said.

I saw the lightbulb go on in Lace's head immediately, her silver eyes flashing to my weapons and pack again, but Miko missed the context entirely. The synossian chewed her way through some more fish before nodding.

"Yes. I returned a glass or so ago. Lace pointed out our room but didn't—*I* didn't—want to risk waking you." She cocked her head. "Why do you have your pack with you, nest-brother?"

"I'm pretty sure he was going to go get you," said Lace, "which would have been a disastrously stupid thing to do on his own."

"That's why I went looking for you first."

"Oh."

Miko looked between us. "Why do think—argh." She switched to the High Tongue. "Why did you think I needed rescuing? We have done a service for this duke. We are here to be rewarded! What have you seen that I missed?"

"You weren't back by the time I went to bed," I said lamely, keeping my reply in Trade, so Lace could understand. "And then still weren't there when I woke up. I got worried."

"That is all?"

"Yeah." I didn't have to say I felt like an idiot. The looks on their faces—reptilian sympathy from Miko and mild amusement from Lace—told me they already got it.

"The examination of Wilhemina took longer than expected," said Miko, swapping back to Trade. "When all was done, guards and arbiter brought me back here."

"What about Wilhemina?"

Miko brightened like her goddess had just parted a cloudy sky. "Is still asleep but cured."

"Really?" That was from Lace. "Just like that?"

"Not *just* like that. But Iris is fabulous healer. And famous too. High Copper trying to break through to Iron. After hearing story and examining Wilhemina, she tried several different blessings. Last one succeeded; none of us can sense corruption in girl's body anymore."

"But she's still asleep?"

"Will—*they* will—let her wake naturally," said Miko. "Remember, healing takes from patient too, even for such a high-ranked healer."

"Still, that's done," said Lace. "And well timed too. A few days living in northern luxury, an audience to receive whatever rewards we're going to be given, and we can be on our way again."

"Would like to see enclave of my people," said Miko.

"Humber said he'd take us when he was done with his duties." I scratched my head. Neither Darcie nor her unnamed daughter had shown up yet, and I couldn't tell if that was the quiet professionalism of not wanting to intrude on our conversation or a less than subtle way of showing their displeasure that the inn's only guests were already awake and wanting food. "If not tonight, then maybe tomorrow?"

"I would like to rest," agreed Miko. "Have not even had time to meditate."

"Should we ask them to prepare the baths? The water heats up all by itself, but someone still has to fill the tub."

"Is fine. I bathed before examination. Iris is strict about cleanliness and contamination in her…" She paused, switching to the High Tongue again. "Facilities?" she asked me.

"Facilities," I replied, making sure I said it in Trade.

"Yes, facilities. But I will meditate and sleep, if is okay."

We both turned to Lace, who paused, mug halfway to her mouth. "Is this city infecting both of your brains? You've never asked me for permission to *sleep* before."

"I think she just wanted to know if you had any plans that she'd be disrupting by going to bed."

"I already *told* you my plans. Food. Drink. That stupidly comfortable bed. And then, before the softness can steal away our strength and our hate, we'll be on the road."

I met Miko's gaze.

"Will go to sleep then."

"Good luck," I told her. "If you level, let us know."

"Is possible… and of course."

She carried her empty bowl over to a low table outside the inn's kitchen and headed up the stairs, a certain lack of fluidity and grace the only thing that showed how tired she must have been.

"She's close to leveling?" asked Lace.

"Yeah. Just needs a few skill gains."

"Good. We're going to need all the levels we can get."

"Levels are only part of it," I said. "We need all the *everything* we can get."

"Then we should probably avoid invading palaces to rescue people who don't need rescuing, don't you think?" Even as my cheeks started to burn, Lace tossed back the remnants of her drink. "Still, it would have made for quite the tale. Hashoggath knows, you don't lack courage, Brian Fieldings."

Darcie's daughter, Miko's age and a head taller than I was, finally made an appearance, making her way over with a long-suffering expression any service worker would recognize.

"Does the Night Hag *care* about courage?"

"Of course. It's one more thing that must go before the fall."

○○○

As nice as the inn was, it didn't take long for it to go back to feeling like an absurdly comfortable prison. Miko's return meant we now had a second arbiter parked outside our door and while they hadn't *said* we couldn't leave, their focus had spiked to deeply concerning levels anytime I so much as wandered in that direction. So, we sat and we waited, and we ate and at least one of us drank like a fish while playing a little bit too freely with the surplus of knives she kept on her body.

We remained the only guests at the inn. I couldn't tell if that was because other guests were being warded off, or if this place *only* dealt with dignitaries and *they* preferred to travel in the warmer months.

By mid-afternoon, Miko had finished both her meditation and her nap. As she came back down, she gave me a small shake of her head.

Still no level, then.

I'd have offered to let Lace use her knives on me to give Miko a chance to hit her needed skill gains, but three things stopped me:

First, I didn't like pain.

Second, I'd already maxed out *Pain Tolerance*, so I wouldn't get anything from doing so. Outside of new patches of slightly tougher, differently colored skin, I supposed.

And third and most importantly, Miko had maxed out her *Field Dressings* skill on the trip from Madea, so a chance to wrap and treat new wounds wouldn't help anyway.

According to the Priestess, Humber didn't even have that skill. While they had the same base class, the Tin-ranked healer had chosen a career path that would keep him far away from battlefields. Our recent misadventure very much excepted. I had to assume that lack of combat would stunt his growth eventually, but he had decades to get wherever he was going and no real penalties if he never got there.

It was hard not to envy that. We didn't have the same luxury. Not as adventurers, and not as people trying to save Miko's species.

"What skills do you still need to level?" I asked. It was a rude question, by Eosian standards, but Lace was on her fifth ale and both Darcie's daughter and our jailers were studiously *not* paying attention.

Also? I was speaking the High Tongue, because information was gold on Eos, and I had to believe that included *our* information. The hell with giving anyone anything for free.

"One point in *Counseling* or *Ceremonies* would do it," she said. "I'm a few points away in *Oratory* as well, not that it's necessary for leveling."

"Oratory? Like public speaking?" I knew Miko had combat-related skills, too… she'd just already leveled those. Still, I hadn't realized quite how broad her class skills were. So far, *Leadership* was about the only class skill *I* had that wasn't directly related to combat or physical activity.

No wonder Humber was able to level without constantly being thrust into situations likely to get him murdered.

"Yes. Sermons and readings, mostly. Depending on what we find at the enclave, there might be an opportunity for me there."

There was just as much chance there wouldn't be. So far, the few native synossians we'd encountered had abandoned Miko's pantheon entirely. In fact, they hadn't even known the gods' names. And while I didn't doubt that those gods would approve strongly of their Priestess proselytizing on their behalf… we didn't have the time, the energy, or the overwhelming military might for whatever holy war doing so might kick off.

"*Ceremonies* is like the funeral services you've led?"
She nodded.
"Well, hopefully, we won't have another of those anytime soon. Which leaves *Counseling*, I guess, if you want to get to level seven."
"Are you in need of counseling, nest-brother?"
The answer was almost definitely yes. Would always be yes until the disease in me was rooted out or it killed me like it had my dad. But that wasn't something I wanted to talk about. My feelings about all the blood we'd shed and the people we'd lost along the way fit into that category too; something to stuff into a box and hide away in a deep, dark corner until some future date. After all, guilt and anger and grief were just parts of the human experience, weren't they?
Lace drained her mug and waved it in the air.

Darcie's daughter, whose name I still didn't know and whose professionalism had eroded over a full day of the Marauder's drinking, pretended not to notice.

"I don't need counseling," I told Miko, deeply regretting the point of *Deception* I *wouldn't* be gaining from such a bald lie thanks to the stupid General skill cap. "But I think we both know someone who's struggling. And she might be drunk enough now to finally let her guard down too."

Miko stared at me for a moment, followed my gaze to Lace at the far end of our table, and then snapped back.

"Oh!"

"Exactly."

"If you will excuse me…"

"Good luck."

She made her way over to the Marauder, approaching the other woman like an overconfident Earth man sliding into a stranger's DMs. Unlike in that scenario, however, her approach seemed to work. Soon, the two were deep in conversation. I couldn't hear much of what they were saying, but Lace hadn't laughed, spit, or invoked her goddess yet, so I was hoping progress was being made.

I was pretty sure the amazon didn't *want* counseling and wouldn't accept it if she knew it was being offered… but that would just increase the difficulty level, right? And in turn, that might boost Miko's chances of getting her last needed skill point.

I had a hell of a lot to learn about the Framework still and, as of yet, no way to do so, but it felt like I was getting a handle on bits and pieces of it. And if I could help Miko in the process of proving out one of my theories?

Victimless science had a nice sort of ring to it.

In the meantime, *I* needed something to do. I made my way over to Darcie's hovering daughter.

"I'm Brian," I told her, pretty much brute forcing an introduction.

"Della." Even after enduring multiple glasses of Lace's drinking, she had enough professionalism left to manage a curtsey.

Darcie and Della. I wondered if alliterative names were a thing some families did here, like back on Earth.

"I'm sorry for Lace," I told her, "and I'm happy to help you clean up any messes she makes."

I thought that might win me a smile. Incorrectly, as it turned out. So, I pressed on.

"She just lost someone and is having a difficult time with it."

Something shifted in the waitress' expression. "A friend?"

"The man she's loved ever since she was your age."

Whatever walls Della had erected came tumbling down.

"That's awful," she breathed. "What happened?"

"He died saving a town on the frontier from blighted."

"Gods… I can't even imagine."

"It was hard on all of us." If there was a skill for *honesty*, that statement right there would have earned me my first rank, even *without* sitting down to meditate afterward. "But as you can imagine, she's struggling with it the most. So, please… try not to hold it against her."

"I would *never.*" She tore her eyes from Lace's suddenly tragic figure. "Should I bring out more ale? Would that help her forget or just deepen the pain?"

That was a way more insightful question than I'd expected.

"Maybe split the difference?" I suggested. "Bring her a drink, but water each new mug more and more?"

"We don't water our ale at all."

"Really?" Lomas, the dunsman Brewer back in Harborton, had seemed convinced that *everyone* but him heavily watered their beer.

And given the thin taste of the ale served at the Night's Sky, I'd assumed he was correct. "Do you brew it on site?"

"Of course not. We purchase from Brewer Camlin."

Right. Because pseudo-medieval societies favored specialization… and the Framework did too.

"I can help water the ale then, if you want. I have some skill in *Brewing*."

Two skill points, to be precise. It was nowhere near what I'd need to make even something as bad as one of Caleb's worst experimental brews back in Madea, but for adding water to an already-brewed beer? I figured those skill points couldn't hurt. And if doing so might net me a *third* point in the skill…

Well.

Progression was still progression, even when it came in a skill I only had because of my barista past.

Later that night, I sat down on the floor Miko watching from her bed. I'd dumped both of our coin purses out and the thin copper bits mingled with the handful of fatter plugs in an untidy pile in front of me. If there'd been a poker game on, Kenny Rogers would have been horrified by what I was about to do. As it was, it was just one more experiment and I thought the Gambler would understand.

I closed my eyes and sank into meditation. And then, as the day's admittedly limited experiences trickled through me, I reached down and started sorting the coin pile into bits and plugs, counting each as I went.

It was hard to split my focus that way and even harder to retain my meditative trance, despite an Uncommon-tiered version of the skill. I lost my hold on meditation twice and lost my count three times, and Miko later told me the whole thing ended up taking half again as long as normal. Still, any proper experiment required more than one test subject… and if upping the difficulty of something *did* raise the possibility of skill gains, I was going to do so any chance I got.

When I opened my eyes, I had two stacks of coins in front of me—a squat column of four plugs and a teetering tower of seventeen bits—and a familiar glowing screen in front of my face:

```
You have increased the following skills:

Minor skills:
Leadership (U) [+1]: 7/35

General skills:
Brewing [+1]: 3/10
Diplomacy [+1]: 2/10
```

Well, that was frustrating. Not the increase in *Leadership;* even if I still didn't understand how the skill worked, it *was* a class skill and that mattered *way* more than the gain in *Brewing*. And *Diplomacy* had been shockingly difficult to level, so getting another point there was great. What was disappointing was the lack of a change in *Meditation*. Now, even if Miko *did* end up getting a point in *Counseling*, we wouldn't know for sure that the increased challenge had had anything to do with it.

With a sigh, I banished the window.

And immediately received another:

```
You have increased the following attributes:

Discernment [+1]: 11
```

I didn't know if that was because of my dealings with Miko, Lace, Della, or even Darcie. What I did know was that I freaking loved seeing numbers go up. And I no longer had any attributes stuck at the bog-standard human average of ten. Which meant *I* was no longer a strictly average human.

Miko offered me enthusiastic congratulations on my increase in Discernment—*suspiciously enthusiastic,* if I was being honest—and then in for her own meditation. Her skill was still Common-ranked and she didn't try anything fancy with it, so I sorted our money back out into two piles—two plugs and nine bits for her, two plugs and eight for myself—and dumped it into our respective coin purses.

After a few minutes had passed, I retrieved one plug and one bit from my stash. I hadn't seen a skill gain in *Juggling* since before our ambush, mostly because I hadn't been practicing the skill at all. But this was as good an opportunity as any to do so.

And who knew? Maybe there were professions on Eos that could make good use of the skill. If Miko could cure my disease, I would have a long life ahead of me after helping to save her people and avenge Skaal. Something less deadly as a post-retirement gig didn't sound all that bad.

I wasn't sure *circus performer* was high on my list of future jobs, especially once I was old and crotchety, but I'd be happy just to live long enough to have that option.

I dropped more coins than I juggled, owing to the fact that my skill was still stuck at one and plugs and bits were significantly different in weight, but it helped the time go by. And I was in enough of a flow by the end that I snatched both copper pieces out of the air with one hand when Miko's eyes finally snapped open again.

She didn't have to say a word, not with the smile spreading across her reptilian face.

Level seven!!!

○○○

I waited as Miko read through the screens she was no doubt being presented. Chief among them would be the selection of new abilities or upgrades to the ones she already had. There was nothing that said she needed to share those choices with me—I still only knew a handful of Lace's techniques, and those were mostly just from observation—but if she needed someone to talk through things with, I would be there for her.

"Hmm." The synossian mouth changed the shape of some sounds in indescribable ways and that was one of them. Orange, sclera-less eyes narrowed.

I couldn't help myself. "Good or bad?"

"Good. I think." She rocked back and forth a bit, forked tongue flicking in and out through her sharp teeth. "There is an Uncommon-tiered upgrade to *Flare* called *Abiding Light*. I have not seen that one before, but I would guess it allows me to summon flares that last for a greater length of time."

I could see the value of that, especially when we delved underground. Then again, torches *were* a thing.

"While it might lead to other, more interesting upgrades for *Flare*, I would rather expand my abilities," she added. "Thankfully, my other two offerings are both new. There is the Uncommon-ranked *Light Healing*, which is not an upgrade to *Minor Healing* but an entirely new blessing that can be used side by side with it."

That was a hard one to turn down. I was a big fan of healing.

"And then there is the Uncommon-ranked *Dawn Strike*."

"Have you heard of it before?" As a Priestess, the abilities Miko was offered were largely taken from the domains of the goddess she worshipped. Aurea was a goddess of healing, the sun, and fire.

She idly tapped her left arm. "Yes. It is a short-range attack that does light-based damage. One of Mother's guards received upgrades that both extended its range and provided a chance that the blessing would ignite the target and cause fire damage as well." She paused and looked over at me, past the dialogue window I couldn't see. "I am sorry that I was not offered a blessing to cure your condition, nest-brother."

"It's okay. We knew it would probably be something in Tin or even Copper." I hesitated. "Do you think maybe this Iris person…?"

Miko dropped her eyes. "I asked her already. She has been offered blessings to cure poison, infection, and even plague, but nothing like what you have described. Not just disease but something that is passed from parent to child."

I tried not to show any reaction.

And failed.

"I am sorry, Brian Fieldings. Truly. But it is my belief that the Framework—and the gods themselves—responds to need. Aurea hears my prayers. I know it. She will give me the tools to heal her Chosen."

"We've got plenty of time," I said, trying to mean it. I stuffed the disappointment away and rallied. "This isn't about me anyway. This is about you and your new level. If *Abiding Light* is out of the running—?" I waited for her nod. "Which of the remaining two are you going to pick? You've said you wanted something to boost your offensive capabilities, right? *Dawn Strike* sounds like it would do that."

"Yes. But… there are injuries that *Minor Healing* cannot address, even with multiple castings. *Light Healing* would not only offer me greater flexibility, it would enhance that which makes me most valuable to you and our party."

"You're valuable for a lot more than just your healing. You should pick what *you* want. Isn't that what the Framework is about?"

"The Framework is about giving mortals the opportunity to grow, nest-brother. How we grow is up to us, but every choice has consequences. I would very much like to fight side-by-side with you, to use Aurea's light to cleanse the dark spaces in this world, but…"

"You can do that, whatever you choose," I reminded her. "You *will* do that. You'll watch my back, and I'll watch yours, and Lace will… do her thing."

She tapped her left arm again. "*Light Healing* will help us now and in the future. With luck, I will be offered *Dawn Strike* again at level nine." Her eyes flickered momentarily, the inner membrane flashing shut then open again. "Oh."

"Oh?"

"I've now been offered an advanced class."

Seeing her muted reaction, I had to ask: "I'm guessing it's *not* Battle Medic?"

"No. It is called Faith Healer." She couldn't frown, but I could *hear* the expression in her voice. "I already *have* faith. I am already a healer. I do not know what this means."

"It sounds like something that would take you further down that path."

"Yes." She leaned back against the bed, clawed hands fidgeting with her robes. "I know I just chose *Light Healing* because it would benefit the party most, but…"

"But you don't want to *just* be a healer."

"I do not."

"Then don't be. Specialization's not a bad thing, especially within a party, but neither is flexibility. And judging by what Riok and Kacellius told me, if your path doesn't fit what you truly want to be, then breaking through to Tin will be all but impossible."

"It feels selfish, somehow. Yet there is truth in what you say. I can feel that as well." With a deep sigh, she double-blinked again and straightened up. "It is done. I will remain a Priestess for now and wait to see how I can better serve the Bright Lady in the future."

Half a glass later, she was asleep, worn rather than energized by her new level. I lay awake in my bed and stared up at the darkened ceiling, thinking of the choices we had made and the ones we'd have to continue making in the future.

Between the two of us, we'd now *both* rejected our first class evolutions. According to everything I'd read, the Framework didn't have true sentience. It didn't play favorites, and it didn't judge.

Hopefully, that meant it didn't get frustrated either.

14

The next morning, we sat around in the dining hall waiting for Priest Humber—first name, Rollin, according to Miko—to show up and take us on the tour he'd promised. While we waited, Lace heard I'd been practicing my juggling and after a very early, not-watered-down-at-all beer, I found myself agreeing to demonstrate.

With knives, at the Marauder's insistence. After all, while we had yet to prove that *difficulty* increased the likelihood of a skill gain, we knew for a fact that *danger* did.

Soon after, Miko got to show off her new healing spell and I had a fresh patch of tough, olive-tan skin on my left thigh. I'd have to wait until meditation to see if a skill point in *Juggling* came with it. Given that I'd dropped *both* knives, I wasn't feeling optimistic.

I idly tapped that new rough patch of skin as I swapped from beer back to water. I regretted taking *Beast Skin* for more reasons than just the aesthetics. The piecemeal way in which it spread, manifesting only where my human skin had been broken, made for a piss-poor defense. Between the bandits outside Madea, the blighted, the supposed Zarisian ambushers, and simple training, a good portion of my chest, shoulders, and arms had at least partially transformed, but that left a lot of ground uncovered.

If I was offered an upgrade to *Beast Skin* when I reached level seven, would I take it? I'd almost have to, right? Just to make it more useful? Or would that be, as our home economics teacher had loved to say back at Jefferson High, throwing good money after bad?

This was why I wanted an actual advancement path. Techniques came along far too rarely to waste them on a bad choice.

By mid-day, we were *still* waiting for Humber to show up when a clatter of hoofbeats outside was swiftly followed by one of our two assigned arbiters poking his head indoors.

"Lord Hawthorne is here to take you to the palace for your audience," he said.

It seemed Humber would have to wait.

"I'll get Miko," I told Lace. "Before we go, she can sober you up with *Touch of the Dawn.*"

"Why would you think I'm drunk?"

"Because you've had like seven beers since I came down?"

The Marauder gave me a look and lowered her voice. "I have a twenty-eight Vitality, Brian. A little bit of beer isn't going to get me drunk, even before you convinced our hosts to start watering it down." As if to prove that point, she hopped lithely to her feet.

"But yesterday, you—"

"Chose to give little Miko a chance to say what she's been dying to say since Madea? And in the process helped her to reach her new level?" As ever, Lace's smile was mostly just a baring of teeth. "Why yes, yes I did."

Now I *really* didn't know if my *amp up the difficulty to improve skill gains* theory held any water.

I encountered Darcie in the upstairs hallway. With only two of the inn's ten suites occupied, I wasn't sure what she did most of the time. Especially with a cook on staff. Surely, dusting and cleaning wasn't a full-time job? Something told me that that wasn't a good question to ask if I still wanted to have a room when we returned from our audience. So instead, I stopped her and motioned to the spear in my hand.

"The lord arbiter has come to take us to the palace. I'm going to guess that I won't be allowed to carry *this* in with me?"

She wrinkled her nose while she looked at the corroded, seemingly decrepit weapon. "Those such as me and mine don't warrant invites to His Grace's palace, but no. No weapons longer than one's forearm are permitted, and even those that qualify must be peace-bound."

I didn't know what peace-bound meant, but I guessed we'd be finding out soon enough. After all, I was *definitely* bringing my knife, and Lace would be too. But my spear… Riok's spear…

I don't know if Darcie's long years of running an inn for dignitaries kicked in then or if I just was doing a particularly poor job of hiding my expression, but the older woman's face softened.

"Your belongings will be safe here at the Night's Sky. I will lock the doors to your rooms myself and none shall pass through until you return."

She was an innkeeper, not a wizard, but somehow, I believed her anyway. I curled my free hand into a fist and pressed it against my heart in the synossian version of a salute.

"Thank you."

Five minutes later, our party was escorted by the two arbiters to a carriage that was both larger and significantly fancier than the one that had barely survived the trip from Madea. It had space for three men up front with the horses—one of whom I recognized as Hawthorne's personal guard and driver—and the interior was fancier than anything I'd ridden in on Eos or Earth. Even though we were all freshly clean and wearing our best clothes instead of armor, I hesitated before sinking into a plush bench seat wrapped in velvet.

The carriage was wide enough that Miko, Lace, and I could all fit together on one side. Lord Arbiter Hawthorne sat on the other, somehow even fancier than the carriage in a black velvet vest, puffy-sleeved tunic, and black pants tucked into boots so shiny they must have literally been polished on the way over. Cold eyes scanned each of us in turn, head to toe, and when he nodded, I couldn't tell if it was in approval or resigned acceptance.

"As I was the one who brought you all to the capital, I have been tasked as your escort to and from today's audience. We will arrive there in a quarter glass, but if there is anything you wish to know beforehand, this is the time."

"Has Wilhemina awoken?" asked Miko.

The lord gritted his teeth. "*Lady Willerton* remains asleep, but the duke's healer is confident that will change once her body finally recovers from its trial. I will warn you that it is unlikely you will ever meet with the duke's daughter again, even should you stay here in Trynfall."

"Why's that?"

"She is the heir to the duchy," he said simply. And then, when none of us seemed enlightened, he added: "Even if she wasn't going to be occupied with matters of the state, His Grace will likely take significant steps to ensure something like her kidnapping never occurs again. That means less freedom, additional security, and far fewer guests of an uncertain provenance."

"Meaning non-nobles," guessed Lace.

"You understand exactly."

"Are there any protocols we should be aware of when meeting the duke?" I asked. I wasn't sure if I was asking because of my recently improved Discernment attribute or because I was aware that same attribute was still only an eleven.

"You won't be meeting with the duke."

"What?"

"His Grace only returned a seven-day ago from a multi-moon campaign—a *successful* campaign—against Zaris. He has barely even had the time to meet with his council. A direct audience with him would be sometime in the distant future, if it happened at all. No, you'll be meeting with his seneschal, which is why this audience is occurring so quickly."

Our party exchanged glances. To come all this way and *not* see the man whose daughter we'd not just rescued but kept alive seemed… disappointing.

"His Grace *has* spoken to Seneschal Douglass regarding your rewards and I believe you will be satisfied."

"You know what we're getting?" That was Lace, fully engaged in the conversation for the first time.

"I do, but I will leave it to the seneschal to tell you all. However, on the subject of rewards…" He reached into his vest and pulled out a pouch that clinked pleasantly. "Payment for services rendered on the road to Trynfall."

Lace took the pouch, both because she was the party leader and because she was a hell of a lot quicker than Miko or me. She didn't count the coins inside but instead tucked it away under her jacket. If I did my math right, it would have twenty-four copper bits inside, with six of those going to Lace, six to me, and twelve to Miko. We'd been on the road for twenty-four days, all in, after I'd negotiated salaries for us, but I suspected Hawthorne was one of those people who didn't round up for partial seven-days.

It was something to think about the next time I played the role of Human Resources recruiter. I didn't think there was a lower currency unit than copper bits, but future contracts could have some kind of acceleration clause or at least account for smaller slices of time.

I wasn't sure if it was *Mercantilism* that had me thinking that way or my increase in Intellect. Or hell, maybe both. If I ever found myself back on Earth—and frankly, I hoped I wouldn't—I might figure out a way to buy out Pritchard's Coffee & Baked Goods and fire *Mike's* pasty white ass.

But that was a dream for another day. In the meantime, we had a seneschal to meet. Whatever a seneschal was.

ooo

Whether it was the comfort of the familiar setting, relief at being back home, or gratitude that he'd be rid of us soon enough, Hawthorne was actually helpful during our short ride to the Upper City and then on to the palace that perched at its top. We were instructed on protocols to follow with the seneschal: *no bows, but keep your hands clasped behind your back and maintain a respectful distance from the man and his station.* We were informed of what would occur after the audience was done—a return to the Night's Sky for a single night, after which our futures, fates, and lodging expenses would be in our own hands. We were even told what a seneschal was, which satisfied both Lace's and my curiosity.

Miko, it seemed, had already known that last part. The now fallen synossian empire had been nothing if not highly regimented.

With the wooden shutters closed, we didn't see any of the streets we rode through and only the slight chill seeping in from outside kept the carriage from being oppressively hot. Hawthorne seemed impervious to temperatures and Miko was Miko, but I think Lace sweated almost as much as I did. At least it was clean sweat, in both of our cases; Miko wouldn't have too much to complain about by the time we were done.

Not that I wouldn't take a bath immediately upon our return anyway. The whole *human stench* thing had taken up residence in my brain, but even more importantly, I didn't know when we'd have ready access to hot baths again once we left. I was going to soak up every second of the Night's Sky's luxury, and if that made me soft, well… the road would beat that softness right back out of me soon enough.

Our carriage finally slowed to a halt, but Hawthorne remained seated and motioned for us to do the same. A minute or so passed before there was a tap at the door.

"All is well, my lord."

The head arbiter nodded, as if to himself, and then we all disembarked. There were four guards—three men and a woman— waiting for us in bronze chain with tabards in the duke's colors. Behind them was a thin, balding man whose well-fitted tunic, vest, and pants screamed *rich person* even as his demeanor and deep bow whispered *servant.*

His voice, on the other hand, neither screamed nor whispered. "Lord Hawthorne. Adventurers Fieldings, Nesari, and… Lace. On behalf of His Grace, I wish you all welcome. If you will do me the honor of following, I will escort you to the Chamber of the Sun."

Miko had gotten excited when the lord arbiter had told us about the Chamber of the Sun, but it had nothing to do with her goddess. Instead, it was an audience hall in the depths of the palace, leveraged for lesser meetings or when the duke's larger, grander reception hall, the Chamber of the Sky and Sea, was already utilized.

We rated an invitation to the palace… just not an audience with the duke or even time in his fanciest hall. I'd have been annoyed, but if even the servant was better dressed than me, I didn't want to even think about how out of place I'd feel in the fanciest room inside.

At a nod from Hawthorne, the man bowed again and spun about smartly on one heel. Two of the four guards detached to follow us as an escort, falling in with Hawthorne's bodyguard and an arbiter, and our party of nine entered the ducal place before I'd gotten more than a glimpse of the exterior.

Back on Earth, Ohio had a surprising number of castles, but the closest had been hours from Midton and privately owned, besides. I wasn't entirely sure if the palace qualified as one—or what criteria were needed to qualify, for that matter—but it was big and impressive enough. We passed from the courtyard where the carriage had been parked into a grand hall. At the far end of the hall, a set of equally grand stairs led a short way up to double doors that would have made even Skaal look small. Columns lined the hall's sides, the arches in between indicating either shallow alcoves with gleaming marble statues or smaller hallways leading off to the left and right. High above us, the painted ceiling was vaguely barrel shaped, adding even more volume to a space that dwarfed our oversized group.

My first thought was to wonder how expensive it was to heat the place. My second was to realize we wouldn't be taking the stairs, as those almost definitely led to the main audience hall. Sure enough, our guide took us to the first of the half-hidden hallways on the left. There were a handful of doors off this hallway, but they were closed and we were past them before I could ask about the rooms they contained. We didn't encounter any additional servants as we proceeded, but guards were plentiful, that one hallway more secure than all of Baron Sakeld's mansion.

This didn't appear to be where Miko had come with Wilhemina, judging by my friend's wondering expression, but it *did* put my haphazard rescue plan in perspective. I'd have been caught and killed before I even reached the Upper City, most likely.

The hall we were in didn't run straight, but continued to curve to the right, like the outer edge of a half-circle or the road in the Lower City that had circumnavigated the market. We were about two-thirds of our way around that half circle when the exterior wall was replaced with a banister, more columns, open air, and a view worth dying for.

"Oh!" murmured Miko, the delight in her voice unmistakable.

We'd spent most of the day before our arrival at the Night's Sky climbing. First to Trynfall, and then *through* it. That had continued with today's carriage ride taking us up the remaining tiers of the Middle City and into the Upper City. But it wasn't until that moment that I really understood how far we had climbed and why.

Trynfall was built into and atop a mountain, each level shadowed by the one above it or by the mountain itself. But there were no more levels here, at the peak, and the rear half of the duke's palace opened onto the ocean that lurked behind that mountain. Nothing but water for leagues, with the faint scent of brine drifting up from far, far below.

I leaned out over the edge of the banister and saw nothing but space beneath us, this part of the palace apparently cantilevered out over the edge. Behind us, the walls of the palace sprouted out of the stone like they'd been grown rather than built. Ahead of us, the mountain protruded again, giving space for more of the palace, but for this brief stretch, it was just us, the cloud-filled sky, the angry ocean, and a cold wind tugging at our not-so-fancy clothes.

And that was enough of that.

I retreated even before Lace could tug me back. I wasn't afraid of heights, but I was pretty sure someone could sing two *Happy Birthdays* on the way down and that was far too many by anyone's estimation.

"Below us is the harbor," said our guide, sounding more than a little bit proud. "The greatest in the kingdom and perhaps even any of the nations that have sprung from the remnants of the Endless Empire. If you are staying in Trynfall for any length of time, I highly recommend giving it a visit. In the meantime, we should not dally. The seneschal has been in audience for a glass at least and it would not do to be late for your appointment."

With those words, he got us moving again. It was both a relief and a tragedy when our path took us back indoors. Without the expansive vista distracting us, our pace improved. We passed a half-dozen additional rooms and finally turned to the right, stopping outside a set of double doors that seemed like the younger siblings to those in the main hall. Two more guards were present, this time flanking those doors. After exchanging words with our guide, one stepped forward.

"Any weapons must be peace-bound before entry," she said, nodding to the daggers visible on all of our waists. In one hand, she held out a selection of short pieces of braided rope. "If you need assistance, we are here to provide it."

Peace binding apparently involved taking one of those lengths of rope and weaving it around your sheathed blade so that the weapon couldn't be easily drawn. It wasn't as easy as it looked, and even after I'd wrapped my blade, I looked at it dubiously. It would make pulling the blade more difficult, yeah, but not *entirely* impossible. On the other hand, it would slow me down enough that any guards would be able to cut me down before I started something… which was probably the real point.

Of course, I now owned more than one knife, and it hadn't occurred to me to *not* bring the one tucked into my boot. Rather than risk it, I asked for another piece of rope, pulled the hidden blade out, and repeated the process. That won me an approving nod from the guard, although I wasn't sure if that was because they appreciated my attention to detail, honored the old cliché of a knife in the boot, or had simply already spotted the knife and were glad I wasn't trying to sneak it through.

Miko only had the one blade and was done long before me. Lace, on the other hand…

"You might need more rope," she said, a half-dozen knives into the lengthy process. Her smile was almost as cold as her eyes.

The two door guards traded glances with our escort and then looked to Hawthorne.

"She's a blood-scorned amazon," he said simply, as if that explained everything, "visiting from beyond the Waste."

A few expressions cleared. Others went hard. Having traveled with Lace for literal months now, most of it in the shadow of a reaver, I'd forgotten that her people, too, had a reputation.

"I can fetch more rope," said the second guard. "Or she can leave her extra weapons here to be returned upon departure."

In the interest of time, we went with the latter. Several minutes later, an impressive array of blades and needles had been piled to the side. I was pretty sure the tightly corded rope Lace had used today to tie up her braids could serve as a garotte in the Marauder's hands, but I didn't mention it to the guards. I didn't know how you peace-bound something like that anyway. Tying *more* rope on didn't seem productive.

When we were done—*finally* done—the guards swung the doors open. We passed between them and got our first look at the Chamber of the Sun.

It wasn't huge, not by the standards of the grand hall we'd seen when first entering the palace. Still, you could have fit the entirety of Sakeld's garden inside, with space left over. The chamber was circular, with a balcony above us ringing half of that circle. Above the balcony, the walls curved inward but stopped before they met. The gap between was filled with a latticework of metal and glass, natural light streaming into the chamber even on a cloudy day like this one. On a clear day, especially in the spring or summer, I could see how the room would earn its name.

Ahead of us was a line, organized into small clumps of people, and ahead of them, a man stood behind a pulpit on a raised platform. He was tall and spindly, rich clothes hanging loose on a skeletal frame, but when he spoke, his words rolled around the chamber like thunder.

There were a handful of others in the chamber, spread out along the sides. They seemed content to watch and talk amongst themselves as the seneschal gave out his pronouncements for each subsequent party.

Looky-loos or whatever the equivalent was here on Eos. Maybe this qualified as entertainment in a world without television.

Hawthorne guided us to the end of the line, then stepped away. His part in this elaborate production was done until our audience had been completed. The guards and his men joined him, leaving us on our own, at the rear of the line.

"When they said *audience*, I did not think they meant there would actually *be* one to watch us," murmured Miko in the High Tongue, mindful of the faces turning our way.

"Just pretend it's your congregation."

"I will try."

Apparently, a number of people had done things of value during the duke's absence. Things that merited acknowledgement by the duke's man, if not the duke himself. We'd arrived toward the end of the audience but stood as a merchant family from the Lower City was honored for its outstanding contributions to the Zarisian war effort. They were granted temporary trade rights in the Upper City and seemed thrilled by it.

Next came a recently married couple from two minor noble houses; the seneschal passed on the duke's blessings and gave the newlyweds a small amount of money. *His* words... without knowing if the purse contained copper, silver, or gold, it was impossible to judge what a small amount of money meant to the noble class. Regardless, the newlyweds seemed happy with it. A lupine in clothes almost as fancy as Hawthorne's was granted permission to expand his business in the Middle City and when his tail wagged in response, nobody pointed or took exception.

Finally, it was our turn. We'd received our own share of looks, as Miko had noted, but most of those were reserved for the women in our party. While female warriors weren't all that rare here on Eos, Lace's blue-black skin, braids, and eyes set her apart as something other than human. Meanwhile, Miko was the only synossian I'd seen today; she towered above most of the crowd, resplendent in the orange and crimson robes I'd had made for her all the way back in Harborton.

Next to them, I looked even shorter than normal. A servant or maybe a particularly splotchy child. I felt naked without my spear, my hands wanting to tighten around something… anything. With a lot of effort, and at least some credit to my recently improved Discernment attribute, I kept both hands away from the peace-bound dagger on my belt.

I'd been feeling put out that Grand Duke Willerton hadn't even bothered to show up to speak to the people who saved his daughter, but honestly, even this lesser and sparsely populated audience chamber was almost too much for me to take.

"You can pretend it's my congregation too, nest-brother," murmured Miko. "The Bright Lady watches us from above and the Trickster safeguards us from the shadows."

Given my relationship with God—or gods, even—that shouldn't have helped, but I pulled my shoulders down from my ears and rotated them back, feeling a little bit of tension leak out of me in the process.

When it came to skills, *Counseling* might be almost as amazing as *Deception*. Up close, the seneschal looked like a sneeze could blow him over, but his eyes were as sharp as the lord arbiter's. If there were any notes on his pulpit, he must have memorized them in advance, as he never once looked down.

"Lastly today," he began, voice rolling in a way that would have made voice actors back on Earth green with envy, "we have three adventurers from the frontier who have done this duchy, this kingdom even, a great service, in defeating an army of blighted and a sect of Zarisian cultists while securing the safe return of Lady Wilhemina Annerose Lakesia Willerton, eldest daughter of Grand Duke Willerton and heir to the duchy of Trynfall."

It was easy to see who had already heard the news and who hadn't. A chatter arose from the latter, while the former simply leaned in, eyes intent and metaphorical knives sharp.

We hadn't seen anything suggesting the cultists were *Zarisian*, but I was betting the duke and his seneschal already knew that. Politics were in play here and my recent gains were woefully insufficient to the task of navigating those waters.

Thankfully, Miko's gods hadn't brought me to Eos to defend the reputation of some small mountain nation that had already been conquered. I could just shut up and listen instead.

"Such a great service…no, such a *grand* service, requires an equally grand reward. And I am honored to be the conduit for that reward."

For the first time, I started to actively worry. This was *significantly* different from when he'd given the newlyweds money.

"For almost a hundred cycles," continued the seneschal, "the Trynfall Ducal Academy has helped the noble children of this duchy develop their gods-given gifts. Some students have gone on to serve valorously in our kingdom's armies while others have returned to their noble houses to take up the mantle of leadership. All have emerged from our hallowed institution greater than they entered. Now, for the first time, the academy's doors will open to those who are not of noble blood."

Both groups were murmuring, eyes turning from the seneschal back toward us.

"Miko Naseri and Brian Fieldings, you are officially welcomed as students of the academy, where you will be granted training for a period no greater than two cycles."

Wait. What?

Book 6: Initiate

*"What beauty there is to be found in so simple, so pure,
so transformative a thing as education!"*

-Excerpt from *The Unfinished Diary of Mordecai Callus
na'Mezzari, Adept of the Crimson Needle*

15-INTERLUDE

From the balcony above the pretentiously named Chamber of the Sun, she watched the seneschal dole out rewards to people who would likely never set foot within the palace again. Too many of them were being praised for the roles they'd played in the invasion of her homeland. *Indirect* roles, because those whose actions had been truly pivotal merited audiences with the warmonger himself.

She knew *those* people's names. She kept a private list, chiseled in stone and blood.

It had been more than a glass since the audience had begun, and she hadn't stirred even once. The man at her side made up for that stillness in spades, his nervous shifting only increasing as the length of their stay continued to grow. Finally, he couldn't hold his peace any longer.

"We should move on. Our presence here has been noted."

"Our presence anywhere is noted, Ardalan. That is what life will be like for the foreseeable future."

They spoke softly, for all that they used a language rarely heard in the kingdom of Elthor. After all, *rarely* was a mountain's breadth from *never*, and it was all but certain that any assigned watchers would have at least a passing familiarity with their language.

"I am well aware of our circumstances," replied Ardalan, his voice tight. "But to take a position out in the open like this and then maintain that position beyond reason is to make yourself a target. I am but one person. I cannot guarantee your safety."

"Then it is a good thing the warmonger has assigned so many watchers to us," she replied. "I have more value to him alive than dead."

"How can you be certain?"

For the first time she turned from the tableau to meet Ardalan's ever-anxious eyes.

"Because we still breathe." She shook her head and looked back to the Chamber of the Sun. "Father always said a lever only works as long as it remains intact."

"Still, some risks are necessary and some are not. Why are we here?"

As she made to reply, a final group entered the chamber below, escorted by guards in the warmonger's colors as well as the city's head shadow and two of his men.

"We're here for them," she said.

Ardalan peered over the balcony. "A strange group. A scaled who carries herself like a queen. A human barely taller than a child of dust. And… I'm not even sure what the last one is, besides intimidating."

"She's a blood-scorned amazon. They are a warlike people from the jungles beyond the Waste. Archaeus wrote of them in the journals of his ill-fated expedition to the southern sea. Reavers and amazons and stranger things besides."

"I see." He studied the group in silence. "Who are they?"

"That is what we are here to discover." She felt the other man's gaze on her and gave, just a little. "They are adventurers, arrived two days ago from a frontier town named Madea on the fringes of the barony of Sakeld."

"Sakeld. Madea." Ardalan stiffened. "The party that found the missing heir?"

"The same." She studied the trio as the warmonger's seneschal spoke to a recently married pair of humans wearing the heavy layers of fabric favored by the city nobility.

The black-skinned amazon stalked the hallway like some sort of jungle cat, all controlled fury and thinly disguised impatience. Beneath that lurked another emotion, deeply buried. Grief, though who or what the amazon grieved for had yet to make it into the Upper City's rumor mill. Provoke her and she would erupt.

The scaled woman wore robes dyed like the earth's own heart blood: bright fire and ruddy magma. Where Ardalan had seen pride in the reptilian woman, she saw confidence, mixed with uncertainty. Age was difficult to discern with that species, but her instincts told her the scaled was young. Young but with a story to tell.

And then there was the small one. Dark of hair, skin bronzed by the sun, he was a head shorter than the amazon, and laughably tiny next to the scaled. Still, there was something about him that belied his size. Maybe it was the way he stood, body unconsciously angled to shield the scaled woman at his side. Maybe it was the way his eyes roved the chamber, touching upon everyone and everything in it like a merchant judging his rival's wares.

Some people, she had been taught, were like copper, soft and swift to give way. Some were poorly wrought iron, plentiful but brittle. Others were hardened bronze, better than the first two, yet prone to failure with time and usage. Only a rare few were forged from more resilient ore, from precious veins locked away deep within the world's secret domains.

If this human was one of those kind, if the scaled at his side could rise above her people's lowly state, if the amazon's fury could be harnessed and redirected…

She shook her head, admonishing herself. So many ifs. So many possibilities. All of them *useless*, given her status as political prisoner, as a living totem of her country's demise. She needed to focus on what mattered. These people had found and rescued the heir. They held the information needed to absolve her country of the crime for which it had been accused. The crime used to justify a war only one side had ever been able to fight.

She was young but not so naïve as to think that even unassailable proof would change anything. Not in the short term, at least. Still, a rockfall that began with a single cast-off pebble might, by its end, bury an entire city. An entire *kingdom*, even.

"Do we know what their reward will be?" asked Ardalan.

"We don't. Nor do we care, to be honest. But I must find a way to speak with them before they depart Trynfall."

Ardalan had worked with and for her father for almost three decades. As stuck in his ways as he too often was, he was also far from slow. "Your father would not wish you to jeopardize your safety, Zamira."

She let the low rumble in her voice communicate her feelings on that. "My father knows the people come first. More importantly, *my father is not here.*"

He accepted that with his usual frustrating grace and simply changed tack. "While we *can* request an audience, it is unlikely that such a request will even reach the adventurers. You know that as well as I do. Once they leave this room, you will never see any of them again."

Below, the adventurers finally stood before the seneschal. Zamira listened as the man spoke of the heir's rescue, of grand deeds undertaken, and then, of a reward commensurate with those deeds. At the end, she turned back to Ardalan, and if the smile that crossed her face was small and crooked, it was still the first she'd had since being brought to this horrid city.

"You were saying?"

Ardalan nodded, his eyes still fixed on the trio of unwitting adventurers below.

"Perhaps the Wanderer has not forsaken us after all."

16

As the seneschal's words rolled through the Chamber of the Sun, the world seemed to slow. It wasn't like when Shan had literally stopped time to save my life, breaking a cosmic rule that dated back to the Godswar in doing so. This was just me, just my brain kicking into overdrive when faced with the unexpected.

I had heard of and read about the kingdom's academies, one for each duchy. Unlike Mordecai's beloved Crimson Needle, the *academies* weren't universities dedicated to higher learning and the pursuit of knowledge, no matter how esoteric. No, they were more like… vocational schools for nobles. Hands-on training for renowned instructors and all the knowledge a second- or third-born noble child would need to make something of themselves.

Adventurers, especially common-born adventurers, weren't allowed to enroll.

Until now, apparently.

On the one hand, it wasn't the kind of reward we'd been hoping for: a rich patron, noble titles of our own, or even literal chests of gold crowns. In the short run, it didn't solve any of the very large-scale problems we'd be facing upon the arrival of a fleet of synossian refugees.

On the other hand, it was *everything* I could have asked for in a vacuum. Training *and* teaching. Guidance to rank up to Tin. A safe and stable place to finally create a foundation for my new life on Eos. And while none of *that* was helpful for the task Miko's gods had assigned me, every one of our classmates would be from the duchy's noble houses. What if we could build alliances from the bottom up instead of the top down? Befriend the sons and daughters and the parents would hopefully be inclined to follow. A dozen houses willingly on our side would be far more effective than any one patron *assigned* by the grand duke.

Unfortunately, none of those great points mattered, because we wouldn't be staying.

We'd sworn to help Lace get her revenge against Arrius. I'd even gotten a quest for it, given by the brother to Miko's goddess Aurea. A god named Kal who was *literally* known as the Oathkeeper. School was a dream, but unless we could have that dream deferred to some distant point in the future, we would have to let it go.

With that realization, time clicked back into motion. The seneschal turned toward Lace, not so much looking at her as through her, like she was a ghost, like we were all ghosts, spirits summoned to receive his words and then dissipate into the air.

"Admission into the Trynfall Ducal Academy is limited to those who possess twenty cycles or less. Instead, we offer you a single lesser boon of your choosing. Speak with the lord arbiter and if the stated request is deemed satisfactory, it will be done."

I wasn't sure what qualified as a *lesser* boon, but that didn't sound terrible. If we'd all gotten the same, we might really have had something to work with.

The guards swept us away shortly after, but I could feel eyes on us as Lace reclaimed her weapons. Whatever happened, the story of our reward would spread, and the little voice in my head told me that would end up causing trouble in the end.

I called that voice *bitter experience.*

With our former guide long gone, Hawthorne took the lead now. Rather than returning to the carriage, we passed back through the open-air hallway and then turned into one of the rooms we'd passed on the way in. It was set up as a study of some sort: a gleaming wooden desk in the middle with shelves behind, chairs and low couches along two walls, and a single window that showed nothing but cloud-stricken sky and ocean.

The guards took positions out in the hall, but the arbiters and Hawthorne's driver swept past us and into the room. After they gave the all-clear, we joined them.

"What is this?" asked Lace, the first words she'd spoken since entering the Chamber of the Sun.

"On most days, it is a waiting room," said Hawthorne, taking a seat behind the desk. "Right now, it is a space for private discussions instead. I am sure you have questions about the lesser boon you have been granted."

"Several."

"Ask and I will answer them so that you may decide upon your boon. It is unlikely we will ever see each other again after you are returned to the Night's Sky; I would prefer to settle the matter here and now."

"What about us?" I asked.

"My orders are to deliver you and Priestess Naseri to the academy. I will do so as soon as your belongings arrive."

My recently improved Discernment attribute told me now was the time to raise the most important question. "Is there any chance of us deferring our studies at the academy? We have things to do as a party, and this was not part of those plans."

"My orders are to deliver you and Priestess Naseri to the academy," he repeated, roughly twelve degrees cooler than the first time, "and I will do so." He turned back to Lace. "I'm waiting, amazon. You'll find that here in the north, time is money."

"We sat for two days before we saw the seneschal," she said.

"His Grace has both time and money to spare. I do not."

The amazon gave Miko and me an unreadable look and left to join Hawthorne at the desk. The lord arbiter nodded to his bodyguard, who made a gesture with his right hand, index and middle fingers skyward. Just like that, we couldn't hear a word he or Lace were saying.

Some sort of summoned privacy field? As undeniably useful as it was, I couldn't ever see burning one of my prized technique selections on something like that. Not until Gold or whatever came after, maybe.

Clearly, a bodyguard had different priorities than an adventurer.

"What is happening, nest-brother?" whispered Miko in the High Tongue.

"How much of all of that did you understand?"

"The words? All of them. The situation? Much less, I think." She looked down at me, orange eyes wide. "You know I have nothing against study or learning. I would have chosen to be a scholar if Aurea had not called me to her service. But we do not have the time for this, and we cannot abandon our friend."

"I know." I tried not to be obvious as I scanned the room, but every time I looked over, Hawthorne's bodyguard seemed to be looking straight back at me. "And we're not going to. When we get to the academy, we can try explaining our position. I just want to talk to Lace first and see how she wants to play this. The academy could be useful for us if we're allowed to come back and enroll *after* dealing with Arrius."

"True training would be a dream," she said. "But my people…"

"We'll need money and help and a lot of other things to be able to handle their ships as they arrive," I reminded her. "If we can't get an audience to speak with the duke about it, we can instead reach out to the duchy's nobility."

"Many of whom will have children at the school."

"I think so. Or hope so, at least. I don't know how many houses there are, but those that are here in the capital almost have to be wealthier and more influential than Baron Sakeld. Get a few of them on our side and we could at least have the start of something."

And who knew? Maybe delivering Eustace's note to Elina d'Kay would net us another ally, fifth daughter or not. After all, her parents would be happy to see her spending time with a baron, right?

Miko tapped her left arm. "Bring Arrius to justice, deliver Mordecai's belongings to his estranged love, and then return to Trynfall for study?"

"Yeah. Although we *might* be able to find someone to take the Mage's inheritance to the Crimson Needle on our behalf. I don't know how long a trip that is, and like you said, we don't have a lot of time."

That wasn't *totally* accurate. Our best estimates, based purely on Miko's readings of the journey her ancestors had made when fleeing this continent for their new home had the ocean crossing taking upwards of two cycles. Even if the first ships had left before Whitehall's fall, that still gave us around a cycle and a half. With each cycle consisting of eleven moons of thirty-five extra-long days, that *was* a lot of time… and yet I wasn't sure it would be enough. Infrastructure, supply lines, land, even sufficient building materials and craftsmen… the list of needs to support potentially *thousands* of refugees seemed to grow every time I thought about it.

That was what made finding allies so important. The noble houses of the kingdom of Elthor would almost have to be better suited for organizing this sort of thing than an ex-barista who'd balanced his budget with a pen and a prayer and still left behind literal drawers full of bills.

Lace's silent conversation with Hawthorne continued for a while. The Marauder had ignored the offered chair and paced back and forth as she spoke. Hawthorne, by contrast, was a study of stillness, as comfortable behind the desk as if it was his own.

I didn't know *why* Hawthorne had had his guard erect some sort of privacy barrier, but that was kind of par for the course with the lord. The bigger question was why Lace had chosen to leave us out of their conversation. I added it to the list of things to talk to her about. Which… wouldn't do me any good if we couldn't find a way to carve out time for that discussion.

Miko took a seat on one of the couches, careful not to poke the fabric with the claws on her hands and bare feet, but I was too amped up to sit. Much like Lace, I paced back and forth as I looked for my opportunity to speak.

Before that opportunity could arrive, the door cracked open and another arbiter in black slipped in. It was strange how that uniform seemed to anonymize them. Each arbiter we'd seen so far had been visually distinct from each other—if all human—but all I could remember after they were gone was *a person in black*. This one was a woman, slim and shorter than Lace. She crossed the room and bent to whisper something into Hawthorne's ear.

At least I thought it was a whisper; her addition hadn't affected the privacy field at all. Still, whatever she said got the lord arbiter's attention. He motioned to his bodyguard and just like that, we could hear him again.

"It appears we will be taking a side trip to the Night's Sky *before* delivering you both to the academy."

That sounded very much like the opportunity I'd been looking for. Still, I had to ask: "Is there a problem?"

"The proprietress insists that she will open your room only to its occupants."

Okay, maybe Darcie *was* a wizard.

"She's just one woman," said Lace, not helping matters at all.

"Who is well within her legal rights." Hawthorne pinched the bridge of the nose, looking disconcertingly mortal as he rose to his feet. "You will discover as you travel this kingdom, amazon, that a quality inn is worth its weight in gold crowns. And unlike many of those inns, the Night's Sky has the *political* stature to match. An extra trip there and back will have ripple effects, upon scheduling if nothing else, but remains a small price to pay to keep the peace."

I hid my frown. After working retail for years, I thought I'd gotten pretty good at reading people, but Lord Arbiter Hawthorne didn't seem to want to fit neatly into any of my boxes.

ooo

The trip back to the inn was undertaken in silence. Hawthorne seemed off in his own world and Lace was stewing about something. Probably the thought that we were going to abandon her. The amazon's upbringing hadn't left her big on trust even *before* you factored in the goddess she worshipped or the fact that she'd lost her name and her clan both.

I waited until we were inside and upstairs—Darcie letting us pass like the benevolent authority figure she apparently was—and pulled the Marauder aside.

Figuratively pulled her aside… I wasn't stronger than she was, and I sure as hell wasn't quick or skilled enough to keep her from stabbing me if she felt like it.

"We need to talk," I said in Gorash, the language of the south.

She gave me another of her patented looks but led me into her room. With only one bed, it was substantially more spacious than the already palatial suite I shared with Miko.

"What is there to talk about?"

"We're a party," I reminded her for at least the second time since our arrival in Trynfall. "And you're our leader."

"And?"

"And Arrius is waiting out there somewhere. But we also need to plan for the post-Arrius future. So, assuming the school won't let us defer our studies, how are we going to get out of the city? And more importantly, how can we do it *without* angering the duke who just broke with tradition to enroll Miko and me in his prized school?"

She stared at me for long enough that I worried I'd accidentally lapsed into some other language. Maybe the *words of stone and wind*, as the dunsmen poetically called their tongue.

"You're not going anywhere," she finally said. "And neither is little Miko."

"What?"

"I *know* you understood me. Hell, there isn't a language I could speak that you wouldn't understand."

"The words, yes. The meaning, not so much." I frowned at her. "There's a Copper who needs killing."

"More than killing."

"…right. So, what am I missing?"

"The fact that he *is* a Copper. A Tin and two unranked? We'd have to get very lucky to even have a chance. Even luckier than 'oh look, here's a convenient wall with stakes at the bottom.'"

"It worked once."

Her voice went serious. "It did and the Night Hag probably laughed a storm because of it. But luck is every bit as fickle as

Hashoggath's own black heart. The old man's memory deserves more than just a suicidal roll of the bones."

The *old man* being Skaal, who had *maybe* been a few years older than Lace when he died.

"Now, *three Tins* against a Copper?" she continued. "Especially a Copper who has been hounded to the ends of the world by a hunter of men? A Copper who has been stripped of all protection and shelter? *That* has promise."

"You *want* us to attend the academy?"

"I want you to grow stronger. My plan was for us to join an adventuring company here in Trynfall and level that way, but a school for nobles will teach you more than I ever could on the road. And maybe you and little Miko will find allies to help deal with your *other* insurmountable problem."

Lace, I constantly had to remind myself, was neither as dumb nor as barbaric as she liked to pretend.

"But what about you?"

"What part of *hounded to the ends of the world by a hunter of men* was unclear?" Her smile was savage in the room's dim light. "I doubt I can kill Arrius alone, any more than I could with the two of you as you are now, but harry him from the shadows? Make misery his daily bread? Let him understand what it feels to have no one and nothing? That much I can do."

Okay, so she wasn't as *dumb* as she liked to pretend. The jury was still out on the barbarism.

Still, something about how she'd said *to have no one and nothing* caught my ear.

"You're not alone, you know."

"I was talking about him."

"Of course." One more piece of what she'd said suddenly made sense. "So, the boon you were offered?"

"Announcements will go out tomorrow exiling Arrius Vitellius from this duchy. The northern lord says the other duchies will follow suit as a matter of principle. The man will find himself without a guild *or* a home and I will track him down and harry him, pecking away until death seems like sweet release. By the time you and Miko are ready to join me, all that will be left to take will be his name and his life."

"That's a *lesser* boon?"

"Copper or not, he is only one man. In cities and kingdoms as large as this, a single life doesn't even register."

"You could have just asked them to kill him then."

She snarled. *Actually* snarled, sending me back a step. "He is *mine* to kill, Brian Fieldings. I may not be Chosen, like you, but I am a devotee of Hashoggath, blessed since my Dreaming. Vengeance is my birthright."

I wasn't going to argue with that, and not just because she looked a breath away from murder. The truth was, *I'd* been the one next to Skaal when he breathed his last. I wanted a hand in Arrius' death too, and if that said bad things about my moral character, I couldn't find it in myself to care.

"I guess this is goodbye then."

"Get your pack," she told me. "I won't spend a silver tower or whatever it costs to stay here another night. We can say our farewells below."

∘∘∘

Miko was already in our room and packed. She gave me a look I had no trouble interpreting as I came through the door.

"She wants us to stay," I said, switching seamlessly to the High Tongue. "To train up and reach Tin while she makes Arrius' life miserable from the shadows or something."

"We're… separating?"

"I know… I know. Never split the party, right?"

Miko didn't have the pop-culture knowledge to truly get that reference, but in a world of literal adventurers and parties, it made plenty of sense on its own.

"Wouldn't it be wiser for her to remain in the city with us?"

I shrugged, calling on *Deception* to mask my own concerns. "Probably. But who's going to make her do anything she doesn't want to do? It'll be fine."

"Yet you are as concerned as I am, nest-brother."

I spent the next few seconds silently blaming *Deception's* low skill cap. And wondering if the Spearman advanced class I'd rejected would have changed the skill's classification.

It didn't seem likely, but not knowing would eat at me.

"Of course I'm concerned," I eventually admitted. "But she's a lot better equipped to survive out there by herself than we are, and I think she needs to feel like she's doing something."

I still wasn't entirely sure what that something would be, but between the Night Hag and Lace herself, I was willing to accept it would be appropriately awful.

"I understand." Miko hung her short staff from a hook on her worn leather belt. "Then we must make sure to use the time she has sacrificed for us wisely."

"Tin and beyond and we'll even gather some allies for your people along the way."

"Yes."

I slung my pack over one shoulder and took up my spear, immediately feeling more prepared to deal with whatever came our way. Downstairs, we found Lace trading stares with one of the arbiters in the street. Hell, maybe both of them; all the talk about Arrius after we'd sidestepped the subject for days had clearly gotten her fired up.

Miko moved toward the other woman, then paused, just a few feet away. "Friend Seanna and her people express gratitude through touch. Would like to do same, if is okay."

I thought for a moment that Lace was going to say no. But as she looked up at the taller synossian practically radiating earnestness from every scale, she cracked.

"This once."

Despite those scales and the sharp weapons on the end of her fingers and toes, Miko gave really good hugs.

"How can we contact you when we're ready?" I asked, once their embrace was over.

"Send a bulletin through the adventurer's guild," said Lace. "I'm going to stop by Trynfall's chapter on my way out to give them Carlson's letter. If you can, you'll both want to check in sometime in the next moon or two to keep your status as guildmembers."

"We will." I added it to my mental list of things to do, a list that might soon be long enough to eat its own tail. "And we'll figure out how to do the bulletin thing when it's time."

"Good enough. Stay safe. Don't take any grief from these soft northerners; I have a name again and a reputation to uphold. Now, go. We will see each other again and bathe in the blood of our enemies."

That got a reaction from one of the two arbiters, but we paid it no mind. I didn't offer Lace a hug—nor did she show any signs of wanting one—but saluted her instead, synossian style, and turned to leave.

Lace caught me before I could. "Brian," she said in Gorash, "there *is* one more thing."

"What is it?" I replied in kind.

"Should things not go my way, this task will be left to you."

"Don't say that. Things—"

"I'm not interested in false assurances."

I tried not flinch from the rebuke.

"This task will be left to you," she repeated. "That man's life *and* his name must both be taken from him. Do you understand?"

"Yes." That didn't seem sufficient given the sheer intensity in her gaze, so I added on. "Whatever else happens, he's a dead man. We'll make sure of it."

"A dead man with no name." Her nod was a swift thing, as sharp as any of the many daggers on her body. "And if it does come to that, there is something you must say when you face him."

Her eyes, like the seneschal's seemed to stare right through me.

"Tell him this: *I come with hate in my heart and spite in my soul to cut you out of the Weaver's web. What was left of a man will now burn forever, nameless and forgotten, adrift in the void between stars.*"

"That's..." I stopped myself a moment too late.

"Yes?"

"Kind of a mouthful. Can I say it *after* we've taken him down?" I held up my hands. "I'm just saying... I'm going to want the element of a surprise and I'm not sure a speech like that, as badass as it is, is conducive to surprise."

"I will not miss you at all, Brian Fieldings." Her smile came and went, one more sharp edge added to the mix. "Just make sure he hears it when he dies. Swear it."

"You have my word. On the nine rosy breasts of the Night Hag herself." I waited, for just a second, to see if I'd get another quest from the Framework, but apparently the one I already had to kill Arrius was enough for Miko's gods. Or maybe they didn't like that I'd sworn by Lace's demon goddess. "But in less than a cycle, I'm going to listen to *you* giving him that speech instead of me. And then you're finally going to teach me *Lockpicking* like you promised."

She switched back to Trade. "We will see. Take care of little Miko."

"Am still not little," said Miko.

"Not in form or heart," agreed the amazon. She gave me a solid thump on the shoulder and then was past the carriage and striding down the street, Tempest on her back with her pack, hands free to produce bladed weapons on demand.

"We need to go," said one of the arbiters.

"Yeah." I watched the Marauder until she'd turned the corner and vanished from sight. "I guess we do."

Before we left, and much to Hawthorne's thinly veiled irritation, I went back into the Night's Sky and thanked both Darcie and Della. I don't think either of them cared that much, but when I added, in absolute honesty, that it was by far the nicest place I'd ever stayed, I got a half-smile out of the mother and a look of frankly insulting disbelief from the daughter.

I really *did* need an *Honesty* skill.

We were halfway to the Upper City before I realized Lace had slipped Mordecai's belongings into my pack.

ooo

The Trynfall Ducal Academy, which I had to assume was always spoken of in caps unless you were a noble who could afford to shorten it to *academy*, was all the way back in the Upper City. That explained why Hawthorne had tried to have our stuff packed up and moved while we were dealing with the seneschal. It also explained why the school was nobles-only, because on our return trip, the carriage's wooden shutters were open, and we got an eyeful of Trynfall's uppermost tier.

If I'd been British, I'd have called it posh. Since nobody on Eos knew what *either* of those things were, I didn't. Not even in my head. I was trying to acclimatize to living here and part of that was thinking in local terms.

Then again, my *Speaker of Tongues* trait would just tell me that *fancy* in English was *fancy* in Trade, Gorash, the words of stone and wind, the reaver language I'd never gotten the name of, Common, and of course, the High Tongue.

I didn't include the essoli or irkonnen languages in that mix, mostly because I didn't want to even think of them.

Regardless, I'd thought the Middle City and the Worshipper's Ascent were something, but *this* was another level entirely. And not just literally. The palace was at the far side of the Upper City, perched at the edge of the cliff for its amazing view. To its right was an amphitheater-like building, all curves and rounded edges, and opposite it, forming a sort of plaza outside the palace's guarded courtyard, was…

Well, it kind of looked like another palace, with two slightly shorter towers to the duke's one, but I was informed it was, in fact, the Trynfall Ducal Academy. Still all in caps.

To get there, we followed an absurdly wide street past literal mansions. Meaning twenty, maybe thirty rooms, multiple stories, expansive estates, and, I had to assume, entire gardens of elaborate animal topiary. This was where the nobles lived when they weren't away in their ancestral homes on their ancestral lands doing no-doubt ancestral things.

They were *summer homes* twice the size of Jefferson High back in Midton, basically. It broke my brain a little bit. *These* were the people whose grown children we'd be going to school with?

It was late afternoon when we reached the school grounds. I was pretty sure Hawthorne was seething about the delay behind his cold mask… but only pretty sure. We waited for his bodyguard to give the all-clear and then followed him outside to find two people waiting for us on the front steps.

One was a woman, slim, stiff-backed, and grey-haired, dressed in a charcoal doublet and pants as black as any arbiter's. Next to her was one of the largest humans I'd seen on either world, as broad as Arrius and maybe a little bit taller. He too wore charcoal and black, but it was the scars that covered one side of his face and much of the visible skin of his left arm that got my attention.

Both because they were intimidating as hell and because I couldn't imagine how much the wound had hurt when it happened or how much healing it had taken to keep him alive.

Hawthorne ignored the man, which took some serious balls in my opinion, but favored the woman with a nod. "Dame Credence."

"Lord Hawthorne. Are these my new students?"

"By His Grace's order, yes."

She looked us over, visually dissecting us in a way that made Hawthorne's original appraisal back in Madea seem almost amateurish. Miko's bright robes and scales, my patchwork skin and the decrepit spear in my hands.

"Interesting," she decided.

"I leave them in your care." Hawthorne gave another short nod, and returned to his carriage with his driver, arbiters, and a unit of the duke's guard, leaving just the four of us standing there.

"Always in a hurry," rumbled the monster of a man.

"And too clever for his own good," agreed the woman. She turned to us. "Make no mistake, what we provide here is *instruction*. If it's care you want, there are painted houses in the Lower City where the women will give you all you can take and a couple of unwanted extra gifts besides. But within these walls, you are mine."

The giant man's smile was a thing of ghastly beauty.

17

The first thing we learned was that we were late. Not just for our meeting with Dame Credence, but for enrollment in general. We'd missed orientation at the Trynfall Royal Academy by almost a moon, and an extended orientation period had been underway for three full seven-days. Which made us not just commoners in a school full of nobles but something even worse: *transfer students.*

It was the headmistress who filled us in as she escorted us through the facilities. With orientation ending, classes would begin in three days. According to her, they ran the gamut from weapons training to history to survival to politics.

As someone who had never enjoyed school, I was surprised to realize how much I was looking forward to it. Part of that was that the Framework would let me actually *see* any improvements I made, but the bigger part was that we would be learning stuff that *mattered…* not just for our future success but our continued survival.

Room, board, and three sets of uniforms were included in enrollment, but any spending beyond that would come out of our personal finances. That wasn't a problem for the nobles, but Miko and

I would have to budget when it came to weekend excursions and keeping our other gear in good condition.

"Sixth and Seventh Day are usually free," said Dame Credence, as we swept through the southern wing of the building on our way to the initiate dorms. "But you have ground to make up. Tomorrow, you will join our other new student on a tour of the facilities and receive the reading materials covered in orientation. On Seventh Day, you will report to my office for your official curriculums." She turned on Miko without breaking stride. "I understand you are not a native speaker."

"No. But I am learning," Miko said carefully.

"If you need assistance with your reading, I'd advise you to hire a tutor. My staff do not have the time for such things."

"I'll help her," I said.

"I doubt *you* will have the time either."

"I'll make the time."

That got me a long look from the headmistress, but she continued on.

"All students are housed here at the academy. While the rooms themselves are restricted by gender, the common spaces are not. You are all adults in the eyes of both the law and the Framework and are expected to behave accordingly. Fieldings, you will be sharing a room with one of our existing initiates. Naseri, we have an odd number of women, so you will have your own space."

"Would prefer to share room with Brian," said Miko. "If possible. Please."

For the first time, Dame Credence downshifted from the brisk pace that had kept me practically jogging through the school. "Is there something that I should know about? Fraternization may be common within adventuring parties, but it has no place in my institution."

"It's not like that," I said. "But we're from the same town and we work best together. In a party and otherwise."

"You won't always have that option here. Nor should you. Growth requires discomfort." She shook her head and resumed her punishing pace. "Still, one must sleep. The room assignments are intended to maintain modesty and reduce possible friction. As that is not a concern here, I will note the change in your sleeping arrangements. Young Donaghey, at least, will be happy to continue having a room to himself."

The hall we'd been walking down finally terminated in an oversized door. Above it was a wooden sign with a single word painted on it in no-nonsense block letters.

"Dorms," I read aloud.

That got me another look from Dame Credence.

"You read ancient Caserian?"

"I was a scholar before I was an adventurer," I said, hoping *Deception* would help me hide my wince. "And I did some translation work while we were operating out of Madea."

That last part was true. In fact, I was pretty sure the language on the sign matched the language of some of the books I'd deciphered for the ritual performed after we found Wilhemina. I just… hadn't had a name for it until now. Or realized that I wasn't seeing Trade in time to avoid blurting the word out.

"Interesting," the headmistress said for the second time in the past quarter glass. "Very interesting."

I didn't love the sound of that.

Despite its size, the door opened easily on well-greased hinges. Inside was a small common room with a fireplace and several tables and benches, and doors in each of its four walls. The one across from us opened onto a long hallway with doors on either side. She took us to the first of those doors, a few feet from the common room, and handed Miko the key.

"This is your room. I will send a second key shortly. I will also have someone deliver dinner to your room, but this is a one-time occurrence. You will be expected to attend meals at the designated times in the mess hall when it is open and to find your own fare out in the city when it is not."

"Got it."

"Since it hasn't been said yet, welcome to the Trynfall Ducal Academy. Whatever your origins, you will be treated the same as any other students. This will be a cycles-long trial by fire, but if you survive the experience, I believe you will find that the lessons taught here will take you to places you never dreamed possible."

Given that I'd already changed literal realities, I was pretty sure I was way ahead of her on that one.

Once the headmistress was gone, Miko used her key to unlock the door, and we entered the room we'd be living in for the foreseeable future. It… wasn't the Night's Sky. That was immediately clear. What furniture was there—two beds, two dressers, one shelf—was simply made and without any ornamentation at all. The walls were bare, the windows narrow, and if feng shui was a thing on Eos, this was the place it might come to die.

On the other hand, it was spacious enough that I'd be able to practice my knife forms without Miko having to duck aside. There were candles next to the beds for nighttime, one dresser could easily hold all my clothes and most of my supplies, and the narrow windows brought in natural light while offering a partial view of some sort of grassy interior courtyard.

Best of all? A door, set where the second bookshelf would have otherwise stood, led to a small bathroom and that bathroom had both a mirror and one of those fancy enchanted chamber pots we'd seen at the inn. It looked like actual bathing would happen elsewhere, but we weren't without *every* possible comfort.

I couldn't decide if I was happy at how quickly I'd acclimatized to life on Eos or sad that *chamber pots* were somehow now my bar for comfort.

Dinner that night was bread and cold slabs of meat. Extremely basic fare that was, at worst, on par or better than what we'd had on the road. Noises from the hallway told us some of the other initiates were up and about, but even Miko was exhausted after the eventful day. We decided to leave introductions until the next day's tour.

So: dinner, the last bits of unpacking, and then meditation before sleep. I let Miko go first but when she was done, she smiled and shook her head. Despite all that we'd done that day, very little time had been focused on self-improvement; it wasn't a shock to not see a single skill gain.

No, the shock came when *I* finished my meditation and saw I'd earned a point in *Knife*. How was that even possible? I hadn't practiced my weapon forms that morning… and Caleb had made a point of telling me that *those* were more to limber up my wrists than actually improve my skill.

So then…

I scanned the rest of the dialogue window and bit back a groan as things became clear.

```
You have increased the following skills:

Major skills:
Knife [+1]: 29/35

General skills:
Juggling [+1]: 2/10
```

When I told Miko, she giggled for three minutes straight before I managed to extract a simple, unbreakable oath from her:

We were never, ever going to tell Lace about this.

○○○

I was up early the next day. Miko, as usual, was not. My nest-sister had no difficulties pulling an all-nighter healing but give her a proper bed… or even a tent and a bedroll, and *morning* somehow became the secret identity of one of Eos' nine demon gods.

To be fair, it might even be the *real* identity of a demon god. Hashoggath was the only one of the nine I actually knew about. Was it weird that I was excited to learn about the other eight in class?

It *seemed* weird.

I used the chamber pot and then wandered down the hallway to the common room. Another sign in ancient Caserian led me to the bath halls. These *were* segregated by gender, which was just as well as the one I entered was one big room with steps leading into a pool of steaming water that might easily fit a dozen people. It wasn't until I was submerged that I realized there was a current; water flowing in from somewhere and then back out again.

I wasn't sure if someone on Eos had actually cracked indoor plumbing, or if there was a magical explanation for both the heat and the circulating water, but the net effect was pretty much the same. I scrubbed down—using an actual sponge, not the stiff-bristled brushes synossians used to scrape the dirt from their scales—and then simply soaked in the warmth.

With apologies to the Night's Sky, *this* one part might actually be better. So far, the Trynfall Ducal Academy was a study in contrasts. It tried really, really hard for a military-like asceticism, but if you scratched the surface, everything beneath was the sort of luxury you'd never find in border towns or, I had to assume, in the Lower City.

Maybe for nobles, *this* was considered roughing it?

After a half-glass or so passed in the bath, I figured Miko would be ready to string multiple syllables together. So, I climbed back out, dried myself with a towel I'd pulled off the stack by the door—again, *luxury*—and then dropped both that towel and my used sponge into designated receptacles on the way out.

All of the signs were in ancient Caserian. Hopefully, I'd find out why at some point.

Upon my return, I pointed Miko to the baths (explaining which side was for the women) and got dressed. I did some brief stretches, an even briefer run-through of my knife forms, and even a half-dozen juggling passes. *With* knives, because sometimes, you have to stick with what's working. Thankfully, Miko was back quickly enough to take advantage of yet another opportunity to train her *Field Dressings* skill. She followed that up with a *Minor Healing* that made the bandages she'd just applied redundant.

One more day until we'd get *real* training, but hell if we were going to let chances to improve ourselves pass by in the meantime.

We were back to discussing what little I remembered from *Meditations on Mortality* when there was a knock at the door. I traded glances with Miko and we both went to meet our tour guide.

"Oh! Well, that's different." The speaker would have been short next to anyone but me. He wasn't wearing the uniforms we'd been given—white tunic, black trousers—but instead an unlaced shirt under an old and badly worn jacket, paired with what my earthborn mind immediately categorized as harem pants. The shirt was lemon yellow, the jacket had probably started its life bright red, and the pants resisted any casual interpretations on a color wheel. His dark, shaggy hair looked like it hadn't seen a comb or a barber in far too long.

"How did you two get a room together?" The stranger peered at Miko, looking her up and down in a way that would have been offensive if he wasn't swaying slightly and blinking furiously, as if trying to bring her into focus. "This is going to come off as incredibly rude but… you *are* female, right?"

Miko straightened, staring down her suggestion of a nose at the human.

"Yes," she said simply.

"And…" He turned to me. "You're male?"

I couldn't help myself. "Clearly, this *is* a place of learning."

Beneath the streaks of dirt across his face, the other man cracked a smile. It was hard to be sure given his current state, but I thought he was probably several years younger than I was.

A cycle or two, by local time units.

"I had to be sure," he confessed. "How in the twenty-seven hells did you two manage to get a room together?"

"We're related."

He looked back and forth between us blearily and then shrugged. "You know what? I'm not going to argue with that. I'm Wilf, one of your fellow initiates and the *only* person dumb enough to volunteer when the Iron Lady went looking for tour guides last night."

The mark of a good nickname was that I knew exactly who he was talking about.

"Is nice to meet you," said Miko, thawing just a bit. "Am—*I* am—Miko Naseri."

"A pleasure. We don't do family names here unless you're one of the faculty," said Wilf. "Too easy for certain someones to put on airs, if you know what I mean. But I'm guessing *that* won't be a problem with either of you."

"Probably not." I kept my right hand on my spear and offered him the left. "I'm Brian."

He stared at my hand for a moment, then winced. "Sorry; I can't even begin to remember what my hand's gotten up to last night and this morning. Let's do the arm clasping another time, yeah?"

"I am excited for the tour," said Miko diplomatically.

"Really?" Wilf seemed taken aback. "Well, that's alright then. We'll have a good time and get you all sorted before the faculty do their best to murder us on First Day."

"Murder?" asked Miko.

"Academically speaking."

I had no idea what that meant, so I pivoted. "Dame Credence said something about another new student?"

He wrinkled his mud-spattered nose. "We don't use titles or names for the faculty either. Not unless they're in hearing range."

"The Iron Lady then," I said.

"Right. Yeah, three new students showing up a moon late has caused a bit of a stir, and not just with the initiates either. But from what I hear, you've all got your reasons." He paused, as if inviting us to fill in the blanks, then shrugged. "Anyway, the new girl's waiting outside the common room for us. Don't take anything she does, says, or thinks too personally, yeah?"

"I'm sorry?"

For a moment, the levity dropped from Wilf's face. "She's had a tough time of things. I know we're not supposed to feel sorry for her, but I do anyway. At least that's what I remind myself every time she opens her mouth."

With that, he did a four-point turn—something I'd never seen performed by someone on feet instead of in a car—and headed back down the hall to the common room.

I traded glances with Miko.

"He is strange," she said in the High Tongue.

"Yeah. I think I like him."

The common room was still empty as we passed through, but I could hear voices from the bath halls, suggesting other initiates were finally up. Wilf seemed to pick up momentum as he went and by the time we exited the dorms, he was no longer staggering nearly as much.

Of course, he *still* almost ran into the woman waiting for us outside.

She was… strange. And not in the way that Wilf was strange, with clothes seemingly thrown together at random and at least one night of drinking highlighting every eccentricity. She was roughly the same height as Wilf, and slim, but there was a solidity to her that didn't match her build. She wore the academy's initiate uniform, like Miko and me, and her long white hair would have blended perfectly with the shirt if she hadn't arranged it in an elaborate braid that ringed her head like a circlet.

"Hello again," said Wilf. "These are Miko and Brian. She's Miko and he's Brian," he added, putting peculiar emphasis on our pronouns.

"I am Zamira," she said, but I was distracted by my latest realization.

Her eyes were stone.

Not 'I can't believe you forgot my birthday and will never forgive you' stone, but actual stone. Tombstone grey. Hard granite. The way they flicked about told me she saw out of them anyway, and that was almost as weird as the eyes themselves.

"Is pleasure," said Miko, bringing a clawed hand to her chest in a sharp salute.

"The pleasure is undoubtedly mine," replied Zamira in a voice as smooth as the seneschal's silk doublet. "I am relieved to not be the only late arrival, though of course you arrived under your own power while I was brought in a cage."

"What matters is that we're all here," said Wilf, blithely ignoring the woman's comment, "and you've all got me for a day to show you about."

"Because you volunteered," said Zamira.

"That's right."

"*Why*, exactly?"

He shrugged. "Information matters. Here, especially. Anything I learn about you all is something I can sell to the other initiates when they get back."

I had to ask. "Is there an *Honesty* skill?"

"Not that I know of. But just by you asking that, I'm pretty sure you already know that's not true of the opposite."

"*Everyone* has *Deception*," said Zamira. "It is, by far, one of the most common skills."

"And the sages wonder why we can't just all get along."

She stiffened. "If that is a comment on—"

Wilf held up a hand, one that I couldn't help but notice didn't waver at all. "It was not. There are people here who will delight in reminding you of your situation, and there's not much you can do about that, but I'm not one of them."

The two of them stared each other down for a bit until Zamira nodded and relaxed, just a shred. "Very well."

"What *is* situation?" asked Miko.

"I am Zamira Lachesia na'Jafani," she announced, seeming to draw strength from the sheer length of her name.

"Am Miko," said my nest-sister. "Miko Naseri."

That seemed to confuse Zamira.

"We're not from around here," I added.

"My father is…" She stopped. "No, you apparently would not know *his* name either."

"Her father is the merchant king of Zaris," said Wilf. "Or was until a few moons ago, I guess."

"Not *king*. The people of Zaris do not have kings, for all that the blood in our veins is as thick and rich as the lakes of living light deep in the earth. He is the first, yes, but the first among equals. And I, his youngest daughter, have been chosen to stay here in this city and this school as a guarantor of his continued good behavior."

"A political prisoner," I concluded, as much for Miko's understanding as for mine.

"Yes."

This was exactly the kind of trouble Miko and I *didn't* need.

"They will train you?" asked the synossian. "An enemy?"

"And in doing so maintain their pretense of a moral high ground," said Zamira, sarcasm heavy in her voice as she stared at us through stone eyes. "After all, look how they are helping the daughter of their loyal new vassal!"

For the first time since we'd met him, Wilf looked nervous. "Maybe we should focus on the tour and leave politics for another day, yeah?"

Zamira took a deep breath and seemed to settle again. "Certainly." And then, in a guttural voice that seemed to emanate from her chest rather than her mouth. "Why should anyone care about the death of a country when there are classrooms to see and gardens to make much of?"

I used my apparently very common *Deception* skill to keep my face still but not *too* still. Nobody else had reacted at all, which meant two things. First, they hadn't heard her. Second, and given that Miko's senses remained maddeningly better than mine, Zamira must have spoken in a language that only my *Speaker of Tongues* trait allowed me to even hear.

I let the timbre of those words roll around in my head. The only language I'd encountered that bordered on telepathy had been the essoli foulness, but this had none of that stench to it. A hidden language that *didn't* make me want to hurl might be a really valuable tool one day. For now, it just gave me a little bit more insight into Zamira's state of mind.

Understandably, that state of mind wasn't great.

"Nest-brother?" asked Miko. She and the other two had started down the hall only for her to realize I wasn't following. "Are you coming?"

"Sorry. Yeah. Let's go."

"Nest-brother?" asked Zamira as we turned down a hall I only vaguely recognized.

"They're related," said Wilf. "Got their own room together in the dorms and everything."

"They are… *what?* How?"

"Couldn't tell ya." I could hear Wilf's smile even if I couldn't see it; in a handful of steps, he had regained the rolling sway and swagger of someone at least two sheets to the wind. "Now then, if you'll all turn your eyes to the left—that's port-side for you seafaring types—you'll see the first of our designated classrooms. Drones On teaches the Bestiary courses there, which are handy if you want to be able to identify the thing that's busy chewing your legs off." He pantomimed a bow in the room's direction but kept walking. "Next up is a classroom I can only hope none of you will ever be forced to step foot in. He calls it Theology, but *I'm* pretty sure Saint Sermon is here to save our souls instead of teach."

"Is good," said Miko. "Souls are important."

"Then I'll surely pray for yours."

Miko shot back a sharp-toothed smile. "And I will ask Saint Sermon to pray for yours."

"I'd… uh… prefer you not mention me to him at all. And especially don't tell him his nickname. Not that you're likely to speak with him anytime soon. Theology class is for adepts—second-cycle students. When it comes to us lowly initiates, he only has times for the Priests."

"Am Priestess," said Miko, going for the verbal KO.

Wilf's smile lost a lot of its brilliance. "Really?"

"Really," I said.

"Well, now I'm regretting this entire conversation."

It took more than a glass to walk the school grounds, with Wilf slowly regaining steam as we went on. There were classrooms, training halls, two different places to eat, the inner courtyard we'd seen from our window, and at least a half-dozen places that we were told were off limits for now.

"Most aren't particularly hard to get into and are far less interesting when you do," confided Wilf. "But the Iron Lady's got a few of them locked up tighter than a—" He coughed and looked away. "A lockbox."

Nobody called him on the obvious change of metaphor.

"Anyway, as you've all probably heard, orientation ended yesterday. The faculty are going to use whatever information they gathered from it to assign us each curriculums that better fit our needs."

"Needs?" asked Zamira.

"Almost everyone here is noble," explained our guide, "but only a few are their family's designated heirs. Those will go back home, show off a little, and get on with learning how to run the house. A few others are spare heirs, but most are even further down the pecking order. We've all got different futures waiting for us when we graduate, and it's the Tryn's job to make sure we're prepared for those futures."

I frowned. "The Tryn?"

"The Trynfall Ducal Academy. Don't tell me you've been using the full title, even in your head? Life's too short, yeah?"

"So, coursework will be structured according to what we're going to end up doing with our lives?"

"That's how they've explained it. You and Miko are adventurers, right? I don't think there's a specific track for that—it's not a particularly popular calling for people with more than a few towers to rub together—so you'll probably be lumped in with the soldiers, like me."

"*You're* going to be a soldier?" asked Zamira.

"An officer, but yeah. Off to mud-boot training following my time at the Tryn, then I'll serve my ten, collect my earnings, and return home." He coughed, looking anywhere but at the other woman. "Most of the time, military duty just means manning a garrison somewhere."

"*Most* of the time." For a moment, the Zarisian woman's voice was stone, just like her eyes.

ooo

We stopped at the mess hall for lunch, and I learned the place closed early on Sixth Day and Seventh. Since this would be our last meal of the day, we made it a big one, and as we all sat and ate, I let the others' conversation wash over me.

Zamira was strange in more ways than just her eyes and the alien language nobody else could hear. She had little time or patience for Wilf but went out of her way to be pleasant to Miko. I appreciated that, but I also had a hard time trusting it. It felt like the other woman had been primed to befriend us even before we'd made our appearance.

And she, unlike Wilf, hadn't been surprised in the slightest at the reveal of Miko's class.

I spent a few idle moments wondering what class Zamira had, but I was far more concerned with what sort of game she was playing. She was a prisoner in the capital city of the nation that had invaded and conquered her own. She was alone and without allies. Did she think *we* could change that somehow?

If so, she was going to learn otherwise soon enough. Miko and I had a lot of things to accomplish, and rocking the boat wouldn't help with any of them.

As for Wilf? I'd bet every copper bit I had that he was a Rogue or some variant of it. *Definitely* not a Marauder like Lace; he seemed to favor a lot of the soft skills that she had moved away from. And his sobriety had come and gone on demand. But *why* pretend to be drunk at all? Did he think we'd let some profitable bits of information slip if he could get us to lower our guard? Since when did a *noble* need to worry about money?

I let those questions rattle around in my head as we returned to our dorm room. The questions were still there when a runner several cycles short of their Dreaming brought us a stack of books and scrolls that covered the orientation we had missed. They were still there when I finished a round of ultimately unsuccessful meditation. Still there when I got back from a second, impractical but undeniably luxurious trip to the bath halls, and even as I read the first few pages of a handwritten journal on multiple carnivorous species of giant bugs. In fact, those questions might have followed me to sleep if Miko hadn't leaned in and asked a question of her own.

"Brian," she asked quietly and in the High Tongue, "do *you* have this *Deception* skill that the others were talking about?"

It was a true sign of just how much our relationship had progressed that I didn't even think about using the skill in question when I replied.

18

Seventh Day started much the same as Sixth, with a trip to the chamber pot and the baths, followed by what little training was possible in our dorm room. Once Miko was awake, we dove back into our reading. I finished up the bug journal while she started in on a history tome. Every now and then, she brought it over to me when she encountered a word she didn't recognize, but language issues aside, I think she learned more than I did.

My mind kept wandering to the academy itself. Wilf had said there were forty initiates in total. That seemed a lot but if there was one thing that Trynfall, and the Kingdom of Elthor in general, had, it was nobles. Still, only a few of the initiates were heirs, and only two of those were from houses of any renown in the capital: House Marchon and House Darish.

A surprising number of titled families didn't have much more land than what they lived on, yet their children were still eligible for enrollment and happy to take advantage of that fact. Add in the handful of children from houses in other duchies—exchange students, basically—and our initiates group was a sort of a melting pot of backgrounds and attitudes.

Not that we'd met any of them yet. I'd encountered a few in the bath houses—a return to high school locker rooms was going to take some getting used to—but in time-honored fashion, we had all minded our own business. Miko said the handful of women she'd bumped into had been too busy pointing and staring to introduce themselves.

Got to be honest, I didn't like that one bit.

We ate a late breakfast in the mess hall, where the staff were professional but distant, and then were individually summoned by the Iron Lady to discuss our forthcoming training schedules. Unlike the rest of the Tryn, Dame Credence's office was a real showcase of bare-bones minimalism. Just a desk, a bookshelf, and two chairs so uncomfortable it almost had to be intentional.

"Initiate Fieldings," she said, "I see you've survived a full day as an initiate."

I was pretty sure that was supposed to be a joke… but only pretty sure.

"Yes," I said.

She waited and then shook her head. "We are not out in the field. There are no medals given here for operational security."

"I'm sorry?"

"Don't be sorry. Just give me your first impressions of my institution."

"It seems nice."

"Nice?"

I nodded. "Roomy. The food is good, and the bathing facilities are amazing. Obviously, we haven't had any classes yet, but this all feels pretty fancy."

Dame Credence tilted her head. "You'd be one of the few who thinks so. Every cycle, I get a half-dozen new initiates in here complaining about the *abhorrent and unlivable* conditions."

"We were on the road for multiple seven-days, eating dust and scaring the horses with our smell. I mean… this isn't the Night's Sky, but it's easily the second-nicest place I've ever stayed."

"Interesting."

That word was going to give me a complex.

"Do you think you are ready for classes to begin tomorrow?"

For a moment, I wasn't sure whether she meant *emotionally* ready or was obliquely referring to the mountain of study materials we'd had delivered to our dorm. I decided it had to be the second one; Wilf wouldn't call her the Iron Lady if she was known for having a softer side.

"I think so. Miko and I come from a small town outside the kingdom," I said, sticking to our long-established story. "Information was hard to come by, growing up, and what we *were* taught has turned out to be wrong half the time. We'll be behind on some of the academic stuff, but we'll get there."

"If you do not want to hire an outside tutor, I suggest leveraging your fellow initiates."

I didn't even have the *names* of my fellow initiates yet, but I was pretty sure she knew that.

"What about your scaled friend?"

"Synossian," I corrected.

That won me a hard stare. "What?"

"That's what Miko's people call themselves. Or used to, anyway. We were surprised to find even that had changed here in Elthor."

"Synossian." She seemed to chew on the word. "That is the first I have heard of it though I've traveled beyond this kingdom. Still, I will make a note."

"Thank you." Even if *scaled* hadn't been commonly used as a slur, I didn't care for it. It was like calling the kithrizal *furred* or the corbin *feathered*. Reducing an entire species to their base description was lazy bullshit.

"The question stands, however," she said. "How is Initiate Naseri doing with the reading material?"

"It turns out she reads Trade better than she speaks it. Writing is… still a bit of a challenge, but Miko's smart. Smarter than I am, at least. You don't have to worry about her."

"I suppose we'll see." She leaned back in her chair. I think she was going for a more relaxed demeanor, but her *Deception* skill was sadly lacking; she still looked one move away from cold, dispassionate mayhem. "We use the first few seven-days at the Trynfall Ducal Academy—"

The Tryn, my mind supplied.

"—to take the measure of our initiates. While some students' futures are set in stone before they arrive, the roles in their respective houses fully defined, others are more fluid. It is our task to help determine, within the boundaries of a house's needs, what career each student would be best suited for upon graduation. Once we know where someone should go, it is my staff's job to get them there."

"Yeah, Wilf said something about that."

A minor twitch of her lips. "So, you actually *have* spoken to a classmate."

"One or two. That'll change once classes start, I hope. After all, making personal connections is half the value of enrollment here, isn't it?"

"I suppose that depends on your goals." She moved a handful of what looked like wooden coasters from one side of her desk to the other, leaving a stack on each side. I didn't know what they were used for, but my instincts told me she could kill me with them as easily as I breathed. "When I was told that we would be getting three initiates even after orientation was functionally over, I was less than pleased."

My nerves spiked, just a bit.

"I do not like unexpected alterations to my process," she continued, "especially when that process has been proven to work and work well. Still, running a school is not unlike orchestrating a military campaign: things change, and you must adjust or die."

I nodded. I'd never been in a military campaign, but our battles had been pretty much the same way: careful tactics and a lot of improvisation.

"Without the orientation period, we are unable to gauge what prospects best suit you from the array of options available. Thankfully, those options are already quite limited."

"Adventurer, adventurer, or adventurer," I supplied.

"Yes, unless you choose to enlist in the army or retire and pursue a profession as a Dedicated. However, we do not *have* an adventurer's curriculum at this institution. I can count on one hand the number of nobles who have ever pursued the path, and four of those had already been banished from their respective houses."

"Who was the fifth?"

"A man named Denarius Calison. The heir and eventual head of House Calison some three hundred cycles ago. You'll learn about him eventually, should you take our history courses."

I made a mental note of the name. Denarius Calison. Anyone who went off adventuring and *still* managed to lead a noble house had to have had their shit together, right?

"Thankfully, the curriculum for our future military assets is not very different from what an adventurer requires, at least at this stage of the journey. The real distinction will come after graduation, when would-be officers head to the army's finishing school while you and your *synossian* friend return to running missions for the Adventurer's Guild." She took the left-hand stack of wooden coasters and fanned them out in front of me. "Each cycle at my school will be divided into two segments, culminating in exams that will determine whether your study here continues. These are the courses we have assigned to you for the first segment."

I read them, one after the other.

Basic Conditioning. So… gym? I really *was* getting high school flashbacks. But if it could improve some of my physical Attributes, I was here for it.

Next up, *Basic Weapons Training.* I didn't know if that was a universal course—Humber had shown us that Priests could level without weapon skills—but it was another no-brainer for me. Especially with *Spear* still a point away from my level's current max.

Third was *Small Group Tactics.* I perked up at the course name, and not just because I had a Major skill with a similar name that was creeping towards *its* max. Adventuring was *all about* small group tactics. The better we worked together, the more effective we'd be, and the less likely we'd ever have to bury a future party member.

The Beasts of Eos, 101. This felt like an extension of the books I was already reading back in our dorm room, and I didn't hate it either. So far in my adventuring career, we'd spent most of our time in the wilderness. Knowing what was out there ahead of time would be invaluable. And it would be way safer than relying on Lace to teach me.

Wilderness Survival 101 was a winner too. In fact, those two courses pretty much went hand in hand. I'd always *prefer* to have a bed in an inn, with warm food and hot baths, but being able to stay alive while roughing it in the wilds would be invaluable. So far, Miko and I had both been relying on the vastly more capable people around us for all of that.

I frowned at the next course name. "What is *Dungeon Delving 101*?"

"Exactly what it sounds like. The world is ancient. Hundreds of lost civilizations came and went before ours and many of them left remnants that have yet to be explored. Ruins, abandoned cities, and fallen towers abound. And then there are the holes in the world, the dark places in the depths where things that hate the light invariably seem to gather."

I thought of the underground cave system where we'd retrieved the nilwort and then of the marsh-locked island where we'd first encountered the blighted.

"I'm familiar."

"When such places are discovered near a town, it falls to the local garrison to clear them of whatever creatures have taken up residence within. In locations where the army has less of a presence, that duty falls to adventurers. The course will cover all aspects of that experience, from traveling underground to fighting in closed spaces."

I nodded to show I understood and watched as she flipped over the seventh and final wooden tile.

It was... blank.

"We are a place of learning," she said to my confused look. "While most of our instruction is dictated by your future role, it is important that students be able to broaden their horizons. Each time we meet to discuss your coming courseload, you will be permitted to choose one class to add to that curriculum." She pulled back the blank tile and fanned another stack of tiles across the table. "These are your current options. If you have questions about any of them, I am—"

"That one," I said, pointing at the third tile from the left.

Only a slight tightening around her eyes betrayed her irritation at being interrupted. "Be certain of your choice. You'll be stuck with it until exams."

"I'm certain," I said.

"So be it." She swept the rest of the tiles to one side, leaving only the six courses I'd been assigned and the one I had selected.

As much as I was looking forward to Small Group Tactics and Dungeon Delving, I found it hard to tear my eyes away from the final tile, the course I'd picked from the pile:

The Framework: Questions and Theories.

It wasn't an advancement path or leveling guide—those no doubt remained locked away in the vaults and archives of the city's wealthiest houses. But it might be the next best thing: education and information on how the Framework functioned.

With knowledge came understanding. And with understanding…?

Maybe I could forge my own path.

○○○

Miko had the same basic courseload as me, although her Priestess class meant she'd been given a choice between Basic Weapons Training and Sectarian Ceremonies. Given that she'd taken *Light Healing* upon reaching level seven, that choice was easy; her short staff and natural weapons remained her only real source of offense.

For her elective, the Priestess had gone an unexpected route. Political Relations wasn't a course that would offer much value to us as adventurers. On the other hand, the attendees would almost exclusively be the higher-ranking nobles in our class. Sons and daughters who'd be expected to navigate the ever-murky political waters upon graduation. Miko was thinking about the alliances we'd need to make before her people's arrival and taking the necessary steps to find those allies.

There were times I wondered if my *true* role as Chosen was simply to guard her back while *she* saved the synossians.

If so, it was a role I could live with.

We spent the rest of the morning in our room, studying the material for our new courses. Beasts of Eos really *was* a continuation of the journals I'd already been perusing… pages after pages of hand drawn images and accompanying notes. And if some of those pictures looked too bizarre to be real, I just had to think of the essoli to remind myself I was not on Earth anymore.

With magic in play, some things on Eos had been created as weapons and others had evolved in spectacularly strange ways. A three-headed lizard the size of my forearm that spat necrotic juices out of two of those heads? Sure. I mean… why not? Having already faced gyr beasts, it wasn't particularly hard to imagine a smaller, multi-headed version. And bipedal cannibalistic humanoids called *leshra* who wore their skeletons on the outside of their skin weren't half as off-putting as the sluthari on Miko's home continent.

Still, if we were going to ever cross the Stoneknife mountains in the far west that the leshra called home, I'd make sure we did so in the summer when the creatures were supposedly sluggish and less apt to swarm.

Miko had abandoned her previous book and was now working through a primer for her politics class. Our plan was to do a little bit of advanced study each day and to share what we had learned with each other. So far, we hadn't made much progress, but it had only been a day and a half. These things took time, both for born scholars and high school graduates who had yolo'd themselves into another universe.

Once the studying was over, I practiced juggling again, Miko practiced her bandaging skills, and we *both* practiced our meditation. She still hadn't been able to rank up her *Meditation* skill to Uncommon, and I hadn't seen any fresh gains in the skill, but that didn't stop us from trying. Epiphanies and enlightenment only came around so often. The rest of the time, we just had to grind.

It was Seventh Day, so lunch was the last meal that would be provided, but the mess hall remained conspicuously empty. When we went back for seconds, Miko got the cold shoulder from one mess hall worker and a tentative smile from another. I did my best to mark both of their faces in my memory.

When we returned to the dorms, we found a familiar figure standing outside our room.

"Friend Rollin!" cried Miko, sweeping past me to greet the man I still thought of as *Priest Humber*. "You are here!"

"Yes, quite." Humber offered both of us a short bow and a relieved smile. "I wasn't sure if this was your room or if someone had played a prank at my expense. I'm sorry it's taken me so long to find you. I spent a full day being debriefed, first regarding the heir's condition and then the difficulties we encountered on the road home. After that, Bishop Highquill had a mountain of tasks that all naturally had to be completed the instant he assigned them to me. By the time I had managed *that*, word came that you had been made initiates here. How exciting! Anyway, when I finished my morning duties, I hurried on over to see you. Gods know, you won't have the time for visitors soon."

He said all of that in one breath, and so fast that I wasn't sure Miko got it all. Still, she gave him a comforting pat on the shoulder. "Is okay. You are here now. Is good to see a friendly face."

"Are they not treating you well?" He glanced from the synossian to me.

"So far, we don't have any complaints," I said. "Honestly, we've barely seen any of the other initiates."

"If they're anything like prior classes, I suspect they're spending their free days carousing down in the Lower City."

There was a brief pause while I translated *carousing* for Miko.

"Anyway, if you have the time, I came to finally give the tour I promised." He beamed. "It's a beautiful day out. Relatively warm for this time of year, and the morning marine layer is finally burning off. I figured we could start at the Worshipper's Ascent in the Middle City and then work our way down?"

"Would like to see enclave for my people," said Miko.

"And the Adventurer's Guild, if possible."

"Of course! While I don't think either stop would be at the top of most people's lists, I'm at your service for the day. Both are in the Lower City, so we could see them and then stop back by the market square for dinner?"

I traded glances with Miko. She was as cost conscious as I was when it came to our limited funds. Maybe even more so, because she didn't come from a tipping culture. Still, I didn't think it would hurt to at least see what options were out there.

She apparently agreed. "We have already eaten big lunch, but if we are hungry by dinner and there is something—" She paused and switched to High Tongue. "Affordable?"

"Affordable," I said in Trade.

"—yes, affordable."

"Street vendors," said Humber. "Cheap, hot, and the portions are small so you buy only what you can eat."

"Street vendors?" That got my attention. "Do you think they'll have kebabs?"

Miko huffed in mock disapproval. We'd only eaten at the kebab stand in Madea a few times a week, so I didn't know what she was getting at, really.

"It's the Trynfall market. They've got everything."

"Then what are we waiting for?"

ooo

I took all afternoon to work our way down to the Lower City. That was less a factor of distance than it was the tour itself. Humber was very proud of his birthplace and wanted to show it off, especially the temples and storefronts in the Middle City.

As much as I'd enjoyed our short stay at the Night's Sky, the rest of the district kind of wore on me. Starting with the temples. Religion and I had long had an uneasy relationship, and while the existence of genuinely good clergy members like Miko and maybe Humber were helping to change that, my brief exposure to Shan, an actual god, hadn't left me feeling warm and fuzzy. Even if he *had* saved my life. The temples we saw were interesting for just how wildly they differed from each other, but it was hard for me to not fixate on the sheer amount of money flowing into each church's coffers. Money that would no doubt get spent on gold leaf for another statue of a three-legged chicken with wings.

"Blessed Avariel," said Humber, when he saw me looking.

Yeah…

As for the shops, they kind of reminded me of the perfume section at Macy's, the closest thing we'd had to a high-end department store. Lots of *look but don't touch* vibes, served with extra helpings of *are you sure you're in the right place, sir? Because there's a 7/11 down the street that's running a special on Slurpees.*

I mean… we passed a *millinery* that literally occupied half a city block. Nobody needed that many hats and not just because the few we saw in the window cost six towers each, roughly the annual GDP of all of Madea. Hell, Harborton's entire charter had only cost eight towers!

I did my best to take a page from Miko's approach. She delighted in everything she saw but it was the act of seeing things that she valued. The fact that we couldn't afford those items was immaterial. She wasn't invested in the idea of ownership and so she simply let each go in turn.

As much as I tried to follow her lead, I just couldn't. I appreciated the craftsmanship on display in the stores we walked past, but it was also very much a reminder of what it was like to be poor. And I'd gotten plenty of that back on Earth.

We passed through the gates to the Lower City and after descending several tiers, things started to feel more normal. The district was divided into multiple neighborhoods. Each orbited around the main shopping hub which, in turn, held the market square at its center. Here, the stores were well kept but small and often squashed together; a leatherworker sharing a wall with someone selling handmade trinkets who in turn shared their other wall with the local grocer.

Off the main path, the streets were narrow and often crooked. There were no carriages or wagons, just pedestrians. Some of them browsing, some chatting with neighbors or friends, and some with their heads down as they hurried to jobs or appointments or homes. Humber warned us to keep our purses in hand, but I was way ahead of him on that front. Left hand on my coin purse, right hand on the oversized spear that got me looks everywhere we went.

Most of those looks were thinly veiled amusement or even pity, but at least one shopkeeper back up in the Middle City had seemed fascinated. I couldn't decide whether to seek out that shopkeeper again or to steer as far clear as I could.

I had even considered leaving the weapon back at the Tryn, but the truth was, Miko and I were going to stand out, regardless. I might as well be fully armed while doing so.

On our first trip past the market, Humber bought us a round of some sort of non-alcoholic mulled cider, served in a hard-shelled bread cup dusted with sugar on the outside. The sugar got everywhere and I had a minor issue when I made the mistake of eating part of the cup before the cider was completely gone… but that was part of the experience. By the time we reached the Adventurer's Guild, I was having fun.

The guild hall in Madea had been a two-story building conveniently located between two different taverns, and the one in Trynfall didn't buck that trend. It was, however, almost twice the size, and when we made our way in, we found it packed in a way that Madea's hall had never been.

We made our way past tables of adventurers, several of them blasting the auras that branded them as Tin. There were a few groups in matching colors, like the medieval version of sports teams, and I could only assume they represented the adventuring companies Lace had originally been keen to join. As with everywhere we'd been in the duchy so far, humans were a large majority, but we also saw turbingas, lupine, and a handful of the elf-like species that Humber said were called fiorlans. No kithrizal, no blood-scorned amazons, and no reavers, but those species all hailed from south of the Waste, so that wasn't too shocking.

The lack of synossians *was* a bit of a surprise until I remembered the attitude of the family Miko had tracked down in Madea. They'd been unwilling to even consider anything that might raise their stock in life; if that was representative of the greater whole on this continent, it was easy to imagine that something as dangerous as adventuring would be a path never taken.

Miko got her share of attention as we came in, and I and my spear did too, but nobody did more than stare or, in a few cases, comment in languages I almost definitely wasn't supposed to understand.

Short as a dunsman was a phrase I was starting to get tired of in any language.

The keeper was away on business according to one of the black-feathered clerks who stood behind a long table at the far wall. Her badge, pinned to her collar rather than hanging around an overly long neck, marked her as a full member of the guild.

"Brian Fieldings and Miko Naseri," I told her, fishing out my provisional badge as Miko did the same. "We wanted to check in. We'll be studying at the Trynfall Ducal Academy."

"Provs, eh?" If she was impressed by our enrollment at the duchy's pre-eminent school, the corbin woman didn't show it. She simply held out a hand, the fingers abnormally elongated, and waited for us to pass our badges over. Each was carefully examined in turn, first visually and then by passing a small crystal above. Satisfied with their authenticity, she finally reviewed the numbers carved into their backs. "Oh."

"Oh?" asked Miko, leaning in.

"Did you have a party member stop by recently?"

"Lace, yes."

"Pretty as a picture with blonde hair and crystal green eyes?"

I frowned. "She's a blood-scorned amazon... so *no* on all three of those things."

"Maybe just the last two," the corbin corrected. "I guess you're who you say you are then. Your party member brought in a communique from the deputy keeper in Madea."

"Right. Deputy Keeper Carlson, regarding Arrius—"

"The rogue Copper, yes. She also requested that both of you be made full members of the guild. Apparently, you were involved in the defense of Madea. While there was no official mission related to that action, Keeper Omudsen has magnanimously agreed that it should qualify as one."

She pushed our badges to the side, pulled out two new badges from a drawer, passed one to each of us, and made a careful note in her ledger.

As we waited for her to do... whatever it was she was doing... I examined my new badge. It was almost identical to the last one, a wooden plaque on a rawhide cord. A crossed hammer and blade had been carved on one side, and the P from our previous badges was missing. On the reverse side, an eight-digit number could be found. I was guessing that was my employee ID, which was a little more dystopian future than I'd have expected here on Eos. It was hard to believe that the guild had tens of millions of members, so there had to be some sort of matrix to determine each number.

"Congratulations on becoming full members of the guild," said the corbin, sounding anything but celebratory. "You are now able to select missions from the board on your own. Furthermore, your future successes or failures will be logged to your records and factor into any instances where you and another party both seek to claim the same mission off the board. Reputation and service go far in this guild," she added.

"Is only right," said Miko.

"Well said." Corbins couldn't smile, not with beaks instead of mouths, but you could *hear* the tone in her voice shift from cool to friendly as she turned to Miko. "And I must say, it is refreshing to see one of your kind at the guild. Don't let anyone keep you down or tell you what to do, do you understand?"

"Will not," said Miko, offering a salute. "And thank you."

"Yes, thank you," I added.

Eyes that could pin a squirrel to a tree at a hundred paces drilled into me, and just like that, all the melody leaked right back out of the corbin's voice. "If that will be all…?"

As we turned away, Miko leaned down. "Am thinking she does not like you, nest-brother."

"She can get in line."

"Is strange. Maybe city people have different tastes than women in small towns."

○○○

Our next stop was the synossian enclave. It turned out to be located somewhere in the center of one of the worst parts of the Lower City. I could feel Miko shrinking in on herself as we walked past dilapidated houses and alleys whose dead ends seemed like metaphors for the people forced to live there. Trash was everywhere and even the houses were filthy.

I hadn't seen this many synossians since Miko's home city of Whitehall, but the discrepancy between those proud people and Trynfall's version was so large that it was almost hard to consider them the same species at all. I couldn't imagine someone like Riok or Berys or even Niaci sprawled out in the street in front of a house that lacked both windows and a door, chewing something that had their sclera-less eyes rolling back in their heads.

Humber's cheer dwindled almost as fast as Miko's, and I wasn't far behind either of them. I was used to poverty and bad sections of town, both back home and in Madea, but this was something else.

"I'm sorry," said the Priest, in a voice that faded the longer it went. "It's been a few cycles. I had no idea things had gotten so terrible."

Miko narrowed her orange eyes, nostrils flaring, and walked on. I took up a space on her right, spear in hand, ready to shield her if anyone took exception to our presence.

We picked our way past a burned-out shell of a building, moved down three streets under the sullen gaze of a handful of underdressed and overly aggressive synossians, walked past the aftermath of a fight that had left the loser dead and stripped of clothing and valuables, and eventually found ourselves in front of a warehouse-sized building. It stood out from the squalor around it only by virtue of its size and the sign that read *Enclave of the Scaled*.

Actually, it read *clave of the Scal*, because someone had taken a weapon to it at some point and left pieces of the sign scattered in the street.

"This will not stand," said Miko, softly and in the High Tongue. "Not if I have to journey into the void and bring back Synos with my bare hands."

The door wasn't locked or even latched. I took the lead and nudged it open. There was an awful lot of empty space inside, none of it being used for anything, and the best that could be said was that it was well lit, thanks to both the lack of interior furnishings and the ponderance of windows high up on every wall.

In the center of the cavernous room was a circle of chairs of all sizes and makes. There were eleven of them, if you counted the one lying on its side, but only three were occupied.

"We have to do more!" said one of the synossians, a young male who had at least remembered to get fully dressed.

"A petition," said another of a similar age. "Enough signatures and we'll show the city we are a people to reckon with."

"Petition," scoffed the last synossian, larger than the other two, one eye as milky as his scales. "Signatures. Talk. All you *do* is talk and where has it gotten us?"

"I don't see you suggesting anything!"

They had yet to take any notice of us. Miko turned to me with the synossian equivalent of a frown.

"Is this… is this it?"

I nodded, eyeing the dialogue window that had just appeared:

```
QUEST COMPLETED: Help Miko Naseri make contact with
          the synossian enclave in Trynfall.
```

"It is," I told her.

She bowed her head for a long moment, then returned my nod. "Is what is. Will do what must be done."

Squaring her shoulders, my nest-sister bore down on the bickering trio like an army marching to war.

19

Basic Conditioning found us out in the Tryn's massive interior courtyard at a time best described as *ungodly*. Miko and I were used to waking up early, even without the city's system of bells to announce each new hour, but we'd returned to the dorms well after dark and it had taken a very, very long time after that for my nest-sister to calm down enough to sleep.

Hell, we hadn't even gotten our meditation in.

So, the mood as we stood in a row with other uniformed initiates was one part disgruntled and three parts just plain tired. Not that our instructor seemed to notice or care.

'Stick' was a member of the same elf-like species as Tantalas and Lissiana, tall and thin as his name, with a perpetual smile that made it seem like he was the only one in on the joke. He ran us through a series of stretches that saw about a third of the class collapsing halfway through. I only made it through on account of the Vitality gains I'd made through leveling, and even then, I was drenched in sweat.

Which was when we switched to running instead.

When Stick finally called a halt to the marathon, Zamira slowly made her way over. She'd been one of those who had faltered during the stretches, though she'd made it further than some other initiates. She'd also been in the rear of the pack for our many, many laps around the courtyard. Miko and I had kept to the middle while a few brave or really dumb souls had done their best to keep up with the indefatigable instructor. Two of those were dry heaving off to the side, even now.

"This is ghastly," said Zamira. Her white hair had been wrangled into three braids instead of one, exposing ears every bit as pointed as Stick's. She was somehow even sweatier than I was and taking big, gasping breaths in between each word.

"I knew it would be bad when I saw the instructor was a fiorlan," said Wilf, flat on his back a few feet away. "Everyone knows they're basically tireless." He hadn't graced Stick with a nickname, announcing that the man's given name was already perfect.

Wilf hadn't been one of the initiates on Stick's heels, but he'd mostly kept up with us. He didn't look *fresh*, but he wasn't nearly as wrecked as Zamira either. I wasn't sure if that was because he was higher level than her, had a naturally higher Vitality, or had some sort of skill related to running.

Hell, maybe it was a combination of all three.

Zamira was too tired to react to Wilf's unexpected presence. "I'm not sure I can do this again tomorrow."

"Can," said Miko. "And will. Come to dorm room tonight and will heal tired muscles."

"Can I get in on that?" asked Wilf.

She gave him a steady look. "Do not seem so tired."

"Never let them see you suffer, Miko. I've got skill points in *Performance* and just enough energy left to make use of them."

That perked me up. A complimentary skill to *Deception*? Yes, please. "Is that why you flip-flopped between being drunk and sober while giving us our tour?"

He nodded. "It's not an easy skill to level. Not at all. I have to get practice in whenever I can."

"Can come to room too," Miko decided. "But need to teach nest-brother skill."

"I can try," said Wilf, "but no promises. It's even harder to learn than it is to level for some reason."

"The Framework will do what it will," said Zamira. From the sound of it, she might have been quoting someone.

"Is it just me or is it hotter over here than it should be?" asked Wilf waving a hand in the air above him.

"Some of us sweat to cool ourselves off," I said. "Others just dump heat."

"No mess, no smell," said Miko, and if she sounded smug, well… that smugness was both earned and a welcome change from her unhappiness the previous night.

A crack like a gunshot got our attention; Stick had clapped his elongated hands together. The fiorlan gave the class an arch look.

"This is Basic Conditioning. It is *not* run a little and then lounge about in the grass like lazy ticassoles!"

I hadn't made it very far in my Beasts of Eos course work, so I had no idea what a ticassole was. And by the looks of confusion on the faces around me, I wasn't alone.

"Up!" cried Stick. "Now that you have *finally* warmed up, class can begin!"

A chorus of groans broke out across the courtyard; I think one of the initiates even cried.

I forced myself to my feet and pulled Miko to hers. And when Zamira and Wilf both reached out, I helped them up too. They were close to the same size, but somehow, Zamira outweighed Wilf by a significant margin.

Thanks to my augmented Discernment attribute, I knew better than to point that out.

∘∘∘

Basic Weapons Training took place in a vast chamber I'd never seen before, deep in the heart of the school. Like the courtyard, it was open to the sky, but here, there was dirt instead of grass. The center of the arena was a circle, twenty-five feet wide and flat, but the rest of the terrain was uneven, designed to better mimic real life combat environments.

Thirty of us had gathered, forming into three rows. Before us stood the massive man who'd been waiting with Dame Credence when Miko and I were delivered to the Academy. Next to him were two smaller human men with hard eyes.

Once again, Wilf was with Miko and me, but this time, Zamira was nowhere to be found. There were ten students missing overall, and I was guessing those were all Priests or Mages who didn't feel a need for weapons training.

Because they had *magic* and magic was awesome.

I wasn't the only one who'd brought his own weapon—Miko had her short staff and a tall, muscular blond man had a long blade on his hip—but my spear stood out, given both its appearance and its size. I'd gotten quite a few looks when I carried the damn thing all the way through Basic Conditioning, but here, nobody seemed to care. After all, weapons training class needed a weapon, right?

The scarred instructor stood in silence for just long enough that people started to get nervous. When he did speak, it was in a voice that was surprisingly soft for someone Wilf called the Hammer.

"For those who I have not met, my name is Merrick. Outside of this classroom, I am Sir Merrick Thorne. My assistants and I have been entrusted with teaching you all so that you won't die the first time you enter true combat. Whether we succeed or not in that task is entirely dependent upon your effort and diligence over the next half-cycle." He scanned our two rows, eyes landing on each of us. "I know that some of you have already received training, some of you have not, and a very, very few of you have faced death on the battlefield and made it through to the other side."

There were some murmurs from our classmates, trying to decide who fit that last box. Surprisingly few eyes turned our way.

"Which of you lack any weapons skill at all?"

Two people raised their hands: one, a heavyset woman only a few inches taller than me, the other, a hatchet-faced man who could have been called Stick if the name wasn't already taken. Neither looked happy to be in the spotlight, and the mocking laughter from the sword-wielding blond and some of his friends didn't help.

"That *isn't* a bad thing," said Merrick. "You'll have to work harder, yes, especially if you want to catch up to the other initiates, but you're also coming into this fresh. Unlike some of your classmates, you won't have any bad habits for us to break before you can learn." He scanned the rest of us. "Natural ability varies from person to person, and growth rates within the Framework will too. That much is beyond your control. Effort, however, is not. Give all that you can, and I promise that your effort will be rewarded."

Miko nodded, as if to herself. It *was* her kind of speech.

Another slow review of our lines. "I see a few of you have brought weapons. While I commend such initiative, we will not be using live blades yet."

"Live blades?" squeaked the hatchet-faced student, sparking more laughter from the same group of students.

"Not at first, though they will come. It is vital to familiarize yourself with the actual thing, and even with different variants of each weapon. While the Framework treats weapons within a given class as the same—every knife a knife—reality strays from that idea quite a bit.

Weight, balance, edge, and hardness all depend upon a weapon's style and material. Learn to adjust for those differences and the Framework will reward you accordingly. There are limits to how far you can take *any* weapon skill without the proper foundation. We are here to give you that foundation."

Merrick rolled his giant, scarred head around on his equally giant neck and a series of disquieting pops filled the clearing. "That's my speech," he concluded. "Don't expect another. We'll be splitting you into groups based on the respective reach of your preferred weapons and will be working with each of you on initial forms for that weapon. But first we have some business to take care of."

That got the murmurs going again.

"You," said Merrick, pointing at the golden-haired initiate who had laughed earlier. "Introduce yourself for those who might not recognize you."

"Lucius Darish." I recognized the surname as one Wilf had mentioned; this was the heir to one of the two largest houses in the duchy. If he was surprised to be suddenly made the center of attention, he didn't show it. He seemed utterly relaxed, surrounded by a half-circle of his friends.

"Lucius, it seems to me that you've had something you want to say since the moment you walked in here. If so, now's the time."

"Not at all, Sir Thorne." Lucius' voice was smooth as silk. "I was taught that it is a lord's responsibility to look out for his lessers and I honor my duty. I am thus entirely in favor of an approach that helps the neophytes of our class attempt to improve their lots in life."

"That… is *deception*, yes?" murmured Miko.

"If so, nobody's buying it," I told her, watching the faces of the two skill-less initiates crumble.

"I just hope," continued Lucius, "that there will be something of actual interest for the rest of us."

"Ok, no… I think he might just be an ass," I decided.

One of the teaching assistants seemed to share my point of view. Face darkening, he opened his mouth, only to be waved off by Merrick.

"It's true that not everyone has had years to benefit from a blademaster's personal instruction, Lord Darish. Perhaps you would like to demonstrate those skills for us."

"I'd be delighted. Which form do you wish to see?"

"I'm not talking weapon forms. I'm talking a spar."

Lucius cocked his head. "Against you or one of your assistants? Weapon skill notwithstanding, I suspect I am still a few levels yet from being any of your matches."

Wilf lapsed into a fit of coughing.

"You're righter than you know," said Merrick. "While there *are* things to be learned from a one-sided ass kicking, it's generally only the loser who learns that lesson. I'd prefer to find a more equal match so that your whole class can benefit."

"I am, of course, your humble servant," said the increasingly less humble lordling. "Who shall I face then? Packard? Klaus? Surely not dainty little Mireille?"

A short-haired brunette who I took to be Mireille made a rude gesture in response. Tall and rangy, she hadn't been one of those who tried to chase Stick in Basic Conditioning, but she *had* been up near the front of the pack along with Lucius and the others he'd just mentioned.

"I was thinking him," said Merrick, pointing in the general direction of our group. I turned to find that Wilf had faded away at some point, leaving me standing alone with Miko. "Spear versus sword. A newcomer to Trynfall against one of the city's vaunted young elites."

"I thought you wanted an even match?" Lucius looked me up and down and smirked as he moved into the center of the ring. "I suppose I could limit myself to keep things interesting."

Riok's spear in hand, I went to meet him.

"Nest-brother," called out Miko in the High Tongue, "it will hurt our cause if you kill a child of a noble house."

"You haven't even been to a single class yet, and already Political Relations is paying off," I replied in the same tongue, keeping my eyes trained on my would-be opponent. It had been a long time since my teenage years, and while the young lord's disrespect rankled, just a bit, I wasn't here to lose my head. This was a training match, nothing more.

"I'll make this quick," Lucius announced to his followers, "but not *so* quick as to rob the lesson of any value."

"On the other hand," added Miko, her voice gaining an edge to go with the sibilance of her native tongue, "Kal teaches that strength, too, will open doors."

Lucius gave the synossian a look, getting the gist of her tone even if he didn't understand the words themselves. His sword sang as he unsheathed it, the blade unlike anything I'd seen. It wasn't bronze or iron or the metal the synossians had used on the other continent, and it didn't look anything like the steel we'd had back on Earth. It was polished silver married to burnished gold and seemed to glow even under a cloudy sky.

In the silence that fell, I could hear an unseen Wilf's curses.

"This is my family blade," Lucius told me. "Called *Sever*, it has been passed from father to son for generations since its forging."

"It's very pretty," I said blandly, sparking some surprised laughs in the crowd.

The lordling took a step toward me, features twisting in anger, but Merrick was already there, a human wall between us.

"When we spar in this class," he said, "we do so with discipline and purpose. You will end the fight when I say so or I will end it for you. No death blows or attempts to permanently maim. No techniques. No allies. Just weapon and skill. Am I understood?"

"Naturally," said Lucius.

"Yes," I echoed.

"Very well." The mountain of a man stepped away. "Begin."

I brought my spear into a guard position, but Lucius stayed motionless for a moment, balanced on the balls of his feet, the blade in his hands still a distraction with its glow.

"I am sorry you must be made an example of," he said in a language I'd never heard before.

I could hear his insincerity as easily as I could parse the unknown tongue and couldn't help but rely in kind.

"And *I* hope Sever will find a worthy wielder someday."

As his eyes widened, either from the implied insult or in surprise that I knew the language, I flowed forward into my attack.

Sadly, the lordling's arrogance was earned. He slipped back and away from my thrust, footwork impeccable, then danced in to return a swift blow.

My spear was already in his path, darting forward again, short-circuiting his lunge and forcing him to sidestep a second time.

He mostly hid his surprised frown and got down to business.

We went back and forth for one minute, then two, our weapons contrasting blurs that never quite made contact. Lucius was taller than I was, of course, and faster too, but my spear gave me the advantage of reach, and that limited his options. On the downside, the flat, open terrain of the arena made it all too easy for him to evade my strikes. There was no way for me to trap him, no wall to pin him against and take away his escape routes. And while he *was* using a lot more energy than I was, if our conditioning class was anything to go by, he might also have more to spare.

Still, I thought the advantage was mine. A stalemate would be a blow to his reputation where I had none yet to speak of. And even if there wasn't any higher ground for me to hold, he had to find a way past my weapon's reach if he wanted to even attempt a blow.

Another three passes, streaks of darkness split by light, as our classmates watched. Finally, the lordling changed tactics. As I thrust forward again, he stepped to one side, spun, and chopped downward with both hands, striking not at me, still well out of range, but at the exposed shaft of my spear.

Sever struck the corroded weapon ten inches behind the spearhead and rebounded with a gong-like noise that sent Lucius staggering. I let my hands slide down my oversized weapon, spun it about, and drove the butt end hard into his chest. Air whooshed out, almost lost beneath the sound of *something* cracking, and he was sent tumbling in the opposite direction.

To his credit, Lucius was back on his feet before I could reach him, and while he was clutching his ribs with one hand, he had Sever in the other.

Still, it was over, and we both knew it.

This time, *I* was the one advancing, my footwork nowhere near as precise as his, but ultimately implacable. Part of me expected Merrick to call the spar, but it looked like I'd have to disarm Lucius first. Which would take roughly two moves and three seconds.

I had just moved into striking range when the lordling's wide eyes flashed gold. My steps inexplicably slowed of their own accord, air thickening, gravity doubling, then tripling. Just like that, the lordling was inside my guard, stepping easily past a painfully slow strike. Sever arced through the air, drawing a shape that would paint the dirt beneath us with my life blood.

Whatever Lucius had done was already fading before the strike fell; I was moving at half speed now, then three-quarters. I let my spear drop. One part of me watched the weapon return to normal speed as it left my grasp, but the rest of me was reaching for my knife as I tried to bend out of the way of a blow that would separate my head from its body.

Ninety percent of my usual speed now, but still far too slow.

Light filled my vision and sound faded to nothing. For a long moment, I thought that light came from Sever, that my brain and my nervous system were caught trying to catch up to the moment of my demise. Then, I blinked and realized the light was ruby rather than silver or gold and that I could see through it to where a mountain of a man had driven Lucius to the dirt. Sever lay a few feet away where it had fallen.

I stepped forward and through the ruby light and sound rushed back in: Miko's startled cry still fading away, the gasps of initiates, at least a few angry shouts. And above it all was Merrick's voice, still too soft for his frame, but cold as ice.

"'No techniques', I said, young lord. And no death blows either. Surely, someone of your *impeccable* lineage can understand basic Trade?"

Lucius had gone limp beneath the other man. His voice came out in a croak. "Quite right. In the thrill of battle, it seems I lost my head." I couldn't see his face, but when he switched back to that other unnamed language, I knew his next words were meant for me. "We very nearly *both* did." Back to Trade. "I naturally accept any punishment you wish to dole out, Sir Thorne."

"I will have an apology to your opponent and a word from you both that it ends here."

"Of course." There was a pause. "Assuming you let me up?"

Merrick moved aside and Lucius climbed to his feet, only the set of his jaw betraying the pain from where I'd, at the very least, cracked one of his ribs. He turned to me and sketched out the barest semblance of a nod.

"Well fought," he said. "It is with the greatest of humility that I seek your pardon for straying beyond the imposed limitations of our mock battle."

His delivery was smooth, his tone sincere, and his expression entirely free of artifice, but *Deception* was a skill that worked both ways and I knew a lie when I heard one.

Of course… I *also* only had a Discernment of eleven, and recent history had proven that to be, at best, bog-standard, and at worst, wholly insufficient for high society. And House Darish was one of the most powerful noble families in the duchy.

He'll never be an ally after this, I told myself, *but we can't afford him as an enemy either. Not with the synossians' future at stake.*

I buried my reaction and gave him an easy smile, flexing *Deception* for all that it was worth. "Not at all. That was fun."

He matched my smile. "Yes. Yes, it was."

We stood there for a few seconds, beaming at each other like LED bulbs, with about two percent of the matching warmth, before Merrick intruded again.

"What can we take from their spar?" he asked, turning to the rest of the class.

"Spears are a reasonable substitute for skill," said one of the initiates standing next to Mireille. Packard, I thought.

"In some ways, that is true," admitted the instructor.

"Both of them were *plenty* skilled," said Wilf. "And after watching that fight, I'm thinking I'd like to learn the bow instead, yeah?"

"Bows are great," said a baby-faced initiate with blond curls.

Their exchange netted a few laughs, this time genuine, and the tension in the room faded. One of the teaching assistants approached Lucius and a glow I recognized as *Light Healing* enveloped the lordling.

I tried to convince myself that readily available healing was a *good* thing. It meant Miko could preserve her energy and removed at least one reason for Lucius to hold a grudge over this whole thing.

Not that *he* was the one who'd nearly just died.

"Every weapon has its advantages and disadvantages," said Merrick. "You saw some of those on display just now and will see more over the course of this class. In fact, I invite you all to rotate between weapon groups over the coming seven-days. Maybe you will discover a weapon type that resonates with you more than expected or maybe you will simply learn what to do should you ever face a wielder of that weapon. You don't need to earn a weapon's skill to learn how to fight against it."

"Well done," murmured Miko, as I rejoined her.

"I've got a lot to learn," I admitted.

Somehow, Merrick heard me, a reminder that *anything* we wanted kept secret should be said in the High Tongue.

"You've *all* got a lot to learn," he told me. His gaze swept over the thirty of us—some excited, one recently healed, and at least a few clearly questioning why they'd enrolled in this class at all. "But that's why we're here. Now, let's get started."

ooo

I was a very tired Warrior as Miko and I headed to our next— and last—class of the day. If our first Beasts of Eos class involved us facing off against some of the continent's man-eating monsters, I was sorely tempted to just lie down and let them eat me. Between the conditioning drills that morning, my spar with Lucius, and almost *two* glasses of weapons training, I was a mess. A *Minor Healing* from Miko had removed any bruises and aches I'd acquired but done nothing for the mental drain. Worse, because healing took some of the energy of the patient, it had left me *more* tired.

Not that I was going to complain about the lack of pain, especially with *Pain Tolerance* already capped for my level. Living with a healer was a massive advantage for anyone. That healer being Miko just made it so much better.

Wilf didn't accompany us to Beasts of Eos and we didn't find Zamira waiting there either. It was just Miko, me, and seven other initiates, six of whom had been in the Basic Weapons Training class with us. The seventh was one of our class's rare non-humans, golden skinned, androgynous, and with two sets of batlike wings sprouting from the exposed skin of their back.

"Is that a skyborn?" I asked Miko.

"I don't think so. Their wings are feathered. Or at least they were said to be back on Issandryl."

Needless to say, we were back to speaking in the High Tongue. If talking about someone's class, level, or skill was considered rude, I could only imagine the pitfalls of openly discussing someone's species.

This classroom was indoors and had stadium seating, but there were so few of us that we all fit on the bottom row. Up front and facing us was a desk and behind that was the first chalkboard I'd seen since coming to Eos. Normally, the sight of that chalkboard might have sent a chill racing up and down my spine, with dull premonitions of *high school* haunting my tortured psyche. After the day we'd just had, I welcomed a return to the mundane.

Hell, seeing as how I'd read ahead, I wouldn't even care if our teacher hit us out of the gate with a pop quiz. As long as it was a *written* quiz and not something practical.

We were all seated by first evening bell, meaning the first bell after the fifteen morning bells had elapsed, but our instructor didn't show for several minutes after. She arrived in a rush with an armful of scrolls and what appeared to be some sort of paper-wrapped sandwich on top. I felt more than heard Miko's shocked inhalation at that sight. Scrolls meant knowledge and sandwiches meant messes and putting the two anywhere near each other offended every individual cell in her ex-scholar's heart.

When the teacher reached her desk, the sandwich went down on one side, the scrolls on the other. My nest-sister breathed a little sigh of relief to see that their union had at least been a temporary thing and one with no lasting ill effects.

We traded glances. Wilf had said this class was taught by *Drones On,* and it was hard to square that nickname with the energetic woman in front of us.

"Hi," squeaked the instructor. She was dark-skinned but human, black hair a cloud around her face, eyes wide behind the only set of spectacles I'd seen on Eos. She cleared her throat and tried again. "Hello! I'm Professor Maxine Weathers, but you can just call me Professor." She paused for laughter, and when none came, deflated just a bit. "Well, *I* thought it was funny. Anyway. This class is normally taught by Professor Dronassi, but he was called away on an exciting research venture, and I volunteered to step into the role this half-cycle. We're here to talk about the wonderful world we live in and the equally wonderful, terrible, horrifying, magical, *and* mundane creatures that outnumber us literally millions to one. Although that ratio is quite a bit less uneven if you don't count the insects. Which we will! Count them, I mean. Because honestly? They're *amazing.*"

She turned to the chalkboard, knocked her sandwich off the desk, and spent a solid minute both picking it up and making sure it remained intact.

Miko cracked a sharp-toothed smile, the professor's earlier indiscretions already forgotten. "I do not understand all the words she uses," she murmured, "but I like her very much!"

○○○

At dinner, you could tell which of the initiates had only attended Basic Conditioning and which had gone on to a second active class like Basic Weapons Training… because those of us in the second group were all dragging. Miko and I seemed the most energetic of that smaller group, along with Lucius, Mireille, and one of the Darish lordling's cronies. That was both a very low bar and a sign that the rest of our classmates were likely lower level. I'd seen just how much difference an extra few points of Vitality made while on the road and that clearly remained the case here at the Tryn.

Zamira, for example, *still* seemed tired from Basic Conditioning. That was a surprise. Even if the daughter of Zaris' merchant king hadn't been an Aspirant before her country's invasion, the sense of solidity her species gave off had me assuming her Vitality would be higher than a human's.

As we'd agreed, both she *and* Wilf would be coming over that night for Healings. I was confident I'd be able to figure out why a political prisoner and a noble's son had decided to make our acquaintances.

Or… not. By the time they left our dorm room later that night, I was none the wiser, all my subtle and not-so-subtle efforts notwithstanding. Zamira had departed first, with a sharp, poorly disguised look of frustration at Wilf's back. A few minutes later, it was Wilf's turn, the presumed Rogue saying he needed to check in with *his* roommate on whether there'd be any parties the coming Sixth Day.

His promise to let us know felt a lot like a threat, but that could have been my exhaustion talking.

I trudged down the hall to the baths, where I got a few odd looks, due to either the spear in my hands or the splotches of darkened skin that stood out even against my farmer's tan. Someone whispered that I looked like a kithrax—which may or may not have been some sort of evolutionary offshoot or even precursor to the kithrizal species—only for a second initiate to respond that even kithrax juveniles were half again my size.

Both shut up pretty damn fast when one of the initiates from Basic Weapons Training reached them. Hushed words were exchanged, and the looks sent my way afterward were at least twenty or thirty percent less condescending. It seemed that nearly getting killed by Lucius' cheating had had *some* positive effects. After Wilf's third rendition of the story for Zamira, each successive version increasingly divorced from reality, I'd started to wonder.

When I returned to our dorm room, I didn't bother trying to raise the difficulty of my meditation practice. As tired as I was, just concentrating at all would be challenge enough. I took a seat on the floor with my legs crossed, placed my hands on my knees, palms up, and let the day's deeds cycle through me.

By the time I was done, Miko was back. I waved at her past the dialogue window filling my field of view.

```
You have increased the following skills:

Major skills:
Knife [+1]: 30/35
Spear (U) [+1]: 35/35

Minor skills:
Avoidance [+1]: 34/35
Focus [+1]: 27/35
```

I hadn't picked up the *Performance* skill, but I hadn't really expected to. If Wilf *had* been trying to teach it to me, he was an even worse instructor than Lace.

But *Spear* had finally maxed out for my level! Completing the quest to reach the synossian enclave—such as it was—had pushed my energy levels right to satiation, and that meant I was only two points in *Tactics* or five in *Knife* from a level.

Better yet? Small Group Tactics was one of tomorrow's classes.

I settled in to watch over Miko as she meditated and despite my exhaustion, I found myself smiling. Level seven was so close I could taste it.

And it tasted kind of like victory.

20

I spent my first ten minutes of wakefulness the next morning making sure I still had control of my mind and body. Fine motor skills? Check. Memory, short term and long? Check. Sensation in all my extremities? Check. By the time I sat up, I'd run through the full checklist I'd created almost a decade earlier and found nothing.

It was Second Day, I was still me, and I had a level to gain.

By the time seventh bell woke Miko, I'd already been to the baths, made it through my daily round of juggling with only a half-dozen drops and two near-misses, and swapped to my knife forms. A sixteen Vitality wasn't sufficient to keep me from getting drunk, but it did make a real difference in my recovery times. Lately, I'd found myself doing fine on an hour or so less sleep a night.

Why Miko, who almost definitely had a Vitality every bit as high as mine, still slept like the dead and woke like a bear emerging from hibernation remained one of life's great mysteries.

We hadn't spoken about the synossian enclave since we'd left it on Seventh Day, but I knew that situation couldn't last. At some point, she'd want to go back and before that happened, we needed to come up with a plan that *wouldn't* get us tossed right back out again.

And that meant talking, even if it was a painful subject.

Still, the earliest we could go to Lower City was in four days. There was plenty of time for Miko to raise the subject on her own without me trying to force the issue.

For now?

I had a level to gain and a class that would hopefully help me do so.

By ninth bell, Miko was ready, and we had left for class. I had my spear with me, both because that was the first rule Riok had taught me and because it made no sense to go unarmed after the confrontation with Lucius. Trying to jump us seemed very out of character for the lordling, but having a paid hireling do it for him?

That didn't seem nearly as unlikely.

So, I had my spear and leather gambeson and Miko had her short staff and vambraces, and if that extra weight slowed us down in our second morning of Basic Conditioning? Well, it probably also improved the chance of a natural attribute gain. Or even the chance of acquiring some obscure calisthenics-related skill *other* than *Athletics*.

Fewer initiates threw up this time, which was mostly because everyone had an idea of what to expect. Still, by the end of class, Miko was the only one of us *not* drenched in sweat, and she was practically a walking furnace with scales.

Given the winter chill, I would normally have welcomed that extra heat, but for those first few minutes after conditioning class, it was a lot. Still, if there was a *Silent Suffering* skill, I was willing to earn it. And not *just* out of morbid curiosity about how such a skill would impact future technique choices or class evolutions.

Small Group Tactics was scheduled a bell later than Basic Weapons Training, so we lingered a bit at lunch. I didn't see Lucius or his crowd, but Mireille made an appearance, loading up a plate with meat, meat, and more meat. The tall brunette and I traded nods from across the room, and for a second, I thought she might join us. Instead, she headed for a far table where she was welcomed by other initiates.

At some point, I'd learn those other initiates' names. Right now, I mostly lumped people into groups based on the classes we shared.

Both Wilf and Zamira had had things to do after conditioning class, so it was just Miko and me in public for seemingly the first time since the seven-day had started. I waited for my nest-sister to finish tearing her hard roll into shreds and then broached a potentially sensitive subject.

Not the enclave. That could wait still.

"We need to talk about Zamira," I said in the High Tongue.

Miko finished chewing, drained her cup of water, and nodded. "It is clear she wants something from us," she said. "And also does not want Wilf to know. Do you have any thoughts on what that thing might be?"

I was starting to shake my head when a thought struck me. "She's *Zarisian.* Grand Duke Willerton invaded her country in retaliation for the loss of his heir. And we're the ones who found that heir alive if not well on the far side of the duchy. I don't know how she'd know our part in that or what she'd want from us, even so, but… it's the only connection I can think that we have."

"We are also foreigners, much like her. Among the only ones in the class. In normal circumstances, that might be sufficient to forge a bond on its own." She stole a crispy tusker strip from my plate and tossed it into her mouth. "But these are not normal circumstances, are they?"

"I think normal stopped applying after that plate of pot brownies," I muttered.

"I don't know what those are, nest-brother."

"That's for the best." I slid my plate between us, so she'd have easier access. My appetite had barely survived Stick's idea of a *fun game* to finish class. "I guess the bigger question is what we want to do about her?"

Miko picked up her water cup, realized it was empty, and turned covetous eyes toward mine. "Why must we do anything now? There are many other bites of the thegar to be taken, with classes, and politics, and…" She looked away. "Other things."

I handed her my cup. "It's the politics part I'm worried about."

"Oh." She hesitated, cup halfway to her mouth. "I didn't think of that."

I nodded. I was the furthest thing from a brilliant politician, as my history on two worlds had made abundantly clear, but life in a small town had given me experience with cliques and how they worked. And if that translated to a duchy's noble class…

"You worry that a relationship with Zamira will impact our ability to acquire allies here."

"She *is* the princess of a nation that was just conquered. That makes her more than just a political prisoner… it makes her the enemy, right? Will houses want to support our cause if it means being associated with her, even indirectly through us?"

The synossian sighed, my cup still in hand but now forgotten. "I have not even had a single Political Relations class, and the subject is already frustrating. I know that she has ulterior motives, but she is also alone, she is clever, and I quite like the different things she does with her hair."

I blinked. "Uh yeah. Her hair."

As if the universe had been waiting for that moment, the woman in question entered the mess hall. She stepped inside, stopped, and looked about until she spotted us. With a wave and a smile, she headed for the food line. Her white hair was in a series of dangly loops.

I thought it looked like something out of a 70s sci-fi movie, but something told me Miko would be delighted.

"Maybe I'm overthinking things," I said. "Maybe the houses we find to ally with won't care about our other associations. But it's something to consider. I don't want to risk your people's futures."

"I understand, and you are right to be concerned. I just—Oh!" Miko had spotted Zamira and today's new hairstyle. "*That* is different! Never did I wish my people had hair until I met first Lace and then Zamira. I wonder if I could achieve something similar with ribbons?" She finally remembered my water cup, drained it dry, and passed it back to me. "Perhaps I am naïve, nest-brother, but I want to believe there is a way to save my people without turning our backs on others who are also in need."

That *did* seem a little bit naïve, but it also seemed very Miko. And very much in keeping with her goddess' teachings too.

"We don't have to make a decision now," I admitted. "I just wanted to raise the concern. I'd meant to talk about it before class, but…"

"But I am like an overfed phloxl when first waking up." She patted my arm. "I know. My fellow acolytes used to tease me for it. In fact—" She stopped, dropped her head, and looked away.

I took her clawed hand in mine and gave it a squeeze, finding those pebble-like scales now cool to the touch. It was almost certain that the acolytes she was thinking of were all dead, casualties of Whitehall's fall. As much time as we spent talking about saving Miko's species, it was sometimes easy to forget that the coming refugees would just be the small percentage who had survived.

I'd lost my world, but Miko had too. Was it any surprise that a part of her wanted to find new friends here in the continent her people called the Great Wilds? Even friends with unfashionable origins and still-murky motives?

"*Light shared is light spread,*" murmured Miko, as Zamira headed our way with a half-filled plate of food. "So Mother once said. We will find a way."

I squeezed her hand again. "Okay."

○○○

"Over six hundred cycles ago, Armsmaster Quintillius Briglin famously defined military tactics as the art and the science of maximizing one's effectiveness against the opposition. Needless to say, we have made *countless* advances in that field since Briglin's day. Nevertheless, it is, I suppose, an adequate starting point."

Small Group Tactics was taught only three doors down from Beasts of Eos and in a virtually identical classroom, but Ebenezer Florras couldn't have possibly been more different from our bug-obsessed zoology professor. The too-thin old man stood at the front of the classroom like a scarecrow tied to a post—stiff-backed, stern-faced, and with all the dynamism of a three-day-old corpse.

"Who wants to tell me some of the key precepts when it comes to implementing tactics for a small group?"

Everyone from Basic Weapons Training was present, as were a few others, filling up four rows of chairs. We all looked blankly at each other. Wasn't this the sort of thing we were there to be taught?

"If nobody volunteers, I will start calling on you instead," warned Florras.

A hand went up.

"Good. Stand, give your name and your answer, and then rctakc your seat."

"Uhm." I recognized the initiate from our Basic Training class. He'd been the baby-faced, curly-haired guy who agreed with Wilf on the value of bows. "Barth," he said. "And I think—"

"Think? Or know?"

Barth colored. "Just think, professor."

Florras waved a hand. "Carry on."

"I think a key precept would be… teamwork?" The words were barely out of his mouth before Barth was back in his chair.

"Is good answer," murmured Miko.

"The professor doesn't seem to think so," replied Zamira.

"Skipping lunch was a mistake," said Wilf, seated to my left.

"Shhhh!" said someone sitting in the row behind us.

"Teamwork," said Florras, somehow drawing the word out like it contained a hundred letters instead of just eight. "Not the most daring of guesses, but I suppose it is accurate nonetheless. To function efficiently as a group, you must operate as one and not a collection of individuals. Does anyone out there want to dig deeper than the blindingly obvious?"

After watching Barth's treatment? *Hell no.*

Florras sighed, disappointment wafting off him like a year's supply of menthols and Old Spice. "This is not a class where you will be spoon fed the truth. The world does not need more people who have learned to mindlessly regurgitate facts. It needs those who have been taught to think for themselves. Adventurers consider four to be the minimum viable number for a party for reasons we will go into at a future date. The kingdom's military orders set that number at seven instead. Today, you are all adventurers. Separate into groups no smaller than four. You will spend the remainder of class working with your group to come up with a list of precepts you believe form the core foundation of small group tactics." He swept our entire class with a withering look. "Teamwork has *already* been given as an answer."

With that, he turned away and took a seat at the desk, apparently done with his instruction for the day.

I was *never* going to reach level seven at this rate.

"We've got four of us right here," said Wilf. "I suppose the question is if we want a fifth or sixth member, yeah?"

"We should get Mireille," I said.

"Mireille?" Wilf gave me a sly look. "Don't tell me you're looking to climb *that* mountain."

"She seems better prepared than most of us. And anyone willing to talk back to Lucius can't be bad."

"Spoken like someone new to Trynfall's court politics." He held up his hands. "I'm not saying she's a terror or anything like that. From what I hear, she's a perfectly normal scion, if overly competitive and serious-minded. But she does come from one of the few families in our duchy with a similar stature to Lucius'. Wealth and power offer them both a degree of latitude that the rest of us will never know."

He seemed to recognize the bitterness that had seeped into his tone and shook it away with a smile. "Regardless, your future conquests will sadly have to await another day. Power also *attracts*, and yon Mireille is already forming a group of her own."

"Should get Barth," said Miko. "Is young but brave. Spoke up and spoke well."

"I don't think we'd have to compete with anyone for *his* addition," admitted Zamira. The young initiate was an island unto himself down in the first row, seeing nothing but the backs of his fellows as he looked about.

"Let's do it," I agreed. "Unless you know something about *his* family that suggests we shouldn't?"

"All I know is that he's from the duchy of Apsa." Wilf shrugged and ran a hand through hair in need of a cut even worse than mine. Somehow, it had gotten even more unruly in the two glasses since Basic Conditioning. "His family can't be too highly placed, or he'd have stayed there for his education. But they can't be too low in the pecking order either or they'd never have been able to afford to send him across duchies."

"Good enough." I stood, cupped my hands around my mouth, and yelled down. "Barth!"

The teenager spun to look up at us, went big-eyed for no reason that I could determine, and pointed at himself.

"Yes, you! Come on up!"

Florras' voice was a whip crack that cut through the general hubbub with almost frightening ease. "There will be no yelling in this class. This is the Trynfall Ducal Academy, *not* a village market. Understood?"

I *would* have replied, if it hadn't required more yelling. Instead, I just waved an apology that Ebenezer promptly ignored.

"What's *his* nickname?" I asked Wilf.

"Ebb and Flow," replied the presumed Rogue. "I know, I know. Clever wordplay, but it doesn't fit, yeah? Not unless we're talking about the old man's chamber pot habits… which is something I try to never do. I'll keep working on it."

Barth reached us after having to weave his way up past a handful of still-forming groups. "Hi!" He squeaked. "I'm Barth. But you know that already."

"Am Miko," said my nest-sister. "These are Zamira, Brian, and Wilf."

"I saw your fight," Barth said to me, perhaps forgetting that he'd spoken up in that class as well. "It was exciting!"

"Thank you?"

He was taller than Wilf or Zamira, with blonde hair that curled down to his shoulders. Unless the baby face was fooling me, he was also at least a few cycles younger than the rest of us. If we'd been on Earth, I would have thought him about fifteen years old, a sophomore in high school, and the kind of guy who would be amazing at anything he tried only to then get embarrassed about that.

"Should discuss and determine answers before professor yells again," said Miko.

"I've already got the first one figured out," said Wilf.

"Really?" Zamira's stone eyes gave away nothing, but it sounded like she wasn't sure whether to be suspicious or impressed.

"Yeah." He looked smug. "*Teamwork.*"

There was a moment of silence.

"Meister Florras said we couldn't use that answer," said Barth.

"No, he said it had *already been given*. And it was. By *you*. And now that you're a part of our group, I don't see any reason we all can't profit accordingly."

Our newest addition frowned thoughtfully. "I… guess?"

"Excellent." Wilf covered his mouth for a burp that was, I thought, seventy-percent *Performance* and fifteen-percent alcohol. "My work here is done. I can't wait to hear what the rest of you come up with."

He closed his eyes and leaned back in his chair. Within seconds, he was snoring quietly.

"You're not asleep and we all know it," hissed Zamira.

Wilf cracked open one eye. "What gave it away? And please… be specific. I need to know if I'm going to ever improve."

"You fell asleep way too fast," I told him.

"Is that all?"

"And your lips were twitching. I don't think that's a thing, normally."

He sighed. "Noted. Who's up next?"

I looked to Miko. "Do you have any ideas?"

She nodded. "Was tapping his foot too. Is not normal for sleeper to do."

"I meant regarding the exercise we've been assigned." Miko had trained in the military before I'd met her, even if it had just been part of her country's compulsory service.

"Oh." She pondered. "If was larger group, would say supply lines. For small unit, maybe where the fight occurs?"

"In retail, location matters," agreed Zamira. "In battle, I imagine that would still be true. A defensive position or even just elevation might give an advantage. It's hard to climb a wall and fight at the same time, right?"

That brought back flashbacks of Madea. The defense of the town had been on a much larger scale than a single group, but the underlying theory made sense.

"It works the other way too, like when you fought Lucius," added Barth. "You had the reach advantage, but the open terrain allowed him to avoid your attacks."

"So, part of tactics is finding an environment that gives your group an advantage?" Wilf nodded. "I hate to say it, but that does seem foundational, yeah."

"Maybe it's also about creating that environment if it doesn't exist," I said. "If Miko had been part of the fight with me, she could have flanked Lucius to help box him in."

"And would have cracked him in head when he dared to cheat," my nest-sister said, orange eyes serious.

Wilf's smile turned a little bit sickly.

"Cooperation to make best use of our respective strengths and minimize our opponents'." Zamira ticked one finger. "Find an advantageous location or create one through maneuverability and positioning." She ticked another finger. "What else?"

"Adaptation," I said. "Things go wrong in battle. A group has to be flexible enough to adjust when necessary and to cover each other's backs when the plan suddenly changes."

"And the other side of that coin is planning at all," agreed Wilf. "Scout out the enemy, then go in with an objective and a plan to pull it off."

"That's four," said Zamira. "Are we missing anything?"

"Ten thousand cycles of military doctrine and a professor willing to teach it to us." Wilf shook his head. "Other than that, I think we're good."

I was replaying the battles our party had waged in my head, not just up on the walls of Madea but before that. The bandits who'd raided the Maris family farm. The blighted in the tunnels beneath the swamp ruins. Even our desperate fight against the monstrous centipede south of Harborton.

"Decisiveness," I said. "You make a plan, if you can, but when the time comes, you go in fast and hard. Not just surprise but shock and awe."

Okay… *some* of that I'd stolen from my home world.

"They all kind of fit together, don't they?" asked Barth. "Like planning without teamwork or adaptability won't work. Adaptability is great, but it won't always make up for lack of scouting or information. Or… maybe it does? I've never been in a real battle."

"No," said Miko. "Are—*you* are—right. Need most together. All, if possible. Otherwise, it increases risk and battle is already enough of a risk."

"Is there a way to minimize that risk entirely?" asked Zamira.

I traded glances with Miko. Neither of us had said anything about our experiences, but Barth and the Zarisian were deferring to us anyway.

"I think it depends on the objective," I said. The faces of the dead came to me unbidden. Friends, allies, protectors, heroes. All gone now, leaving behind only memories.

"The relative strength of the forces matters too," said Wilf. "Even if tactics *are* about maximizing effectiveness, there's a point where the opposition is so overpowered that tactics don't matter anymore."

"And then what?" asked Barth.

"You run," said Wilf, "and hope you're faster than they are."

"And when that's not possible," I added, mind flashing to Mordecai's sacrifice in the tunnels, and then a reaver's lonely death in the fields of Madea, "you try to take as many of the enemy with you as you can."

There was a moment of silence.

"Is that what happened when you saved the duke's heir?"

It was the *wrong* time for Zamira to finally act on her agenda. The merchant princess shrank back from whatever her stone eyes saw in my face.

"We're not talking about that," I said, the jagged edge in my voice attracting attention from the groups around us. "Not here. Not now."

"Lost much," said Miko, her voice a soothing counterpoint to mine. "Lost friends. May tell the story, if you wish, but is private matter. Deserves setting to match."

"And maybe a few bottles of wine, by the sounds of things," said Wilf, his voice for once devoid of humor. "In the kingdom of Elthor, we drink to the fallen."

"Yes," said Miko. "Is good."

I said nothing, staring into the distance, my hand not *quite* touching the spear at my side.

Maybe a few bottles of wine wouldn't hurt.

And maybe I didn't have quite as tight a grip on my feelings as I'd thought.

ooo

Things weren't exactly *weird* after that, but they weren't normal either. We made it through class, submitted our answers, and split up to go to our next courses.

No idea what Barth thought of the whole thing. He'd kind of gotten dropped in the deep end right from the start, and I was betting he'd find himself a different team the next time Ebb and Flow split our class into groups.

Wilderness Survival class was entirely drama free, at least. Including us, it had all of the students from Beasts of Eos, plus a handful of extras, and while the aptly named Professor Greenwood was nowhere near as charmingly eccentric as Maxine Weathers, he at least came with a lesson plan beyond *split up and figure things out yourself.*

For the first half-cycle, we'd be studying in the classroom, but the eventual possibility of field trips out into the countryside was dangled before us like some sort of carrot. Of course, I'd already *been* out in the countryside, and knew we'd have to travel for a lot more than a day to find true wilderness. Still, I knew I'd be very ready to get out of Trynfall at some point.

Just… not until winter was over.

Miko was her usual self: interested in everything and quick with a kind word or a thoughtful observation. We ate dinner at the mess hall with Wilf and—surprisingly—Barth and then the two of us retired to our room to study and train.

This time, I dropped more knives than I caught; two of those drops required healing. I tucked the knives back away with all the others we still needed to sell and buried myself in another bestiary journal instead. Flipping through, I found that the ticassoles Stick had mentioned were fuzzy caterpillar things the size of large dogs. For the most part, they lounged about in the sunlight, digesting their food, but once or twice a seven-day, they were known to swarm vastly larger prey, injecting the target creature with venom that both killed it and rendered its meat into a sort of paste suitable for ticassole consumption.

Eos never missed an opportunity to be gross.

I was moving on to our Wilderness Survival reading when Miko set aside her tome and turned to me.

"Do you wish to talk about it?"

It, of course, being the very minor blowup I'd had in class.

"We do not have to speak on the matter," she added when my silence showed no sign of breaking. "But it might help."

Truthfully, this wasn't a conversation I wanted to have right now, but life didn't care about wants or wishes. And as I'd said in class, there were times you couldn't just run away.

"I think…" I began, before realizing I hadn't figured out what exactly to say. "I can't decide if I'm more tired of good people dying around me or of those deaths just being minor footnotes in everyone else's personal ambitions."

"Around *us*, nest-brother."

"What?"

"They have died around us. You are not alone in your grief. We have each other to share this burden."

That wasn't true for one of those deaths, but she knew that.

"It feels almost like a wound," I said, fumbling for a fitting analogy. "Every time I think it's healed, someone new dies and rips it open again. Or someone we've literally only known for a handful of days starts picking at the scab instead.

"By now, Lace could be anywhere. Hunting a Copper that all three of us would have almost no chance of killing. If she dies, will we ever even know? And will it make it better that we're not there to see it or worse?" I shook my head. "I don't know. I think I'm just over tired. I'll feel fine again tomorrow."

"It is okay to be angry."

"You're not."

"Sometimes, I am. Mostly, I am too busy being afraid."

"For your people?"

Miko tapped her left arm. "For myself, for the refugees from the primacy, for you and Lace and those we left behind in Madea, even for my people on this continent who have, over a thousand cycles, chosen to let others dictate their worth. Most of all, I am afraid of failure, of an ending even more devastating than that which already fell upon my homeland."

I stared across the room into her bright eyes, into her open soul, and shook my head.

"And here I am, having a tantrum."

She made a clicking noise. "You always do this."

"Throw tantrums?" That didn't seem *entirely* fair.

"Make light of your feelings. It is a disservice to who you are and what you have endured."

"I don't know what else to do."

"*This.* This is what we do. We talk, you and me. Moons ago, we agreed to watch each other. Help each other. To talk and think and share. I cannot help if I do not know it is happening."

That had been before Skaal. Before Mordecai even. Back when I was first grappling with feeling nothing but satisfaction from having killed two men. We'd spoken since then, of course, but maybe I'd built a few walls too.

In fact, maybe we both had.

"Do *you* want to talk about last Seventh Day and what happened at the synossian enclave?"

"No." She sighed. "But I should. I need to walk the talk."

That wasn't *quite* the phrase I'd taught her, but I supposed it was close enough.

"However, I think I need to speak with Aurea about it first."

"Even though she never speaks back?"

"Even so. The Dawn Maiden lives somewhere beyond the spiritual realm, nest-brother, but she also dwells in my heart. A prayer is more than just an unanswered cry; it is a process of discovery. I will speak to her and maybe I will find that the answers have been waiting inside me all along."

Even in a world with actual gods, I just didn't *get* faith.

"If not, you'll at least have someone literally chosen by those gods here and willing to lend an ear."

"Thank you." She grinned suddenly, breaking the mood. "We have not resolved anything, have we?"

"Not really. I feel better though. At least a little bit."

"That is how it goes, I think. Mother said progress is a thousand infinitesimally small steps that add up to what feels like nothing until you think to look back at where you started."

"She was wise."

"She was the Voice of Aurea." Miko spread her hands wide. "And it wasn't until she was lost that I realized she was also just a person. She had her own flaws and fears and a handful of trusted friends to help see her through."

Which brought us back to our burgeoning social group. I wasn't sure if Miko had planned it that way or if there really was no escaping the subject.

"When it comes to Zamira and even Wilf," I finally decided, "I think we should put our cards on the table."

"Please explain. We have cards here, but I was never one to play. Is this like when something is *in the cards?*"

I'd completely forgotten teaching her that phrase.

"Sort of. In card games, putting your cards on the table means showing what you have to the other players. The way I'm using it, it means being open and honest."

"And we would ask them to put their cards down in turn?"

"Yeah. I'm not suggesting we spill our secrets, of course. Not to people we just met. But we *know* Zamira wants something and she knows we know. And Wilf has some reason he's associating with us too, I'm sure."

"And Barth?"

"I'm pretty sure he's exactly what he seems."

"Good. I would hate to have been fooled by him."

"I know it's only been four days. I know we just talked about it this morning, even, but I think this whole situation is wearing on me. I don't want to waste time and energy on people who won't be honest with us."

"We will put our cards on the table," agreed Miko, "and if their doing the same is not in the cards, we will find another way to take a bite from the thegar."

I *really* needed to stop teaching her Earth sayings.

She gave a decisive nod. "Yes, I like this path forward. And when we have time alone, I will speak to you of fear, and you will speak to me of anger, and a thousand such conversations from now, we will look back and see how far we have traveled together. Yes?"

"Yes."

My meditation that night was different. Instead of trying to challenge myself or turning the soul spigot on and just letting things flow, I split my focus. Part of me communed with the Framework while the rest thought about our conversation, about our renewed resolve to have even *more* conversations.

Mr. White, our high-school gym teacher, had loved to tell us that talking never solved a thing and my life on Earth had often proven him right. Words hadn't kept my father from dying. Words hadn't convinced my mother not to abandon us both shortly after my birth.

Words hadn't done a thing to make me feel better at Dad's funeral or to keep me from getting canned in the hours after.

Actions mattered. Actions would *always* matter.

But maybe words had their place too. And maybe the trick was to think of them like one of Miko's prayers… not something that produced an immediate result, but something that built slowly over time to a resolution.

When I finished meditating, a dialogue window was waiting:

```
You have increased the following skills:

Major skills:
Tactics [+1]: 33/35

General skills:
Juggling [+1]: 3/10
Meditation (U) [+1]: 9/10
```

Any increase in *Tactics* seemed overly generous given that Ebb and Flow hadn't taught us a thing. But an improvement in *Juggling* after I'd spent the whole night dropping knives?

Sometimes, it felt like the Framework had a sense of humor.

21

Third Day was the first of the week where we *didn't* have Basic Conditioning. In fact, we didn't have any classes at all until after lunch, when Basic Weapons Training would be followed by Dungeon Delving 101. Fourth Day would then revert back to the three-class format and Fifth Day would finally include our elective course.

That made Third Day a kind of rest day in the middle of the week, and we were fully going to take advantage of that. Eos' thirty-hour days sounded fine, in theory, and then sucked once people started filling all those hours. When ninth bell rolled around, Miko had only *just* gotten out of bed and was in the process of her morning prayers. It was an open question whether we'd make it to the mess hall in time for breakfast or if lunch would be our first meal of the day.

I was debating wearing my full hauberk to weapons training. I'd be the only one in armor, would sweat like a dog, and probably earn a few snide comments too, but the chance to gain points in *Medium Armor* seemed worth it. I was also going to focus back in on *Knife* if I got the opportunity, since *Spear* was already capped for my level.

If I explained to Merrick, he'd understand… right?

Of course… if *Juggling* had taught me anything, it was this: the more knives the better. Maybe training with a knife in each hand would increase my chances of leveling up the skill. Or maybe it would net me a new skill.

"Miko, is there a skill for wielding two weapons?"

My nest-sister's yawn showcased her full assortment of dangerously sharp teeth. "I don't know," she admitted. "Why? Are you ambidextrous?"

"No… but maybe I could learn—"

A knock at the door interrupted us both.

"Are we expecting anyone?"

"I don't think so."

I picked up my knife, just in case, and went to answer the door. "Zamira?"

The Zarisian stood in the hallway, wearing a deep blue dress instead of our academy uniforms and with her hair loose and falling past her shoulders. She was accompanied by an older human man I'd never seen before.

"Brian." She craned her head to look past me. "And Miko. I don't mean to intrude, but I was hoping we could talk."

"Is fine," said Miko, coming to join me.

"Who's this?" I asked.

"This is Ardalan. He's a very long-time friend of my family's and was permitted to accompany me to the kingdom as a chaperone and aide. He escorts me to and from the Tryn each morning."

"You don't sleep here?"

"Not yet. I'm hoping that will change soon." A door opened and slammed somewhere down the way, and she shifted uneasily. "Is it okay if we speak inside? Ardalan will wait in the hall until we are done."

"Of course," said Miko, tugging me out of the way. "Enter and be welcome."

There weren't any chairs in the dorm room, so Miko and I both sat on our respective beds while Zamira stood between us, showing a nervousness that seemed at odds with her usual demeanor.

"I wanted to start with an apology," she said. "I have bungled much of this past seven-day and it came to a head yesterday." She turned to me. "I have lost people too, and recently. If I had known, I would have not phrased things so thoughtlessly."

Which was a long way from saying she wouldn't still have asked, of course.

"I would like for us all to be friends. Truly and irrespective of any other concerns. But I think I should clear the air first."

"Would be good," said Miko supportively.

"I was at the Chamber of the Sun when you and your other party member were rewarded for returning the duke's heir. If you hadn't been enrolled here, I would have sought you out anyway. Given that we were all being brought in as late initiates, I thought it would be better for our meeting to happen organically instead."

"Why did you want to meet us at all?" I asked. "Obviously, it's something to do with Zaris, but what made you think we could help?"

"It's not so much about help. It's about information. What do you know about Zaris?"

"Almost nothing," I answered truthfully.

"My country was born out of the early stages of the Kingdom Wars and has always been small. Our military, such as it was, consisted primarily of a local peacekeeping force and a trained escort service for merchant caravans. We achieved a certain level of prosperity through purely economic means, by being useful as a trading hub for our larger neighbors without also presenting a threat."

She frowned, stone eyes still staring off into the distance. "And then the grand duke's heir vanished, and we inexplicably found ourselves blamed for it. I promise you this: nobody on Zaris' council had anything to do with the kidnapping. My father included. Business is about profit, and there's no profit in something so foolish. Yet no sooner had the news of our supposed involvement reached us than there was an army on our doorstep. Surrender was the only way to avoid outright destruction."

"Have sympathies," said Miko. "*Our* sympathies. But what does this have to do with us? Zaris had been conquered before word of Wilhemina's survival could spread."

"I know. What was done is done. I'm not trying to change the past, as much as I wish I could. What I want to do is find a better path forward. I want to prove that Zaris was *not* behind the heir's kidnapping, that we had nothing to do with how and why she came to be on the eastern frontier. I might be able to use that to gain concessions from Willerton. Perhaps my nation could regain some of its independence if not full sovereignty. We will *not* go the way of Hybellus!"

"You want to blackmail a grand duke?"

"No. I want to make a business deal with him for the betterment of my people. But I must first have something of value to trade. I am hoping that the two of you will be able to provide that."

I traded glances with Miko. This was *exactly* the sort of thing I'd been worried about. Hearing everything laid out clearly made it hard not to sympathize with Zamira and her people, but she'd already acknowledged there was no undoing the past. Was her one-person public relations crusade worth putting a second nation's people at risk? I'd been brought to Eos by Miko's gods to save the synossians, but they were ultimately *her* people. I tried to tell her without words that I'd back whatever she decided.

As the silence grew, Zamira shifted. "Like I said, I do want to be friends. But I am happy to approach this from a transactional perspective instead, if you would rather. What can I give you for the full story of Lady Willerton's rescue?"

"Should start by putting all cards on table," said Miko. "And we will do the same."

"I'm sorry? I don't… cards are not a Zarisian pastime. I could have Ardalan fetch some dice instead if that would suffice?"

My nest-sister shot me a look that didn't need interpretation… even if the saying she'd borrowed from me apparently did.

"She means she wants you to be honest and open with us."

"That was already my intent." She gave a little curtsey. "I am Zamira Lachesia na'Jafani, a loyal daughter of Zaris, come before you without artifice or guile to ask for your aid."

"Without artifice or guile?" I clarified.

"Indeed." It shouldn't have been possible for someone with stone eyes to lower their gaze demurely, but somehow, she managed it.

"So, coming here with your hair down and wearing a dress *wasn't* an attempt to soften your look and make you seem more sympathetic?" I asked.

"Oh, come on! That's not *guile*, that's basic business! Presentation is everything when it comes to such deals. Or are you telling me you go everywhere with that giant spear just for *protection*?"

"Is fine," said Miko. "Am told everyone has *Deception* skill anyway."

Zamira blew out a long breath. "What do you *want* from me?"

My nest-sister took her time, choosing her words with care. "I preferred your first offer. I would rather put faith in a friend than trust in a transaction."

"Are you sure?" I asked her, swapping to the High Tongue.

"No," she replied. "But that is when faith matters. And I do not think there is anything in our tale that will make a difference anyway."

That did put things into perspective. If we'd found anything that conclusively proved the Zarisians *hadn't* kidnapped Wilhemina, we would have presented that evidence to Hawthorne. All we had was an unknown signet ring and even that wasn't directly linked to the kidnapping.

"That's... a really good point."

"Soon I too will have the *Deception* skill." She didn't sound happy about that.

"Languages were a pastime of mine back in Zaris," said Zamira, "but I am struggling to place yours. There are parts that round off like post-Empire Agrissul, and some of the intonations remind me of ancient Caserian, but the words themselves are the next best thing to gibberish." She stopped, aware that we were both staring at her. "What? You wanted the real me! Here I am!"

"Is nice to finally meet you," said Miko. "Am Miko Nesari, daughter of Synos and Priestess of Aurea the Dawn Maiden."

"Brian Fieldings," I said, leaving a whole bunch of other stuff unsaid. "Human, obviously. And Warrior."

Zamira took a moment. "Zamira Lachesia na'Jafani, as I've said. And I'm a Mage, if barely."

"If barely?"

"I told you; we are not a warlike people in Zaris. I was a Merchant by profession and choice."

"You're a Dedicated?" I had trouble wrapping my brain around the idea of someone being given the class of Mage and choosing *not* to pursue the art and science of unraveling the universe.

"Yes. Or I was, I suppose. I reached level three as an Aspirant and realized I vastly preferred pretty things to books and life-threatening circumstances." She swallowed. "Recent events have forced me to reconsider that stance. In ages past, my kind were renowned for their battle prowess. Wanderer willing, we will be again."

"Your kind?"

"The o'naseri. Scions of stone."

"Like the dunsmen?"

She sniffed. "Hardly. They are the flesh and blood children of the Waste, however they might claim otherwise. The o'naseri come from stone and return to it when our heart gems finally dim."

"Huh." That explained the eyes, at least. "I have a lot of questions."

"And I will happily answer all of them. But first…"

"Will tell you the story of Wilhemina Annerose Lakesia Willerton," said Miko, "but on Fifth Day, not today."

Zamira swallowed her disappointment with admirable swiftness. "May I ask why?"

"Can always ask. Is part of friendship."

"We want to have a similar conversation with Wilf first," I said, realizing where Miko was going with this.

"I suppose it would be ridiculous for me to tell you not to trust him, given everything?"

"That's what the talk is going to be about." I managed a smile. "But if you have any knowledge that can help shape that discussion…"

"I guess I can't complain about having to make a show of faith. I know that he comes from a small noble house. His father died under mysterious circumstances, and his older sister—the heir—vanished less than a cycle after. There are questions as to both the long-term health of the house and the fitness of the only remaining son."

"Seems fit to me," said Miko. "He runs well."

"I think she means emotional fitness," I told her.

"Still seems fit enough."

"What I don't know is why Wilf has spent this past seven-day with us rather than aligning with either Mireille or Lucius' factions," continued Zamira. "At first, I thought it was about me, but he seems fixated on the two of you instead."

"That'll be part of the conversation too. Either we'll end up telling you both about Madea or Wilf will be out of the picture and you'll be the only one to hear the story."

She glanced over in the direction of my spear. "And when you say out of the picture…"

"I'm not going to kill him, Zamira."

She took in a deep breath and blew it out again. "Thank the Wanderer. I didn't want to assume, but I *did* hear about your battle with Lucius."

"It was a friendly spar," I said.

The Zarisian sent me an arch look. "And here I thought we were being honest."

ooo

Basic Weapons Training came and went. True to my plans, I rotated out of the polearms group and got in some practice with my knives instead. I asked the training assistant if there were any two-weapons forms but his response was to have me first do my existing knife forms with my offhand instead.

It went… poorly. So poorly that I was glad I'd stuck to only juggling two knives so far. A third would have required me to use my left hand, and that would have been bloody.

Bloodier than normal, even.

Once again, Wilf and Barth were in our weapons class while Zamira was not. That made a little bit more sense now that we knew her class, but at her level, she'd only have two spells at most. A weapon seemed like a good backup plan.

Still, it was her life and her class, and I wasn't going to tell her what to do with either.

Our second and final class of the day was another that I'd been looking forward to since meeting with the Iron Lady: Dungeon Delving. And I was *still* looking forward to it… right until I walked through the classroom door and found a certain crusty old bastard standing at the front.

Ebb and Flow didn't wait for us to take our seats.

"I'm not going through introductions again, because every one of you in this class was in my Small Group Tactics class too. I already know who you are and I'm not particularly impressed. Maybe today will be the day you manage to change that."

I tried using my maxed-out *Deception* skill to keep any expression off my face and failed. It would have been a hell of a lot easier if I'd also had *Performance*.

"You know the drill, so hop to it, initiates."

Nobody moved.

"Uhm… Meister?" Barth, bless his soul, decided to take the hit for us all yet again.

"This is not Apsa, initiate! Here, the correct term is *Professor*."

"Yes, Professor. Sorry, Professor. It's just… I don't think we know what drill you're talking about?"

Ebb and Flow's sigh was loud, performative, and maybe twelve percent phlegm. "I asked for bright minds and this is what they sent me? I want you all to break into groups. The same groups from yesterday's class. Assuming any of you can remember that long ago."

"I am starting to think he is not a nice man," said Miko, smartly choosing to say so in the High Tongue.

A few minutes later, and after at least one loud complaint from our sainted professor, we were back with our group. Wilf looked from Zamira to Miko and me and tilted his head.

"Huh. I thought this would be a lot more awkward, yeah?"

"Whyever for?" asked Zamira, in a tone of studied innocence.

"Past is past," agreed Miko. "The future waits."

"To quote the Iron Lady herself: interesting. Very interesting."

"Good. You've all found your ways to one another," said Ebb and Flow. "And it only took a quarter of the class too. Out in the field, exploring ancient ruins or delving into a true dungeon, lollygagging about like that will get you killed. Now that you've all taken your seats, stand up if you've ever been in any kind of dungeon."

To my surprise, almost a dozen people stood, including Miko and me. Somehow, I wasn't surprised to see both Mireille and Lucius on their feet. We all kind of side-eyed each other as we waited for the next shoe to drop.

It came quickly.

"Only remain standing if you've been to a dungeon *other* than the one beneath Trynfall."

That set the class abuzz, especially when nine of the twelve sat back down. From what I could hear of the mutterings, I wasn't the only person surprised to hear that Trynfall had a dungeon.

The professor eyed the three of us still standing—Miko, me, and Lucius—before settling on the noble.

"Lucius. Where did you go and when?"

"The Nebkash Ruins, a seven-day's ride from our ancestral home in Estear. I accompanied the guard last cycle on their semi-regular sweep of the place."

"That is the thing about dungeons, even the mundane variety," said Ebb and Flow to the rest of us. "They seem to attract the undesirable. My esteemed colleague, *Meister* Falcone of the Apsa Training Academy, believes the fallen places of the world have a kind of metaphysical allure to the darker elements of Eos... that like calls to like. He has, of course, failed to produce so much as a shred of evidence to support that theory. Shelter and isolation are strong enough enticements on their own in my far more considered opinion. You may take a seat, young Lucius."

That left just Miko and me.

"You!" the professor barked, pointing a crooked finger in my direction. "Give your name and explain why you have brought a weapon to my class."

"Brian," I said. "And the spear goes where I do."

A few derisive comments arose from other groups. Mostly from those who *hadn't* been in Basic Weapons Training.

"*That* is the proper attitude for a dungeoneer," said Ebb and Flow, surprising me and quieting the class at the same time. "Anticipate danger and prepare yourself accordingly. Brian, when and where did you delve your dungeon."

"A few moons ago, in a set of ruins in the swamps southwest of Madea."

"Madea, for those of you who think the duchy begins and ends with Trynfall and your own ancestral lands, is on the kingdom's eastern frontier. Did these ruins have a name?"

"If so, we didn't know it."

"Unfortunate but also unsurprising." Again, he addressed the class instead of me. "The so-called Endless Empire encompassed more land than all of today's northern nations put together, and yet even it only reached so far. Our knowledge of the greater world is as incomplete as our history of it. Nations rose and fell out there in the uncharted wilderness, and it is only through what they left behind that we may learn about them. What did you find in your swamp ruins, Brian?"

"Blighted, mostly."

One of the men in Mireille's group snickered. "There hasn't been a blighted sighting in the kingdom in almost a dozen cycles."

"Untrue," said Lucius, standing without being asked to. "A minor force assaulted Madea not long ago. I assume they chased Brian and his party all the way back from these ruins."

Miko stiffened at my side at the dismissal of thousands of blighted as a *minor* force, but I just nodded.

"They did."

"When exploring unknown ruins," said the young noble, "always bring sufficient forces to deal with what you might find, lest you put innocent civilians at risk."

"Well quoted," said Ebb and Flow, "but dungeon explorers do not always have the luxury of an army at their sides. Which brings us to today's exercise. Within your groups, discuss how *you* would prepare to explore a newly discovered dungeon. What would you bring? How would you go about your delve? And what steps would you take to prevent a tragedy like the one that almost befell Madea? I want your answers by the end of class. As with everything in this class, those answers *will* be graded, with your groups ranked accordingly. When I deem you ready, the top three groups will be given the opportunity to delve the Echo. The rest of you will have to wait."

"The Echo?" asked the winged person I recognized from Wilderness Survival.

"Pay attention, initiate! I'm talking about Trynfall's dungeon."

o o o

"Does Trynfall really have its own dungeon?" asked Zamira as we gathered after class.

"It does," said Wilf. "A true dungeon too, not just another collection of ruins or dark caves."

Miko leaned in. "What does that mean? *True* dungeon?"

"A world fragment," said Barth. "A remnant of before."

"That *is* one explanation." Wilf shrugged. "One of many, yeah? There are places in the world that operate differently, bound to our reality by only an entry point and a tether. The Echo is one such place. Located in the tunnels deep below Trynfall, it is an ever-changing realm, both one of the early keys to the city's success and the reason this lovely place was built at all. I've never seen it myself, of course. That privilege is for those in power."

"And what's inside?"

"Conflict, always. Treasure, sometimes. The exact nature of what is found shifts with the passing of days. Over the cycles, patterns have emerged that make it possible to determine what level of danger will be presented by the current permutation. Which is how the Echo went from an unknowable and unpredictable threat to something useful."

"A training grounds," I guessed. "With real, if carefully managed, stakes."

"Quite right. If we five are going to be a group for the remainder of class, we'll need to determine if access to the Echo is something we desire."

"On that note, I need to talk to you, Wilf."

"Oh?" He looked intrigued.

"Will see you at mess hall, nest-brother," said Miko. "Have offered to help Zamira with hair before dinner."

"And I accepted that offer, with gratitude," added the o'naseri.

The two women headed down the hall, leaving Barth standing awkwardly next to Wilf and me.

"Is she… really your sister?" asked the youngest member of our class.

"By choice, not blood."

"Oh. That makes more sense. I'll see you all at dinner!"

I watched the foreign noble walk away.

"Did he really think Miko and I were blood relatives? The lack of scales should've been a clue."

"Between your… skin condition, your size, and your singular choice of companions, there is a story going about that you are not entirely human."

"And how did *that* story get started?"

"This once, it wasn't me. Crone's oath," he said. "But for a small fee, I could track down the source, yeah?" He read the answer in my face and shrugged. "Another time then. Now, I'm guessing this talk you want to have would best be handled in privacy?"

"You really are a credit to the powers of education," I told him.

"Don't let anyone hear you say so. I have a reputation to uphold."

Wilf led me down several hallways, through a heavy wooden door, and then up a long and winding flight of stairs to an empty room that had to sit at the top of one of the Tryn's towers. The lack of glass in its narrow windows meant the room was cold and smelled of the sea.

"Sound will carry up here," he warned as he slouched against the wall, "so you'll want to keep from yelling. But even if anyone realizes the door is no longer barred, we'll hear them long before they reach us up here."

"It used to be barred?"

"There are quite a few places in the Tryn like that. As I told you when we first met, most are similarly boring."

"You're a Rogue then."

"I am a gentleman of good breeding and unimpeachable moral character. To discuss my class would be unseemly." He ruined his speech with a lazy smile. "Perhaps we should proceed to the meat of your inquiries instead, yeah? What is this about?"

"Trust."

His smile flattened. "A dangerous word in most circles."

"Dangerous for who?"

"For *whom*. And that depends on who is being trusted and who is doing the trusting."

"Me. And you. And vice versa, I guess. We all came up with a good list of tenets for our Small Group Tactics class, but none of those things work without trust. And I'm not going into a dungeon, *true* or otherwise, unless I trust everyone in our party to watch each other's backs."

"Only adventurers call it a party," said Wilf, with a theatrical roll of his eyes. "It's one more indication that you've all got something seriously wrong with you."

"Unit then. Or group. I'm not blind or dumb. I know you have ulterior motives for associating with us. I want to know what they are."

"And this will magically create a bond of trust between us?"

"No. Trust has to be earned. And I mean that for me as well as for you. But… it'll be a starting point, at least, which is a lot better than nothing."

"It's been less than a seven-day, Brian from somewhere beyond Madea. For this to become an issue so swiftly tells me one of two things. Either you are properly paranoid, which seems unlikely, given all your talk of trust, or you have been listening to stories. Stories about the sinister Wilfred McCall and the dire fate that he has perpetuated upon family and house."

"Wilfred?"

"There's a reason I go by Wilf." He smiled, but his eyes were flat, like unpolished glass. "Given how small *your* social circle is, I must assume the source of those stories is none other than the foreign-born elemental whose hair your *sister* is so fascinated by. Tell me, have you interrogated Zamira regarding *her* motives?"

"Yes. This morning."

"Oh." That took the wind out of his sails. "And she told you?"

"Not everything, I'm sure. Which is fine; we're not offering to do that either. But it was enough that we at least understand where she's coming from and what it is she wants."

"And in exchange, you will provide information on the rescue of one Lady Wilhemina Annerose Lakesia Willerton. Yes," he added, reading my reaction perfectly, "I am also neither dumb nor blind."

"We're willing to share that information with you as well. A story for a story."

"The difference is that *I* don't need that story. Though I am sure it is fascinating, yeah? Especially if the blighted you mentioned in class are somehow involved."

"I thought you were looking for secrets to sell."

"Information about new arrivals is one thing. Harmless, cheap enough to barely merit mention, and entirely safe. I don't trade in information on the grand duke's immediate family because I value both my life and the future of my house." He turned away, wandered to the other side of the small room and then came back again. "Now, if you want to share details about the town you and Miko purportedly grew up in together… I'm sure I could find at least a few repeat buyers."

That was obviously never happening. But repeat buyers suggested…

"People seriously paid for information on us?"

"You, Miko, and our exiled Zarisian princess, yes. I'd offer a share of some of the money earned in the deal, but it is sadly already earmarked for revelries. What comes easily goes just as easily."

It was nice to see *some* sayings translated.

"If the money is so minimal, why do this at all?"

"*In the game of politics and the art of blades, neutrality always comes at a price.* Some ancient philosopher said that. Long dead and entirely lacking in vision, if you ask me. I would rather have that price paid to me."

"I see," I lied.

"As for why I joined your circle? Where else should I go? Neither I nor my house will remain neutral for long once I start working with Lucius' faction or Mireille's, and both have spent the past moon pressuring everyone in our class to make that choice. You, Miko, Barth, and even Zamira are outsiders, and that makes you the safer option. For now, at least. Does that answer your concerns regarding my motives?"

Wilf, I couldn't help but notice, got a lot more formal with his speech when he was pushed. I wondered if this was a reflection of the real person or it was just another performance.

"It does," I said.

He looked up at the swiftly darkening sky. "Zamira wants information from you to further her personal mission. Barth, I suspect, is simply happy to find somewhere to fit in. And I am looking for a reprieve, no matter how temporary, from the necessity of choice."

"And your family?"

"You've heard the stories. What more do you need?"

"Your side, maybe?"

"Someone recently told me that trust had to be earned, and so deep is my respect for that person that I've chosen to make their phrase my own." When he turned back to me, his easy smile was back in place, showing no indication of what might be lurking beneath. "If there's nothing else, I'm feeling a bit peckish, yeah?"

"Just one more thing."

He sighed. "I'd sell our class the truth of your tedium if I thought it would bring me any coin. What is it now? Shall we share blood and swear an oath? Entwine our pinky fingers like children daydreaming of future greatness? Toss bones in an ale-stained alleyway to determine our fortune?"

"None of that. But if you want to hear the story of Madea, we'll be sharing it with Zamira in our room after classes on Fifth Day." It was my turn to shrug. "It might not be information you can sell, but that doesn't make it worthless."

"Sadly, I have plans already. The revelries I mentioned." I thought he was blowing me off until he continued. "Shall we do it Sixth Day instead? In the afternoon or evening, preferably?"

"Sixth Day could work."

"Excellent." Wilf's smile was practically cherubic and entirely untrustworthy. "I'll bring the wine."

○○○

Another night of practice and study, combined with *two* hard conversations in the same day, left me almost too tired to meditate. I forced myself to do so anyway, and when I was done, the fruits of my efforts were apparent.

```
You have increased the following skills:

Major skills:
Knife [+1]: 31/35
Medium Armor [+1]: 26/35

General skills:
Diplomacy [+1]: 3/10
```

Between *Deception* and now *Diplomacy*, I almost wondered if I should have joined Miko in the Political Relations class.

22

Fourth Day had us back at Basic Conditioning, where Stick finally had us doing something beyond stretching and running until we wanted to die. Although… after experiencing Eos' version of strength training, I decided I would have been fine sticking with cardio. Pushups, sit-ups, isometric exercises… by the time the class was over, my heart felt like it was up in my ears and my arms were dead weights from the shoulder down.

If we'd had to go to Basic Weapons Training after that, I would have been utterly useless, a barely mobile training dummy for even Barth to beat around the courtyard. Thankfully, we instead had Beasts of Eos, followed by Wilderness Survival, and those were both still purely academic studies. My mouth still worked, and my brain was only a half-step slow for the first glass or so, letting me give a decent enough accounting of myself.

It didn't hurt that Miko healed me before Wilderness Survival. We didn't see the rest of our erstwhile group until dinner that night, where both Wilf and Zamira at least gave the impression of being perfectly at ease as Barth talked, at length, about the Leadership class he was enrolled in as part of his exchange program.

I hadn't seen *that* course on the options Dame Credence had laid out for me. It seemed nobility had its perks.

Beyond just the money, wealth, lands, and titles, of course.

Zamira visited with us in our room for a glass or so after dinner, derailing my plans to see if I could squeeze in *three* visits to the bath halls. For the most part, it was just her and Miko talking while I practiced my juggling and read another bestiary journal, this one written by an explorer who'd ventured into the Waste. He wasn't much of a writer, but the subject matter was almost interesting enough to make up for it, descriptions of fascinating and exotic creatures mixed in with entirely too much slice-of-life nonsense and, oddly enough, recipe reviews.

When Zamira left, met by a still-silent Ardalan at our door, there was barely enough time for a bath and meditation before I passed out. No skill gains this time, but I couldn't complain about that. Frankly, the increases I'd already seen since coming to Trynfall were shocking. With all respect to Caleb back in Madea, the level of instruction at the academy was a cut above, and that was already making a huge difference.

Which made getting to level seven even more imperative. I could have been seeing gains in *Pain Tolerance, Athleticism,* and *Spear* too, but they were stuck at their current cap.

It hasn't even been a full seven-day, I reminded myself. *Level seven will come before you know it.*

Which was fair. The problem was, I needed level eight to follow as quickly as possible after that. And level nine and ten too. And once I broke through to Tin... well, I still had two quests left to complete, and one of those involved helping our party leader with her revenge.

I let that cheery thought chase me to sleep.

ooo

Fifth Day gave us another break from Basic Conditioning. That was the good news. The bad? We had Small Group Tactics and Dungeon Delving 101 back-to-back without even a lunch break in between. Three glasses, all told, of Ebb and Flow's unique brand of teaching by not teaching, and the fact that our group ranked well in both of the assignments we'd completed didn't ease that pain very much. Nor did it keep the professor from calling on Zamira in the middle of class and then reading her the riot act when she couldn't analyze our most recent reading with the savvy of a veteran campaigner.

Even Wilf took a turn making her feel better after that, which was nice to see. The Rogue—and I was certain he was one at this point—remained an enigma, but I could see how he might fit well in our group if we continued working together. I just wasn't sure if he was a class clown with a brain, or a brain who chose to be a class clown as a defensive tactic.

We left Dungeon Delving with yet another group assignment, this time to pick a known dungeon, research it, and present our findings to the class the following week. It was Miko who suggested we also put together some sample group tactics for that dungeon, in case Ebb and Flow tried to trip us up in his other class. My nest-sister still didn't have *Deception*, but she *had* gained *Tactics* as a Minor class skill a few days earlier and seemed intent on applying it to academic and social situations rather than just combat.

Obviously, I did my best to emulate that behavior. Two more points in *Tactics* would change everything, and I didn't much care how I achieved that.

Lunchtime was a noisy affair. We remained largely ignored by the two main factions in our class, but some of the fringe initiates had drifted into our general orbit, pulled in by Wilf and even Barth. Miko still got a lot of looks, and I wasn't very far behind, but for the first time, I had hope that both realities might eventually change.

And then, finally, it was time for our electives. I said goodbye to our group. Zamira and Wilf headed off individually, while Miko followed Barth to Political Relations class. I went down the hall to a new classroom. Unlike the others I'd been in so far, this one lacked stadium seating and even a chalkboard. It was just a room with a dozen chairs arranged in a circle. Eight of those chairs were taken; I nodded to two of the friendlier nobles from Small Group Tactics. Their presence in this class instead of Political Relations told me they were either powerful enough to not need the other class—unlikely, given that Mireille and Lucius were the acknowledged heads of their respective factions—or that they or their houses were so low on the power rankings totem pole that they wouldn't be having cause to engage in politics at all.

As far as I was concerned, they'd lucked out. Of all the classes we'd had this week, this was the one I'd been looking forward to most, even before Ebb and Flow's teaching style had stolen the shine from *his* courses. This was The Framework: Questions and Theories; I was finally going to get some actionable knowledge!

"Welcome, one and all!" Our teacher for the class couldn't be much more than a few cycles older than me, human and bright-eyed, with his hair shaved on the sides for unknown reasons. Professor Lunsford—please, call me John—didn't have the manic energy of Beasts of Eos' Maxine, but his enthusiasm for the subject had been apparent since he'd walked into the room, and that enthusiasm was infectious.

"You have all chosen to take the first, vital step into the realm of academic theory and I applaud you for it. In this class, we're going to peek behind the curtain, to examine what the Framework is, review theories of its behavior, and how we might put that knowledge to use for ourselves and our communities. This is one of the oldest fields of study in history. Long before the Endless Empire, there were farmers, there were hunters, and there were those who wanted to know how things worked. Not just the natural world around them, but the spiritual world that lay beneath, and the mechanism the gods had created for us to bind the two together.

"Because make no mistake," he continued, "the Framework *is* a mechanism. There are rules that we can learn and apply to our own growth, whether as Aspirants or Dedicated."

"I was taught that the Framework was ultimately unknowable, Professor Lunsford," said the initiate to my left. Georgie, if I remembered correctly. "Because of the number of Chaos gods involved in its creation."

"That is one theory," admitted our teacher. "The one I subscribe to is that the Framework is so expansive that it is impossible for mortals to grasp it in its entirety. What others see as randomness or even capriciousness are instead orderly operations occurring based on criteria we simply have yet to perceive."

"What's the functional difference?" asked a woman with cropped dark hair and shoulders like a linebacker. *Ames*, I thought.

"If the first theory is correct, the Framework will always be unknowable. But with the second, we can approach it like a puzzle. We might not have all the necessary pieces, but if we can assemble what we *do* have, we will get a better image of the larger whole, and can use that to direct our search for new pieces. Over time, the gaps and spaces will fill in."

"What if the gods don't want us to know?" That was a woman next to Ames, looking overly blonde and bouncy beside her more straitlaced companion.

"Whatever our respective species, our gods gave us brains. They gave us imagination and curiosity. Most importantly, they gave us freedom of will. To be a Scholar is to question, to seek understanding.

That the Framework itself recognizes the profession tells me my path is part of the divine plan. The unknowable exists to one day be known."

The blonde didn't look convinced, but there were nods from around the circle.

"Before we can work to expand our knowledge, we must examine where we've come from. While there might be older records in private collections across the land, the first *publicly* available treatise on the Framework was written seventeen hundred cycles ago, by a fiorlan Scholar by the name of Lanthalei. A noted theologian, her research on the Framework began as an attempt to establish the primacy of her species' pantheon. While many of her theories have since been disproven, the work she did in that failed pursuit laid the groundwork for what became modern Framework studies."

I settled back and listened to the history of someone who'd died long before Miko's people had even fled the continent. It wasn't the step-by-step guide I'd hoped to receive for building my own advancement path, but that didn't keep it from being *fascinating*.

○○○

Miko was buzzing after her first Political Relations class and filled me in on it during dinner and all the way back to the dorms. There had only been ten students, including her and Barth, but those numbers had included Mireille, Lucius, and the other nobles Wilf had pointed out as the movers and shakers in our initiate group. All were either the heirs to their houses or belonged to houses of particular renown. Mireille and Lucius were unique in being both.

"Our first class was what the professor called a meet and greet," Miko chattered in the High Tongue as we headed down the hall to the wing that held the initiate dorms, "but I think it went well. Everyone was nice—even Lucius!—and when there were words I did not know, Barth was happy to help me understand. There will be study, yes, of politics and dealmaking, but it seems the course is primarily a social exercise. A means for nobles to develop their own networks of contacts and potential allies."

That explained why Wilf wasn't taking it. I doubted he would want to put himself in yet another situation where House McCall's neutrality was threatened. But for Miko's needs?

"That sounds kind of perfect."

"Yes. I must, of course, take my time and build each relationship with care. It is as Wilf wisely said several times this morning: trust must be earned. I will not speak to anyone of my people's plight until then. But this, even more than the academy itself, feels like it might be the answer to our problems."

We passed into the common room and nearly collided with Wilf, heading in the opposite direction. He was back in his street clothes, though this time the color combination had been scaled back from an unholy offense against nature to something merely eye-searing.

"See you all tomorrow," he said. "Sixth evening bell or thereabouts, yeah?"

"That's when Zamira is coming over."

"Alright. I'll try to get back early enough to wash up first."

"Hey, Wilf!" A half-naked initiate had just emerged from the men's bathing hall. "I thought I heard you. Give me a few ticks and I'll be done. Tonight can finally be the night you introduce me to those women of yours."

"I've told you before, Gareth, it's not going to happen. I've got a good thing going on; why would I muck it up for myself by bringing competition to the party? I'd go to pour myself an ale and turn back around to find you making off with all the women!"

"Making off or making out?"

"One's pretty much the same as the other, yeah?"

Gareth grinned while dripping all over the common-room rug. If this was what college was like, I hadn't missed much. "One of these days, I'm going to wear you down."

"It's good to have dreams." With a clearly performative cackle, Wilf slipped past us and out into the hall.

"Women?" I asked Gareth. Dark haired and built like a fire hydrant, he was in half our classes.

"That man's got himself invited to a secret brothel down in the Lower City. Leaves every Fifth Day with a full purse, comes back the next day penniless, smelling like a perfumery and smiling the blissful smile of someone who spent the night dipping his wick. One of these days, I'm going to just follow him down."

For the first time, Gareth seemed to take notice of the puddle growing at his feet. With a shrug, he turned and swaggered back into the bath hall.

"*Dipping his wick?*" asked Miko.

"You don't want to know."

"I assume it has to do with a *brothel?* What is that?"

I'd never had the birds and bees talk with my dad, and I'd for damn sure never given it to a humanoid-lizard religious figure either. Thankfully, Miko already knew about sex. But synossians had mating seasons that were dictated by their biology; I had to think a brothel would be a foreign concept.

"It's a place people go to when they want to pay for sex."

She gave me the slow double-eyelid blink that said she was trying to process something outlandish.

"Humans are very strange sometimes."

"I don't think it's just humans." I'd overheard enough commentary from the soldiers we'd marched to Trynfall with to know that the synossians were an outlier among Eos' species. "Wilf mentioned he had plans tonight, but I'd assumed he meant an actual date or maybe even just simple petty crime."

"Crime is *never* petty and rarely simple, nest-brother."

Lace might have argued with that, but I wasn't going to.

○○○

Another day ended without any gains.

Can't say I loved it. All the juggling I'd been doing should have earned me *something*. And then there was the schoolwork. Even if my assigned classes didn't correspond to specific skills under the Framework—and I wasn't convinced of that—I'd been hoping to see an attribute bump. Intellect, maybe, or even another increase to Will. I mean… I'd sat through *two* classes taught by Ebb and Flow! Back-to-back! If that wasn't the kind of soul-crushing trial that triggered growth, I didn't know what would be.

Instead, nothing.

With a sigh, I went to sleep.

○○○

Sixth Day was our first time off since school had started. Miko took advantage of it by sleeping in, while I read ahead in the textbook for Professor Lunsford's course.

Textbook made it sound more impressive than it was, really. It was a pamphlet, basically, a collection of pages with passages from some of the Framework scholars we'd be studying in class. I went straight to the back, looking for appendices with titles like *500 skills and how to earn them all in a single night*, but came up empty. Like all books I'd found so far on Eos, this one was handwritten and loosely bound. The scribe responsible had either been new to the profession or coming off a three-day bender, because their penmanship was atrocious.

Was that an elitist thing to think? It *felt* elitist. One week into noble person's college and I was already putting on airs. That didn't seem right.

The handwriting didn't really matter anyway. *Speaker of Tongues* was the only reason I could read the words at all, and headache notwithstanding, it handled legibility almost as well as it did translation.

I really needed to find a way to monetize the trait.

There wasn't much useful information in those early scholars' notes, but it was interesting to see how they'd approached the task of categorizing the uncategorizable. In some ways, research didn't feel all that different from dungeon delving: you needed an objective, the proper tools, skills suited for the task, and, if possible, plenty of backup. In the case of this research, the backup had occurred over the span of generations, one scholar picking up another's work to either further it or disprove it.

One phrase that was repeated regularly with a maddening lack of clarity or elaboration was: *strong foundation*. I didn't know what it had to do with numbers going up and it wasn't clear the scholars did either. Which didn't keep them from endlessly pursuing metaphors about trees and root systems or castles made on sand.

On our next trip to the Lower City, I would see if I could buy some paper and a writing utensil. Or a slate and chalk if that was all I could afford. The more I studied, the more I wanted to take notes. Maybe with an Intellect of twenty, I could have just memorized everything instead, but for the time being, physical notes were my only viable option.

Or they would be if I had any of the necessary materials.

Remember to ask Lunsford about foundations, I told my brain. *And to* never *mention brothels again around Miko.*

I also wasn't going to think about how I missed sex. Now or ever. Not until I was cured anyway.

I set the textbook aside and looked for something else to distract myself with. Juggling was out; my latest attempt at tossing three knives had gone very, very wrong, and I needed that experience to fade just a bit before I tried again. I'd already studied. Miko was asleep. And there was a limit to how many baths I could take a day without getting the wrong kind of reputation.

With no other options occurring to me, I pulled up my personal record for the first time since leaving Madea.

Name: Brian Fieldings
Class: Warrior (Common) – 6
Profession: None
Deity: None
Ideal: Freedom

Attributes:
Strength: 12 [+1] / **Finesse:** 12 [+2]
Vitality: 16 [+2] / **Intellect:** 13
Discernment: 11 / **Will:** 15

Skills:
Major: Formations: 16/35, Knife: 31/35,
Light Armor: 25/35, Medium Armor: 26/35,
Spear (U): 35/35, Tactics: 33/35, Throwing: 1/35
Unarmed Combat: 5/35

Minor: Acrobatics: 3/35, Athleticism: 35/35,
Avoidance: 34/35, Focus: 27/35,
Leadership (U): 7/35, Pain Tolerance: 35/35

Professional: None

General: Animal Behaviorism: 10/10, Brewing: 3/10,
Caretaking: 7/10, Danger Sense (R): 10/10,

```
Deception: 10/10, Diplomacy: 3/10, Hunting: 2/10,
Juggling: 3/10, Meditation (U): 9/10,
Mercantilism: 5/10, Orienteering: 1/10, Riding: 2/10,
Scribing: 3/10, Stealth: 10/10, Tracking: 5/10

Techniques: Beast Skin (C), Deceptive Strike (U),
Lunge (C)


Achievements: None
Titles: Agent of the Wild
Traits: Speaker of Tongues, ???, ???

Quests:
    • Find the owner of the crest ring.
    • Deliver justice for a fallen brother.
```

I'd spent ample time staring at my skills every night and had no interest in repeating that exercise. The same went for my attributes. It had been a long time since my improvement in Discernment, and three classes a day hadn't done a thing for any other attributes yet. When something changed, I'd know it.

I *could* have spent another glass or so pondering my Ideal, freedom, but frankly, I didn't think I had any fresh insights to consider. Zamira and Wilf's respective situations added new wrinkles to the question of freedom in general, but I wasn't sure they had any bearing on what freedom meant to me.

Or maybe they did, and I just didn't want to think about them. I didn't fully grasp Wilf's situation, which was entirely his fault, but it was an example of how politics could muddy the idea of personal liberty even within the limited arena that was the Tryn. Whereas Zamira's recent history spoke to the impact of politics on freedom at the international level.

Still, I was just one person, and I wanted to keep the scope of my Ideal similarly narrow. So, pondering my Ideal again was out, at least until we covered the subject in Lunsford's Framework class.

My techniques were what they were. A part of me badly regretted *Beast Skin*, but if I was offered an upgrade to it, I might end up taking it anyway. Would that be pouring good money after bad, or would it be making a diamond from coal? And would I end up still being recognizably human when all was said and done?

As for achievements? I didn't have any, which felt like a personal indictment, given all that Miko and I had accomplished since coming to the Great Wilds.

My quests were a mixed bag. Arrius was out of reach for now, literally and figuratively, which left the quest to kill him similarly off the table. But the signet ring… that was something I could start looking into more at any time. I hadn't decided yet whether to mention it in tomorrow's story time but was leaning toward keeping it secret. While we'd found the ring among the possessions of the High Cultist of the Ever-Hungry, we didn't know anything else about it. It was entirely possible it didn't have a thing to do with Wilhemina or her kidnapping, especially considering Baron Sakeld hadn't recognized it.

Wait. Baron Sakeld.

I groaned loudly enough that Miko stirred in her bed. The Framework hadn't created a formal quest for me to deliver Eustace's letter to Elina, the fifth daughter of House d'Kay… and I'd completely forgotten about it as a result.

Add it to the list of non-Framework-promoted things to do: sell the knives we looted from our assassins, buy some sort of writing supplies, find this Elina d'Kay, help Miko with whatever her eventual plan for the synossian enclave will be…

Was there anything else? I felt sure there must be.

Oh, yeah. Reach level seven.

I was tired just thinking about all of it, and it didn't help that I hadn't gotten a dopamine hit from seeing numbers go up in multiple days. Still, I was pretty sure I'd now covered my quests, official and unofficial.

Which left only the title and traits.

I added 'monetize *Speaker of Tongues*' to my ever-growing to-do list, but otherwise, my frankly overpowered gods-given ability was doing just fine on its own. The second and third traits were still represented by question marks, something Miko and Lace didn't understand, and I didn't dare ask anyone else about in case it was a detail that would out me as being Chosen.

My title though… *that* I might be able to openly investigate. After all, I'd earned it in Madea, and it almost definitely had nothing to do with my Earthly origins or the ritual that had summoned me across an entire reality.

Agent of the Wild.

I'd gained the title after using the berries of the false dawn bush to summon the swarming carnivorous bugs known as lurkers. A lot of blighted had died in the process, which might have been the only reason we survived that first day of the town's defense. But what *was* the Wild, and how had my admittedly ingenious and only partially suicidal trap made me an agent of it? Or… them?

I added it to the list:

Research the Wild. Find out if it's a place, person, organization, or country. Try to do so without letting anyone know you're an agent of them in case that's a bad thing.

I closed my personal record as Miko decided eleventh bell was an appropriate time to wake. I wasn't sure that I'd accomplished all that much, but at least I had a bunch of things to work on.

Gods willing, I'd even remember all of them long enough to write them down.

◦◦◦

"…and then we met with the seneschal in the Chamber of the Sun and were told we'd been enrolled here. We need to level and there's a lot about the duchy and the kingdom at large for us to learn, so it seemed perfect."

"Not perfect," said Miko, "but close, I think. Am worry about Lace."

"Me too," I admitted. "Anyway, that's our story. Any questions?"

Wilf and Zamira shared a look… maybe the first time those two had shared anything.

"Yeah," said Wilf, looking rumpled and more than a little stained after a night at his secret bordello. "What gods did you piss off in a past life?"

Zamira chimed in, nodding. "King snakes, thunderbirds, horse-sized centipedes, gyr beasts, bandits, irkonnen…"

"Don't forget the essoli and shadeweaver," said Wilf.

"I was getting to them. And the cultists of a dead god."

"Not dead," said Miko. "Just banished, I think."

"Well, that makes it all better, doesn't it?"

We'd told them the whole story, with a few creative edits, starting from our journey through the forests to Harborton and ending with our arrival in Trynfall. Anything Chosen-related had gotten snipped, obviously, along with my talks with Eustace Sakeld and his knight, Kacellius.

"And then you got attacked *again* on the road to Trynfall? And this Hawthork—"

"Hawthorne."

"Hawthorne blamed it on Zaris? *Again?* It's like something out of a story. A *horror* story. How did you even survive?"

"Luck and the sacrifice of friends much stronger than us."

That brought the mood *all* the way down.

Wilf looked away, but Zamira took the subject head on.

"It sounds like this Arrius deserves what's coming to him, but… three people, even if you both make Tin, against a Copper? Those aren't good odds." She looked to Wilf. "Right?"

"Normally, I would say no. But then I think back to twenty seconds ago and the litany of fiends we just listed… and I have to wonder, yeah? No wonder you held up against Lucius so well, Brian. Man's had incredible trainers all his life, but I don't think he's ever been down in the muck like you two."

"Literal muck," said Miko. "Swamp was filthy and disgusting. Thought I might have to burn my robes after. But had to give funeral services for Mordecai."

Zamira softened, as much as someone supposedly born from stone could do, at least.

"He sounds like he was a good man. Skaal, too."

"World is colder without them," said Miko.

Wilf pulled a bottle of wine from his pack along with four only slightly dirty glasses. "I wish I had a better vintage to toast their memories, but this was all I could find."

"It's Zarisian!" Zamira plucked the bottle from his hands and turned it over. "See the etchings in the glass? How did you get this?"

Wilf coughed and looked embarrassed for the first time I could recall, running a hand through hair perpetually in need of combing. "There's a lot of goods flooding the Lower City as the duke's personal army returns from—"

"From taking Zaris." She scowled. "Well, that makes an ugly sort of sense. Still, this is a good wine and a better year. I think the vintner would find some small comfort in us using it to toast fallen heroes."

I dropped my eyes. I'd been the last person to see Mordecai *and* Skaal. The last to trade words with them. The one who bore witness to their sacrifices. I didn't know that wine and toasts could possibly live up to their memories.

On the other hand… Mordecai *had* liked to drink.

I took the glass Wilf handed me. With the sun beginning to set outside and our candles the only light within, the wine looked an awful lot like blood.

"To the fallen," said Wilf, as solemn as a man who'd apparently come straight from rolling about in an alleyway could be. "To memories that never fade."

"Even in darkness, there is light," said Miko, voice hushed as she stared into her glass. "May theirs shine forever."

We drank and my nest-sister's face twitched with an expression I recognized as surprise.

"Oh! This is good!"

"I wasn't going to bring something subpar to this meeting," said Wilf, conveniently ignoring that he'd said just the opposite, moments earlier.

"Did our story help you at all, Zamira?" I asked.

She glanced over at Wilf.

"I've got eyes and ears," he told her. "Two of both, yeah? I figured you were looking to hear the story of Lady Willerton's rescue from day one."

"Of course you did. When options are so limited, predictions become child's play." She took a long sip and closed her eyes as she rolled the wine about in her mouth. "Uhm… I'll have to discuss it with Ardalan. If that's okay?"

"Just parts about Wilhemina," said Miko. "Please."

"Of course. Trust me, that man has a shocking level of disinterest in the world at large. Anyway, I don't know if it will help or not. I've never heard of this Khamani the Ever-Hungry, so I can't imagine he has any devotees in Zaris."

"So, how would the supposedly Zarisian kidnappers have the connections to get the heir to the cult," said Wilf.

"Exactly. I mean, that's far from proof of innocence, of course. As is the obvious fact that Zaris and Madea are literal moons' travel away from each other. Even if my people had had a means for infiltrating the palace, a motive for the kidnapping, and an established relationship with this cult, why would we send her to the far side of your duchy instead of doing whatever it was we kidnapped her to do?" She tossed back the rest of her wine and held the glass out for a refill. "No offense to you and the rest of your friends, Wilf, but the only reason anyone would believe this story is because they wanted to."

"Profit makes believers of us all," said the noble.

"I hate that quote and I really hate that it's so apt." She shook her head, disturbing the delicate crown of hair that she and Miko had spent almost two glasses styling. "I'll wait to hear what Ardalan thinks, but it feels like a dead end. But the attack you suffered on the road from Madea? That's something else entirely."

"It seems like someone—maybe Zaris, most likely someone else—panicked when they realized Wilhemina was alive and being returned to Trynfall," said Wilf, topping up Miko's glass.

He held up the mostly empty bottle and sent me a questioning look, but I shook my head. I'd rather have had some of Lomas' ale.

"And managed to get agent into rescue force," added Miko.

"Right. That takes access and foresight. But it also opens up an avenue of investigation—" Wilf caught himself. "I mean, *interested parties* might want to dig into that. As long as they realized they could be kicking a hornets' nest in the process."

"Admit it," I challenged him, passing Miko my mostly full wine glass. "*You're* an interested party."

"I do like puzzles."

"You should be in my Framework theory class then."

"A local with knowledge of both the city and its power players might be better positioned to find relevant information than a political prisoner whose movements are no doubt watched," said Zamira.

"Or two foreign adventurers," agreed Miko.

Wilf looked at me. "You've got something to say too, yeah?"

"Not really." I was being honest too. As much as I felt for Zamira's plight—and the more we got to know her, the harder it was to remain unaffected—I wasn't sure I wanted *us* getting further involved in this mystery. I certainly wasn't going to try to convince *someone else* to do so. "Although, I *am* curious about your class."

"I don't think you really want to know—"

"He's a Rogue," said Zamira, bright spots of color in her pale cheeks as she finished the last of the wine. "It's blindingly obvious."

"I *was* a Rogue," corrected Wilf.

"You advanced your class!" said Miko.

The nobleman licked his lips, looked at the empty bottle in his hands, and sighed. "I suppose I'd come off as an ass if I didn't tell you this much after you three spilled your guts just now."

"It's going to be something awful, isn't it?" Zamira looked equal parts horrified, fascinated, and drunk. She was *seriously* lacking in Vitality. "Back Alley Backstabber? Underworld Enforcer? Or just a conniving Poisoner?"

"Only two of those are even a thing, and if I was the last one, you'd all be doomed after drinking the bottle of wine I just brought in. Except for Brian," Wilf allowed. "He only had a few sips."

"Can cure poison," said Miko, only the slightest bit tipsy.

Wilf's reaction was significant enough that I almost thought he *had* poisoned us all. "What kind?!"

"All kinds, I think. Alcohol too. But is more effective just after poison is administered."

"Ah." His excitement drained away. "Figures. Anyway, I'm not a Poisoner. And it sounds like your party leader has that position covered anyway."

"Then what are you?" I asked.

Wilf licked his lips again, looked about as if to verify nobody had teleported past Ardalan and into our dorm room, and lowered his voice.

"I'm a Spy."

"I see!" said Miko. "Only… what is that?"

23-Interlude

"That does it for the adepts." Credence moved a scrap of parchment from one side of her desk to the other. "With two more graduating to Tin, that frees up an extra day for our initiates to begin their patrols. When does Ebenezer think the students will be ready?"

Merrick was far too large for the only chair available but made do anyway. "He says two or three groups will be ready within the next moon. And the Echo might be viable a moon after that. At the lowest challenge rating, of course."

"Of course. This institution does not exist to get its students killed." It had been a long time since Dame Credence's smiles had held any warmth, and this one didn't break that trend. "Which brings me to a rumor I heard about a recent Basic Weapons Training class."

"I had it under control. The Darish scion was pushed more than he expected and forgot himself and the rules."

"Pushed by one of our three new students?"

She knew the answer and he knew that she knew, but Merrick nodded anyway. "Yes. Brian Fieldings. The little adventurer."

"What are your impressions of him?"

"Solid, if not exceptional. His choice of the spear for a weapon makes up for some of his obvious physical shortcomings, but he's no prodigy, let alone a dragon in waiting. Still, pair earned competence with actual battlefield experience…"

"And the heir to one of this duchy's most powerful families found his ego checked. Good."

"Is it?"

"If it gives that class's two noble factions something to focus on rather than each other? Yes. I assume that's why His Grace invited the adventurers to my institution in the first place."

"A distraction? Or a common enemy?"

"Either will suffice, don't you think?"

"Maybe. You know how I feel about politics. To be honest, Fieldings' spear concerns me more than the man himself."

Dame Credence gave him a look. "Elaborate."

"The Darish boy was wielding his family's ancestral blade."

She sucked in a breath. "*Sever?* In a spar?"

"Like I said, I had it under control. Any truly dangerous strike from either side would have been stopped before it landed."

She made a gesture of acknowledgment.

"But during the spar, Lucius struck at Brian Fieldings' spear instead of the adventurer himself."

"Remove the weapon's threat and end his opponent's reach advantage at the same time." Credence nodded. "Reasonable, if unfortunate. Have you replaced the weapon? From what I recall, it looked to be well past its service anyway. Even if that spear had sentimental value for Mr. Fieldings, something basic from the armory would be a marked improvement."

"I didn't *have* to replace it. As far as I could tell, the weapon wasn't even damaged by the blow."

She stilled. "Are you sure it made contact?"

It was Merrick's turn to give his longtime superior a look.

"Of course you are. So, how did an adventurer's decrepit spear survive a direct hit from a weapon famed for its ability to cut through anything?"

"I don't know."

"You don't know? *You?*"

"There are no visible runes or sigils. Nothing about the weapon suggests an enchantment. If it's instead a technique that Fieldings has to strengthen his weapons, I would have seen the activation with *Eyes of the Warlord*. Which would mean it's either a *passive* ability or something specific to the weapon itself. As highly enchanted as Sever is, and given Fieldings isn't even Tin, the first is hard to imagine. And the second..."

"Would require a nascent artifact, at minimum."

"Yes. Which raises the question of how something like *that* ended up in the hands of an unranked adventurer from some unknown town beyond the kingdom's easternmost borders."

"A family heirloom, perhaps? At least now I understand why the boy takes the weapon with him to classes. If *I* had an artifact, even one still in the early stages of its evolution, I wouldn't let it out of my sight either. Has it done anything else yet?"

"Not that I've seen. But it's only been a few days."

"Keep me informed. And look out for any initiates who might be taking too great an interest in the weapon. We don't want to be dealing with artifact theft on top of the political nightmare of having the Darish and Marchon heirs in the same class."

"The first rankings will be posted soon. If history is any indicator, everyone will be focused on those instead."

"Or they'll be the spark that ignites a greater conflagration. And on that note, we should discuss the na'Jafani girl and what we can do to prevent an incident with the duchy's newest vassal state..."

ooo

"Your father will see you now, young master Lucius." The speaker was old—had been old for as long as Lucius could remember—but impeccably dressed in the uniform of House Darish, the ornate pin on his left breast signifying his rank and status among the house servants.

"Thank you, Ingles." Lucius gave the other man a nod—*always be polite in public, especially to the people who actually matter*—and stepped past him to the door of the study. It was dark wood, elaborately carved to feature an array of hunting scenes, and older than the house itself. As a child visiting the capital, he'd spent hours tracing the carvings, imagining the stories behind each image.

Now, it was just another thing. Expensive. Old. Irreplaceable. Further proof of House Darish's ascendancy in the duchy. He entered the room, closed the door again behind him, and stood at attention, one hand clasping the other's wrist behind his back.

Robash Alexander Callum Darish, Marquess of Estear, sat behind his desk, examining the reports arrayed before him. Even seated, his height was apparent. In his forty-third cycle, he remained as thin as a dueling sword, greying hair trimmed at a length that would have been unfashionably short for anyone of a lesser stature.

A true lord does not kneel to trends, or fashion, or even the will of the masses, he had told Lucius more than once. *Instead, he redefines them.*

Thankfully, Tabitha, Robash's senior wife and Lucius' mother, had taken a more… enlightened view on the first two subjects, ensuring that Lucius' early introductions to high society hadn't been a *complete* debacle.

"Lucius." His father's voice was quiet and even. In seventeen cycles, Lucius had never heard him raise it. "Do you know why I summoned you?"

The first trickle of unease followed a drop of sweat down Lucius' spine, but he kept that spine straight and his face impassive.

"You want an update on my activities at the Trynfall Ducal Academy."

"No." For the first time, Robash looked up from his reports. His eyes were dark and cold; coupled with the Darish hooked nose, they gave him the visage of a hunting bird. "I want an explanation."

Another drop of sweat followed the course laid by the first. "Sir?"

"My heir saw fit to involve himself in a public spar, using the blade passed down our family line over six generations." He let the silence build, eyes never blinking. "And then *lost*. To a commoner. In front of the scions of both our allies and our rivals."

"It was—" Lucius' words were cut off by Robash's slashing hand.

"I said I wanted an *explanation*. Not excuses. Refocus if you must and then speak."

Lucius took a breath and let it back out again, centering himself. "There are no excuses, sir. I failed to adequately scout my opponent and allowed his size and background to sway my estimation of his abilities."

"And what should you have done instead?"

"Waited to act until I had all of the necessary information."

"Forbearance and cowardice all too often arrive at the ball in the same doublet."

"Sir?"

"There are times when you must act, even with insufficient information. What you do not do, what you must know *better* than to do, is risk assets of significance in the process. Children from ten of our vassal families attend the academy with you, and according to past reports, you have made inroads on several others, yes?"

"Yes."

"Then why would you not have one of *them* represent you in the spar? Take the measure of your opponent while risking only the reputation of those who barely matter in the greater scheme of things?"

Lucius bowed his head. The fact was, Merrick had called him out specifically, likely as some sort of payback for the man's own low birth and limited career prospects when he'd been in the duke's corps. But saying so would simply be seen as another excuse.

"Thank you for your instruction, sir."

"Show your thanks by doing your job and representing our house well, Lucius. You are my heir, but I have other children. If a change must be made…"

"That won't be necessary."

"We will see. Now, tell me what you have observed of House Marchon's whelp. Then, we will discuss what to do about this most recent embarrassment."

In a way, Lucius was grateful to remain standing for the next glass in his father's study. If nothing else, the military's ready position, which his father had adopted for his family's own, kept his clenched fists out of sight.

○○○

The Marchon estate in Trynfall, rebuilt after the Middle City fires eighty cycles earlier, stood as a testament to the region's Revivalist style. Unadorned white stone, all the more eye-catching for its simplicity, soared skyward to form the manor's single tower, an exterior wall curving around the property in a way that felt organic rather than purely functional. Even the guards, visible at the estate's main gate and sprinkled here and there throughout the property, seemed almost like adornments in their crisp white and blue tabards.

It was very much in keeping with her family's history, thought Mireille, as she circled the manor and headed for the training grounds that occupied much of the backyard, to use beauty to mask their strength. It was a strategy that had served them well long before the kingdom had essentially split into four grand duchies, and one that continued to prove out even now.

It was also a strategy that fit her poorly. She was a head taller than all but one brother, and strong enough to hold her own with any of them, even if she hadn't been higher leveled. Oh, she was fit enough and had some of her mother's slimness, sure, but even if that made for a striking overall effect, the next person who called her beautiful would be the first.

Mask strength with more strength was a much more apt motto, as far as she was concerned.

Her father was out back, training with Gerhardt, her baby brother and the pet of most of the family. Mireille winced as she watched the youngest Marchon wade in with a wide, looping swing that a blind beggar could have not only seen but handily dodged. Her father was, of course, no longer anywhere in the vicinity when the strike finally arrived, but off to the younger man's weak side with a wide-open target to attack.

"You need to at least *try* to bait him, Ger," she called out. "Father's getting old; he might fall for it."

Cassius Aurelius Barium Marchon, Earl of Locasil, sent her an arch look as he parried Ger's next swing without even looking. "Old, am I? Is that my daughter and heir I hear or some loudmouth braggart from the Docks?"

"I think it might be both," laughed Gerhardt, attempting another attack that was an abject failure before it began. He'd had his Dreaming the previous summer, and why someone like him had been given the Warrior class remained one of the Framework's great mysteries. Thankfully, he'd never have to pursue that class when the family had her and her brothers… not to mention multiple thriving businesses in need of a talented money manager.

"Once I finish off papa, I'm coming for you, little one," she threatened, patting the hilt of one of her axes. They weren't enchanted like the monstrosity Lucius Darish toted around, but the Smith who had forged them hailed from the far western nation of Te-Rel and could do miracles with alloys far stronger than bronze or iron.

"You'll have to catch me first," said Ger, waving his training weapon about like it was a baton and not something still fully capable of breaking bones or at least leaving bruises. Like most of the family, he was devastatingly pretty for a boy, with tousled blonde hair and eyelashes Mireille would have killed for.

"Gerhardt, judging by the particularly mulish expression your sister has on today, I think she and I need to talk," said Cassius, plucking the weapon from the younger boy's hands. "Why don't you go find Chef Sara and let her know we're having one more for supper tonight?"

"Yes, Papa!" He sprinted off in an explosion of floppy limbs and far too much enthusiasm, streaking for the door that led to the manor's solarium and then kitchen.

Mireille watched him go, shaking her head. "Was I ever that young?"

"Of course not. You came out of your blessed birthmother with a ferocious scowl and a demand for winterchill brandy." Cassius' smile was gentle and open, one of the many reasons so many opponents had underestimated him over the years. Opponents now dead or ruined. "But come, I didn't expect a visit from you for at least another few seven-days. What brings my heir back to her house?"

"Politics."

The easy humor slipped from her father's handsome face. "House Darish? Already?"

"Yes and no." She tapped one of her axes again, a nervous gesture she'd been warned about more than once. "What do you know about the Tryn's newest initiates?"

Cassius headed for the open shed behind them and stowed both training weapons in their requisite barrel. "The daughter of one of Zaris' merchant council, publicly a new ward of His Grace when everyone knows she's really a hostage to assure her father's continued allegiance."

"Zamira." Mireille nodded.

"I would suggest caution when it comes to forming any kind of relations with her, no matter how informal. The pretense of wardship carries with it responsibilities that Willerton must at least pay lip service to, but such fictions can and will be discarded at a moment's notice."

"That's not a problem. She doesn't interact with most of us anyway and seems prickly at best."

"There are some who would call *you* prickly, my dear."

"Not where I can hear them."

"Quite right." A grin came and went. "As for the other two… they are adventurers, yes? Nominally involved somehow in Lady Willerton's return and rewarded accordingly, though your mothers think His Grace has ulterior reasons for enrolling them at the academy."

"And? Does he?"

"He's a duke. Assume he has ulterior reasons for everything." No smile this time. "Given how quickly you moved on from the Zarisian, I assume these adventurers are at the center of your concerns?"

She nodded. "They're not much to look at. The woman is scaled, believe it or not, but seems diligent and intelligent for all of that. A Priestess of some goddess I've never heard of. The man is full-grown but shorter even than Ger, with strangely patchy-colored skin and a spear that looks like it lay forgotten in a barn somewhere for cycles and hasn't been cleaned since."

"So, what is the issue?"

"He fought Lucius in a spar. And won."

This time, Cassius' smile had an edge. "My heart bleeds for the Darish heir. When was this?"

"First Day."

"That we haven't heard of it suggests the news is actively being repressed, lest Robash's golden child see his reputation tarnished. I will set your mothers on the task. You know they are more adept with that side of things." He tilted his head, ignoring the breeze that ran through golden locks shared by four of his six children. "I assume the news ran rampant through the academy, at least. How has it impacted your recruitment?"

"Not as well as I'd hoped. A few holdouts have taken steps to our side as a result, but a greater number are holding firm."

"To House Darish?"

"To neutrality. Neither adventurer is impressive enough to be inspirations or anything, but together, they *are* examples of a third path, one separate from both Darish and Marchon."

"They are commoners, for whom such a stance is acceptable. With the rest of your classmates being nobility, even if only in name, I'd expect them to understand the distinction."

Mireille didn't say anything, and the Middle City's noise seeped in, muted but never entirely silenced by the estate's wall. Her life had taught her that expectations were like appearances; blindly trusting in either was a mistake.

"Well," decided her father, after a moment's consideration, "the solution seems obvious. You must offer a better example for your peers and potential vassals to follow. Which means you'll first have to do something about these adventurers…"

○○○

Wilf stood in the uncertain light of his dorm room, examining his reflection in the free-standing mirror. The night's outfit was another carefully calibrated riot of color and style; ridiculous enough to not be taken seriously, but not so much as to call undue attention. The coin purse on his belt had a handful of copper bits, the one hidden under his doublet nothing but silver.

His roommate, Shamond, had already left for a night on the town with a half-dozen initiates from both camps, each promising to outdo the other in drinking and wenching. Gareth Donaghey had, yet again, pressed Wilf for the location of his secret brothel and left unsatisfied; he gave it one more seven-day before the nobleman tried to follow him through the Lower City.

Won't that be fun?

Wilf ran his hands through his brown hair again, disrupting its wave into something approaching chaos, and nodded at what he saw. He was ready.

Almost ready.

He twisted his lips into a smile, adjusting the expression until it looked natural instead of forced. Next, he took hold of the rumbling emotions that so often filled him, the rage, the despair, and the helplessness, and forced them down, squeezing everything into a tiny ball at his core. When he was done, all that remained was silence and stillness, and just like that, the eyes in the mirror were smiling to match his mouth.

The *Performance* skill had its uses, and he'd done his best to master them all. With a jaunty salute to his reflection, he headed out into the night.

24

We settled into things relatively quickly at the Tryn. Multiple classes, five days a week, with two free days at the end; it was almost like I'd finally gone off to college, especially with us living in dorms. Although so far, there'd been a lot less drinking and a much greater focus on violence.

Over the course of the next few seven-days, I earned three more points in *Knife*, two in *Medium Armor*, and one in *Tactics*, *Avoidance*, and *Juggling*. I was still short of what I needed for level seven by an agonizing single point in either of two skills, but that would almost definitely take care of itself with time.

Even better was the dialogue window I'd seen toward the tail end of our third week in school:

```
You have increased the following attributes:

Strength [+1]: 13
```

I'd honestly expected an improvement in Vitality first, given how much cardio Stick had us do in Basic Conditioning… or maybe even an increase in Finesse, given my continued juggling efforts. But Strength? I would take it. I'd improved the attribute twice naturally and once via leveling since coming to Eos, and the difference was substantial. My iron hauberk, which had been almost impossibly heavy when I first wore it, was now a comfortable weight, and the blows I landed in training were noticeably harder. If ten was an average Strength attribute for humans, a thirteen put me solidly into above-average territory. I was a long way from superhuman—that would be somewhere in the high teens or even low twenties—but the muscles in my arms were evident and for the first time in my life, I had abs rather than just a stomach.

The only downside was that I hadn't grown even a fraction of an inch. I was starting to lose hope that attribute changes would be the key to a newer, taller me. Then again, being a mini-Hulk wouldn't be horrible. I'd learned growing up that there was *short* and there was *small*, and for men at least, the first was almost always better than the second.

My Framework-related gains aside, school continued to offer a mix of interest and challenge. All the studying Miko and I had been doing at night helped close the gap created by our late arrival, and while I didn't think we were going to challenge for the top spots in any of our classes, we were settling in comfortably somewhere in the middle.

The two exceptions were our team-based classes: Small Group Tactics and Dungeon Delving 101. Between our real-world adventuring experience, Zamira's outsider perspective, and Wilf's tendency to subvert situations to seize an unanticipated advantage, we were one of the few groups Ebb and Flow seemed to find promising. Hell, even Barth added something to the group beyond youthful energy and a stubborn willingness to respond to the teacher's questions even when he didn't have an answer.

On the third weekend, I followed Miko down to the Lower City. We stopped at the market and finally offloaded our collection of looted daggers, though even *Mercantilism* was insufficient to convince the merchant that most were worth more than the metal they'd been cast from. One plug and five bits, all in, minus the four bits we then paid for food from a streetside vendor.

That meal was some sort of meat on thin bread, this time. It wasn't a kebab, but it was tasty enough, and if the vendor wasn't telling us what kind of meat it was, well, I'd learned better than to ask.

We kept our actual knives, of course, two for me and one for Miko, and I held back a fourth, just in case I reached a point where juggling two knives in each hand would feel like something other than attempted suicide. And then it was onward, past the market to our true destination.

I'd known we'd be heading back to the synossian enclave eventually. I just wasn't sure what we'd be doing there when we arrived. Our last visit had ended with us being escorted out of the warehouse-like building soon after Miko lost her temper and started telling the three self-appointed community leaders the very many ways they were failing their people and their gods.

Gods that even the *scaled* here in Trynfall didn't seem to know... which was at least part of why she'd lost her temper in the first place.

The neighborhood hadn't gotten any nicer as we moved into the heart of winter and the streets hadn't gotten any cleaner either. Still, Miko led the way unerringly, a blaze of color in the robes I'd had made for her way back in Harborton. It was those robes, worn instead of her academy uniform, that had told me she'd finally reached a decision regarding her people.

We reached the enclave, the streets quiet enough that we could hear the argument happening—again—inside, but the Priestess didn't force her way in this time. Instead, she took up a position to the left of the door, back to the building. She clasped her clawed hands in front of her and scanned the intersection like a thief looking for his next mark and then, in a voice pitched to carry, she began to speak.

"We gather here today," she said, ignoring that *we* consisted of just her and the soft-skinned human standing nearby with a spear, "to speak of Synos, the Father. Of the Creator and his role amongst the Elder Gods in carving reality from the void. We come to speak of the celestial children born of Synos' soul—mighty Kal the Oathkeeper, Aurea the Dawn Maiden, Etriska the Pure, and Shan the Trickster. In the Father's absence, they are the keepers of the pact with his mortal children."

She launched into a sermon regarding the universe's creation, the smooth intonations telling me it was a story she'd told many times before. Maybe even when she'd led ceremonies as a shrine keeper. But this time, every word of it was in Trade and every word of it was perfect, telling me just how much time and effort she'd put into the translation.

After a half-glass or so, one of the men in the warehouse behind us stuck his scaled head out, shook it, and disappeared inside again. At another point, a synossian woman emerged from a nearby building— windowless, its door more a suggestion than an obstacle—to throw a pot of something foul into the street.

Still Miko talked, moving from one story to another, touching not just on the gods these people didn't know, but on the history of their mortal children. Three bells passed and by the time she was done, the sun was almost gone from the sky, shadows transforming the neighborhood around us into something as foreboding as any of the dungeons we'd studied in class.

During that entire time, Miko had been preaching to an empty street, but if she was disheartened by that fact, she didn't show it. The Priestess looked about her, gave a sharp nod, and came over to me.

"Thank you for watching my back, nest-brother."

"Always. I'm sorry that nobody came to listen."

"A fire begins with a single spark." Even in the coming twilight, she practically glowed. It wasn't just the orange and crimson of her robes either, but the conviction inside of her. Whatever one-sided conversations she'd been having with her goddess, she'd found what she needed. "When that spark catches, it spreads. Before long, there is enough light to see."

Something told me we'd be back again the next weekend.

Turns out I was half-right.

We were back again the next *day* instead.

And this time, we brought food.

ooo

Nine days later, I finally received the message I'd been working toward for so long:

Congratulations, Warrior.

You have reached level 7!

I must have made a noise of some sort, because beyond the floating screen obscuring most of my vision, I saw Miko look up from her studies. She correctly guessed what had happened and launched into a little dance of celebration, right there on her bed.

We traded grins and I turned back to my all-important messages. That first window was naturally followed by another:

```
You have increased the following skills:

Major skills:
Knife [+1]: 35/35
Tactics [+1]: 35/35
```

There was something uniquely frustrating about the fact that I'd been waiting for months for either skill to reach their cap, only to have them *both* do so at the same time, but for once, I didn't let the Framework's oddities bother me. Because seven was an odd-numbered level, and that meant I had choices to make. *Exciting* choices.

Sort of.

```
Congratulations, Warrior.

Select your level 7 advancement option:

-  Upgrade: Lunge (C) -> Liberating Lunge (U)
-  Upgrade: Beast Skin (Passive - C) -> Beast
   Hide (Passive/Active - U)
-  New technique: Fueled by Pain (U)
```

I stared at the dialogue window for a long while. It wasn't fair to say I was *disappointed*, per se, but... I'd been hoping for something new and singularly transformative. Instead, I'd been offered all three of these abilities before.

In fact, *Liberating Lunge* had been offered up *three* times now. If the Framework had a bias, it was making that bias pretty damn clear. I didn't know what the ability did, exactly, but it was an upgrade to my only movement technique and that made it worth consideration. *Liberating* suggested an association with my Ideal, but whether that meant a shorter reuse time, greater freedom in how I used it, or something else entirely remained frustratingly opaque.

Beast Hide was an upgrade to my level three technique, *Beast Skin*, which had been making my skin slightly tougher and distinctly pigmented one wound at a time. I'd originally chosen the ability because it was passive, and an always-on defense had seemed like an easy win for a Warrior; I'd been regretting that choice ever since. Would *Beast Hide* address the ability's shortcomings? Would it just make the healed patches of skin that much tougher, leaving most of my purely human flesh as vulnerable as ever? Or would it take me further down the road towards something not quite human? And what did it mean that it was both passive *and* active?

Hell if I knew. The Tryn had a library, but I'd been disappointed to discover it was filled with history books and not advancement paths or even technique primers. And Professor Lunsford's Framework class so far remained entirely mired in history and esoteric theory rather than offering up anything even vaguely actionable.

My third advancement option was the only *new* ability on offer, but it was one I'd already rejected once before. I *did* know what *Fueled by Pain* did, because Lace had recognized it when it was initially offered to me four levels earlier. When activated, it added some portion of the damage I received back into my outgoing strikes.

I'd hated the idea of the ability then and I *still* didn't like it all this time later. The point of using a spear wasn't only to make up for my natural reach disadvantage; it was also to keep the enemy at a distance so I *wouldn't* be hit. Berserkers had been an attractive enough concept in the games Bug favored back on Earth, but that allure faded significantly when the pain being suffered was real. Even with *Pain Tolerance*, I didn't know if I wanted to base my advancement around getting hurt.

On the other hand? I had yet to make it through a fight *without* suffering some damage. Maybe I should accept that reality and try to get some benefit from it?

I talked over all three options with Miko until the next bell, but ultimately, she didn't have much in the way of advice to give. The choice was mine and one I would have to live with.

On the bright side, the last few levels had made it clear that rejecting a technique *didn't* mean I wouldn't see the ability offered again. The real risk wasn't loss of opportunity; it was choosing something I might end up regretting forever.

That was what decided me in the end.

Beast Skin had a lot of downsides already and I had no idea if *Beast Hide* would redeem literally any of them. *Fueled by Pain* had the potential to be great, but it would also set the path I followed for the rest of my career. Meanwhile, *Lunge* had been my first technique and remained a vital part of my build. An upgrade to something useful that fit my fighting style was, on the third offering and with no better options available, something I couldn't pass up.

And it meant the Framework would have to give me *something* different when I reached level nine.

I made my selection and immediately went to work.

I spent the next bell triggering *Liberating Lunge* in our dorm room, where nobody could see. Even more than their level, a person's techniques were best kept private; the less someone knew, the harder it was for them to game plan against you. By the time I ran out of energy, I felt I'd gotten a handle on how the upgrade differed from its common-ranked predecessor. To my dismay, the changes were far from impressive. The recast time had lowered by a fair amount but remained lengthy enough to end my dreams of chaining together multiple Lunges to streak across a battlefield.

Mostly, what had changed had to do with the technique's built-in restrictions. With *Lunge*, I'd needed an entirely clear path between me and my destination. Anything that blocked that path, even a little bit, kept *Lunge* from triggering at all. With the upgraded version, those restrictions had been loosened. But only slightly. Anything large enough to block me from physically walking somewhere—like, say, a solid wall or even a bed—was still a problem for *Liberating Lunge*. But something like a chair or Miko's pack on the floor? Well, now I could lunge straight through, like a poor man's Shadowcat from the comics.

It was… something… but I'd expected more from upgrading a technique from common to uncommon. In fact, I spent a few nights beating myself up over what felt like *another* bad leveling choice. But the more I thought about the improvements, minor as they were, the more my initial disappointment faded. One thing both Basic Weapons Training and Small Group Tactics had hammered home was the importance of battlefield mobility. This upgrade addressed one of the weak points of the original technique and that mattered.

Now, I just needed to learn to incorporate those changes into my fighting style.

ooo

"Wilf will scout ahead," I said, reiterating decisions that had been made three classes ago. "Then me, Zamira and Miko. Barth…"

"I'll guard the rear," agreed the nobleman from Apsa, patting his bow. "I will need support if something creeps up on us from behind though."

Miko touched her fist to her chest. "Will help."

"And I'll do my very best not to die pitifully," said Zamira.

"Nobody's dying," said Wilf. "That's what our adept is here for, yeah?"

Adept Basil rolled his eyes. He was a sour-faced man around my age, decked out in ornately worked leathers with a curved blade on one hip. "You're supposed to pretend I'm not here, initiate."

"Right. I keep forgetting that part." Wilf's grin was entirely unapologetic, and when Zamira took her first real breath in minutes, I couldn't blame him. The Mage was our lowest-level party member by far. It was good for her to remember that we weren't down here alone.

Down here because we'd left the academy as a unit for the first time. *Down here* because Small Group Tactics had moved beyond theory into practical exercises. Down here because we'd *literally* gone down via a heavily guarded lift from the Tryn and now found ourselves below even the Lower City, in the tunnels that honeycombed the mountain.

"It's a simple patrol," said Basil. "If you encounter anything more dangerous than a few tunnel rats or maybe a pygmy gyr, you'll fall back and let the real guards handle it. Now, let's get a move on. I'm being graded on this too, you know."

He was kind of bossy for someone we were supposed to pretend wasn't there, but as a second-cycle student at the Tryn, he was also Ebb and Flow's stand-in for the exercise. I shrugged and turned to the others.

I wasn't sure how or why I'd taken a leadership role with our squad. Maybe it was because I had an uncommon-ranked Framework-given skill for it… or maybe it was because Miko and I were the only ones with practical experience, and my Trade was still better than hers. Or maybe it was because I was the oldest initiate in not just our party, but our entire class. Whatever the reason, Wilf had been the one to suggest it, and Zamira and Barth had been almost *too* eager to have someone take up the mantle.

Most of the time, being our party leader didn't amount to much. Down here in the tunnels, I felt the weight of responsibility for the first time.

There were a handful of ways in and out of the tunnels, and guarded checkpoints stood at each of them. Our lift had deposited us a few minutes' walk from the even more heavily guarded entrance to Trynfall's true dungeon, but our patrol route led in the opposite direction. The good news was that the upper tunnels were well lit, with lanterns hanging from wall hooks every fifty paces. Part of our patrol duties were to relight any lanterns that might have gone out, but mainly, we were there to stamp out vermin and look for disturbances that suggested incursions from further below. The tunnels predated Trynfall by hundreds of cycles and there were rumors they both descended halfway to Eos' core *and* ran the whole length of the duchy. I wasn't sure how much credence I gave those rumors but given what we'd learned in Dungeon Delving 101 about dark and deep places, the permanent guard presence made sense.

For the students of the Tryn though, this was just a way to get real-world experience in a relatively controlled environment, sprinkled in with the kind of conflict we needed to advance our levels. Ebb and Flow had said it was practice for the Echo, where we'd be on our own. In fact, our performance on patrol directly impacted our chances of getting to experience the dungeon early.

"Let's move out," I finally said, realizing everyone was waiting for my order. "Wilf, lead the way."

I was the nominal leader, but I wasn't going to tell our Spy how to do his job. I didn't know his level, but *Stealth* was a class skill for all Rogues, and it was immediately apparent he'd put some time into leveling it. Lace might have had some pointers to offer, but to me, he was a ghost as he slipped down the corridor.

We gave him about thirty seconds lead time and followed. Basil was a shadow behind us that likely made Barth's position at the back unnecessary, but we held our formation. As the adept had said, we were supposed to pretend he wasn't there. And as a Warrior, albeit one who'd focused on the bow, Barth was the best choice to play rearguard.

Healers and Mages to the center, I quoted from one of our classes. That calculus changed in open spaces, where it was important to spread out so that a single area of effect spell or technique didn't wipe out your most vulnerable party members in a single strike. But in tunnels like these?

Spot the enemy with a Rogue. Funnel them toward the Warriors. Hold the Mage in reserve for situations that require her intervention. And let the Priestess put everyone back together afterward when necessary.

On paper, we had the perfect unit composition. In reality, once you considered our respective levels, weapon choices, and builds, perfection didn't even begin to enter the picture.

Our first patrol went for a long while, though it was hard to tell time when we couldn't hear the city bells. We followed our assigned route through the tunnels, stopping to confer as we reached each new intersection, and all the while Basil watched in silence. After a while, even Zamira stopped jumping at every noise and shadow, but a combination of nerves and discipline kept our chatter to a minimum. Wilf spent half his time ranging ahead and the other half waiting for us to catch up; if the solitude bothered him, he hid it well.

Lace had been the same way, so maybe it was a Rogue thing.

We were circling back around to what I thought was our starting point when we found Wilf waiting in a pool of darkness. A lantern had gone out, only the third such we'd encountered out of almost fifty.

"Will take care of it," said Miko, pulling out the fire-striker she'd brought all the way from her home continent. She opened the lantern door and struck her implement, sending a shower of sparks toward the wick.

I took the moment of downtime to touch base with Wilf, although by then, it felt almost like we were just going through the motions. We hadn't even seen one of the rats Basil had listed dismissively as potential dangers.

"Anything we should be wary of?"

For the first time since we'd started our patrol, he hesitated.

"Wilf?"

"I'm not sure. There's an intersection up ahead and one of the tunnels leading from it is dark."

"A second lantern went out?" That seemed unlikely, given how rare that had been so far.

"Maybe? Something feels… off about the tunnel. I was thinking once Miko relit this lantern, we could bring it with us and go look? I didn't see anything, but it *was* dark."

"I could take a look now," said Barth, joining us. "If need be?"

"You never said you could see in the dark."

"I didn't want to boast." Proving the truth of his revealed ability, he read my confused face easily despite the lack of light. "It's an enchantment, not a technique."

"Item or adornment?" asked Wilf, suddenly interested.

"Adornment. Even if items weren't easily stolen, my family would never have let me leave Apsa with something so valuable."

"You've both lost me," I said. "*Adventurer from a village in the middle of nowhere*, remember?"

"Items can be enchanted." It was Zamira's turn to join us. "But the enchantment has only a set number of uses, depending on both the quality of item and the level of the enchanter."

"Right." That much I knew. "And adornments?"

"Are inscribed onto the body instead. Like a tattoo. They pull energy from the owner when used. Like when you use a technique or a spell, but far less efficient. As a result, they're only suitable for minor tasks, and even then, they're still temporary."

"Enchantment fades and the tattoo does too." agreed Wilf. "It's still a painstaking process… *and* it requires access to an Enchanter and Inscriber pair with the relevant skills."

"Like I said, I didn't want to boast," said Barth. "My adornment lets me see in the dark for two glasses in total, although I can restrict each use to a single minute. And no matter how sparingly I use it, it will fade on its own within the next cycle."

All the drawbacks they'd listed went in one ear and right out the other. The truth was simple: I wanted an adornment of my own. In our delves with Lace, darkness had been one of the biggest issues we'd faced beyond the monsters themselves. Either you had to pack and carry torches—and in doing so, announce your presence to anything in the tunnel, while *also* depriving yourself of a free hand—or you needed a technique like Lace's *Night Eyes*. An adornment sounded like the perfect solution.

It also sounded expensive. Which was a problem. I was already growing concerned about our dwindling finances, given the cost of buying even low-quality food every weekend for the synossian enclave.

But still… I wanted one.

"We've already got a lantern," I said, as Miko finally got it lit. "Let's use it to check Wilf's tunnel and keep the expensive enchantment in reserve. And no," I told Barth, before he could open his mouth, "none of us thought you were boasting."

"But we are going to have a talk about your family's connections after all this, yeah?" added Wilf. "I'm not swimming in gold crowns or anything, my rakishly stylish outfits aside, but an

Enchanter is a good person to know. Even one living in another duchy entirely."

I had a moment of wondering just how many crowns it took to have enough to swim in. Cut that number by ninety-nine percent and it would *still* dwarf the amount of money I'd seen since arriving on Eos. Hell, even before we'd started spending our money, Miko and I together hadn't had a single gold crown.

Put simply, nobles were *not* like the rest of us.

A minute or so later, we stood in the tunnel Wilf had mentioned, with the lantern Miko had relit now held by Zamira. The tunnel had curved slightly as it descended, and without our borrowed lantern, the darkness would have been all-encompassing. As it was, we had brought sufficient light to see the first of two concerns: the hook where this section's lantern should have been hanging was empty.

That was enough to get even Basil's attention.

Our second discovery had the adept outright frowning.

"I don't have the *Tracking* skill, but those don't look like rat *or* gyr prints," said Wilf.

I *did* have the skill, for all the good it did me.

"Webbed feet, I think," I finally said, pointing to where the print was blurred. "Is there water down here?"

"There is water everywhere," said Zamira. "In the peaks, the valleys, and the deep places of the world."

"Can you sense anything?" I asked her, not sure if I was referring to her Mage abilities or her innate senses as an o'naseri.

"*Stone, ancient and forgotten, touched by wind, wave, and flame,*" she said in that strange rumble only I seemed able to hear, let alone comprehend. After another moment, she shook her head. "Nothing relevant."

"Could be cave crawler," said Miko, studying the same tracks. "Learned about them in class last seven-day, didn't we? But these are bigger. And crawlers would not know to take lantern."

"Not common crawlers, anyway," I agreed. Beasts could advance and evolve in their own way, as we'd seen in our travels, from dueling stags to an overgrown centipede all the way up to the Thunderbird and Nikkaali, the titan snake. Although a blind tunnel crawler gaining both the intelligence and the means to recognize and dispose of a light source felt like a real stretch. "We'll mark it down, regardless. The question is, do we want to push deeper and try to see what's down here, or just alert the guards so that they can handle it?"

"We're not down here just to take in the sights," said Wilf.

"Agreed." Miko's voice was resolute.

That left Barth and Zamira.

"Maybe at least as far as the next lantern?" suggested Barth. "One missing lantern could be a freak accident. Two is a pattern."

"This is why I wanted to stay a Merchant," muttered Zamira. "Fine. Let's do it."

I'd honestly expected her to be the voice of dissent. Or maybe reason, even. "I guess it's unanimous then."

"Not quite." All eyes turned to Adept Basil, who was still staring at the tracks we had discovered. "I'm going to pull rank here. Patrols are meant to get your feet wet, not to dump you into the drink, head-first."

Miko sent me a confused look, and I knew I'd be explaining yet another saying later. At least this once, I wasn't the one confusing her.

"You've done what you were supposed to," continued Basil. "You've spotted a disturbance. Now, we'll report that disturbance so that a full guard patrol can be dispatched." He caught my expression before I managed to smooth it out. "Do you have a problem with that, initiate?"

"No," I lied easily. "It's just different from how we would have handled it as adventurers. The change will take some getting used to."

"That's the advantage of serving a cause other than yourself." I wasn't sure the words were meant to come out as snottily as they did, but… I wasn't sure they weren't, either. "Allies. Backup. Support. None of us are ranked, not even me. We'll leave this to those better suited for the task."

I bit my tongue, smiled, and said nothing as we headed back up the tunnel to return our lantern and resume our patrol route.

○○○

Later that night, I was looking at my latest skill gains—plus one to *Formations, Leadership,* and *Tracking*—when a knock got our attention. Miko was up first; she opened our dorm room door just enough for Wilf to slip inside.

"Is everything okay?" she asked.

"Not for long. News just leaked," he said.

"They found something in the tunnels?"

"What? No." He shook his head at me. "At least… I don't think so. I don't have any contacts among the guards down there, although I'm working on it. No, this is about the initiate rankings."

Miko and I exchanged looks as she took a seat on the edge of her bed. We were familiar with the concept, of course… in addition to the per-course rankings that would grant access to the Echo, there was a wider set of rankings encompassing the initiates as a whole. Those rankings hadn't been released yet, but we'd been working to ensure we'd fall somewhere in the middle. High enough to avoid any censure, but low enough so that we could continue skating through school without making any waves.

"They've released the numbers?" I asked.

"Yes. A full moon earlier than expected, for reasons I can only assume have everything to do with politics. You're eleventh. Miko is nineteenth." His face twisted. "With the numbers public, ranking duels will be swift to follow."

"Ranking… duels?" Miko cocked her head, forked tongue flicking out as if to taste the words.

"Academic performance matters, but strength does too. If someone wants to move up, they can challenge someone for *their* rank. And earn their house some honor in the process, while costing another house the same. They can challenge someone who is five or fewer places above them, but even so, this is where my fellow nobles start to show their teeth."

"Will stay out of it," said Miko. "Need allies, not enemies."

I nodded, agreeing. "We've got nothing to gain and—"

Another knock sounded on the door, this one loud and firm. With a look to us for permission, Wilf went and opened it.

"Actus? What can I do for you?"

"I'm not here for you, Wilf." I recognized the deep-voiced initiate from several of my classes. He was tall and broad shouldered with a chin carved from granite. "I'm here to make a challenge."

"A little bit eager, yeah? As far as I heard, duels aren't on the table yet."

"You need to check your ears then, McCall. The word just came down from on high. Dueling season is officially open. I wanted to be first in line."

Wilf threw a look over his shoulder at us both, half frustrated, half helpless.

So much for us staying out of things. I shook my head and rose to my feet. I'd seen Actus fight and unless he'd been holding back or his techniques were something truly special, he'd picked the wrong first target.

Make an example of him, whispered a voice inside of my head. *Teach the other initiates to seek softer targets.*

"Alright. How do we do this?" The size difference between us was extreme, bordering on parody, but my voice was as steady as the spear in my hands.

Actus shook his head and something too ugly to be called a smile marred the squared lines of his face. "I'm not here for you either. Not yet anyway."

He shouldered Wilf aside and pointed to my nest-sister, still seated on her bed.

"I'm here for her."

25

I don't know what Wilf saw in my face, but he got between me and Actus before I had even taken a step. Maybe I could've gotten past him with my newly upgraded *Lunge*, but before that had occurred to me, the door was shut again, and Actus was gone.

"What the hell, Wilf?"

"Duels are sanctioned." There was no trace of the Spy's customary humor, and that brought me up short even through my anger. "Fights in the dorms are not. And attacking a noble will get you thrown out of more than just the Tryn."

"Friend Wilf is right, nest-brother. Must act, not react." Miko turned to the Spy. "How do duels work?"

"It's like I was saying earlier. You can only challenge someone who is five ranks or fewer above you in ranking. That's to keep anyone from charging straight to the top in one duel and the top students from overtly bullying their lessers." Wilf gave me a long look, and then, apparently convinced I wasn't going to do something stupid, started pacing. "All duels take place on Sixth Day in the training hall. You can only be challenged once per seven-day. Let's see… what else?"

"Can a duel be refused? Or forfeited?" I stopped. I'd been with Miko long enough to be able to interpret the growing outrage on her reptilian features. "I'm not saying you *should*. But we're not nobles. Rank doesn't mean much to us, right?"

That won me a grudging nod, but Miko's metaphorical hackles were up. There were times I forgot she had her pride and a temper of her own under all that piety and responsibility.

"Forfeiture will only invite more challenges," said Wilf.

"Predators hunt prey," said Miko.

"Exactly. Show you're not an easy target and a lot of the potential challengers will look elsewhere."

"Is that why Actus challenged me? Because I seem weak?"

"Maybe? I don't know. He's from an unaligned house. It could be he's just trying to work his way up the rankings without getting on the bad side of either House Darish or House Marchon. That doesn't leave a lot of options. Zamira is a ward of the Grand Duke, whereas you two are..."

"Commoners," I finished.

"Exactly. And anyone who didn't watch your spar with Lucius has at least heard about it."

Which was good for me, and bad for Miko.

"Who sets terms?" My nest-sister bared sharp teeth at the looks we sent her. "What? Am familiar with idea of duels, if for honor, not rank."

"Right. The good news is that, as the person being challenged, you get to set the terms. The bad news is there are limits on what you can do."

"Is fine." Miko leaned forward, voice going hard. "Have two days to prepare. Will make them count."

∘∘∘

Sixth Day was normally a day everyone spent off campus, but the training hall was practically full when we arrived. Miko's duel was just one of four—and the second on the schedule—but most of the initiates were there for the free show, I thought. That or the equally free peek at the competition.

Merrick and his assistants would be running the duels, but there were two Priests on loan from Middle City too. The one from the Temple of the Weeping Crone was paradoxically young and more handsome than any human should be. The other, from the Church of the Radiant Divide, was middle-aged, with a face like a Shar Pei.

I was never going to understand religion.

"Is there anything I can get you?" I asked Miko.

"No, nest-brother. I am ready."

She looked it too. She had her school uniform on instead of her robes, and her armored vambraces on top of that. Her half-staff was in her hand instead of dangling from her belt; it practically hummed as she casually wove it through the air.

We'd spent much of the last two days training and strategizing for her fight, but there was a limit to how much you could cram for a duel. Last night, she'd stopped early, taken a bath, communed with Aurea, and gone to bed.

"Do not worry for me, Brian Fieldings," she said, lapsing into the High Tongue. "The teachers are on hand to make sure nobody goes too far. Win or lose, this is training, and I will come out the other side of it stronger."

"I thought we weren't going to use the L word?"

Miko grinned, not even noticing the nearby initiate who recoiled at the mouthful of teeth she'd just exposed. "I keep forgetting."

"Stick to the plan and you'll crush him."

"Yes." She took a deep breath and let it out. "Yes, I will."

"Spectators need to take their places in the viewing area," said one of the teaching assistants. "Duelists, come with me."

"Win or win, I'll see you on the other side," I told her, sparking another grin.

Zamira and Wilf had saved me a spot on one side of the arena. I squeezed in next to them.

"Will she be okay?" asked the Zarisian.

"She's ready," I said, not really answering the question. Miko had a few big handicaps when it came to a fight like this. As a Priestess, her weapon skills were less effective than a Warrior's equivalent. Some of that might be mitigated by her species' superior strength and natural defenses, but *I'd* been able to beat her more often than not when sparring.

The second handicap was far, far bigger… but we had a plan for that, at least.

But we had another duel to get through first. Once Merrick had met with the duelists, the first pair took the stage.

"I still think they should have saved this one for last," muttered Wilf. "It's against every law of showmanship to start with the biggest fight."

In the center of the open space, Lucius squared off against a much larger man with a massive maul in his hands.

"Do we know what Lucius has against…"

"Derry?" Wilf nodded. "There's the obvious: as the top score in our class, he's currently ranked higher than Lucius, which is of course unforgiveable. And second…"

"Darishal's family are vassals to House Marchon," answered a new voice, rough and deep for all that it came from a woman. Then again, Mireille was taller than Wilf and likely far stronger too.

"Politics?" I asked. I wasn't on *good* terms with the noblewoman, but I wasn't on bad terms with her either. This was the first time she'd ever sought me out.

"Everything in Trynfall is about politics."

"I'm guessing you don't make it down to the Lower City very often. I'm pretty sure the people there care more about where their next meal is coming from."

"And who makes that food possible, if not the duchy's nobles?"

"The farmers. And probably the merchants and warehouse owners and…"

Wilf coughed. "Zamira and I are going to go find a better vantage point for the duels." With that, he and the white-haired Zarisian moved deeper into the crowd.

Mireille watched them go. "If you'll take some advice from a woman you barely know? Be wary in your dealings with Wilfred McCall and what little remains of House McCall."

I finally turned and gave her a direct look. The short-haired noblewoman loomed over me, but I was frankly used to that from all this time with Miko. "Is there something you need, Mireille?"

"Not at all. I'm simply here to watch the duels, like everyone else." She nodded back to the field.

"Do you think Darishal has a chance?"

"If he did, Lucius wouldn't have challenged him."

"Yet you don't seem concerned."

"Politics are more about strategy than tactics. If you're only planning five steps ahead, then you're unavoidably behind."

"Well, *that* clears everything up."

"There's a reason we made sure it was Darishal who was in a position to be challenged."

It took me way too long to figure out what she was getting at, but then, *I* hadn't slept nearly as well as Miko last night.

"You're sacrificing him to draw Lucius out. For what? Information?"

That won me a look of consideration. "Yes."

"That seems kind of callous."

"Not at all. Ultimately, Darishal has little at stake. He earns valuable combat experience and makes a public proclamation of his allegiance to House Marchon. Of us all, he will gain the most here. Still, it should prove an illuminating match. As will your companion's, no doubt."

That tore my attention from the preparations. I leaned hard on *Deception* to keep my tone conversational.

"Wilf thinks Actus is acting on his own. Just an unaligned noble trying to better his position in our class."

Mireille's eyes were brown and surprisingly big. Something flickered in their depths. "It has been known to happen."

"I'm sure. Except I keep returning to something he said when he came to challenge Miko."

"What's that?"

"That he wanted to be first in line."

She looked away. "Ah."

"Doesn't sound like someone acting alone, does it?"

"No." Mireille gave a short shake of her head. "No, it doesn't."

"Which makes me think he's doing it as part of some grander… let's call it *strategy*. Maybe this is *his* way of showing his allegiance."

"That's not—"

I kept going, voice turning cold. "I don't know if it was you and your house that put him up to it, or Lucius and his, but after all this talk of politics, I'm starting to lean in a particular direction. So, I'm going to ask again: is there something you need, Mireille?"

Bright spots of color bloomed in her cheeks. Anger, rather than embarrassment, I was pretty sure. "Neither I nor my house had anything to do with Actus' challenge."

Which would have been great to hear if I thought I could believe it. But so far, Mireille's best quality had been that she *wasn't*

Lucius. That didn't buy her an ounce of trust. Not with Miko being targeted.

"However," she added, in a slightly calmer tone, "in clinging to neutrality, you're exposing her, yourself, and those around you to further such machinations. Align yourselves with me and I swear to you that I will personally give you both House Marchon's protection."

I let the silence build between us for just a moment.

"How's that working out for Darishal?"

Her nostrils flared, but she bit back whatever it was she was going to say and took a breath of her own.

"My nursemaid had a saying: some phloxls are so stubborn that they will only drink if they are drowned."

"That sounds terrible for the phloxl."

"And even worse for the farmer dependent upon its bounty. I'm not here to be dragged into an argument. I'll leave you to watch the duels in peace."

I watched her push her way back through the crowd, headed for the large knot of initiates on the far side of the field who publicly supported her house. She was halfway there when a sudden realization had me cursing.

"What is it?"

Somehow, I wasn't surprised to turn and find Wilf back at my side like he'd never left. Zamira was still making her way back over to us, looking as annoyed as someone with stone eyes could manage.

"I just realized something," I said.

"That diplomacy means *not* lashing out at an earl's heir?"

"No." I sighed. "I realized why House Marchon has sounded so familiar all this time. Does Mireille have any handmaidens?"

"Again, she's the daughter of an *earl*. She has several."

"And is one of them named Elina d'Kay?"

"A child of House d'Kay? I… think so? Why?"

"No reason. No reason at all."

Delivering Eustace's letter had just gotten that much more difficult.

○○○

Contrary to Mireille's prediction, the duel between Lucius and Darishal was far from illuminating. Or maybe it was, but not in a way I'd anticipated.

It was twelve moves, start to finish, and it ended with Darishal wrapped in one of the healers' protective shells as the other worked to put him back together.

Lucius flicked the blood from Sever and accepted a cloth from one of his sycophants to wipe the blade fully down. All the while, he stared not at his downed opponent but at Mireille and then, in one of those uncomfortable moments that reminded me how strange my life had become, at me.

"There's no way he improved that much in a single moon of training," I said to Wilf.

"Techniques *were* permitted this time, yeah?"

"Still." Maybe *Deceptive Strike* would have allowed me to take down Darishal that cleanly, but I wasn't willing to bet on that. "He's not Tin ranked; that means he should have at most five techniques."

"The ring on his left hand is enchanted," said Zamira. "As is the earring and what I think is a necklace under his tunic."

"Multiple enchantments? That is *so* unfair," muttered Wilf.

He wasn't wrong. Lucius had moved like lightning and hit like a titan, and it was entirely possible he hadn't given away any of his techniques at all. I turned to Zamira.

"How can you tell? About the enchantments, I mean?"

"I was a Merchant. *Appraisal* is one of my profession's skills, and the value ranges it's giving me are wildly off for gemstones that small."

I added yet another skill I badly wanted to have in my repertoire. "I'm guessing your *Mercantilism* skill is sky high too?"

"I am a daughter of Zaris." She said it like it was answer enough… and I guess it was.

"We need to bring you with us on our next shopping trip."

"Aren't you spending most of your money on simple food?"

Not even *Deception* could help me hide my wince. I was grateful that Miko and Zamira had bonded the way they had, but revealing the dire state of our party finances seemed like a bridge too far.

"Once we have money again, I mean," I said instead. "Especially since I want an adornment like Barth."

"It cost him two crowns," said Wilf. "That's a significant cost even for some noble houses."

"Really? We were well on our way to having a crown between us when we arrived in Trynfall." I shook my head, not wanting to think about how that coin had dwindled so fast. "Easy come, easy go, I guess."

"You've spent almost a gold crown since you arrived a *moon* ago? How?"

"Okay, not a whole crown. Or even a half one, technically. But we had over two towers. *Had* being the operative word."

Zamira and Wilf exchanged bewildered looks, and it was the Zarisian who leaned in.

"Brian," she said, "how many towers do you think are *in* a crown."

"Ten. Ten copper bits to a plug, ten plugs to a silver tower, ten towers to a—"

"To a castle," finished Wilf.

"A what?"

"A silver castle. Ten towers to a castle. Ten castles to a crown."

"I… what?" I asked again. It seemed inconceivable that I would have missed an entire unit of currency in the lesson I'd gotten back in Harborton.

Then again… the village had been as poor as it came, with most of the families counting their wealth in bits instead of plugs. Even Erlund and Val, the village's founders had only had eight towers between them, and they'd spent all of those on Harborton's charter. It was entirely possible they'd never *heard* of a silver castle because they'd never had that much money.

I suddenly knew what that was like.

"I'm feeling really poor all of a sudden," I admitted. "And maybe we'll have to put off that adornment purchase for now."

"If it helps," said Zamira, "it's unlikely any level of *Mercantilism* skill would convince an Enchanter to budge on their prices anyway."

It didn't help. It didn't help at all.

○○○

When the healers were done, Darishal was able to walk off the field under his own power. Head down, he made his way over to where he was welcomed by Mireille's cohort. The noblewoman herself gave him a hearty slap on the back and leaned in to whisper something that lifted both his head and spirits.

Lucius, meanwhile, stalked back to his space, accepting the congratulations pouring his way with the barest hint of a smile. And just like that, our initiate class had a new top-ranked student.

House Marchon and House Darish. It was just bad luck that Miko and I had ended up at the Tryn in this cycle and with this class. I didn't want any part in their political power struggle, but neutrality clearly had its costs too.

As if to prove the point, Miko took the field against Actus. She moved easily, balanced on the balls of her feet like a boxer as she stared the other man down.

"I forget how *tall* she is, sometimes," said Zamira. And then, after a quick, almost apologetic glance my way: "No offense, Brian."

"I've known synossians that make her look like she's my size, comparatively," I said. "Men and women both."

I wished one of *them* was here, fighting this duel in Miko's stead. And not *just* because it would mean they were still alive. Riok would have smoked Lucius… Actus wouldn't have even been a speedbump. And Niaci would have hit the burly, unaligned nobleman so hard she launched him all the way across the arena.

Miko could take care of herself. But Actus' weapon of choice was a trident, and that gave him almost as much reach as my oversized spear…

"Breathe," said Wilf, leaning down to murmur in my ear. "Unclench your jaw, unwrinkle your forehead, and breathe."

"I'm not—"

"If this duel *is* politically motivated, it's an attack on you as much as Miko. Don't let them see that the blow landed. Any more than you already have. This is a training exercise. Nothing more. Nothing less. Breathe."

I latched onto his voice like it was a lifeline. Miko was tough, and including her, there were *three* Priests available. Even if she lost, the only lasting hurt would be to her pride.

"I'm good," I said, calling on *Deception* to keep my voice light and my face relaxed. "But he had better hope he doesn't climb high enough in the ranks where I can challenge him."

Wilf started to say something, then swallowed it, and simply nodded instead. Miko and I were both in the middle of our class's hierarchy, but my performance in Basic Weapons Training and my leadership in Ebb and Flow's two classes had me just outside the top ten, whereas Miko was half a dozen ranks lower. Actus would need to win a lot of duels, or dramatically improve as a student, to pass me.

But if he did?

Well, it was a brother's job to fight for his sister, and a warrior's job to protect their healer.

Merrick finished speaking with both duelists and took a step back and away. For a moment, there was silence.

"Break him, nest-sister!" some idiot called out in the High Tongue. "You've got a sermon to give in the Lower City!"

Miko's answering smile was savage.

Unlike the duel between Lucius and Darishal, Miko's fight took a while. Part of that was that neither she nor Actus were anywhere near the level of a Lucius with multiple enchanted items. A bigger part was the terms Miko had set for the ranking duel.

No techniques.

We hadn't been sure if that would be permitted—unlike on Earth, something like specifying weapon type was not—but there'd been no pushback from the instructors. And that helped to balance the playing field considerably, given that Miko had no offensive spells at all.

Even so… it was close. Miko had a slight edge in strength and possibly level, Actus a more evident edge in skill. Her scales and vambraces protected her better than his leathers did him, but that trident left her at a reach disadvantage. She had to bait the Warrior into strikes with feints and then capitalize whenever she could get inside his guard.

It didn't always go smoothly.

I did my best to keep my face impassive as more of Miko's blood splattered onto the dirt. She'd only taken two hits so far and twisted just enough to be grazed instead of impaled, but both wounds were bleeding freely, and the terms she'd set meant she couldn't heal herself.

I tried to comfort myself with the fact that Actus didn't look any better. He wasn't bleeding, but he *was* limping from a blow he'd taken to the hip, and Miko's last strike had only missed taking his head off by a fraction of an inch.

Even better, he was slowing down.

"I can't watch this," murmured Zamira, voice thick with anxiety and—I was pretty sure—nausea.

"It's almost over," I said.

That was more of a prayer than a prediction, admittedly. Still, as a Chosen of the gods, it was possible my prayers held a little bit more weight than most, because the next move proved me right.

Miko stumbled.

Actus lunged forward, trident leading the way, only to find Miko spinning forward, her half-fall a feint that brought her in close. One clawed hand wrapped around the trident's shaft, pushing it out wide. The other hammered her short-staff into the Warrior's side.

We could hear the impact all the way across the field, accompanied by the sound of ribs breaking, but Miko didn't stop there. She spun Actus about, using his trident as a fulcrum, and when the Warrior clung to his weapon, she brought her staff down on it.

The sound of that arm snapping was almost lost under a *third* hit, as Miko landed her final blow, this one to the leg that was now the only thing keeping her opponent upright.

Actus tumbled to the dirt.

"*Oh*," breathed Zamira, as the healers headed for Miko's downed opponent. I'd never heard someone be simultaneously sick, proud, and relieved, but somehow, she managed it.

Miko stood above Actus, and only our long association let me see she was *dying* to help heal him. But if this duel had been about sending a message—to us or the other unaligned initiates—then we needed to send our own message back.

So, she stood there and said and did nothing in a show of impassivity, her scaled features masking the mixed emotions she was no doubt feeling. And when Actus was on his feet again, multiple bones healed, she waved the healers off, healing her own damage with a single spell, as if to remind everyone watching what she was.

I was unreasonably proud.

"Well fought," I told her in the High Tongue when she rejoined us.

"That is not as easy as you made it look." She accepted the rag I offered and wiped both blood and bone fragments from her weapon. "I am glad it is over."

"Hopefully, that'll be the end of things." I scanned the crowd as best I could, given my lack of height. Mireille was looking our way, face set, while Lucius didn't seem to have paid any attention to the fight at all. Whichever of them had set Actus after Miko—if, in fact, *either* of them had—I could only hope they'd gotten our message:

Priestess or not, Miko wasn't as vulnerable as they thought.

ooo

Zamira was too busy to come to the Lower City, but she sent Ardalan with us to help buy food for Miko's next sermon at the enclave. By now, word had gotten out, and a line of synossians, many of them only half-dressed, were already waiting when we arrived. Two of the three community leaders were there too, ready to help us organize the distribution. The third had called his compatriots fools, Miko a zealot, and washed his hands of the whole affair the last time we saw him.

Most of the food we set out was day-old baked goods that we'd been able to get for a song, but Zamira's aid had allowed us to bring a half-pot of still-warm stew with a mystery meat that I was almost positive *wasn't* tusker. It wasn't a lot, but it was more than most of the people here got, judging by the way the audience had grown each successive seven-day.

They were here to eat, not listen, of course. Most people scurried away as soon as they had their fill—whether to try to get back in line for seconds or to retreat to what passed for their homes—but a handful stayed behind, listening as Miko carefully wove words about Synos, his celestial children, and the species who had been created in their image.

Last week, there'd been four listeners, including one of the two community leaders. Today, there were seven. *Not* counting Ardalan.

It was progress. Toward *what* exactly, I couldn't say, but even separated by a thousand cycles and uncountable generations, these were still Miko's people. If I'd been called to save the synossians, there was nothing to say we couldn't start with those who'd never left the continent in the first place.

Or so I told myself. Really, it was Miko's play, and I was just backing it.

Which would have been easier if our resources had been anywhere near infinite. As it was, feeding so many people cost us almost a plug a day, even buying food that was well on its way to spoilage. At two days of sermons a week, we were burning through our finances fast. Zamira's help was sorely needed, but away from her home and family, her resources were even more limited than ours. As a so-called ward of the Grand Duke, she was granted a stipend of a single copper plug a week. It was income, where Miko and I had none, but it wouldn't support our charitable activities on its own.

That was why, after the sermon was over and Miko had traded words with the handful of synossians who had stayed through the whole thing, we didn't follow Ardalan back up to the Middle City. Instead, we returned the empty stew pot to the street vendor we'd purchased it from and then made our way over to a building we'd only been inside once before.

The Adventurer's Guild.

The people in the hall had changed, but the atmosphere was the same: tables full, voices raised, and at least two encounters of the… *blatantly sexual* variety happening in plain sight. The corbin at the front desk was different than the one we'd met before, her feathers stiped grey and white instead of black, and far too absorbed in whatever she was doing to even say hello as we walked past. To the left of the desks, next to the stairs leading up to rooms we wouldn't be able to afford, a large board had been hung from the ceiling. It was half covered with scraps of parchment, each bearing a title, a presumed ranking, and a reward.

Adventurers very rarely stumbled upon secret treasures in undisclosed and unexplored locations. Most of them made their money by working for the guild, either directly as a clerk or Keeper, or by taking on jobs that non-adventurers had sent in. The guild served as middleman, pocketing a portion of the proceeds in the process, but it was adventurers who saw those jobs done and walked away with the greatest share of the reward.

And as full members of the guild, Miko and I no longer needed Lace or someone else present to choose our own missions.

There were a *lot* of tasks on the board. We outright ignored anything that was ranked Tin or above, of course, as well as anything that would take us out of Trynfall for more than a day. That left everything from in-city escort services to dockside security to a handful of tasks that looked suspiciously like manual labor and paid almost nothing.

Interestingly, there were a few that involved the tunnels under Trynfall, either hunting for underground herbs, winnowing the hordes of low-level monsters beyond the patrolled areas, or even hunting for specific creatures whose parts were themselves valuable ingredients in various forms of crafting pursuits. I took one of those and wandered back to the nearest clerk.

"If you're claiming a mission, I'll need your badge," she said, with the air of a cashier too busy browsing TikTok to bother with customer service.

Hide the beak and the feathers, and I'd have felt like I was back at the Quick Mart in Midton.

"I actually had a question about it first."

"If it's regarding specific details about the mission, you'll have to take it up with the mission giver, not us."

"No, it's not…"

For the first time, she looked up. Her eyes were more human than the corbins I'd met previously, even if her plumage made no bones about her species.

"What can I help you with, adventurer?"

I'd worked retail long enough to recognize boredom—and burnout—when I saw it, but… I *did* want to know.

"These missions are for the tunnels down below. How do we get access to them? I thought access was controlled by the guards."

"It is." If bubblegum had been a thing on Eos, she'd have been chewing hers as desultorily as possible. "But half those tasks come *from* the guard. They focus on security above and below ground. The rest gets outsourced to the guild." Because I clearly wasn't getting it, she sighed and added: "Show up with your badge and they'll let you in. Just don't expect support. And be prepared to be searched on your way back through. Smuggling cuts into the city taxes and taxes pay the guards' wages."

That made things easier. If Adept Basil wasn't going to let us seek out danger on our school patrols, we could do so on our own instead. *And* profit from the experience.

My nod of thanks was promptly ignored, so I headed back over to Miko. "It sounds like our badges will get us into the tunnels on our own," I told her. "We should each take a mission and see if we can get them both done at once."

"Good," she said, handing me a parchment. "This is mine."

The first thing I noticed was the posted reward. One copper bit wasn't going to get us anywhere. Hell, I didn't even know how the guild would get their cut, considering that was the smallest unit of currency the kingdom had.

The next thing I noticed was the difficulty: unranked. That, at least, was good news, although I knew those difficulties were, at best, estimates.

Unranked. Worth a single copper bit. And it would involve us going into the tunnels? Even the manual labor jobs made more sense… until I finally reached the top of the parchment.

Missing child. Last seen near the lower tunnels. Answers to Greshal, Gresh, or Little Fuzz.

And then the real kicker:

Lupine. Four cycles old.

That explained everything. We'd known some lupine back in Madea, including three little cubs that were the cutest balls of fluff I'd ever seen in my life. The wolf-like humanoids were famously loyal to their mates and protective of their offspring. If a single copper bit was being offered, it was because that was literally all they could afford. And the fact that they weren't down in the tunnels searching even now told me they physically couldn't.

"Yeah," I said, swallowing a lump in my throat. "That's a good one."

We paired it with a gathering mission: retrieving twenty sprigs of something called Last Breath, which grew only underground in damp places and which Miko said could be used as a local anesthetic. I brought both mission tags over to the disaffected corbin clerk and slid them across the desk with our guild badges.

"What can you tell us about this one?" I asked, tapping the mission Miko had found.

Whatever the clerk had been planning to say died twice, first at the seriousness of my tone, and second, when she scanned the parchment itself. She went to the shelf behind her desk and pulled down a folder of loose papers, flipping through until she found what she was looking for.

"It was posted a day ago. The gentleman who came in asked for his name and address to be kept private until Greshal was found."

"Did he give anything more?"

Her too-human eyes sharpened. "The reward is what was posted."

"I mean information. Where to start looking. That sort of thing."

"Oh." I'd never gotten an apology from a corbin, but some of the annoyance leaked back out of her. "There's nothing else recorded. Let me ask Lettie. She was on duty that day."

She left and returned a few minutes later with the corbin who'd originally swapped out our provisional badges almost a month earlier for the new versions. I don't know if Lettie recognized us, but she gave Miko a friendly nod.

"Ulla says you wanted to know more about the missing lupine child?"

"Yes," said Miko. "Please. If you remember anything."

"It was just yesterday; I remember. He was an older fellow, fur more white than black. His grandpup had been playing out in the streets, not far from the dockside entrance to the deeps. Old man stopped paying attention for just one moment and his pup was gone."

"How did he know he went into the tunnels?"

She tapped her beak. "Lupine can smell better than you or me, dunsman. He followed the scent trail as far as he could before it petered out. The guards stopped him soon after."

"They didn't help?" I decided to let the dunsman comment slide. Hell, maybe it was an *improvement* to be taken for one. If Lomas back in Harborton was any indication, I was tall, hairy, and kind of handsome for a dunsman.

"Helping would mean admitting that some little furball had made his way past them without them realizing it." Lettie sniffed. "Oh, I'm sure they looked around a bit, eventually, but if you want to get something done, you hire adventurers for the task."

"Has been a day," said Miko. "Yet mission is still on board."

Lettie looked away. "It's a single copper bit."

"No." My nest-sister shook her head. "Is a life."

"We'll take both missions," I said.

Ulla nudged Lettie aside, picked up a quill, made a notation on the parchment in front of her, and slid our badges back across the desk. Her too-human eyes were bright.

"Good hunting, adventurers."

ooo

It was late by the time we left the guild hall. Far too late to go down into the deeps, no matter how much we wanted to do so. Instead, we made the long hike back up to and through the Middle City and then up again and west to the Tryn. Through the school's front gates, to the left through the entry hall, down the network of halls that eventually terminated in the common room for the initiate dorms. The common room was empty as usual, but as we left it behind and came upon our room, we found a tall figure waiting. He was dark haired, built like a fire hydrant, and one of the better fighters in Basic Weapons Training.

"Miko," said Gareth, "I'm here to offer challenge."

My nest-sister offered a single, sharp nod in reply. "Will meet you in combat next Sixth Day."

"Yes, you will. Feel free to ban techniques again if you think that will help you."

Ignoring me entirely, Gareth headed deeper into the dorms.

I shared a look with Miko.

Breaking Actus hadn't been enough.

We needed a new strategy.

26

On the one hand, two gold crowns for an adornment that would fade all on its own within a cycle was a *lot*. Especially now that I knew each crown was worth a hundred towers, rather than *just* ten. On the other hand, could you really put a price on being able to see in the dark?

I mean… *technically*, the answer was yes, and that price remained two gold crowns. But after at least an hour or two of delving the tunnels beneath Trynfall, money was the least of my concerns.

Even if it was the need for money that had driven us down there in the first place.

Getting into the tunnels had been easy enough. Like Ulla had said, my guild badge had worked like a ticket of admission for all of us. Which… was good, because our whole party was in attendance. Miko had told Zamira about the missing lupine, Wilf had heard we'd come up with a way to make money, and Barth had been sitting in the common room and hadn't wanted to be left out.

So, there were five of us, instead of just two, and one of those five could see in the dark for brief bits of time, which was huge. Or… would have been huge, if Barth had been our scout. Unfortunately, he didn't even have *Stealth*, which made him a poor fit for the role. Wilf was easily our best scout, but once we'd left behind the well-lit upper tunnels, he couldn't see a thing.

Running a party was way harder than Lace had made it look.

We doubled back and took the last lantern off its hook to bring with us. The light would almost definitely attract some creatures, but Barth was the only one of us prepared to fight in the darkness. Relying on his hearing and sense of smell more than his eyesight, Wilf continued to scout ahead but he shortened the distance between us in case he ran into trouble, just ahead of our small traveling circle of light.

It wasn't ideal, but it worked.

Until it didn't.

A twinge from *Danger Sense* was my only warning as something leaped out of the shadows in near-perfect silence. I didn't have time to dodge, let alone get my spear into position, so I just punched out instead, hand wrapped around my weapon's shaft.

White-hot pain sparked as something popped in my knuckles, the agony only partially masked by *Pain Tolerance*, but my punch sent the vastly smaller attacker flying to the side. It landed on all eight of its furred feet and scurried forward again, two furless tails waving behind it like tentacles, but this time, I was ready.

My first thrust missed. I blamed the hand whose knuckles I'd almost definitely just cracked. Still, it sent the thing skittering to the side, and that gave me more time to measure my next attack. This time, I hit, Riok's spear piercing all the way through the creature's body. It kept coming anyway, spider-like limbs churning as it climbed the length of the spear to get at me. I spun, hoisting the thing into the air along with my weapon, and smashed it against the wall. It was still moving afterward, if a bit more sluggishly, so I did it again. Something squished and fluids—black in our lantern's dim light—sprayed across the stone.

A squeal erupted from behind me as Miko and Barth finished off a second creature. Wilf reached us too late to help with either foe.

"What the hells are those things?" demanded Zamira.

"Tunnel rats," I said. Roughly the size of a small dog, they were larger than what had been described in our class, but the eight legs and hairless tails were a dead giveaway.

"Stay alert," added Miko. "Come in swarms, not pairs."

Zamira swallowed. Wilf slipped to the rear to join Barth, daggers at the ready, while Miko and I looked ahead.

Nothing came.

"Is strange," said Miko.

"You can't always trust what you read, I guess."

My nest-sister sent me a look like I'd just insulted puppies.

Right. Former Scholar. Loves books.

"Or maybe something else is going on," I offered.

"Yes. Must be so." The lantern light was just enough to see her eyes flare as she caught sight of my right hand. "Your hand…"

"I think I cracked something when I punched the rat." I peeled that hand off my spear and held it out. Two of the fingers were slightly off-kilter, despite my best efforts.

"I'm going to be sick," said Zamira.

"*Pain Tolerance?*" asked Barth, sidling up to me. At my terse nod, he pursed his lips. "I've never had much opportunity to level the skill."

Of course he hadn't.

Miko hung her half-staff from her belt and extended both her hands over my injured one. Moments later, the warm glow of *Light Healing* washed over me.

Light Healing because *Minor Healing* didn't do well with bone damage.

When the spell was done, I squeezed my hand into a fist. It still hurt, but everything moved the way it should. And given both how much energy *Light Healing* took out of Miko and how few times she could cast it without rest, that would have to be enough.

"I'm good," I told her, taking back up my spear. "Thank you."

"Do we want anything from the bodies?" asked Barth. "I've never harvested anything for ingredients before."

I shook my head. Even if I hadn't splattered my attacker all over the wall, I didn't remember tunnel rats having any body parts of alchemical value.

"Should take tails," said Miko. "Saw a mission to return twenty of them. Not for recipe, but for proof of kill."

"Here's hoping it will still be on the board when we go back."

We let Wilf do the honors since he had his knives out anyway. He stored the bloody trophies in Miko's pack, wrapped in the parchment-thin hide she used to separate different kinds of herbs.

"Sixteen more to go, I guess. Shall we press on then?"

"I don't know what good me scouting is going to do if things can just creep right past me in the dark," said Wilf.

"Maybe you should focus on looking tastier." Zamira's stone eyes were cold stone and her grin was shaky, but she was trying.

"I keep *those* outfits for when I'm out on the town, yeah?"

A little bit of tension went out of the group at their banter, weak as it was. The problem was, Wilf was right. Putting him out front when he couldn't see what was coming not only left him vulnerable, it also offered us very little value in terms of scouting.

"Formation change," I said. "Miko will be carrying the lantern just behind me. Then Zamira and Barth. Wilf will watch our backs."

"Are you sure you don't want me up front?" asked our archer.

"I do, but... we don't want to burn through your adornment. And you need space for your bow."

After a moment's consideration, he nodded.

"Let's keep it fairly tight though?" suggested Wilf. "Stop at every intersection we find and make sure nothing's waiting in ambush."

"I should be in Zaris, sipping ice blossom tea and discussing upcoming fluctuations in the spring market for spider-silk weave," muttered Zamira.

"Can still discuss it," suggested Miko, "when child is safe."

The Zarisian looked away. "Of course. I'm sorry."

"No," said my nest-sister, patting the other woman on the arm. "That was an offer, not a…" She turned to me and swapped to the High Tongue. "Admonition?"

"Admonition," I translated into Trade.

"Yes, admonition. Would very much like to hear about spider-silk and more."

"Oh. Well, yes. That would be fun!"

"Can maybe braid hair as well?"

Barth was oblivious, but I traded glances with Wilf.

Regardless of species, sometimes women were just plain weird.

○○○

Either our Beasts of Eos book *was* wrong, or something else was going on; we were attacked another two times by tunnel rats, but they never came in groups larger than three. Fighting more than two at a time was instructive; while we'd quickly adjusted to their ambush tactics, there was a limit on how many we could take at once. A swarm would've presented real problems.

Other than two heals from Miko, we'd been keeping our techniques in reserve. *Shepherding our resources*, as Ebb and Flow had once inexplicably called it. There were worse things than tunnel rats lurking below Trynfall, and none of us wanted to be out of energy—or on ability cooldowns—if we encountered them.

Wilf couldn't scout for us, but he still had the best *Pathfinding* skill in the group. Or… the only one, really. I hadn't been aware there was a different skill for finding your way below ground, but the Framework could be remarkably specific at times. So, *Orienteering* was great if you were aboveground, but *Pathfinding* was required below.

Mostly, it just meant he kept us going in the right direction—down—and made sure we didn't accidentally loop back to tunnels we'd already explored.

We'd gone at least a glass past the patrols now, and some of the tunnels we encountered were little more than cracks in the stone. Others were wide enough that all five of us could have walked side by side if we wanted. We found the occasional support, old, heavy wood frames bracketing the tunnel walls, but most of the tunnels appeared natural instead, carved out of the mountain by water, or wind, or maybe even beasts.

The further we went, the less optimistic I was about finding the missing lupine cub. Even if the tunnels hadn't run for literal miles, they were a maze we had very little chance of solving.

We should've brought the grandsire, I realized. *Just because the initial scent trail was gone doesn't mean he wouldn't have been able to pick up something deeper in.*

Instead, we were just wandering. Wandering and hoping. I didn't need tactics class—or another abbreviated lecture on strategy from Mireille—to know how well that usually worked out.

I don't think any of us expected Zamira to come up with an idea, least of all the merchant princess herself, but at a certain point, she pulled up short and came to a halt.

"Lupine need water, just like other species, right?"

"Not as much as dryads," said Wilf, "but a lot more than dunsmen, and slightly more than humans or fiorlans, yeah."

"How do you even know that?"

He gave her a look. "We had a lupine guardsman when I was growing up. Before…" He shrugged. "Anyway, what was your point?"

"It's been two days. If this Greshal is still alive…" She winced. "I know, I know! But *if* he's still alive, he'd have to have found water, right?"

"Yes," said Miko.

"So maybe we should look for water down here instead of just wandering the tunnels?"

It was a great idea, in theory.

There was just one big problem with it.

"How are we going to find water *without* just wandering the tunnels?"

I don't think she had any tear ducts, but Zamira blinked anyway. "I'm a water Mage. I can sense it."

"Water Mage? But… you're an o'naseri," said Wilf.

"And you're a human. So what?" She scowled. "Just because I'm born of stone doesn't mean that's *all* I am."

Wilf looked to the rest of us for help and found none. Like him, I'd assumed she'd have some sort of earth-based magic, but my Discernment attribute was just high enough that I knew better than to admit it. Besides, someone needed to keep an eye on the shadows around us. It'd been a while since our last attack, so we were due.

"Is blessing or skill?" asked Miko.

"*Water Sense?* It's a skill that came with my attunement."

I'd done enough Framework study by that point that I at least sort of knew what she was talking about. Mages, being obviously the *best* class on Eos, began with an attunement to an element or sub-element, and that attunement shaped the Major and Minor skills available to them. As they leveled, they could add a second attunement, although the process for doing so was mysterious, indescribably complex, and almost definitely involved a lot of study and experimentation.

To me, it seemed unfair they could double up on something as profound as *mastering an element of the physical realm*, but what did I know? Thanks to the gods and the system they'd created, I was just a Warrior with a pointy stick.

On the plus side, *I* could juggle. Sort of.

Nobody had any better ideas, so we started following Zamira's plan, letting her choose the direction whenever we reached an intersection with multiple usable tunnels. Two more attacks later, we'd finally reached twenty of the tunnel rat tails we needed for the guild mission, although that last attack had only been a single rat, and it had seemed almost reluctant to attack.

We found out why a few minutes later, when we came across a scene that could only be described as carnage.

"There's your swarm," said Wilf, doing a better job of holding back his queasiness than Barth or Zamira. "Or what's left of it."

Tunnel rat remains filled the tunnel, so thick that you couldn't see the stone floor beneath them. Nothing was in one piece, leading to a strange landscape of severed legs, shredded tails, and pulverized forms.

"A cave crawler didn't do this," said Miko. "At least I don't think so."

"Pygmy gyrs seem unlikely too," I said, "unless the pack was enormous. And a pack that size would need food, so it seems unlikely that they'd just leave this all behind."

"You don't think… the lupine cub did it?" asked Barth.

"According to the note, Greshal is four cycles old."

"So, probably not then?" His voice made it into a question.

Apsa, I would find out later, did *not* have a lot of lupine within its borders. It was one of the many things that separated Grand Duke Willerton's duchy from the rest of the kingdom.

"Whatever did this, they either took their dead with them, or didn't have any to leave behind. Either way, we don't want any part of them," I said, using my spear to clear a path so I could cross the tunnel without further ruining one of my sets of pants. "Nest-sister, can you bring the lantern over here?"

I had gained one *Tracking* point on our last patrol and still had the highest skill of us all, but it didn't take much talent to see multiple sets of bloody prints leading away from the battle.

The stone and lack of indentations made it impossible to judge things like weight distribution, but there appeared to be multiple markers to either side of something large that dragged along the floor. Like a snake with legs, maybe? I didn't remember anything like that from class. Assuming each set was one creature—and in that mess, it was a bold assumption to make—there'd been at least three of the creatures and they'd wiped out almost six times as many tunnel rats.

Of course, the tracks said they were also a *lot* bigger than the rats had been. A lot bigger than anything that should've been down here.

I pointed the tracks out to the rest of the party.

"Anyone have any idea what could make these?"

Barth started to shake his head, blinked, and leaned back in.

"The scale is off, but… when I was growing up, I briefly had a pet that the menagerie manager called a deathclaw? Eight legs, two claws, and a long tail with a stinger."

"Did it have an armored carapace?"

"I think so." He shrugged apologetically. "It got out of its cage one day and my brother's falcon tore it to pieces."

"Yes," said Zamira. "We had them up in the mountains south of Zaris. Their sting is venomous."

It was always dangerous to rely on Earth knowledge when it came to Eos, but it *sounded* like they were talking about a scorpion. And I had to admit that kind of fit the tracks we were looking at, now that I gave them a second look.

The problem was those same tracks told me *these* scorpions would have to be the size of mastiffs. Or even ponies.

"I don't want anything to do with them," I said again, nodding to the very edge of the lantern's light, where the tracks headed down a side tunnel to our left. "Hopefully, they'll head off one way, and we can go the other."

Zamira cleared her throat nervously. I knew even before she opened her mouth that I wasn't going to like what she had to say.

"The water's in the same direction that they went," she said.

Yep, I knew it.

Part of my brain spent the next fifteen minutes talking itself into a sort of cautious optimism. The slaughter of the tunnel rats had happened at least a few glasses earlier. The blood of the scorpion's trail had long since dried. It was not just possible but almost *reasonable* that the giant alien killing machines had long since vacated the general area.

The rest of my brain knew better. Since I'd arrived, Eos had been trying to kill me. Why would this be any different?

And so, when our tunnel opened up into a cavern, the pond on its far side illuminated by some sort of glowing pale moss, I wasn't at all surprised to see the dark, monstrous silhouettes of the creatures we'd been following.

Or even that there were *four* instead of three.

I was, however, more than a little surprised to see that these scorpions had upper halves that were humanoid enough to wield primitive weapons in addition to their claws and stingers.

○○○

The smart thing to do would have been to quietly make our way back up the tunnel to the nearest intersection and pick a new direction. There were almost definitely other bodies of water down here in the depths and they almost all had to be better destinations if we wanted to find the cub called Little Fuzz.

Two things stopped us though.

First, two of the four monstrous scorpion-people things were prowling back and forth along the far wall, just past the pond. One had a twisted piece of wood it used as a spear, and it appeared to be trying to find an angle to thrust it *into* that wall.

Second, the phosphorescent moss was enough to show a different kind of liquid, not far from that wall and the pond's edge.

Blood. Fresh enough that it hadn't yet dried.

We withdrew as quietly as we could, and I relayed my observations to the rest of the party.

"Those things have *something* cornered," I said in hushed tones, going off both what I'd seen and what my maxed-out *Animal Behaviorism* skill was telling me. "Maybe it's another tunnel rat or a pygmy gyr, but…"

"Could be cub," said Miko. "And if so, is injured."

"Exactly. The question is, do we risk what will almost definitely be a tough battle on the mere possibility that we've found Greshal?"

"What does our party leader think?" asked Barth.

"That this is something we all need to agree on," I replied flatly. I already had too many deaths on my conscience.

"Vote yes," said Miko. "I have *Touch of the Dawn* to help with venom, and plenty of energy for heals as well."

"I've only got two spells." Zamira looked pale in the lantern light. "But ample energy to cast both multiple times, as long as someone keeps the things off me."

Barth nodded. "The armored lower halves might be a problem for my arrows, but the torsos are another thing entirely. Like Zamira, I just need space."

"But do you want to attack them?" I asked them both.

"I don't know what they are," said the young nobleman, "but I don't think they're supposed to be here. And anything that would make a mess like the one we waded through doesn't seem like the kind of neighbor Trynfall wants to have."

Zamira shook her head. "I don't *want* to attack them, but I also don't want them coming up behind us in the darkness either. And honestly? I don't know if we'll find any other water sources before we have to turn back."

All eyes turned to Wilf, who shrugged.

"It's a nobleman's duty to die for his country, yeah?"

Barth either didn't detect the sarcasm or just plain ignored it, clapping our party Spy on the shoulder. "Well said."

"Okay." I blew out a breath. "We'll need to come in fast and make use of the advantage of surprise to kill or cripple at least one of the things. Two, if we can manage. In the absence of literally anyone else, I'll lead the charge, but we should set up at the entrance first. Zamira and Barth, pick out targets; when you see me move, let them have it. Wilf and Miko…"

"Will be right behind you, nest-brother," said Miko.

"Okay. Just… let them focus on me. Attack from the flanks."

"Yes. Will be like with sluthar."

Honestly? I could have done without the reminder of the last horrific beast/insect hybrid thing we'd fought, especially since we'd had to be rescued from *it* by Riok.

"I don't know what that is, and I don't think I want to either," said Wilf. "Between their tails and their weapons, I'm going to have to dart in and out. If you can keep their attention though, I should be able to land some hits."

It was not a great plan. A great plan would have had Skaal up front, weathering attacks the way only a Copper reaver could, while Lace danced the shadows in the service of her twisted goddess, and Mordecai rained down fire from afar. A great plan would have had Miko and I guarding the Mage's flanks and otherwise keeping out of trouble.

But two of those people were dead and the third was a long way away. We had to roll with what we had.

Dance with the one that brought you, as some old Earth song had once famously put it.

"We need to reduce their numbers as quickly as possible," I repeated. "Use your big abilities early. We'll deal with any cooldown issues as they arise."

"I really hope it's not another tunnel rat they've cornered," muttered Wilf.

That seemed as good a line as any to end it on. We crept back to the cave entrance, where our plan immediately went to shit.

Maybe we'd been too loud, or maybe the scorpion things could detect vibrations the same way their Earthborn equivalents could. Either way, as we made it to the cave entrance, we found one of the monsters clicking its way toward us, massive stinger poised to strike.

I didn't think. Thinking was death. I triggered *Liberating Lunge* and was there before the creature could react. Driven by the technique and my own growing strength, Riok's spear drove deep into the spot where the humanoid torso met the scorpion-like lower half.

I didn't stop, but yanked my spear out and thrust again, this time calling on *Deceptive Strike*. As the scorpion's pincers tore through the illusory image of my assault, I found myself behind the creature's torso, riding its carapace like it was a surfboard, my spear tearing through what passed for a humanoid head.

Deceptive Strike always did its best to put me in position for a critical strike and this time, its best was plenty. The tail just starting to unfurl sagged, and the monster did too, legs splaying outwards in uncontrolled, spasmodic motions.

The good news was that these things were much, much weaker than the centipede we'd fought south of Harborton. Weaker even than the gyr beasts in that same forest. They were dangerous, but they hadn't ascended.

The bad news was that there were still three of them, and I'd just blown through my techniques.

A stream of water tore through the twitching chest of the scorpion I'd already killed, but Barth at least managed to hold his fire. I leaped off the back of the collapsing scorpion, fumbled the landing, but managed to get up to my feet again to meet the first of the coming monsters.

No techniques now, just skill, as I tried to press a creature that had three massive weapons to my one, even before you counted the twisted length of wood in its hands.

It was a losing battle. Thanks to its long, armored tail, I didn't even have the advantage of reach.

Thankfully, I *did* have allies.

Something with only vague similarities to an arrow tore through the air past both me and my target, a silver nimbus wrapped about its form. It was answered, a heartbeat later, by a strangled screech of pain from a creature that clearly hadn't mastered speech. Splashing from somewhere beyond my opponent suggested Zamira had used her second spell, and if it wasn't the big damage dealer the first had been, it seemed to at least slow one of the three remaining enemies.

And as I gave grudging ground to the whirlwind of death that was my oversized opponent, Miko came in from its left flank, her half-staff beating a drum beat against oversized legs. Ironwood met chitinous armor, and I couldn't tell which got the worse end of things. Still, it was a distraction, and that allowed me to weave between pincers to strike at one of the inhuman arms of the humanoid upper half, forcing it to drop its only non-natural weapon.

If I could have, I'd have gone for the head instead. As it was, I still wasn't quite quick enough; a snapping pincer just missed severing my outstretched arm but hit me hard enough to hurl me to the ground. I held onto my spear and tried to roll with my fall, now having to dodge stomping pincers as well as everything else.

Then, Wilf was there, surrounded by a shadowy aura that made his movements difficult to follow. The scorpion reeled back from blows I couldn't see, and that was enough for me to find my feet again. Wilf darted back away, and I pushed in. My arm hurt but nothing seemed broken, and my spear practically thrummed through the air as I resumed my attack.

There was a snap to my left, and the mystery of ironwood vs. chitin was finally solved, as one of the creature's legs gave way to Miko's blows. The tail struck in a movement almost too fast to see, but Miko was already dodging aside. I whipped my spear about like a staff, batting one of the pincers down, then using the momentum of that collision to send my weapon streaking, point-first, toward the humanoid torso.

It was stopped cold inches from its target, caught by the second pincer, trapped between serrated edges that could snip off a limb as easily as they could tear a tunnel rat in half.

But if there was one thing I'd learned about the spear I'd inherited from Riok Diocil, it was that it didn't break. As the scorpion brought its might to bear on the weapon in its grasp, I pushed forward, putting all my Framework-enhanced strength to the task.

There was a horrendous screeching noise, coming not from the scorpion itself but from the contact points between spear and pincer. The weapon slid forward. An inch, then another. Pieces of carapace cracked and flecked away, unable to hold against the corroded-looking spear.

And then there was a squeal instead of a screech. The final inch of space disappeared, and the weapon's head slid smoothly into the monster's unprotected chest. The one pincer spasmed and fell away, even as the second came back around to bat at me. Thankfully, Miko was there with an overhand swing to smash it to the ground.

I took another step forward, pushed the spear all the way through the creatures' flailing humanoid body, pulled it out again, and this time drove it up under the weak chin and half-formed mandibles.

It wasn't *Deceptive Strike*, but the technique had already shown me where to hit, and that was enough. I barely got my spear out before the creature collapsed.

Two down, two to go, and I could already tell the difference our conditioning classes had made in the past moon. I was breathing heavily, but I wasn't relying purely on adrenaline to keep me moving.

As I rounded the two pony-sized bodies, Miko and Wilf fell in beside me.

The remaining monsters were advancing. The first had a hole, blackened and scorched, torn through both its scorpion body's right pincer and the humanoid torso above. Seven additional arrows sprouted from the unarmored form like pins in a map, though I hadn't seen any of them fly past us in the battle. Still, it was easy to separate the normal attacks from Barth's first technique-powered strike.

Until the young nobleman triggered his second technique.

Six of the seven arrows in the scorpion twitched, arresting the creature's movement. Those twitches sped up, creating a hum of vibration that widened the wounds each arrow had made. Two of the arrows snapped and stilled, but the others kept going, digging deeper into the target, turning impact points into craters and sending rivulets of black blood to splatter against the floor.

Behind us, Barth wheezed, his voice barely audible over the thing's piercing screams. "Who gives a child a deathclaw as a pet anyway? I was six!"

The last scorpion, the one that had been closest to the pond's edge, was moving slower and it took me a moment to see why: tendrils of water stretched out of the pond to tangle three of its too-many legs. Zamira's second spell was already fading, unfortunately, and it had done no damage at all.

Two scorpion monsters left, one on its last legs, one still whole. I was maybe fifteen seconds away from another usage of *Deceptive Strike*, but *Liberating Lunge* was ready again. I didn't use it but held my ground, letting the enemy expend their energy coming to us.

"Aim for the head, Barth!" shouted Wilf.

"What do you think I've been doing?!" came the reply.

Battle was a strange thing. Sometimes, it was a blur. Other moments stretched like taffy in the summer sun. We had plenty of time to eye the half-dead scorpion, its ravaged torso, its missing arm, and its entirely undamaged head. Wilf even had time to shake his head and mutter something under his breath.

Then the world was back in motion again, and two more killing machines were headed our way.

"I've got Barth's target," said Wilf, running past us. "You two take the other."

So far, Wilf had done the least damage of *any* of us, but there wasn't time to question him. The undamaged scorpion was coming in fast now, but it had enough intelligence to use its badly wounded companion as a partial shield.

That would have protected it against *Lunge*, but my very first technique had recently gotten an upgrade. The world blurred around me as I streaked *through* the first scorpion's extended pincer like Casper the unfriendly ghost.

My target reared back onto its hindlegs, spoiling my aim, and what should've been a strike to the head instead caught the creature in the chest. Maybe we could cut Barth some slack. Headshots were harder than they looked.

The more immediate problem was that I was left dangling from my spear, my feet off the ground.

Lesson #1 was *don't leave your spear*, but I was a sitting duck for the pincers already coming in from either side. If I'd been five inches taller, my feet would have still been on the ground. As it was, I lacked the leverage to pull out my spear. And that gave me no choice but to—

Wait.

I had one of those mid-battle epiphanies that Merrick had talked about in weapons class… brief moments crystallized in time where a thought emerged, one that would quickly prove to either be brilliance or folly.

It was time to find out which.

Instead of letting go of my spear, the only weapon besides Barth's bow that had proven truly effective against these things, I gripped it tighter. I jackknifed my body upward, kicking my legs up and out to find the one surface that, unlike the ground, *was* still in reach.

The scorpion's body.

As my boots thumped into its abdomen, I bent my knees to absorb the impact, then pushed out again, tugging on my spear as I used the creature as a springboard.

It turned out that Merrick was wrong. Some ideas were both genius *and* folly. It worked; I got my spear free and launched myself away before either pincer could close in on me. But then I landed, a few feet away and flat on my back, and the air blasted out of me from an impact neither my hauberk nor the gambeson underneath could nullify. I looked up to see a fist-sized stinger at the end of an armored tail, already lashing down.

I rolled but already knew I would be too slow, that the best I could hope for was to turn a sure death blow to something crippling. I caught a flash of red and orange out of the corner of my eye, Miko still rushing in, if far too late.

And then the stinger came crashing down and my world devolved into agony.

27

I had rolled just enough that the stinger didn't hit dead-on. Looking back, that was the only positive that could be taken from the situation. The stinger had driven into my side instead, breaking at least a few ribs as it drove a bone tip as sharp as any blade into my flesh. The venom came while my body was still reacting to those first agonies; a wave of burning spread out through my body from the impact site.

I don't know what I'd have done without my least favorite skill. Even with *Pain Tolerance*, my body seemed on the edge of locking up, going into shock, or just plain shutting down.

My spear was useless in this position, so I pulled my knife instead and drove it into the scorpion's tail just behind the bulb of the stinger.

It penetrated maybe an inch.

I could *feel* more venom being dumped into my body, but I was pinned. So, I stuck my blade back in the small hole I'd already made and wiggled around, trying to widen it. Hell if I was going to be able to actually sever the thing, but maybe I could inconvenience the scorpion enough to pull its stinger back?

Only, the wave of burning reached that arm and it went limp, leaving the blade sticking out of the tail like a stubby version of one of Barth's arrows. The scorpion loomed above me, insectile lower body next to its outstretched tail, and once again brought its pincers to bear.

A stream of concentrated water tore through the air above me and burrowed a hole through the creature, but it wasn't anywhere near enough to kill it. Next, a *Flare* burst into existence in front of the creature's face. It didn't have eyes, as far as I could tell, but it reeled back anyway, just as Miko finally arrived. She ignored the pincers that now threatened her as much as me, and even the makeshift wooden spear in the scorpion's humanoid hands and swung her half-staff at the tail instead.

It had taken her multiple blows to break even one of the previous monster's spindly legs; I could have told her she'd have far worse luck with the armored, muscular extra appendage.

Except… instead of hitting the tail, she struck the dagger still embedded in it, both momentum and synossian strength on her side. She drove the blade in up to its cross guard, and *that* finally forced the creature to react.

The stinger hurt just as much coming out as it had going in, but I was free. My arm wasn't working, I was bleeding like a stuck pig, and all that venom was doing whatever the hell it did as it spread, but I was free.

I was free and *Deceptive Strike* was off cooldown.

The technique could do a lot of things, but it required me to at least attempt an attack. I got my feet under me, one of them so numb I could barely feel the tingling in my toes, and surged upward, spear in the hand of the arm that still worked.

My thrust would have gotten me laughed out of weapons training. It was slow and weak and aimed at nothing vital, but it was still an attack, and that's all I needed.

Deceptive Strike.

My spear blurred and I blurred with it, reappearing a few feet away, not on the scorpion's back this time, but outside of its pincers. Something else inside of me tore with the movement, but my attack took it in the armpit, right below one of its outstretched human arms, and carved a path through.

Still, it stayed upright and on its feet, one of those waving pincers catching Miko in mid-swing and hurling her across the cave. I ignored the pain and pushed with my spear, trying to arrest the creature's momentum if I couldn't flip it over entirely.

The half-formed head turned to focus on me, and the tail that still had my dagger buried in it flicked back into motion.

And that was when Barth finally hit his shot.

An arrow sprouted out of the inhuman face, followed by another, a heartbeat later. The third struck the throat, triggering a fresh shower of blood, but the scorpion was already sagging, its tail hitting the ground like a localized earthquake, its legs going stiff.

It took me far too long to realize I was the only thing still holding it up. I tried to pull out my spear, failed, and just let it go instead, staggering to the side as the corpse followed its tail to the floor.

I didn't know what Wilf had done to finish off the final scorpion, but we were the only things still standing. The Spy reached me before Miko, hissing as he saw the state I was in. My nest-sister was there, moments later, and for the second time that day, *Light Healing* washed over me. A few bones knitted back together, the blood flow slowed noticeably and that was it.

It wasn't anywhere near enough.

"Will cast again as soon as I can," she told me, clutching her own side where she'd been hit. "But first, should treat venom."

"Wait, Miko!" Zamira had reached us too, and she was pointing at the far side of the cave, where a small black lupine had emerged from its hidey hole. It crawled forward on four paws, moving in an uncertain wobble, and then collapsed.

We'd found Greshal, and by the looks of things, he was near death.

"Go," I told Miko through gritted teeth. The cub wasn't even half my size. If he'd been stung…

She left me with Wilf and hurried over to the fallen lupine. A sharp gasp and the look she sent told the story.

"Do it," I said, in a voice so quiet Wilf had to repeat my words. "I'll hold until the cooldown is over."

The light that formed around Miko's clawed hand was golden, the first touch of the sun on the sea. It moved from her to Greshal's chest, surrounding the lupine cub.

Touch of the Dawn.

I didn't get a chance to see the results, because Wilf had gone from supporting me to trying to staunch my bleeding.

It was the right idea.

It was probably even necessary.

But it also sent me spiraling into darkness.

○○○

I woke to Miko's face, orange, sclera-less eyes looking down at me worriedly. When she saw I was awake, she breathed a sigh of relief.

"How are you, nest-brother?" she asked in the High Tongue.

The most accurate answer was *not good*, but that wasn't a productive response. So, I went with the runner-up option.

"Better. I think." I winced as I sat up and looked down at the torn rings in my hauberk and the rip in the underlying padded vest. I wasn't actively bleeding anymore, as far as I could tell, but I was a long way from full health. One thing notably absent, however, was the burning sensation that had been sweeping through my body. "*Touch of the Dawn?*"

"Just finished casting it." She looked exhausted. "Once for Greshal, once for you. And a *Light Healing* for each of you, followed by a *Minor Healing* to at least get your wound to clot."

"But it worked? With Greshal, I mean?"

A tired smile, not at all terrifying, made its way onto her face. "It did. He is still asleep. Zamira is watching him, while Wilf and Barth watch the tunnel."

Apparently, I'd been out longer than I realized. Still, I couldn't help but notice that she was still slightly hunched over. "What about you?"

Miko looked away. "Both *Light Healing* and *Touch of the Dawn* are expensive. I only switched to *Minor Healing* for the last casting because I was almost out of energy."

"We need to get out of these tunnels before something else comes calling," I decided. "Can you walk?"

"I am in better shape than you are. And sorely tempted to yell at you even though I know this is not entirely your fault."

"What?"

"This is not Madea, nest-brother. We are a team. You need to stop running ahead and getting yourself hurt." She pulled her soiled robes around her, then winced at the motion. "I barely reached you in time there at the end. We should have waited and taken on that last monster together."

That was…

I scowled. She wasn't wrong. I'd seen a chance to use *Liberating Lunge* and I'd taken it, but if there was one thing Ebb and Flow had continuously railed on, it was that nobody in the early ranks was an army unto themselves. Small Group Tactics was about leveraging everyone's strengths to minimize our weaknesses. Charging ahead solo was the opposite of that.

"You're right," I said, the admission hurting almost as much as my side. "I'll do better."

"*We'll* do better," she corrected. "I have much room for improvement, and not just when it comes to managing my energy levels."

"Something to work on," I agreed, "*after* we make it safely back to the city."

Miko handed me my spear and helped me to my feet, where I simultaneously appreciated how much better I now felt and how low that bar apparently had been set. The synossian's pack was lying nearby, suspiciously overstuffed.

"Trophies from the scorpion things?" I asked in Trade.

"No, but that's not a bad idea, yeah?" said Wilf, coming over to join us.

"Found Last Breath herb growing at water's edge," said Miko. "Was one of plants that provided glow. Used some to numb wounds, left enough to regrow. Now have twenty sprigs and twenty tails."

"I'd say that was convenient, but given that we all nearly just died, I'll take it." I took a few experimental steps around. I wasn't doing great, but I thought I might be able to fight.

I also really, really hoped I wouldn't have to.

The four scorpion things lay where they'd fallen. In death, they didn't look that tough. Horrifically alien, yes, but not tough. In fact, they were small enough that it was amazing I'd been able to ride that first one's back after using *Deceptive Strike*.

With an effort, I keyed back in on what Wilf had said.

"You think it would be worth it to bring trophies back?"

"The venom in the tails might be worth something," he said, "assuming it doesn't go bad after their deaths. But I was thinking more so we have something to show the guards."

That got Miko's attention. "Why?"

"These things, whatever they are, aren't supposed to be here."

"Yes. But now they are dead."

"Agreed. Only… I don't see a nest around here, do you?"

That brought us both up short. He was right. The cavern, lit by the phosphorescent plants and our still functional lantern, was empty of anything that would qualify as either a nest or a camp.

Which meant they might have been staying elsewhere.

And that there might be even more of the things out there.

"If this is an actual incursion, the guard needs to know. Even if it's not, it's clear it's been too long since the last sweep." Wilf tapped the hilt of one of his daggers. "Maybe it'll be another Adventurer's Guild mission, or maybe they'll come down themselves. Either way, nobody's going to believe us without proof."

That made sense. A lot of people were making sense since I'd woken up.

"Okay. You're right. We should bring at least one of the tails back with us. I'd want all four if I thought we could carry them." As it was, Zamira was the only person other than Miko who'd brought a pack for what we'd assumed would be the work of a few glasses.

"Just one would be best," agreed Wilf. "If there are any more tunnel rats out there, I don't want to have my arms full when they attack."

His even saying that made me tired.

"I'll carry Zamira's pack so she can carry Greshal," I decided. "I'm not sure the weight's going to make a difference to how I fight anyway."

"Warriors," said Wilf, shaking his head. "Always tougher than the rest of us put together."

That… hadn't been what I meant at all, but I let it go. Morale was a thing, and if he and the others thought I was in better shape than I really was, it would only help.

Miko, as our party healer, and the one person even more familiar with my wounds than me, gave me a long look that said absolutely everything. Still, she held her peace. My nest-sister clearly had a higher Discernment stat than me.

Anyway, we ended up fitting two of the tails in Zamira's pack instead of just one.

ooo

Wilf hadn't been wildly effective in our battles, but he proved his value again once we started out, leading us back up through the maze of tunnels with only a handful of wrong turns and miscues. He stayed up front with Miko and the lantern, with Zamira and Greshal close behind, followed by me and then Barth.

In retrospect, my place in the formation made it clear everyone knew I was a mess. At the time, the thought never even entered my mind.

Healing took energy from the patient as well as the healer, which was half of why I felt like a truck had run me over. The other half, of course, was the unfinished nature of my healing. The longer we walked, the more I drifted. Things hurt, especially once the anesthetic properties of the Last Breath wore off, but *Pain Tolerance* handled that, for the most part. Thoughts, on the other hand, remained slow to come by and swift to fade, leaving me trudging along like an automaton.

At some point, Greshal stirred in Zamira's arms, asking half-formed questions in a confused series of yips, and without thinking, I responded in kind.

The cub settled back to sleep, and I didn't even notice the looks sent my way by the rest of our party. Yeah, I spoke the lupine language. So what?

We didn't get attacked a single time on our way back. I didn't know if it was the scorpion stench warning other creatures off or if the tunnel rats had just been cleared out of this section, and *Animal Behaviorism* wasn't giving any answers.

Once we reached the well-lit, regularly patrolled upper tunnels, we had to backtrack a bit to find where the lantern we'd *borrowed* had come from. It had gotten banged about a fair bit in some of our fights, but we hung it on its hook, secure in the knowledge that some initiates would come by, refill the oil, and light it again if it went out in the interim.

Hell, we might even end up being those initiates.

After that, it was a half-glass to the nearest guard post. I stood like a zombie as Wilf spoke with them, the Spy being our group's only local noble. Both the scorpion tails were removed from the pack on my back, triggering a reaction from the guards that mostly just washed over me like a spring rain.

Something was said about the guard captain and an investigation, but like most of the noises around me, those words kind of just floated by. Soon enough, we were on our way again. Wilf and Barth headed for the lift up to the Middle City, while Miko, Zamira, and I found the exit that led back out to the Lower City.

The afternoon sun hit me like a hammer between the eyes. It seemed wrong for it to still be daytime, like when Bug and I would see a matinee movie and then emerge from the theater's darkness to find the world heading off to lunch. It helped wake me up though, as did the crisp, cold air of Trynfall in winter. Even the smell of the docks helped in its own way: fish and the sulfur-like smell I recognized from our time in Harborton.

I was awake enough and alert enough to notice the way the crowds in the Lower City peeled back to make way for the three of us. Even Zamira was splattered with blood and far grosser liquids after our many battles down in the tunnels, and I was later told I marched like a man headed to do murder.

Given I was using my spear as a walking stick as much as a weapon, I don't know how that was possible, but the reactions of the crowds seemed to bear it out.

We encountered several guards and at least one arbiter on our way through the Lower City, but Zamira's status as an official ward of the duke who'd kidnapped her helped us smooth the way. Eventually, we reached the Adventurer's Guild, where our entrance was… largely ignored. After all, it wasn't *every* day that adventurers returned bloody but victorious, but it wasn't exactly uncommon either.

"Will get rat tail mission," said Miko, peeling off. It was my turn to take the lead, heading for the clerk desks at the rear of the guild hall. I spotted Ulla on duty behind one of the desks and headed for her.

"Adventurer Fieldings!" She made a show of looking me up and down. "I guess I don't need to ask where you've been!"

With effort, I strung my words together.

"We wanted to turn in some missions."

"You know, once a mission is claimed, it's yours. You don't have to worry about anyone swooping in and stealing your reward." When I gave her a look as blank as an unwritten page, she leaned in. "I mean turn-ins can generally wait until *after* you've visited the baths."

"Not this time." I stepped to the side, revealing the lupine cub in Zamira's arms.

"*Oh.*" She peered closer with her too-human eyes. "Is he…?"

"Just sleeping," Zamira assured her.

"We'll need the address of his grandsire," I said.

"Also must turn in Last Breath sprigs," said Miko, joining us and hefting her pack onto the desk.

"The mission called for only twenty sprigs," said Ulla, checking her notes and eying the overfull pack.

"Might have enough items to complete third mission too." Miko had the parchment for the tunnel rat elimination mission in her free hand.

By guild rules, we couldn't actually *claim* a third mission until one of our first two had been officially completed. Thankfully, Ulla didn't seem to care, so long as we did things in the proper order. She called over another clerk—this one the first male and non-corbin we'd dealt with—who immediately set to counting out the sprigs of Last Breath that had been gathered during my nap.

"I'll need to verify this is the lupine cub specified," said Ulla, the feathers on her long neck flaring briefly in what I thought was embarrassment. "Not that I think you'd just nab some child off the street and try to pass it off, especially for a single bit…"

"It's fine." I turned to Zamira and the ball of fluff in her arms. "Greshal," I said borrowing the lupine language I'd only just learned, "it's time to wake up."

"Hungry," he yipped in reply, trying to burrow deeper into Zamira's chest. "Tired."

"I'm sure you are. We'll get you some food on your way back home."

That got through to him, and he cracked open one wolf-like eye. "Food?"

"Soon. Do you speak any Trade? This nice corbin needs to verify who you are."

The cub yawned, exposing a maw that was somehow adorable despite all the sharp teeth, and looked about until he spotted Ulla. "HellomynameisgreshalandIamnotmean," he said in squeaky Trade. Closing his eyes again, he switched back to his native tongue. "Warm and soft."

"*And to think Papa said I didn't have a maternal vein in my heart gem,*" rumbled Zamira in the secret tongue that nobody else seemed able to hear. "*By the Wanderer and the Wild, he is so* cute!"

If I'd been fully conscious, my reaction would have been impossible to hide, even with *Deception.* In all my time on Eos, this was the first mention I'd heard of the Wild other than the title I'd earned on the walls of Madea.

I just… needed to figure out a way to ask Zamira about it, without admitting that I'd been listening to her private speech.

That sounded like a task for future-Brian to figure out.

"Is that enough to count as identification?" I asked Ulla.

"Of course it is. We just needed to follow protocol." She gave me another look, one that I could recognize as odd even on her bird-like features. "You know, I don't think I've ever met a human who spoke the lupine tongue."

"I wanted to be a Scholar before I became an adventurer," I said, falling back on the old lie. "Languages were one of my passions."

"If you want to learn corbin, I might know a girl." Her too-human eyes sparkled.

"Hmmm," murmured Miko in the High Tongue, "Maybe city women are not as immune as I'd thought."

"Twenty-one sprigs of Last Breath," announced the unnamed clerk who'd been counting out our haul. He left them laid out and returned to his own desk, unprompted.

"We can return the extra sprig?" said Ulla.

"Yes, please," said Miko. "Can use in tinctures."

"Of course." Ulla picked up a quill and wrote down a note. "That will be one plug, six bits for the herb retrieval and…" she coughed. "One bit for the successful rescue and retrieval of the lupine cub. Of Greshal," she corrected.

Greshal, hearing his name, opened one eye, then let it drift shut again.

"Would like to claim new mission," said Miko.

"Before you do…" Ulla turned to Zamira. "Are you a member of the Adventurer's Guild, miss?"

"Me? No."

"Would you like to be? The guild welcomes people from all walks of life, and you wouldn't be our first o'naseri member."

"I… don't know?"

Ulla moved into sales mode like it was a career she'd been looking for her entire life. "There *is* a nominal fee for membership, but the reason I'm asking is if we get you registered as a provisional member *before* these upstanding guildmembers claim their new mission, you could get credit for its completion as soon as they turn it in."

"That's kind of brilliant," I admitted, winning me another ruffle of feathers. This one was… *pleased*, I thought?

"How much is the membership fee?" asked Zamira.

"A one-time payment of a single copper plug."

The Zarisian winced. "Is there any way of lowering that?"

"I'm afraid not. But if you three keep running missions, I think it will pay for itself in no time."

"And once you've completed enough missions to become a full member, we could take three missions at a time instead of two," I realized. "That really *is* smart."

I didn't know what sort of bird species was in Ulla's family tree, but I was starting to think it was a bird of prey, because she was looking at me in a way that made me feel distinctly like a snack.

"Are we *going* to keep running missions?" Zamira asked Miko.

My nest-sister nodded. "Need the money. And the experience."

"That's true. If I don't level from today's…" She shuddered. "Well, I'll be very surprised. Still, I almost got us all killed today by panicking and wasting my first spell."

"Nothing ever goes entirely right," I told her. "That's why we train as a team."

Ulla leaned in over the desk. "It sounds like there's a story there."

"There is," I admitted. "But we should get Greshal back home as soon as we're done here. Another time?"

"I'll hold you to that."

In short order, we had Zamira registered for the guild. Shortly after that, we turned in the tunnel rat tails, completing our third mission of the day and her first.

It paid out far more than the gathering quest had, netting us an additional two plugs and three bits.

We'd earned four plugs, all-in, if we counted the single copper bit for Greshal's retrieval. I wouldn't say it had been *easy*, but the scorpion things also hadn't been part of the plan. With them gone now, this seemed like a great way to grind for money and levels.

Hell, maybe two crowns isn't entirely out of reach.

That thought lasted just long enough for basic math to rear its head and squash it flat again. If a single golden crown was a hundred towers, it was a *thousand* plugs. At four plugs a seven-day, that would take us two-hundred-and-fifty such hauls to get a single crown. And *five hundred* to get two.

And that was *before* I realized we'd have to share our proceeds with everyone in the party. I wasn't sure about keeping a party share, like Lace did, since we weren't *actually* roaming around adventuring, but everyone had played their role in today's delve, and everyone deserved to profit from it.

Once again, the dream of owning an adornment to see in the dark died a pitiful death.

∘∘∘

Address for Greshal's grandsire in hand, we made our way back out into the Lower City. On the way, we bought meat on a stick from one of the few vendors who *didn't* seem convinced we were going to rob him, kill him, and wear his skin as a hat, only possibly in that order. Two bits got us enough meat for everyone. Even Greshal woke up just long enough to nearly take Zamira's fingers off as she fed him before he drifted to sleep again.

We had to stop for directions a few times, as the Lower City was a mishmash of neighborhoods and alleys once you got past the market, but eventually found our way to a dilapidated shack on a rundown street. The best thing I could say about it was that it *wasn't* the synossian enclave. There was a vague sense that the people there cared at least a little bit about *their* community. The inhabitants weren't all lupine either, which was a refreshing change from some of the single-species ghettos we'd encountered so far.

Still, the deeper we'd traveled, the more Zamira's face had closed itself like a fan. She and Miko had traded a few quiet words back and forth while I trudged along.

The door to the shack opened before we reached it. An old lupine in what could have been a bathrobe back on Earth limped outside, eyes closed and wolf-like nose twitching.

"Gresh? Little Fuzz?" he called.

The ball of fluff in Zamira's arms stirred to life and just like that, Greshal was leaping down to charge his grandsire. He ran first on four legs, then on two, and wrapped his arms around the older lupine's leg. His *good* leg.

Zamira and Miko looked to me to translate the yipping that followed, but I just shook my head. It wasn't anything they needed to hear; just a scared little boy telling his grandsire the terrifying tale of his journey into the deeps.

When the tale was done, the old lupine looked our way.

"You… has… gratitude," he began in halting Trade.

"Grandsire, it's okay! The short one speaks Cantus!" said Greshal with a laugh, giving me the name for their language.

"We were glad we were able to find him," I said. "And return him home to you."

"I am Cailus. My hearth is yours to share, now and forever," he said, including Zamira and Miko in the gesture. "Greshal is all I have left of my son, his sire. He means everything."

I translated the words so the others could understand. Miko and Zamira exchanged glances and my nest-sister stepped forward.

"He is a brave child," she said carefully, "and deserves a bright future."

As I translated her speech, she knelt next to Greshal, took his paw in hers, and closed it around something that glittered copper in the late afternoon sun.

"Will not take money to do something that needed doing," she told Cailus, rising back to her feet.

Again, I played the role of translator, and Cailus gave a strange sort of bow, front paws crossed in front of his chest and wolf-like head tilted to one side. When he straightened, there was a strength to his voice that suggested the man he might have been in his prime.

"For his sake and his alone, I will not refuse your generosity. But a debt is owed. Please, give me your names, all of you." We did so, and he nodded solemnly. "Know that if you call, I will come."

"Me too!" yipped his grandpup, earning himself a pat on the head. "I'll help!"

"Would like to return another day and look at leg, if possible," said Miko. "Might be able to help."

"She made my hurts better," agreed Greshal, tail wagging as he swapped between Trade and Cantus in a flow that was bewildering even *with* my *Speaker of Tongues* trait.

"There are wounds and then there is simple age," said Cailus, once I had repeated Miko's words. "You have done enough. There is only so much debt one such as I can hold."

"Aurea does not see debt," said Miko. "Only what has been done and what should be done."

It was pure Miko and undeniably heartfelt, but I gave her a nudge. Cailus was clearly overwhelmed and just as clearly doing his best to hide what he perceived as his weakness.

"Another time," I said. "I think we should leave these two to their reunion."

"Go in peace with our gratitude," said Cailus. "And may your hunts be forever successful."

We were a few blocks away before anyone spoke.

"How much did we give them?" I asked.

Zamira dropped her eyes, but Miko knew me well enough to predict my reaction. "Ten bits," she said. "Did not think giving plug was wise in that neighborhood. Bits are easier to spend."

Leaving us with three plugs, to be split between five people. Midton Brian would have had to call on a non-existent *Deception* skill to keep the wince from his face, but *he'd* been dealing with a mortgage, medical bills, and more credit card debt than anyone should ever see. Trynfall Brian just nodded. We were still up for the day, and my share would likely pay for the repairs to my hauberk.

"Worth it," I decided.

○○○

It was still Seventh Day, and after we found a guard to safely bring Zamira back to the Middle City, I insisted on following Miko to her people's enclave. The crowd melted away like snow in the rain when it became apparent we *hadn't* brought food this time, but still, a handful stuck around to hear her sermon.

That sermon was short, because it had been a very long day and neither of us was entirely whole. One of the two community leaders—the young firebrand whose name was, unexpectedly, Joshua—was concerned enough about our condition that he actually escorted us back out of the neighborhood.

Considering he'd been the one to kick Miko out of the warehouse on that very first day, that meant something.

By the time we reached the dorms at the Tryn, I wanted to do nothing more than sleep. Instead, I headed for the baths, where I walked straight into the steaming water. The current rinsed the filth from both my clothes and body, carrying it elsewhere.

"Commoners," muttered someone, my first clue that I wasn't the only initiate in the baths. "Can't take them anywhere civilized, can't harvest the fields without them."

For the first time in a while, I let myself appreciate that Wilf and Barth were the rare nobles who *weren't* dicks.

I used my spear to help myself climb back out of the baths—because of course I'd brought it into the massive basin with me—and hobbled back to our dorm room once I was dry again.

Meditation was the last thing I wanted to do, but that was how life worked sometimes. I gingerly lowered myself down to my bed and did my best to block out the pain of my ribs as I let the experiences of the day, the battles fought and wounds taken, the fear and the hope and the *satisfaction,* all flow through me. There were lessons to be learned from all of it, I knew, but we could leave those for class. For now, I just wanted to see if and how my soul had grown from the experience.

When I opened my eyes again, the answers were clear:

> **You have increased the following skills:**
>
> **Major skills:**
> Formations [+3]: 20/40
> Knife [+1]: 36/40
> Medium Armor [+2]: 30/40
> Spear (U) [+3]: 38/40
> Tactics [+2]: 37/40
>
> **Minor skills:**
> Acrobatics [+1]: 4/40
> Athleticism [+1]: 36/40
> Avoidance [+1]: 36/40
> Focus [+3]: 30/40
> Leadership (U) [+3]: 11/40
> Pain Tolerance -> Pain Tolerance (Uncommon)
> Pain Tolerance (U) [+5]: 40/40
> Toxin Resistance (U) [+1]: 1/40
>
> **General skills:**
> Diplomacy [+1]: 4/10
> Tracking [+1]: 7/10

Holy crap.

Not only had I gained points in virtually every Major and Minor skill I had, *Pain Tolerance* had both upgraded from Common to Uncommon *and* once again become my first skill to cap out for the level. *Spear*, *Medium Armor*, and *Tactics* were all just a few points away too. And I'd even picked up a new Uncommon skill: *Toxin Resistance*.

There was no question how I'd earned that one. I just... really hoped there'd be an easier way to level it now that it was mine.

28

"Which brings us to one of the least-understood aspects of the Framework: ranking. Why is it that the otherwise orderly progression of power from one to a presumed infinity gets interrupted by these breakpoints every ten levels? And if a level ten, unranked Aspirant and a level ten, Tin-ranked Aspirant are both, by their very definition, the same level … how can they be so very different?"

Professor Lunsford didn't wait for any guesses. "The answer is that the Framework does not process advancement purely on a quantitative level, but also a qualitative one. Who here has a skill ranked above Common?"

About half of us raised our hands.

"And above Uncommon?"

The number of raised hands dropped to two, one of them mine.

"And what did you notice, as you progressed your skill from Common to Uncommon to Rare and above? Mr. Fieldings?"

I cleared my throat. "I don't know. The only skill I have at Rare was already at that rank when I got it."

"*Bullshit*," coughed Ames, the only other person with her hand raised.

"It has been known to happen," said Lunsford, "albeit rarely, if you'll pardon the pun. What about you, Ms. Thasker?"

"A Rare-ranked skill is more effective than the Uncommon-ranked version of that skill, and both are more effective than the Common-ranked version." She shrugged her heavy shoulders.

"Even though the numbers are the same?"

"Of course. Everyone knows that."

"I would warn you not to underestimate the world's ignorance, but this class focuses upon the Framework and not the inadequacies of Eos' many education systems."

The professor, I had noticed over the past few seven-days, made an awful lot of points while telling us he was going to refrain from making those same points.

"The existence of ranks, even when it comes to skills, demonstrates exactly what I am talking about. There are aspects to our advancement that remain only vaguely represented in the personal records the Framework provides. Which may be why so many aspects of that underlying system remain open to interpretation. Let's return to the subject at hand, however. What does being a Tin-ranked Aspirant mean?"

After a long moment of silence, he looked around our circle of chairs. "That was not a rhetorical question."

"It means being better," said Georgie, still seated to my right, all these classes later.

"True, if remarkably vague."

"It means being more," I offered.

Our professor raised an eyebrow. "More what?"

"More… you?" I shrugged. "That's what I was told anyway."

"Correct," said Lunsford.

"Wait. How was that less vague than *my* answer?"

"It benefits from being more *accurate*," said Lunsford. "A Tin-ranked individual has a greater metaphysical weight in both the physical and spiritual realms. A Copper even more so. And if you are ever fortunate or unfortunate enough to feel Dame Credence's aura, you will understand that this progression continues through Iron and beyond."

"Even if that's the end effect of ranking, I still don't understand how the process works," said Prisa, Ames' blonde friend. "How do you reach Tin in the first place?"

"You'll be happy to know that your confusion has long been shared by many scholars in the field. Shai Mulvinus spent a full ten cycles of his life interviewing ranked Aspirants for their takes on the process and came away with only anecdotes instead of answers." The professor shrugged. "All these cycles later, we do know a few things. First, in order to increase in rank, you must have first reached the maximum level for your current rank, in much the same way that leveling requires a certain number of capped skills. Second, you must have earned an Ideal, the Framework's acknowledgment of some concept you hold in your heart and soul. Third, once you reach the requisite level, you can rank at any time. It is the *sole* form of progression that does not first require some form of focused communion with the Framework."

I knew for a fact that the last part of that wasn't true, not that I was going to share that knowledge with the class. The quests I got from the Framework also happened outside of the meditation loop. And I was pretty sure I'd ranked up *Spear* in the middle of a battle, even if the notification hadn't come until later.

"Lastly," continued Lunsford, "ranking requires that you develop an understanding, not just of yourself or your Ideal, but of how those two coincide. Who are you, who do you want to be, and how does your Ideal factor into that?"

"Stefan calls it spiritual navel-gazing," said Ames.

"Your lord brother is many things," said Lunsford with a smile, "but I think you will agree he is a count first and an Aspirant second."

"I'm not sure he's considered himself an Aspirant at all since graduating," she said with a broad smile. "Good thing he's so skilled at making pretty speeches."

"Yes, well." The professor cleared his throat. "Even with this knowledge, most people find their progression ends at level ten. If leveling is the process of strengthening your soul, ranking is the act of reshaping it. Every rank requires you to improve both your understanding of who you are and your image of who you will become. The act gets harder each tier."

"Does that mean that people are better the higher ranked they are?" asked Roban, a dark-haired, serious-faced man I only ever saw in this class and Basic Conditioning.

"Better in what way? A scholar must be precise in their words."

"Morally."

"Definitely not," I said.

"Trust our resident adventurer to have experience with such things," said Lunsford. "Mr. Fieldings is correct. Just as the Framework is neither good nor bad, progress within its structures is not tied to morality. A killer who is certain in themself might rank just as easily as a knight hero. More easily, even, as certain kinds of mental maladies lend themselves to extremely strong senses of self."

I had a lot more questions, and I wasn't alone in that, but the bells were already ringing, signaling the end of class. As I waited to speak to Professor Lunsford, Ames made a show of pushing past me on her way out the door.

I traded glances with Prisa, trailing behind Ames as always. "Did I do something to irritate her?"

She hesitated and lowered her voice. "Yes."

I waited.

"Ames is a Mage."

"And?" Given the other woman's build, that was a surprise, but I still didn't see what it had to do with me.

"And she's in the bottom third of our class. She had planned to make up some of that ground through ranking duels."

"And *I* changed that, somehow?"

"Everyone knows it was you who told your scaled—"

"Synossian."

"Whatever. You're the one that told her to set 'no techniques' as the terms for her duel, right?"

In actual fact, Miko had been the one who came up with the idea; I'd simply supported it. Regardless, I nodded.

"Sure."

"Well, anyone that *Ames* challenges gets to choose terms too."

I thought those ramifications through.

"Oh."

"Exactly. How is a Mage supposed to win a duel if her opponent decides to disallow techniques?"

That was a really good point. Still, even if Ames wasn't as fit or as skilled as, for example, Mireille, she was plenty physically imposing.

"Can't she just beat them up?"

Prisa sniffed and turned away. "You really *don't* know anything."

I watched her go, not sure what to say. It's not like we had *invented* the loophole. Surely, there were ways around it? Or were Mages usually either content with their rankings or academic-minded enough to not find themselves at the bottom?

The room emptied out, leaving only Professor Lunsford and I behind. He gave me a look as I approached.

"Is there something else I can help you with, Mr. Fieldings?"

"Sort of. When I was doing some of the pre-class readings, I kept running into a few mentions of *foundation*. What is that?"

"Either utter nonsense or the secret to long-term progression, depending on who you ask." He grinned at whatever expression popped up on my face. "Welcome to academia. But to answer your question *less* succinctly, there are those who believe there to be another aspect to progression under the Framework. We should not just strengthen and reshape our souls but broaden them as well. As any housewright would tell you, the taller the building, the wider and stronger the foundation that is required." He shrugged. "Does the same hold true for the soul? I don't know. Studies have proved inconclusive, but that's often the problem with a course of study where there are so few high performers. Give me a hundred Gold-ranked Aspirants and I might better be able to test the hypothesis."

I had a hard time imagining that many Golds. Nobody living in the kingdom of Elthor had ascended past Bronze. Still …

"Any suggestions on how to develop that foundation?"

"I have many, all of them unproven." He ticked them off on his fingers. "Learn more skills. Visit more places. Experience more things. Love someone, lose them, then love again. Perhaps one of the easiest things to do would be to learn a profession."

"But… I'm an Aspirant, not a Dedicated."

"Which defines only your focus. As you know, there is no reason you cannot have both a class and a profession. A large number of your fellow initiates have professions already."

"They do? What?"

"Nobleman or Noblewoman. It's something that is theirs by birth. A bare handful will swap that profession out for Baron, Count, or other such professions once they take over their houses." He shrugged again. "That's not an option for you, of course, but there's nothing preventing you from earning a profession yourself. And you're going to eventually need something to do when you have downtime as an adventurer. The way I hear it, it's either that or drinking yourself into an early grave."

I gave that some thought as I headed out. Miko had at one point been trying to earn a profession as an Herbalist and I'd thought about using my trait to become a Scribe, but those ideas had been more about income than anything greater. Still, if it somehow fed back into giving my soul the foundation I'd need to grow as an Aspirant too?

Well, that seemed worthwhile.

ooo

It was too early for dinner, so I headed back to the dorms to read and maybe juggle. Miko was going to spend the afternoon with Zamira after her elective, which meant I'd have the room to myself… and also meant I wouldn't risk moving up to four knives just yet.

In some ways, Lunsford's Framework class had been a disappointment. I'd gone in expecting answers and guides and instead gotten history lessons, popular theories, and even philosophy. At the same time, I left every class with more to think about, and today's session was no exception. Between what Riok, Kacellius, and now Lunsford had all said about ranking to Tin, I felt like I had a pretty good grasp on what I'd need to do to get there. And it involved a lot of self-reflection, one of my least favorite activities.

I had three levels to go before ranking became a concern, but something told me it would be worth it to put in the work long *before* I hit level ten.

For once, there were people in the common room: Mireille, Darishal, and another of the nobles in her faction. If the Political

Relations students had already had time to return to the dorm, my talk with Lunsford must have gone longer than I realized.

Whatever conversation the three were having cut off as I came in. I wasn't sure why. If they'd been spilling secrets, they'd have done it somewhere other than the common room. And Mireille didn't seem the type anyway. Unless she *was* that type and seeming otherwise was part of her strategy. The one thing I knew after my time at the Tryn was that I didn't know a damn thing about nobles or how they operated.

I started to walk by, trading a nod with Darishal while the others studiously ignored me, then forced myself to stop. It had been almost a week, and I still needed to take care of something.

"Mireille," I said, stepping over to the cushioned couches, "can we talk?"

She gave me a look and then turned to her cronies. "Give us a moment, please? I'll see you at the Stag."

"The Stag?" I asked, once they were gone.

"It's a restaurant on one of the Lower City's upper levels." Her voice was even, her tone somewhat clipped, but that didn't mean much. She seemed to approach most conversations as, at minimum, sparring contests, and was as economical with her emotions as she was her attacks. "I had nothing to do with Gareth's challenge, but something tells me you're not going to believe me."

"Would you, if you were in my shoes?"

"Knowing as little as you do? Probably not." She ran a hand through her cropped hair. "Of course, I'd take steps to combat that ignorance, rather than whatever it is you've been doing."

"Keeping to ourselves, mostly."

"How's that working for you?"

"Not great, but probably still better than the alternative."

"I heard you went down into the tunnels last Seventh Day."

"We're adventurers," I reminded her. "We have to make money somehow."

"Well, whatever you found there has people stirred up. I'm told they might send the guard on a deep sweep for the first time in more than a cycle."

I hadn't heard that, but then, we hadn't heard *anything* since turning in our scorpion tails five days earlier. I was really hoping that would change soon… and that a reward of some sort was coming.

But that wasn't what I'd wanted to talk to Mireille about.

"You have handmaidens working for you, right?"

As subject changes went, it wasn't my smoothest.

Seated on the couch, she had to look up at me for probably the first time in our mutual existence. "I'm a lady of Trynfall and the heir to House Marchon. I have *several* handmaidens, though none reside here at the Tryn with me. What of it?"

"I wanted to speak with you about one of them."

She sighed. "Carmella is taken. Or so she claims. For now. Until next seven-day probably, at which point, she'll pull a name from a hat and be taken once again. Honestly, I had thought better of you, adventurer. And of her."

I genuinely had no idea what she was talking about.

"I don't know a Carmella. I was asking about Elina d'Kay."

Mireille's already-hard gaze went positively arctic. "Elina is a sweet girl, but she only has twelve cycles to her name. It would be one thing for her house to promise her to another, but if you are suggesting what I think you are suggesting, we will have words, and those words will be followed by an honor duel to *more* than just first blood. I can promise you that."

I held up both hands. "That's not what this is about. At all." Before she could find some new way to read terrible things into my words, I continued. "I have a letter for her. From Baron Sakeld."

"What would *he* want—" She trailed off. "Wait. Baron Sakeld passed away, didn't he? Are you talking about his heir?"

"Yes. Eustace. We stopped in Sakeld on our way from Madea. He asked me to find Elina and give her his letter."

She digested that for a few seconds. "A letter that he chose not to send through official channels."

"I don't think he felt his mother would approve."

"And now you want me to be a part of this subterfuge?"

"I mean…"

"Elina has spoken of Eustace a time or two. As a mere fifth daughter of the d'Kay family, it seems unlikely that they will be judged a match, even considering Sakeld's limited prospects. Still, she could use a friend." She nodded firmly, as if to herself. "I will deliver the letter."

"Just like that? You don't want anything in return?"

"If I asked for something, it would only reinforce your negative impressions of House Marchon. At least this way, you must waste energy wondering if my generosity itself is a ploy."

It was like she was reading my mind.

"I'm guessing *you* have a plenty-high Discernment attribute," I muttered.

She flushed, stoic mask dissolving into a scowl. "Hand over the letter and be done with it."

"It's in my room."

"Make haste then. I *do* have places to be." Mireille made a show of stretching out her legs and leaning back on the couch.

Twenty seconds later, I was back.

"This is Sakeld's signet," she admitted, examining the letter. "If Elina has a reply, should I deliver it to you?"

"I… don't think so? I don't have any way to get it to Eustace."

"Hopefully, he will have thought of the issue and enclosed instructions. If not, I suspect my handmaidens will have ideas of their own." She hopped up off the couch where she immediately towered over me. "And now we have had a conversation where you did *not* accuse me of some form of malfeasance. Congratulations, adventurer."

"Enjoy dinner at the Stag," I offered.

I had to say it to her back, as she was already on her way out.

○○○

Later that night, I finished my meditation without any new gains. Over the week of classes, I'd only picked up one point in *Spear* and another in *Tactics*, but we had plans to go back into the tunnels on Seventh Day to complete some more guild missions. With any luck, I'd be able to start maxing out some skills, leaving me only with the experience gap before I reached level eight.

It was a shame that Eustace's letter *hadn't* been a Framework-supported quest. Judging by my energy satiation, I was somewhere around thirty percent of the way through level seven, even after our battle against the scorpions. A quest completion could have boosted that to seventy percent or even higher.

Instead, I'd have to grind.

Miko was late coming back from visiting with Zorana. By the time she finally returned, escorted by Ardalan, I was too tired to do much more than say hi. I drifted off before she'd even begun her meditation.

Sometime in the middle of the night, I woke up to a sound I hadn't heard in quite a while but would never forget.

Miko was crying.

"Miko? Are you okay?"

Her sobs didn't so much stop as kind of soften a bit, just enough for her to offer a strangled "No."

It was pitch black in our room, and I had no idea where the firestick *or* candles were, so I fumbled my way over to her bed, aiming for the darker shadow that I assumed was her. I sat down and wrapped my arm around my friend. She was all scale and muscle, as usual, but melted into my touch, slumping against me, hip to hip, shoulder to head, as she continued to cry.

"Hey." I kept my voice gentle. "What's going on?"

That just ignited a fresh round of tears, so I did the smart thing and kept my mouth shut for a good long while. Miko was heavy and the larger scales on her torso and shoulders were rigid, digging into the parts of my face and flesh that hadn't already been changed by *Beast Skin*, but I didn't budge. I just held her and waited.

Finally, her tears slowed to a trickle, and she managed a few words in the High Tongue. "I received a new Title tonight," she said, in a voice far too small for her frame.

"Is that a bad thing?"

"This one is." Her breath caught and the tears resumed.

The darkness hid my troubled look. "Whatever it is, we'll face it together, nest-sister. You and me. You know that, right?"

"There is nothing to face. There is only reality."

Again, I waited.

"My new title," she finally said, voice still too small, "replaced the previous one."

I only knew of one title she had. "Hand of the Dawn Maiden?"

She nodded against the top of my head. "It has been replaced. My new title is Voice of the Dawn Maiden."

"But… that's good, right?"

"Aurea has many hands, Brian Fieldings, but only one voice."

Right. Because the head of her church was known as the Voice. Still, I wasn't entirely sure I saw the problem. Yeah, Miko was young, but she'd been preaching to a whole community of synossians who were totally ignorant of their original gods. If that wasn't high priestess behavior, then what was?

I think my silence spoke for itself because Miko, in the midst of the grief I still didn't understand, forced herself to explain.

"When Mother was killed in Whitehall, her successor gained the title. When that successor died, both title and position would be passed to the next in line." She choked back another sob. "And on and on down the chain until it reached someone like me, a former shrine keeper, barely above even acolytes in the church hierarchy.

"I cannot even count the dead," she added, "the number of senior brothers and sisters of the faith who had to perish for me to gain this mantle. The last of them died sometime today."

"That's…"

"*How* are they still dying all these many moons later? Did none of the Bright Lady's servants make it to the ships in time? Am I truly all that is left?"

I didn't have any answers. Not about what was going on back on her home continent, or how many ships had successfully launched from Issandryl's southern shore, or even how many of the refugees packed into those ships would survive the treacherous, cycles-long journey across the ocean.

"I don't know what it means," I said. "To be honest, I can't even grasp the scale of the genocide, of the tragedy involved. But we *know* ships made it out; they had already left long before Whitehall fell. And maybe those ships didn't have higher-ranked members of your clergy on them, but they definitely carried believers. Of Aurea, of Kal, of Etriska, and even of Shan. Your people will survive and so will their faith."

"Theirs, maybe. I don't know if mine is up to the task."

I wasn't sure what to say to that. *If not you, then who?* came to mind but even my Discernment was high enough to know it was precisely the wrong thing to say. But Miko's faith was the strongest of anyone I knew. Maybe she was young, maybe she was inexperienced, and maybe she was naïve, but she was also *worthy.*

I opened my mouth and just let the words spill out.

"I didn't believe in God back on Earth. I still don't. And frankly, religion in general hasn't been something I cared for since shortly after my dad's diagnosis. I know gods are real here, but I can't see myself ever worshipping any of them. I've met Shan and didn't care for him. I've seen Hashoggath and she scares me to bits. And the less said about Khamani, the better. Gods are for someone else, not me." She started to pull away, but I held on. "But you've changed my mind on religion. You've shown me that it can be about helping others, about sharing community. Berys helped with that. Even Humber has helped a little, but mostly it's just been you. And if Aurea really has picked you to be her Voice… despite the circumstances, despite the tragedy of what it means… I can't imagine anyone better suited for the role."

"I'm not ready," she said.

"You have time," I reminded her. "You have time and you're not alone. We *will* be ready."

I'd love to say she stopped crying, that my words patched up the hole in her heart, but that wasn't the way the world worked. Not Earth and not Eos. So instead, I held her until she cried herself asleep, tucked her into bed, and sat next to her until morning.

○○○

Miko was the third duel this time.

She looked like a shell of herself, barely put up a fight, and got utterly demolished by Gareth. After her lengthy healing, I handed her off to Zamira and went in search of Wilf.

I don't know what the Spy saw in my face, but he took a careful step back.

"I'm putting an end to this bullshit," I told him. "And I need your help."

"You're talking the ranking duels, yeah?"

"I'm talking whoever is targeting Miko."

"I don't know what you think I can do about them."

"You can get me information. Isn't that what you do?"

He looked away. "It's just rank, Brian. In the end, it doesn't mean anything unless you let it."

"It's never *just* anything. Given all the stories about you, I think you'd understand that."

All expression dropped from Wilf's face. "We should talk about this elsewhere."

I followed him out of the arena, down a hall, and up into the tower where we'd had our last heart-to-heart. When we reached the top floor, he turned on me.

"That's a hell of a thing to say to someone whose help you need. A *hell* of a thing."

"Am I wrong? From what I understand, you've put up with this sort of nonsense a lot longer than we have."

"And yet I'm still here. Still surviving. Because I play things smart. I don't make waves. I find ways to be useful enough that I don't get squashed."

"Yeah, well that's—"

He cut me off. "Can I ask you a question? Why don't you just ally with House Marchon? Or hells, with House Darish? I don't know why they both seem fixated on you, but it's a problem with an easy solution."

"I don't know which of them is behind Miko being targeted."

"Who cares? Kiss some noble ass for a cycle or two and it won't matter anymore. If the house you ally with is responsible, the challenges will stop. If it's the opposing house instead, you'll have the protection of your new faction."

"If they'd just asked at the beginning, maybe I would have. Hell, I definitely would have. But this isn't just about school. I can't ally with a house I don't trust."

Something in his voice told me he understood, maybe even agreed with me, but he asked anyway. "Why?"

I hesitated. It wasn't my secret to tell, *especially* to someone who had already admitted to selling information. But I'd fought with Wilf. We'd bled for each other. I wasn't sure if I *trusted* him. But… would I have asked for his help if I didn't?

"It's fine," he said, voice flat. "I don't need—"

"There's something big coming," I said. "In a cycle and a half or so, we think. And we're going to need support from the nobility to help deal with it."

"What kind of support?"

"Logistics. Supply. Organization. Political aid. Money. Maybe even land." I shook my head.

"You don't ask for much, do you?"

"We wanted to reach out to the duke directly, but—"

"But that's not how things work. Not in Trynfall." He frowned. "Is *that* why Miko is taking Political Relations class?"

"Yeah. To try and meet people and make friends."

"There are no friends in politics. Only the enemies you halfway trust and the enemies you don't. A commoner taking that class is just a joke to the other initiates." He sighed and rubbed his face, looking momentarily ancient for all that he was maybe twenty Earth years old. "What exactly is it that you want from me?"

"I want to know who's behind Actus, Gareth, and the rest of them."

"And then?"

"I'll figure something out."

"You know it really *could* be either, right? Mireille comes off alright by comparison because Lucius is an arrogant ass, but they're the heirs to the two most powerful houses in the duchy. Darish, by virtue of Lucius' dad being one of only three marquesses, Marchon, thanks to the sheer web of alliances Mireille's father has willed into existence. No house reaches that level of power without blood on its hands."

"That's why I need your help."

"Then I'm going to need yours in return." He hesitated, then turned to the stairs. "But first, I need to show you something. Let's go."

"Where?"

"To the Lower City."

"Now?"

"Now." His tone hadn't changed since we reached the tower. Hard and flat and totally unlike the Wilf I'd spent so much of the past moon with.

As bad as his pretense at being drunk had been when he'd first shown up to give us our tour of the Tryn, I'd assumed Wilf's *Performance* skill was every bit as low as he'd let us think.

Now, I had to wonder if even *that* had been an act.

Who *was* Wilfred McCall?

"Alright," I said, following him down the stairs. "Let's go."

Only… when we got to the bottom and stepped out into the hall, we found a scarred mountain of a man waiting for us, arms folded. His eyes flicked to the spear in my hands and then back to our faces.

"Dame Credence wants to see you both," said Merrick.

29

Merrick didn't comment on the fact that we'd been in a section of the Tryn that was supposed to be locked and he didn't share how he'd known to find us there either. Instead, he shepherded us to the office I'd already visited once before.

Dame Credence was waiting, and she wasn't alone. Barth, Zamira, and Miko were already present, as was a middle-aged human man wearing a guard tabard over armor heavier than anything I'd seen.

"Thank you, Merrick," said the Iron Lady, voice crisp as usual. "Please stay for this. I'll want your thoughts as well."

"Of course," he rumbled.

There was one chair other than the one the headmistress was sitting in, but nobody had taken it. I decided to follow their example and remained standing, if leaning on my spear. Unless Wilf had done something illegal, I was pretty sure I knew what this was about.

I was right.

Dame Credence leaned forward in her chair, grey eyes finding each of us in turn. "I have been informed that the five of you went on a delve recently in service of the Adventurer's Guild."

The others looked to me, so I nodded. "Yes. Miko and I are full members. Zamira is a prov. The rest of our party came along so we could practice our small group tactics."

"And it is good that they did, given what you all encountered. This is Guard Captain Hutton. He has some questions about your experience and about the trophies you delivered upon your return."

What followed was a lengthy examination of our sojourn into the tunnel depths. The tunnel rats, the dead swarm, the scorpions, and even our rescue of Greshal. I answered questions where I could, but the others pitched in too.

It all felt kind of like an interrogation, but that did seem to be the Iron Lady's style.

Finally, we were done. She leaned back in her chair and traded glances with both Merrick and Hutton.

"Interesting."

I was starting to hate that word.

"The creatures you encountered do have some distant links to the hand-sized deathclaws you'll find in the low mountains of Apsa," she continued. "They are known as ishi-ka, an invasive species that predominantly live underground."

"In small groups, they're not too much of a menace," said the guard captain, glossing over the trouble *we'd* had with just four. "But where there is one, there will often be many."

Dame Credence took back over. "Initiate McCall's concerns about the lack of any visible nest or campsite were well founded. Over the past few days, the guard conducted several sweeps down on the levels you ventured to. They encountered additional ishi-ka, with signs suggesting a colony has taken root even further below."

"How can we help?" I asked. Being part of a joint operation to wipe out a threat to the city sounded like an ideal way to gain experience and skills. Especially if we'd have the safety and security of high-level backup.

"You can stay out of the tunnels until otherwise notified."

"I'm sorry?"

"Initiate na'Jafani is a ward of Grand Duke Willerton. Initiate Ceelos is a visiting noble from our sister duchy of Apsa. And you took both of them into mortal danger."

"My parents sent me here because they feel Apsa is too civilized," said Barth. "I think danger was half the point. Maybe more than half."

For the first time, Miko stirred from her funk, giving the young noble a look caught between horror and outrage.

"Be that as it may, I am not interested in dealing with the political and diplomatic ramifications of either of you dying under my watch."

"Always good to know where the rest of us stand, yeah?" Wilf was back to his usual self, and for the life of me, I couldn't tell if he was pretending.

"All initiate lives matter, McCall," said Credence. "However, you were born to this game just like I was. You know some lives matter more than others."

"Quite right," he said easily.

"So… what? You called us in to tell us we weren't going to be allowed to continue operating as members of the guild?" I frowned. "With respect, I don't think the Adventurer's Guild answers to the Trynfall Ducal Academy."

"The guild may not, but as long as you attend my school, you will."

The threat there was unmistakable.

"How long will this ban last?"

"Until the guard and soldiers from the duke's personal army can destroy the new colony. No more than a moon, I'm certain."

"With luck," added Hutton, "and depending on how entrenched that colony already is."

"I have an alternate suggestion in mind," Dame Credence continued smoothly. "One that will allow you to continue testing your skills, albeit in a more controlled environment."

"More patrols?" asked Zamira. "I don't mind marching around relighting lanterns, but I gained a full *level* from our delve. A patrol is just busywork by comparison."

"It was my understanding that you had no interest in pursuing the life of an Aspirant," said the headmistress.

"That was before Zaris became a *loyal vassal state to the Grand Duke and his duchy*," replied the Mage, in a tone far too sweet to be believable. "How will I ever *properly* show my appreciation if I remain this weak?"

The sarcasm was so thick that I thought someone might drown in it. And since I was, per usual, the shortest person in the room, that someone would be me.

"Patrols will continue for you and the rest of the units in your class," said Credence, "but your assigned adept will ensure you do not go below the second floor."

I didn't bother trying to hide my frown. It wasn't even the skill gains I'd miss—those were at least replicable through training, if more slowly. But there was no substitute for real, life-threatening combat when it came to strengthening your soul. I'd started to think level eight might only be a few seven-days away, but this set that timetable back immensely.

Miko seemed to feel the same way. "With apologies," she said, voice subdued but gaining strength as she continued. "Must grow.

Patrols suffice for practicing basic formations and tactics, but battle is essential to advancement."

"I'm normally just as happy to hang out and do nothing at all," agreed Wilf, "but it seems like a lousy way to reach Tin."

Credence pinched the bridge of her nose, for the first time looking almost human. "This is a school, not the army, but the next person who speaks before I am done will get to run through Merrick's idea of a conditioning course."

"It involves each of you lifting a lot of very heavy things until you pass out," said the large man.

"I don't hate it," murmured Barth, unknowingly saying what I was thinking. "I could use more Strength."

"If you would prefer, you could double up on one of Stick's conditioning courses instead."

That shut us all up in a hurry.

"What I was *going* to say," continued the Iron Lady, "was that, while the lower depths will be off limits until such time as the Guard Captain Hutton has completed his sweep and declared them safe again, there *is* another alternative available to students at my facility. We had already planned to open access to the Echo earlier than usual. For your group, we are moving that up even further."

Our party traded excited glances. I'd heard a lot about Trynfall's true dungeon since arriving at the academy, but Ebb and Flow had suggested we wouldn't even sniff it until summer.

"A true dungeon is safer than the tunnels under the city?" asked Barth, either deciding that Credence had finished speaking or already forgetting the exercise-related threats she'd levied.

"Yes. The Echo's threat level varies regularly, but there are means to divine that level before sending in a group of delvers. And once an instance has begun, it will not change until the delvers have re-emerged. I have reserved access to the Echo for your group tomorrow."

Hutton cleared his throat. "I'd advise arriving early. You may have to wait a glass or two for the Echo to cycle through to an acceptable threat level for your first delve."

"Still," added Credence, "once entered, the true dungeon offers a stable, consistent challenge. You will have your danger without the risk of coming across a horde of ishi-ka who tear you to pieces before you can do so much as scream." She let that sink in, in case we hadn't already gotten the point that the lower tunnels were off limits. "Early access to the Echo is a privilege and one the city guard and I have agreed to extend your group as a reward."

"Knowledge of the enemy on Trynfall's doorstep allows us to act before the situation further deteriorates," agreed Hutton. "It will ultimately save lives. I have also spoken with His Grace's seneschal, who has authorized a finder's fee of five copper plugs, to be paid out to each of you for your service."

Nobody, not even Zamira, was mad about that. Twenty-five plugs, all-in, or two and a half silver towers, was a hell of a payout. Throw in access to the Echo, and everyone looked a lot more excited, even Miko.

"That will be all," said Dame Credence, as Hutton placed five stacks of five plugs on her desk for us to take. "On behalf of the Trynfall Ducal Academy, the city guard, and the people of Trynfall, I thank you. Let's make sure something like this never happens again."

○○○

I still had somewhere to go with Wilf, but he told me he'd meet me in the common room in a half-glass. So instead, I joined Miko and returned to our dorm room.

"Are you okay?" I asked her, reverting to the High Tongue as I always did when we had potentially sensitive topics to cover.

She looked down. "I fought terribly."

"You weren't at your best," I said, which had the benefit of being both supportive and undeniably true.

She nodded, more to herself than to me. "Next time, I will do better."

I wanted to tell her I was working with Wilf—would hopefully be working with Wilf—to make sure there weren't any more *next times* but didn't. Getting her hopes up before Wilf agreed to help, and long before I found out if the Spy even *could* help, felt needlessly cruel.

Especially if she was going to get challenged again tomorrow.

"Do you still want to go the enclave today?" I asked instead.

"Now more than ever! If I am the Voice, I have a responsibility to spread Her word."

"Something you were already doing."

"Yes. And I will need to warn Joshua that we might be late tomorrow, if our delve into the true dungeon goes too long." She paused. "I would ask him to arrange food in the event of our absence, if I wasn't concerned that he and anyone he chose to help would be robbed of it. While most of my people in the Lower City are Dedicated, he says there are a few Aspirants, largely on the wrong side of the law and hungry."

"We could try setting something up with the city guard, maybe? Or even some of Hawthorne's arbiters? I'm pretty sure they would charge for their services though."

"And the silver tower we have just earned will go quickly without the ability to complete new missions for the next moon," she agreed.

"We should see if there are any missions involving the Echo. I know it's unlikely, given that access is restricted, but you never know."

"Yes. Maybe we can do so after this afternoon's sermon?"

"Actually, I'm going out in just a bit. I can try to swing by the Adventurer's Guild while I'm away."

Miko froze and turned to me.

"You are going out? Where? Would you like me to accompany you? I have schoolwork to do, but it can wait."

"I'm not sure where I'm going." That won me a wide-eyed look and I sighed. "Wilf asked me to come with him."

"That is—oh."

"Oh."

"Go and enjoy yourself, nest-brother. You deserve it."

"Deserve… it?"

"In fact, I will see if I can catch Zamira before she departs the academy. She and Ardalan can accompany me to the enclave, and you won't have to worry about such things for one night."

I wasn't sure what she was talking about, but she seemed almost happy as she turned and slipped back out into the hall, so I let it go.

It was twenty or so minutes later when I met Wilf and found him dressed in another of the mismatched and garish costumes he wore for his nights out on the town that it finally sank in.

She thought he was taking me to his secret brothel.

I *really* needed more points in Discernment.

○○○

Wilf was practically breezy as we made our way out and down to the Lower City, filling the air with a constant stream of chatter on any number of entirely inconsequential topics, from initiate gossip to winter crops to news trickling in from the kingdom's capital Elthoris.

I studied him as we walked, looking for any hint of the serious, audibly bitter man who'd traded words with me in the tower. There was nothing. Either that had been a performance or this was. Either way, he had no tells that I could find.

It was the sort of thing to make an ex-barista nervous, but I'd seen Wilf fight. I had my spear, I had *Liberating Lunge*, and I was *mostly* confident he wasn't luring me away to knife me in a back alley.

At the same time, I was glad I'd told Miko who I'd be with.

We passed through the gate from the Middle City to the Lower City and started down the series of switchbacks that led to the lowermost tier. Before we reached the market, however, Wilf led us off onto one of the connecting streets and into what appeared to be a commercial district. If the market primarily had stalls or single-room storefronts and the Middle City had shops that could double as five-star hotel lobbies, the stores here fell somewhere in between. A little higher end than in the market, significantly less so than what could be found above.

We passed a tavern, already full despite the sun's presence. I checked, just to be sure, and verified it was *not* the Stag where Mireille and her faction had gone a night earlier. Past the tavern, a bakery and a brewery faced each other across the street, and past them, on the side of the road that overlooked the next tier, was a two-story building without signage. I thought it might be a home at first, from the curtains I could see in the upper windows, but the man lounging outside the door suggested otherwise.

I knew a bouncer when I saw one.

Wilf traded nods with the man but didn't slow as he led me past and inside, where I was hit with a variety of perfumes and enough incense to immediately make my head spin. Still, it wasn't until we reached the small room just off the foyer and saw a half-dozen women of differing species in varying states of undress that the truth hit me.

Wilf really *had* taken me to a brothel.

Before I could say anything, he led me deeper. There were more than just barely clothed women in the place; there were a few barely clothed men too. Equal opportunity sex workers, I guessed. As a kid from Midton, Ohio, that didn't make me any more comfortable. A few were playing some sort of dice game, while the others simply lounged about in little bits of nothing while talking quietly to one another.

Past the foyer and sitting room was a long hallway with doors on either side of it. There, we were met by a fiorlan woman in a corset and long skirt, pale green hair piled atop her head. Fiorlans were rumored to age slower than humans, which meant she could've been anywhere between my age and that of the grandfather I'd never met.

"Wilfred," she said, in a voice like warm honey that sent tingles up and down my spine. "I did not expect to see you again so soon." Angular eyes, gold and alive with intelligence and curiosity, shifted to me. "Or with company."

"Something came up," said Wilf. "Is she available?"

"For you? Always. Adriana was going to check in on her shortly."

"We won't be that long, I promise. Thank you, Telidra."

"Go along then. I trust you to inform your companion on the rules of this house."

She slipped past us in a rustle of skirts, headed for the sitting room.

"Rules?" I asked Wilf.

"Ware your eyes and hands both," he said. "The Velvet Fist has a small and very select clientele and no patience for anyone who is less than respectful."

"Why are we here, Wilf?"

"You'll see." He led us down the hall, past doors that I could only assume led to bedrooms. At the end of the hall, we ascended a spiral staircase whose filigree steps appeared to have been cast from solid bronze to reach another hall, this one with only a handful of doors. He stopped outside the second one on the left.

"I want your word that you will not tell anyone about this."

I wasn't sure what *this* was but shook my head anyway.

"I'm not keeping secrets from Miko."

Any more than I already had, at least.

Something dark crept into Wilf's brown eyes, as if a predator was peeking out from behind the mask his *Performance* skill gave him.

I didn't back down. "That's non-negotiable."

"Fine," he eventually said. "But her and nobody else. You want to talk about trust? About *truly* working together? This is where that starts."

In some ways, it felt like a ludicrous discussion to be having, given where we were and what would no doubt soon be going on all around us, but I nodded anyway.

"Okay."

"I mean it, Brian. Tell anyone other than Miko and I will find a way to kill you both."

Anger bubbled up inside of me as I mentally added *being threatened by a would-be friend* to my list of new experiences for the night. The hallway was too narrow for my spear to be of much use, so I shifted it to my off hand, leaving my other free to draw the knife on my belt.

"I *said* okay. And don't you ever threaten Miko again."

Wilf's smile was thin and sharp. It reminded me of Lace's somehow. "Protective of your 'sister'? Yeah. I know what that's like."

With a flourish, he produced a key seemingly out of nowhere and inserted it into the door's lock. Two twists to the right and then, bizarrely, a single twist back to the left, and I could hear the mechanism unlatch. He turned the handle and pushed inward, stepping into a dimly lit room.

"This door closes again in five seconds," he said. "Stab me or come inside."

I never thought I'd be torn between those two choices. I blew out a long breath, trying to send my rampaging emotions with it, and followed Wilf into the room. He turned back and closed the door behind us.

There was a single bed against the far wall, a small circular window with colored glass above it, a wooden chest at the bed's foot, a nightstand to the left, and a mostly empty bookshelf to the right. It wasn't what I'd expected a prostitute's bedroom to look like, although I wasn't sure why. Not enough frills maybe? Everything was clean but drab and ordinary.

Except for the woman sleeping in the bed.

She had dark brown hair, long, curly, and tangled. Her bed had a surplus of comforters—three, at the very least—but she had kicked all of them off and lay sprawled out and sweaty in a thick sleeping gown that covered her from wrist to ankle. In the light provided by the small window, her face was mottled, not unlike what *Beast Skin* was slowly doing to me. Her eyes were shut, but her mouth was open, teeth bared, jaw clenched as if she was in pain.

"What the hells is this, Wilf?" My voice was hushed. If there was one thing I knew from my life on Earth, it was unwell, and this woman was unwell.

"This, Brian Fieldings, is Ellisha Primrose McCall." His smile flashed again, still entirely without warmth. "My sister."

○○○

I looked from the woman in the bed to the Spy at my side and couldn't find much in the way of a resemblance.

"I thought she was dead?"

"Everyone does. Which is why she's still alive." He lost even the poor facsimile of a smile. "Or as close to it as I can keep her."

"I don't understand."

Wilf made his way over in silence to his sister's side, gently tugging some of the hair out of her snarling face.

"House McCall has never been powerful, rich, or even large. My lord father spent some of his time trying to change that, and the rest working to make sure we stayed unremarkable. A growing house can be perceived as a threat to those above it. A stagnant house attracts neither attention nor malice. Or so he thought."

I was slow, especially when it came to politics, but I wasn't entirely stupid.

"Someone attacked your house."

"Yes. It started small. Business deals gone sour. Investors pulling out at the last minute. A warehouse fire. A wagon lost in transit. Then there were the so-called accidents. Our captain of the guard was found drowned in a river. My father died when he fell from his horse riding on our land. Middle of the day, a handful of others with him, and somehow not a one of them saw it happen."

"And your sister?"

"Came down with an unknown illness. The first two healers sent from the capital were all too happy to take our money and do nothing. The third told us she thought it was poison and then disappeared shortly after. Another 'accident', no doubt. By that point, Ellisha was like this, and we were ruined as a noble house. We sold our winter home in Trynfall so we could hold on to our ancestral lands and pay, clothe, and feed the few servants we had remaining."

I'd heard—and seen—a lot of horrible things since I'd arrived on Eos. Too many, in fact. Something about Wilf's story hit hard though, even if the scale was comparatively small. Maybe it was the emotionless way he had recounted it. I'd spent enough time in a post-Dad emotional funk to know that the absence of emotion was sometimes a defense mechanism, something done to keep the ocean of feelings from swallowing you whole.

"I'm sorry," I said. "That's awful."

"It's life. And death. It's politics. Anyone who doesn't recognize that has no business getting into the game."

His words, cutting as they were, didn't seem to be aimed at me.

"Why are you both here in the capital then?"

"It is every noble's right to attend the Ducal Academy of Trynfall. When I heard who would be in this class, I decided to avail myself of that right."

Again, I put two and two together.

"You think whoever was behind the attacks on your house is in our class?"

"Maybe. Even in this duchy, justice is not usually so willfully blind. Whichever house was responsible would have had to have powerful backing. And there are few houses more powerful than Marchon and Darish. Do I think Lucius or Mireille were directly responsible? Of course not. Do I think enrollment at the Tryn provides both access and opportunity to dig deeper into the matter? I do." He turned back to his sister. "As for my sister, it was safest for her to disappear. Telidra was once aided by my grandfather and the fiorlans honor their debts, even across multiple human generations. She and a couple of her girls care for Ellisha when I am away, though only Telidra knows who she truly is. To the others, she is Millie, an old friend of mine who fell afoul of the lord she was working for."

"What about your mom?"

"Her daughter might as well be dead. Her son's reputation has been so tarnished that there are open questions as to who will inherit House McCall when she is gone. She does what she must and no more from within the walls of our ancestral house. It's up to me to find out who did this."

"And when you do?"

His smile then was simple, bright, and impossibly cheery. "I'm going to kill every single gods-cursed one of them. And when they're dead and buried and every house involved is in ruins, I'll take Ellisha to their tombs. I'll tell her that it's over and that she can finally wake up again."

I looked from Wilf to his sister and back, imagining their mother sequestered in their house, the Spy carrying his sister from grave to grave.

I had no idea what to say. "This is… this is a lot."

There was a knock at the door. Wilf's hand dropped to one of his blades, then fell away again when a second knock followed the first a few seconds later. He moved past me and opened the door a crack.

"Master Wilfred." The voice was young, female, and unfamiliar. "It's Adriana. Can I speak with you? Lucia overheard something last night about one of the lords on your list. I thought you might be interested in speaking with her before the evening rush begins."

He hesitated, looking back at me and at his sister. For once, there was no mask or act to hide the uncertainty in his eyes.

"Can I trust you, Brian? To protect my sister like she's yours?"

The answer rose from my chest, unbidden.

"Yes."

Another long breath and then he nodded. I had to assume that *Deception* was a class skill for a Spy, much like *Performance*, and that he therefore knew I was telling the truth.

Still, after he slipped out into the hall, I heard the distinctive rattle of the key in the lock, ensuring I wouldn't have an easy way out if his trust was misplaced.

And that just left me alone with a young woman who hadn't moved since we'd arrived and yet *still* seemed like she was writhing in pain. I waited, long minutes, trying to focus on anything other than Ellisha, and then finally gave up.

First, I shifted her into a more comfortable position. Her limbs were stiff, but also oddly pliant, any muscle tone she'd once had lost in what had to be multiple moons of being bedridden. I didn't check her for bedsores, both because she was a woman and because they'd be obvious whenever they next gave her a bath, but did collect a jug of water and a towel from the nightstand. I dipped the towel into the water and wiped the sweat from her face. Her skin was almost papery; the lines carved into it from her silent snarl deeper than they should be for someone only a cycle or two older than me. In the absence of a brush, I followed Wilf's earlier lead and used my fingers to comb the rest of her hair out of her face. I tucked her hands down and brought the lightest of the three comforters up to cover her, folding the other two neatly so they would be a reassuring weight on her lower legs and feet.

Her eyes never opened, and her expression never changed, but by the time I was done, I thought she was breathing a little bit more easily.

I looked up again to find Wilf staring at me.

"You've done that before." His voice was quiet, almost as if he was only now afraid of waking his sister.

"I used to be a caretaker."

"Can you show me? It's been more than two moons since we came to the city. I do my best, and I know Adriana and Telidra do too, but none of us have the skill, let alone the profession."

I didn't have the profession either—and I thanked every one of Eos' gods for that—but despite the lack of use, my *Caretaking* skill remained at seven, all these months later. So, I nodded and walked him through what I had done and why, as well as what should be done daily.

"Keep the linens clean and reposition her regularly so she doesn't develop sores," I said. "If you can do some sort of light massage to keep the blood circulation going and maybe even keep the muscles from atrophying too, it would be helpful for when she wakes. Regular baths would be good, if possible; hygiene is even more important for someone in her situation." I nodded to the bookshelf. "And I'd suggest reading to her whenever you have the time."

"Do you think she can hear?"

Oddly, between Erlund, Wilhemina, and now Ellisha, all of my experience with semi-comatose patients had been since coming to Eos. For all of the ways Huntington's had ravaged my dad, he'd remained conscious until the end.

Out of his mind and trapped in his own body, but conscious.

I shook my head, banishing those memories.

"I don't know. But if she can, it might help to give her something to focus on."

"I do speak with her already, every Fifth Day, but reading… reading is doable too." It was his turn to shake his head. "So. Now you know my secret."

"Yeah. And next time, we should come with Miko, to see if she's able to help your sister."

"That's… yes, okay. That's a decent idea. But she would be the fourth healer to see Ellisha and the only one who wasn't even Tin. I don't have much hope on that front."

I frowned. "Then what did you want from me?"

"Information."

"I've given you—"

"Not now. In the future. I'll help you find out who is behind Miko's succession of duels, and you will no doubt join their rival faction for the reasons you stated back at the tower. If it was House Darish, you'll ally with House Marchon, and vice versa."

"Right. And?"

"And that means you'll be in position to observe your new ally's dealings. Maybe you'll even get invited to their estate here in Trynfall at some point. Maybe someone there will let something slip about House McCall. Something of significance."

"You want me to be an informant. On whichever faction *isn't* coming after Miko."

"Yes. The Framework offered me Spy as a class evolution on my very first level after my sister's unexplained illness. Things don't get much clearer than that. Every scrap of information adds to the greater tapestry, but I need to grow my network of eyes and ears. If you want my help, this is the price."

To be honest, the price seemed *way* out of proportion to what was on offer, but it was hard to say that with Ellisha in the room with us, snarling at nothing. The ranking duels were an annoyance, a mild harassment that only chipped away at Miko's resolve, and yet I'd already come close to losing my shit multiple times.

For the first time since we'd met, I felt like I had seen the real Wilf. I felt like I understood him, and it was hard to blame him for wanting more. If I was in his place, I was pretty sure I'd want to burn everything down too.

"Agreed," I said. "But Miko's not a part of this."

"I wouldn't ask her to be." For the first time, a smile that was vaguely familiar emerged. "I'm not sure she even *has* the *Deception* skill. Either that or she's mastered it, yeah?"

"I think we both know which one it is."

He nodded, as if that was obvious. Which… it kind of was. "We should be going before the johns start trickling in. I'll pass on your suggestions to Telidra on our way out."

"Okay." I gave his comatose sister a bow that didn't feel quite as dumb as it had when we first arrived in Trynfall. "It was a pleasure to meet you, Ellisha. I'll see you aga—" I stopped.

"What is it?"

"Sorry. I hadn't noticed that." I pointed to the slender chain around her neck that disappeared under the nightgown. "You'll want to take that off. If she moves at all, even unconsciously, it could be a hazard."

"Of course." He hurried to do just that, revealing a small silver pendant on the end of the chain. "It was a gift from our father on the day of her Dreaming. I thought it would be good for her to have it nearby at least. And nobody in this house would recognize the sigil anyway."

"The sigil?"

He showed it to me: a stylized bird, flames rising all around it. For some reason, it looked familiar.

"The firebird," he said. "The crest of House McCall."

And just like that, I felt my soul shiver as a dialogue window opened before me:

QUEST COMPLETED: Find the owner of the crest ring.

30

From the outside, the Echo didn't look like much. Just a large door, set in stone, walling off the tunnel behind it. Two lanterns were mounted to either side of the door and, oddly enough, another three hung from the ceiling above, though only two of the latter group were lit.

We'd had to pass two guard checkpoints to get here, and there was a third set up about five feet in front of the door. Like the other guards, these ones checked our names, even though we'd been escorted down by Merrick.

"It'll be a bit still," said one of them. "Right now, the Echo's scaled for Tins."

"How can you tell?" asked Miko. My nest-sister looked and sounded immeasurably better after her trip to the enclave and a good night of sleep.

He waved at the lanterns above the door. "Those are sensors tied to the dungeon. Don't ask me how it works; all I know is it took dozens of cycles, multiple Enchanters, and at least as many Mages. Two lights mean Tin, one means unranked, none means it's not operational."

"But… there are three lanterns, yeah?" asked Wilf.

"One of the head Enchanters was convinced it scaled past Tin and I guess nobody felt like arguing with him. That third lantern's never lit." The guard shrugged. "Anyway, with nobody currently delving, it should be a half-glass or so before it changes."

Merrick was already on his way back to the Tryn, leaving the rest of us to just wait until the Echo was ready. I spent a few minutes trying to get comfortable despite my gambeson and recently repaired hauberk, laid my spear down next to me, and leaned against the tunnel wall. I hadn't spoken to Wilf about the signet ring. Not yet. Not until I had time to think things through. After hearing his life story, I had a hard time believing he, personally, had ever had anything to do with the cult of the Ever-Hungry, but the jury was still out when it came to the rest of his family.

It felt like a conversation we had to have, but it could wait until sometime *after* the dungeon. I at least trusted that Wilf would have our backs while we were inside. Everything else was another problem for future-Brian.

"It's strange to get all dressed up only to then sit and do nothing," said Zamira, seated to my left.

"Isn't that what they say about army life? It's all hurry up and wait?"

The Zarisian gave me an arch look. "I've never heard that said before, but then, we didn't *have* an army in Zaris." Our party Mage wore a quilted leather jerkin that extended past her hips, heavy wool pants, and boots that were as nice as any I'd seen since coming to Eos. If there was one thing I'd quickly learned as an adventurer, it was the value of good footwear. Blisters out in the wilderness could lead to infections, and infections made for a really bad day if there weren't any Priests conveniently parked around the corner.

Or… parked just to the right of you, in my case, I thought, glancing over at Miko. My nest-sister had her eyes shut and was either napping, meditating, or praying. Knowing her, it was somehow a mix of all three. I wasn't going to disturb her.

Barth and Wilf were across the tunnel from us, having their own conversation, so I turned back to Zamira. This was as good a time as any to finally ask her about the Wild. I'd even figured out a way into the conversation that *wouldn't* reveal I could hear her inner... not thoughts.... Did it count as speech if almost nobody else could hear it?

"Does everyone in Zaris worship the Wanderer?"

"No. Many o'naseri do, of course, but Quinn-Koln has her share of worshippers too, being one of the better-known goddesses of commerce. And I'm sure the guards and city folk have their own deities as well. We don't have as many temples as Trynfall, but gods don't *need* buildings to be worshipped." After the encounter with the ishi-ka, she'd found herself a staff, longer than Miko's, if made from ash instead of ironwood. She shifted it around as she turned to me. "Why do you ask?"

"Just curious. I don't really know a lot about the Wanderer."

"That's not surprising. Despite being one of the Elder Gods, he was never interested in developing a mortal following. The o'naseri honor him, like I said, as do some dryad communities, but he's not a deity interested in institutions."

"Is he a nature god then?"

"Not in the way you mean it, no. He's a loner, the sole god in his own pantheon. The stories passed down through stone say he was the first to find Eos out in the void. When the other gods arrived and began to influence this world with their wills, his efforts were instead bent on preserving what was already here."

"The Wild?" I asked, taking what was, in retrospect, a significant leap.

Zamira stared at me for a long moment, her stone eyes making it difficult to tell what she was thinking.

"There are *very* few who know of the Wild. I'm surprised you are one of them."

"All I know is the name," I said, which had the benefit of being entirely true. "I read it once and heard it another time."

"The Wild is Eos-that-was, before the elder gods' arrivals. Before words. Before labels or structure. Not a deity unto itself so much as a primal force. Much of the world was irrevocably changed when the gods came, and much of it has been changed again many times since, but there remain places, above and below, that still contain traces of the Wild. The stone remembers and some ascended beasts do too."

That… didn't *really* explain anything to me, but I'd read enough Earth-based mythology to know that's how such things went sometimes. Sometimes, a story was a parable or a *kōan*. Other times, it was just a story about a god transforming into a bull to get laid. It sounded like the Wild was some kind of unformed chaos… except if Eos had already existed at that point, then it would have been anything but unformed.

Frankly, the story about the bull made *more* sense.

"So, the Wanderer was a kind of protector of the Wild?"

"I think he was less a protector of it and more of a voice or advocate for it? But I'm not entirely sure. Following the Godswar and the resulting covenant for the gods to no longer meddle with the physical realm, it all became pretty abstract. And *that* was hundreds of thousands of cycles ago. Maybe even more."

"Interesting."

Damn it, now Dame Credence had *me* doing it. But it *was* interesting. Both because I'd seen Shan break that covenant to save my life and send me—and Miko—to this continent and because the title in my personal record suggested the Wild still mattered enough for the Framework to take it into account.

As usual, every answer only spawned more questions. I now knew, sort of, what the Wild was, and had a vague confirmation that I'd gotten my title for the trap I'd set using the false dawn outside Madea, but that was the extent of my understanding. How could you be the agent of something that didn't seem to have agency? And why would the Framework recognize that? What purpose did it serve?

I spent the next ten or so minutes trying to come up with a subtle way to slip that question into Professor Lunsford's next Framework theory discussion. Preferably without incriminating myself in the process. Maybe I could use Priest titles as a starting point, and then ask if there was something similar for secular classes?

Between actual school and all the mental work I was having to do outside of it just to stay afloat *without* revealing anyone's secrets, it was a wonder I hadn't earned another point in Intellect.

Finally, the second lantern went dark, all on its own. After monitoring it for a few minutes, the guards waved us to our feet. "Looks like it's stabilized," said the same guard from before. "You can enter when ready."

We knew from class that the true dungeon's instances all had a staging area, so we wouldn't be attacked upon entry. Still, we got into formation before we entered, something that won us a nod of approval from the guard who'd been doing all the talking. I was in front, the only person in anything heavier than leather, followed by Wilf, Miko and Zamira, and finally Barth. The second guard undid the lock on the door and pulled it open.

I hadn't been sure exactly *what* the entrance to a true dungeon would look like, but given its nature, I had assumed it would be some sort of a portal. So, I wasn't too shocked to find swirling mists in place of anything tangible. They gave off an almost ozone-like smell that cut through the tunnels' more earthy fragrance and the temperature noticeably dropped as I approached.

You've been teleported before, I reminded myself. *One of those times was across realities or universes, and the other was across continents and after you'd been stabbed. This is nothing to worry about.*

My lizard brain didn't buy that for a second, but thankfully my body was moving forward anyway, one foot in front of the other, spear in hand. I reached the mists and kept going, letting them swallow my form.

Another step brought me back out of the mists and into a well-lit room, maybe ten feet by ten feet. The walls were worked stone and windowless, with two torches each to our left and right. Directly opposite me, two more torches flanked stone stairs leading down.

I moved forward and then to the right to make sure Wilf wouldn't run into me. He cut left instead, and then it was Miko's turn to emerge, her inner eyelids flickering back open as she did. She followed me to the right.

The others continued to emerge from what, on this side, appeared to be another solid stone wall, if one lacking brackets for torches. Barth was the last. He shook his head as he pulled his bowstring from its pouch and unhurriedly strung his weapon. "That was unpleasant."

The others nodded, leaving me to wonder what I had missed. Maybe my *Toxin Resistance* skill had done something for me, even though it still only had a single point?

"At least this instance is an inside dungeon and one that's lit," said Wilf. "Those are both positive signs, yeah?"

"Any guesses on the theme?" I asked.

"Yes," said Miko. She'd wandered over to the stairs to take a peek down. "Are cubbies in the wall. It looks like these might be catacombs."

Wilf's curses were both heartfelt and impossibly filthy. "Catacombs mean we'll be facing risen, most likely."

Zamira groaned.

Risen was short for the risen dead, which came in two forms, both nasty. The more common type, which Miko and I had been unfortunate enough to encounter, were corpses who had been reanimated from a Mage specializing in necromancy, or a Priest who worshipped a god of death. Zombies and skeletal warriors were the most frequently encountered of this type.

The less common kind of risen were those who, through magic, or accident, or even their own will, had used their deaths as a catalyst to transform into something else. Severed from their own souls, they were neither truly dead nor truly living but something in between… monsters who lost any morality they might have once had but retained their free will and mental functions. I didn't think Eos had vampires, but if it did, they'd be included in the second group along with ghosts.

Regardless of type or origin, risen were often far more dangerous than they had been when wholly alive, and not *just* because killing them took a whole lot more effort.

"Go for the head if you have the opportunity," I said. "Focus on the joints otherwise. Disable them and we can finish them off after the battle is over."

"Might not be risen," said Miko hopefully. "Could just be bats or cave creatures."

"Or *risen bats*," said Barth. "That would be something to see."

"I worry about you and everyone else from Apsa, Barth," said Wilf. "I truly do."

The visiting noble grinned.

"Does this change our tactics?" asked Zamira.

I shook my head. "I don't think so. According to Ebb and Flow, an unranked dungeon will only have one level." Looking at the stairs, I amended that. "Staging room aside, I guess. Make it to the end and we'll find the way back. If everything stays lit, it means Wilf can scout and we should spot any attack before it happens. Just don't go too far ahead," I told the Spy.

"Not for all the treasure in the fabled Dar," he agreed.

I added *fabled Dar* to the list of topics I needed to research at some point. It sounded like a place but hadn't come up in any of my studies so far.

"We'll stop and reassess after every battle," I said. "There's no time limit, so I'd rather be slow and careful."

"Slow, careful, and alive," agreed Zamira.

Barth frowned. "Depending on what we find, I might have to lean more heavily on techniques than normal. The risen are a bad matchup for arrows. Except for the kind that need to be put down with a once-living material, I guess."

"Just keep an eye on your energy levels. We don't know if this is an instance where the difficulty builds or stays steady throughout."

"Just as long as it's not a horde defense," muttered Wilf.

"You're full of pleasant thoughts today." Zamira nudged the nobleman. "Stay in your lane, McCall. *I'm* the party pessimist."

That sparked a surprise smile out of Wilf and he offered a deep, almost flagrantly extravagant bow of apology.

"We should get started," I said. Just because there wasn't a time limit didn't mean we should waste time either. And I had a feeling that the longer we stayed in the staging area, the harder that first step would be. After all, this was everyone's first true dungeon and only Miko and I had even been to the more standard variety.

Wilf nodded and stepped forward. He drew one of his daggers, the blade blackened so as to not catch the light. "Watch my back."

"That's what we're here for."

I watched him ghost his way down the stairs, gave him a twenty count, and then started down after.

ooo

"I'd officially like to retract my earlier positivity," sighed Wilf as the glow from Miko's *Minor Healing* slowly faded. "Maybe next run, the Echo will give us something easy. Like cosmic wyrms or something from the demon pits."

Barth, for once, was too tired to pipe up with some other horror he'd like to see.

It had taken us almost two glasses to travel this deep into the catacombs, through a mix of tight halls and large, open spaces. I honestly wasn't sure which was worse. The cubbies Miko had initially noticed each contained at least one body, and while most of those bodies remained dead, a few did not. Which meant, after the first time something crawled out and attacked us from behind, that we had to clear each hallway thoroughly before we could progress.

The open chambers, on the other hand, seemed to have been designed as rest spaces for mourners to congregate or even honor the dead. There were statues and occasional benches and even artwork celebrating a god Barth recognized as Sie, the Burning Child. What a child, let alone one on fire, had to do with dead things was something I didn't want to know.

Regardless, without any mourners and with the risen having taken over, all that space was simply an opportunity for the enemy to attack us in a rush. With his bow, Barth was the only one who benefited from the wide-open sightlines.

The good news was that we'd faced only zombies and a few skeletons that had long since lost their flesh. The bad news was that this was Miko's fourth heal spell, and while they'd all been *Minor Healing*, she was nearing the point where she'd have to go into conservation mode in case *Light Healing* or *Touch of the Dawn* became necessary.

Neither Barth nor Zamira were much better off. Zamira had a long way to go to learn to wield her new staff, which meant she'd been relying on her spells to contribute. And Barth's earlier concern had proven prophetic; his arrows were poorly suited for putting down the risen. Even headshots often were insufficient unless they came empowered with a technique.

I was pretty sure Miko and I were the two highest level Aspirants in the group, and the bulk of the killing had fallen to us. Oh, Wilf had done his part, like the others, but daggers weren't a great weapon of choice against creatures strong enough to crush their opponents with their bare hands.

Miko, on the other hand, was wielding a blunt weapon, and the past few weeks of duels and duel preparations had pushed her weapons skill to new heights. Occasionally, she'd land a blow that smashed right through a zombie's head, sending the rest of the body crashing to the floor, but mostly, she focused on the joints, like I'd suggested. A zombie without knees wasn't out of the fight, but they were far less mobile, and that made a huge difference.

And with the skeletons being nothing *but* bone, her ability to smash them into pieces was invaluable.

For my part, I had my spear. It wasn't the perfect weapon against the risen, but the reach it gave me was damn near a cheat code in the long, straight tunnels, and only slightly less valuable in the open chambers. I'd only had to use *Liberating Lunge* twice so far, both times in the mourning spaces, to reposition myself and take down an opponent who had flanked one of my party members. I hadn't used *Deceptive Strike* at all, leaving me plenty of gas still in the tank for when we'd use it.

My body, on the other hand, was getting tired, the spear a far heavier weight than when we'd started, my breath coming in short gasps no matter how much I tried to even them out. And as much as my hauberk had done to protect me, it felt like an anchor, weighing me down.

"Should rest," said Miko. "Will try to recover some energy too."

"Agreed," I said. "Stick to the center of the room in case anything new comes calling, but let's take a break for now."

"How much more do you think we have?" asked Zamira. She was already at work on her hair, unwinding two of her braids that had lost their shape and redoing them again.

"We've got to be nearing the end," said Wilf, not looking over from where he'd flopped onto his back. "The better question is: since the difficulty has mostly remained static, will it continue that way, or is there going to be some final battle. Against a skeleton knight and his squires or something?"

"Oh, that would be—"

"Yes, something to see. We *know.*" Wilf shook his head as he cut off Barth. "Did your lord parents really send you to Trynfall because of the danger you'd find here?"

"They did." Barth was seated, leaning back on his hands as he surveyed the chamber around us. "My father said I needed to toughen up if I was ever going to make anything of myself in Apsa. And everyone knows this duchy is the wildest and most primitive of the four. No offense, of course."

Since only one of us was native to the duchy and *he* had some seriously negative views about it, nobody took offense. Barth seemed surprised, then gratified.

"What about your mom?" asked Zamira.

The young nobleman looked away. "She's considerably less optimistic about my chances."

"Of surviving at the Tryn?"

"Of making anything of myself." He grinned then, shocking me, and shrugged. "My older brother, Bastest, is a duelist of some renown. My younger, Barolo, killed his first assassin when he was nine cycles old. He hadn't even had his Dreaming yet." The young nobleman's sigh was almost wistful. "The family is very excited to see what Barolo becomes."

"Gods," murmured Zamira. "Is Zaris the *last* bastion of true civilization?"

"Bastest?" Wilf flopped over to one side to look at Barth. "Why is that name familiar?"

"He's better known by the name he duels under: Bloody—"

"Bloody Bones! Gods, he's *Iron*, isn't he? I had no idea you were so famous."

"Not me. Just my brother. But here at the Tryn, I'm sure that will change. I've already gained one level and now I'm delving a true dungeon! By the time we're done with school, we'll all be Tin and have exploits of our own to share."

That triggered a fresh round of comments from both Zamira and Wilf, but I tuned them out and turned to Miko.

"Are you okay, nest-sister?" I asked in the High Tongue.

"Yes, of course. Just a little bit drained."

"Okay. You just seem kind of down still. Are you fixating on the duels?"

"I wasn't until you mentioned them." She patted my arm before I could apologize. "It's fine. I lost yesterday and the world did not end. I even improved one skill in the process, despite my poor showing. If all advancement costs me is rank and some embarrassment, that is a small price to pay."

"So you're *not* unhappy?"

"I am… worried," she admitted. "About Wilhemina."

That came out of left field. "Wilhemina? Why?"

Miko gave me the slow double-blink of her people, something that sometimes meant astonishment, and other times meant she was focusing inward.

"Did I not tell you? Zamira, Ardalan, and I encountered Neesa on our way to my people's enclave yesterday."

"Lady Willerton's maid?" I hadn't even thought of Neesa—either Neesa—in a very long time, which hopefully said less about me and more about how busy we'd been.

"Yes. She said that Wilhemina still has not awoken."

"But it's been…"

"Yes. Priestess Iris has tried everything to awake her. Neesa said she has even sent a message to Mordecai's former school, requesting aid."

"The Crimson Needle?"

She nodded. "They are the most respected institution of knowledge in the kingdom. They might know something about the nature of the Ever-Hungry's curse, and how to end this last, lingering effect. But in the meantime, Wilhemina continues to sleep. Friend Neesa is beside herself."

"Huh." I guessed that explained why Wilhemina hadn't made any public appearances. Zamira had been opining on the subject the other week; our classmate was trying to set up a meeting with Lady Willerton through official channels to discuss her kidnapping and how Zaris couldn't possibly have been responsible. "Well, to hear Mordecai talk, there was nothing the Crimson Needle didn't know. I'm sure they'll have the answer."

"I hope so," agreed Miko. "But it's hard to think of her still asleep. After all we went through to rescue and heal her, I feel protective of her. I *want* her to be better, to succeed." She made the synossian equivalent of a frown. "I just hope *her* version of success is healthier than Barth's."

○○○

We stayed put for a half-glass or so. Long enough for everyone to recover their breath, not quite long enough for Wilf to take a nap. It took a substantial amount of rest to replenish the soul—if not a full night's sleep, then something close—but at least our bodies were ready again.

Four fights later, including one particularly nasty encounter in an intersection where we were attacked from three directions, we found ourselves at what almost had to be the final location in the dungeon. The door was twice my size, cast from bronze, and showcased varied scenes of battle across its surface. All featured the same simple figure, a knight in heavy armor. Sometimes, the knight was supported by allies, other times, it battled alone against creatures straight from Cthulhu's worst nightmares.

"A separate tomb," said Zamira, voice hushed, "for someone important or powerful or both." She turned on Wilf. "You just had to make that comment about the skeletal knight, didn't you?"

"That was Barth, not me."

"Was it?" Barth gave it some thought, then shrugged, offering Zamira a courtly bow. "My apologies."

The Zarisian's death stare never wavered from Wilf.

"Gods, Barth, I was *joking*, and now you're making me feel bad. You can't just go around apologizing for things you didn't do."

"Of course," said Barth, turning his bow on Wilf. "My apologies."

The Spy frowned. "He's doing this on purpose, isn't he?"

"You deserve it," said Zamira. "Regardless, if there *is* a knight, we'll likely have to defeat it."

"Not just the knight," I said. "Most likely, he'll have been buried with his retainers."

"We haven't done that for hundreds of cycles," protested Barth. "It didn't help with loyalty at all, and retainers are entirely too valuable to the house to just kill them off when their lord dies."

"But Echo comes from before-times." Miko gave me a nod of acknowledgment. "Would likely be based on customs from its time instead."

We, at least, had been keeping up with our reading assignments.

"A skeletal knight and his squires," said Zamira, biting off every word. "Just like *someone* said."

"And they will be guarding a chest of gold crowns and enchanted items," intoned Wilf, as if reading from a terrible novel. He met our confused looks with a shrug. "I might as well use my powers for good, yeah?"

"We don't know what kind of knight it will be," I said, cutting through the banter, "but I think it's a pretty good guess that it *will* be one, and will have allies. Do we want to focus on those allies first or the knight?"

"Allies," said Barth, all business. "You can only be in one place at a time; we can't let the squires get past you and swarm Miko or Zamira."

Or *him*, technically, although even with a bow, he was less of a concern than our Priestess and Mage.

"If there's a water source, I can try to restrain some of the squires," said Zamira.

"Should bring water with you, friend Zamira," said Miko.

"I would, but I can't carry sufficient amounts to make a difference." The Zarisian frowned. "I picked *Water Control* as a spell to play with the fountains in Zaris, not as some kind of combat tool. Next level, if I can get *Create Water*, it will really help rescue my path."

"Okay," I said. "So, Zamira will be on crowd control if she can, and stick with *Water Blast,* if not. Barth will focus on the retainers too, and Miko and Wilf will work to keep them from reaching either of you. And I'll keep the knight busy until you guys can join in."

"Nest-brother…"

"I'll play it smart," I said. "No risky plays until some of you are there in support."

"It makes sense," said Wilf. "Divide and conquer. The retainers should be weaker than their knight. Once they're dead—again—we can focus on the main threat."

I hoped he was right. We were really just making a plan based entirely on assumptions, which Small Group Tactics class had made clear was a terrible idea. Still, with the massive door in our way and enemies almost definitely waiting on the other side, I didn't see much choice.

"Follow us in and split off to the sides," I told Barth and Zamira. "We'll retreat into the halls, if we have to. We already know *those* are clear."

For the first time in a long while, Miko grinned and nobody in the party reacted poorly.

"Luck to all," she said. "The Bright Lady will see us through to victory."

I took off my pack and set it aside. It took two of us to pull open the massive door and I kept expecting the hinges to squeal like in a horror movie. Instead, they rotated quietly, if not easily, revealing the room beyond.

Whereas the catacombs had been lit by the occasional torch, casting shadows that too often hid the risen dead, this enormous circular room was bathed in wan light that poured down from above. It created a dappled circle of illumination, like a God ray back on Earth, and in the center of that circle was a massive stone coffin. Its lid was shut and the exterior had additional scenes carved upon it, though we were too far away to make out what they were. A mosaic on the floor was mostly damaged, extending out from the coffin to four archways along the chamber's walls. Unlit torches were mounted beside each archway.

"Watch the arches," whispered Wilf.

Arches for the retainers, tomb for the knight, I told myself. It was pretty straightforward, and better than if the risen had just been waiting for us, ready to attack.

I started to take a step, then stopped again as *Danger Sense* twinged. *Something* was wrong, but I couldn't tell what.

I held up a hand and let my eyes do another slow sweep of the chamber. Arches with unlit torches. Tomb in the center. Broken mosaic on the floor. Light coming from above, dappled and ever-shifting.

Wait.

I craned my head up, looking for the source of that light.

Unfortunately, I found something else.

"Did you all see any scenes on the door," I asked, voice as quiet as I could make it, "where the knight fought a thegar-sized spider?"

I wasn't sure anyone but Miko even knew what a thegar was, but my nest-sister sucked in a breath as she followed my gaze and spotted what I had. The light was coming down through a hole in the ceiling, and that hole was mostly choked with webbing. An arachnid that made the ishi-ka look like toy poodles was picking its way down toward us.

I'd seen bigger; I'd seen a shadeweaver. I'd also stood back and watched multiple Coppers and an all-offense Tin struggle to destroy it.

"What about the knight?" asked Zamira, voice shaking.

"A red herring," murmured Wilf. "The one thing in this place that didn't rise."

And then the spider was moving, its speed insane for something so massive. It squeezed through and dropped down, landing so lightly it might as well have been a cat. Eight legs straddled the tomb, the massive hairy body not even touching the stone below.

"New plan," I said. "Kill the giant spider before it eats us."

31

A few things quickly became obvious, even as the room devolved into chaos. One, I needed a bigger spear when my opponent's legs were even longer than the weapon. No idea how I'd *wield* a spear that big, but that was a problem for future-Brian. Two, eight legs were too damn many weapons for any one creature to have, even before you included the fangs. Three, something was seriously off if *this* was supposed to be an unranked fight, because now that we were in combat, I could feel the spider's aura, slippery and alien, swelling around us almost like a chittering wave. And unranked Aspirants and unevolved beasts both had one thing in common.

They *didn't* have auras.

This thing was Tin or the ascended monster equivalent.

I waited to use *Liberating Lunge* this time, advancing in lockstep with Wilf, Miko a little bit further behind us. A spider raised the possibility of even more venom and that meant we needed to preserve her spells and energy, if possible.

I just... wasn't sure how it would be possible.

A glowing arrow streaked through the air, but where Barth's technique had blasted through the ishi-ka, it just left a small crater on the giant spider's form. The thing hissed but otherwise seemed unaffected. Zamira's watery blast had even less effect, though she'd aimed it for one of its dozens of multifaceted eyes.

"*Flare!*" called Miko, turning words into action as a burst of light erupted in front of the spider's face.

I took the opening and ducked past the dripping fangs to strike with my spear, but any hopes that my blows would be more effective were quickly ended; the spearhead barely penetrated, skidding off and digging a shallow furrow along the spider's underbelly instead.

In response, the creature skittered sideways and three massive hairy legs, each as thick around as I was, thundered down. I ducked and dodged and finally rolled and still would have found myself pinned or impaled if Wilf hadn't attacked from the other side.

I'd never seen the technique Wilf had used to kill the final ishika, but I was pretty sure I saw it now; the Spy threw himself into the air and lashed outward with both knives. He was a good five feet short, but darkness gathered around his blades and lashed outward again, striking the spider's flank.

It shifted, just a bit, the final of its leg attacks on me twisting to the side, and I was back on my feet again, still whole but wracking my mind for what we could do.

Barth had used another technique to fill the air with arrows— five, then six all in flight—but most broke on the spider's hide. If he was trying to set up his third technique, the one where arrows he'd already landed all bored deeper on their own, it wasn't working.

"Go for the eyes!" I shouted.

Unfortunately, everyone but me had used their biggest techniques already, to laughably little effect. This battle wasn't a test, it was a trap, and we'd walked right into it.

Which doesn't make sense, I thought as I tried to keep the spider's attention despite being too busy dodging to launch much offense on my own. *The guards said the Echo was scaled for the unranked. And every fight before this supported that.*

So, what had changed?

I attacked one of the massive legs instead of the spider's body and the impact was so jarring that I almost lost my spear entirely. There was no weak spot there. Miko had just as little luck with her staff and took a return hit that sent her flying across the room to crash against one of the arches. Wilf was impaled by a leg, prompting a strangled scream from Zamira, only for the body to fade away, revealed as an illusory clone. The Spy came back into view, creeping to try to flank the spider.

The twang of a bowstring announced yet another arrow in flight. This one took the spider in an eye. For the first time, it found purchase, sinking in all the way to its fletchings, but if anything, the spider only amped up its aggression.

If Barth could land a dozen arrows in as many eyes, and *then* use that other technique, maybe...

The Apsa nobleman dove back through the open doorway to avoid the spider's counterattack. It spun around, still far too fast, one leg coming within a breath of decapitating Zamira. If the partial loss of one eye bothered it at all, I couldn't tell. And with it turned about to fixate on Wilf and me, its only semi-vulnerable spots were hidden from our two ranged attackers.

We're screwed, I realized. I hadn't used either of my techniques yet, but I knew what *Deceptive Strike* could do, and it wouldn't be anywhere near enough. *How the hell are we supposed to kill this thing?*

I couldn't find an answer, which was an answer all on its own.

Maybe *we* weren't supposed to.

"The arches!" I shouted, struggling to make myself heard when my lungs were already on fire and the chamber was filled with the sounds of desperate battle. "Light the torches!"

I bull rushed Miko to the side knocking her out of the way of another sweeping leg. My nest-sister came up limping, still wobbly from the earlier hit, and this time, I swung Riok's spear like a nine-iron to block the incoming second leg. In the battle of irresistible force and a very movable object, I came out on the losing end. I think I lost consciousness for a moment, coming back to myself only when I smacked hard against the knight's stone coffin.

Riok's spear as a crutch was the only thing that got me to my feet again. Even so, I cast it aside to push on the coffin's lid.

Nothing. I wasn't sure even *Skaal* would have been able to move the thing. My thirteen Strength sure as hell wasn't up to the task.

Light appeared at the doorway, ruddy and golden, as Barth reappeared with one of the torches from the outside hall. He'd dropped his bow and now charged forward toward the nearest alcove.

The spider spun on a dime and this time, it attacked with something new; a massive glob of sticky glue sprayed out and took the young nobleman off his feet entirely. Barth went down and the torch in his hands went flying.

Zamira appeared at the door with a second torch, but even if my desperate last-second strategy was correct, the spider was more than capable of keeping anyone from reaching the arches. Which meant *someone* needed to try to distract it.

Probably the person who hadn't used any techniques yet.

Wilf was already sprinting toward Barth to free him while Miko was headed for the fallen torch. I retrieved my spear, focused on a spot at the very end of *Liberating Lunge's* range, and triggered the technique.

The world blurred about me. I found my head inches below the webs that ringed the natural skylight. Any taller and I'd have been stuck, which was definitely the first short-man win I'd had in moons. As it was, with the technique ended, gravity was already reasserting itself. I was falling, and it was all I could do to orient myself so that I fell feet first, spear pointed downward toward the monster beneath me.

Riok's weapon wasn't anywhere near as long as one of the spider's gargantuan legs, but it *was* a lot taller than I was. It struck first, all my weight and momentum behind it.

Every doubt I'd had about our ability to kill the thing was confirmed, then and there; I did more damage than anyone else had so far, but it didn't make a damn bit of difference. My feet made contact next, rattling the teeth in my mouth, as I let gravity and inertia pull me down the spear shaft. Yanking the weapon back out, a truly distressing quantity of fluids spurted forth from the flesh wound I'd just exerted so much effort to make.

I took a step and struck down again. Without the extra momentum, my damage was even more paltry. Still, it was something.

Another step. Thrust.

Another. Thrust.

And then, finally. *Deceptive Strike.*

For the first time ever, the technique didn't alter my position. Maybe I wasn't in range of anything that *could* be considered critical. Maybe what I was already doing was as good as it was going to get. Regardless, the technique still boosted my damage; this time, the spear drove a solid four or five inches into the creature's armored hide.

It wasn't enough to do more than annoy it, but sometimes annoyance is Plan A, B, and C. The spider crouched down under me, almost tossing me from my perch, and then sprang upwards and a little bit forward to smash against the ceiling.

For the second time in this battle, *Danger Sense* proved why it was a Rare-ranked skill. I was already in motion before the thing jumped and flew clear of the creature's back a fraction of a second before impact.

Which… left me in one piece, but also twenty feet up in the air, arms and legs spread like I was a skydiver only now realizing he'd forgotten his parachute.

Lunge wasn't back yet, but it was close.

I just… wasn't sure if it would arrive before the rapidly approaching ground.

I tore my eyes from the tomb's floor and focused on a spot a few feet off the ground, not far from where Miko was just now reaching one of the arches.

Either I was dead or…

Liberating Lunge sent me flashing forward, redirecting all that momentum horizontally instead. I emerged *completely* out of control, flying forward to crash onto the floor and skid my way across the broken mosaic. I smacked into another of the arches just in time to see *its* torch light of its own accord, one of three pinpricks of light lighting up in response to the sixth torch that now burned merrily thanks to first Barth, and then Miko's efforts.

From the emptiness of the alcove, something stepped past me, a man in heavy plate, a greatsword held in two hands, pointed downward like a cross. He had no eyes, his face was entirely featureless except for the hint of a nose, but he moved with a smooth, certain grace as he closed in on the monster in our midst.

Every alcove birthed a figure, and every one of them was different, linked only by their origins and the faded, tattered tabards they wore. An unarmored woman waved hands that were missing three fingers, and another figure blurred, gaining impossible speed as he danced through a forest of legs to tear into the spider's underbelly with hands suddenly transformed into hooked claws. The fourth figure raised a stringless crossbow and fired, sending motes of pale light streaking through the air to explode like firecrackers in the spider's face, even as the Mage cast a second spell, one that slowed the spider's movements to a crawl.

And then the greatsword wielder in heavy plate reached the beast. One swing cut through a leg that had seemed invincible to our party; a backswing took out two more. It wasn't until a sense of inevitable heaviness gathered around both the wielder and his weapon that I realized those first strikes hadn't even involved techniques.

The eyeless face looked at the staggering arachnid above him. He shifted his two-handed grip then struck upward. The air itself seemed to scream, as if it was being cut; the spider above fared no better. Steel and then energy tore through a body too large for even a sword of that size to have fully impaled and cleaved the massive spider in two. Both halves crashed to floor.

Silence fell, broken only by the sound of innards oozing out of the dead beast.

"Tell me we *don't* have to fight them now," begged Wilf.

Three of the four figures turned; for a moment, I worried the Spy had just killed us all. Instead, they returned to their respective arches and faded away again, leaving only the faceless man in the center, greatsword still pointed skyward, the spider's remains surrounding him almost like a web.

That massive sword swung down again and then came to a perfect stop halfway through its arc, as if weight and momentum had no roles in the scene we were witnessing. Arms fully extended, the figure held his enormous weapon perfectly parallel to the floor, pointed at the only other object in the room.

A crack came from the stone coffin, and then the lid fell away to either side, split down the middle by a force I couldn't see.

Without a word, the knight—because I was almost positive this was the knight in all the scenes—pulled his weapon back into the position he'd first held it in, gauntlets wrapping the blunt portion of the blade just below the hilt, sword held to his chest like some kind of cross. He stepped past me again, still smooth, still implacable, and disappeared into an archway that was once again just stone.

I took a long breath and wished I hadn't.

We were alone. We were alive. We were safe.

But spider guts *reeked*.

Zamira looked at the second torch still in her hands and frowned.

"So, should I put this back then or what?"

○○○

The first rule of dungeon delving is: if there's a coffin in a tomb, *don't* open it; you'll just unleash whatever is probably lurking within. But I was pretty sure that rule went out the window when the coffin had *already* been opened, and by the thing that would presumably otherwise have been lurking within.

Meaning whatever was in there was fair game for our party.

First though, we had some recovery to do. Two castings of *Light Healing*, separated by its almost unfair five-minute cooldown, saw to Miko and me. The Priestess' remaining energy went to casting *Minor Healing* on the others. When she was done, only Zamira and Barth were anywhere near a hundred percent, but the worst remaining injuries were bruises.

Mostly, people were just exhausted. That one fight had been brutal enough, but it had come at the tail end of a lot of other fights, if more manageable ones, and Miko wasn't the only one out of energy for techniques or spells. Nor were our bodies and souls the only things to have been depleted; one thing I was rapidly learning about life as an adventurer was that even the battles everyone survived had a cost.

Often, a *literal* cost. Equipment maintenance and repair was a never-ending money sinkhole. Of us all, my gear had weathered the delve the best. My spear remained far less breakable than my body, there were only a few rents in my hauberk and the underlying gambeson, and I hadn't had to rely on my daggers even once, so they remained pristine. Meanwhile, Barth had all of two arrows left in his quiver, Zamira's staff had cracked at some point along the way, *both* of Wilf's daggers had been blunted and bent on the spider's legs, and Miko's favorite robes were yet again badly in need of a Tailor's needle and thread.

We were a tired, filthy, blood-spattered group, and the pool of spider guts was only smelling worse the longer we sat there, but ultimately, none of that mattered.

We had done it. We'd faced down something we couldn't kill, had figured a way past it anyway, and had come out whole on the other side. And we'd done it all as a group. I was sure Ebb and Flow would have had some things to say about our performance if he'd been there to see it, but since he wasn't, we could just all lie back and soak in the glory of our success.

To a point.

"Gods, that really *does* smell foul, doesn't it?" said Wilf.

"I want a bath, a massage, a nap, and food, in that order," said Zamira, wrinkling her nose. "Something with vegetables."

"Bath then nap," said Miko. "Might even take my nap *in* bath."

"First, we have to finish here." Suppressing a groan, I pushed myself to my feet and helped pull Miko to hers. Barth detoured back into the hallway to collect our packs, and then the four of us headed for the coffin, now surrounded by pieces of its stone lid. Even those fragments were heavy; I picked my way around them after failing to push one aside.

The coffin was large enough to hold the knight we'd seen, but mostly empty. At the top, where the body's head would normally have rested, sat a pile of items.

Because that was one of the *other* things that differentiated a true dungeon from the mundane variety. Places like the Echo? They almost always had treasure, waiting at the end.

I'd been dreaming of this shit since I became an adventurer.

We moved everything out of the coffin and down onto the floor back by the door and sorted things into piles. There was a small mound of copper bits, three pieces of jewelry, a sheathed blade about the length of Miko's forearm, and a hooded cloak that looked fresh from a Tailor's shop.

It wasn't… quite the exciting loot haul I'd imagined, but I wasn't going to complain either. We'd found a few bits and bobs on the dead we'd killed on our way over, including a pair of copper hoop earrings dangling precipitously from a risen dead's ears, but nothing like this.

Zamira counted the copper, sorting it into stacks of ten bits. There were two plugs as well, but it quickly became clear that the reward we'd gotten from the guard exceeded our dungeon coin by a considerable margin. Twenty-three bits and two plugs, or forty-three bits in total. Split five ways, that wasn't even a plug for each of us.

Thankfully, we hadn't *just* gotten coin.

Even better? We had a merchant with us, and her *Appraisal* skill was topnotch.

"A plug at most for this," she said, putting the first piece of jewelry—a ring with a cracked green stone—back down. "Two plugs for the necklace. Those earrings we found earlier are only worth the weight of the copper, so maybe a few bits?" The Zarisian picked up the last of the pieces of jewelry, what would have been something like a tennis bracelet back on Earth. "Oh."

Something in her tone caught Wilf's attention. "Oh?"

"This appraises for anywhere between six and nine towers."

I frowned at the bracelet. It had been made from copper and silver links, the work delicate but nowhere near enough to merit that sort of valuation. A single copper charm dangled from the bracelet; shaped like a kite shield, it featured a stylized sun inlaid with silver thread.

That inlay was intricate enough to bump the price up a bit, in my unprofessional opinion, but even a single tower seemed like an enormous stretch. Unless…

"Ah," said Barth, leaning in to take a look.

"I move that we all start using multiple syllables, yeah?" said Wilf. "The suspense is killing me."

"It's a standard protection charm," said our visiting noble. "I don't recognize the god's emblem, but the style's familiar enough. Single-use enchantment. Given the materials and the tier of dungeon we just faced, it'll completely protect its wearer against a single unranked attack or partially protect them against someone who's Tin."

"How does it work?" asked Miko.

"You put it on and will it to activate." Barth grinned. "Before they added the activation step, the things were an enormous waste of coin. Assassins knew to always start with a weak attack to burn the charm's charge and follow it up with the real killing blow."

Apsa, I was increasingly starting to believe, was not a nice place.

"You know a tremendous amount about enchanted items." Zamira tore her eyes away from the charm to give Barth a considering look. "Do you have a fourth brother you haven't told us about? An Enchanter, perhaps?"

"Unfortunately not, but… enchantments are a lot more common in Apsa than they are out here on the frontier. And I wanted to *be* an Enchanter, growing up. I even studied extra and everything."

"What happened?" I asked.

"The Dreaming." He shrugged. "I was made a Warrior instead of a Priest or Mage."

"Sometimes the gods are unfair, aren't they?" I'd never felt closer to the young nobleman than at that moment.

Miko turned to give me a look.

"Not *all* gods though," I added. "Some are great."

"It's impossible to be an Enchanter, if you don't have any magic," said Barth. "The closest you can get is probably some variant of Runesmith, and that's more of a supplementary role; you inscribe the rune but it still takes an Enchanter to activate it."

"What rune?"

He flipped the charm over and showed me the back of the stylized shield. There was a single sigil on it, and thanks to my trait, I could read exactly what it said.

Shield.

Nothing earth shattering, especially given that Barth had been able to recognize the bracelet's purpose even without reading the sigil, but still…

I added *Runesmith* to my list of potential professions. Being able to innately read—and presumably write—the language of runes *had* to give me a leg up over other people, right?

Plus, I knew both a Priest *and* a Mage. If Zamira wanted to swap from Merchant to Enchanter, or Miko gave up her pursuit of Herbalist…

"If Enchanters are so heavily in demand, why aren't there more of them?" I asked. "And why aren't *they* the ones running things?"

"Some of them *are* running things," said Zamira. "The One Alone is rumored to be the greatest living Enchanter on Eos, and they rule their own domain. But the truth is, it's hard to even *get* the profession, let alone level it."

"It's not enough to just have magic," added Barth. "Learning the requisite skills is hugely difficult, even with another Enchanter teaching you. And then leveling the profession is just as difficult. It's like the Framework resists progression along those lines. There are *maybe* ten Enchanters in the entire kingdom who can make adornments or simple charms like this one. And only two who could have made something like House Darish's Sever."

"Only one now," said Wilf. "Qi-Ran the Enlightened died this past fall."

"I hadn't heard." Barth made a small gesture, drawing a triangle in the air in front of him. "May her soul be at peace."

That… put a different spin on things. Something told me the road to becoming a Runesmith was only slightly less expensive and difficult than the road to becoming an Enchanter, with both being entirely out of our grasp for the foreseeable future. But it was nice to dream.

"Do we sell it or keep it?" asked Wilf, more focused on practical matters. "Nine towers is an awful lot to give up for a single-use charm."

"It only holds one charge," corrected Zamira, "but that doesn't mean it's single use."

"Right, but it's not like any of us have an Enchanter waiting to do our bidding." The Spy sent Barth a look. "Right?"

"Not here," admitted the other nobleman.

"How much is it worth with the charge used?" I asked.

All eyes turned to Zamira, who shrugged. "I can't appraise hypotheticals. But since it will still be capable of holding that same enchantment, I'd guess… maybe three to four towers?"

The Spy frowned. "So, hold onto it, use it, and then sell it if and when we can't find an Enchanter?"

I nodded. "We'd be giving up three to five towers instead of nine while still granting one of us a chance to save their own life."

"That's harder to argue with," Wilf admitted. "It should probably go to Miko or Zamira then, yeah?"

"What? Why me?" asked the Zarisian.

"Because you have the defensive instincts of an infant and the Vitality of wet parchment," he told her.

"I'll be level five before you know it. Once my skills start catching up at least. Maybe I'll take *Water Shield* if it's on offer instead of *Create Water*. Or I'll use the latter to make my *own* shield." Zamira shook her head. "I think it should go to Miko. She's the one who keeps putting us back together after every battle."

"Always protect the healer," agreed Barth.

"Have scales. And vambraces." Miko held her long, lean arms up to show off both. "And staff that is not broken. You must live long enough for me to be able to heal."

Zamira looked at all of us, then sighed. "Fine. And thank you. I'll pay you all back somehow."

"We're going to be delving the Echo at least once a moon for the next half-cycle," I said. "I doubt most instances will have an enchanted item, even a single-use, unranked one, but we'll have lots of time to find out for sure."

"On the topic of that future, let's maybe downplay the difficulty of this instance if the Iron Lady asks," added Wilf. "I don't want to have her take away our access to *protect* Barth or Zamira from themselves again."

The two people in question nodded vehemently.

"We can just say we figured out the puzzle a little bit faster than we did." I shrugged. "Once the torches were lit, everything was under control. It was just the stuff before that that was a little bit hairy."

"If that was a spider joke, I'm not ready for those," said Zamira.

"Poor choice of words," I admitted. "Anyway, what do we have left. A cloak and a short sword? Is there anything special about them?"

"I don't think so. The cloak looks to be oiled, so it'll at least be water resistant. It only appraises for five bits though." She pulled the short sword out of its sheath with the air of someone who'd literally never held a sharp object in her life. The blade was bronze and double-edged, its cross guard cast to look like the twisted branches of a leafless tree. "This appraises for multiple plugs. It's well-made but mundane."

"I'd like the sword, if that's okay?" asked Barth. "I need a secondary weapon if I run out of arrows or we encounter something else they're less effective against. I had meant to buy one in the Middle City when my requested spending money arrived, but it seems to have been delayed."

"How delayed?" asked Wilf.

"We've been at the Tryn for… three moons now?" the other nobleman asked.

"You all have. The siblings and I got here just over two moons ago," said Zamira.

"Right. And I was here for a moon even before that, which was when I realized they'd accidentally sent me with far less money than promised." He nodded. "Factoring in the time to deliver my request, I'd say it's been delayed at least two moons so far then."

We all traded glances.

"My parents are very busy. I promise I'll pay everyone back when it does show up."

"You don't have to do that," I said. "You're party. Everyone gets a share, and if there are specific items someone needs more than the rest, then so be it."

"In the military, every item is turned in," said Wilf, "and then needed gear is requisitioned from the quartermaster. But this works for me too. And speaking of me…"

"You want the cloak," I finished for him.

"It has a hood. Spring is rainy and nobody loves a soggy Spy."

"Because they're soggy or because they're a Spy?" asked Zamira.

He grinned and tapped his chin. Like me, Wilf needed a shave in the worst of ways. "You know, it could honestly be either one."

"Does anyone object to Wilf getting the cloak or Barth getting the sword?" I didn't have a problem with either. It *was* a nice cloak, nicer than the one I'd bought in Madea, but I could already tell it was too long for me. And as for the sword, I wasn't sure adding yet *another* weapon to my list of skills to not just advance but also maintain was smart.

Nobody objected, so they all took their loot. A less reasonable or less experienced man might have had an issue with the fact that Miko and I were the only two *not* getting new items. *I* was just looking forward to the next time we ran the Echo.

"Once we sell the mundane jewelry, we will have netted around seven plugs, five bits in total," said Zamira, focused on the shinies in a way my *Mercantilism* skill couldn't help but appreciate. She turned to Barth. "I'm not going to take a cut of the coin since I got the charm. What about you?"

He shook his head. "No, I'm good."

"You just said you don't have any money," pointed out Miko.

"That was before we got paid for the ishi-ka," he reminded her with a bright smile. "I've got plenty to tide me over until my parents' shipment arrives."

Wilf and I traded looks. Judging strictly off what we'd heard of Barth's parents so far, I don't think either of us expected there to even be a shipment.

"Take six bits," said Zamira. "It will make the rest of the math easier."

My math skills were decent enough to know she was being generous rather than honest, especially since seventy-five divided evenly by three. But I wasn't going to begrudge Barth some spending money, given that his parents had sent him to a foreign duchy and then effectively abandoned him.

"That leaves twenty-three each for Miko, Brian, and Wilf." She glanced down at the bracelet she'd already slipped onto her arm. "That seems a bit imbalanced."

"That's what future delves are for." I gave Zamira the mundane jewelry to sell, confident her *Mercantilism* skill was a lot higher than mine. Miko took fourteen bits to make up the difference, and Wilf got the rest: two plugs and three bits. "As fun as this has been, should we look for the exit?"

"Yes," said Miko, whose sense of smell was far more sensitive than mine. "Bright Lady, yes."

ooo

It took some searching, but we found the portal out hidden in an almost invisible alcove just past the knight's archway. One short step later, we were back in the tunnels, and soon after that, we were back in the Upper City. Zamira split off to head to her assigned quarters while the rest of went into the Tryn and made our way back to the dorms for much-needed baths and a change of clothes.

I think Barth and Wilf might have gotten the naps we'd all been talking about, but Miko and I headed back out soon after, down to the Lower City and the synossian enclave for another afternoon of sermons and food. Joshua had been joined by a synossian woman named Yuna, her scales cloudy and cracked with age. The two of them helped a few other volunteers organize the food line and settle the disputes that almost inevitably erupted as the day wore on.

Admittedly, Miko's words and my spear might have helped keep those disputes small too.

By the time we returned to our room at the Tryn, Lakshi and Tyrsa, Eos' two moons, were in the sky. I took a second bath and then got to the all-important business of checking in with the Framework. A short meditation later, the day's *real* gains were made clear:

```
You have increased the following skills:

Major skills:
Formations [+5]: 25/40
Medium Armor [+4]: 34/40
Spear (U) [+1]: 40/40
Tactics [+2]: 40/40

Minor skills:
Acrobatics [+4]: 8/40
Athleticism [+2]: 38/40
Avoidance [+1]: 37/40
Focus [+1]: 31/40
Leadership (U) [+3]: 14/40

The following skills have decreased:
Riding [-1]: 1/10
Scribing [-1]: 2/10
```

It seemed pretty dickish for the Framework to choose today, of all days, to decrement two of my skills, but admittedly, I hadn't used either for a very long time. And the other gains more than made up for it. I already had the needed Major skills capped for my next level, and either *Athleticism* or *Avoidance* would get me there for my Minor skills too.

Add in the experience I'd gained from completing the signet ring quest *and* the experience from our last two, very eventful delves, and level eight was already shockingly close.

Which made the next popup even sweeter:

```
You have increased the following attributes:

Finesse [+1]: 13
Intellect [+1]: 14
```

Two more natural gains to attributes that could really use it. Unlike the improvements allocated through even-numbered levels in the Framework, natural attribute gains were both limited and subject to reversal, just like skills, but it was nice to see both my studying and juggling were paying off.

And hell, maybe surfing the back of a giant spider and solving the tomb's mini puzzle before we got obliterated had both helped too.

While I waited for Miko to finish her own meditation, a knock came at the door. I opened it to find Prisa, from my Framework class, standing there, dark hair damp and sticking to her face.

"What is it, Prisa?" It was deeply weird to see her without her constant companion. "Do you or Ames need help with something?"

She coughed, looking uncomfortable in her academy uniform. "I'm not actually here to speak with *you*, Brian."

"Oh? *Oh.*" There was only one reason I could think of for someone to seek out Miko, especially on Seventh Day. I heard my voice go flat. "She's busy."

"That's okay," she said, not meeting my eyes. "Let her know I'll see her next Sixth Day in the dueling circle."

"If someone is making you do this…" I began.

"Nobody makes a Lothis do anything," she said, stiffening as she referred to her noble house. "Rank *matters*. I need to improve mine."

I didn't believe her as far as I could throw her with a thirteen Strength, but it didn't matter. Prisa was only mid-level, based on her performance in weapons class, but she was still a Warrior and would be a tough fight for Miko.

"I'm eleventh in our class," I told her. "Keep climbing and we can have a duel of our own. In the meantime, maybe we'll get paired off in weapons class."

The right application of *Deception* might have been able to hide the threat in my voice, but I would never know as I hadn't bothered calling on the skill. Spear always in hand, I stared the noblewoman down.

"That's *never* going to happen." Prisa scowled and spun away, not quite running back down the hall to her room.

A half-glass later, when I broke the news to a now conscious Miko, she surprised me with a sharp-toothed smile.

"Prisa picked a bad time to make her challenge. My *Staff* skill is higher than it has ever been, my defenses are too, and best of all…?"

"Yeah?"

Another grin, this one savage.

"I just reached level eight."

Book 7: Oathkeeper

"*…and though I go to meet my fathers*
with weapon bent & shield shattered

with flesh rent & savaged
into bloody strips

I will not fear to meet their gaze
for my word
at least
remains unbroken"

-Excerpt from *Meditations on Mortality*

32-Interlude

Eccol watched out of the corner of his eye as he collected empty mugs from the tables. The big man had pushed his way into the tavern that morning, covered in snow from the road, a scowl splitting the wild black beard that covered his features from the cheeks down.

Beneath the now-melted snow, beneath even that overgrown beard, was a face that looked like it had been roughly hewed from stone and then left unfinished. It was, Eccol knew, the face of a criminal. The face of a traitor. The face of a wanted man.

Arrius Vitellius. Copper. Armed and extremely dangerous. That's what the notices had said, notices that had been posted across town just a seven-day prior. Grand Duke Willerton himself had signed the order, and that meant something, even this far south, even in a town like Shamburg.

Fat Tam, who'd been the closest thing Eccol had to a father, was in back, in his tavern's kitchen with his long-time woman, Em. He'd been there since they'd sent their other cast-off boy out the back door to find the constable. Tam was many things—a good cook, a strict taskmaster, and a surprisingly funny storyteller—but a brave man wasn't one of them.

And that left Eccol to serve the entire room.

Constable Niccols was Tin, and everyone knew a Copper could squash a Tin like a phloxl stomping on a mountain hare. But everyone also knew that numbers mattered. Niccols was almost definitely gathering every Aspirant he could find for the task.

At twelve cycles of age, Eccol wouldn't be one of them. His part was to keep refilling the killer's mug, to keep the big man happy even though he himself was so scared he could barely speak.

With a heavy swallow, he carried another mug of unwatered ale to the table. This close, he could feel Arrius' aura, brutish and overpowering, angry and somehow primal all at the same time. He squeaked as he dropped the mug off and scurried back to the bar, cheeks burning at the derisive chuckle from the Copper who watched him go.

Between the weather and the man's bloody aura, it was a wonder there were any other customers at all, but winters in Shamburg were long and gray, and that was reason enough for some to seek warmth in their cups. There were four tables in total to wait on, and if all were a good distance away from the criminal, their occupants showed no signs of leaving for home.

So, Eccol did his rounds. Unwatered ale for the brute. Something considerably less potent for the others. Tam wasn't sure if a Copper even *could* get drunk but had made the call anyway. Whatever advantage they could give Constable Niccols and the others might be the difference between justice and slaughter.

It was another glass before the end of Eccol's lingering service nightmare finally came.

"Arrius Vitellius!" rang Constable Niccols' voice from outside. "You are wanted by Grand Duke Willerton for crimes against the duchy. Come out and submit to justice and you have my oath that you will be treated fairly on the way to your sentencing."

For a long moment, it seemed like the big man didn't even hear the constable, though everyone else in the inn had gone quiet and still. Then, with a heavy grunt, the Copper stood. Beneath his beard and unkempt tangle of hair, he was sweating despite the cold, eyes somehow both furious and too wide. He released his aura, and it drove Eccol flat, the clatter of pots from the kitchen and the strangled gasps coming from the other customers announcing they had all been similarly affected. It felt like Arrius' head brushed the ceiling of the tavern, like he'd have to duck and turn sideways just to squeeze out through the door. He rotated in that direction, hand on a bronze mace that seemed too small for its owner, took a step that shook the walls of the inn…

And then stumbled, dropped to one knee, and spewed his insides out all over the inn's floor.

For a brief moment, all Eccol could think of was the fact that *he'd* be the one who had to clean up the mess. Next came the thought that the ale had been far more successful than even Tam could have hoped… followed swiftly by the fear that the Copper might blame *him* for his own sickness.

When Arrius stood again, his aura had guttered out. His face was ashen beneath the sweat that saturated his beard, and veins throbbed in the hand now clutching his stomach, so thick and wide that Eccol could see them even from his position on the floor. With a roar, the Copper lowered his shoulder and smashed through the door, charging out into the street.

The sounds of combat erupted, then faded just as quickly. It was followed by Constable Niccols' ringing voice, rallying the men and women to chase after their quarry, but Eccol had eyes only for the fragments of the inn's door and the snow flurries drifting inside. Villainous Coppers fleeing from the duke's justice were all well and good, but how were they going to get a *new door* in the heart of winter?

Somehow, Eccol just knew Fat Tam was going to make this *his* problem to solve.

Neither he nor anyone else in the common room ever saw the woman who slipped out of the kitchen, a cloth-wrapped weapon on her back, and set off in pursuit. Frankly, Eccol thought she might just be another of his boss' stories, invented after spending the entire day hiding in the back and sampling his own product.

After all, what kind of woman was black as a starless night, with braids to match and a smile as sharp as the winter wind?

33

That first run of the Echo set the pattern we'd follow for the next moon: school during the week, followed by duels, sermons down in the Lower City, and a delve whenever both scheduling and the Echo permitted. As productive as our time at the Tryn was, it was impossible to overstate how heavily the true dungeon factored into our progression.

Each of the next four delves we went on was different and the victory conditions were too. We defended places that hadn't existed for thousands of cycles, explored ruins that predated the creation of the blighted, and fought as a single unit amidst battlefields that stretched to the horizon. Once, we were even tasked with escorting a funeral procession of slope-backed, three-armed sapients whose single eyes stared blankly out from beyond layers of brightly colored veils. Every scenario involved combat. A lot of combat. And that meant more than just chances to test out what we were learning in class.

It meant Miko wasn't the only one to make progress.

Four seven-days after she hit level eight, I got the message I'd been waiting for:

> **Congratulations, Warrior.**
>
> **You have reached level 8!**
>
> You have one point to allocate to an attribute of your choosing:
>
> **Strength:** 13 [+1] / **Finesse:** 13 [+2]
> **Vitality:** 17 [+4] / **Intellect:** 14
> **Discernment:** 11 / **Will:** 15

Before I did anything more, I pulled up the skills portion of my personal record:

Skills:
Major: Formations: 29/45, Knife: 38/45,
Light Armor: 25/45, Medium Armor: 40/45,
Spear (U): 40/45, Tactics: 40/45, Throwing: 1/45
Unarmed Combat: 6/45

Minor: Acrobatics: 9/45, Athleticism: 40/45,
Avoidance: 39/45, Focus: 31/45,
Leadership (U): 19/45, Pain Tolerance (U): 40/45,
Toxin Resistance (U): 1/45

Professional: None

General: Animal Behaviorism: 10/10, Brewing: 3/10,
Caretaking: 8/10, Danger Sense (R): 10/10,
Deception: 10/10, Diplomacy: 4/10, Hunting: 2/10,
Juggling: 5/10, Meditation (U): 9/10,
Mercantilism: 5/10, Orienteering: 1/10,
Performance: 1/10, Riding: 1/10, Scribing: 2/10,
Stealth: 10/10, Tracking: 7/10

I'd been seeing a crazy amount of skill gains over the past moon, most of them earned on the days we ran the true dungeon. *Medium Armor* had joined *Spear* and *Tactics* in being capped for level seven, and Avoidance was only a single point behind *Athleticism* and *Pain Tolerance* in my Minor skills. My General skills hadn't seen nearly that level of explosive growth, but *Juggling* had gained a point and I'd finally picked up the ever-elusive *Performance* skill to go along with my maxed-out *Deception*.

I'd also, somehow, gained a point in *Caretaking* from the times I'd accompanied Wilf to look after his sister, but hell if I was going to let *that* harsh my level-up buzz.

Not when I had a decision to make.

Unlike skill improvements, attribute gains had been hard to come by after our first trip to the Echo. I wasn't sure if I was already starting to run into the soft cap the Framework imposed on natural improvement, or if I needed to find new ways to push myself. Either way, training alone was providing less than stellar results.

Which made my level-up choice as important as ever.

Thankfully, that choice was pretty easy, this time around.

Ignoring the part of my brain *convinced* another point in Discernment would somehow solve all my problems, I increased my Strength to fourteen. That pushed it past Finesse and brought it in line with Intellect. Vitality remained my highest stat, thanks to the free increase it received at every level, while Will was becoming an increasingly distant second.

The more we explored the Echo, the more I realized early access to it had been, by far, the most valuable reward we'd gotten for discovering the ishi-ka's encroachment. Five copper plugs was a decent sum, but progression was the name of the game on Eos, and the true dungeon was the key to that progression. And while we hadn't seen an enchanted item since the very first instance, our share of the sellable loot had been more than sufficient to cover both the cost of repairs and our weekly trips down to the synossian enclave.

Hell, I almost had enough put aside for the pair of vambraces I'd been eyeing. *Bronze* vambraces, rather than the strange metal of Miko's looted pair, but still a damn sight better protection than the nothing I currently had.

Unfortunately, with our second moon at the Tryn almost over, two other parties from Dungeon Delving 101 would soon be added to the dungeon rotation. And that meant our delve-time would be impacted for the foreseeable future. It was *still* a hell of a lot better than patrolling the tunnels—especially since that duty had largely been curtailed as the city guard moved more troops down to defend against the ishi-ka—but it felt like our easy path to power was over.

Still, I was pretty sure we'd *all* gained at least a level so far. As the least experienced of our group, Zamira had gained two and thought she was a quarter of the way now to level six.

Progress in other arenas had been significantly slower. Miko had won two of her last three duels as the pool of available talent ranked below her thinned out, only for those rankings to be updated *en masse*, adjusted for our continuing academic performance. Which had pushed some of the initiates who had already challenged her once back down to a point where they could do so again.

While I waited for Wilf to provide any actionable intelligence, I'd been doing my best to sabotage my own rankings, hoping to drop far enough that I could at least avenge Miko's losses if not prevent them entirely. Our professors weren't cooperating though; we were a seven-day away from the next update, and I was pretty sure I remained in the top half of our class.

All those successful trips into the Echo didn't help, since they factored into the grades we received in both Small Group Tactics and Dungeon Delving.

I was starting to think I needed to increase my class rank instead and then go after the head of the snake behind Miko's continued struggles.

I just… needed to know which snake to target.

○○○

Another two seven-days later, we were on our way back to the dorms from Beasts of Eos class when Wilf caught us.

"Brian, do you have a moment?"

I caught Miko's eye.

"Am meeting with Zamira and Shiloh for study and dinner. Will see you after?"

"Sounds good." She headed on to our dorm room and I turned to follow Wilf, spear in hand.

Muttering something about the abandoned tower now having been compromised, the Spy took me to a new spot deep in the Tryn; what appeared to be an old, rarely used storage room. No doubt it spent most of its time securely locked.

"Have you found something?" I asked, once Wilf had finished inspecting the area and given his okay.

"Maybe. House Thompsen—"

"Who's that?"

"Rustik's family."

I nodded. Rustik had challenged Miko and won handily. His name was now inscribed on my shit list right next to Gareth's.

"House Thompsen appears to have come into some unexpected wealth over the past few days. Lady Thompsen was seen at Domasai's just yesterday, ordering a new gown. That's a tailoring shop in the upper Middle City," Wilf added. "*Very* posh. Out of the reach of most minor houses, *especially* one whose mining interests have badly faltered in recent years."

"So, House Thompsen got paid," I summarized.

"They're *all* getting paid, I suspect," he corrected. "In favors, if not coin. Rustik's family are just the first ones dumb enough to show it."

"Any leads on *who* paid them?" That was the whole point of this, after all.

Wilf gave me a look. "I'm a Spy, not a miracle worker, yeah? The only thing tougher to crack than a house's security is the kingdom's banking system."

I nodded, acknowledging the point. Framework-given skills only went so far, especially for someone who wasn't even Tin.

"However…" He flashed a smile sharp enough that I almost believed it. "With the White Sails celebration just a moon away, it takes more than just coin to shop at Domasai's. It takes *influence*."

"If you can't follow the money, you follow the influence instead," I concluded.

"Exactly. When Octus Domasai founded his store twenty cycles ago, he did so with the help of a few private investors. And one of those was Robash Alexander Callum Darish."

"House Darish. *Lucius'* house. I knew it."

Wilf shrugged. "Maybe? All signs point to Darish, yeah, but I need to do more verification. Signs can be faked, after all. Clues can be planted. And I don't trust any answer that practically falls into my lap."

"Still…"

"Yeah. It's *something*. If I find more, we'll know for sure."

"At which point, I'll ally with House Marchon, and you'll get your mole."

The Spy's eyes glittered. "And my own answers."

"Right." The idea of using the other house as a shield against Lucius' influence while simultaneously spying on them for Wilf didn't sit particularly well with me, but a deal was a deal. And if House

Marchon *had* had anything to do with the series of calamities that befell Wilf's family, they'd have it coming.

The enemy of my enemy is my friend was a saying that seemed to lose all validity when applied to politics.

"That's not what I wanted to talk to you about though," said Wilf, all affectation gone from his voice.

"No? Did you want Miko to take another look at Ellisha? Because until she gets a new spell at level nine—"

"No. I want to know why you've been treating me like a plague vector ever since you met my sister."

I blinked, unfortunately knowing *exactly* what he was talking about. Apparently ten points in *Deception* and one in *Performance* weren't sufficient for fooling someone who specialized in both.

"I thought trust had to be earned?" I managed.

"Really? *That's* what you're going with?" Wilf skewered me from across the room with a look. "I told you my family history. I took you to my sister, someone whose continued safety depends upon people *not* knowing she is alive. Hells, we've been on how many delves as a unit now? And you don't think I've earned your trust?"

The hurt in his voice was obvious. The problem was that there was no way to tell if that was just another performance.

"Some of it is your class," I admitted. "It's hard to know who the real you is: the drunkard, the social butterfly, the thoughtful friend, or the angry revenge seeker."

"I contain multitudes." He shrugged again. "We all wear masks. We all have secrets. What else?"

"I'm sorry?"

"You said *some* of it is my class. There's nothing I can do about that. I had a need and the Framework provided, and I'm not going to apologize for my choice. But meeting Ellisha should have helped *build* trust between us, not tear it down."

"Yeah," I agreed, finally coming to a decision I'd been putting off for way too long… since the night in question, in fact. "And it probably would have. Except for this."

I ignored the decoy coin purse on my belt, with its handful of copper bits, and reached into my shirt for the money belt that carried my actual valuables. Most of what was in there was copper too, of course, if plugs instead of bits, but what I pulled out was a silver ring with a faded crest on it.

Any doubts about Wilf's proficiency with *Performance* were forever put to rest; his expression didn't change a bit as he took in the signet of House McCall.

"Look familiar?" I asked.

"That's my father's ring." His voice was calm as one hand almost idly dropped to a knife hilt. "How did you come by it?"

I was second-guessing my decision, but it was too late now.

"I found it in the possessions of the Ever-Hungry's high priest. None of us knew the sigil until—"

"Until I took you to the Velvet Fist and you saw Ellisha's pendant." He nodded. "That was over a moon ago. Why didn't you tell me?"

I gave him a look. The *last* person I should have to explain this to was him.

Sure enough, he got there just fine on his own.

"You thought we were involved? House McCall, I mean?"

"Yeah. Maybe not you, but your family…?"

"My father was murdered almost two cycles ago, Brian. His heir has been an invalid since shortly after. My mother spends more time in bed than out back at our country estate."

"And the ring?"

"Went missing around the time of my father's death. *Stolen.* Not sent by one of us to some fringe cult on the far side of the duchy."

"How can you be sure?"

He waved a hand dismissively. "If my father was making those sorts of deals, my sister would have known about it as his heir. She'd have taken steps following his *accident*, and as *her* heir, I would have been informed of those steps."

"So, why was it—"

"There for you to find? I don't know. Our house is already broken. We're no threat to anyone. Although…" Inexplicably, a small smile broke through his scowl. "With no ability left to defend ourselves, we *would* make an excellent patsy if that ring was to be discovered."

"Why do you seem happy about that?"

"Because I just realized our white-haired Mage and I might have more in common than I realized. And maybe our respective investigations do too, yeah?"

It wasn't a new thought for me. Since we'd first found the ring, I'd assumed that its owner had had *something* to do with Wilhemina's kidnapping. If House McCall *was* innocent, then they, like the Zarisians, had almost definitely been framed by the responsible party.

Still…

"It *could* be a coincidence."

"A coincidence is you and me accidentally wearing the same colors for a night out on the town." He shook his head. "My lord father's signet ring showing up along with the duke's daughter in a dungeon of the blighted many seven-days from here? That's something else entirely."

"What now then?" I asked.

"I'm going to have to bring Zamira in on at least some of this."

That felt like a big step. "You trust her?"

"To look after her country's best interests, if nothing else." For a brief moment, he looked almost as young as Barth. "It's an odd thing, having to rely almost exclusively on foreigners, but for now, her goals and mine align."

I found myself frowning. I understood his need for secrecy—and it wasn't like I didn't have secrets of my own—but still, it seemed like a hard way to live. And for the first time since we had reached Trynfall, I realized something.

It wasn't the sort of life I wanted for myself.

It was an epiphany I hadn't sought and didn't want. Since we'd arrived in Trynfall, I'd done my very best to play the game, even if I sucked at it. Neutrality or at least the pretense of such. Cold, calculating logic. Navigating a path toward putting Miko's people first while leveraging those around me to get what we needed.

The problem?

That wasn't who I was.

Not on Earth and not here on Eos either.

I just hoped Miko would understand.

"This is yours," I said, handing over the ring.

Wilf studied my face. "I'm not going to say no, but… are you sure?"

"Yes."

For a long while, he turned the ring about in his hands, letting his fingers trace the slightly blurred lines of its crest.

"I'm not a noble, a politician, or a merchant," I told him. "I understand this whole *trading favors* and *goals that are aligned* thing, but I'm not… I don't *want* to live my life transactionally. Miko and I need allies, but we need friends too. Where better to find them than in our party?"

He dropped his eyes and looked away.

"Only adventurers call it a party, Brian."

"Then maybe we know something the rest of you don't."

ooo

Later that night, I filled Miko in on my personal epiphany.

It went… a lot smoother than I'd expected.

"Of course we should help Friend Wilf and Friend Zamira," said Miko. "To do otherwise would be to turn our backs on the Bright Lady."

"Still… I know we need allies and money and power to help prepare for your people's arrival," I said. "That's half the reason we agreed to attend the Tryn. I've been trying to balance that need with everything else."

She did the double eye-lid flick thing synossians did when they were processing and then leaned in from her side of the bed, voice serious.

"Nest-brother, I'm not taking Political Relations class to ingratiate myself with anyone, no matter how large their houses. I'm there to sort the good people from the bad. Yes, we need allies with influence in certain areas, but if a noble or their house treats others poorly, how could I ever trust them with my people's fate?"

"Do you think we should tell Wilf and Zamira about your people?"

"And Friend Barth. Yes. I've been thinking just that but did not want to pressure you if you disagreed."

"Really?"

She nodded, shakily at first, and then again, with more certainty. "I trust Zamira. You trust Wilf. And Barth's heart is pure, despite what appears to be a continued pattern of poor treatment from his blood family. I don't know how or if any of them can help, but—"

"Zamira obviously still has contacts with her father and the rest of Zaris," I said. "A merchant country, even one that's been forcibly annexed, has to understand logistics. Which would help us with routing your people from wherever they land to wherever they're going to stay. And as horrible as Barth's family sounds, it's clear that they're also wealthy, and that Apsa is a much richer duchy than Trynfall. As for Wilf…"

"Friend Wilf knows local politics. While his house lacks power of its own, he can point us to connections we will need to make."

"Assuming he agrees, yeah."

She paused. "For all my talk of friendships, I immediately move to discussing how they can be of service to us. Are we *using* them, nest-brother?"

"No." This much at least I felt confident in. "Using them would be what we were doing. Not telling them the truth and trying to get something out of them anyway. Asking for help once they understand what is at stake is the opposite."

After a moment's thought, she tapped her left arm in agreement. "Still, even if they join us in this, we *will* need the support of a noble house that is not fallen from grace."

"Shiloh?" I asked. I didn't know the dark-haired girl well, but Zamira and Miko had made numerous expeditions into the city with her as of late.

Miko shook her head. "She is the fourth child of a house only recently raised to the nobility for their actions during the last plague."

"The one that ended the Kingdom Wars?"

"Yes. She is friendly and kind, but her house has little influence amongst their fellow nobles. However…" Here, she broke out in a grin that would have absolutely terrified any human that didn't know her. "There are extended members of her family who still work as crafters."

It took me far too long to put the pieces together, maybe because we hadn't talked about it for a very long time. When I did, I couldn't help but smile.

"You found someone to apprentice under as an Herbalist?"

I don't know how she managed it, but her arm tap this time felt almost… victorious.

"A distant cousin of Shiloh's, who only recently set up his shop in Trynfall. He is in the Lower City until he can build up his business, and will not be able to pay me for my work, but…"

"But you should be able to learn the other primary skills needed to gain the profession."

"Yes." She grinned again. "I will report to his shop two nights a week."

After the night's meditation was over—no gains whatsoever, though I could at least feel my energy levels creeping slowly closer to the level nine would require—I let our earlier conversation replay in my head. We hadn't told the others yet but had made plans to do so during the next delve when there would be no chance of anyone overhearing.

Just making that decision helped.

I felt… lighter. Cleaner, somehow. Instead of drifting off into sleep, I spent a glass or so digging into that feeling. Both the epiphany that had triggered it and the sense of relief I'd felt even before speaking to Miko. I didn't know how any of it tied into my Ideal, if it *did* tie in at all, but Professor Lunsford had said self-knowledge was a key part of breaking through to Tin. Not just an awareness of who you were, but of who you wanted to become.

Something told me *this* was as much a part of all that as Kacellius' poetry book, as my hours training with the spear, and even my dream conversation with the god who'd helped bring me to Eos.

It sure would have been nice to have some sort of numerical progression to track my progress though.

ooo

With other groups from our class now having gained access to the Echo, we only got to run the dungeon every other seven-day. Loot and experience both slowed down accordingly, although it was honestly the former that hurt more. Miko's apprenticeship with Herbalist Jesher was free, thanks to Shiloh's connections, but the equipment she needed was not. Glass vials and tubes, a mortar and pestle, scales for weighing out measurements, even cheesecloth for straining some tinctures and concoctions. The good news was that we didn't have to buy Miko a burner as she was permitted to use Jesher's. The better news is that he cleared some space in his workroom for her to store her stuff, so it wasn't sucking up all the oxygen in our dorm room.

The bad news was the expense. Once she had the profession, I was pretty sure it would start paying for itself. In the meantime though? Startup costs were a bitch, even without having to rent a workspace of her own. Tack on the twice-weekly trips to feed what seemed to be a growing crowd of synossians, and our finances were shrinking for the first time since we'd gained access to Trynfall's true dungeon.

Which made the mangled bronze knife in my hands even more of a problem. Today's delve had involved us defending one wall of a city against winged creatures that looked like a cross between gargoyles and drakes. None of us recognized them, suggesting they were a species that had either never existed or had gone extinct hundreds of cycles earlier, but of course that didn't matter at all in the Echo. The damn things had been fast too, swarming us like bloodhungry imps. Barth had been next to useless, forced to switch to the short sword he'd gained from our first delve, and I hadn't been much better, laying about with my knife when everything slipped past my spear's reach without even trying.

Of course, the things hadn't just *looked* like gargoyles. They'd been almost as tough as them, too, and our various weapons had fared far worse than Miko's ironwood short staff.

Even worse? The chest at the end, all alone by itself in the middle of the dusty courtyard, contained nothing but coin. And even then, there were barely enough bits to make up a single plug for each of us.

"Is it just me or are the rewards getting *worse* the more we delve?" asked Zamira, twisting her hair back into a braid as she eyed her cracked ash staff mournfully.

"It's a hazard of it being run too often," said Wilf. "With three groups from the Tryn delving the unranked tier, it quickly becomes more about the experience than the loot. But that was the point all along, yeah?"

Which was easy for him to say, as a noble. Even one whose house was falling apart. He wasn't *wrong;* Miko swore she was a seven-day or so from leveling, and after two full moons of delving, I wasn't that far behind. But money mattered too.

"We might have to start doing some missions for the Adventurer's Guild again," I said, tucking away my ten bits into an increasingly anemic money belt. "Any word on the ishi-ka?"

Wilf shook his head. "Last I heard, they'd crushed one nest only to find another. And then realized *both* were offshoots of a larger nest entirely. I wouldn't be surprised if they brought in your guild to help out the guard, but…"

"But school will not permit Zamira and Barth to participate," finished Miko.

"Which remains patently absurd," added the Zarisian. "Some of the fights were way worse than our fight with the ishi-ka. And I think most of us have leveled since then anyway. Three ishi-ka should be a joke."

"I think they're more worried about us running into thirty of them," offered Barth. "Or ascended versions, even."

That quieted the rest of us pretty fast. I didn't want to even picture an ascended ishi-ka. The closest our party had come was the giant spider in our first dungeon delve, and *that* would have annihilated us without the undead knight and his retainers.

"We should head out," I said. "I don't know how long that took, but Miko and I need to head down to the enclave again tonight." And I needed to find a food stall owner that my *Mercantilism* worked on. Even getting our spend down by a few bits would add up over time.

I took a step and stumbled on a knee that had swollen up since we'd stopped moving. I didn't remember getting hit there, but the lump would make a baseball jealous… if baseballs existed on Eos.

Miko hurried forward and *Minor Healing* took down some of the swelling. *Light Healing* might have addressed it entirely, but I'd waved off the offer. One of the things Ebb and Flow had hammered home in Small Group Tactics was the value of keeping things in reserve, and our healer's energy was one of those things. Even with the delve done, we were trying to internalize that lesson.

I was healthy enough to walk and that was good enough. I could wait until tomorrow to get fully healed.

The castle we'd been defending was an odd thing, mostly shrouded in mists that resisted our attempts at exploration. During the battle, we'd seen shapes in those mists that almost had to be other defenders, but only the courtyard and our section of the wall had remained clear. With the defense complete, it felt like we stood in someone's dream of a place that never was.

Thankfully, the path out was clear. I led the way, doing my best not to limp; that would just make Miko want to heal me again, and we needed to get past that sort of thing.

Moments later, we emerged into the tunnels to find the Echo's two guards were no longer alone. In fact, there were four men, all in black, flanking an older man Miko and I knew well.

"Lord Hawthorne?" I stepped to one side out of habit, clearing the way for the next of our party to emerge. "What are you doing here?"

"Priestess Naseri is needed," he told me.

The woman in question had been a half-step behind me and heard the nobleman's response. "What is wrong?" she asked, sketching out a salute.

"Priestess Iris requests your immediate attendance," he told her. To his credit, Hawthorne no longer looked like he was sucking on a lemon every time he spoke to one of us. "I've come to escort you there."

Miko and I traded glances. The lord arbiter wasn't giving any hints, but there was only one thing either of us could think of that would link Iris, Miko, and Hawthorne back together.

Something was wrong with Wilhemina.

"Should I come with you?" I asked her in the High Tongue.

She tapped her right arm. "They did not allow it last time. I do not think they will this time either."

I was pretty sure she was right but pressed the issue anyway with Hawthorne. It was almost as productive as debating a tree.

"Will see you back in the dorms, nest-brother," she told me before the arbiters whisked her away. "Can you bring my apologies to Joshua and Una? I don't know if I will make tonight's sermon."

Most of the synossians *still* seemed more interested in the food than anything Miko had to say, but I nodded anyway.

"I can help with the food tonight," offered Wilf.

That was big. Of all our party, he'd been the one most skeptical when it came to the reveal about Miko's origin, people, and the boatloads of refugees headed to the continent. This felt like an olive branch of sorts.

Misreading the look on my face, he was quick to add: "I'll help with the purchasing *and* carrying."

It was good to have friends.

And that was how Wilf and I found ourselves at the synossian enclave that night, helping pass out food and listening to a few would-be orators who tried to fill the void left by Miko's absence.

Back on Earth, I'd have told them not to quit their day jobs.

Here on Eos, I wasn't sure they had any.

Late that night, with Miko still missing, I emerged from meditation to discover that I was one point away from maxing *Knife* for my level and had once again capped out both *Pain Tolerance* and *Medium Armor*. For the first time, *Spear* was lagging behind just a bit, the skill's Uncommon ranking finally having an impact on its leveling speed. Meanwhile, *Tactics* had been capped out since our last delve, and *Athleticism* and *Avoidance* weren't far behind:

```
Skills:
Major: Formations: 36/45, Knife: 44/45,
Light Armor: 25/45, Medium Armor: 45/45,
Spear (U): 43/45, Tactics: 45/45, Throwing: 1/45,
Unarmed Combat: 6/45

Minor: Acrobatics: 11/45, Athleticism: 43/45,
Avoidance: 44/45, Focus: 35/45,
Leadership (U): 23/45, Pain Tolerance (U): 45/45,
Toxin Resistance (U): 1/45

Professional: None

General: Animal Behaviorism: 10/10, Brewing: 3/10,
Caretaking: 8/10, Danger Sense (R): 10/10,
Deception: 10/10, Diplomacy: 4/10, Hunting: 2/10,
Juggling: 6/10, Meditation (U): 9/10,
Mercantilism: 5/10, Orienteering: 1/10,
Pathfinding: 1/10, Performance: 1/10, Riding: 1/10,
Scribing: 2/10, Stealth: 10/10, Tracking: 7/10
```

I'd picked up *Pathfinding* a few seven-days earlier, but we hadn't run any delves since that seemed suitable for improving it. *Toxin Resistance* was also still stuck at the first rank, but Miko had plans on how to fix that once she became an Herbalist. She thought she could level her profession while feeding me toxins to increase my skill. It would be a win/win for everyone except my stomach and probably a few other vital internal organs.

It was sometime after third bell—meaning three glasses past the thirtieth hour that made for an Eosian midnight—when our dorm room door finally rattled with a key in its lock. Seconds later, a very tired synossian let herself in, still carrying her adventuring gear.

I hopped up to help lighten her load only to remember my knee wasn't healed yet. *Pain Tolerance* helped swallow my shriek, and *Deception* must have kept the anguish from my expression too, as Miko didn't react. She even let me take the pack from her shoulders once I'd made it over to her.

"Is everything okay?" I asked as she flopped back onto the bed, more liquid than lizard.

"Yes. And no." She propped herself up on elbow and turned in my direction. As tired as she clearly was, she'd also apparently managed a bath at some point. Likely, Iris had insisted on it before granting Miko access to her patient. "Wilhemina is not getting better."

"She's *still* asleep?"

The synossian was too weary to even tap her arm. "Worse. The contagion has come back. Priestess Iris needed my help to cleanse it again."

A High Copper needing help from an unranked healer was almost as worrisome as a ducal heir sleeping for five moons... and not *nearly* as worrisome as a cult-given infection that came back even after it had been cured.

"She is at a loss," Miko continued. "Both to why my blessings are effective, and to how we can permanently break the curse."

"They haven't heard from the Crimson Needle?"

"No." She sighed. "I don't know how this will impact our delves, Brian. If I am necessary to Wilhemina's survival…"

It was my turn to flop back onto my bed. That would make her more important than Zamira or Barth to the duke, which might mean risking her even in the rank-defined Echo was a bridge too far.

"We'll figure something out. For now, you should get some sleep. Apparently, Stick's got something special planned for tomorrow's Basic Conditioning class."

Miko's groan was remarkably similar to the one I'd made, a few glasses earlier, when Wilf had given me the same news.

34

Another ten days passed. One trip to the Echo. Two duels, neither of which Miko won, but which still pushed her closer to level nine. Multiple sermons down at the synossian enclave, our continuing classes at the Tryn, and four sessions a week for Miko with Shiloh's Herbalist relative. I gained a point in *Spear* and another in *Athleticism* but otherwise, gains were hard to come by.

We'd been at the academy for almost three and a half moons, or roughly a third of the eleven-moon cycle. To hear everyone talk, spring was right around the corner, but I couldn't tell. Trynfall's location on the coast meant winter landed with a lighter touch there than elsewhere in the duchy but the nights were still cold enough that our breath fogged on the way back from visiting Wilf's sister or preaching to Miko's people. Not that that reality seemed to matter much: the coming White Sails celebration, intended to celebrate the season's departure, had both the Middle and Lower City in a state of near-frenzied preparation.

Either everyone will drink to protect themselves from the cold or they'll drink to celebrate the end of that cold, as Wilf had put it. *Either way, the festival will be a success. A drunk populace spending their money is good for the merchants and happy merchants are good for the duke.*

While Trynfall lost its collective mind over the coming festival, I was a lot more interested in something *else* Wilf had discovered: a second of Miko's challengers had revealed ties to Lucius and House Darish. The connections Wilf had uncovered might have easily been dismissed as circumstantial on their own. Taken together with House Thompsen though?

It was a pattern.

And that was what led to me waiting alone in the dorm hall's common room on Second Day. Miko was away for her apprenticeship, Zamira was back in her appointed quarters in the duke's palace, Barth was off having a formal dinner with some noble house his family had decided he should evaluate, and Wilf…

Well, Wilf had his pretense of neutrality to maintain.

When Mireille came in, she was, as always accompanied by a handful of other nobles. Ames being one of them gave me some pause, given that her friend Prisa had been one of many to challenge Miko. Still, it was hard to imagine the blunt-faced and blunt-tongued Mage being involved in some sort of secret conspiracy.

Now, *beating me to death with a rock for annoying her?* That would be more Ames' style.

All five were sweaty and wearing rumpled academy uniforms. From the look of it, they'd all just come back from private training, something available only to those with both money and connections. Hell, they might even have gotten an extra delve in the Echo on one of the six days the Tryn didn't have access. And if the rest of our class was any indication, they'd be washing up and heading back out soon for dinner.

That didn't give me much time.

I stood and headed their way, trading nods and/or grunts with a few of the initiates I'd gotten to know in class. As my target became obvious, they all closed ranks about Mireille, like they were part of her honor guard rather than nobles by their own right.

There were *some* downsides to carrying my spear everywhere.

"Mireille," I said, locking eyes with House Marchon's heir, "I wanted to talk to you."

The brunette eyed the spear in my right hand. "You're thirteenth in the initiate rankings, you realize? That means you can't duel any of us in the top seven."

"I'm not here to challenge you."

"You'd lose even if you could."

"Whatever you say."

Judging by the narrowing of her eyes and the flaring of her nostrils, that had been the wrong response. Wonderful.

"I just want to talk," I repeated.

"*Someone's* looking for a White Sails party invite," said Darishal, who'd been a lot more likable when Lucius was wiping the floor with him in their first and only duel.

"Commoners don't *get* invites," added the dusky-skinned woman hanging off his arm. Sky was one of the few healers in our class other than Miko and, like most of the others, one of Mireille's party members. According to Wilf, she hailed from one of House Marchon's smallest vassal families. Still, if there was one thing an eleven Discernment stat and all my time at the Tryn had taught me, it was that the gulf between noble families was a crack in the road compared to the world-swallowing abyss between nobility and commoner.

Of the five, only Darishal was as tall as Miko, which naturally didn't prevent the whole group from looming over me.

Mireille turned to the others. "I'll speak with Initiate Fieldings. Meet back here in a half glass or so?"

"I can wait with you," said Ames, the Mage's flat-eyed stare never leaving me.

"There's no need but thank you. Go on ahead."

We watched the burly woman follow the others down the hall to the dorm rooms.

"I didn't realize you and Ames were close," I said.

"Amelia? She joined our unit last seven-day," said Mireille, "after Farrell bowed out."

Farrell was another Mage, this one male. I think I'd heard him say a total of five words in all the classes we'd had together.

"What happened with Farrell?"

"I would have thought McCall would've told you all about it. Or perhaps Euphrates?"

Wilf and Shiloh, respectively, although I only knew the latter's house name by accident.

"We've been more focused on our own progress than anything," I said, shading the truth like only someone with a maxed-out *Deception* skill and a point in *Performance* could. "I'm an adventurer. All this politics stuff is your domain, not mine."

"Naturally."

I didn't think she believed me. Nor did she give me any further information on why Farrell had fallen out of their dungeon rotation.

"What can I do for you, Brian? If you're here to accuse me or my house again, get it over with and move on. I've got things to do tonight. Vastly better things."

I wasn't sure why everyone on Eos always had to make things so difficult. The only thing I could be certain of was that it *definitely* wasn't my fault. Still, I *was* the one who'd asked to talk.

"I wanted to see if your offer was still open."

"My offer?"

"To ally with House Marchon."

She blinked at me for a long moment, either a vastly superior performer to Wilf or completely incapable of masking her surprise. When she finally schooled her features again, a new sentiment colored her expression: suspicion.

"Why now? You all seem to be doing fine on your own. The way I hear it, your synossian friend is almost level nine, even."

I would *dearly* have loved to know where she'd gotten that little nugget of information. I could count the number of people who knew Miko's level and progress on one hand, and they were all in our party.

"The duels are becoming a distraction," I said, again leaning on *Deception*. "I'm tired of them and want them to stop."

That prompted an exasperated sigh from the distractingly straightforward noblewoman. "I can only tell you this so many times: we are not responsible."

"Yeah. House Darish is."

She rocked back and gave me another long look through surprisingly long lashes.

"How do you know that?"

"We haven't been *entirely* focused on our own progress." My smile would have done Wilf proud; cold and sharp as one of his knives. "You said you could put an end to this if we joined you?"

"Yes. I… think so."

"You *think* so?"

She looked away. "You've been targeted because you're unaffiliated. That made you a threat to the status quo."

"You have eyes and ears in House Darish?"

Mireille shook her head. "If so, I wouldn't divulge that information to you. I have a noble father of my own. If my lord father could see your threat, old Robash definitely did. *Especially* after you embarrassed Lucius in that initial spar."

"Which brings us back to us allying with your house."

"A lack of affiliation doesn't just make you a threat, it also leaves you vulnerable. House Darish *should* back off once your affiliation is made public. If not, we would have our own vassals in the lower tiers of the class make their own ranking challenges as reprisals. Nobody wants a war, not even Lucius. However…" Mireille's frown marred the lines of a face that would always be a shade too severe to be considered pretty. "You asked the question. Are you even listening to me?"

I wasn't, because a dialogue window had just appeared in the air before me, and while that in itself wasn't *entirely* unprecedented, the specific text had my attention.

NEW QUEST: Save the Voice of the Dawn.

[Accept | Decline]

"I've got to go," I said, accepting the quest as fast as I'd ever done anything in my life. "Miko's in trouble."

ooo

Mireille caught me before I made it to the hall, her grip like steel.

"What do you mean she's in trouble? How do you know?"

"I just do." I strained for the door, dragging her with me. She was bigger than I was, but no stronger. "I have to go."

"Where's your unit?"

"Not here."

"Then give us thirty seconds. Mine will come with us. Heading into danger alone is stupid."

She… wasn't wrong, as much as I hated to admit it. I tightened my fingers around the shaft of my spear, gave a terse nod, and waited.

It was more like a minute, but the same group that had been accompanying Mireille re-emerged, some of them pulling on armor over their uniforms. The head noblewoman herself tugged a bronze helmet nicer than anything I owned down over her short hair and strapped on a belt with two hand axes of a different metal dangling from loops.

"Where are we going?" she asked me, all business.

"There's an Herbalist in the Lower City. I don't know where exactly, but he's a distant relative of House Euphrates."

"Zelig's. I know the place," said Darishal.

"Since when do *you* care about herbs?" asked Sky.

"Since *you* started dragging me out on the town every Sixth Day. Man sells the cheapest hangover cures in town."

"Nobody said you have to drink your body's weight in ale."

"Do we have any idea what's going on?" asked Ames, interrupting the two.

The whole group looked to me; I shook my head.

"Just that Miko's in danger."

"Lovely. I've got energy for one, maybe two spells."

"That will have to do." Mireille turned to Darishal. "Lead us out. As fast as you can, but we need to be in condition to fight when we get there."

"It'll be faster if we can take the lifts," he said.

She hesitated for a second, glanced at me, then nodded. "Do it. I'll get ex post-facto approval from my house."

Any other time, I might have taken notes from her leadership style to see how I could improve my own. At that moment though, getting to Miko was the only thought in my head.

We made it to the lifts in record time, and any resistance the guards there would have mounted crumbled as soon as Mireille started throwing her house's name around. Minutes after we'd left the dorm halls, we were exiting out into the Lower City. To the north, stairs led down to the docks I could smell but not see. To the right, the road curved around to the first tier of Trynfall's bottommost district.

We went right. Three blocks down, up a stairwell to the second tier, then another two blocks over, to a large stone building with a slate tile roof and a sign out front with a carved sprig of some kind of plant on it.

Everything was quiet. If anything, our presence was the only real disturbance on the block; more than a few passers-by cautiously crossed to the opposite side of the street to avoid us on their evening walks.

"Watch the street," Mireille told Darishal and the slim, hook-nosed man who was their fifth group member. Kamet, I thought. "Sky and Amelia, you're with us."

I went first, spear at the ready, and cut to the side as soon as I was through the door, clearing space for Mireille and the others. We'd never worked together as a group, but we'd all been attending the same classes for more than three moons now. And while none of us were Tin, we were still some of the Tryn's best initiates.

We'd make do.

Except... what awaited us in the herbalist's shop was a single man in long sleeves, gloves and a leather apron, a combover doing a terrible job of masking his baldness. He stood behind a counter that held a handful of glass jars of dried vegetation; a cloth spread before him presented other herbs, sorted and bound in discrete bundles.

"Welcome to Zelig's Herbal Emporium!" he said, offering up a practiced smile. "I am Zelig, proprietor and the Herbalist responsible for the goods you see on display. What can I do for..." He sized us up, eyes drawn almost by accident to Mireille's gear. "...the noble scions of Trynfall?"

"We're looking for Miko," I said. "Your apprentice."

"My soon-to-be *former* apprentice, you mean." His smile slipped. "A nice enough girl, no doubt, but when I agreed to take her on as a favor to my third cousin, twice removed, I had one hard and fast requirement. She would *always* show up on time."

"She was late today?"

"Late?" He gestured around his shop. "She never showed at all! I had thought better of her, to be honest."

I traded glances with Mireille, who turned to Ames and Sky.

"Back outside. Tell Darishal and Kamet. Check the streets in either direction on this block for any signs."

For once, Ames didn't even argue.

"What's going on?" asked Zelig. "And who are you?"

"I represent House Marchon," said Mireille. "We have reason to believe that Priestess Naseri is in danger. This is her brother."

The Herbalist sent me a confused look. "*You're* her brother?"

"By choice, not blood," I said, though that was kind of obvious to anyone with eyes. "When I last saw Miko, she was heading down here for her lesson."

Zelig swallowed heavily. "She… she never arrived. I've been here since just after lunch."

Mireille turned back to me. "Thoughts? Otherwise, I'd suggest we work our way back up the path she likely took from the Tryn and look for clues."

The only thing keeping me from freaking the hell out was that I hadn't *failed* my quest yet. And that meant, Miko was still savable. We just had to find out what had happened to her.

No, I told myself, *we just have to find her. What happened can wait until after she's safe.*

Mireille was still waiting… which was problematic because I didn't have an answer. I opened my mouth to tell her so, then stopped again. I didn't have an answer, but I *did* have an idea.

"Miko keeps a change of clothes in your workshop, right?" I asked the Herbalist.

"Yes. We both do. Some solvents we use can be tough on fabric. Why?"

"Because it'll have her scent." To hear Miko talk, synossians didn't have any odor whatsoever, but I'd spent enough time with my nest-sister to know otherwise. They didn't *sweat*, per se, but that was another thing entirely.

"We can track her with bloodhounds!" said Mireille.

"Do you *have* bloodhounds?" I asked.

"I'm a noble of Trynfall. Of course I do. Just… not here in the capital," she admitted. "This city's not a place for their breed. They need room to run and lots of it."

Sky ducked back in from the street. She gave Mireille a slow shake of her head. "Nothing. Kamet even double-checked our alleys. He doesn't see a sign of a struggle or even any indication that the scaled was here."

"Synossian," I said, echoed by Mireille a half-breath later.

"Right. Synossian."

"Okay." Mireille turned to Zelig, who had just emerged from the back with Miko's spare set of robes in hand. "If Priestess Naseri shows, please send word to the Tryn. Direct it to Mireille of House Marchon."

Somehow, the Herbalist went even more pale. "Lady Marchon. Yes… yes, of course. You have my word."

It took him an extra-long second to realize I was there and to hand over Miko's robes. By the time I emerged, Mireille was already conferring with her group.

"There's a breeder on the east side of the market," the presumed Rogue I now knew as Kamet was saying. "I can't guarantee that they'll have any bloodhounds in stock at all, let alone properly trained ones, but…"

"We don't need a bloodhound, trained or otherwise," I said. "We have something better."

"What's that?" asked Darishal.

"Two lupine who owe me a favor."

ooo

It took us a quarter-glass to reach Cailus and Little Fuzz's house in the southeast quadrant of the Lower City, but only a minute for the lupine to agree to help. With speed being of the essence, Cailus sent Greshal with us after securing a promise from his grandpup to keep out of danger and stay focused on the task at hand.

As it was, I still carried Greshal on my back as Mireille and I ran back through the Lower City to where the others had been working to identify Miko's route from the Tryn. Every time I glanced over, mid-stride, the noblewoman was giving me odd looks.

"What?" I finally asked.

"How on Eos do you speak lupine?"

"It's called Cantus," I replied, getting a yip of agreement in my ear from the cub. Between all my stat increases and conditioning training, the Lower City's dirty streets were positively flying past, yet neither of us was out of breath.

"And how do you know *that*?"

The short answer was that Greshal had inadvertently told me when we returned him to his grandsire, but that answer would just open a whole new can of questions, so I wasn't going to give it.

"Languages are a passion of mine," I said instead. "Maybe it comes from growing up with Miko."

"That's right. You speak her tongue as well." The considering looks didn't lessen in the slightest. "Some day, I'd really like to visit this foreign town you both came from."

"Unless you like titan snakes, I'd wait until you're at least Copper," I said. "Or maybe even Iron."

That was the wrong thing to say, apparently; Mireille's focus only intensified.

Thankfully, we spotted Sky and Darishal not long after, up near the gate to the Middle City.

"It's a good thing Miko's a sca—synossian," said Sky. "There aren't a lot of her kind coming down from the Middle City, so one of the guards on duty remembered her. Kamet and Ames are checking the route the guard said she took."

They led us a handful of blocks away, where we found Ames standing watch on a corner. Behind her, in what passed for a dark alleyway this close to the Middle City, Kamet was squatting down, examining something.

Mind suddenly full with unwanted possibilities, I forced myself to approach until I saw it for myself: an ironwood short staff, one end of it covered in dried blood and what looked like bone fragments. On my back, Greshal had gone quiet and still.

"She didn't go easily," said Kamet, nodding first to the remnants of whatever Miko had hit and then to our surroundings. As my eyes adjusted, I picked out blood spatter on the nearby building's back wall and even a still-wet pool of the same beneath. "I don't know how much of this blood is hers, but whoever attacked her had enough people left over to remove any bodies."

"I don't want to say it," said Darishal, "but—"

"She's still alive," I said.

"How can you be sure?"

As much as I appreciated their help, I wasn't going to tell them or anyone else about my Framework-given quests. The last thing I needed was to end up on the Eosian version of a dissection table.

"I just am."

"No offense, but—"

"He knew she was in danger from halfway across the city," said Mireille. "If he says she's alive, she's alive."

"There's no body," added Kamet. "So, either way, they took her somewhere."

"Somewhere down here," added Ames. "The gate guards would have noticed anyone trying to smuggle a body back into the Middle City."

"Gresh will help find pretty one," squeaked the cub on my back. He hopped down to the street, landing softly on all fours, and sniffed about. "Which scent is hers though?"

Mireille handed over the spare robes we'd taken from the herbalist. Greshal went back and forth from fabric to alleyway a few times before his tail started wagging back and forth.

"I have it!" he exclaimed, yipping excitedly. "Follow me!"

I caught him before he could dart off into the darkness.

"Slowly, Little Fuzz," I said in Cantus. "So we can all keep up."

That won me another tail wag. He darted to the opposite end of the alley and then turned and waited for us.

"He speaks *lupine?*" Ames sounded like she'd discovered Eos had four moons instead of two.

"It's called Cantus," corrected Mireille, handing Miko's bloody short staff over to the Mage to carry. "And yes, he does. Now, let's go. Kamet out front. Darishal, take rearguard. Amelia and Sky, the cub is your priority. Brian and I will deal with any threats we encounter."

I had to wonder how high Mireille's *Leadership* skill was. Or, more accurately, if it was tiered higher than my own Uncommon variant. Because it was remarkably easy to go with the flow when she handed out orders.

It's her party, I told myself. *It makes sense to let her take command.*

Strangely, the thought that I'd been a barista less than a year earlier while she'd been trained all her life for the task wasn't part of that internal debate. I'd already changed so much that Bug and Kate might not even recognize their long-lost friend.

Frankly, they'd probably be more focused on the spear in my hands.

Whoever had taken Miko didn't leave any kind of trail that my *Tracking* skill could follow once we had re-emerged onto the city's main streets, but Greshal didn't have that problem. We followed him back down all the way past the Velvet Fist and Zelig's shop to the first tier of the Lower City and the passageway leading to the guarded city lift. But instead of turning inside, the lupine cub kept going, down the slowly descending street that led toward the docks.

The further we went, the more the anger inside of me grew. Miko wasn't perfect, any more than the rest of us were, but she was one of the best, most genuine people I'd ever met. And someone had attacked her. Jumped her in an alleyway. Kidnapped her and spirited her away. Someone was going to pay for all of it.

Trynfall's harbor was as much a key to the city's success as the Echo and the tunnel systems under the mountain, making Grand Duke Willerton's capital one of the primary centers of maritime trade for the entire kingdom. I tried to remind myself of that as we climbed down a set of stairs. In our entire time in Trynfall, I'd only been to the docks once. They smelled exactly like I remembered: a mix of fish, alcohol, and far less savory things.

I almost hoped Miko was unconscious. Otherwise, the odor would just be insult added to her obvious injury.

Thankfully, any worries I had that that same odor would prevent Greshal from following my nest-sister's trail were quickly proven unfounded. The cub continued to scamper along, fast enough that I wondered why I'd carried him in the first place, leading us down through the maze of shops, taverns, warehouses, and tenements. The streets were full with a mix of early revelers and dockworkers, but even the hardest among them steered clear of our armed and armored unit.

"Does your sister have any enemies who would want to take her?" Mireille asked me during a brief pause as Greshal and Kamet surveyed the next intersection.

"I can only think of one."

She gave me a look I couldn't interpret. "Kidnapping is a hell of an escalation from ranking duels, Brian Fieldings. I think this is a little much even for Lucius."

"And yet you knew exactly who I was talking about."

She huffed, but our little tracker was on the move again, and so were we.

As we got closer and closer to Trynfall's enormous piers, the thought occurred to me that Miko's kidnappers might have taken her onto a ship. I didn't know a thing about sailing… or the ocean, in general, but they wouldn't have had time to already head out, would they?

If they *had*, I would beat Miko's destination out of Lucius with my bare hands. And then I'd hand him over to Zamira and Wilf. Something told me they both had plenty of anger to work out.

Instead, the trail led us to a harborside warehouse, two stories tall, with dark windows and a pair of doors large enough for heavily laden wagons to travel through. Greshal made a circuit around the building then scampered back over to where we waited, mostly out of view.

"The pretty is inside, *nihuwa*," he told me in his broken Trade.

"Nihuwa?" asked Mireille.

I had to sound it out in my own head, mentally swapping to Cantus before my *Speaker of Tongues* trait would properly translate.

"It means something like older brother," I said. Which… was *mostly* true. There was a whole bunch of other stuff too. Stuff about responsibilities in the family pack and for the hunt that didn't apply to human interactions.

"A synossian sister and a lupine brother." The noblewoman pursed her lips. "You have an interesting family." She turned to Kamet, who had just made his own circuit of the warehouse. "Exits?"

"Two. These doors and a smaller one in the back."

"Do you have enough energy left to see what's inside?"

The Rogue gave a reluctant nod. "Yes, but that won't leave me anything if we get in a fight."

"Today's delve was a long one," Mireille told me, explaining why basically everyone in her party was running low. Then, to Kamet again: "Do it. Once we know what we're facing, we can decide on the next step."

Kamet's perpetually sour expression grew even more so, but he nodded again, crossed the street to the warehouse, and placed one on its wooden wall, palm flat and fingers splayed outward.

"What is he doing?" I asked, keeping my voice low.

"House Inshalla is famous for producing Infiltrators," said Sky, her own voice a quiet song. "Kam's only just started down that path but he's far enough along to be useful."

The Rogue—no, Infiltrator—sagged as his technique finished. When he came back to us, the circles beneath his eyes had somehow deepened. "Six people inside," he said, words hushed. "Four upright, two prone. One on the ground is significantly warmer than the rest. There are shelves in the warehouse but it's a clear path to whoever's inside. That's all I can see."

"Synossians run hot," I said. "Especially after exertion."

"Guess that settles things. Four's easy enough," said Darishal.

"Unless one or more is Tin," replied Mireille.

"Doubt the sca—that *Miko* would have put up so much of a fight if they were." The bulky Warrior looked to me for confirmation.

I shrugged, less certain. Miko would have fought, no matter what, and she was a lot tougher than most people realized.

"We need to make a decision then." Mireille scanned her party members and then me. "I can send word to my house's troops here in the city, but it will take time for them to arrive and attract a lot of attention. Or we can go in as a group, here and now, and take care of things ourselves."

"We didn't get to be the best unit in the whole Tryn by sitting on our hands," said Darishal.

"We didn't get there by taking stupid risks either," countered Kamet.

I wasn't sure they'd gotten there at all, but this wasn't the time or place to say so. Not when Miko could very well be bleeding out in the warehouse.

"I'm going in," I said. "You're welcome to join me or not."

"One on four—or even five—doesn't make for good odds," said Sky, her voice oddly diffident.

"I'll make do."

"I've seen you spar," said Darishal. "You're not *that* good."

I shrugged again. "Sparring's a lot different than killing."

Mireille studied my face and sighed at whatever she saw. "When this is over, we're going to sit down and review how the chain of command works."

I nodded but said nothing, prompting another sigh.

"I'm going in with Brian." She turned to the others. "We'll need at least one of you to stay back and watch over the lupine. Sky?"

"Yeah, happily. But you all need to stay in one piece. I'm talking to you, Derry. I don't have enough spells left to put you back together again today."

Darishal just grinned.

Mireille nodded. "Kamet, watch the rear door and take care of anyone that tries to flee that way."

It would keep him out of the thick of the fighting and the Infiltrator seemed happy about that.

"Darishal, Brian, we'll go in together." She turned to the last member of her unit. "Amelia, we're going to need whatever boost you can give the three of us."

The Mage shot a look my way but nodded. "Okay. But divided three ways, that's only ten ticks of haste for each of you."

"It'll have to do."

"Haste?" I asked.

"My Mage school is kinetics," said Ames. "That's—"

"Motion and force." I *had* finished high school, after all.

"Right. I have a spell to accelerate your movements. The difference isn't huge, but..."

"Speed kills," finished Mireille.

I wasn't going to argue with that. But party loyalty meant I also wasn't going to admit that that single spell was already a hell of a lot more useful than anything Zamira brought to the table.

"Darishal, you're on entry, as usual," continued Mireille. "Make it big, make it loud. Brian, I'll go left."

I nodded. "I've got right then."

"And I'll bring the pain right down the middle." Darishal cracked his knuckles and unlimbered the heavy maul.

The big man was talking a big game for someone who'd gotten dismantled by Lucius in roughly a minute, but I wasn't going to say that either. While I *would* have still gone in by myself, three on five was a lot less likely to get me dead.

"Prioritize casters, as always," said Mireille. Kamet had already left, headed for the building's rear door, but she gave him a thirty count, then nodded. "Let's go."

35

"Thank you," I said, as we marched across the street, heading directly for the warehouse's double doors. "All of you. Seriously. Neither Miko nor I will forget your help today."

"House Marchon looks after its own," said Mireille.

Darishal didn't add anything, but he was suddenly ahead of us, not moving faster, but stepping further with every stride as his already oversized form swelled to vastly larger proportions.

I'd seen the technique before and considered it one of Eos' greatest sins that, despite my frequently remarked upon lack of height, I'd yet to be offered it by the Framework.

By the time he reached the doors, Darishal was seven feet tall and almost as wide as the obstacle he faced. He took the now absurdly large maul in both hands, cocked it back and then smashed it forward.

The doors were large, sturdy, and barred from the other side.

That didn't matter at all.

Wood cracked, splintered, and, closer to the point of impact, absolutely exploded inward. The remnants of one door swung open, the other simply ceased to be, and Mireille and I rushed in.

One of the four standing figures Kamet had seen was down with wood shrapnel in their back. The other three were already in motion, turning to face us. I had the brief impression of short, sharp blades coming to bear, but I was already in motion.

Lunge.

My spear caught an unarmored foe right in the armpit and drove on through. As Ames' spell settled on me, the world seemed to slow down. I had all the time in the world to cross-step, using my weapon as a fulcrum, and to move the impaled man into the path of a second attacker's swing.

The damage I'd done with *Lunge* probably wouldn't have killed my target. But when the other kidnapper's club made a mess of that same target's face?

We suddenly had one less person to kill.

I took a magically swift step back and my spear slid smoothly out of the dead man even as he fell. Another step forward and I drove my weapon toward my second opponent.

He got his club up to deflect my thrust wide, just in time for Darishal's maul to come crashing in from the side. Even with the noble's size buff having already faded, the kidnapper only fared slightly better than the doors had.

Two down already. Three, given the short work Mireille was making of *her* opponent, carving bloody patterns through the air with an axe in each hand.

And then things went very wrong.

An aura flooded the warehouse, slippery like oil, like grease, like shadow. It wasn't anywhere near as strong as Skaal's or Arrius', let alone what we'd felt from Nikkaali or the Thunderbird, but it didn't need to be either.

Nobody who had an aura was less than—

"Tin!" cried out Mireille, as the fourth kidnapper, the one who'd been knocked down by fragments of the warehouse's door, rose to his feet. Visually, he was of a piece with the others we'd just cut down--unshaven, dark-haired, overly tan, and poorly dressed—but he had a hauberk like mine over a padded leather vest. In his hands, he held two kamas, their short wooden handles giving way to a sharp, sickle-like blade jutting out perpendicularly at the end.

I'd tried to wield a single kama in *Weapons Training* class and come away with a new appreciation for my spear. But *I* wasn't Tin.

To make matters worse, Ames' enhancement took that moment to finally fade. The world around us sped up, and the Tin did too.

Still, if my time up on the walls of Madea had taught me anything, it was that Tins were mortal too.

Lunge wasn't back yet, so I simply thrust instead, a measured strike more about gaining information than about doing any damage.

The man's parry nearly taking me off my feet told me plenty. He was strong and fast. Worse, he either had eyes in the back of his head or was simply skilled enough to detect Mireille's attack, timed just after mine. He spun easily, used his second kama to trap one of the noblewoman's axes just behind its bladed head, and effortlessly yanked the weapon out of her grasp, sending it flying towards Darishal.

An impact and a grunt told me it had landed, but not how bad the damage was.

With Mireille overextended, she was in no position to dodge or parry the Tin's second kama, but as it slashed through the air, it rebounded off a golden nimbus surrounding the Marchon heir. That nimbus cracked and faded after a single hit, but the defensive technique or enchanted item had done its job.

Then it was my turn to weather the onslaught. The kidnapper turned back to me, and his form went smoky and indistinct, making it hard to spot in the warehouse's shadowed interior. I parried one strike, then two, but he was gaining speed with every exchange too, kamas a blur as they prescribed impossible angles through the air in my direction.

Before long, it was all I could do to keep my spear between us. Even as I backpedaled, he closed that distance, kamas beating a drumbeat against the shaft of my weapon. As he forced his way inside my guard, I twisted away from a strike that came within a hair's breadth of landing. I choked up on my weapon and swung the butt of it low to take his feet out from under him.

That was the plan anyway.

Unfortunately, that plan didn't say anything about the other man simply dancing over the outstretched shaft of my spear, avoiding the sweep as easily as if it wasn't there, even as he sent one of his kamas flashing toward my throat.

Plan B wasn't a plan at all, really. I dropped to one knee, drew the brand-new knife at my belt with my free hand, and thrust upward. And then, for good measure, I triggered *Deceptive Strike*.

The pain radiating up my arm, moments later, told me, long before my mind had caught up with my body, that the Tin had somehow parried even my best technique. My knife fell from fingers gone numb from the impact to clatter noisily to the floor, and only a panicked, second usage of *Lunge* got me out of the way of the man's second kama, the one that had nearly torn my throat out moments earlier.

Even so, when *Lunge* expired, I could feel the line of fire he'd carved down my side through hauberk, gambeson, and flesh.

A quick survey of the battlefield told me Mireille was on her way, Darishal was fighting his way back to his feet, and our opponent had so far not even been touched. His expression was hard to make out with whatever defensive technique he'd triggered, but he looked almost... bored.

And that was some serious kind of bullshit.

He was just too fast. As slippery as his aura. This was like fighting Lace, just without all the poison and jumping around.

I met Mireille's eyes as she approached the Tin from behind. She gave a slight nod to one side.

Go left. That was a hard one to misinterpret.

I didn't know what her plan was, but it had to be better than mine, so I followed her lead, pressuring the Tin from the left even as I tried to maintain my reach advantage. A kama in each hand, he dodged rather than parrying, still as elusive as smoke.

Mireille attacked from behind, but also to the left, the sharp edge of her axe glowing crimson. Another handful of glowing auras came and went, protecting her from our target's deadly counterattacks, and between the two of us, we forced the Tin the other way.

Where Darishal finally rejoined the battle. His massive maul came crashing down just as our enemy danced into range. Off-balance for the first time in the fight, surrounded by enemies, and with his own acceleration starting to fade, the Tin *still* managed to brush the descending maul's head aside. He trapped the weapon with both of his kamas and started to pull—

—which was when *something* streaked through the air through the space I'd only vacated and embedded itself in his back.

It wasn't an arrow or even a dagger but a sliver of metal, like an oversized needle. Still, it struck exposed flesh, and for half a breath, the Tin froze in a rictus of surprised pain.

It was Darishal's turn to pull on his maul, yanking the Tin's arms outward. And then Mireille was there, blazing axe cutting through flesh and bone to leave blood fountaining from suddenly handless stumps… and I was there, too, spear finally finding purchase, piercing armor, then flesh, then armor again to emerge in a second eruption of blood out of the Tin's chest.

Handless, weaponless, and impaled on an unbreakable weapon, the man finally did the right thing and died.

Darishal's eyes rolled back in his head, and he collapsed. Mireille was there to catch him before he hit the ground, but she sent a thankful nod for the man behind me, the man who'd thrown the dart that had given us our one and only break in the fight.

The man who'd come in through the back door he was supposed to be guarding.

"I thought you were totally out of energy," she said.

Kamet's face was poorly suited for smiles, and he didn't bother attempting one here, contenting himself with a shrug instead.

"*Almost* totally out."

With the two of them dealing with Darishal, I turned my attention to the two bodies that hadn't moved since our entry. One was clearly part of the same group; dressed like a sailor, armed like a kidnapper. The mess that was left of his skull told me he must have been the one Miko took down in the Lower City alley.

The second body was Miko and only the fact that she was breathing kept me from losing my shit entirely.

Her robes were bloody and torn, as were some of the scales beneath, and dried blood covered the lower half of her face. Almost as bad were the shackles—large, heavy, and iron—that bound her at wrist and ankle. Several of her long fingers had been broken, and I was guessing only some of that had happened *during* her capture.

I'd just helped kill four people and it was nowhere near enough.

Dimly, I heard Sky and Greshal entering the warehouse, the latter on four paws instead of two, but I had eyes only for my nest-sister. I didn't know if there was anywhere to touch her that *wouldn't* hurt, but I also knew Sky was almost out of heals.

Like it or not, waking Miko was the quickest route to ending her pain.

Wincing, I reached down and shook her awake.

Or tried to. She didn't respond at all.

"Miko," I called, shaking her a little bit harder.

Still nothing. I'd had to wake my nest-sister more than a few times in the past, and knew what a challenge it could be, but this was something else entirely. I checked the dried blood on her mouth and found the faint residues of something else.

I didn't know if they'd drugged her or poisoned her, but it was going to take more than just me to wake her up.

"Ribs are broken, for sure," Sky was saying, her voice tight as she looked over Darishal's injuries. "If you'd been hit by the axe blade instead, you'd be dead, you idiot."

"Can you heal him? Heal them both?" asked Mireille.

"With only enough energy for one spell? No. But I can at least take the edge off." She glanced over at Miko and paled. "A little bit anyway."

"Hopefully, Initiate Naseri will pitch in when she's awake."

"That's going to be a problem," I said, explaining what I found.

"I don't have any cures, even if I had the energy to cast them," Sky told Mireille.

"We can bring her to one of the temples once she's in shape to be moved."

The healer nodded. "Okay then. Help me get Derry closer to Miko then. You know how small the area of effect for this spell is."

Kamet had disappeared again, but between Mireille and I, we helped move a quietly cursing Darishal over. As soon as he was down again, Sky took up a spot between the two injured and placed one hand on the warehouse floor. I waited for the glow of light that accompanied Miko's healings, but instead, the vague outline of a stone fountain formed between them, spectral water cascading down from the top in an endless flow to splash in a circle around it.

"*Waters of Renewal*," said Sky. "A blessing of the Anointed Trio."

Its effects weren't nearly as instantaneous as *Light Healing*… or even *Minor Healing*, but it persisted and impacted multiple targets. I was watching Miko's injuries start to heal when Mireille, coming up beside me, let out a gasp.

"You're *bleeding*, Brian."

"Right." I gritted my teeth as the pain I'd been unconsciously repressing came flooding in like a black-watered tide. "I forgot."

"You *forgot* the Tin nearly carved off a piece of you?" Mireille gave me another in a long series of strange looks.

"You don't have the *Pain Tolerance* skill?"

"Of course I do, but it's incredibly difficult to level."

"I haven't seemed to have that problem," I admitted.

"Strange."

"Sit next to the fountain," instructed Sky.

I blew out a breath as the fountain's waters washed over me, easing at least some of the agony.

Minor Healing would have mostly taken care of my damage, while *Light Healing* would have healed it entirely, but when *Waters of Renewal* finally faded, several minutes later, its limitations became clear. At best, Darishal was breathing more easily and not quite as ghostly pale in the face, while Miko still looked a wreck. My bleeding had stopped and part of the long cut in my side had stitched itself shut, but with *Pain Tolerance* no longer doing its thing, it hurt to even move.

Still, we had bigger things to worry about.

"We need to get out of here," I said. "In case these assholes had any friends."

"Slavers don't have friends," said Ames, speaking up for the first time since the battle.

"There is no slavery in the kingdom," said Mireille. "It was outlawed during the reign of King Leopold II, over a hundred cycles ago."

"Someone forgot to tell these people that." The Mage held up a ring of keys and a set of shackles like the ones currently binding Miko. "There are dozens of these hanging beyond the shelves over there, next to what look like makeshift pens."

"That explains the proximity to the docks," murmured Sky. "Ships get searched far less regularly than wagons, and almost never when *departing* Trynfall."

The rage in me kicked up another notch. As Mireille herself had said, ranking duels were one thing. An attack on the city streets followed by a kidnapping was another. And Miko being sold into slavery? Whatever line there was in politics, Lucius and House Darish hadn't just crossed it. They'd obliterated it.

"Brian is right; we need to leave," said Mireille, helping Darishal climb to his feet. "Now."

I used my spear to stand on my own and looked down at Miko. Despite our absurd size difference, I *was* strong enough to carry her... I just didn't think I'd be able to do so through the breadth of the docks and Lower City. Not while also holding my spear. And especially not without tearing open my partly healed battle wound.

"I can take her," offered Mireille, the only Warrior in our group who *hadn't* been injured.

Ames cleared her throat. "Better let me do it instead, I think? If we do run into any reinforcements, you're going to need to fight."

"Our first step will be to find members of the city guard to secure this compound and escort us to safety," said Mireille, "so I don't think it will matter."

Still, she stepped back and let Ames remove the shackles and scoop Miko off the floor. I was pretty sure the Mage hadn't put any of her levels into Strength, but she still managed as easily as I would have. More so, even, given that Miko's legs dangled in the air from her grip rather than dragging on the ground as they might have from mine.

"She's heavier than she looks," Ames admitted, "but I'll manage."

"Great," said Kamet. "Let's get the hell out of here."

○○○

Either the docks were a no-travel zone for the city guard, or they were all on an early White Sails holiday; we didn't see any uniforms while making our way from the warehouse. That might have been the time of day too. Night had truly fallen at some point during our fight and recovery, and if the streets were no less busy, they still had a different energy to them. More dangerous, if equally smelly. The bubble of space we'd been granted on our way down was gone; either the darkness hid the blood and gore from our battle or the streets' present occupants were used to such things.

I could hear Ames huffing and puffing as she carried Miko, but the rest of us weren't faring much better. Even Sky and Kamet were moving slowly, bogged down by fatigue instead of injuries. Only Greshal remained fresh, scampering about underfoot while throwing the occasional concerned glance at the still unconscious Miko.

It was only as we neared the ramps back up to the Lower City that the crowds finally started to clear. And that's when we ran across Lucius Darish, accompanied by almost a dozen of our classmates.

The nobleman was dressed down from his usual finery but had made up for that with enough golden chains around his neck to pass for an 80s rapper back on Earth. His eyes widened as he looked from Mireille and then to me.

"Picking up strays are we, Marchon?"

I took a step forward, only to be stopped by a grip like steel. Mireille. "This isn't the time for your pettiness, Lucius," she said, voice hard.

Lucius' frown came and went so quickly it seemed a trick of the lanterns.

"Pettiness? From me? I'm simply offering a friendly warning. When you lie down with hounds, you must be prepared for them to bite."

I felt myself settle, heart rate dropping like a stone as I took in the forces arrayed against us. Lucius' whole party was present, of course, along with a half-dozen other initiates and at least two older people that were probably guards tasked with babysitting him. But the Darish heir was out front on his own, he was unarmored, and my paltry few techniques were all off cooldown. Mireille's grip on my arm wouldn't be enough to stop my upgraded *Lunge*, and that meant I could be on him before anyone reacted. One thrust to trigger and dispose of whatever defensive enchantment he might have, and then *Deceptive Strike* to put him down for good.

It wouldn't be a fight. It would be an execution.

Mireille's grip tightened. "Brian, don't," she hissed.

"Speaking of mongrels," Lucius continued, peering past Mireille and I to where the rest of our small group stood in the darkness, "where *is* your hideous so-called sister, Initiate Fieldings? I would hate for anything to happen—"

Lunge.

Spear extended, I streaked forward, leaving Mireille holding onto nothing but air. A glowing nimbus appeared around the young nobleman, deflecting my attack, but I'd been ready for it. I got my feet back under me, took a step, and—

A grip far stronger than Mireille's caught the haft of my spear before I could trigger *Deceptive Strike* and I was hurled aside. I rolled back to my feet and found myself faced with one of Lucius' two guards. Eyes burning, he stepped forward and his unfurled aura crashed down upon me like a meteor shower.

Not Tin, but *Copper*, at the very least.

Behind him, Lucius screeched like a flightless bird. "You all saw that! An unprompted and malicious attack on a nobleman! I'll have him thrown out of the duchy for that!"

The Copper scanned me from head to toe, and something in the hard lines of his face shifted, just a bit. "My lord, it looks like your fellow students have had a hard night already. I'd suggest that you let this—"

I shook my head. Any chance I had of killing Lucius here in the open was gone, had probably never existed in the first place, given the unexpected strength of his escort, but hell if I was going to let the asshole just *walk away* either.

"Lucius Darish," I said, interrupting the Copper who stood between us. "Consider yourself challenged to a duel. You and me. Sixth day."

"I'm first in our class, adventurer. You're eleventh. You *can't* challenge me."

"Not if we're dueling for rank," I agreed. "This is for honor."

Dimly, I heard Mireille's quiet cursing from further down the ramp.

"Honor duels can only be initiated between the nobility," said Lucius, sneering. "You don't—"

"I'll sponsor him," said Mireille.

The Darish heir lost his smile. Eyes narrowed, he turned on the other woman.

"You're going to involve House Marchon? For this?"

"My house has nothing to do with it. I'm exercising my right as an independent noblewoman on behalf of a cause I deem just."

"I always knew you were a blunt instrument," he said to her, seemingly having forgotten me entirely. "Somehow, the reality of it is even *more* disappointing."

Turning back to me, he ran a hand through perfectly coiffed blonde locks. "The challenged has the right to choose both the time and the place, but I won't have there be any excuses for when I destroy you. Sixth Day it is, at the Ducal Academy of Trynfall following the ranking duels."

"As the challenged, you may choose the terms as well, my lord," said the other guard.

"Oh. Right." Lucius' smile twisted. "No terms. Anything goes. We fight until one of us is dead or has surrendered."

The Copper between us stirred. "Lord Darish—"

"I have spoken, Decimus." Lucius looked past his bodyguard to me. "You have four days left to live, commoner. Make of them what you can."

With that, he led his friends and sycophants down the center of the ramp, forcing Mireille's group to step aside to let them through. The Copper was the last to leave, and though he never once touched a weapon, his aura alone kept us all in check until long after he had disappeared.

"What in the nine hells just happened?" asked Darishal, his deep voice threaded with confusion.

"Nothing good," said Kamet. "Nothing good at all."

"Keep going." Mireille sounded worse than tired. "We still need healers for half of you." As we all lurched back into motion, she fell in beside me. For a long moment, she said nothing, as if desperately searching for words. When they finally came, they were hard. "I am deeply regretting that I agreed to speak with you in the common room today."

With the adrenaline draining from my body, it felt like my higher processes were functioning again for the first time since we'd encountered Lucius. I hid a wince, imagining what Wilf would have to say about me attacking Lucius in the city streets, right in front of a dozen-plus witnesses.

Not being cut out for politics was one thing. Squandering every advantage because I was pissed off—even righteously so—was something else entirely.

"I'm sorry," I managed. "That was dumb."

"Yes. It was."

I nodded but had to ask. "Why back me against Lucius then?"

"Because he's an ass and apparently you're not the only fool among us." She cursed again, quiet but heartfelt. "If my father strips the succession rights from me, I will have only myself to blame for it."

"But you kept your house out of things."

"Legally, yes. Practically? Not at all. I am the heir to my house. The city will know House Marchon has chosen to back you in this, and that means we will face the consequences of your duel."

"What does that mean?"

"It means you *must* win."

Given that the duel was to the death, I thought that part was pretty much a given, but she didn't give me space to say so.

"And when you do, you must also avoid killing him. Force his surrender."

"Miko was kidnapped, beaten within an inch of her life, and poisoned or drugged by would-be slavers! And you want me to let him live?"

"The scion of one of Trynfall's most powerful houses, who may or may not have had *anything* to do with tonight's events? Yes. Yes, I do. If you can manage that, we will revisit the possibility of an alliance.

It will start with you attending the White Sails opening banquet with me."

"As a… date?"

The darkness mostly hid the color that came to her cheeks, but the look she unleashed on him nearly brought back winter all by itself.

"As a show of your alliance with House Marchon."

That made a whole lot more sense.

"And if I lose the duel?"

"You will be dead, and this mess will be mine to deal with."

I swallowed. "And Miko?"

"Will become irrelevant. The ranking duel scheme—which Lucius *was* responsible for—was a weapon aimed at you in retaliation for the very public embarrassment of your initial spar. With you dead, the synossian's usefulness as a lever will be gone. Assuming House Darish does not push for her expulsion after the fact."

I chewed on that as Kamet left to follow Greshal home. As the rest of us made our way to the lift and Mireille, yet again, abused her authority as the heir to House Marchon to get us a quick ride up to the Middle City. I kept chewing on it as we made our way to one of the temples—the Shrine of the Blooded Shrike—where a Priest on duty took a substantial donation to mend our wounds *and* cure the toxins flooding Miko's unconscious form. We walked from the Middle City to the Upper and over to the Tryn that occupied the western margins, and by the time we made it to the dorms, where Ames gently laid the still-sleeping Miko onto her bed, I'd made my peace with the corner I'd backed myself into.

Everything was riding on my forthcoming honor duel… so, I'd just have to win it.

As for Lucius' ultimate fate?

I'd deal with that when the moment came. Because Lace, along with all my experiences on Eos, had taught me one thing: you didn't leave an enemy alive to stab you in the back.

I thanked Mireille and her party members, getting weak smiles or stiff nods in return, and closed the dorm room door after they left. It was then, and only then, that I got the message I'd been waiting for:

```
QUEST COMPLETED: Save the Voice of the Dawn.
```

The rush of energy that filled my soul shook me. Like a river overflowing its banks, it flooded my very being, sending tingles down nerve endings that didn't even exist in the physical realm. I'd been maybe twenty or thirty percent of the way to my next level, but now…?

Now things were different. Very different.

Miko was still unconscious, so I dropped into a meditative pose on my bed. For once, I didn't try to press the boundaries on what activities I could manage while also meditating. Instead, I just dove deep into the flow, reaching out to the Framework and the realm of the spirit that it served to connect us to.

A glass or so later, I was rewarded by a succession of dialogue windows.

```
Congratulations, Warrior.

You have reached level 9!
```

Next was the now-familiar skill-up window:

```
    You have increased the following skills:

    Major skills:
    Formations [+2]: 38/50
    Spear (U) [+1]: 45/50


    Minor skills:
    Acrobatics [+1]: 12/50
    Athleticism [+1]: 45/50
    Avoidance [+1]: 45/50
    Focus [+2]: 37/50
    Leadership (U) [+1]: 24/50


    General skills:
    Diplomacy [+1]: 5/10
```

The gain in *Diplomacy* almost *had* to be a joke, but I'd ponder the Framework's comedic inadequacies some other time. The completion of my gods-given quest had leapfrogged me past Miko all the way to level nine, and that meant a new technique choice.

Honestly, three levels in as many moons felt ludicrously fast after my time in the wilderness and Madea. But that was the value of academies, coupled with the availability of the Echo. Endless training, coupled with more deadly combat than any average adventurer would see in a cycle on their own, added up.

And my time at the academy had had one other benefit; I'd finally been forced to accept that, whatever my defensive abilities, whatever advantages my spear's reach gave me, I was *still* always getting hurt in battle. It was stupid to ignore that reality, and even more so to avoid the technique that let me turn that into something of a positive.

This time, I was going to take *Fueled by Pain*.

Except it seemed the Framework wasn't done with its one-man comedy routine:

> **Congratulations, Warrior.**
>
> **Select your level 9 advancement option:**
>
> - Upgrade: Beast Skin (Passive - C) -> Beast
>   Hide (Passive/Active - U)
> - New technique: Leap (C)
> - New technique: Hold your Ground (C)

When Miko woke, tired and confused, it was to the sound of her nest-brother cursing up a bloody storm.

○○○

The next three days passed in a frenzied blur of preparation. I'd spent much of that first night speaking with Miko, filling her in on what happened while she did her best to do the same for me. One of us had more information than the other; all she remembered was being jumped in an alleyway on her journey down to her apprenticeship with Zelig. She was frustrated by how easily they had taken her until I informed her a Tin had been involved. Then, she'd focused all her worry and attention on my forthcoming duel instead.

After the talk with Mireille, I expected some level of recrimination from my nest-sister. For putting my life at risk. For putting our mission to rescue her people at even greater risk. Instead, she just nodded.

"I was not there. You did what you felt you must, and I will always support you in that. Now, we must simply make sure you win, as Mireille said."

On that front, we had some allies. First, there was our party, of course. Wilf kept his distance publicly, but in private, he joined the others in helping however he could, mostly feeding me whatever bits of information he had regarding the House Darish scion.

Not all of that information was welcome.

"You're not the only one who's been leveling like a madman," said Wilf. "Lucius hit level ten just a seven-day ago. Word is he's had no luck breaking through to Tin yet, but you have to be prepared if that happens, yeah?"

"How do you know that?"

He gave me a look. "Which part?"

"All of it." A person's level, like their ranking and everything else on their personal record, was private information.

"Reese has the *Analyst* trait and a terrible habit of leaving his notes in a locked chest in a locked cabinet in his locked office where literally anyone could find them."

"That would do it." Reese was one of Merrick's two senior instructors. Unlike his boss, he'd apparently never warranted a nickname, but suddenly, he was a whole lot more interesting to me. The *Analyst* trait was rare and represented one of the only ways to see any part of another individual's personal record. Even if that glimpse was often deeply limited, it offered a huge advantage in any conflict.

"What else could he read?"

"Just that." Wilf winced. "Slightly *less* than that, to be honest. He can only see someone's level, as far as I know. But if Lucius had already made Tin, you can bet we'd have felt his aura at some point."

I mentally added another worry to the pile. The difference between level nine and ten wasn't substantial enough to concern myself with. But the difference between unranked and Tin?

I could only comfort myself with the thought that Lucius didn't seem the type for self-awareness *or* personal enlightenment.

Mireille's aid was more overt. She rented a training hall for three full days, and I skipped classes for all those days as I fought one-on-one against every Warrior in our combined groups as well as a handful of duelists House Marchon had on retainer.

I won most of the fights against Mireille, Darishal, and Barth, and lost *all* the ones against the professional duelists, even the one who *wasn't* Tin. At a certain point, Mireille must have realized morale was more important than whatever I might learn from my defeats; the duelists quietly disappeared between the second and third days.

Last but not least was a masked woman in a hooded robe who never spoke but spent almost two full glasses blasting me with a spell similar to the technique Lucius had used in our spar, the one that had stunned and slowed me for those critical few seconds. If I could learn to resist the ability—or, better yet, earn a *skill* that helped me do so—then it would remove one weapon from the noble's arsenal.

That didn't go well either. As high as both my Will and Vitality stats were, they were apparently insufficient for resisting the effect. The best I could manage was mitigating my vulnerability by turtling as soon as the ability hit… and that wouldn't help me at all against Sever. At the end of the session, the woman walked away with a small bag of coin and all I had to show for it was a splitting headache.

Skill gain had slowed even more since I hit level nine, but I picked up another point in *Spear* and *Medium Armor* as well as two in the ever-popular *Pain Tolerance*. I thought the fact that I'd weathered three days of brutality without losing my shit would've gained me another point in *Diplomacy* or maybe *Focus*, but apparently, I only got *those* for challenging noble assholes to duels to the death.

At least I'd gotten the opportunity to test my new technique while training. In the end, my choice had been surprisingly easy. *Leap* hadn't offered me anything I couldn't already manage with *Liberating Lunge*, and the latter's cooldown was short enough that I didn't *really* need a second option. That had left two options, and I'd spent a brief while debating between *Hold Your Ground* and *Beast Hide*.

Ultimately, I realized I'd rather make an existing ability more useful than add another potentially mediocre technique to my repertoire. *Beast Hide* was ranked Uncommon, after all, and seemed like it had a better chance of being useful in the coming duel.

Three days later, I still *thought* I'd made the right choice, even though the reality of the upgrade hadn't quite matched expectations. *Beast Hide's* passive component just built on what *Beast Skin* had already been doing, thickening the skin that grew back when healing from an injury. Whereas that new skin had once been differently colored and mildly tougher than my normal flesh, now it was almost leathery. Which I knew because the change was retroactive. There were swaths of skin across my body as tough as boiled leather, and while they wouldn't keep Sever from cutting me in two, they didn't suck either.

What *did* suck was that the change in texture and consistency was somehow even more apparent than *Beast Skin* had been. One glance in a mirror without my shirt on introduced me to whole new levels of body dysmorphia. The Brian I saw was no longer simply particolored like a calico cat, but someone that stretched the boundaries of humanity. From the neck down, at least, and given my luck, my face would get torn up soon enough too.

In my new life on Eos, I'd met a lot of alien species, from synossians to kithrizal to lupine, fiorlans, dunsmen, amazons, and even reavers. I'd befriended a surprising number of them and found them to be no worse—and frequently better—than the humans that made up most of the duchy's population. Still, seeing myself in the mirror and not immediately thinking *human,* let alone *me,* was far more disquieting than I could have anticipated.

It *should* have prepared me for the *active* component of my newest technique.

It didn't.

It really, really didn't.

36-Interlude

On the day of the honor duel, Mireille dressed herself as if going to war. Every article of clothing was a piece of armor, every choice a weapon added to her arsenal. Far too much of her immediate future rested on the day's outcome and the only thing more terrifying than that was that the person in control of that outcome wasn't her or her family but a foreign-born adventurer whose gaps in knowledge were almost as strange as his facility with languages.

Brian Fieldings did not fit neatly into a box, no matter how much she'd tried to allocate him to one since his arrival in Trynfall. He was difficult to understand, difficult to predict, and difficult to dismiss.

She only hoped he was also difficult to kill.

If not, she might pray to the Weeping Crone for him to be resurrected so she could kill him again herself.

Like almost every student at the Tryn, she shared a room, but her roommate had left campus to spend time with her brother, freshly returned from Elthoris. Kima was a nice enough girl, if every bit as chatty as Mireille's youngest handmaids, but she had no interest at all in politics and even less in blood sports. Upon graduation, she would happily settle down with whichever husband her family had picked out for her from among the list of many, many suitors.

Sometimes, it felt like the Iron Lady had been trying to make a point when she'd made the two of them roommates, but what that point was continued to elude Mireille.

The tap on the door came on schedule. She opened it to find her unit waiting. Darishal and Sky were on one side of the hall, the latter draped over the arm of the former, while Kamet and Amelia were on the other, the distance between them greater than mere space could account for. Their families had had bad blood between them a dozen generations earlier, and some of that continued to well up from time to time.

It was part of the reason Amelia hadn't been in her group to begin with. Unfortunately, Farrell had proven a disappointment, and the number of Mages in this year's class was disappointingly low. Feuds notwithstanding, both houses belonged to her father's coalition, and thus Amelia had been the obvious choice of replacement.

Mireille stepped out into the hall, gave both her Rogue and her Mage a pointed look, and then turned to Darishal.

"Brian and Miko?"

"Already went ahead." The man shrugged. "I figured that was for the best."

She wasn't sure what to think about that, so simply nodded. "Let's go then."

It was a short walk, as always, to the training grounds where school-sanctioned battles took place. As the cycle had worn on, the initial allure of the ranking duels had faded. The duels themselves still happened, of course, but once-large audiences had dwindled to small groups of friends, allies, or particularly bitter rivals eager to see their enemy fall. On a normal Sixth Day, at least three quarters of the school's initiates would be gone. Maybe more, with the White Sails festival so close. But word of the day's honor duel had spread, and Kima might be the only initiate missing from the Tryn's hallowed halls.

Even some of the second-year *Adepts* could be seen, pushing their ways through the crowd of their juniors to find the best views for the coming fights.

No sooner had Mireille entered than she was spotted by Miko Naseri. The woman waved a long, muscular arm, flashed her horrific smile, and gestured to an empty space at the front that she had somehow held despite the crowds.

In many ways, the Priestess was even more of an enigma than her so-called brother. Mireille had never seen a scaled—or synossian, as Brian insisted she be called—take on the role of adventurer. Even the few who became Aspirants instead of Dedicated tended to end up as low-level enforcers for the street gangs that so often ran the less desirable portions of the kingdom's larger cities. But Miko did not carry herself like a typical member of her species and she seemed immune to the antipathy of her fellow initiates. House Marchon had detailed reports on the woman's sermons in the scaled encampment, on the charitable work to bring food to people used to begging for every scrap. Her father's advisors were convinced there was some ulterior motive at play and maybe there was, but Mireille couldn't see it.

Most interestingly of all, Miko had been seen entering the ducal palace a few seven-days earlier, accompanied by the lord arbiter and without Brian at her side, and for all her father's many spies in the Upper City, not a one of them knew what the synossian had been doing there.

More mysteries, thought Mireille, following the movable wall that was Darishal until they reached the woman in question. *I'm really tired of mysteries.*

"Miko," she said in greeting.

"Friend Mireille." The synossian offered a strange salute, as seemed to be her custom. "Well met."

"How is Brian?" She hadn't wanted to ask that right away, had wanted to wait until a suitable amount of time had passed, but it had slipped out anyway, exposing her anxiety as surely as the hunch in Kamet's shoulders demonstrated his.

"He is ready." Miko, by contrast, seemed unruffled, her strange, sclera-less eyes calm and still. "All will be well."

With her unit creating a buffer around her, Mireille felt comfortable enough to voice at least some of her disquiet.

"The past three days were not encouraging."

"There is difference between fighting and killing," Miko said simply, the statement even more horrible for the mildness of her tone. "Nest-brother's story does not end here."

"I hope you're right."

"Hope is good." She patted Mireille's shoulder, dangerously sharp claws safely turned away, then smiled that awful smile again. "Faith is better."

○○○

Three ranking duels went by in a flash, and Mireille couldn't have said who won any of them. The biggest surprise was that Miko *hadn't* been challenged this week. Even if House Darish had hired the slavers, the smart move would have been to plan a duel anyway rather than potentially reveal their advance knowledge of the plot. So either Lucius wasn't that smart—a possibility, if not a likely one—or something else was going on.

It could even be that they were running out of people to challenge her. Many of those beneath Miko in the class rankings were either friends of House Marchon or stubbornly clinging to neutrality like Wilfred McCall.

Regardless, the Priestess remained by their side throughout all three duels, double eyelids flickering as she followed the action. When

Amelia's former friend, Prisa, was healed from the beating Packard had given her, Miko stiffened again, rising to her full height.

Brian Fielding and Lucius Darish were being escorted forward by Merrick's head instructors.

On the other side of Miko, the Zarisian sucked in a breath. "He's got enough enchantments on him to pay for a new expedition into the Waste."

He, Mireille was pretty sure, was Lucius, not Brian, but she didn't ask for confirmation. Ward of His Grace or not, Zamira was a dangerous person to know, let alone spend time with, and she'd risked her house's standing enough as it was.

"Is fine," said Miko. "Will be fine."

Mireille would never have the Priestess' faith, and not just because religion was something she'd been raised to see as a tool rather than a calling. And right now, seeing the difference between the two duelists, not just in size but in equipment, hope was a hard thing to find as well.

Lucius topped his opponent by almost a foot and whatever her personal feelings towards the spoiled noble, it was impossible to ignore the fluidity of his movements or the strength in his arms and legs. The scion once again had Sever riding in a sheath on his hip. On the other hip was a long-bladed knife that lacked a name but likely had enchantments of its own. His armor was finely crafted—a chain vest of blue-tinged ethasium alloy above thigh greaves of the same material. Two rings, a medallion, and even an earring were all items she recognized from reports on House Darish. Three were defensive enchantments. The fourth granted a one-time boost to strength upon activation.

Next to him, Brian looked small and poor, the survivor of some wasting sickness that had left his skin discolored and patchy. A simple iron hauberk showed signs of regular repair atop a worn leather gambeson, and a single copper charm dangled from the bracelet on his right wrist. He wore a brace of daggers across his chest and a longer knife on his hip, but even sheathed, those weapons looked like a Smith's discards. His spear, too, looked like something stolen from the scrapheap, though Mireille had seen it in action too much to doubt its efficacy. Any weapon that could withstand Sever was more than it seemed.

Still, if any of the attending students had been gauche enough to bet publicly on a fight like this, she knew where all their money would have gone.

"Will be fine," said Miko again, but this time it sounded like she was trying to convince herself.

"Yes," said Bartholomew, sandwiched between the Zarisian and Miko. "I see what you mean."

Mireille badly wanted to ask what the hell the young Apsan meant, but *he* was almost as dangerous a potential acquaintance as Zamira. Thankfully, Amelia had the tact and political awareness of a family who had first risen to prominence through horse trading; she leaned in and asked for herself.

"What are you talking about?"

The noble looked over his shoulder and up at the taller Mage.

"Brian," he said. "We've delved the Echo six times now, and fought in hundreds of encounters, but I don't think I've ever seen him really *angry* until now."

Mireille glanced again at the man who held her own future in his hands and frowned. *Lucius* looked angry. And smug. And supremely confident. Brian just looked… empty.

"Angry?" Again, Amelia gave voice to Mireille's own thoughts. "He doesn't *look* angry. He doesn't look much of anything."

"Yeah," said Bartholomew. "My brother looked the same right before he cut the Red Serpent into bloody quadrants and slew all seven of his risen retainers."

Amelia's mouth fell open then snapped shut again. Apparently, even she had her limits when it came to asking questions.

On the field, Sir Merrick Thorne approached the two duelists, going through the terms of the honor duel as Lucius had set them. When he finished, he turned to each of them.

"While there is honor to be gained in battle, history has taught that honor can also be found in the thoughtful avoidance of battle. This can end here and now, with no blood spilt. All it takes is a word from each of you. Will you give that word?"

Silence. Lucius even had the temerity to roll his eyes.

The weapons instructor nodded. "Then I will instead have each of you retreat to your designated positions." Once they had done so, a solid ten feet of space separating them, he turned to Lucius. "Is the challenged ready?"

"Ready and eager." Lucius rested a hand on the hilt of Sever.

Merrick turned to Brian. "Is the challenger ready?"

For the first time, Brian smiled, a sliver of cold ice that never reached his eyes and sent shivers down Mireille's spine. "With hate in my heart and spite in my soul."

The scarred older Warrior, called the Hammer by those who knew his story, swallowed, looking a dozen cycles older.

"Then begin."

ооо

Anyone expecting a replay of the first fight was doomed to disappointment. Although perhaps *disappointment* wasn't the right word. The addition of techniques changed everything, the addition of enchantments changed more, and the impact of multiple moons' worth of training and experience made even the early stages of the duel something entirely new.

There was no feeling out process. No careful dance.

Instead, they both did their level best to kill each other.

Despite her efforts, Mireille still hadn't gotten a complete list of Lucius' techniques, but the Darish heir activated one right off the start, gaining a golden halo that floated above his head. A second technique, which she *did* recognize as *Double Strike*, triggered moments later. One cut from Sever became two, both deflected by the shaft of Brian's strange spear, and the halo's glow strengthened.

Whatever that halo did, it seemed to be growing in power every time Lucius landed a blow.

Brian must have realized that too as he dodged the next blow instead and then thrust forward in a picture-perfect lunge that belonged in a textbook and not on a battlefield. Mainly because it left him *wide open* for retaliation. Only when Sever swept down, it passed right through a figure who was no longer there.

Instead, Brian was somehow behind Lucius, weapon already in motion.

A nimbus of light appeared and cracked, and just like that, one of Lucius' defensive enchantments was gone. Yet the halo above him glowed even more brightly, absorbing energy even from the blow the noble would have taken.

More exchanges, many of them so quick that even Mireille, a level eight Warrior trained by the best House Marchon could hire, struggled to follow them. Thrown knives accounted for a second of Lucius' defensive enchantments, but a moment later, Brian's own charm shattered, lost when the other man baited him into a bad position.

The ability Mireille recognized as *Lunge* got Brian the angle he needed to attack, but this time, the nobleman dodged past that strike;

only a last-second parry by the adventurer kept his head from leaving his body.

And even that parry added more energy to the still-active halo, which was now pulsing all on its own.

Brian dodged a second, lightning-fast strike and responded with a kick that Lucius took on his hip instead of his knee… and that was apparently the final piece needed; the halo above Lucius' head erupted in an explosion of light.

Even in the front row, Mireille and the others were far enough that they could simply blink away the afterimages. Brian, on the other hand, reeled back, clearly blinded. Lucius took a half-step to the right, quiet and smooth, then struck.

Somehow, Miko's brother got his spear up in time to block a strike he couldn't see coming. He staggered back, ducked aside from another attack, and then *changed.*

Mireille had already had the misfortune of seeing this ability in action a few times, but for the rest of the class, it was like witnessing a nightmare come to life. Thick fur sprouted over the spear-wielding adventurer's body, black and coarse. It wouldn't hold up to Lucius' enchanted knife, let alone Sever, but that wasn't the point either.

The transformed Brian opened feral eyes that were clear and vibrant and went back on the attack, moving faster than ever before.

In the span of the next few seconds, Lucius lost his last defensive enchantment. In turn, Brian took a glancing hit from Sever that carved right through his armor and removed a stretch of bestial hide from his flank.

First blood had gone to House Darish, but whatever Brian had been doing to train *Pain Tolerance* was clearly working because he didn't even slow.

Not for the first time, Mireille wondered just how far he'd taken the damn skill. And if it was even Common-ranked anymore.

It had taken Lucius only twelve moves to dismantle Darishal two levels earlier and with far fewer enchanted items, but Mireille had long since stopped counting even the moves she could follow in this duel. Instead, she held her breath, as one attack chained to the next and her future teetered precipitously on the edge of a blade.

When Lucius stumbled awkwardly, the feint was so obvious to Mireille that she almost laughed… until she saw Brian darting forward again to take advantage. His corroded spear hissed through the air… and then slowed and slowed and finally came to a halt, along with the man wielding it.

Lucius' trump ability had finally come into play, and for all their recent training, Brian still couldn't stop it.

The House Darish scion wasn't foolish enough to take even a second to gloat. The earring in his right ear flashed, doubling the strength of his next blow, and then Sever was arcing down in an eerie reenactment of the death blow that Merrick had stopped moons earlier.

Next to Mireille, Miko's mouth had dropped open to reveal those needle-sharp teeth, part snarl, part scream. Meanwhile, Sever's enchantments left a glowing path in the air as it swept down in a picture-perfect strike—

—where it hit nothing but air.

Somehow, even frozen, Brian had used *Lunge*. He appeared just past Lucius, facing the wrong direction, and drove the butt of his spear back into the other man's side.

Lucius' expensive chain vest held. The ribs beneath did not. Even so, Brian was dangerously close and off-balance, and Lucius, showing his own grit, was already spinning on him, Sever again a blur.

Instead of dodging yet another decapitating blow, the adventurer planted his spear in the earth vertically and dropped to one knee. Sever struck the weapon for at least the twelfth time that battle and was once again denied. Meanwhile, the small, fur-covered Warrior at Lucius' feet drew the knife on his hip and lashed out.

Armor could only protect what it covered; blood fountained out of Lucius' inner thigh. As he staggered back, Brian rose again, reclaiming his spear. His lips twitched, saying *something* that Mireille couldn't hear or understand, something that froze Lucius as surely as any technique. And then that spear, that shabby, corroded, utterly terrifying spear leaped forward like a living thing, charting a pathway that could only terminate in Lucius' exposed throat.

It was too quick for Mireille to curse. Too quick for her to shout a reminder that Brian needed to leave Lucius alive if he wanted to avoid some kind of war. Too quick for her, an unranked Warrior, to do anything, for all that she was the heir to the second most powerful family in the duchy.

For others though, it must have been an eternity, and in that eternity, that long, endless space between living and dead, someone finally acted.

The training hall shook as an aura was unleashed, an aura that whispered of long marches and empty battlefields, of blood shed and spilled, allies and enemies alike left to fill pits instead of graves. It drove Mireille to her knees, and she wasn't the only one; around her, initiates and adepts alike toppled like uprooted trees. And in the arena, a blackened spear strained futilely to cross the last inches of space between it and its intended target.

"This duel," said Dame Credence, in a voice like spring thunder, "is over."

37

The Iron Lady's aura fell upon us all like an avalanche. Lucius collapsed where he stood and it was all I could do to remain standing at all. I wasn't unique in that, but those of us on our feet were in the extreme minority: Miko, Merrick, one of the other instructors, a couple of second-year adepts, and Barth.

I didn't know what the rest of them had gone through to be able to withstand an aura like this one, but for Miko and me?

We'd felt worse.

The Thunderbird, for one. The Buried necromancer for another. Shan, in my Dreaming, in those desperate moments where he'd stopped wearing my dad's body like a suit. Hell, after Lace had taken us all into her goddess' embrace, I'd watched Hashoggath herself crawling towards me across miles of broken glass.

Judging by her nickname, Dame Credence might be the first Iron-ranked Aspirant I'd ever met… which put those others, deities notwithstanding, somewhere at Bronze or above. Or, in the case of the Thunderbird, whatever the equivalent was for ascended beasts. And that made me finally understand that the necromancer who had killed Riok and the rest of his squad had been playing with her food.

If she'd wanted, she could have crushed us with her aura alone.

Dame Credence couldn't do that, but just because I was still standing didn't mean I was in control. And even as I strained to complete my attack, I knew my opportunity to kill him as part of the duel had passed.

It was harder than I could have ever expected to withdraw my spear, to flip it about so that I could use it as a crutch to hold myself up as *Beast Hide* faded, taking with it the stat boost it provided. *Pain Tolerance* was one thing, but blood loss was another entirely. I'd taken a half-dozen hits during the fight, though only the cut to my side was of any real consequence, and my gambeson was doing very little to staunch the bleeding. I sagged, clinging to my weapon with a bloodied, sweaty hand, but kept my gaze fixed on the noble frozen at my feet.

Dame Credence's aura faded as she approached us. "This ends now," she said, voice quieter.

The world spun when I tried to shake my head, so instead I held still. "Those weren't the terms. And not even the duke has the authority to end an honor duel."

"He doesn't," said a voice I vaguely recognized, "but I do."

Lord Arbiter Hawthorne swam into vision, the very image of the man who'd appeared in Madea to retrieve the duke's missing heir.

"Why?" I managed.

"The position of lord arbiter is an apolitical one. My family can never rise or fall from the status we had when assigned this role, and so we are not considered a political entity. That gives me the right to act where others may not."

"No," I said, words coming slowly. "Why… stop?"

The taller man gave me a sharp look, eyes widening as he saw the blood pouring down my side. "We need a healer—"

"Am here," said a voice I *did* know well, followed by the warm light of Miko's spell washing over me. "Rest now, nest-brother. Is over."

That would have been a great time to pass out, but the truth was, it *wasn't* over. So, I stubbornly resisted, straightening up as my legs firmed beneath me.

That… was a mistake. *Light Healing* had stopped the bleeding, but the gash was wide and deep enough that multiple healings would be required to close it entirely. And the spell didn't do anything to address the blood I'd lost. Worse, like most direct healing spells, it took at least some of its energy from me. Only Miko's arm, swiftly wrapped around me, kept me from face-planting in front of the whole damn school.

"Stupid phloxl," she said. "Lean on me and be still."

I closed my eyes and leaned against her, borrowing from her strength. She couldn't be *too* angry, I knew, because she'd insulted me in the High Tongue.

When I felt steady enough to stand on my own, I opened my eyes again. A pale-faced Lucius, pants drenched in blood, was getting healed by Merrick's training assistant rather than the Priestess in his own party. Initiates and adepts were both slowly climbing back to their feet now that Credence's aura had been lifted, but nobody seemed sure what to say or do. Meanwhile, Hawthorne, Credence, and Merrick were conferring. From the look on Merrick's scarred face, his role in the honor duel wasn't winning him any accolades.

Finally, Dame Credence turned to address us all. While she didn't raise her voice, it carried easily across the arena.

"This institution is a place of learning, but by the nature of its students, there is an inevitably political aspect as well. I have chosen to permit such behavior both because it, too, is a part of your education, and because I trusted the next generation of our noble class to be wise enough to understand this truth: *there are limits.* Limits to what is permitted. Limits to what is legal. Limits to what will be stood for."

Her voice hardened.

"It seems I overestimated all of you. Rest assured: I will not make that mistake again. There will be changes here, and you will each bear the responsibility of those changes. But a few of you must be singled out for your specific roles. Brian Fieldings, Lucius Darish, Mireille Marchon. You and your units will stay. The rest of you are dismissed. If I see any of you in my halls before First Day, you will learn exactly what happens to those who test my patience."

In the front row, Mireille, who had just opened her mouth to protest being singled out, swallowed those words.

Wilf made his way down to join the rest of our party, and then we all waited as the arena slowly cleared out. Ironically, three full parties represented almost half the initiate class anyway, so the chamber didn't feel *that* much emptier when they were gone. Despite the duel that had just taken place, there wasn't a lot of congratulating or commiserating going on; everyone seemed focused on whatever hammer Dame Credence was prepared to drop on us.

First, Hawthorne motioned to one of his black-clad arbiters, standing by the exits. The woman raised her hands, whispered some words, and the air around us seemed to thicken.

"We are shielded from any listeners," Hawthorne announced.

The Iron Lady nodded but her eyes never left us. "I leave the academy for a seven-day," she said, "and come back to near calamity."

"It was an honor duel—" began Lucius, his words cut off when she raised a scarred hand.

"I have both eyes and a brain, initiate. I have also seen more honor duels in my life than you have cycles to your name. And that experience gives me something you and your generation seem to sorely lack: perspective."

She waited for an argument, but none of us were dumb enough to make it. Not even Lucius. With another nod, she continued.

"What would have happened to the academy… to the duchy, if the heir to House Darish had died here today? Or," she added, "if you had instead prevailed and killed one of the first three commoners ever enrolled within these walls? Enrolled by the order of His Grace himself? Your lord father should have taught you that actions have consequences, even for a marquess' son. Perhaps *especially* for one."

"The *adventurer* challenged *me*." Lucius sent me a cold glare.

"After *you* had Miko kidnapped off the street by slavers!" Only my nest-sister's hand on my arm and my overriding exhaustion kept me from getting in his face.

Lucius rolled his eyes. "What are you talking about? Slavery hasn't been legal in Elthor for more than a hundred cycles. And House Darish would *never* associate with individuals of such low repute."

Hawthorne stepped forward. "My arbiters were first on the scene after House Marchon reported the kidnapping and have been following the leads ever since. While it is clear there *was* a slavery ring operating in the Docks district, nothing we have uncovered so far suggests a connection to one of Trynfall's noble houses. Including House Darish," he added.

"Wonderful! It must have just been a truly unfortunate coincidence that someone who has been targeted for harassment since her admission was then singled out, attacked in the streets, and smuggled to the docks then." suggested Wilf. "I'm glad that's all cleared up then, yeah?"

The look the lord arbiter turned on Wilf was cold enough that Zamira, a few feet away, actually shivered.

"The last thing I'd expect from someone with your family history would be to jump to the obvious conclusion, Lord McCall."

Wilf held up both hands. "I wasn't even there when the challenge was made. The only conclusion *I've* jumped to is that this little conference is about more than just the honor duel."

Dame Credence and Lord Hawthorne exchanged glances, but I wasn't going to let the conversation go off the rails.

"You're saying you can *prove* that House Darish wasn't behind Miko's kidnapping?"

"Accuse my house again, and *I* will be the one making the challenge!" snapped Lucius.

"With all your defensive enchantments gone?" I bared my teeth like I was still under the effect of *Beast Hide*'s active ability. "Bring it."

"Be silent or you will *be* silenced," hissed Dame Credence.

"Proving a negative is all but an impossibility," said Hawthorne. "My agents can only follow the evidence and there is none that leads to House Darish or, as I said, any other noble house."

"Then why was she targeted?" asked Zamira.

Mireille and her team, I couldn't help but notice, had stayed quiet this whole time. Diplomatic? Maybe. But the lack of support wasn't filling me with a great deal of warm fuzzies either.

"The answer to that is why we are here," said Hawthorne, "and why I asked Dame Credence to cut her family visit short and return to Trynfall."

It was hard to imagine the Iron Lady *having* family. I turned to trade looks with Miko, but she was staring at the lord arbiter.

"Wilhemina," she said, voice a quiet breath.

"Lady Willerton," corrected the lord. "But yes."

"What does this scaled have to do with His Grace's heir?" That was the fiorlan in Lucius' group, tall and green-haired in her academy uniform. *Anthasa,* I thought her name was, though we'd never spoken even once.

"The adventurers were part of the group that returned Lady Willerton to the capital," said Lucius. "It's the sole reason they're sullying these halls instead of out scavenging through old graveyards and ruins."

"True enough," agreed Hawthorne, reminding me why I didn't like the man. "However, it is not the whole story."

"Before he gives that story, however," cut in Dame Credence, "I will have both of your words that this conflict is over." In case there was any question who she was speaking to, she pointed first at Lucius and then at me.

"And if it isn't?" asked Lucius.

"Then you and your unit will be sent back to your dorm rooms here and now and will have to watch as Initiates Fieldings and Marchon take their units on the mission Lord Arbiter Hawthorne has brought to our doors."

The mention of a *mission* got everyone buzzing, even Mireille's group, but Lucius frowned.

"My unit, specifically? Not mine *and* his? Even though *we're* at the top of the class?"

"Yes. Rank has its privileges, which is why all of you are here, but what is being offered today is an opportunity, and ultimately, that opportunity can be withdrawn. And Initiate Fieldings' unit is vital in a way that yours is not."

That sparked a fresh round of murmurs.

"That's not fair! It means *he* could prevent my unit's inclusion regardless of what I say or do."

"Initiate Fieldings?" asked Dame Credence.

Frankly, I didn't see any downsides with Lucius' idea. Although if he *hadn't* had anything to do with Miko's kidnapping… if the attack *was* somehow related to Wilhemina instead…

Beyond Lucius' group, Mireille seemed to be trying to push words into my head through the force of her stare alone. I sighed.

"The honor duel is over," I said. "I won."

"You didn't win," argued Lucius. "I never surrendered."

I ignored him and turned to Dame Credence. "That's the end of it, as far as I'm concerned. Until or unless the arbiters find out his family was connected to the kidnapping after all."

"Initiate Darish?" asked the Iron Lady.

"While I may have encouraged some of the ranking challenges the scaled faced, that is all I have done, and even that was only over the course of the first moon. Frankly, there was never any *need* to do more; everyone in my unit ranks among the class's top ten. The strength of House Darish and the rewards given to its loyal vassals have been made more than apparent." He gave me some serious side-eye and kept going. "Should this unwashed animal restrain himself from making further unwarranted accusations, I, as a gentleman of good breeding, will consider the matter settled. However, I insist that the results of our duel be correctly labeled as inconclusive."

For the first time, Merrick spoke. "He is within his rights there, Fieldings. The terms of the duel were that it would be fought to surrender or death. Neither eventuality occurred."

Pride had me wanting to point out that we'd been about a half-second and two inches from a very fatal conclusion and that this *unwashed animal* had still spilled Lucius' blue blood all over the arena's floor… but I refrained. Maybe it was the weight of Miko's clawed hand on my shoulder, or the pleading look on Mireille's face, or even just the memory of my first life on Earth and how poorly *that* had gone.

Or maybe I was just tired as hell and could see past the haughtiness on the nobleman's face to the fear and pain underneath.

"Fine," I said. "We can call it a draw."

Dame Credence let the silence build for a bit as she studied each of us in turn. Whatever she saw must have satisfied her because she turned to Hawthorne. "Very well. Please proceed."

"What I am about to tell you has already been conveyed to the heads of His Grace's council," said the lord arbiter. "It is, however, not to spread beyond these walls. If the whisper of a rumor arises, my arbiters have been instructed to trace that whisper to its origin, and I will bring the full weight of the law and my position down upon the individuals responsible. Is that clear?"

It was interesting seeing Hawthorne operate amongst his so-called peers. Even with twelve of the fifteen initiates present being nobles and two of *those* being from high-ranked houses, nobody seemed eager to test the lord arbiter's convictions.

Fifteen heads nodded.

What followed was a brief, mostly accurate if not entirely forthcoming, retelling of Wilhemina's retrieval from Madea, her condition when we'd found her, the attack we'd faced on the road, and her eventual delivery to Priestess Iris. Somewhere in the middle of all that, Miko hit me with another *Light Healing*. Most of my more minor wounds were gone completely when it was done, but the wound in my side stubbornly persisted.

"Your sources in the palace," said Hawthorne, giving both Mireille and Lucius significant looks, "have no doubt told you that Lady Willerton has remained unconscious since her return. The healing she received and continues to receive has kept her body in reasonable health, but her state otherwise has proved troubling. A little over a moon ago, His Grace even raised the possibility of making his son heir instead."

For some reason, *that*, more than anything else, got Lucius' attention. And he didn't seem happy.

"Shortly after Lady Willerton's return, Priestess Iris requested aid from the researchers at the Crimson Needle. Given the season and that school's location in the mountains, we have only just now received a reply: rather than send one or two specialists to Trynfall, they have asked that the patient come to them instead."

"You're putting together an expedition," said Mireille. "And you want us to be part of it?"

"What does this have to do with *their* unit?" asked Lucius, not quite pointing at me or the rest of my party.

"Lady Willerton recently had a relapse. The contagion thought to be banished returned. And this time, Priestess Iris was not able to cure it. Nor were three other heads of their respective churches. Where they all failed, the unranked Priestess who initially found and rescued the duke's heir succeeded."

"Is temporary measure," said Miko, ignoring the wide-eyed looks coming her way. "Know now will reoccur."

"Yes," acknowledged Hawthorne. "If Lady Willerton is to survive the long trip to the Crimson Needle, she must be accompanied by Priestess Miko Naseri. And Brian Fieldings—"

"Goes where Miko does," I finished idly, my eyes on the dialogue window that had just appeared in the air before me:

```
NEW QUEST: Escort the Voice of the Dawn and Wilhemina
   Annerose Lakesia Willerton to the Crimson Needle.

              [ Accept | Decline ]
```

With nobody the wiser, I hit *Accept*.

"When Lord Hawthorne raised the possibility to me more than a seven-day ago, I recognized the opportunity it presented," continued Dame Credence. "Your three units are the best in our initiate class, but the Echo, for all its benefits, is a designed and constrained reality. An expedition like this would give you real-world experience."

"And free up yon true dungeon for the rest of the class, yeah?" asked Wilf.

"Indeed."

"The expedition, led by myself, was intended to leave after White Sails," said Hawthorne. "Recent events have changed our timeline."

Things finally clicked into place. "You think Miko was kidnapped because she's the only person who can heal Wilhemina?"

"I think the timing is too suspicious to ignore, yes."

"Why not just kill her instead?" Surprisingly, that was Kamet, on Mireille's team. He shrugged at the looks we sent him. "I'm not saying I *want* that. I'm just saying it would have been more effective than selling her into slavery."

"We cannot answer that because we don't know who is responsible or what their ultimate goals might be," said Hawthorne. "My assumption—which is only that, at the moment—is that the perpetrator wanted to keep their options open for now. With that initial plot foiled, my concern is that they will next opt for harsher means."

"We need to safeguard both Lady Willerton and the sca—and Priestess Naseri," said Lucius, oddly earnest. "And that means… an earlier departure?"

"It does," said Dame Credence. "You leave tomorrow, before the rest of the initiates return."

"Apologize to your family tailors," added Hawthorne. "None of you will be attending White Sails this cycle."

"Your classmates will be informed that Merrick has taken you out into the wilds as penance for your recent misbehavior," said the Iron Lady. "You will be scrubbed from the rankings and re-inserted at the bottom to start the next half-cycle, so that tale will not be entirely false."

That sparked some more muttering from both other parties, but Lucius and Mireille just nodded. And I don't think anyone in my party cared at all about rankings. Hell, being at the very bottom would save Miko from any further challenges when we came back. *Especially* if Lucius really wasn't pushing people to go after her anymore.

"One day's not a lot of time to prepare for a journey of that length," said Mireille.

"Half a day," corrected Merrick. "We leave in the morning."

"And you will travel like soldiers not nobles." Dame Credence's tone never shifted, still hard as granite, but something told me she was taking a small bit of pleasure in this bit of news. "One pack a piece. No mounts. No servants. Treat this as a moons-long delve."

For the first time since Hawthorne had mentioned Wilhemina's illness, Lucius lost a little bit of his fervor.

"What about *our* party?" I asked.

One of Lucius' team's two mages scowled. "Like any of you have horses. No offense, Barth."

Barth just shrugged. "My parents kept my horses with the family herd in Apsa; they didn't want me putting on airs out here on the frontier."

"That's not what I was asking," I said. "We weren't even allowed into the tunnels anymore because of Zamira's status and Barth's position as a foreign noble. Is the Grand Duke—"

"His Grace," murmured Wilf.

"Is His Grace going to allow them to go on this expedition?"

"Things change when it is His Grace's own daughter at risk," said Dame Credence.

"Some lives really *do* matter more than others." Wilf's smile was beatific and, despite all his skill in *Performance*, as false as a three-dollar bill. "It's always nice to see, yeah?"

"Does House McCall have any complaints to make?" asked Hawthorne, voice low and dangerous.

"None whatsoever. A little bit of fresh air will do the body good… and should whoever was responsible for these attacks on Lady Willerton seek to strike at her again, I would dearly like to be present."

For some reason, Lucius sent Wilf an approving nod. Meanwhile, Zamira started to say something, then stopped. I was pretty sure she'd arrived at the same conclusion as Wilf. If everything that had been going on *as* connected, this trip might further *both* of their investigations.

Hawthorne cleared his throat. "Settle your affairs and pack your bags. Initiate Naseri, we will have to ask you to remain on campus tonight, so have someone from your unit tackle any errands you might have. The rest of you should be back here by twelfth bell tonight, because we leave bright and early tomorrow. And remember what I said: speak to no one about what you have been told. If anyone asks, all you know is that you are being punished for your stupidity."

"That much will be readily believed by anyone who witnessed today's debacle," added Dame Credence.

"I don't *have* a room here," pointed out Zamira.

"Can stay with nest-brother and me," said Miko.

The Zarisian glanced my way and frowned. "That wouldn't be proper."

"Stay with Sky and me then," said Mireille. "You and Miko both can. We'll make it a girls' night and paint our faces while speaking poorly of the weaker sex."

"Can braid hair too," said Miko.

"And Master Bartholomew and I will have a boys' night with Brian," declared Wilf.

"We will?" asked Barth.

"Yes. It will be great fun. You'll see. Vicious gossip and ritual floggings, yeah?"

Wilf, I reminded myself, hadn't had any friends for a long time.

Lucius' group was the first to depart. Their golden-eyed Priest, Ivar, traded surreptitious glances with Wilf on the way out. Next was Mireille's group, and this time it was Kamet giving Wilf a nod when he thought nobody was watching.

If our party Spy survived long enough to avenge his family and revive his house, he would likely grow into a complete terror, but in the interim, I had to wonder just how successful Wilf's attempts to play every side against the other really were. Surely, nobody bought his act?

Then again, *I'd* almost lost my head a second time to the exact same trick Lucius had used during our original spar. I was in no position to throw stones.

Dame Credence and Hawthorne were next to go, trailed by no less than four arbiters in black, leaving just my party and a stone-faced Merrick in the training grounds.

"Will need to send message to Zelig," Miko was telling Zamira. "And coin to synossian enclave as well, so they can carry on gatherings in my absence." She paused. "Coin too, so they have food. But need supplies…"

"I'll take care of it all," I told her. "We can figure out our finances when we get back to the dorm and then I'll run all of our errands for us."

"I'll go with you," said Barth. "I'm already mostly packed."

The four of us gave him a wide range of looks.

"How?" asked Zamira.

"I only ever unpack what I need. In the event of fire or plague or invasion, it's important to be ready."

"Wine," announced Wilf. "We're going to need some wine to go along with the vicious gossip tonight. Something dry that tastes like berry-soaked dirt."

Agreeing to meet back at the dorm common rooms, we were dispersing when Merrick finally stirred.

"Fieldings. A word?"

Somehow, he made it a command rather than a request.

"I'll see you all in a bit," I told the others. Miko's second healing had done me a world of good; I barely even hobbled as I made my way back over to the instructor. Up close, our size differential bordered on the comical. The man was a mountain in human form, scars notwithstanding, and I had only ever been tall compared to dunsmen or pre-pubescent children.

"I want to talk about your duel," he said.

That could go a *variety* of ways, so I just nodded and waited.

"Sloppiest thing I ever saw," he added.

"I *won*."

"Unofficially, but sure. Still, I've seen you train. My instructors and I *helped* you train. Today was a discredit to our efforts."

He awaited my protests, a light in his steel-grey eyes. When none came, he grunted with something like approval and continued.

"Techniques are our most powerful tool, but they are *just* a tool. Weapon skill is what carries a Warrior through combat. There are differences between a duel and a delve. In the former, you don't have anyone but yourself to protect. That makes mobility your ally. You should be using your footwork and your weapon to their greatest capabilities. You should *not* be trying to strike them down like some sort of hero from a bard's song." He scowled. "If you're fighting a horde of weaker things, by all means go for the kill with every strike. Against a skilled opponent though? All that will do is expose you. Stay balanced. Stay protected. Make them come into your domain and bleed them every time they do. Letting someone like Lucius bait you into his style of combat is a good way to end up dead."

They were hard words to hear, considering I *had* won, but that didn't make Merrick wrong. More's the pity.

"Second," he added, because apparently he'd had ample time to write a whole dissertation on my performance, "when facing a named blade, try *not* to showcase your own weapon's impossible durability. Sever is not an artifact, let alone one of the Twelve, but it still has a reputation that is well deserved. And you don't have the power or the backing to deal with the thieves who might be dispatched when word spreads of a nascent artifact in the possession of a commoner and unranked adventurer."

"A nascent what?"

He blinked, slowly, looking strangely bovine in his confusion. "You don't know?"

I just cocked my head.

"That," he said, pointing at my spear, the spear of Riok Diocil, that had been forever transformed by the blood of the necromancer who killed him. "It has no enchantments that we on the faculty can see, and yet it easily withstands a weapon whose entire purpose is bent toward cutting."

"Artifacts are dangerous," I said, thinking of Tempest, which even Skaal couldn't wield without paying a ruinous price.

"To their target and their wielder both," agreed the big man. "Yours hasn't reached that point, yet. Maybe it never will. But there's a seed of something in it, and that alone is worth killing for. Entire houses have fallen for less. So, stop showing it off where anyone can see, or prepare yourself for the consequences of doing so."

That, more than anything else, felt unfair. I only had the one weapon. I carried it everywhere I went, which felt even more necessary now that I knew some people might try to steal it, and I wasn't going to *not* fight with it when my life was on the line.

"Anything else?" I asked.

"Yes. I don't know what that technique you used was, but you should be cautious of even partial transforms. Travel down a given road far enough and there might be no returning to your starting point. If you ever want to rank, you need to do more than just see yourself; you need to be okay with what it is you see."

I knew he meant well, but the truth was, Merrick hadn't lived my life. *Either* life. He hadn't seen what I'd seen in the past half-cycle and he definitely hadn't been saddled with the same responsibilities or choices. I met his gaze.

"Yeah. But I also need to stay alive long enough to get there."

○○○

That conversation was still playing in my head as I spent my afternoon running around the Lower City with Barth, doing errands. The truth was, I'd been as taken aback by *Beast Hide*'s active component as anyone. It wasn't a true transformation ability, of course… those were the province of Coppers at the earliest, but that knowledge didn't make it any less horrific to look in the mirror and see a creature crouched in my place, with thick black fur and eyes too feral to be human.

The boost it gave to my Finesse was invaluable, but the tradeoff was… extreme. The first time I'd used the ability in Mireille's rented training hall, I'd canceled it again almost immediately after, only to find myself stuck with a multi-hour cooldown. The second time, I'd forced myself to maintain it for its full minute-long duration and then spent ten times that long trying to come to grips with not just how it had felt, but the looks I'd seen in the eyes of the people around me.

Miko had been supportive, of course. Barth had been weirdly enthused. But Zamira and literally everyone in Mireille's party? Horror and disgust had been the prominent traits, for all that they'd each spent time with Greshal. Then again, a lupine looked natural in their own way. I looked like something else entirely and that created a cognitive dissonance that repelled.

Still… I'd be dead without *Beast Hide*, assuming that Hawthorne and the Iron Lady hadn't been secretly waiting in the wings the whole time to stop our duel. And I couldn't help Miko or her people as a corpse. Power was power, no matter how disquieting.

As for my spear being an *artifact*, or more accurately, being in the process of becoming one? As long as I could still wield it, I didn't see a downside.

My first stop in the Lower City was at a Smith that had taken far too much of my money over the past few moons. Unfortunately, his assistant confirmed that the damage to my hauberk was too extensive for overnight repairs. Rather than leave it behind, I decided to hold onto it; some protection was better than none, after all, and the broken and torn links didn't dig *too* much into the worn, increasingly padding-free gambeson beneath.

I had that gambeson restuffed and stitched back up at my next stop, where I also picked up some more simple but sturdy traveling clothes, a new cloak for Miko, and a sewing kit for on-the-road repairs. Upon Barth's suggestion, I also bought a new pair of gloves for myself in case the winter was still lingering by the time we reached the southern mountains.

Zelig's shop was only a few blocks away from the tailor. He kicked up a fuss when we passed on Miko's apologies but that ended as soon as Barth name-dropped Lord Arbiter Hawthorne. Then, the Herbalist was all smiles and rueful chuckles; he assured us his apprentice would *of course* retain her position upon her return and then did his best to kick us out of his storefront.

Politically neutral or not, the arbiters, I had noticed, made an awful lot of people in Trynfall nervous.

I moved on to the guild hall. Our trip to the Crimson Needle and back would take multiple moons, and while that made doing any missions pretty much impossible, I wanted to verify that the ones we'd already completed would keep us in good standing until our return. Ulla, manning one of the desks, as usual, confirmed that to be the case, although she spent most of that time staring in fascination at Barth's blonde curls. Once she remembered I existed, she made me promise to pass her goodbyes and well wishes onto Miko.

Lastly, we made a stop at the synossian enclave, bringing with us the food that should have accompanied Miko's sermon that night. I handed over a truly painful percentage of the money my nest-sister and I had accumulated to Joshua and Yuna, the two synossians who'd taken on leadership roles in Miko's burgeoning enterprise. I didn't think those funds would last until our return, even if the two followed our recommendation and scaled back to a single gathering every Seventh Day, but there were limits to what we could do.

The synossians had been merely surviving, and only barely, before we came along. Hopefully, the community Miko and the others had worked so hard to establish would let them do more than survive until our return.

Miko had faith.

I… had doubts.

The only thing Barth bought on our entire trip was a bread bowl containing what looked like baked scarab, shell included. As we traveled about, the Apsan noble crunched his way through the bowl. He seemed cheerily excited and blissfully unconcerned about the coming trip and as usual, I couldn't tell if that was naivete, or a result of his alien and deeply disturbing upbringing. Either way, he was good company, and not *just* because he bought me a kebab on our way back.

○○○

When we arrived back at the dorms, Wilf was waiting outside my room, a bulging pack in his hands. That much was expected, if not exactly invited. Mireille's presence, on the other hand, was not. Nor was the heavily wrapped bundle she'd set down by her feet.

"Fieldings," she said, voice brusque.

After multiple moons, I had realized Wilf's welcome speech about how the initiates all called each other by first name rather than house had been, at best, aspirational, and at worst, an outright lie.

"Marchon," I said, to drive home that reality.

"Barth," said Wilf, making his counterpoint, "shall we head in and leave these two to their discussion?"

Barth had carried his pack and bow with him throughout the entire trip. He shrugged and nodded.

"Give me a second to unlock it," I said, digging into my money belt for the door key.

"No need," said Wilf, turning the handle and ushering Barth inside with a sweeping bow. "I've taken care of that small concern."

"Then why were we waiting in the hall?" demanded Mireille.

"We are members of the noble class, Lady Marchon." Wilf's expression was damn near pious. "It would have been unspeakably rude to enter before either of the hosts had arrived, and we must always remember our manners."

When both Barth and Wilf were safely ensconced in my room and the door had shut again, Mireille turned to me.

"I don't know how you deal with him."

"Wilf? He's not all bad."

"You know he's selling your information to Darish, right?"

"*Just* House Darish?"

At least she had the grace to look away. "That's different. We're allies now." She kicked the bundle at her feet, causing a metallic clank. "Which is why I brought this."

"May I?" At her nod, I knelt down and unwrapped the bundle in question. It was… another hauberk, this one significantly fancier than the one Seanna had made for me in Madea. Most of the links were iron still, but a few were some other metal, almost rust-colored. "This is for me?"

"It was supposed to be done for the duel, but even my family's Smiths don't work that fast, regardless of the money you throw at them." She scowled. "Still, White Sails celebration aside, you held up your end of the deal. You won the duel and Lucius is still alive."

"I'm pretty sure the duel was a draw."

The look the noblewoman sent me was scathing. "There are two realities in this world, Brian. The political one and the actual one. In one of those realities, your duel with Lucius ended inconclusively and nobody lost any honor in the process. In the other, everyone saw the killing blow that would have landed."

I wasn't going to argue with that, so I held the hauberk up and then against me. It was heavier than the one I had on. I wasn't sure if that was the thickness of the new armor's rings or all the pieces mine was missing. Perhaps the most surprising thing wasn't that House Marchon had made me armor... it was that that armor seemed to fit.

"I had a Smith and Tailor come by while you were training," she admitted. "They have skills to judge sizing by eye rather than tape."

The Smith part made sense, given the hauberk in my hands, but... "Why a tailor?"

"If you survived to join me at His Grace's White Sails feast, you would have needed to dress the part."

"Even though it wasn't a date?"

"Appearance is everything in politics." She looked me up and down. "In some ways, I'm glad we will miss the festival. After witnessing your duel, I think the Tailor's outfit was poorly chosen. Better to lean into your warlike aspects and lack of civility."

She turned and headed down the hall to where she, Sky, Miko, and Zamira would soon be braiding hair or putting together grand strategies for bloody conquest.

I hadn't seen any wine in Wilf's hands. Hopefully, that didn't mean there wasn't any, because I really, really needed a drink.

ooo

Two bottles of wine and a shocking amount of vicious gossip later, I emerged from my meditation to see the results of the day's actions. I'd gained some experience from the duel, even if nobody had died, but it was my skills that should show real growth. And for once, the Framework didn't disappoint:

```
You have increased the following skills:

Major skills:
Medium Armor [+1]: 47/50
Spear (U) [+1]: 47/50
Tactics [+1]: 46/50
Throwing [+2]: 3/50
Unarmed Combat [+1]: 7/50


Minor skills:
Athleticism [+1]: 46/50
Avoidance [+1]: 46/50
Focus [+2]: 39/50
Pain Tolerance (U) [+2]: 49/50


General skills:
Mercantilism [+1]: 6/10
```

The point in *Mercantilism* was a nice and unexpected bonus, but as always, my eyes drifted of their own accord to a particular skill's location on my personal record. Even with skill gains slowing dramatically, *Pain Tolerance* was somehow only a point from the level cap.

It blew my mind that Mireille didn't have hers maxed.

38

Lord Arbiter Hawthorne had clearly learned something from the previous expedition, and the inclusion of our teams from the Tryn was only a small part of that. While the carriage had no doubt been fully repaired, it didn't make a reappearance, instead replaced by three covered wagons, each one identical at a glance.

There was no way of knowing which one Wilhemina was inside, which would add another layer of safety in the event of an attack on the road. Unless the fake Zarisians sent enough mercenaries to just wipe us all out, of course. That didn't seem likely, but a lot of unlikely things happened on Eos.

In addition to our fifteen initiates and Merrick, Hawthorne brought along his bodyguard, three wagon drivers, a chef and her assistant, and a full baker's dozen of soldiers. When two Mages showed up in lemon-yellow robes, followed by a Priestess in a pale blue dress wearing a mask of white bone, it all started to feel less like a caravan and more like a traveling circus.

Still, all three of the final arrivals were Tin, and one of the soldiers was too. Add in Merrick, who was Copper, and we were a well-armed group. Any bandits along the trail would take one look at us and decide it was a great night for hanging out and telling stories around the fire somewhere far, far away.

As for the unnamed enemy who may or may not have been behind Miko's attempted kidnapping?

If they wanted to try something, we'd be ready.

We would have made quite the sight if we'd traveled through Trynfall as a group, but Hawthorne had us departing separately. Our party joined up with the other initiates outside the gates just after seventh bell. A few minutes later, Merrick came through with Hawthorne and the wagons, followed eventually by the rest of the soldiers and then the three colorful Tins.

No Priest Rollin Humber this time. No Samhill or Jenkins either, although I was kind of okay about their absence. I didn't want to see if any hard feelings might re-emerge with Lace away.

Most of the day was spent with Trynfall the city slowly fading away in the distance, though it would take well over a moon to leave Trynfall the duchy. It was odd; I'd spent more time in Trynfall than anywhere on Eos except Madea—and even that was close—but the frontier town had felt a lot more like home. Maybe it was because we'd spent most of our time at the academy and not wandering the streets. Maybe it was because the only real friends I'd made outside of Greshal and his grandsire were on the road with me. Or maybe I'd been so focused on leveling that I hadn't made time for anything other than helping Miko.

Hell, at least *she* had started working toward a profession. I'd watched my *Scribing* skill actually deteriorate instead.

Either way, I had mixed emotions looking back at what little we could see of the city. Pride at how far Miko and I had both come in so short a time. Reluctance to leave a place so well suited for our goals and advancement. Excitement to see something beyond cobblestone streets and the walls of my dorm room. I even found myself missing

Earth for the first time in a very long while. Without cars, trains, or planes, the round-trip journey would take more than three moons. By the time we made it back, it would be late spring, and the school's first half-cycle would be long over.

It took a day and a half for a new emotion to join the others: regret that I hadn't figured out some way to bring a bathtub with us. The ready access to the dorm baths had made me forget just how filthy marching on the road was, and having three wagons and the commensurate number of horses just added to that.

For those first two days, we mostly stuck to our individual parties. Or our units, as everyone else insisted on calling them. Three groups of five carefully orbiting each other within the larger mass. Mireille and I exchanged a few words, Wilf did his best to flit between all three groups when he wasn't in deep conversations with Zamira, but Lucius kept to himself, quiet and withdrawn.

I didn't trust it. The longer it took Lucius to start something, the more I became convinced that his passivity was a ploy, that whatever he had planned was going to be that much more devastating.

Instead, he showed up at our tent after we'd finished making camp. He wasn't alone—their team's fiorlan Rogue, Anthasa, seemed to shadow the nobleman wherever he went—but he *was* unarmed.

"Initiate Fieldings," he said, then turning to Miko. "And Priestess Naseri. I have come to put the recent unpleasantness behind us."

"Which part?" I asked. "The honor duel, the way you had Miko targeted for ranking challenges, or her kidnapping?"

He drew himself up to his full height, which was a lot more impressive in relation to me than Miko. "You were the one responsible for the honor duel, and I had nothing to do with the kidnapping, as Lord Hawthorne himself already attested to."

"He said his arbiters hadn't found any evidence," I corrected. "That doesn't mean there wasn't any."

Lucius took a step toward me, visibly caught himself, and stepped back again. "Believe what you will. I have come here to put an end to our feud."

Miko stirred at my side, but before she could accept, I spoke up again.

"Why?"

"Because there are more important things at stake than school rankings or even my own reputation."

I'd spent remarkably little time with Lucius despite the fact that we'd tried to kill each other twice… but he *seemed* sincere. Despite that being a sentence I would never have expected to pass his lips.

"Things?" I asked.

"Lady Willerton. Her life and her future hang in the balance and I will do all that I can to preserve them both." He turned to Miko. "If that means defending you until Wilhemina is well again, you have my sword."

You don't even have your sword, I just barely managed to avoid saying. Sever had been left in Trynfall with House Darish, and while the weapon he'd brought in its place was a thing of beauty, it was still a far cry from his family's treasured relic.

"Will accept peace accord," said Miko, once again taking a higher road I wasn't sure even existed. "But only if nest-brother does too."

And just like that, the ball was back in my court.

I shrugged. "I guess I'm just surprised. I didn't realize House Darish was so devoted to His Grace."

"His Grace?"

"Grand Duke Willerton, then." I was *never* going to get these terms of address correct.

"We are loyal, of course, to both castle and crown, but my concerns center on Lady Willerton herself, given how intertwined our futures are set to be."

I gave him my best blank stare. It seemed to work.

"When she is of age, we will be promised," he clarified.

"Promised what?"

For the first time, some of the old Lucius re-emerged as he sent me a withering look. "To *each other*."

It still took me way too long to get it, maybe because I'd been born on another planet entirely and in a time where marriage rates in general had fallen off a cliff. When I realized what he was talking about, I couldn't keep the reaction off my face.

"She's… six or seven cycles old."

"Which is why any official announcements will necessarily wait until she is of age." His scowl grew to match mine. "I did not *ask* to be promised to a child, adventurer. But we of the noble class must think beyond tomorrow to all the cycles yet to come. Combining House Darish's line with that of His Grace's is the best thing for Trynfall's future, and as the heir, that duty falls upon my shoulders. To eventually wed, Lady Willerton must survive. To survive, she must be cured. For that to happen, she must reach the Crimson Needle, which depends upon both our escort and your… sister's… efforts. And that means that I and those who owe allegiance to House Darish will focus all our efforts upon protecting both the lady and her healer."

Miko stepped in again while I was still unpacking everything Lucius had just said.

"Can agree that Wilhemina is what is most important."

"Lady Willerton."

She gave him a long look.

"Allowances must be made," he muttered under his breath, either thinking my nest-sister and I were deaf or not caring if we overheard. "We are in agreement then?"

"Yes. The past is past," agreed Miko. "Would like to speak more on the subject in days to come."

"Of course. Given that we will all be sharing each other's dust for the next quarter cycle or more, that goes without saying." He offered her a nod and me an even shallower one. "Initiate Naseri. Initiate Fieldings."

"Initiate Darish." I looked past him at the silent fiorlan. "I don't know your last name, so I guess I'll just have to call you Anthasa?"

"For now." Her grin exposed teeth almost as sharp as Miko's. "And who knows? Maybe you can give me some instruction in the spear at some point?"

"I didn't know *Spear* was a class skill for Rogues."

"It's not," hissed Lucius, shooing Anthasa a glare that seemingly made no impact whatsoever.

The fiorlan's smile widened. "I suppose we could *also* talk weapons."

We watched them both depart before Miko turned to me and spoke in the High Tongue. "I think that one might be in her mating season, nest-brother."

"Considering she's never even spoken to me before today? It seems unlikely."

"Past is past," she said again in Trade, grinning. Then in her native tongue: "Do you believe what Lucius was saying?"

"Sort of. I'm pretty sure he wasn't lying about his plans to marry Wilhemina, although I'm guessing it's a lot more about strengthening House Darish than the duchy as a whole."

"Human customs are strange and unknowable, like the people themselves. But if he and his house *are* looking for this wedding to advance their status, I can believe they would want to protect her."

"Yeah, that makes sense."

"We should tell Wilf and Zamira."

"Because Darish wouldn't have been behind her kidnapping, if so," I concluded. "Yeah. I think you're right."

The problem was that suddenly made House Marchon the most likely candidate for Wilhemina's kidnapping, the framing of Zaris, and maybe even the downfall of House McCall. Not only were they one of the few other houses that had the resources, but wanting to prevent the ascension of their primary rivals made for a hell of a motive.

Only… if *they* were the guilty party, why had Mireille helped free Miko from the slavers? And why had she both put her name and money on the line for me? Miko's disappearance would have been a death knell for Wilhemina and *my* death would have left my nest-sister that much more vulnerable.

I blew out a frustrated breath.

I was missing something. I knew that much.

I just didn't know what it was.

○○○

It took those first two seven-days for the initiates to adjust to the schedule of being on the road. Early mornings were a fright for more than just Miko, and I'm not sure *any* of the nobles in our class had *walked* for more than a few hours in a day before this. Still, nobody wanted to appear weak before the other parties, let alone the soldiers Hawthorne had brought, and that kept the complaining to a minimum at first. Blisters, pulled muscles, and one odd case of sunburn all popped up as people learned what to do and not do on the road instead of in a carriage or on horseback, but with four healers, those minor maladies were all easily addressed.

This close to Trynfall, there was no shortage of villages along the road to spend our nights at. However, Hawthorne seemed to pick and choose from them according to an algorithm none of the rest of us were privy to. And that meant we still spent half our nights out under the stars. Under Merrick's watchful eye, we all pitched in with the soldiers to make camp, and soon, our parties were included in the watch rotation, if always paired with at least a few veterans. I think it was the lack of sleep that really started to wear on the other initiates, more even than the dirt, the tedium, and the constant travel. That was when a few of them started publicly wondering if the Iron Lady's story about this being a punishment detail had carried with it a nugget of truth.

I'd like to say our party fared better than most, but that would be a lie. All that time in Trynfall eating food someone else cooked for us, taking free baths, and sitting in class had spoiled Miko and me, and it took us a few days to reaccustom ourselves to life on the road. Meanwhile, Zamira and Barth's only real travel experience had been their respective journeys to Trynfall and those had been under vastly different circumstances. Wilf was a little bit more worldly, but as unused to traveling by foot as the other nobles.

We'd left Wilf's sister, Ellisha, at the Velvet Fist under the watchful eye of Madame Telidra. There hadn't been any choice in the matter and no time at all to arrange anything else. Still, while Barth and I had been running errands, Wilf had been visiting the brothel to pass on my instructions for her long-term care. He'd also put quill to parchment to draft a comprehensive list of his sister's symptoms, from initial sickness to prolonged coma. That list was in his pack and on his person at all times; if the sages at the Crimson Needle could help cure Wilhemina's curse, maybe they could help identify Ellisha's too.

Even so, I caught Wilf looking back behind us more than once, toward the city that had long since vanished behind rolling hills and the not infrequent winter clouds.

News of House Darish's plans for Wilhemina helped distract him, for a time, at least. Most days, he and Zamira marched together, and while I was pretty sure at least some of their conversations revolved around their dual, potentially complimentary investigations, I was starting to think the stone-eyed political prisoner and the scion of a broken house just enjoyed each other's company.

Eventually, my fellow initiates seemed to reach a kind of equilibrium with life on the road. The complaints didn't stop, precisely, but instead became largely indistinguishable from those of the soldiers in our midst.

By the end of the first seven-day, I'd adjusted well enough to start training again after dinner and before we broke for night watch. Miko would check Wilhemina each night, just to make sure she didn't need a new Healing, and then join me off to the side of the camp. There was insufficient light for proper sparring, but we could at least go through our respective forms.

During the next seven-day, the rest of our party joined in. Even Zamira, whose facility with the long staff had yet to progress beyond *questionable*. And soon after that, the two other initiate groups joined in. At first, we all trained in separate clumps, like rival companies finding themselves on the same corporate retreat. That haphazard arrangement ended when Merrick pulled Mireille, Lucius, and I aside. The scarred man's giant strides made talking to him while on the march an exercise in frustration.

For me, at least; I was practically jogging to keep up.

"If you and your units have the energy to train, we're going to do it properly," he said. "I've spoken with Lord Hawthorne and we're going to stop early three times a seven-day, while there's light still to see by."

"Won't that delay us further?" asked Mireille.

"No, because we'll be making up that lost time on the other days by traveling later into the night. I've asked two of our assigned detachment to assist with the effort, but this is weapons training, not small group tactics. Your units are going to be broken up based on weapon type, and we'll rotate between those groups. Understood?"

It was phrased like a question and sounded like a question, but we'd all attended enough classes with Merrick to know it wasn't, in fact, a question. My nod followed Lucius' and Mireille's.

"Good. I want you to speak to your Rogues too. As we move toward the duchy's southern borders, we're going to want to increase our complement of scouts. Now's the time for them to get some practice in."

Mireille frowned. "I think this is the first significant stretch of time Kamet has spent in the wilderness."

The fact that she even called this the wilderness suggested it was Mireille's first time too, but I didn't say that.

"Wilf too," I admitted.

"Whereas Anthasa practically grew up in the wilds."

I reminded myself that punching the smugness off Lucius' face would do more harm than good.

To my hand, that is.

"They'll each be paired with an enlisted scout," said Merrick, "and be the better for it. Woodcraft is not a bad skill to have, even if just for traveling between capital and family estate."

Woodcraft was *not* actually a Framework skill, but a summation of all the skills like *Tracking* and *Orienteering* that Lace had been teaching me. I knew that, but I wasn't sure the others did.

Nobility had its perks, but I'd noticed it also made for some thegar-sized holes in their upbringing.

But speaking of skills…

"I was trained as a scout before arriving in Trynfall," I said. "I'd be happy to join in."

That got me odd looks from both party leaders. I wasn't sure if it was because I was volunteering for work or because I was a Warrior who ran around in the woods.

"I'll find a fourth scout to vet you," agreed Merrick. "Better let all your people know that today's a day we'll be pushing long. If they can manage, it would do my old head some good to not have the endless murmur of their complaints serenade me to sleep."

That wasn't much of a dismissal, but the Hammer didn't do dismissals. So, after a moment, we started to drift back to our respective units' places in line.

"Fieldings." Merrick's voice stopped me cold.

"Yeah?"

"This person who trained you to scout… who were they?"

"A friend and the leader of our party. Adventuring party," I clarified.

"The blood-scorned amazon you entered Trynfall with?"

"Yes."

"Is she the same person who taught you the Night Hag's oath?" He smiled at my reaction, exposing teeth like granite slabs. "Some of us have traveled, adventurer. The phrasing is hard to forget."

"Yes, she taught it to me." I shrugged. "There's a rogue Copper out there that needs to hear those words before he dies."

Not that I could remember *all* the words, but still. That was what Lace was for. One of many, many reasons she needed to stay alive until we were ready to join her.

"Arrius Vitellius." Merrick nodded.

"You know him?"

"He never served, but I know *of* him. And I've seen the wanted posters." The older man said nothing for a long while as I jogged along trying to keep up. "That friend of yours should have warned you to keep the oath to yourself. Trynfall's a duchy that allows all types, but there are some people who would react poorly to even the few words you uttered. And Hashoggath herself isn't known to have patience with those who speak her words lightly."

I *hadn't* spoken them lightly, but I was pretty sure Merrick knew that as well as I did.

"I'm aware," I said.

"Okay." Another long pause. "I'm not here to speak on what you do after you've graduated, but if you want to kill a Copper? You'd best *be* one. That or bring a damn army with you."

I flashed back to the memory of Arrius, Skaal, and Khamani's High Priest, fighting on Madea's southern wall.

"…yeah."

I gave Wilf the news, which he took with his usual modicum of grace and tact… meaning enough swearing that the nearby Zamira couldn't hold in her laughter. That drew Barth over and the ensuing explanation somehow ended with the young Apsan volunteering for scout training too. Which led to Wilf giving Barth such a look of abject concern and horror that a nearby Miko rushed over to offer healing.

Zamira was still chuckling about it by the time we stopped for dinner that night and somehow, her good humor infected Wilf and through him, the rest of the party. We had the first watch anyway and spent it in pairs—with one roamer—out under a blanket of stars and Eos' two moons, Lakshi and Tirsa. Miko even spotted some of the constellations she knew—the Tears of the Lady and the Shield of Kal—though Corros' Black Heart was thankfully nowhere to be seen.

It was the first night on the road that felt almost peaceful. We might have been back in the Echo, running an escort mission, just our party against the world.

Except the Echo would have almost guaranteed skill gains, whereas I hadn't seen a single one since leaving Trynfall. It would have guaranteed some form of loot too, where my money belt was now almost as empty as my decoy coin purse. And it would have guaranteed a night in our beds when we were done instead of a bedroll in the tent I continued to share with Miko.

So maybe this wasn't like being back in the Echo at all. Still, our party of cast-offs had weathered this unexpected change in circumstances as well as anyone from the academy and that didn't suck. And we'd been on the road for twelve days already, without even a whiff of an ambush; Hawthorne's decision to sneak out of Trynfall ahead of schedule had clearly paid off.

The lack of combat wasn't great for progression, but after all the bloody work I'd put in, patrolling the tunnels, delving the Echo, rescuing Miko in Trynfall, and fighting my duel, I kind of thought it might be good for the soul.

Just… not in a way that the Framework chose to reward.

○○○

The next morning, I went in search of Lucius long before we'd broken camp. He saw me coming, paled a bit for no reason I could discern, and then marched over to meet me. Somehow, even after twelve days on the road, he looked ready for a photoshoot. A little dirtier than normal, sure, and wearing travel gear rather than court finery, but still… it was obnoxious.

"Initiate."

Some days, he remembered I had a name. Apparently, it was not going to be one of those days.

I nodded. "Lucius. I wanted to talk."

"With respect," he said, giving me none, "I don't know what you and I could possibly have to talk about."

"Wilhemina's safety."

Just like that, he was all ears. "What is it? What have you heard? And how?"

"I haven't heard anything. But when we transported her from Madea, we were attacked on the road."

"By Zarisian mercenaries. I heard."

"Mercenaries, yes. The Zarisian part is unconfirmed."

"So you came to warn me of the possibility of attack?" He frowned. "We are all aware of that possibility. That's why we're here along with a detachment of soldiers."

It had been a lot easier to deal with Lucius when I could just treat him as the enemy. He made for a particularly shitty would-be ally. And talking to him this early in the day had been a mistake. Nonetheless, I rallied.

"What is less known about the attack we suffered is that the lead scout might have been working *with* the mercenaries."

"I hadn't been informed of that."

"Yeah, that's what *less known* means," I said. "My point being…"

"That if it happened once, it can happen again. We need to be aware of the same possibility on this expedition."

"Right. If you could tell Anthasa to keep an eye on whichever scout she is paired with for any behavior that seems suspicious…?"

The nobleman nodded. "That makes sense. And it was a deft move to inform me instead of reaching out to her directly. Best to limit the contact between the two of you."

And just like that, he'd lost me. "I told you because you're the group leader."

"Oh. Well, of course."

"In fact, I've only even spoken with her once. And that was when you came over to apologize."

"To end our feud," he corrected. "No apology was issued, formal or otherwise. And Anthasa's conduct during that meeting is precisely why I think distance and decorum should be maintained. Lady Willerton's security is paramount. The time for dalliances is over."

I blinked. It had been a while since they'd met Miko and me at our tent and honestly, I barely even remembered—

Oh.

"I guess I didn't realize that was a serious proposition."

"Anthasa is the third daughter of a fiorlan house." When it was clear I didn't have any idea what that meant, Lucius rolled his eyes. Charmingly. "Fiorlan nobility give their third daughter to the forest, so she can serve as a living connection to their species' cultural past. That childhood made her a capable scout, but when it comes to civility and etiquette, she might as well be one of your kind."

"A commoner?"

"Or an adventurer. Take your pick."

"I like her better already."

"Be that as it may, I ask that you—"

"I'm not going to hook up with her."

"Hook... up?"

"Get together. Sleep with. Whatever you call it here." Anthasa was attractive, in an alien sort of way, but until Miko or someone else could cure the disease I carried with me... no. Just no. Also? Anyone who expressed interest in me *after* watching my partial transform with *Beast Hide* was seriously suspect.

"I am glad you understand the situation," said Lucius, misunderstanding the situation. "And will convey your message as requested."

Enemies or not, talking to the man was exhausting. So, I just nodded, waved, and went in search of Wilf. Since *he* already knew the story behind our trip from Madea, convincing him to keep an eye on his assigned scout partner was a lot less hassle. Even better, he promised to pass the word on to Barth.

Which left only Kamet, in Mireille's group.

Ten days later, I still wasn't sure what to think about House Marchon, given the revelations of Lucius' marriage plan. I'd been keeping my distance, although I doubted anyone had noticed in the chaos of our class's adjustment to the road. Still, as much as I *wanted* to be suspicious of the scion and her house's motivations, I was having a hard time convincing myself.

For all that she was a noble and the heir to one of Trynfall's most powerful houses, Mireille wore her emotions on her sleeve. And her face. I had a substandard Discernment stat, yeah, but *Deception* was capped out; surely, given all the time we'd spent together before the duel, I'd have gotten *some* sort of hint if she was something other than what she presented?

Unless she'd evolved her class into something that promoted *Deception* to a Major or Minor skill.

Which… was always a possibility.

But there was also the matter of my new armor. While the hauberk crafted by Seanna, our kithrizal Smith friend, had been just as well made, I couldn't deny that the new one fit perfectly… or that the materials used were a step up from plain iron. It was hard to distrust someone who had had something like this crafted for me, especially after spending her own money to rent out a training hall to keep me alive.

Maybe that was naïve. Maybe I was letting a minor gift sway my judgment. But actions mattered, and so far, Mireille had played things straight with me. I'd do the same with her… and rely on Wilf and maybe Zamira to warn me if I got it wrong.

I headed over to the circle of tents that Mireille's party was swiftly dismantling.

In contrast to Lucius, Mireille was a very long way from camera ready. Dirt marred one cheek, tan skin glistened with a layer of sweat, and she had a truly epic case of bedhead going on. She ran a hand through the increasingly long hair, not fixing things in the slightest, and smiled as she came over to greet me.

"Finally got tired of avoiding us, have you?"

Okay, so maybe my behavior had been noticed.

"We literally just saw each other yesterday."

"When Merrick pulled us aside, sure. But whenever I go looking for a sparring partner who's *not* Darishal, you're nowhere to be found."

"What's wrong with Derry?"

"Ever since he gained another point in Strength, he's taken to one-handing that maul of his and training with a kite shield. Do you know how *annoying* it is to fight a shield bearer? It's not bad practice, maybe, but a woman needs variety in her life."

"And Lucius?"

'You'd make me spar *him?* Here I thought we were allies, if not yet friends." She gave me a level look, grin falling away. "Speaking of House Darish's golden boy, is there something I should know?"

"He has taken steps to end our feud."

"Huh. What did he offer?"

"I'm sorry?"

"Coin? Land? Property?"

"None of that." I frowned. Had a bribe been on the table? Because as my new hauberk had proven, I was totally okay with being bought.

"Don't tell me he actually deigned to offer an apology?"

"No, he just wanted to clear the air and start over."

"Of course he did. You nearly killed him, which makes you a person of consequence. And your sister is the key to keeping his intended fiancée alive. For now at least."

"You know about that?"

"Everyone does. It was publicly announced almost five cycles ago."

"When Wilhemina was… two?"

"Welcome to what it means to be noble." There was no cheer in her smile. "Alliances must be made, and power must be grasped lest someone else make it theirs."

"Does that mean you're promised to someone too?"

She reacted much like she had when I'd asked her if going to the White Sails feast with her was a date: spots of color appearing on her cheeks as her eyes flashed with anger. She took a long breath and then let it out again, and when she spoke, her voice was calm. Ish.

"Thankfully, my lord father does not subscribe to such customs. When I marry, it will be by my choice."

"That's good," I said, looking to fill the silence.

"Yes. Yes, it is. So, you and Lucius Darish are… what now? Friends?" She snickered at whatever look I sent her. "Allies then?"

"A bit less likely to try to kill each other, I think. But Miko and I already made our choice of allies. That doesn't change."

It was clearly the right response, but she wanted more.

"And?"

"And I'll spar with you tonight when we stop to train."

"Good." She slapped me on the shoulder hard enough that I'd have toppled over back when I'd only had a ten Strength. "Now, what was it you came to say?"

I informed her about the possibility of traitorous scouts, praying that she and her house hadn't been behind those scouts in the first place. She listened carefully until I was done and then nodded. "I'll tell Kamet, though I'm not sure he requires the warning. He might be the most paranoid person I've ever known."

"It seems like a common trait among Rogues." My mind unwittingly turned to Anthasa. "Most of them anyway."

○○○

My assigned scout was *Bruce*, the first person I'd met with that name since coming to Eos. If he'd been born on Earth, Bruce would have liked driving trucks, chewing tobacco, and never saying a word. Probably in that order. In the absence of the first two activities, he seemed to have put all his energy into the last. After scouting a full day with him along as an observer, I was convinced it would take a team of phloxls to drag more than a grunt out of the other man.

To be fair, he was damn communicative with those grunts. In that same span of time, I learned to differentiate surprise from disapproval, impatience from caution, and even *let's check that out* from *it's time we returned to camp*. Basically, Bruce had turned grunting into an artform. Any more fully developed, and it would have been an entire language, and my *Speaker of Tongues* trait would have translated it for me.

Instead, I just had to hope this counted as Discernment training.

Sadly, when I communed with the Framework that night, body freshly healed from the bruises left from sparring with Mireille, my hopes were dashed again.

Twelve days on the road.

No gains at all.

I never would have thought I'd miss school so badly.

39

The lack of skill gains didn't last forever. Days spent out in the hills and then woods scouting netted me a point each in *Orienteering* and *Tracking.* Merrick taking over our thrice-weekly training sessions helped with my combat skills, granting boosts in *Spear, Medium Armor, Avoidance,* and *Athleticism.* I even earned a hard-fought point in *Leadership* as my role in the party solidified outside our delves. And in what seemed to be both a trend and a silent condemnation of my life and lifestyle, *Pain Tolerance* had once again been the first of my skills to cap for the level.

With winter giving way to spring, we'd encountered our fair share of travelers on the road, but most had been traveling merchants on their circuits or locals headed to the nearest town. The few groups that seemed dangerous had given our armed column a wide berth. Not that I could blame them for that. We were a strong enough force that we might have rolled over even a town like Eustace's Sakeld. It would take an army of bandits or a handful of seriously over-leveled opponents to even give us pause.

That had, no doubt, been Hawthorne's intention all along, but it made for a boring trip. The lack of true danger, of events putting my soul under pressure, made experience hard to come by. Three seven-days after leaving Trynfall, my honor duel with Lucius still felt like it had been the only real challenge I'd faced.

I had barely budged from level nine.

I took solace in scouting, in seeing something beyond the backs of whoever was marching in front of me and smelling something other than horses or people. As we progressed south, the land shook off its cloak of civility. I found tracks of wild pigs larger than any of our horses and steered clear of a few trees that had been hollowed out by colonies of what Beasts of Eos class had called emperor ants. The weather was still cool enough that those colonies were mostly dormant, but I passed on the locations to Bruce on my return. Emperor ants were less of a concern than false dawn, but still something nearby villages would need to know about.

Tracking helped me find animal signs, my studies in class helped me identify what had made those signs, and *Animal Behaviorism* helped me understand which represented threats to our scouts if not the column as a whole. There was some real irony in that discovered synergy between skills and education having absolutely nothing to do with my class. Still, I hadn't been on Eos long enough to take anything for granted; class-related or not, two Framework-given skills working in tandem with class-given education was *cool*.

Twice, the real scouts from our company brought back food—a small, russet-colored deer the first time and a flightless bird somewhere between a turkey and a peacock the next—but hunting was never a focus even for those scouts who had ranged weapons. Two of our three wagons carried supplies, and unless something went horribly awry, those supplies would easily see us to the Crimson Needle.

Fresh meat was always welcome though. Salted sailfish and hardtack got us through most of our days, but they were nobody's idea of a good time.

Each morning, while Mireille, Lucius, and I were getting our marching orders from Merrick, Miko ducked into the sole passenger wagon to check on Lady Willerton. After its brief hibernation, the contagion seemed to be coming back with a vengeance; where she'd once been able to go multiple moons between healings, that timespan had already shrunk to multiple seven-days instead. It was far better than when Miko had had to heal the little girl every few glasses, but nobody liked the direction things were heading in. Hawthorne and Merrick both made certain my nest-sister remained nearby at all times. Given the stakes, that was understandable, and Miko never once complained, but I knew she'd have rather been out exploring the wilderness with me.

I did my best to bring her plant cuttings and new varieties of fruit when I encountered them. I didn't have the *Gathering* skill, so what I delivered was in mediocre condition, at best, and completely unusable, at worst—one plant even turned out to be poisonous, causing my hand to swell up like a balloon before *Touch of the Dawn* flushed the toxins from my system—but she appreciated the effort anyway. And the few plants she *didn't* already know were carefully dried, pressed, and stored away as new pages in her Herbalism journal for identification upon our return to Trynfall.

Between that, our weapons training, and the occasional healing, I think she was content, if not particularly stimulated.

Most nights, we were too tired to do much other than sleep when it wasn't our party's watch, but even with my scouting responsibilities, there was time to walk on the march. I did my best to check in with my party, but most of that time was spent with the person I was most comfortable with: Miko. Despite numerous attempts, I'd never found her a copy of *Meditations on Mortality*, and it had now been long enough that I'd forgotten most of what I read, but a lot of our talks centered around thoughts the book had triggered.

In some ways, I thought those discussions were just as necessary as anything we might have been doing back at the Tryn. Miko was almost ninth level, and I was already there, and that meant tenth level and Tin were just around the corner for both of us. If we didn't want to get stuck like Lucius, we needed to put in work on more than just our skills.

Not that I thought Miko would have a problem. As young as she was, as much as she might occasionally struggle under the burden her gods had placed on her, there was a purity of purpose that saw her through every obstacle placed in her path. She ultimately knew who she was. She knew what she wanted. If that's all the test for Tin ultimately required, she would sail right through it.

"Do you have an Ideal though?" I asked her on one particularly dreary day. It had started raining the previous night and while it said something that it was warm enough for it *not* to be snow, slogging through mud wasn't much of an improvement.

"Yes." She gave me a look and dipped her head. "Compassion."

It was somehow both obvious and a surprise at the same time. I didn't have to ask what compassion meant to her, because I saw it in action every single day. She lived her Ideal, so if *that* was the test for reaching Tin, she'd already passed it too.

I wasn't quite so fortunate.

My idea of freedom wasn't chaos. I knew that much. It wasn't control either, which should have been self-evident, but somehow wasn't. I'd decided on the road from Madea that it wasn't *personal* freedom either. Some people might choose the ability to do what they wanted as the rest of the world burned, but that wasn't me.

I felt like I'd had an epiphany during Madea's defense, staring down the horde of oncoming irkonnen, but that clarity had faded with the funeral pyres, leaving behind only smoke and the vague remnants of certainty. I'd spent the months since, the moons since, even, trying to find it again, trying to decide how my Ideal would and should be reflected in the person I intended to become. It didn't feel like I was any closer than when I'd started, and that was starting to gnaw at me.

Seventy percent of the people who reached level ten never made it to Tin. What if I ended up being one of them? I'd been Chosen, yeah, but only because I'd been out of my mind on edibles. There were no guarantees when it came to my future. To my ultimate ceiling.

"Maybe you should focus on yourself first," suggested Miko, several nights later, the rain still beating on the walls of our tent. "Determine who you want to be and what you want to accomplish… and then see how your Ideal fits into that plan?"

I couldn't see her in the darkness, but I nodded anyway.

"That's easy enough." I ticked my goals off on the fingers of my left hand. "Help Lace bring down Arrius. Help you prepare for your people's arrival. Help Wilf figure out who broke his family and help Zamira do the same for Zaris."

"Those are goals, yes," said Miko. "But they're all about helping us with what we need. What do *you* want?"

"I…" I shrugged. "I want to protect the people I care about. I want to give them justice."

She didn't say anything and didn't need to. What I'd said was better, in some ways. In others, it was *still* about other people, not me.

"I want to be someone who matters," I finally said. "Someone who makes a difference. When I die, I want people to know that something of value was lost. There were five people at my father's funeral. Five! The priest and the funeral director. Bob Weatherby, my dad's best friend, who stopped coming to our trailer after he went symptomatic. Ancient Mrs. Applewood, who attended funerals like they were red carpet movie premieres. And me. He was gone and our entire town gave zero shits. I don't want that to be me."

I shook my head, even though she couldn't see it. "I know; that's still about other people in a way. But that's how life works, isn't it? Not even Lace is totally alone. We're defined by our friends or our enemies or even just strangers we've impacted along the way. I don't know how to describe who or what I want to be without factoring other people into it."

"I think we are not so different, nest-brother," she said, voice quiet. "I wish to become a light in the darkness, despite how much both that challenge and responsibility scare me. I want to be someone who others can look to for comfort or an example or just an awareness that they are not alone. To me, compassion is the giving of grace to others, not because they are owed it, or even because they truly deserve it, but because I owe it to myself to try."

"That sounds exactly like you," I admitted.

"We each have a path. I have faith that you will find one that speaks to you."

"In the meantime, I'll fight to defend yours."

We reached across the darkness and clasped hands; hers cool and scaled, with claws capable of tearing through flesh and tendons, mine warm and probably a little bit clammy, with dirt under the fingernails from where I'd dug up what had turned out to be a weed.

Squeeze, release, and silence. Soon after, she was asleep.

I stayed awake, despite my tiredness, staring up at the tent I couldn't see. I'd been right; Miko knew exactly who she was and who she wanted to become. I wasn't there yet, I didn't think. What I'd said to Miko hadn't captured my goals in a way that fully resonated. But something in our short conversation had at least touched on a truth that was mine and mine alone.

Now, I just had to find it and figure out how my Ideal fit.

ooo

By the end of the fourth seven-day on the road, we had passed the halfway point of the journey to the Crimson Needle. The other initiates had settled into their roles, with those who weren't scouts all rotating between marching in the vanguard, the rear, or as security for the wagons. The days were growing visibly longer, and that had led to both longer marches on our off days and longer training sessions the other nights.

Thankfully, that work was starting to pay off. I'd gained another point in *Spear*, bringing me to my cap for level nine, and two points in *Knife* after I'd switched to training my backup weapon. *Avoidance* had stalled out, but all that hiking had taken *Athleticism* to its cap as well, and the constant vigilance while scouting had netted me two points in *Focus*, bringing that skill to a lowly thirty-nine. My *Toxin Resistance* skill had even risen to two, thanks to my ongoing mishaps with gathering.

With both *Athleticism* and *Pain Tolerance* capped, I only needed to level one more Major skill—probably *Medium Armor*, given that everything else was lagging—to be ready for level ten. From a skills requirement anyway. Training *did* net me a little bit of experience, but I was at least a few dozen challenging battles or a handful of near-death catastrophes from where I needed to be.

Meanwhile, my attributes remained unchanged. Given that Discernment was supposed to be more than just an awareness of social cues, I'd been hopeful all my scouting work would net me an increase, but the Framework was choosing to be stingy. And my Vitality was high enough that natural gains were proving harder to come by without some form of near superhuman effort. Pushing *Juggling* to six had allowed me to finally juggle four knives without Miko standing by on emergency watch, but Finesse hadn't budged either.

"What plans do you have when we reach Tradewinds?" asked Mireille, as we left the most recent of our daily briefings with Merrick.

We were less than a day out from the town in question, by far the largest settlement in the region.

"I want a bath," I said firmly. We'd come across more than a few streams in our journey so far, many overflowing their banks with snow melt from the southern mountains, but there was a difference between scraping away dirt in ice-cold waters and luxuriating in hot, scented baths.

Back on Earth, baths had just been a way to help keep my dad sanitary. On Eos, they were a luxury I found myself missing every single day.

"Glad to hear it." Mireille made a show of holding her nose. "I didn't want to say anything, but I think Merrick has you going out in the forest for our comfort more than our safety at this point."

"You've got hair in your face, dirt in your hair, and venison stains on your tunic," I shot back.

"Yes, but at least I don't smell like a sty during summer harvest." She smirked. "Besides, I make this look good."

"Just go with it," chimed in Darishal, as we reached their party's tents. "House Marchon makes the rules of this world. The rest of us just live in it."

Unbidden, I heard Shan's ghostly whisper: *Rules. There are always rules.*

I… didn't think that was what the god had meant.

"Fine. Then she's the prettiest little pig farmer I've ever seen. A real credit to hearth and home." I grinned up at the noblewoman. She seemed caught between shock and anger. "Other than a bath, I don't think my team has much planned. Find a Tailor to make any repairs we couldn't do ourselves, maybe? Money is tight, so I think we'll mostly just find somewhere to enjoy someone else's cooking and having a roof over our heads."

"Not a bad plan," said Mireille, having recovered. She raised her voice to include the rest of her unit in the discussion. "According to Merrick, we'll see maybe two villages after Tradewinds, in addition to the ferry town. Make sure you have what you need for a trip into the mountains. We'll be traveling to elevations where winter might still hold sway."

There was a general chorus of agreement from around us.

"Beyond that, do as you will. But travel in pairs. Yes, even you, Kamet," she added, rolling her brown eyes. "More likely than not, you'll be better armed, better trained, and higher level than anyone you encounter, but that won't help you much if you take a rock to the back of the head when you're not paying attention."

"It's a trading town," said Sky, "not the understreets of Elthoris. I think we'll be fine."

Mireille looked to Darishal, and the big man nodded.

"Yeah, I'll watch her."

That sparked a fresh round of arguments between the couple, and I took the opportunity to slip away.

After all, I needed to pass the word on to my own party.

Also, I was pretty sure calling Mireille a pig farmer had been a mistake. A little bit of physical distance while she got over it wouldn't hurt.

Most of the towns we'd passed in the northern half of the duchy had been presaged by farmlands and cultivated fields. The further south we had gone, the more forests had come to dominate the landscape, leaving those settlements to hack their spaces clear of the surrounding trees. In some ways, Tradewinds fit that latter mold, but much of the forest around it had been cleared, and sunlight sparkled off a ribbon of water just to the south. Our road was one of three that intersected just outside the town, but the river—called the Gellis by mapmakers and the Little Gelly by locals—made for a fourth. It was easy to see why the settlement had been built there, and how it was able to survive without the agricultural base that propped up so many other similarly sized towns.

Trade wasn't just a part of the town's name; it was the reason for its existence and continued prosperity.

Traffic had grown as we neared the town, but this early in the season, that still only meant a handful of other wagons on the road with ours, as well as a small stream of pedestrians heading back before nightfall. Our column got a lot of attention, perhaps justifiably so, and word of our arrival reached the town long before we did. A handful of merchants had even set up stalls just inside the gates, in an unconscious reminder of Madea, but we all stayed in formation until we'd reached a series of warehouses, several blocks in.

Merrick had already told Lucius, Mireille, and me how this would go, and we'd passed that word on down to our respective units, so there wasn't much left to say. With a nod, the big Copper followed one of our three wagons—the one containing Wilhemina, Hawthorne, Hawthorne's guard, and the heir's maid, Neesa—deeper into town, while the rest of us pulled the other two wagons into the open warehouse. One squad of soldiers and one unit of initiates would be on watch at all times, but Lucius had drawn the short end of the straw, and that meant the rest of us were free to do what we wished.

"Bring us back some sweets, spearman!" shouted Anthasa as we left. The forest-gifted fiorlan had found someone else to toy with—an enlisted private who didn't seem to know what hit him—but never let a day go by without making a comment, if not a scene. I did my best not to reward those comments with a reaction. At this point, I was pretty sure her whole campaign was more about needling Lucius than anything, and *that* was a cause I could appreciate.

Tradewinds' public bath house was just inside the southern gates, where the Gellis provided a ready source of water. Our party headed there in a single, smelly group, preceded by Miko who was far too polite to tell anyone but me that she'd taken the lead to stay upwind of the rest of us.

The bath house was a far cry from what we'd had at the Tryn, or even the large copper tubs we'd briefly enjoyed at the Night's Sky, but I don't think anyone cared. Especially when the price came in at two bits per person or six bits for a room. Given that there were five of us, the math was undeniable. A hanging curtain in the middle of our rented room gave Miko and Zamira some privacy, not that my nest-sister cared one way or the other, and after we'd piled our soiled clothes to the side where they'd be given a quick cleaning, we were all climbing down into the heated pools.

Each side of the room had three pools in decreasing levels of temperature. We stayed in the hottest only long enough to whisk away most of the dirt of the road, went to the second to clean the rest with handfuls of fine sand and soap, and then finally ended in the third where we could simply soak for the next half-glass.

Given the darkness of the water in the first tub after our visit, it was clear we'd been even dirtier than we'd realized.

"I vote we stay here for the next few moons and hitch a ride home with Hawthorne when he and the rest come back through," said Wilf, voice slurred with relaxation. "If one of you can just make sure to bring me the occasional ale, that would be great."

"Unless you're carrying around a lot more money than me, I think you'd run out in a matter of days," I said. The pools were so small that I was the only one who could fully stretch out his sore legs. I watched my toes bob up and down a few feet in front of me and reminded myself there were *some* benefits to being short.

And that I hadn't *just* called Mireille a pig farmer but the *prettiest little pig farmer.* Given she topped me by half a foot, at least one of those was objectively untrue. As for the other, I was going to plead road-induced madness and hope she accepted the diagnosis.

I did my best to stretch out the knot that had suddenly developed in my shoulders.

After the baths, we split up. Miko had spotted an Herbalist's sign and headed over there with Zamira and Barth, while Wilf and I went toward the center of town instead. Tradewinds was a big enough town to have a branch of the Adventurer's Guild, and we found it sandwiched between two of the town's more popular inns.

The guild hall was even smaller than the one in Madea, lacking a second floor with private rooms. The task board was on the right side of the common room rather than the left, and in place of a desk, the deputy keeper stood behind a live-edge slab of wood that had been mounted on legs and bolted to the floor, but even so, it felt familiar.

I dug out my guildmember badge, waved it to the deputy keeper—an old woman with hard eyes, boatloads of wrinkles, and arms covered in old scar tissue—and went straight for the task board.

"Are you really going to take a mission?" asked Wilf.

Honestly, I'd been surprised he had come with me instead of going with Zamira. The odd couple had been as thick as thieves since the discovery that their respective conspiracies might intertwine, and I hadn't missed the way his eyes tracked her when she left the bath house.

"No," I said, finally remembering to answer. "We won't be here long enough to complete any of them and I'm guessing most will expire long before we return."

"Then what are we doing here?"

"I'd think that would be obvious, given your specialization." I grinned over and up at the young Spy. It wasn't often I came up with a plan he hadn't already considered. "We're gathering information."

It took him a second, but I could see when it clicked. He looked from me to the board and back.

"That's actually brilliant," he decided. "Guild missions are crowd-sourced, so you can learn the lay of the land just by seeing what needs to be done."

"At least in part, yeah." I scanned the board. In addition to the usual gathering requests, there was a report of some sort of large catlike creature preying on livestock, a message delivery request for a village outside the usual trade routes, word of a gloom spinner infestation many days' ride to the southeast, as well as a half-dozen open-ended scouting missions. There was even one mention of an abandoned tower deep in the southern woods that reminded me uncomfortably of the task that had cost Mordecai and Skaal their lives and nearly wiped out all of Madea. "Obviously, there's stuff that never makes it here, either because people are rich or powerful enough to take it on by themselves or because they're too poor to afford the posting fee, but—"

"But information is a pathway to knowledge, and the more sources for that information, the better," finished Wilf.

That was *not* what I'd been planning to say, but I just went with it.

"Yeah, pretty much."

"I need to join the guild," he decided.

"It costs a copper plug."

Being a noble, even one from a fallen house, that didn't faze him. "Is that all?"

"Yeah, but… I'd suggest waiting until our return trip. There are fulfillment requirements needed to gain full membership, or even maintain your membership at all, and I'm not sure we're going to be able to manage those on this trip."

"Fair." He scanned the mostly empty room and then cocked his head. "And apparently, I don't *need* to be a member anyway, yeah? Not as long as I have one to follow through the door."

"The first visit was free," I said, *Mercantilism* kicking in like a bad habit. "The next one will cost you."

"Half a bit a time?"

"They don't even *make* half bits, Wilf."

"Sure, but Zamira says the key to a proper bargaining strategy is to start with an impossible offer and then be slowly persuaded to that amount you were willing to give in the first place."

Somehow, I was more surprised that Wilf didn't have the *Mercantilism* skill than I was that he was taking advice from Zamira.

"One bit a visit," I said.

"Huh. I would've done two."

"Great. Two bits a visit then."

He scowled. "How about one and my continued friendship?"

"How about one, your continued friendship, and a skewer of something appropriately tasty as we find our way back to the warehouse for our shift?"

"Deal." He grinned. "Trade negotiations are exhausting. This is why I let Ellisha—" He coughed and stopped suddenly. "What did they put in the bath water anyway? If I wake up with a hangover tomorrow, there might be mayhem."

"She'll be there when we get back," I told him quietly. "And we'll figure out who's responsible and how to save her. I'm sorry I haven't heard anything of use—"

"You wouldn't. Not out here on the road. Any conspiracy almost definitely involves the parents, not our itinerant noble classmates, and that sort of information's only available back in the capital. But why are you even fixating on things like that?" he asked, smile patently false. "We've got skewers of meat to buy!"

There were things *Performance* couldn't mask. Not at Wilf's level, anyway. The stiffness between his shoulders and the speed with which we left the guild hall said more than any acting ever could.

The damnable thing was that I was pretty sure getting away from Trynfall was doing our party Spy a world of good. Being somewhere where he *couldn't* do much about his sister's fate had given him freedom to simply live his life, worries notwithstanding. And maybe… just maybe… that would be the difference when we *did* return to Trynfall.

Or maybe it would take a few more levels and a bunch more information sources. In the meantime, all I could do was lead when it was called for and help when it wasn't.

ooo

We had second shift, so our party guarded the warehouse with another squad of soldiers as Lucius and his unit got to go out to play. Normally, I'd have kicked up a fuss about being given middle watch, as it was by far the worst of them all, but the siren call of the bath house had possibly overwhelmed my judgment.

Hopefully, the Framework wouldn't see fit to dock a point from my *Leadership* skill.

It was a quiet watch, which wasn't particularly surprising given our location. Tradewinds was far from a hotbed of criminal activity and it was entirely in their interest to keep what thieves *did* exist from striking the warehouses set aside for visiting merchants or people like us. And the soldiers on watch with us had had long enough to get used to our presence, so nobody gave Miko or even Zamira any trouble either. A private with her blonde hair in braids came over to chat with Barth for a bit, to the catcalls of some of her squadmates, but went back again empty-handed.

Tradewinds didn't have its own bell, so it was hard to judge the time, but at some point, Lucius' unit came back to get some sleep, followed soon after by a visibly cleaner Mireille and her unit to take over the watch. I was laying out my bunk next to Miko's, fully prepared to enjoy having a roof and all the space we never go in our small tent, when I noticed Mireille sitting down under a lantern. More importantly, she had something unexpected in her hands.

I went over to join her and asked the dumbest question imaginable. "Is that a book?"

She looked down at the small, loosely bound book in her hands and then back up. "Surprised a pig farmer can read?"

I winced. I could either apologize or move on, and *Tactics* told me the second option was the safer play. Or… maybe it was Discernment. Either way, I wasn't going to argue.

"Not at all," I said. "It's just the first time I've seen you with a book all trip."

"I only just picked it up. I'd offer to let you read it, but…" She showed me the leather cover and flipped it open to reveal the title page.

"The Pauper's Precious Kiss?" I read.

She damn near dropped the book. "You read Ancient Caserian?"

The obvious answer was yes. For once, this *didn't* come as a surprise to me… the signs at the Tryn were in the same language after all.

"Doesn't everyone?" I asked.

"No. No, they don't." Cheeks flaming, she shut the book again. "Is there something else you need?"

Again, either my skill or my attribute told me it was an opportune time to make my retreat, but this time I ignored the warnings.

"Kind of, yeah. Where was this bookstore located? How was their selection? And… what did their prices look like?" When she frowned, I felt compelled to add: "I want to get something specific for Miko. And I have all of a plug to my name."

"You should have brought more spending coin with you."

I waited for her to get that *all of a plug to my name* meant I didn't *have* any more coin to bring, but apparently, that concept was too foreign for her to grasp.

"Next time I will," I said instead.

"As for the store, it is already closed for the night. But it's not too far from here if you want to try to go there after sunrise." She gave me directions that felt far more detailed than they needed to be, and paused. "Most of what they have will be too expensive for you, I'm afraid, but I could perhaps see fit to loaning another copper plug to the right person."

"I'm sensing there's a condition attached?"

"Two, in fact."

Mercantilism told me asking would give her too much power, so I just waited instead.

"First, that person would have to carry my pack in addition to their own for the next three days."

"Two," I said, "and only on days where I'm not out scouting."

She thought it over. "Acceptable, I suppose."

"What's the second condition? Because if it's some sort of draconian compounding interest scheme, I'm out."

Mireille made a face. "I'm a noblewoman, not a banker. In fact, there are many things I am not, including *little* or a *pig farmer.*"

I was starting to think her *Tactics* skill was higher than mine, but I was going to stick with my plan of avoidance.

"Right. So, what is the second condition?"

"You tell me how exactly you managed to break free of Lucius' slowing ability in the duel. If there's a trick to it, I want to know."

"It's no trick," I told her. "It's a technique."

If I thought the general proscription against digging into someone's Framework-given build would stop the woman I'd allied myself with, I was very much mistaken.

"A technique that you learned in between our training sessions and the duel itself? How?"

"No, it's something I took at level seven. An upgrade to one of my existing techniques, technically. To be honest, I didn't realize quite what it did until that duel."

With her seated and me standing, it was one of the few times she'd ever be shorter than I was. She leveraged it to surprising effect, looking up through lashes I didn't remember being anywhere near that long.

"And will you tell me the name of this technique? I swear on my family name not to reveal it."

It probably should have been a bigger dilemma for me. Knowing a person's build was in many ways key to making a plan to defeat them. But the truth was: Mireille already knew my level. She'd seen me train *and* fight. Given those facts, she could probably figure out which technique I was talking about, especially since I'd used it to not only shake off Lucius' ability but to travel to just behind him.

Still, I wasn't giving something away for nothing.

"Loan me the plug," I said instead, "and I'll check out the store tomorrow. If they have what I want and I can afford it, I'll tell you then. If not, I'll return the plug. Deal?"

She fished a fat copper plug from her purse and handed it over. "You bargain like a merchant."

I was pretty sure that wasn't a compliment, but the Framework clearly agreed with her, because my abbreviated meditation in the warehouse that night netted me a point in *Mercantilism*, bringing one of my very favorite skills all the way to seven.

And the next morning, I returned from my brief outing with two things: a well-worn copy of *Meditations on Mortality* for Miko and a technique name for Mireille.

"*Liberating Lunge*," I told her. I'd thought the ability just loosened the rules on where and how I could lunge. Instead, it seemed to literally liberate me from external effects that hampered my mobility.

"Oh," she said in reply. "Interesting, I guess."

I kept the change.

ooo

Six days later, Tradewinds was just a vague memory of warm bedrolls, hot baths, and fresh-cooked food that didn't taste like it had been rubbed in the dirt and then encased in salt. It had been raining since the afternoon of our departure, and I think we were all feeling it. There was nothing quite like grey clouds, grey rain, and grey moods to suck the color out of life.

The road we were following south was narrower than the one that had taken us to Tradewinds. It was also terribly maintained, more mud than stone in too many locations. Still, even if we had to work to get the wagons past certain bends, it gave us a simple enough route to follow. Without it, I could almost imagine wandering forever in the cold and wet, my two points in *Orienteering* notwithstanding.

Instead, we arrived at the Polemis River, an expanse of water so wide I couldn't imagine swimming it even without the wagons. The only way to cross for leagues in either direction was a ferry, and it was to that ferry, and the village that had formed around it, that the road we'd been following led.

Hobbs' Crossing wasn't much of a place, even by village standards. It was larger than Harborton had been, and quite a bit less smelly, but gave off an aura of age and disrepair, from the leaning exterior wall that ringed the settlement to the roughly thatched homes lurking within. There were no merchant stalls set out for our arrival and no warehouses we'd have trusted to keep the vermin from getting to our supplies, so Merrick asked the sole guard at the gates for directions and then led us straight through, down to the water's edge, a pier as large as any two buildings in the village, and the ferry that floated at its far end.

My ex-girlfriend, Kate, had left Midton to go to New York City for college, and one of the first things she'd sent back were pictures of the ferry ride she'd taken on arrival. The Statue of Liberty, the city skyline, and a double-decker ship with shade, seating, guardrails, and a view from every angle.

This was *not* like that kind of ferry. In fact, outside of its size, it felt more like a raft, massive tree trunks lashed together to form a floating platform. At various spots, iron rings had been installed so that cargo could be lashed down to the ferry, but there was otherwise nothing between its potential passengers and the elements; the sky above and the swift-flowing waters below.

I hadn't had great experiences with rivers since coming to Eos. First, I'd nearly drowned swimming in one in the dark outside Harborton as Miko and I fled from Nikkaali the titan snake. Then, I'd been forced to *Lunge* across one of that same river's far narrower tributaries, up in the mountains, even as the Thunderbird hunted our party.

Baths aside, water was not my friend. And the things in this world's water were even worse. Beasts of Eos class had taught me way too much on the subject, handing out nightmarish creatures like they were party favors. Cutters, freshwater eels, and way too many species of carnivorous fish. The Polemis was even large enough that there might be the occasional leviathan. Or worse, murkdwellers, which would have passed for enormous Earthborn crocodiles if they didn't have two tails and dozens of legs.

I wasn't looking forward to the crossing in the slightest.

I also didn't have any choice.

We stopped at the pier so Merrick could arrange passage with the ferry master. When he returned, it was to tell us that the ferry could transport only a single wagon at a time and that, as a result, the crossing would take all morning. Merrick and Hawthorne were accompanied by a solid half of the soldiers—and all of the Tins—on the first crossing. It was a dead giveaway that Wilhemina was in that wagon, not that anyone but us was out in the foul weather to see.

It took roughly a glass for the ferry to make it to the far side, and twice that for the wagon and passengers to unload and for it to travel back to our pier. The initiates were all part of the second crossing, with the remainder of the guards left to bring the third wagon. I was glad to be next; two and a half more glasses of anticipation might just kill me before the Polemis could.

Even so, I found Zamira on the western side of the ferry as we started to drift out into the water. "You've got plenty of energy for casting *Control Water*, right?" I asked her.

Without a hood for her cloak, the Zarisian's white hair was matted to her head, and her stone eyes were wet from the rain. They glistened as she turned to look at me.

"If you're asking whether I can speed us through the crossing, I can't," she said. "Maybe at Tin or if I get an upgrade to the spell. Sorry. We have nothing but wet misery and tedium ahead of us."

"Yeah. Tedium."

Something in my tone must have tipped her off. She cocked her head and leaned in. "Brian, are you… afraid of the water?"

"Not afraid. Just cautious." The ferry continued to shift back and forth beneath us, wood groaning like it was alive and in pain.

"Huh."

"Huh?"

"I was starting to think you weren't afraid of anything."

That was *so* far off base that I had to laugh, and just like that, some of the tension I was carrying drained away.

"We'll be fine," she continued, patting me on the arm like she was Miko. "If a ferry master can't promise safety, merchants will find someone who will. I'm sure they've done this crossing thousands of times."

By that point, we were a third of the way across, and nothing bad had happened. I gave it a few more minutes, just to be sure, and finally exhaled. She was right; as rundown as Hobbs' Crossing was, it wouldn't exist at all anymore if its ferry wasn't considered trustworthy.

Think of it like a moving sidewalk, I told myself. *You always wanted to try one of those and never got the chance.*

Reassured, I leaned on my spear and tried to move *with* the ferry rather than against it, my gaze turning from the steel-grey clouds above us to the waters below. With the sun hidden, the river was almost opaque, but I could make out the occasional flicker of movement below us, fish swimming east with the current to where the Polemis would eventually either feed into a body of water or curve northward toward the ocean.

Mireille and Kamet had wandered over to join us when something bumped the ferry. That impact wasn't enough to do more than rock it, but even that much was saying something, given the ferry's size. I looked to the east and saw the distinctive double horn of a leviathan, breaching the surface before it dove back down.

"That's something you don't see—" began Zamira, only to be interrupted by a second, even sharper hit.

One leviathan was a surprise. Two? That was a concern. Especially given that the creatures were known to be solitary.

I saw the second leviathan surface, just past our ferry, almost as if it was in pursuit of the first, and then spun back to the west. I didn't see any more leviathans coming our way, but the dark shapes swimming just below the surface toward us were each at least the size of our wagon.

"Is it a migration?" asked Mireille, raising her voice to speak over the suddenly panicked whinnies of our wagon's horses.

"No." Murkdwellers and leviathans swimming together, when they were natural-born enemies? Even the smaller fish I'd noticed earlier were now streaming past us with a fresh sense of urgency. I'd only seen something like this once before, when the creatures of Nikkaali's forest, predator and prey, had left the woods in tandem, ignoring each other as they sprinted for safety. "They're fleeing something."

Whatever Mireille was going to say was lost beneath a noise that drowned out the world, a dull wordless roar greater than any beast I'd read about could make. The sound alone shook the ferry and threw half of us to our knees.

And that was when we saw it.

Not a named monster, like Nikkaali or the Thunderbird. Not even an ascended beast like the stags I'd watched fight for mating rights on the Thunderbird's mountain. In fact, this wasn't a creature at all.

It was a wall. A wall of water. And it was rushing toward us.

"Someone roused the river!" shouted Zamira, and that I could even hear it told me she was speaking in her secret language, in words somehow shaped in stone rather than air. "But how?"

I could have replied in that same language, but I had no words to say and no time to say them. Even as *Danger Sense* finally stirred to warn me of a threat we could all see coming, the moving wall of water was upon us. It blotted out the sky, it shattered the platform on which we stood, and it threw us *and* the wagon into the air like toy soldiers.

Somewhere in the chaos, I activated *Beast Hide*, grabbed hold of the nearest body with my free hand, and triggered *Liberating Lunge.* Then, something heavy struck me and everything went dark.

40

I woke to pain. Head, arms, legs, back chest… even my pelvis hurt, which was weird for the few seconds it took me to remember what had happened. A ferry crossing followed by a tidal wave. In a river.

The good news about hurting badly enough that even *Pain Tolerance* didn't block it out was that it meant I was alive. And apparently no longer in the water either, given the solid surface beneath me. Unfortunately, I couldn't see a thing. I wasn't even sure if my eyes were open or shut. At best, there was a vague impression of light in front of or above me, which did nothing for my splitting headache.

On autopilot, I tried to go through my forms, my brain catching up to my body a fraction of a second too late. If I hurt this much while lying still, actively moving would be— Well, I wasn't sure what it would be, because I wasn't able to move.

Panic surged as my worst nightmare came to life.

I wouldn't be a prisoner in my own body.

I *couldn't* be.

And… I eventually realized… I *wasn't*. A few of my fingers and my toes were wiggling, but even that small movement was constrained. And not by the disease I carried with me, but by some form of binding that had strapped my legs together, my arms to my chest, and seemed to have covered my head as well.

For anyone else, *that* would have been the moment they freaked out. For me, it settled me down instead and let my brain start to function again. I didn't know what was going on, whether I'd been captured and tied up or was just so thoroughly wrapped in riverweed that it felt that way, but both of those were external conditions, and I had a technique that would help free me from them.

Only… I'd never used *Lunge* blindly before. The closest I'd come had been when fleeing Nikkaali, and even then, I'd at least been able to focus my eyes on *something*. The upgrade I'd taken meant I didn't need an entirely clear path to my destination, but I still needed to be able to choose that destination.

Didn't I?

Whatever covered my head muffled the sounds around me, but I couldn't hear anything reminiscent of the river. Which meant I had likely been moved. Now, *maybe* a good Samaritan had come across me, taken me home, swaddled me in bandages, and was doing their best to nurse me back to health, but I kind of doubted it. My time on Eos told me it was far more likely I'd been spirited away to be eaten or infected or in preparation for some new and thoroughly gross defilement.

I needed to escape. The lack of eyesight… hell, even the fact that I was flat on my back rather than upright couldn't be allowed to stop me. Especially if Miko needed me.

Assuming she even survived, whispered the voice in my head. *And what are the chances of that? She wasn't anywhere near you when that wave hit. Anything could have happened.*

Hells, I'd been holding *onto* Zamira… or Mireille… when I triggered *Lunge* in mid-flight, and as far as I could tell, neither of them were anywhere near me.

With a thought, I did one of the few things that *didn't* require movement. I summoned my quest list with a thought:

Quests:
- Escort the Voice of the Dawn and Wilhemina Annerose Lakesia Willerton to the Crimson Needle.
- Deliver justice for a fallen brother.

Thank god. Or gods. Or maybe even just Miko's goddess. If I still had a quest to escort Miko and Wilhemina to Mordecai's old school, it meant both were still alive.

Find Miko. Find the others. Get back to Merrick and the rest of the group.

But first, I needed to get free.

I focused on the light I couldn't quite see and triggered *Lunge.*

When I'd used the ability against Lucius, it had felt like getting unstuck, like I'd pulled myself away from the heaviness his own technique had surrounded me with. This time felt different. The wrapping around me physically strained, stretched, then tore, and suddenly light was everywhere, painful for all that it was indirect. I cracked open dry eyes to see a strange tapestry above me—branches and leaves and something else, spilling between.

Then *Lunge* finished and gravity took over.

I fell back down onto the remnants of whatever I'd torn free of and only *Pain Tolerance* kept me from screaming. I didn't think anything was broken—testament to *Beast Hide's* usefulness against anything that wasn't a magic sword enchanted to *cut*—but even my bruises had bruises. And my back, already in agony from lying on my pack, was done no favors when it landed again on that same pack. By far the greatest source of pain was my right leg, where my pants had been shredded and the exposed flesh was swollen and virulently colored.

I'd had enough close encounters with poison over the past half-cycle that I was pretty sure that's what I was dealing with. At least until I finally had a breath to look at something other than myself. The unknown element of the treescape I'd noticed above me slowly resolved into gossamer threads, threads that drifted down to the forest floor in some locations and stretched taut between locations in others. The distant daylight became increasingly diffuse as it passed through layer upon layer of what could only be webbing. And looking down, I could see the shredded remnants of the web sack *Liberating Lunge* had just torn me out of.

Not poison then.

Venom.

The mission board back in Tradewinds had mentioned a gloom spinner infestation. It looked like I had found it.

Gloom spinners were yet another of Eos' nightmarish creatures; spiders that, at their smallest, were the size of my forearm. Only the ascended variety grew as big as humans, but given their venom, the speed at which they reproduced, and their aggression as they hunted for live flesh to feed their offspring, they didn't need to either.

If emperor ants were an invasive threat, gloom spinners were a full-on ecological crisis.

There were other web sacks around the clearing, the smaller ones dangling from web-strewn branches. The floor of the forest held two large enough to hold a person or person-sized animal. Neither one was moving, which meant either the occupants had died before they could be consumed or had been more thoroughly dosed with the gloom spinners' venom than me. I didn't see any egg clusters, but we'd learned in class that they'd be up in the trees somewhere.

All the better to spill out and drop onto their first meals after hatching.

There was no sign of my spear, the weapon once wielded by Riok Diocil which Merrick had referred to as a nascent artifact. I knew I'd been clutching it when everything went dark, but it was anyone's guess if I'd lost it in the river or afterwards, when the gloom spinners found my unconscious body and took it home for dinner.

At least it's not raining anymore, I told myself. *Now* that *would be bad.*

The truth was, I didn't know what to do about my missing spear. Not just because I didn't want to be the first person in history to misplace an artifact but because I *needed* that spear if I was going to survive. The lack of gloom spinners was a temporary thing, and I had no faith in my ability to fight my way through the woods with only a knife.

Or *two* knives, even. I could feel the reassuring weight of my backup weapon against my right ankle. Add it to the nicer blade in the sheath on my hip and I was halfway to a full set for juggling, yet no more confident in my chances against an entire colony.

A knife helped in other ways though.

Using everything I had learned from Lace, I crept over to the first of the human-sized web sacks. The Marauder would have rolled her eyes if she'd seen—or more likely *heard*—me. Wet boots, clothes, and a waterlogged pack undid both my caution *and* a *Stealth* skill capped at ten.

Still, nothing attacked me, which was as good as I could hope for. I crouched back down and, using the knife from my boot, started to saw through the webbing. It was significantly tougher than I'd expected, giving me a fresh appreciation for the effects of *Liberating Lunge,* but I made my way through multiple layers and slowly peeled it back to look inside.

Since I'd arrived on Eos, I'd seen more death than any one person ever should. One day, I thought I might find myself unmoved by that death, but I couldn't decide if I was looking forward to that day or worried about what it would mean for me.

The blank eyes of Kamet, Mireille's Infiltrator teammate, stared up at me from a pale and bloodless face. A good portion of his skull was simply missing, fragments of bone caved inward to show where something heavy had struck.

Gloom spinners preferred their meals alive, but they weren't above scavenging if the meat was fresh enough. I was pretty sure Kamet had died somewhere upriver and washed up on shore with me. Hells, maybe *he'd* been the one I grabbed back on the ferry? If so, what had happened to—

With effort, I took hold of my runaway thoughts. This wasn't the time. Not for hysteria and not for mourning a man I'd only recently come to know either. The smart thing to do would be to cut him out of the sack and take whatever he had on him that might help me survive these woods.

I just… couldn't. Not yet anyway. So, instead I turned to the second, similarly motionless web sack. Either I'd gotten better at cutting through the webs or I was unconsciously using a lot more force, because it was less than a minute before I'd cut free a space.

Brown hair meant it wasn't Zamira, but it was the length, a few inches shy of reaching the shoulders after a full moon without a barber, that told me I'd found Mireille. She was facing away, but rather than turn her over and hack away at even more webbing, I reached into the hole with my free hand to lay two fingers against her neck.

Her skin was clammy, the pulse as thin as one of the web strands above us, but she was alive.

It took more time than I could afford to cut her out of the web, and the whole time I waited for *Danger Sense* to give one of its too-late alerts that I had company. Instead, the clearing remained quiet and still. I peeled back the shredded webbing and dragged her out of its remnants.

While Mireille was tall and fit, she wasn't a bruiser like Ames; my fourteen Strength was more than up to the challenge of moving her those few feet.

She didn't even stir. Combined with her strange clamminess, that told me she'd gotten a higher dose of the spiders' venom than I had… or that my few points in *Toxin Resistance* had had an outsized impact.

Her continued unconsciousness presented a problem. While I *thought* I was strong enough to carry the noblewoman—she was shorter than Miko, after all, if not quite as slender—doing so would leave me open to attack from the spiders that we'd almost definitely encounter on our way out. And though she *did* still have her axes with her, hanging from leather loops on her pack, they wouldn't do me any good if my arms were too full to wield them. Instead, I needed to find a way to wake her, which meant getting at least some of the toxins out of her system.

I took off her pack and set it aside so the axes were in easy reach and then examined her unconscious form. She looked smaller like this and might even have looked innocent if she hadn't been so clearly afflicted. Any worries I'd had about locating the source of her bite were put to rest as soon as I saw her left arm; it was swollen like a balloon and a virulent shade of red even in the dim half-light. The bite marks themselves were about an inch-and-a-half apart, suggesting a mid-sized gloom spinner, rather than a true behemoth.

Whether that was a good thing or bad was well beyond what I'd learned in Beasts of Eos. All I knew for sure was that the venom had to go.

I dug through my pack and found nothing of use. Not everything in it was drenched, which was the only bit of good news I'd had so far, but any herbs that might have helped were in Miko's pack, and she was… well, hopefully, she was somewhere safe. Although I'd have preferred if she had been with us instead. *Touch of the Dawn* would have had Mireille awake in no time, and *Light Healing* would have meant I could maybe breathe without it hurting.

After watching Miko review my finds, I *thought* I might be able to recognize plants that would help, but searching for them would entail leaving Mireille unprotected. Worse, these woods were basically an entirely new biome. Who knew if what I needed even grew here, where daylight was merely hinted at under the canopy of leaves and webs?

I turned to the still-wrapped bundle that was Kamet's corpse instead. He'd been serving as a scout, just like me, and he hadn't had an apprentice Herbalist to offload his findings to.

Cutting a dead man out of their web coffin wasn't high on my list of fun things to do, but I did it anyway, at least sufficiently that I could get to the man's pack. I couldn't lift his arms, so I cut the straps instead, sliding the pack out from under him and tearing away the few strands of webbing that remained.

Like mine and Mireille's, Kamet's pack was still somewhat wet. I was going to do my very best to pretend all that wetness was from water. I dug through it and found enough clothes to confirm Kamet *had* been a noble, a set of tools I recognized as lock picks, a shaving kit and small hand mirror, a folded piece of aged parchment whose contents had been rendered illegible by the river, and at the very bottom, several bundles of herbs, wrapped in waterproofed leather.

That leather hadn't helped much when both person and pack had clearly been submerged in water. Still, it at least kept the various herbs separate. I spread them out on the forest floor before me. There was a stack of leafy fronds I'd never thought to pick, a few no-longer-dried roots, several grey and black leaves that I was almost positive were poisonous, and what looked to be wildflower petals.

What little time I'd spent with Kamet told me it was unlikely he'd collected those last items out of an appreciation of nature's beauty, but I had no idea what they were used for. On the other hand—

Danger Sense flared and I rolled to the side, dodging a dog-sized spider that had come out of nowhere. For all my carefulness at setting Mireille's pack aside so her axes were accessible, I'd left them—and her—across the clearing while I dealt with Kamet. Because just losing my spear in one day apparently wasn't enough.

Thankfully, my dagger was at hand.

I came out of the roll to find the spider scurrying back up its line, already out of reach of anyone shorter than Miko.

Unless they had a movement ability.

It felt like it had been ages since I used *Lunge* for its actual purpose, and there was a real sense of satisfaction as I blurred through the air to drive my knife into the creature's abdomen. That blow didn't kill the spider, but the combination of the impact and my weight tore it free from its line. As gravity spun us both to the ground, I made sure I landed on top, sharp blade cutting away.

My hauberk deflected several glancing hits, but the outcome was never in doubt. Individually, a gloom spinner of that size just wasn't much of a challenge for a reasonably leveled Aspirant. It was the combination of their venom and tendency to come in swarms that caused problems.

I waited for the spider to stop twitching, stabbed it again, just to be sure, and then scraped the blood and guts off with one of Kamet's wet socks. Some species of creatures on Eos released a scent when dying that attracted others of their kind. I didn't know if gloom spinners were one of them, but as one of the few types of spiders that lived in a colony, it seemed likely.

In other words, time had just run out.

Most of Kamet's herbs went into my pack, but I picked up one of the thick roots. I'd seen Miko boil them in water to make a paste that helped with nausea. Maybe they'd work for venom too?

Without a pot, a fire, or the time to boil anything, I'd have to try administering the root raw instead. I ground it back and forth between my thumb and forefinger, making a powder that wasn't sanitary by any century's measure, and then opened Mireille's mouth to pour the powder under her swollen tongue. What little was left got applied to the bite directly. While the venom had undoubtedly already spread through her body, I hoped attacking it from two directions would be more effective.

I also hoped I hadn't just killed House Marchon's heir.

Nothing happened right away, but herbalism wasn't magic. It took time. So, I finished getting my pack together, adding Kamet's few remaining possessions to what I'd brought on the road. Whatever weapons the Infiltrator had carried were gone, but after a moment of squeamishness, I retrieved a coin purse from his body and added it to the bag.

I'll give it to Mireille. He has… had family, and I'm sure they could use it.

Venom aside, the Marchon noblewoman seemed to be in considerably better shape than me. Whereas I was a walking contusion, she only had a few bruises, including finger-shaped ones where I'd grabbed her arm. I could only assume she'd stayed conscious long enough to avoid whatever had hit me and killed Kamet. In fact, it was entirely possible *she* had been the one to drag us both to shore.

Where we'd then been captured by spiders.

If she ever woke up, I'd have to thank her.

If she didn't, I'd have to survive to find Miko and the others on my own. And with only my knives and two axes I had no skill in wielding, that wouldn't be easy.

Another minute passed and I knew I couldn't wait any longer. If the gloom spinner's death *had* been sensed, more were on the way. I'd just have to carry Mireille and hope for the best. If it came to that, I could always drop her every time I got attacked.

She stirred before I could do more than crouch beside her, opening eyes that were a particularly unpleasant shade of bloodshot. Hands reached for her axes, finding nothing, before those eyes had fully focused on my face.

"Brian?"

"Hey."

"What are—"

"I'm sorry," I interrupted, "but we don't have time. There's an entire colony of gloom spinners in these woods and we have to get out while we can. Can you stand?"

She still seemed confused, unsurprisingly, but her jaw firmed. "Yes. I think. My pack?"

"Behind you. I'll help you get it on if you think you can carry it." I gave her an arm, like we were at the White Sails feast rather than lost in a spider-infested forest and helped raise her to her feet. She swayed, blinked rapidly, and looked like she was about to lose her lunch, but held her ground.

"Pack," she said.

I got the straps around her shoulders, and she immediately slipped both axes free of their loops, seeming to draw strength from having the weapons in her hands. Color was returning to her cheeks and she was already more stable than a moment before.

I'd have to tell Miko about how well the raw roots worked when we found her.

Mentally, Mireille was having a harder time catching up, and things got worse when she saw Kamet's body. For just a moment, grief transformed her features, like a statue cracking in half to reveal something the sculptor had buried beneath.

"I thought—I hoped—that I had dreamed his death."

"You already knew?"

"I pulled both of you to shore. His head was gushing blood and you were a dead weight. I never saw what hit me." She shook her head, winced, and looked to me. "Gloom spinners, you said?"

I pointed at the shriveled corpse and nodded.

She blanched again. "You're right then. We should leave."

"I'd suggest taking Kamet's body with us, but—"

"Do you have his possessions?"

"Yes."

"That will have to do. He was eminently practical about such things. Most things, really. Dead is dead. Best that we not join him."

There wasn't much to say to that. It was already a minor miracle that only one gloom spinner had come upon us. "Let's go then. Do you have—"

"Wait!" she hissed, holding up one axe like it was a signaling flag. "Did you hear that?"

I strained to listen. There was a faint rustle from the left, not up in the trees but down near the ground. For some reason, *Danger Sense* wasn't triggering at all.

I waved in that direction and we both moved, spreading out to flank whatever it was. Mireille was… not very quiet, and by the time we'd arrived at the copse of bushes, the rustling had stopped. The noblewoman went in first, axes at the ready. I came from the other side, knife in one hand, my other arm held horizontally in front of me like a makeshift shield. We met in the middle where we traded confused glances.

There was no gloom spinner waiting. No other creature preparing to pounce. There was just the long shaft of a corroded looking spear that ended in a wickedly sharp leaf-shaped blade.

"You dropped that when I pulled you to shore," said Mireille. "Did you go back and get it *before* you freed me?" Her voice remained hushed, but a little bit of heat had leaked into it.

"No." I sheathed my knife and scooped up the spear. It was covered in dirt, but perhaps unsurprisingly, remained undamaged. "I don't know how it got here."

"Maybe one of the spiders thought to…" She shook her head. "Whatever. You have something more than a dagger now and that's what matters. Let's go."

She headed out without waiting for me. When I followed, moments later, I had a frown on my face. *Tracking* had shown me something she must have missed: a shallow furrow in the dirt, leading from where we'd found the spear back into the woods. It was the kind of track a snake might make when traveling except that it was straight as an arrow.

I shook the oversized spear in my hands, dislodging a few more pieces of dirt. Had the weapon… come to me under its own power? And why did that seem so creepy? Earth mythology had its litany of magical items that did the same thing, but for some reason, this filled me with a sense of foreboding that Thor's hammer never had.

Skaal's artifact, Tempest, had never moved on its own.

Had it?

Mireille marched through the woods like a bull in a china shop. Or… a bull in a forest, maybe. I sped up, passed her by, and cut her off, feeling like Lace must have when she first led *me* through the woods south of Harborton.

"We need to be quiet if we don't want to pull the whole forest down on our heads," I explained. "Gloom spinners track by heat and vibrations, but there are plenty of other things out here that hunt by sound instead."

"How do you know that?"

"I have *Animal Behaviorism* maxed."

"Why?" She looked at me like I was insane.

"I'm an adventurer who moonlights as a scout, remember? Anyway, try to copy what I'm doing," I told her. "Shorter steps, and roll your foot from the outside in. Maybe you can pick up the *Stealth* skill while we're out here."

"Which of course *you* have. Even though you're not a Rogue."

"Adventurers don't get to choose their party members from the ranks of the elite families," I reminded her. "We pick up whatever skills we can wherever we can because you never know when it'll be useful."

She frowned, like I'd said something unkind, but nodded.

It took her a while to catch on to how to walk, and her noise level never dropped much below *person out for a Sunday hike* levels, but there was only so much we could do until she had the skill. With my spear in hand and the Warrior at my back, I at least felt more comfortable about our chances of winning a fight or two. And there were some predators who would avoid a group of two entirely whereas a single target might be considered prey.

We'd traveled for a few minutes, gloom spinners still suspiciously absent despite the webs above and around us, when I slowed to a stop again.

"Where are we going?" I asked.

"You're the one leading."

"Yes, in the direction you originally chose."

"Right." She sucked in a breath, looking far from steady. "I figured we should go west. Back to the caravan."

I dropped my head and did my very best not to sigh.

"We've been headed east."

"Well, *I* didn't know that! There's no sun down here!"

That was a fair point. And she clearly didn't have the *Orienteering* skill either. But even so…

I swallowed my frustration-laden retort. Mireille was as tough as nails, but clearly out of her element. And still suffering from both the venom and the antidote I'd administered. Not to mention that she'd just lost a party member.

She didn't need me making things worse.

"Should we go back?" she asked.

"No. That was clearly some sort of larder, if a small one. Going back there just increases the chances of an encounter. We need to find the other members of our party."

"Do you think any of them survived?"

"Miko did. I know that much."

"Like you knew when she was kidnapped."

"Yeah."

The noblewoman shook her head and muttered something under her breath. "What do we do then? You're the expert in this kind of environment."

If Anthasa had been with us, I was pretty sure the forest-gifted fiorlan would have laughed to hear me described as such. Since it was just the two of us instead, I reluctantly accepted the mantle.

"We should head for the river. It's a landmark any of the other initiates would know to look for. And we can follow it west to Hobbs' Crossing."

She winced. "The wave dissipated not long after it destroyed our ferry, but I remember a whole series of waterfalls. That's where Kamet… Well. I didn't get much of a look because I was trying to stay alive, but I'm not sure we'll be able to climb back up."

That explained some of my bruises. Armor and even *Beast Hide* could only do so much. Still, I shrugged. "We won't know until we get there."

"We'll be exposed on the banks."

If there was a *Follower* skill, Mireille clearly hadn't earned it yet. "Yes," I agreed, trying to hold on to my patience. "But at least we'll be able to see our enemies coming. Right now, gloom spinners could be gathering above us as we speak."

They weren't, of course, because *Danger Sense* wasn't sounding the alarm. But she didn't know that.

Then again, it *was* a notoriously flaky skill.

I gave the trees above us a second, more wary glance, and that, more than anything seemed to convince the noblewoman. I turned north and she fell in behind me.

The webbing in the trees had a way of muffling sound, creating a world that seemed hushed save for the sharp crack of the occasional branch under Mireille's boots. Still, the fact that we couldn't hear the river at all told me we'd been transported a good ways, and the next ten-plus minutes of hiking bore that out.

We came across a few individual gloom spinners along the way, but they were all small, like the one I'd killed. As we dispatched each of them with ease, Mireille regained just a little bit of her confidence, whereas I was only growing more concerned.

Gloom spinners were a social species of monster spider. I knew that from class. To have encountered so few meant most of the colony was elsewhere. And that was bad news for anyone or anything out in the forest.

Like Miko and the other initiates.

I checked my quest log a few more times along the way, just to be sure, but the text hadn't changed by the time we finally heard the sound of rushing water. A few minutes later, we broke away from the trees and found ourselves on the bank of the river that had tried to kill us. The Polemis had narrowed substantially, but the current here was fast. It was good Mireille had hauled us out on the correct shore because I doubted I'd have been able to swim across. Not with how much everything hurt. And especially not with the rocks that poked up like shark fins just above the water line, rocks that would carve a person up even with *Beast Hide* active.

One of the logs that had made up the ferry's base was now lodged between two of those rocks. What was left of it anyway. Looking at what had been done to a tree trunk the size of one of Darishal's legs made our survival that much more astonishing.

I gave Mireille another once-over.

"What?" she asked.

"How the hell did you make it down the river conscious, let alone mostly unharmed?"

"Part of it was my *Shield* technique," she said, "but most of it was this." She reached beneath her own hauberk to pull out a necklace. At its end was a pendant in the shape of a flower, with seven petals that had once been formed by individual gems. Each of those gems was cracked and colorless. "This crafting cost us more than our last house remodel. Refreshing its enchantments won't cost quite that much and I think my life is worth it, regardless. Still, Gerhardt won't be getting that new cutter he's been badgering our father for. Not this year anyway."

"Cutter?"

"The boat, not the creature, although they're equally dangerous to hear some people talk." She sighed and tucked the necklace away again. "Anyway, we've arrived. Now what?"

I'd been scanning the river to find an answer to that question. It was already starting to get dark, and I didn't want to spend the night there. Cutters stayed in the water, but murkdwellers were another story entirely, and we'd just look like lunchboxes with legs to them. I'd originally suggested the river to get away from the gloom spinners, but now I was starting to question the wisdom of that plan. Maybe we should—

Downriver from us, a fiery light split the growing dusk in a burst of red and orange before it swiftly faded.

"What was that?" asked Mireille.

I smiled for the first time since waking up as a human-sized happy meal. "*That* was Miko."

41

We moved quickly along the shoreline, not sure what we would find. *Flare* didn't do any damage, so either Miko had cast it to blind or distract attackers, or she was trying to signal anyone who might be in the area. Either way, we needed to be there.

It wasn't quite as easy as it should have been, of course. As fast as the river flowed at this point, it still wasn't entirely straight. The shoreline wove in and out, adding to the distance we had to travel, and for some of that distance the forest grew right to the water's edge. There were even places where cables of webbing stretched between trees *across* the river, forty feet of open space apparently no true barrier to a truly dedicated gloom spinner.

If the spiders were already expanding to the northern banks, Hobbs' Crossing was under serious threat. Not that we could do anything about it, but… if we survived all of this, we'd have to spread the word.

Travel was much more dangerous in the growing darkness. As the gloom spinners took full advantage of the cover of night, *Danger Sense* became our only warning system. My skill would flare just before the creatures attacked, giving only a split second to react and defend ourselves. It was almost a callback to when Miko and I first arrived on this continent, although then, it had been catosaurs preying on us from above.

And at least this time I had shoes.

Mireille wasn't much help with spotting the gloom spinners before they attacked, but she *was* a hell of a fighter. Not as flashy as Lucius and considerably less mobile than me, but she put her twin axes to deadly use, and her *Shield* technique was both effective and considerably less disturbing than *Beast Hide*. Meanwhile, I leaned into the reach advantage my spear gave me, skewering eight-legged horrors before they could even reach the ground.

We killed almost a dozen spiders as we went and didn't take a single hit in return. Normally, that would have felt like progress, but I knew a colony could have upwards of a thousand spiders. Eleven was basically a rounding error, especially with new hatchlings being born all the time.

It explained why the forest was otherwise so quiet and why the gloom spinners were already trying to move across the river. What it *didn't* explain was where they all were. The creatures weren't precisely territorial, in that their territory was always shifting and expanding, but they were so aggressive that anything that they came across was hunted down and claimed as food. Yet we'd seen, by my count, maybe fifteen of them since waking up.

On the one hand, that was almost definitely why we were still alive. On the other, it felt like there was an enormous shoe just waiting to drop… and that shoe was made up entirely of man-eating spiders.

We didn't see another *Flare* as we traveled, although I wasn't sure if that was because Miko didn't cast one or if our view was just obstructed as we wove in and out. It was possible she was just out of energy too; if I knew my nest-sister, she would have spent most of hers healing anyone she'd ended up with.

I remained a mass of bruises, but moving helped, and *Pain Tolerance* did too. And while I was tired and aching, the energy I used for my techniques remained about half full. I'd used *Lunge* a few times so far that day, *Beast Hide* exactly once, and *Deceptive Strike* not at all, content with relying on the combat skills my class gave me instead.

That was the benefit of being a Warrior and while I *still* wasn't sure it beat being able to throw fire with my bare hands or summon lightning from the sky, it had its moments too.

We heard voices before we found their owners. As we emerged from another copse of trees, the flickering light of a small fire greeted us. Around that fire sat several familiar figures: a synossian woman, a white haired o'naseri, and a hulking figure that I was pretty sure was Darishal.

They were speaking quietly, but voices carried, just like light, and none of the three were keeping watch and the fire they were gathered around was sure to ruin their night vision.

Mireille twitched when I couldn't quite hold back my growl. My nest-sister, at least, should have known better.

We closed to within ten feet before any of the three knew we were there, even with the noblewoman at my side somehow finding every dry branch in the forest to step on. It was Miko who turned first, and as the firelight revealed the tatters of her robes, the mottling across her shoulders and arms, and the cracks in some of the larger scales on her chest, my anger drained away entirely.

She looked even worse than I felt.

"Nest-brother?"

She rose, wavered, and would have almost fallen if Zamira hadn't stood to support her. The Zarisian seemed whole and healthy, but her uniform was torn in too many places to count. The third figure—who *was* Darishal—remained seated, and I realized now that he was hunched over, shield discarded to one side and one arm held to his chest.

"Miko." I stepped into the circle of fire light, ignoring Zamira's gasp at my own sorry state as I went to take the synossian's weight. "Sit down. Please."

"She knew you were alive," said the white-haired o'naseri at her side. "Somehow."

"Yeah. They do that. Both of them." Mireille pushed past me to kneel at Darishal's side. "Darishal? Derry?"

The bigger man barely reacted.

"Has head injury," said Miko, hissing as she returned to her seat. "And broken arm. Will heal when have energy again." Switching to the High Tongue, she told me: "I knew you would survive. I knew it."

"Yeah. The gods aren't done with us yet." In Trade, I addressed the whole group. "How did you all make it? Have you seen anyone else? And why did you make a fire? Do you *want* to bring down the whole colony on you?"

"Colony?" Zamira frowned. "What colony?"

"Spiders," said Mireille. "Gloom spinners. The whole forest is lousy with them, though this one seems to think there should be a lot more than we've already found."

"Hundreds more." I scanned around us. The shoreline was more rock than dirt here, with the trees a good ten feet away, but given how quick gloom spinners were, that didn't mean much.

"We haven't seen any spiders," said the Zarisian tiredly. "Miko set a fire so we wouldn't all freeze to death before we dried out. And Darishal thought he saw someone wash up on the north side of the river as we spun past, but given his concussion, it might have been nothing." She paused and frowned. "What else?"

"How we made it," said Miko.

"Oh. Right." She looked over at me. "After the ferry disintegrated beneath us, I did what you said."

It had been a very long day and I'd been bitten by a venomous spider, so it took me far too long to put it together. "*Control Water?*"

"Yes. Obviously, I couldn't stop the wave, or even myself, but I could… navigate with it at least? A glow underwater helped me find Miko—"

"Was healing," said the synossian. "*Light Healing* to fix head. *Minor Healing* to stop blood flow from arm. Then I repeated whenever possible as fresh wounds accumulated."

"Right. So, the glow led me to her and I was able to keep us afloat until we found a shoreline. Darishal… I don't know. I think he used his defensive abilities, and maybe his shield from the looks of it. We found him half in the water and half out and brought him onto land before the cutters returned. I had no energy left at all, Miko had enough for a few small heals and the *Flare* that I'm guessing brought you all here."

"Where is Sky?" Mireille asked the slumping Warrior.

"She was right next to me," he slurred, not even looking up.

The four of us traded glances. *That* wasn't good.

After that, Mireille shared our story. When she got to the spiders, I took over. Kamet's death was met with deep silence, and our description of the web-strewn forest had both Miko and Zamira nervously eyeing the nearby woods.

"What do we do?" asked my nest-sister.

Mireille was her party's leader, just as I was mine, but she looked to me for guidance.

"It's suicide to travel by night," I said. "Especially if the colony realizes we're here. Once it's daytime again, we were thinking about heading back west up the river. See if we can find anyone else but also determine whether or not we can make our way back to Hobbs' Crossing and the caravan without trekking through the woods."

"I don't think you understand how far we've come," said Zamira. "I was conscious for the whole bloody journey. We're *leagues* away. And there were more than a few waterfalls. Most were low, but a few were basically cliffs. If we want to get back to that town, we'll have to take the long way around."

"I don't think the others will still be there waiting anyway," added Mireille. She shrugged at the look I'd sent her. "I've been thinking it over since we made our original plans. Whatever caused a tidal wave in the Polemis—"

"It was a *who*," said Zamira. "I'm certain of that much."

Given that she was a water Mage, nobody seemed disinclined to believe her.

"*Whoever* caused it then… can any of you see a Tin managing that?"

That was easy enough to answer given that most of us had faced Tins or their equivalents.

Zamira frowned again. "I'm not sure a Copper could either. Those were *leviathans* fleeing."

"Murkdwellers too," I added.

Mireille nodded. "Which means whoever did it might be Iron ranked. Merrick and Lord Hawthorne will have recognized that. They'll want to get away from the water with all speed and hope our attacker is limited to that one element."

"Is even worse than that," said Miko, speaking up despite her exhaustion. "For all they know, we are all dead. *I* am dead."

"Shit," I cursed. "Wilhemina."

My nest-sister nodded. "Without me to heal her, they can only return her to Trynfall to let contagion run course or press on to Crimson Needle."

"And with the ferry out, that's even *less* of a choice than it seems. They'd move on, and as fast as possible."

"Does that mean we're *alone* out here?" asked Zamira. "Alone and abandoned?"

Nobody said anything, which was itself a reply.

"Five of us are alive," I said. "Others might be too. But we can't do anything until morning. So, commune with the Framework and rest up," I said. "I'll take the first watch, but I need a partner. Gloom spinner venom is fast-acting, and those spiders are too damn quiet for us to leave only one person on watch."

"Will join," said Miko.

I shook my head. "You should rest more than any of us. The quicker you can recover your energy, the quicker you can start handing out heals again."

She didn't like that, but it was hard to argue with logic.

"I'll stay up with Brian," said Zamira.

"And I'll take the second watch with Initiate Naseri," agreed Mireille.

"Miko," corrected the synossian. "Please."

"Miko. As for Darishal…"

"Should sleep," said the Priestess.

"We don't need to keep him awake?" I asked. I vaguely remembered reading something about that back on Earth when it came to concussions. Or… had I read that that was a myth?

"No. Rest will help head."

She was our only healer and the closest we had to an expert in the subject, so that was that.

○○○

Our time on watch was long but quiet. Zamira and I were close enough to support each other but far enough apart that we couldn't both be taken down at the same time. That meant talking was all but impossible. Staying awake should've been just as hard, but the memory of what I'd most recently woken up to was still painfully sharp. Hell, I wasn't sure if I'd be able to sleep at all when our shift ended. Other than the river behind us and the wind rustling through branches, it was almost painfully quiet, and my mind couldn't help but conjure a growing army of eight-limbed monsters, slowly gathering within the tree line.

Despite my fears, by the time the second of Eos' two moons was overhead, we hadn't seen a single thing. I woke Miko and went to tell Zamira we were done. The Zarisian had lost her staff to the river, but whirled on me as I approached, hands raised to cast… well, something. *Water Blast*, most likely, although she'd said she didn't have the energy for spells.

Regardless, she dropped her hands when she saw who it was.

"Time to sleep," I told her. Behind me, Miko had woken Mireille and was now headed to cast her first heal of the day on Darishal. "And recover our energy."

She paused, her voice barely more than a whisper. "Do you think Wilfred is okay? And Barth, of course?"

It seemed Wilf had become *Wilfred* to her and had risen in importance so much that Barth had become an *of course*. Any other day, I might have teased her about that.

"Wilf is resourceful, and both he *and* Barth have been training as scouts. They're probably better off than the rest of us combined."

Assuming they didn't drown or bleed out in the apparently leagues-long river ride through rapids and over multiple waterfalls, added the voice in my head.

"Good. I… Good." She brushed past me and took up a seat by the fire.

After checking on Mireille and Miko's respective positions, I joined her. Maybe if I'd ranked my *Meditation* skill up to Rare, I could have communed with the Framework *while* on watch, but for now, there was still only so much I could do at the same time. So, I closed my eyes, rested my hands on my knees, palms-upward, and let the events of the day flow through me. Even if I'd been unconscious for a good portion of that day, there was plenty to cover. Scouting in the morning before we reached Hobbs' Crossing. The ferry ride halfway across the Polemis river. The tidal wave, my desperate leap, and waking up again entombed in spider silk. All the individual battles Mireille and I had had since on our way to the river and then down it to my nest-sister's campsite.

When I opened my eyes, the world was still dark, but a dialogue window awaited me:

```
You have increased the following skills:

Major skills:
Knife [+1]: 47/50
Medium Armor [+1]: 49/50

Minor skills:
Acrobatics [+1]: 13/50
Avoidance [+2]: 49/50
Focus [+1]: 40/50
Leadership (U) [+2]: 27/50
Toxin Resistance (U) [+2]: 4/50

General skills:
Orienteering [+1]: 3/10
Tracking [+1]: 9/10
```

I was still one point away from the cap in *Medium Armor.* Given that that was the last skill requirement for level ten, it wasn't ideal. On the other hand, I'd seen more gains in this one day than in the average seven-day of our journey. Sometimes, just staying alive was enough of a struggle that the Framework couldn't help but reward it.

Which the next popup made clear:

```
You have increased the following attributes:

Vitality [+1]: 18
```

It was the second natural gain I'd gotten in Vitality, and it pushed the stat to unexplored heights. Hell, my next highest stat was Will and *that* was still stuck at fifteen. Vitality's main effect was to increase my endurance, but it also increased my ability to resist damage, whether from weapons or alcohol. It even had a small impact on the size of the energy pool that fueled technique usage.

I didn't know what the Earth-equivalent of an eighteen Vitality would be, but I'd come a long way from the Brian who had been taken down by a plate of pot brownies in Midton.

A very small part of me wondered what my dad would think if he'd been able to see me now.

○○○

I woke to screams, both figurative and literal. The first were in my brain, where *Danger Sense* was sounding every alarm it could. The second came from people I knew.

I was up before I was fully awake, spear in hand as I stumbled over the pack I'd been using as a pillow. My eyes finally cracked open as another voice sounded, this one male and angry.

Darishal was halfway between the burned-out remnants of our campfire and the water's edge, kite shield held in front of him by an arm that was no longer broken. And facing off against him was a creature whose simple illustration had given me nightmares.

A murkdweller. Twelve feet long, from double tail to massive armored head, its gaping maw was large enough to fit Darishal's whole shield within and still have plenty of room left over for the Warrior himself.

Behind Darishal, Zamira was crab walking backwards, blood pouring down her side where one of the creature's claws had struck. Miko rushed to her side even as Mireille burst past me, headed to reinforce her party member.

Darishal doubled in size and his gear did too, shield now large enough to block the murkdweller's monstrous bite. When the man's maul came crashing down in retaliation, it was glowing slightly and struck like a meteor.

The creature staggered and surged forward again, seemingly none the worse for wear.

I hurried to join the two of them, struggling to remember everything we'd learned from class as well as whatever *Animal Behaviorism* might be telling me. Murkdwellers were armored behemoths, the voracious tanks of water both fresh and salty. While there were a few creatures they wouldn't tangle with by choice, they existed at the top of their food chain, without any natural predators. And they were almost as fast on land as they were on water.

"Go for the eyes!" I shouted as Mireille's unleashed one of her techniques, both axes carving shallow lines of fire into the murkdweller's hide. Arriving on the creature's flank, I did the best to follow my own advice.

It *should* have been easy. The creature was so large its three sets of eyes should have made for easy targets, even tucked away behind a ridge in the center of its massive head. But my own strike glanced off that ridge ineffectually as the murkdweller twisted and rolled and snapped again at the meal that had presented itself.

A second strike and this time, my aim was true, only for my spear to strike the eyelid that slid shut like the hatch of an armored car, mere milliseconds before impact.

It was like it *knew* what I was trying to do.

Thankfully, I had a technique for that.

I recovered, sidestepped, and thrust again, motion smooth as silk, power transferring as my weight redistributed from back foot to front. Riok's spear was a blur as it streaked for that same set of eyes.

Deceptive Strike.

I never found out where the technique would have put me, because twin tails batted my blurring form out of the air. Something broke and as I flew backwards, I only took a small bit of comfort in the fact that it was me, and *not* my spear.

For the second time in my life, *Deceptive Strike* had failed me.

Which said terrible things about what we were facing.

Mid-air, I focused on a stretch of free ground near Miko and *Lunged.* I hit the ground under my own power instead of gravity's, and if I bounced and rolled, I was still close enough to my nest-sister for the warm glow of healing to swiftly surround me. Ribs knotted back together, and breath came more easily, if not without pain.

When I rose to my feet again, *Pain Tolerance* doing everything it could to drown out my sorrows, I saw my worst fears realized.

The murk dweller's armored hide was visibly thickening, gaining an almost stone-like quality. Jagged spikes formed across its body and down the elongated head, turning every part of the creature into an even more unstoppable weapon.

This was an ascended beast, much like the spider we'd first faced in the Echo. Worse, it had an earth aspect.

And there were no Risen knights around to help us kill it.

Darishal's next blow didn't even stun the murkdweller. Mireille's *Shield* ability flickered and broke as it was her turn to be hit by the twin tails. Both my offensive abilities were on cooldown and *Beast Hide* wasn't going to do a damn thing to help.

"We have to run!" I shouted. "Zamira, bind it!"

The Zarisian shot me a look of incredulity over her shoulder, but we'd delved enough that she followed orders anyway. Reaching a hand out to the river, she cast *Control Water*. Liquid tentacles formed to wrap around the murkdweller's rear legs and one of its tails.

Unprompted, Darishal triggered another technique and drove his maul into the earth. The ground before him didn't do much more than tremble, but it was enough to drop the already tangled murkdweller to its belly.

He and Mireille backed away, then spun and ran toward us.

"Where?" demanded the noblewoman, one word all she would spare.

She blanched at the look I returned and then nodded, jaw firming.

Where do we run where it won't follow us?

There was only one answer to that.

South.

Into the spider-infested forest.

I followed the others into the woods even as a deep coughing growl, followed by splashes, heralded the end of Zamira's spell. The murkdweller crashed through the first set of trees without even slowing, but we had a head start, of sorts, and the advantage of our size.

Once again, I had flashbacks to Harborton. To Nikkaali, the titan snake who had made even this ascended murkdweller seem small, and our desperate flight through ancient trees.

I quickly took the lead, doing what I could at full sprint to find us clear paths through both trees and webbing. Here and there, the occasional gloom spinner dropped from above, but speed was our ally. Only one judged the angle correctly and it was cut in half by one of

Mireille's axes. The rest were promptly annihilated by the monstrosity on our heels.

Mireille pulled up next to me as we ran. She was breathing easily, long strides eating up the terrain. Of us all, she was probably in the best shape, between general level of fitness and lack of injuries. Still, we'd *all* spent months in Stick's conditioning classes. Even Zamira, who almost definitely was the lowest level person in our group and *absolutely* had the lowest Vitality, was keeping up.

"It doesn't seem to be giving up!" yelled Mireille over the sound of crashes behind us and what my brain interpreted as the screams of the gloom spinners. "What now?"

"Keep going." I stumbled, only to be caught by Miko's strong arm to my left. "Find the colony."

"Is that wise?"

The answer was *obviously* no, but I shrugged. What else out here could possibly give the murk dweller pause?

"If you've got a better idea, let's hear it!"

She scowled but kept running and I turned my attention back to charting our path. Whereas before I'd been trying to *avoid* spiders, I started looking for web clusters, leading our group deeper into what had to be the gloom spinners' domain.

More attacks came from above, and more of those had to be defended against or swatted aside, but still the numbers we were seeing were a tiny fraction of what should've been out here. As the trees thickened, our lead over the murk dweller should have extended, but the increasing number of webs slowed us too. More than once, I found myself encountering almost invisible strands in our path and being forced to use *Liberating Lunge* to break free and clear a path for the others.

Our desperate flight continued.

The night before, I'd wondered to myself just what an eighteen Vitality got me. After thirty minutes of running for our lives through the woods, I had a better handle on the answer. It meant I could lose a fight against a vastly superior foe, sprint as fast as I could for half an hour, and still have ample breath to curse when I realized something.

Zamira was falling behind.

I looked to my left, to my nest-sister, and words passed between us without speech. She dropped back, followed soon by an audible squawk from our Mage as she found herself swooped up in Miko's arms. Even after my levels and training, the synossian was almost as strong as I was, and her size gave her a natural advantage when it came to carrying someone.

Our pace accelerated again, but more spiders were starting to appear, finally reacting to our presence. Most were still the size of lap dogs, but larger ones were starting to make themselves known. I veered away from a group of pony-sized creatures, fell straight into yet another web trap, and used *Liberating Lunge* to tear my way free.

On the one hand, the ability's shortened cooldown had literally saved my life multiple times already.

On the other, I wasn't sure how many more uses I had left. As solid as my legs and even lungs still felt, I was bone-tired, somewhere beyond the physical realm.

Darishal cursed, tearing spiders from his shoulders and back as he ran. The big man had taken at least one bite already and was starting to lag. Mireille swung back around to help, but Zamira, hanging upside down over Miko's shoulder, had cleared the last of the Warrior's hitchhikers with a brilliantly aimed *Water Blast*.

Still, we pushed on.

I used the shaft of my spear to swat one spider out of the air, stabbed a second right between its outstretched probosces, and crushed a third with a flying knee that I never would have been able to even attempt without *Unarmed Combat* and my current level of Finesse. I was the tip of our unit's spear, and I savaged everything in my path, knowing that it was necessary. Knowing also that doing so slowed us even further.

We burst through another webbed section and I could feel I was almost done. *Deceptive Strike* was now out of reach, as was *Beast Hide's* active form. One *Lunge* was all I had left in me and then it would be nothing but normal combat: spear and knife and fist until the inevitable end. A spider hit me from above, throwing me to the dirt, but a kick from Miko's clawed feet tore through its thorax. When I rolled to my feet, there was nothing but wet guts down my back and on my pack to announce it had ever been there. Yet again, my hauberk had saved me from any serious damage.

More techniques triggered from the rest of our party, but the larger spiders we'd started to encounter were far more durable than their younger kin. Blows that had been exploding the smaller versions were simply launching the larger ones instead, and those all too often caught themselves on lines of spider silk and scurried back to attack.

I knew that some of those gloom spinners were turning to face the larger threat of the murkdweller instead, but if things continued as they were, the spiders would kill us long before the monstrous crocodile could. I scanned the forest in front of me, saw a thin ray of hope, and angled our path toward it. Past a twinned pair of trees was something that heralded a possible clearing: blue skies and sunlight.

It wasn't salvation. It was just a place to make a stand without arachnids dropping on us like car-wrecking hailstones.

With a final burst of energy, we pushed past those trees and out into the open, finding ourselves on the ridge of a large valley.

Below us was utter calamity.

"By the Wanderer and the Wild," murmured Zamira in that secret language that I sensed rather than heard. Then, in Trade, she screamed: "Stop! On your lives, don't go any further!"

As we staggered to a halt, as my party members dealt with the gloom spinners who had followed us out, my brain struggled to understand what it saw in the valley. Legs everywhere. A shifting and undulating mass of chitin and hair and torn webs. *Hundreds of gloom spinners*, I'd told Mireille. *Maybe even a thousand in the colony.*

Turns out I'd dramatically undersold their numbers.

But that wasn't what had Zamira cursing in a language nobody but me could even hear.

It was the fact that most of those spiders were dead and the ones that remained were being absolutely slaughtered.

At the center of the colony's metaphorical web was a beast that made the murkdweller behind us look like a caiman. Black smoke in a wolf-like shape, it flowed across the battlefield, leaving devastation in its wake. Crimson eyes, each larger than a reaver was tall, were the only light within its form.

Mireille dropped to a knee next to me, chest heaving. "Anointed trinity, what *is* that?"

I didn't have an answer. Nothing in Beasts of Eos had prepared me for a wolf even larger than Nikkaali and formed of darkness. Not even a thousand irkonnen, backed by essoli, cultists, and a shadeweaver, had evoked this kind of reaction. This was something primal. Something ancient. Something even gold-ranks might quail against.

"If we go down there, we are dead," said Zamira, back on her own feet.

"What is it?" Mireille asked again.

"Death," answered Darishal, voice as grim as the grave.

"Or… an opportunity."

Four sets of eyes turned toward me, three of them incredulous. The final pair, orange and inhuman, latched onto mine.

"What is your plan, nest-brother?"

I told them. Thankfully, it didn't take long.

"That's *not* a plan," said Zamira.

"No," agreed Miko, sharp teeth bared in a smile. "It's a prayer."

○○○

The One Who Rules the River crashed its way through the final line of trees and webs to find a single figure waiting at the edge of a valley. The murkdweller's ascension had come with intelligence far beyond the norm for its kind, and it recognized that the waiting figure was small, even for a two-legged, and strangely colored. The blackened tooth in their hands was long and reeked of potential but remained cycles away from being a true threat. Neither the tooth nor the other two-leggeds, huddled to the side in terrified obeisance, had been worth this time or this hunt.

No, it was the two-legged holding the tooth who had caught the One Who Rules the River's attention, whose very presence had roused it from its slumber. All living things carried a spark to be consumed, but within that tiny, frail form was the flicker of something greater, something divine, something otherworldly.

Chosen, thought the One Who Rules the River, who had never even dreamed of such ideas. It chewed on that word, in the feeding pit of its mind, and found it good. The blackened tooth would grow or not along its path to power as the rules of primacy dictated, but the two-legged's divine spark… *that* was the kind of potential that could be taken, energy that could be stolen for its own use.

Ascension was, after all, a hunt without end.

The two-legged pointed its tooth and made noises with its small formless maw, and The One Who Rules the River sounded its coughing growl in return. Great claws dug into the soil beneath and then it was in motion, sinuous grace despite the added weight of its stone outer shell, bringing all of its power to bear as it charged the two-legged who held the key to its next evolution.

Two bites away from its prey, light erupted in front of it, bright and hot… but such distractions would not have stopped even one of its lesser kin. It closed its eyes and charged through, maw gaping wide to savage its prey, to swallow the spark that awaited.

But jaws that had savaged leviathans, that had torn the tentacles from a so-called king of the deep, closed on only air. It opened its eyes again to see the two-legged above it somehow, like a wingless bird desperately trying to take flight.

The One Who Rules the River tossed its head back to catch the meal already arcing its way back down… and stumbled. The added weight of its earth aspect made such quick stops a challenge, and when the earth beneath it shifted on its own, it found itself slipping and falling down the slope, claws leaving massive rents in the terrain behind.

It rolled once, then twice, and only came back to its feet at the bottom, in a mass of the many-legged. It thrashed about with both of its great tails, clearing space, before it realized that those many-legged were already dead, husks devoid of even the smallest of sparks.

Everything in the great murkdweller's ascended brain told it to charge back up the hill, to claim the prize that had momentarily evaded it, but something deeper, something instinctual, had it turning about instead.

Darkness loomed in the shape of a four-legged. Darkness lurked in the presence of something more ancient than reckoning. Darkness glimmered in a bite that bloodied the air itself.

For the first and the last time of its long life, The One Who Rules the River knew fear.

ooo

For a brief moment, *Liberating Lunge* allowed me to soar like a bird as the murkdweller passed beneath, as Darishal's technique contributed just enough to turn the monster's stumble into a slip and outright fall. But gravity was quick to remind me of my nature. I fell, narrowly missing the tails of the beast sliding irrevocably downhill, and the comparatively softer soil here did little to lessen the impact. Something in my shoulder popped, and not even *Pain Tolerance* could keep the world from whiting out.

When I came back to myself, Miko was there. She didn't have any heals to offer, but she did help me to stand, to turn and see what our desperate gambit had accomplished.

It was already over. The murkdweller who had ignored our best strikes, who had crashed its way through forest and gloom spinners alike, lay in pieces, stone already fading away from the armored hide beneath. Nothing moved in the valley of the dead; even the spiders had ceased their postmortem twitching.

There was no sign of the creature that had caused that devastation, of the darkness in wolf form. There was only death and carnage, the ends of a colony larger than any I'd read about and an ascended beast whose hide could stop even a nascent artifact.

"Did we—" began Darishal, only to cut off with a gasp that sounded strange from someone his size.

We spun to find the darkness behind us now, large enough to blot out the sky. Its growl wasn't truly a noise; it was a whisper of cold wind, but somehow audible for all of that. Its terrible mouth opened, exposing teeth that glowed as red as its eyes—

—and then it stopped, a breath away from devouring Darishal. Darkness flowed, reformed, and the creature was next to me instead, faster than Miko or I could react.

For the first time since we'd seen it, the thing hesitated.

"Whatever you do, *don't* move," said Zamira, in a whisper that carried easily in the silence.

Like all good advice offered after the fact, it was functionally useless. I *couldn't* move, pinned to the earth solely by the creature's intent. It was all I could do to *breathe*.

I stood there for far too long, being studied by darkness. Finally, it huffed—again a soundless noise that I somehow experienced as sensation instead—and flowed back. It headed towards the ridge, stopped, turned back to me, and waited.

"I hesitate to even say this," murmured Mireille in a voice thoroughly broken by awe and fear, "but I think it wants you to follow."

It was hard for me to imagine anything I wanted to do less. Even swimming in the Polemis had more appeal. *With* what I was pretty sure was a dislocated shoulder. But hell if I was going to tell this thing *no*.

"Wait here," I said aspirationally. "I'll be right back."

I'd made it about ten strides before I realized I wasn't alone. Miko, still in tattered robes because she'd lost her pack to the river, met my gaze.

"We go together, nest-brother. Always."

I managed a smile. "I guess we do."

The pair of us followed the wolf creature through trees that had once swarmed with spiders. Now, only shredded webs remained as proof of the colony's existence. The pain of my dislocated shoulder was such that I could almost ignore that I'd turned my ankle in the same fall; I hobbled along as best as I could, alternating between my spear and Miko's arm for support.

Thankfully, we didn't have to go far. We reached a clearing not unlike the one I'd woken in just the previous afternoon. Spider corpses were everywhere, but a space remained empty towards the center, and there a single web sack hung from the tree.

It wasn't *quite* large enough for a person, and whatever was in it was still, but the creature that had led us over fixated on it with an intensity that told me this was why I was here.

Thankfully, this wasn't my first visit to a gloom spinner larder.

"I'm going to need your help with this," I told Miko, setting my spear aside.

"With what?"

"With cutting this down and releasing whatever is within."

I knew Miko well enough to read the myriad questions flashing across her alien features, but she didn't voice any of them. "Just tell me what to do."

With two knives and three working arms, we had the web sack on the forest floor in no time at all. I crouched above it and extended my knife.

A whisper of icy wind stirred the clearing, freezing me.

If the creature had spoken in any sort of language, my trait would have allowed me to reply. Instead, I was stuck with Trade.

"If you want whatever is in this free, you need to let me cut the webs," I said. "I'm not going to hurt it. I did this twice yesterday, and nobody complained."

Granted, one of those two had already been dead, but I wasn't going to say that to a creature that made Nikkaali seem like a garden snake.

I motioned Miko away and waited for a reply from the creature. When none came, I took that as assent and started back in on my task.

This is no different than cutting Mireille out of her web, I told myself as I sawed through strands as carefully as I could with a knife that was increasingly losing its edge. *Other than the fact that you don't know what's in there and can't make guesses as to anatomy.*

That wasn't helping anything.

I slowed down even further as I reached deeper layers of webbing. Whatever was in there remained motionless, and I could only hope that was a result of gloom spinner venom and not something more permanent.

As I finally peeled away the last layer of the section I'd been working on, I found… *fur.* A black furry leg and a body that was still warm for all its stillness. With a better idea of where to cut I started in again only to stop almost immediately.

Darkness wafted off the exposed limb, more shadow than shroud. And just like that, I knew what the gloom spinners had captured and why that had resulted in their destruction.

Another twenty minutes of painstaking work and I'd fully revealed the unmoving form of a slightly larger than average wolf, remarkable only for the way darkness clung to its form.

"It's alive," I announced. "But I'm guessing it's got a lot of venom in it. Miko, I don't suppose you can—"

She shook her head. "I don't have any energy left to cast *Touch of the Dawn.* Should we wait for it to recover?"

A massive paw, more darkness than flesh, made an indentation in the soil next to us.

"I think that's a no."

"Maybe I can gather some herbs then? If I hadn't lost my pack, some of what you found on the journey here would've helped, I think."

That was enough to remind me that I still had *my* pack, as filthy as it now was. I dropped it on the ground and dug through Kamet's possessions to find the herbs I'd originally taken.

"Here," I said, pulling out the roots I'd used to wake Mireille. "We can grind this to powder and feed it to the… wolf?"

"I would *not* recommend that, nest-brother."

"What? Why?"

"In its raw form, it is just as likely to stop someone's heart."

I blinked. Swallowed. Blinked again.

"Let's *not* tell Mireille that?"

"Oh." The Priestess shook herself. "Yes, let's not. With a fire, I can treat the roots and reduce their potency to something less outright toxic. Do you think *it* will allow that?"

The answer, in not so many words, was apparently *yes*. I waited with the two wolves—one largely flesh and blood, the other anything but—as Miko left with the root. Long minutes later, she was back with a wet clump of fiber.

"I boiled it and then drew off some of the solution," said Miko. "What remains should be safe to ingest."

"Should be or is?"

She thought about it. "Is."

Again, she was the expert. I took the root remnant from her clawed hands, carefully pried open the wolf's jaws, and slipped it inside.

"And now I guess we—"

The wolf was already stirring. Eyes like dull embers cracked open and then it rolled over onto unsteady feet. It saw us first and let out a low, entirely normal growl.

Darkness shifted in the clearing and the young wolf froze. It spun about to see the massive creature above it and its mouth lolled open in a very dog-like kind of grin. With a chirp, it danced between the much larger wolf's incorporeal feet, only to be nudged to one side of the clearing by a nose as large as one of our caravan's wagons.

Once again, I felt myself studied, this time by both the primordial beast and what appeared to be its much, much younger descendant. Unsure what to do, I fell back on my Midwestern roots.

"Welp," I said. "We really should be going. Safe travels."

The younger wolf loped off into the forest, while the other flowed after.

I think it was the *welp* that did it.

42

Before we headed back to the others, there were two things to take care of. The first one hurt. A lot. But once my dislocated shoulder was back in place, I moved on to the second thing and gave Miko my pack.

"I have some of Kamet's clothes in here if you want to swap them for your robes? I think they'd fit you better than anything of mine." The Infiltrator had been a long way from Miko's size, but she was essentially wearing ribbons at that point. I figured anything would be an improvement.

Miko nodded and knelt to look through the pack. After a day, most of the contents were mostly dry now, and the pack's waterproof coating had kept the spider guts from soaking through to add to the mess. She pulled out a tunic that would at least reach her waist, pulled it on, and then put the remnants of her robe back on over the top. As she tucked things back into the pack, she smiled.

"You still have Mordecai's possessions. I was worried they would have been lost."

"I think they even stayed dry." Unlike the rest of the items in my pack, everything we had from Mordecai was wrapped tightly in waxed leather. The water that filled my pack hadn't penetrated that much smaller bundle. "At least we'll be able to pass them on when we reach the Crimson Needle."

"Meanwhile, I lost everything. My staff. My herbs journal. Even the book you just bought me." She tugged the drawstrings on my pack shut and looked up at me. "I am sorry, nest-brother."

I offered her a hand and helped pull her to her feet. "None of us planned to get attacked by the river. I'm just lucky I still had my pack on when I went over… and that I didn't drown because of it. Our main focus now should just be catching up to Wilhemina. Everything else can work itself out. That's why we have allies now, remember?"

We didn't dawdle on our way back to Mireille, Zamira, and Darishal, but we didn't hurry either. Vitality notwithstanding, I was *tired*, soul and body both. Five minutes of peaceful walking with my best friend in the world helped ease both, if only by a little.

By the time we reached the others, they were ready to go. Darishal still looked wobbly, but either he had some sort of regenerative technique, or he'd actually dumped points into Vitality, because he had already been shrugging off the gloom spinner venom even before Miko fed him the rest of her root concoction. Like my nest-sister, he had lost his pack, but at least he still had both his maul and shield. Zamira, meanwhile, had her pack but not her weapon, while Mireille and I were the only two with both.

I hoped Mireille's pack included a tent, because mine wouldn't fit all five of us.

And yet shelter was the *least* of our concerns.

"Is it… gone?" asked the noblewoman.

"I think so." I explained what we'd been called upon to do, carefully avoiding any mention of plants that were toxic when served raw. "I don't know what that thing was, but if it had wanted us dead, we'd be down there with the spiders and murkdweller."

"Remember how you once asked me about the Wild?" asked Zamira. "Now you've met one of its emissaries."

"Huh." I wondered if *Emissary of the Wild* was a title like *Agent* was. And whether we'd still be breathing if I hadn't had my own title. The answer to the second seemed like a qualified *maybe*, given that the Zarisian worshipped the Wanderer and had an indirect connection to the Wild. On the other hand, the nightmare wolf thing had come to *me* instead.

"What do we do now?" Darishal wanted to know. "Back to the river?"

Thankfully, Miko and I had discussed this on our way back.

"No," I said. "If you're right and the caravan already left for the Crimson Needle, there's no point in going back to Hobbs' Crossing."

"Especially with an Iron-rank maybe nearby," added Miko.

"Right. With the gloom spinner colony destroyed, the forest should be empty. We have an opportunity to head south instead. A straight line until we hit the road again. Overland travel's not quick, but—"

"Wagons aren't either," said Mireille.

"Right. And the direct route would shave a few leagues off… I think."

"You think?"

"I don't know this land any better than you. And Merrick only showed us the map once."

"So we could end up missing the road entirely," she concluded.

"No." Assistance came from an unexpected source as Zamira shook her head, sending leaves and webs fluttering to the ground. "He's right. I've seen Hobbs' Crossing and the Crimson Needle on trade maps. The road *should* curve around before eventually heading east up into the mountains. If we head south, we'll hit it."

"What about everyone else?" asked Darishal. "Are we just going to leave them to die?"

Mireille sighed. "He's right. We need to at least try."

"I'm open to suggestions on exactly how we do that," I said. The forest was huge and just because it was now also largely empty wouldn't make finding the other initiates any easier. Assuming they had even survived.

"We should check the river," said Zamira. "At least head as far west as the first set of waterfalls and see who or what we find."

"River will be dangerous now that water has returned to normal," said Miko.

"Still."

I wanted to argue, but… two of *our* party members were still missing too. And my beef with Lucius notwithstanding, I didn't wish any of the other initiates dead. It made sense to search for survivors. It was the right thing to do too.

It just… cost us time.

"We should divide and conquer," I said finally.

"Conquer what?" asked Mireille.

I bit back a sigh. How did *that* saying not translate? Eos was a world where conquest was still an actual thing!

"Means there is too much to do," clarified Miko. "Should have different groups tackle different tasks."

"Exactly." I dug through my increasingly jumbled pack to find the empty waterskins, both mine and Kamet's, and then handed them to Mireille. "You three head back to the river and look for survivors and supplies. While you're there, you can fill the skins. And your canteen," I added, eyeing the tin container hanging from Mireille's pack. "We're going to need fresh water and we can't guarantee it'll rain again before we reach the caravan."

The noblewoman passed the waterskins to Darishal. "What will you and Initia—Miko be doing?"

I nodded at the valley of death below us. "Making sure we have food to eat."

"I'd rather starve," said Zamira.

"Spider?" Mireille wrinkled her nose in disgust.

I flashed back to traveling with Lace, Skaal, and Mordecai, and the lessons we'd learned from each of them.

"No. I don't know enough about their anatomy to avoid the venom sacks. The last thing we need is to eat toxic meat. But the murkdweller…"

"Meat from an ascended creature can have unusual effects, even when properly prepared," warned the noblewoman.

"Bad effects?"

She thought about it and eventually shook her head. "Euphoria or an excess of energy, mainly."

"Euphoria might be problematic, but I think we could all use some energy right about now. We'll get a fire going here and then cut and cook some strips of meat to take with us."

"Have *Cooking* skill," added Miko.

"Of course you do," muttered Mireille.

"Will you be able to find your way to the river and back?" I asked.

Darishal pointed behind him at the wide swath of destruction the murkdweller had made crashing through trees.

"I think we'll manage."

Once the others had departed, my bloody work began. Miko rekindled the fire she'd used to make the venom antidote earlier and then sat down to meditate as I descended into the valley.

I made my way down through the piles of dead spiders to the murkdweller's corpse. I didn't know anything about monstrous two-tailed crocodile anatomy either, but I at least knew they didn't have venom. So as long as I stayed away from the organs, I should be able to find edible meat. And given how big the murkdweller was, that meat should be plentiful.

If the thing had still been in one piece, my harvesting efforts would have been defeated before they began. But the wolf creature had torn the murkdweller to shreds, and that meant I didn't have to work my way through an armored hide that even my spear had failed to pierce. Even so, the meat itself was tough; I had to switch to my second knife, the one that still had more of an edge, before I could make any headway at all.

I cut strips of meat, one after the other, resting them on the murkdweller's hide in the absence of a plate or tray, and then cut those strips in half again. It was dirty, disgusting work, enough to tell me whatever profession I chose here on Eos *wouldn't* involve butchering. Still, it was better than starving.

By the time I was done, I had almost ten pounds of meat. Without salt, I didn't know how long that meat would last, but then, I was just the makeshift butcher. Maybe Miko would have a better answer.

I'd rolled back my uniform sleeves before I'd begun the grisly task, but my arms were covered in blood up to the elbows and my clothing frankly wasn't much better. Once the cooking was done, I planned to burn what I was wearing and swap into something halfway clean from my pack.

Somewhere in the back of my brain, the part of me used to running my household budget continued to tally up the costs of the past two days. We didn't pay for our Tryn uniforms, but everything else? There was no way we could afford to replace any of it. A new proper short staff for Miko would cost more money than we had on its own.

Another problem for future-Brian to tackle.

Ten pounds of slippery, bloody meat would be challenging to carry in one hand, but even with the valley empty of life, I wasn't leaving my weapon behind. And not just because that had been Riok's first rule of the spear. Life on Eos had taught me there was no such thing as an unhealthy level of paranoia; I knew as soon as I set my weapon aside, *something* would happen to make me regret it.

Instead, I pulled off my bloody shirt, made a sack out of it by tying the sleeves together, and dumped the meat inside. Carrying both spear and sack, I slowly made my way back up to the ridge and Miko's fire. My nest-sister was still meditating, and the others had yet to return, so I sat down to wait, warming fingers that had gone stiff and achy from all the butchering.

When Miko opened her sclera-less eyes, they shined with an emotion I recognized: satisfaction. Some of the mottling on her scales had faded and since I knew for a fact that she'd spent her heals on everyone but herself, that could mean only one thing.

"Level nine?" I asked.

"Level nine." She visibly scanned the blessings she had on offer and then sighed. "I am sorry, nest-brother."

I shrugged off my disappointment with the aplomb of someone with both a ten in *Deception* and one point in *Performance*. "I think it's clear any spell to cure my disease is going to come from the higher ranks. Did you get anything good?"

"*Dawn Strike* again," she said, naming the short-ranged light-based attack she'd been offered at level seven. "Also an upgrade to *Minor Healing* that extends its range. And a blessing called *Dawnmother's Hearth*, which creates a localized area of regeneration. From what I recall, both the area and the effect are small, but can be improved with further upgrades."

"I think Sky cast something similar when we rescued you in Trynfall," I said. "The healing output was limited, but the fact that it affected multiple people at once made it useful."

"Yes. Especially if we find other survivors." She tapped her claws against the scales on her thigh, a gesture that meant nothing at all because she'd picked it up from me somewhere in the past half-cycle. "They all offer their benefits, but…"

"But you want to take *Dawn Strike*."

"Yes. Perhaps that is a selfish choice for a healer to make, but I worship Aurea, not Etriska the Pure, and the Bright Lady is a goddess of light and fire."

"You wouldn't have been offered *Dawn Strike* twice if it wasn't something she wanted you to have," I said from a place of support and absolutely no real knowledge. "*Minor Healing*, *Light Healing*, and *Touch of the Dawn* will be plenty to carry you to level eleven."

"Yes." Her double sets of eyelids fluttered shut and then back open again. "It is done. And now, level ten awaits us both."

"And Tin."

"Yes." She turned to the strips of meat I'd laid out for her and started to thread one onto a long stick for roasting. "But first, we can see how my *Cooking* skill fares."

I could have used that time for my own meditation but didn't feel any real urgency to do so. I could tell from the sensation in my core that despite the past day of battles, I still wasn't anywhere near what I needed for level ten. Any other gains could wait until nightfall. And on the off chance the surrounding forest wasn't *completely* empty, I wanted to be alert should the fire and roasting murkdweller attract attention.

Eventually, the meat was done. I hadn't tried any—because Miko still lacked the energy to cast *Touch of the Dawn* if things went poorly—but it at least *smelled* good. We'd wrapped the slightly charred pieces in one of Kamet's clean uniforms and I'd scrubbed as much gore from my body as I could—with dirt, ironically enough—before swapping into a fresh tunic and pants.

It was another half-glass or so before the others finally returned. When they did, they brought a surprise.

And that surprise had a name.

"Friend Barth!" shouted Miko.

The blonde Apsan smiled brightly and waved. He had his bow and short blade with him, as well as a quiver of arrows, but no pack. Only a series of fading bruises showed he'd been injured at all.

"We found the other initiates," said Mireille, looking justifiably proud. "Most of them anyway. They're camped up at the top of the western waterfall."

"I was in the best shape, so they sent me down to meet with you all," added Barth. He double-taked as he looked past me to the valley of dead. "It sounds like you guys had it tougher than we did."

"Just a bit," huffed Zamira.

"Who all is up there?" I asked.

"Wilf, Lucius, Ames—"

"Don't forget Sky." Darishal's smile was a whole lot brighter than it had been when they'd left.

"—Sky, and Anthasa. Noxx wound up on the wrong shoreline and said he was headed for Hobbs' Crossing and would hire a carriage and guards there." Barth dropped his voice, still staring at the dead spiders and the carved remnants of the murkdweller. "Shar didn't make it, unfortunately, and we haven't found any sign of Ivar at all."

Ivar had been Lucius' team healer. Noxx and Shar their Mages, so their loss was a serious blow. Not just to Lucius' team, but to our strength as a whole. It felt callous to focus on that rather than the people themselves, but I'd barely known any of them, and hadn't particularly liked what little I did know.

"Two dead," summarized Mireille. "One missing, and one out of the picture unless he rejoins us at the Crimson Needle. It's horrible news, for their families and their houses, but better than I'd hoped for."

"We are Aspirants," said Miko. "Are trained to survive."

"We're also short on food," said Barth, "although Anthasa is working on that. And *something* smells fantastic."

"Ascended murkdweller meat," said Darishal.

"Oh. Nice! There's a restaurant back home that specializes in ascended meals. Although I don't think they've ever served murkdweller." He shook his head. "One time, they served our family basilisk. It can kill you if it's not prepared correctly, which made the whole meal so much more exciting. I even got to try it first."

Mireille gave me a look from behind the blonde noble. I sent her a shrug back. Barth was Barth. I was just glad he was alive.

"Are we headed back to the waterfall then?" I asked.

Zamira shook her head. "I don't even want to think of climbing the cliffs there. I thought Barth was going to fall a dozen times on the way down."

"Me too," said Barth. "Some of those rocks were much more slippery than they looked."

"It was hard to make any plans over the roar of the falls," added Mireille, "which was why they sent Barth down instead. We're going to stick with your idea of heading south and look to join up with the other group once we're past the cliffs."

"Anthasa says she'll be able to pick up any trail we leave," added Barth. "And we can figure things out from there."

We left soon after, hiking our way through the former colony's domain. A few gloom spinners remained, but the ones we encountered were all easily dispatched as we went. Barth's bow wasn't as much help as it should have been, owing to both the webbing in the trees and his limited supply of arrows, but simply having a Warrior who *hadn't* spent the morning fighting for his life made a huge difference.

And he seemed pretty happy hacking his way through arachnids with the blade he'd gotten from our first Echo delve.

By the time we stopped to make camp, it had been at least a glass since our last gloom spinner sighting, and the forest around us was, if not precisely lively, at least less empty than what we had been trekking through. The cooked murkdweller was delicious and every bite sent a wave of warmth through the body, almost like a mug of Lomas' best ale back in Harborton. I almost wished I'd found a way to bring more with us.

With Darishal healthy again and Barth making us a group of six, we had three watch shifts instead of two, promising more sleep than any of us had gotten the night before. I took the first shift with Miko and was happy enough to have it pass by uneventfully. We'd all almost died—again—just hours earlier, and even if I was starting to get used to that sort of thing, it was still a draining experience.

But before I slept, there were gains to be realized. I followed Miko to our tent and while she sprawled out in her bedroll, I settled into my meditation.

An indeterminate amount of time later, I was done.

```
You have increased the following skills:

Major skills:
Knife [+2]: 49/50
Medium Armor [+1]: 50/50
Tactics [+2]: 48/50
Unarmed Combat [+1]: 8/50

Minor skills:
Acrobatics [+2]: 15/50
Avoidance [+1]: 50/50
```

```
      Focus [+3]: 43/50
      Leadership (U) [+2]: 29/50

      General skills:
      Animal Behaviorism -> Animal Behaviorism
(Uncommon)
      Butchering [+1]: 1/10
      Caretaking [+1]: 9/10
      Orienteering [+1]: 4/10
```

It was a hodgepodge of increases, because most of my primary skills had already hit the cap for level nine. *Medium Armor* had been the last one I needed. Now, only experience separated me from that all-important tenth level. *Knife* increasing despite the fact that I'd only used it for freeing the wolf cub and fileting murkdweller meat was a bit of a surprise, as was *Animal Behaviorism*'s jump in tiers from Common to Uncommon, but I wasn't going to say no to either of those unexpected boosts.

As for the change in *Caretaking* and the acquisition of my brand-new general skill: *Butchering?*

I had a hard time squaring the Framework's supposed lack of sentience with the way it seemed to actively work *against* my preferences.

I swiped the screen away and got a more welcome surprise:

```
      Congratulations, Warrior.

      You have earned a new title:

      Agent of the Wild -> Hand of the Wild
```

I still wasn't sure what titles did, but assuming *Agent of the Wild* was the reason we hadn't been eaten by the giant primordial wolf, I was more than happy to see mine upgraded. And I guess I *had* been the literal hands for a creature of the Wild.

I spared a few moments to think of the two wolves, so very different in size and appearance, yet clearly linked by lineage. Of gloom spinners dying in the thousands because they had, in their single-mindedness, trapped the wrong prey. Of the way the five of us had worked together to survive two threats that should have killed us. There was danger and horror aplenty here on Eos, but that was how we grew… and we were doing so together.

Visions of a distant future played in my head: Miko's people safe, Skaal's death avenged, Wilf and Zamira's mysteries solved. The path to achieving any of those things seemed unending, yet every skill gain, every level, every alliance was a new step along that path. And maybe… just maybe… we were making better progress than I thought.

I let myself drift off to sleep.

ooo

It took two days to finally link up with the rest of the initiates, and even then, it was Anthasa who found us. The fiorlan materialized out of the woods, waited for us to spot her, and then led us west to where the others were waiting. House rivalries were forgotten, for just a moment, as everyone mixed and mingled and we all congratulated each other on our survival. Sky took Kamet's death hard and spent the rest of the night wrapped around Darishal. Wilf spoke with Miko and me and then bee-lined for Zamira, while Lucius, Mireille, and I gathered off to one side.

"How much time does Lady Willerton have?" asked Lucius.

"Hello, Lucius. We're glad to see you survived too."

He waved away my words. "Yes, yes. Obviously. Forgive me if my concerns lie with the life of the heir to the entire duchy."

And the key to your family's ascension, I didn't add.

"If we can intercept the caravan, it won't matter," I said. "If we miss them, it gets a bit tricker. Miko healed Wilhemina—"

"*Lady Willerton.*"

"Right. Miko healed Lady Willerton four days ago on the road. At the current rate of the curse's progression, that *should* last at least two seven-days."

"*They* will already be at the Crimson Needle by then. I'm not sure the same holds true for us." He gritted his teeth and looked away. "We've lost multiple days already, and traveling overland has been slower than anticipated. At this rate, it will be another four days before we even reach the road."

"You think the caravan will have already passed by?" asked Mireille.

"Anthasa believes so."

I frowned. "Which would leave us to head to the school as quickly as possible on our own."

"Yes. An unacceptable outcome, for both us and the duke's heir. That is why I want to march from dawn to dusk," decided Lucius. "Maybe even an hour past dusk. We must make up whatever time we can."

"We're unranked, Lucius," said Mireille. "Half of the group is *still* being healed, and the other half is exhausted from their healings these past few days. We need our rest."

"It's worse than that," I added. "We need *food*. Wilf said you've all been living on berries and the occasional bird Anthasa brought down on the fly."

"I was told you've brought ascended murkdweller meat."

"There's very little of it left and what remains is close to spoilage." It was amazing it hadn't *already* gone bad over the past two days, even with the relatively cool weather. I wasn't sure if that was a quality of murkdweller meat, in general, or something having to do with the beast's ascension. "We'll have to take the occasional breaks to hunt and cook along the way."

"That is unacceptable," said Lucius.

"That is reality," countered Mireille.

It wasn't the scowl on Lucius' face, but the thoughts of a little girl dying that had me searching for compromise.

"We've got a few glasses of daylight left today. Why don't we hand out the rest of the murkdweller meat and then press on until darkness? Tomorrow, we can stop a glass or so early to let people rest while Anthasa and I head out and replenish our supplies."

"And after that?" asked Lucius.

"More of the same. Go long on the days where we can, give people an opportunity to rest when we need to stop for supplies anyway."

"That doesn't give you or Anthasa any relief," pointed out Mireille. Which was a lot more consideration than Lucius was giving.

"If it gets to be too much, we can swap other people in. Barth maybe, given he's the only one besides Anthasa with a bow."

"Ivar had a crossbow," said Lucius.

I leaned heavily on my time in the service industry to keep a sigh from escaping. "If we encounter him out there in the wilds, we can add him to the rotation. In the meantime, what do you both think of the plan?"

A Discernment stat of eleven was nowhere near sufficient to tell me how either of them would answer. I just had to hope that my *Leadership* and *Diplomacy* skills, combined with us having no other choices, would be sufficient to sway them both. Because the one thing I knew for sure was that a power struggle wasn't going to help anyone. Least of all Wilhemina.

"If that is the best we can do, I suppose it will suffice," said Lucius, he who had failed to offer any alternate, reality-based solutions.

"Agreed," said Mireille, although I *think* she meant it more supportively.

"Great. Then let's go."

That's how the next few days went. Anthasa proved her value almost immediately, as we moved into forests that had little in common with what I'd seen west of Madea. The fiorlan guided us around more than a few unexpected dangers as we journeyed south. On the second day, I helped her bring down a large blue lizard with vestigial wings and gained a point in *Hunting* in the process. The meat from that kill was enough to fill our packs, and water swiftly became the larger concern. There were ten of us, half as many waterskins or canteens, and the pace we'd adopted was a punishing one that drove the moisture right out of our bodies.

Over the next few days, Anthasa managed to find water in unexpected places, from morning dew to a few not quite ripe fruits, but as our skins and canteens emptied, her ingenuity was barely sufficient to keep us going. With all the rain we'd suffered through earlier in the journey, there was a bitter irony in finding ourselves fighting dehydration now.

By the end of the fourth day, our pace had slowed considerably. When the fifth dawned, with the road still nowhere in sight, we knew we'd have to detour further to find a true stream or body of water.

Instead, Anthasa came back several glasses later with news that she'd found something even better: a small town, ringed in a wooden palisade, smoke rising from some of the unseen buildings within. Zamira, still going off her father's map of trade routes, thought it might be the settlement of Cyrinton, but as far as the rest of us were concerned, it might as well have been called Salvation.

A town meant food, water, supplies, and shelter. We might even be able to buy horses or rent a carriage to get Miko to the Crimson Needle that much faster.

It was everything we wanted and needed.

Maybe that's why I didn't trust it.

The argument with Mireille and Lucius bordered on legendary, but when it was over, I'd convinced them both to give Anthasa, Wilf, and me a single glass to observe the town before we all marched up to its gates. Anthasa, because she was more at home in the forest than any of us. Wilf, because he was a Spy and he might see something the rest of us missed. And me, because… well, it had been my idea.

I was glad I'd included myself in the scouting group when, halfway through our observation, a cold blade materialized at my throat, and a woman's voice, low and full of menace, whispered in my ear.

"Make a move and you die, dirt farmer."

I went still, not out of fear or compliance, but instead surprised recognition.

"Lace?"

43

The blade at my throat didn't move. "I taught you better than to be snuck up on like some fool who's never seen his own shadow, Brian." Something cold entered her voice. "And tell the pretty tree sprite that if she takes another step towards me with that blade in hand, she's going to lose her arm at the elbow."

Lace hadn't changed a bit.

"It's okay, Anthasa," I said. "She's a friend."

The fiorlan didn't respond, but she must have stopped trying to sneak up on the Marauder, because Lace finally relaxed. She tapped my throat lightly with her knife and then released me.

"What I *am*," she said, voice full of thorns, "is disappointed. What are you doing here? The plan was for you and little Miko to reach *Tin* before you sought me out."

I took a careful step away and turned to face her. Lace looked kind of like I felt… like someone who'd been living in the wilds for far too long and just might have gone native somewhere along the way. Her jet-black hair was still tightly braided, but her clothes were dirty, and her obsidian skin was too. Tempest was a wrapped bundle on her back, as always, though she wouldn't safely be able to use it until at least Iron.

"We didn't seek you out," I said. "We're on a… kind of a school trip, I guess."

She sheathed her knife with a frown. "So, you really *were* going to walk right into that town?"

"We need water and supplies," said Anthasa, voice rough with anger, although I didn't know whether it was from Lace's threat or because the Marauder had managed to spot her sneaking up.

"We were watching them first," I said. "Checking for threats."

"At least dirt-farmer school hasn't *completely* ruined you then. We need to talk. And the shaggy-haired one in the tree should probably come down and join us."

"We've already been gone too long, yeah?" said Wilf, climbing down. If *he* was upset about being spotted, he didn't let on. "The others will be wondering where we are."

That was a flat-out lie, but it got Lace's attention.

"Others?" Silver eyes looked from the Spy to me. "What others and how many of them are there?"

"I'd say that's none of your—" began Anthasa.

"Eight more, including Miko," I said.

"All from that school I left you at? All Aspirants?"

"Yes."

Her smile was savage. "Then we might just have a chance. Lead the way."

Anthasa came up to me as we started the short hike back to the others. "Who *is* she, Brian?"

"An adventurer. Miko's and my party leader."

"Lucius said there were three of you who came to Trynfall with the heir."

I nodded. "She's the third."

"And what is she doing out here?"

"Hunting," said Lace, startling the fiorlan.

I grinned. It was nice to see Anthasa on the back foot for once. And even nicer to have someone as capable as the Marauder back with us. "Yeah. That."

In a perfect world, the other initiates, in our absence, would have created a clearly defined perimeter and assigned several people to keep watch. Instead, most were flat on their backs while Lucius and Mireille conferred about who knew what. We'd made it almost all the way to them before Miko spotted us and our guest.

"Friend Lace!" she called, grin sharp and toothy. "Where did you come from?"

"The Night Hag's spiteful embrace, as always," replied the Marauder. She scanned the rest of the initiates, many of whom were only now stirring and sitting up and turned back to me. "The more I see of its students, the more I think leaving you at that school was a mistake."

"Go easy on them," I murmured, as Lucius and Mireille slowly made their ways over. "We've been low on water for days now."

"There's a stream about two leagues due east of here."

Anthasa stiffened. "How do you know that?"

"Because I've been camped nearby for the past few seven-days. It's just a trickle but more than sufficient to refill your skins."

The fiorlan turned to Lucius, who had arrived in time to hear that last part. "I can be there and back in a little over a glass."

"Why bother?" asked Mireille. "Cyrinton's a quarter that."

"Anyone who enters that town's not coming back out again," said Lace. "That's why I'm here. But none of you are worth a damn like this."

Lucius frowned, doing his best to look regal despite dry, chapped lips and a smudge of dirt across his nose. He turned to Anthasa and nodded. "Go."

"Take Barth with you," I said.

"What's that?" asked the Warrior in question. One of the few initiates still on their feet, he wandered over, bow in hand.

"You. Me. Alone in the woods." Somehow, the sharp teeth only made Anthasa's smile *more* lascivious. "How about it, Apsan?"

Lucius sighed.

"There's fresh water nearby," I clarified. "Can you go with Anthasa and refill our skins and canteens?"

"Sure," said Barth. I couldn't tell if he'd completely missed Anthasa's subtext or was just that good at ignoring it. If it was the latter, I wanted lessons.

After they left, I made introductions. Zamira wandered over to join Wilf and the rest of us, but most of the initiates seemed content to wait for water before they moved an inch.

"What's this about Cyrinton?" asked Lucius, as if he'd known the town even existed a few glasses earlier.

"It's been taken over by a certain… unsavory element," said Lace, giving me a significant glance.

"Arrius?"

She nodded. "Along with a handful of bandits he encountered. All of them unranked."

"Arrius Vitellius? From the wanted posters?" asked Mireille.

"The very same."

"Are you sure?"

Lace met Lucius' question with a silver-eyed glare, leaving me to provide actual words.

"She's been hunting him."

The Marauder nodded. "Between your duke's edict and my own efforts, there's been no safe harbor for the walking dead man. So, he decided to make his own. I arrived a seven-day after they started. Found a pile of bodies out in the woods. Town elder and at least two guards, by the looks of it. The remaining dirt farmers inside are little more than slaves. If only there were a near-dozen Aspirants from the duchy's premiere school of fighting who could help change that."

"Arrius Vitellius is a *Copper*," said Mireille.

"He is a bully and a coward. And of the fourteen towns he's visited since leaving Madea, I've found him at eleven and fed him a different one of Hashoggath's tears each time. Those poisons will eventually break down now that they're no longer being actively fueled, but he will never be weaker than he is today."

I traded glances with Miko. Lace hadn't changed a bit.

"Grim talk of an assassin's underhanded methods notwithstanding," said Lucius, "our mission takes priority. The responsibility for this town's safety lies with the local baron; *we* must remain focused on matters that concern the duchy as a whole."

Lace turned to me; I read the question in her look.

"Wilhemina's illness came back," I said. "We were accompanying her to the Crimson Needle when we got separated from the main escort. As the only person who can heal her, Miko needs to reach Mordecai's old school before it's too late."

"We have barely more than a seven-day to reach her," added Lucius. "We might *already* be too late. So, you can understand why the fate of Cyrinton or even this entire barony pales by comparison. We must reach the Crimson Needle as soon as possible."

"It was your duke himself who declared Arrius a wanted man. By this duchy's laws, I am pretty sure that makes you honor bound to bring him to justice."

"Be that as it may, we have our duty."

"Should come with us," suggested Miko. "Can come back from Crimson Needle with allies. Sir Merrick. Others too."

Lace turned on Miko. "I've spent damn near half a cycle hunting down Arrius. I'm not going to leave and let him slip away and recover. And I'm surprised that you, of all people, would even think to leave an entire town of innocents to their fate."

My nest-sister looked down and away.

"Give me *one* day," urged the Marauder. "When we're done, I'll personally escort you all to your destination."

"She's right," said Mireille. "We *are* bound by honor and law to both defend our people and to bring a fugitive to justice."

"These are extenuating circumstances—" argued Lucius.

"These bandits Arrius found," I interrupted. "Did they have horses?"

"Two or three, yes." Lace waved in the direction of the town. "You couldn't see it from your vantage point, but there's a stable just inside the gate. Why?"

"Because Lucius is right. It might already be too late for us to reach Wilhemina and the Crimson Needle. On foot at least. On horseback though? That's another thing entirely."

"Kill the brigands, take the horses? It wouldn't double our speed—not without a series of remounts, anyway—but it would shave multiple days off the total travel time," said Zamira, ever the calculating merchant. "We might even catch up with the caravan that way."

"Except it's not just brigands over there, yeah?" Wilf shook his head. "Bully or not, poisoned or not, a Copper changes everything."

Even more than the Framework-given quest to kill Arrius, I felt the weight of my oath to do the same hanging over me. But still… Wilf was right. I didn't see us killing Arrius. Not without a *lot* more help. And the best way to get that help was to head to the Crimson Needle at the quickest possible speed.

"We can steal the horses," I said instead. "Kill any brigands we see in the process, maybe make enough of a distraction for the townsfolk to get away, and then we run." I turned to Lace. "Break his power base here and he'll run again. But next time you find him, we'll have reinforcements to help you take him down."

For just a moment, Lace's aura unfurled: brambles and hard bronze, cold rain and unseen poisons. Jaw tight, she brought it back under control. "Is *this* what they've taught you?"

I met her furious silver eyes and tried not shiver.

"Yes. If we were all Tin, it would be different. But until then, we're simply not enough. That's why you left us behind in the first place."

"Numbers are their own strength."

"If there were a hundred of us, I'd agree with you."

"I'm with Brian," said Mireille. "We take the horses. And if we can do something to help free the people of Cyrinton at the same time, all the better."

"The man with the caravan is a Copper," I told Lace, speaking in Gorash, the language of the South. "And he has three Tins with him. I'll bring them back with me if I have to physically drag them. I swear that on the names of all the gods who brought me here."

She spat to one side, her phlegm hitting the dirt and sizzling as it ate through the soil. "So be it."

The other initiates stared at us in confusion.

"We're in agreement," I explained, for everyone who couldn't speak Gorash.

"Steal the horses. Bleed some pigs. Leave *that man* fumbling to find a new nest." Lace nodded. "And whoever he kills between now and the next time he is located will have their names forgotten."

"Their… names?" asked Zamira.

"Yes. For it is clear they mattered not, even to those who professed to rule them."

It had the air of one of Hashoggath's curses, and it settled heavily onto everyone in the clearing.

Me, most of all.

"Now then," continued the Marauder. "Did that school of yours teach you how to make a plan?"

Zamira, Miko, and—surprisingly—Mireille all turned to me, to the clear annoyance of Lucius.

"We've got a few glasses until dark," I said, looking to Lace, and then past her, to Wilf. "But first, we're going to need more information."

○○○

By the time night fell, everyone was hydrated, and a plan had been made. There were twelve of us, including Lace, and we all had our parts to play. Barth with his bow and Anthasa with her sling were on overwatch, there to cut down any bandits who left the safety of the town. Sky waited with them as a reserve healer. Lace was responsible for opening the gates and then she, Wilf, and I would sneak to the stables, while Darishal, Lucius, and Mireille, our strongest collection of Warriors, would guard those gates until we were gone again. That left Miko, Zamira, and Ames to get as many townsfolk out as they could.

I'd wanted to put Miko up on the hill with Sky and the others, but I'd been overruled. There was too much value in having a healer in the town with us, and Miko was both higher level and a lot more combat-ready than Sky. She was also the one person we *had* to get to the Crimson Needle. That meant she'd be heading out on the very first horse we freed.

That, as much as anything, convinced me.

Wilf's reconnaissance with Lace confirmed that Arrius and his men were camping out in what had been the town elder's home, a two-story miniature manor just off the main square. Like many smaller towns in the duchy, Cyrinton had a single square at the center with three roads leading from it, representing the three faces of the anointed trinity. The stable was along the eastern road, a block away from the town's only gate, and most of the remaining townsfolk were either keeping their heads down in their homes or serving at the town's only tavern. That tavern was on the opposite side of the square from the elder's home and just as likely to have one or more of the bandits within.

Lace had counted nine bandits, not counting Arrius. There was always one in a guard role on the palisade next to the gate, and Wilf had accounted for six of the others, but that left two who might be anywhere. The hope was that they were in the tavern or even sleeping off their alcoholic excess in the manor.

As for Arrius, Lace had last seen him that morning, heaving his guts out in the back alley behind that same manor.

At the start, everything went well enough. The storm clouds had rolled back in almost as soon as Anthasa had returned with water, as if to mock us, but I couldn't complain about the cover they provided, shrouding not just Eos' twin moons, but most of the star-strewn sky. There was a torch up on the wall by the gate, and a number of lanterns lit within the town, but it was about as close to dark as we could ask for.

Or as I *would* ask for, anyway, still not being able to see in the dark. Wilf and I followed the Marauder to the palisade a good dozen feet south of the gate and waited. A tap on the shoulder was the only indication that she was there at all, and I didn't realize she'd left again until the gates to the town creaked open and a figure, barely visible even within the circle of torchlight, waved us in.

The others, none of whom had any stealth skills at all, would be making their way down to the palisade now, but the three of us had horses to steal.

"The guard?" I asked Lace in a hushed whisper as she ushered us inside.

"Nameless and forgotten."

Fair enough.

Cyrinton was unnaturally quiet, save for the noise from the nearby tavern. I used every bit of my *Stealth* skill to follow in Wilf and Lace's footsteps but felt like Mireille must have when she followed me through the woods. There was just no overcoming the gulf between class skill and general.

The two of them were ghosts. I was a half-drunken badger.

I risked a glance behind us as we neared the stables and saw the unmistakable shapes of Miko and Ames headed to the nearest home, Zamira on their heels. Our rearguard of Lucius and the others was out of sight beyond the gates, but I trusted they would be there if we needed them.

Which was feeling like a pretty big if. Getting into town had been the biggest concern and we'd not only done it but managed it without anyone knowing. As Lace eased the stable doors open, avoiding the creak or horrendous squeal horror movies had trained me to expect, I took my first breath in more than a minute.

We *had* this.

That, of course, was when everything went wrong.

The stables weren't dark. Nor were they empty. There were three horses, yes, but also a man whose abundant facial hair and greasy smile practically screamed bandit. As did the half-clothed girl he had backed into a corner. He spun at our arrival, opened his mouth to yell an alarm…

…and took a hurled dagger right in that open mouth. Teeth shattered and broke, but it was the dagger's blade piercing the back of his throat that really mattered. Miraculously, he crumpled backwards without making a single sound.

His would-be victim looked wide-eyed at the blood now splattered across her chest, then at the man gurgling to death at her feet. I had a painful moment to realize what was about to happen, and then she let loose a scream, high, loud, and piercing, like ten thousand electric kettles left to boil.

"Man plans and Hashoggath laughs," snarled Lace. "Get the horses out. Now!" She darted past us back into the street, leaving her thrown dagger behind, while Wilf and I pushed forward, each headed for a different horse. The stalls here were simple affairs, but the doors needed to be unlatched, and the horses needed saddles and reins if anyone other than Lace was going to ride them.

The woman's scream finally cut off as she sucked in a fresh lungful of oxygen. "Who are you? What is going on?"

"Head for the gate if you want to live," said Wilf.

"But my pa…"

I blocked out their conversation, focused on the task at hand. One horse free and on to the second. With only three horses available, most of us would have to flee into the woods while Miko and two others rode on to the Crimson Needle. But first we needed to get both Miko and the horses out of town, and I could already hear angry shouts from the streets.

There wasn't any fighting, not yet, but it was as inevitable as the dawn.

I had my two horses ready by the time Wilf had handled his one, a testament to both my *Animal Behaviorism* skill and the practice I'd gotten with the dalysi on Miko's home continent and Lord Arbiter Hawthorne's horses on the road from Madea. The blood-spattered woman had left at some point, and I wasn't sure whether she'd gone deeper into town or taken Wilf's advice and headed for the woods. I didn't have time to care either; the first crash of metal on metal, accompanied by a man's roar of pain, announced that at least some of the bandits had reached us.

I handed both sets of reins to Wilf, though I didn't know how he'd manage three horses at once. Especially with them dancing nervously as the noise swelled.

"Get them out of town," I said. "I'll get Miko."

We emerged into light and bedlam: the clash of arms, shouts of anger and hate, and here and there, the sharper cries of children, women, or even animals.

It was only afterwards that I pieced together what had happened. The scream in the stables had been the trigger to rouse, not just the bandits, but the town as a whole. As townsfolk spilled onto the streets, many of them carrying their own light sources, some had seen a half-feral blood-scorned amazon, her weapons bared. Others had found a white-scaled synossian creeping through the streets, followed by a woman with stone eyes and a third who looked like she beat up full-grown adults for their lunch money.

I was used to all those things and more... used to Eos' collection of the strange, the exotic, and the often terrifying.

The people of Cyrinton were not. They were tired, they were scared, they'd seen their homes and their freedom taken from them, and now they were being confronted by entirely new nightmares. Some fled. Others snapped and rioted.

And just like that, our efforts to free them went to shit.

At the time, all I knew was that people were yelling, that I couldn't see Miko *or* Ames, and that, down the main road, Lace was dancing in lantern light with two sword-wielding thugs while a third, wielding a bow, leaned over the rooftop where she'd found a perch.

It took me five running steps to get into range, and in that time, the archer nocked her arrow and drew.

Lunge.

My spear took the woman in the chest. No armor. No defensive techniques. Nothing but cold metal tearing through flesh and bone, the quiet choke of pain lost beneath the noise and chaos. I used my fourteen Strength, pivoted, and threw the woman's dying body off the roof at one of the swordsmen down below.

It wasn't half as easy as it looked, but my target never saw her coming.

Lace darted forward in the distraction, one blade tearing through the throat of the second opponent, even as her longer blade pierced both dead woman and the man briefly buried underneath. She traced the trajectory of the fall back to me, gave me a nod, and started trotting back toward the gates.

Getting down was considerably harder than getting up had been, but I managed. A half-block away, Darishal had come into the town to help Wilf get the three horses out. Lucius and Mireille flanked them both, arms at the ready. A fifth bandit that had somehow snuck behind us lay dead in the streets, wound still glowing silver from Barth's ranged technique.

I was running toward them, toward the gates, when an aura, thick and brutish, filled with rage and hunger, flooded the streets.

Arrius.

He didn't *feel* any weaker than when we'd first encountered him in Madea's streets. He felt like a Copper, and even if he was one with a weak foundation, even if he was one who'd fled from the High Priest of the Ever-Hungry, he was *still* strong enough to destroy the whole town and us in it.

A horse screamed and shook free of Wilf's suddenly slack fingers, galloping the wrong way, back into town instead of away from the threat striding toward us. Its panicked strides took us down an alley and out of sight.

I reached the gates, where the others were already starting to back away, remaining horses in tow.

"We have to go!" shouted Lucius, belaboring the obvious. "Now!"

He was right. We only had two horses left, but the way was clear. The gates were open and Barth and Anthasa could slow down any pursuit with covering fire. Escape was there.

Only… where was Miko?

"Where are the others?" I shouted, even as Lucius leaped into one of the saddles.

Mireille's eyes were wide, but her brain was working just fine. "They went down the sideroad. I haven't seen them since!"

"Forget them!" Lucius' horse danced as he tried to bring it under control. "We have to get away."

I met his eyes and shook my head.

"We can't leave without Miko!"

That stopped him. "Can you get her?"

The street in question seemed choked with people. At least two bandits, with more townsfolk spilling out into the streets. Despite the light spilling out from opening doors, I couldn't even *see* Miko. The only positive was that Arrius might not either.

"No," I said. "Not in time. But if we lure Arrius away, they might get free on their own."

"There are only two horses," said Mireille. "The rest of us can't outrun a Copper. That was the whole point of being sneaky."

"Then we kill him," said Lace. "Here and now."

I swallowed. She was right. "I don't know if it's possible. But if it is," I said, looking up at the mounted heir to House Darish, "it will take all of us."

For a brief moment, Lucius' future danced on the edge of a blade. Escape meant survival, with any shame resulting from that flight easily buried by coin or political might. Staying, even just long enough to retrieve the synossian Priestess key to his ambitions, could cost him everything. And yet...

As Arrius' aura closed in upon us, followed by the monster himself, Lucius closed his eyes, took a breath, and slid from the horse. He passed its reins back to Wilf and met my eyes. "We draw the Copper out to us. Away from the protection of the walls, where we can surround him."

Mireille traded glances with Darishal. "Are you sure?"

"Flee if you wish, Marchon. I am a scion of House Darish, and *Darish does not run.*" As he drew his sword, a sword that, for all its fine construction, was *not* Sever, something shifted in his bearing, like a ripple in a pond or a knot loosening in his soul. An aura unfurled, weak and tremulous like a newborn kitten, but tangible for all of that.

Lucius Darish had just broken through to Tin.

"I'll take the center with Lucius," I found myself saying. "Arrius knows me. He'll come at me. Flank him if you can. Burn whatever techniques you have. If we can plant even a seed of doubt in his mind, he'll break."

"How do you know?" asked Mireille.

"Because I've seen it," I said, eyes on the massive man as he stomped his way down the street toward us. "That's what he does."

Lace faded away to one side, Mireille and Darishal to the other. Lucius and I separated just enough to keep us from both being swatted at the same time.

"I hope you had your defensive enchantments refreshed before we left Trynfall," I told the new Tin.

"I did. And then burned them all just to survive the river."

"Well, shit."

"Spoken like a commoner." He sketched a pattern in the air with his sword, aura slowly thickening. "Don't die, Fieldings. I think I'm ready for a rematch of our duel."

The nobleman had a smile when he said it, but I didn't think he was joking.

"I'll do what I can. And Wilf, you…"

I blinked. Wilf wasn't there anymore, and neither were the horses.

"Never trust a McCall," said Lucius, his words bitter. "Even Mireille should have told you that much."

Any reply I could offer was moot, because Wilf was gone, and Arrius was pushing his way through the gates. The man was just as massive as I remembered, not as tall as Skaal had been but twice as broad, wearing a heavy leather jerkin, stained pants, and boots. The club he'd lost in Madea had been replaced by one of solid bronze, with wicked curved spikes on its bulbous head. A hit from that thing wouldn't just break everything, it would shred it too.

At the same time, the torchlight revealed the ravages of all the many things Lace had poisoned the man with over the past few moons. He moved a step slower than I remembered, with maybe a fraction less implacable might. He had lost all his hair, and his eyes were overly bright, set in a face of pale wax.

Those eyes fell on me and widened.

"You," he rumbled angrily. "I remember you."

"Arrius Vitellius," I said, holding his stare even as his aura did its best to batter us into submission. "I come with hate in my heart and—"

The big man charged.

Hell if I knew how Lace's goddess expected *anyone* to get that whole damn speech out.

○○○

Techniques popped off like multi-colored fireworks, lighting the darkness, but I didn't have time to catalog them. *Lunge* got me out of Arrius' way, but as soon as I landed, his massive club was screaming through the air at me. I ducked, rolled, and ran, but he was too damn big and too damn fast.

Beast Hide lessened that divide, just a bit, thick fur covering my form as my Finesse stat received its boost, but even then, it was all I could do to stay ahead of his strikes. Every step, every dodge was a desperate gamble.

Meanwhile, the others opened up on the Copper. A silver arrow flashed down from above to explode against the man's massive form. One of Anthasa's sling bullets followed with a sound like thunder. Darishal grew and drove his maul into the larger Warrior's knee, Mireille drew a line of fire down his ribs, and the halo above Lucius' head glowed brighter with each lightning-quick slash.

None of it seemed to even faze Arrius.

That was how battles across rank went. Our victory, if it came at all, would have to arrive through a death of a thousand cuts. We had to wear him down, had to *survive* wearing him down.

Lunge came back just in time for me to avoid being pasted all over Cyrinton's palisade. I went *up* this time, not around, and came back down with my spear leading the way. My weapon barely penetrated. Even with gravity's assistance, it was like stabbing concrete.

He spun and threw me off, and when I rolled back to my feet, Lace was there, spitting venom in his face. A second technique sent a noxious green cloud to paint the larger man, every wound on him bleeding just a little bit more freely. For the first time, Arrius reacted, a roar that had taken on physical force, blasting the Marauder away and scattering the initiates in front of him like bowling pins.

Only Lucius kept his feet, the halo above his head now glowing like a star about to detonate. I turned my head away as blinding light flashed, far more devastating than when the same effect had triggered during our honor duel. When Arrius' club smashed down Lucius wasn't there anymore, a shimmering trail marking where he had used some sort of movement ability to dodge. Another swing and it became clear that Arrius had been temporarily blinded.

A part of me dared to believe we had a chance.

That was when the Copper used his second technique.

Arrius grew, doubling in size in a single moment. Where Darishal's version of the same technique only gave him size, Arrius' added speed. Even blinded, his blows were too swift, too plentiful to be avoided entirely. Mireille's *Shield* technique shattered as she flew through the air to impact the palisade with a crunch. Darishal had to abandon his return strike when the bronze club came within a hair's breadth of taking his head off.

Barth triggered the ability that sent his arrows digging deeper into their victim, but even with Lace's cloud still hanging about, those arrows didn't make much more headway than my spear. Anthasa had abandoned her sling and was racing downhill toward us, green hair streaming behind her and a curved sword in her hands, and Sky was on her heels.

Lucius slid between two errant strikes and struck out at what was now the leg of our vastly larger opponent. His sword dug into flesh, followed by a ghostly echo of the first attack that dug the wound deeper, and I took the opportunity to trigger *Lunge* for the third time in the battle, this time using to drive my spear into the small of the Copper's back.

A dozen feet away, Lace's thrown dagger multiplied into three, then five weapons, each dripping with poison. They thudded, one after the next, into the chest of our opponent.

"Ware!" shouted Lucius, using his movement technique again to dodge a riposte. "His blindness will—"

Arrius' aura flared and again, pure force came with it, bursting out of the big man in a conflagration that could be neither avoided nor withstood. Closest to the epicenter, Lucius and I got the worst of it. I lost consciousness, regained it again as I hit ground, bounced, and rolled, every inch of my body smoking like I'd just walked through a bonfire. *Pain Tolerance* got me to my feet in time to see Darishal's *Earth Stomp* do nothing at all, to see Lace activate a new technique that caused her motions to blur with speed.

Beyond them, Anthasa had reached a limp Lucius and begun to drag him toward the waiting Sky. An ethereal fountain of water was waiting, its soft light shining like a beacon, and a second glow surrounded the Priestess' hands, heralding another healing spell on the way.

My *Beast Hide* was fading far faster than it should have and I could barely feel the spear in my hands. Still, I had *Deceptive Strike* at the ready and *Liberating Lunge* would be back in a matter of seconds. I staggered back into the fray as the glow of healing surrounded Lucius, as he took his first breath since his fall.

Deceptive Strike gave me my best hit of the battle, *Lunge* saved me from the return swing that would have annihilated me, and then it was down to footwork and melee. Even with my spear, I lacked a reach advantage, so I did my best to harry the Copper, darting in whenever he focused on one of the others. I'd seen nature specials where wolves harried an elk like this. It wasn't pretty, let alone honorable, but it was our only chance.

Lucius had just reached his feet when Arrius changed tactics. He bull rushed the House Darish noble, tossing him aside, and swatted Anthasa away with bone-crushing force as he closed in on our healer. Sky wasn't fast enough to do more than raise her hands in refutation of the coming doom.

Down on one knee, Lucius' eyes flashed golden and the Copper slowed… for less than a second. His club came whistling down on the defenseless healer.

Somehow, Darishal was there, standing between them, kite shield raised to defend his girlfriend, the glow of some fresh technique causing the air in front of him to harden like stone.

Arrius' weapon blasted right through that technique. Through the physical shield behind it. Through the arm, the armor, and the body of the Warrior beneath, spikes impaling what had already been obliterated. Darishal's corpse hit Sky instead of the club and smashed the healer into the ground.

The healing fountain flickered and faded.

With a scream, Mireille struck the Copper from behind, moving in a blur. Mireille, who *should* have been an unmoving lump at the base of the Cyrinton palisade. One arm hung limply at her side, but the other held a glowing axe. Right before it landed, the axe's force seemed to increase, tearing a line of fire through the back of Arrius' knee.

For the first time that battle, the man staggered.

I moved in, attacked the same leg with far less effect, ate a kick that would have broken every bone in my body if I hadn't blocked it with the spear, and flew backwards for the third time in as many minutes. I landed by Cyrinton's gates and rolled up against a pair of bloody boots, worn by a shaggy-haired man who sometimes liked to pretend he was drunk.

Wilf extended a hand to pull me up. The blade in his other hand dripped gore and more blood was spattered across his clothes, but the Spy was in one piece. And next to him, similarly battered but breathing, were Ames, Zamira, and Miko.

A warm glow surrounded me, knitting together torn flesh and taking the edge off some of my pain. Zamira raised her arms and a small cloud gathered above the Copper. Rain fell in sheets, the water twisting into tendrils that did their best to coil about the man and restrict his movements. And finally, Ames' spell settled around me like a mantle, and the world slowed down.

Arrius tore free of the watery tentacles and spun on Mireille, but she'd been hasted too. She dodged, nearly slipped in the mud Zamira was creating, and then dodged again, the few ticks of acceleration Ames had granted her making the difference as Arrius started to flag.

I came in again, all the time in the world to watch Lucius' vastly slower strike hit the same leg the three of us had damaged, doing the kind of damage that came with being Tin. Plenty of time to see Lace step from the shadows and drive both of her blades into the Copper's back… and then spit even more venom into the resulting wound.

Still, Arrius took everything we gave him and more. Another silver streak came through as Barth fired what almost had to be his last arrow and the big man ignored it. Miko's *Flare* burst into existence right in front of the brute's face and he stomped right through. Crimson energy crackled across the Copper's chest and grotesquely muscled shoulders and he grew again, his attacks growing even wilder and more unpredictable. This time, he caught Mireille, and even though a quick spell from Ames robbed that strike of at least some of its force, the Warrior's *Shield* ability fractured and she went flying.

Miko was already rushing over, a heal at the ready, when the man's aura shifted as he unleashed yet another technique. The ground around us, ground already soaked by Zamira's spells, became a mud pit, more than just gravity sucking us down.

Mireille, on her hands and knees, went completely under. Miko, a few feet away, and trapped in mud up to her thighs, couldn't reach her. Of all of us, only Lace was free, high in the air in the midst of another soaring leap I could only even see thanks to Ames' spell.

As the shortest person on the field, I was chest-deep in the mud. Thankfully, I'd made one *very* fortunate choice two levels earlier. I triggered *Liberating Lunge*, aiming for the small circle of solid earth that surrounded Arrius.

Nothing happened.

No… not *nothing*.

With Ames' haste still active, I could *feel* my technique straining, feel its liberation aspect warring against the effect keeping me pinned. In all my practice sessions I'd never had the luxury of examining a technique that way, of sensing the way energy was molded into the Framework's prescribed forms, into whatever arcane construct was required to make each of our abilities work.

I could tell, in that quiet moment, as I sank deeper into the mud, that the technique would fail. That there simply wasn't enough energy within to break free of the vastly stronger Copper's attack.

So, I dumped more in.

I dumped *everything* in, every shred of power my soul would give me, flooding the technique with light I could feel if not quite see.

Something shifted. Something tore.

And then I was free, blurring through the air while Lace was still in mid-leap. The ground I reached was solid, if not safe, directly in front of the Copper. He raised his foot to stomp me just as my haste faded, and I cursed him in the profane language of the essoli, wordless shapes spoken directly into his brain.

Arrius was a Copper. Mere curses couldn't stop him, even when spoken in that dark tongue. They couldn't even slow him. But for just a moment, they pulled him back to a battle on a frontier town's walls, to the rapacious High Priest of the Ever-Hungry, to the encounter where, in full view of the world, Arrius had turned and fled.

And in that moment, the man above me broke.

Giving Lace time to complete her leap. Blades flashed as she hit the oversized Copper from behind up high. His savaged leg twisted under him, her impact sent him toppling forward—

—and I threw myself flat into the mud, thrusting my spear behind me, down to the solid earth deep beneath so that it stood upright, tall, proud, and forever sharp, to meet the falling Copper.

The mud swallowed me just before an impact drove the air from my lungs. I lost my grip on the spear and my grip on consciousness right after.

I drowned in a darkness where Shan wore my father like a skinsuit, where the wind howled in languages even I couldn't comprehend, and the void cursed my name.

ooo

I was coughing when I woke, lying on one side and spitting out mud and water even as the warm glow of healing surrounded me. Even when oxygen replaced the gunk in my lungs, breathing proved difficult, a sharp pain stabbing me with every inhalation. A wet rag washed more mud from my face and for the first time in what must have been an eternity, I opened my eyes.

Something was flickering in my field of view, but I ignored it, trying to look around me without actually moving. It was still nighttime, but someone had brought out lanterns, and together, they sketched a circle of illumination where the injured had been laid. I recognized Mireille and Ames. The glowing ethereal fountain between them told me that Sky, at least, had survived.

"Rest, nest-brother," said Miko, rolling me onto my back and then placing a hand on my shoulder as if I had any intention of sitting up when everything hurt. "All is well, but we are running out of heals."

"Arrius?" I croaked.

"Dead."

"My spear?"

"At your side." Something shifted in her voice.

"Thank you for bringing it."

"I didn't. Nobody did. Last we saw, it was stuck entirely through Arrius, while Lace whispered something in the dead Copper's ear. I don't think anyone wanted to touch it *or* him, given the toxins in the man's bloodstream."

"Oh." Apparently, the spear coming to me *hadn't* been a one-time thing. When I was less tired, I'd figure out how I felt about that. In the meantime, I had to know.

"Darishal?"

Her voice quieted even further. "Dead."

"The others?"

"Anthasa had her leg broken in four places, Mireille has a spiral fracture in her left arm and at least three cracked ribs. Amelia tore something in her knee when we were beset by bandits in the town streets. Lucius is… better off than I expected, to be honest."

"Sky healed him during battle. And he made Tin."

"That explains it then. Meanwhile, Zamira, Wilf, and I are all in one piece, Lace insists she is fine, and your body seemed desperate to drown in the mud before you could bleed out."

"Yet I'm still here."

"Yes. And you will be stronger tomorrow, once my blessings have returned. But for now, you must rest."

"I think I saw Shan again," I told her, energy fading with each word. "He wasn't happy."

"Then it must have been a dream, nest-brother. For I *know* my gods look down upon us both with pride."

I let my eyes flutter shut, and she left to see another invalid. I was starting to drift away when I remembered the incessant flicker. Opening my eyes, I focused on the dialogue window that swam into view.

QUEST COMPLETED: Deliver justice for a fallen
brother.

The energy that filled me brought me frustratingly close to level ten, like a three-course meal at the Night's Sky that then failed to deliver on the promised dessert. Too tired to complain, too tired to commune with the Framework to even see whatever paltry skill gains I might have managed with almost everything still capped, I closed the notification.

It was replaced by another, one I'd never seen before:

TRAIT UNLOCKED: Breaker of Bonds

I sank into a godless slumber.

EPILOGUE

For a renowned institution of higher learning, the Crimson Needle looked a lot like a castle; all turrets and crenelated walls, built into the side of a mountain. It was visible through much of the final day of our journey, sometimes silhouetted against the low-hanging clouds, other times partially masked by them, looming over us like both a promise and a threat.

The Crimson Needle's founder, Olmithor Sezan the Unknowing, had clearly possessed money, might, and a certain sense of style to go with his lofty title.

The mountain road wove back and forth through lesser peaks still crowned with slim circlets of snow, but as we neared our destination, the incline leveled off, giving our tired mounts as much respite as we could afford. The other initiates had been left behind in Cyrinton to heal, recover, and then follow as a group, leaving four of us to make the climb, squeezed onto three horses.

Four instead of three, because Miko was needed to heal Wilhemina and I went where she went. Because Lace's revenge was done and nobody was going to tell *her* to stay behind. And because Lucius, the Tryn's newest Tin, insisted he be part of the group that delivered Miko to Wilhemina.

We'd never caught the caravan, even with the supplies we'd received from Cyrinton to speed us on our way. Still, we'd found enough tracks to know we'd made up ground on Merrick and the others… that we were, at worst, just a few days behind. Unless the curse had ramped up its timetable considerably, we would arrive in time to prevent calamity.

The heir to House Darish pushed to the front as we took the last switchback and the gates to the school finally appeared. Those gates were famously always open, much like the mind of the founder himself, but led to a short tunnel, easily defended by the guards waiting above and below. The Crimson Needle had its share of Dedicated, Scholars and Sages bent entirely on study, but there were enough Aspirants within its walls to make the fortress façade a reality.

One of the two guards out front stepped forward as we approached, visibly female despite the hooded blue robe and the cloth mask that hid her face. A biting wind whipped through the open space here and either her robes were lined with some kind of fur, or she simply bore the cold better than the rest of us. She offered a short bow. "I bid you welcome, seekers of knowledge, and ask the purpose of your journey here."

"We come from Trynfall," said Lucius, sitting tall and proud in the saddle, "and seek Sir Merrick Thorne and the Lady Willerton, who should have arrived here within the past seven-day."

The guards exchanged glances.

"And if they did?"

"Tell them that Lucius Robash Alexander Darish has arrived, unbloodied and triumphant, and that he has brought with him the lady's salvation."

Resisting the urge to roll my eyes, I urged our horse forward so that Miko could speak.

"Am Miko Naseri," she said simply, "Priestess of Aurea."

The masks hid their expressions, but I could see the news hit both guards like a lightning bolt. The man stepped back to clear the way and the woman turned to lead us through.

"Lord Darish. Priestess Naseri. Word of your impending arrival came down from the Third Circle this morning. If you will follow me, I have been instructed to take you directly to the healers' ward."

"Is Wilhemina okay?" asked Miko.

"I am but an initiate of the First Circle," was the response. "Such matters are left to those better versed in our school's mysteries. I am sure the meisters of the ward will wish to speak to you on the subject."

We followed the guard inside, through the long corridor of darkness, and out again into air that was both fresher and warmer than that found just outside. The storm clouds that had been our ever-present companions these past few days were nowhere to be seen, and golden sunlight streamed down from a sky as blue as the initiate's robes.

"Welcome," she said, "to the Crimson Needle."

As she spoke, a dialogue window appeared before me, one I'd been looking forward to since our departure from Trynfall:

```
QUEST COMPLETED: Escort the Voice of the Dawn and
Wilhemina Annerose Lakesia Willerton to the Crimson
                      Needle.
```

It was accompanied by a rush of energy and, at last, the feeling I'd been waiting for. A sense of contentment, of fullness, of what Miko's people called *energy* satiation in my core.

I would still need to commune with the Framework later that day to make it official, would need to lock in my gains and choose an attribute to improve, but at long last, I knew:

I had reached level ten.

Now?

It was time for Tin.

BRIAN'S PERSONAL RECORD AT THE END OF *AGENT OF THE WILD*

Name: Brian Fieldings
Class: Warrior (Common) – 9 (Level 10 Pending)
Profession: None
Deity: None
Ideal: Freedom

Attributes:
Strength: 14 [+2] / **Finesse:** 13 [+2]
Vitality: 18 [+4] / **Intellect:** 14
Discernment: 11 / **Will:** 15

Skills:
Major: Formations: 41/50, Knife: 49/50,
Light Armor: 25/50, Medium Armor: 50/50,
Spear (U): 50/50, Tactics: 50/50, Throwing: 3/50
Unarmed Combat: 8/50

Minor: Acrobatics: 17/50, Athleticism: 50/50,
Avoidance: 50/50, Focus: 46/50,
Leadership (U): 32/50, Pain Tolerance (U): 50/50,
Toxin Resistance (U): 4/50

Professional: None

General: Animal Behaviorism (U): 10/10,
Brewing: 3/10, Butchering: 1/10, Caretaking: 9/10,
Danger Sense (R): 10/10, Deception: 10/10,
Diplomacy: 5/10, Hunting: 3/10, Juggling: 6/10,
Meditation (U): 9/10, Mercantilism: 7/10,
Orienteering: 4/10, Pathfinding: 1/10,
Performance: 1/10, Riding: 2/10, Scribing: 1/10, Stealth:
10/10, Tracking: 9/10

Techniques: Beast Hide (U), Deceptive Strike (U),
Liberating Lunge (U)

Achievements: None
Titles: Hand of the Wild
Traits: Speaker of Tongues, Breaker of Bonds, ???

Author's Note

So, here we are. Book two in what is definitely going to be a long series. How long? Well, that kind of depends on me, really. Every book in the series so far has broken 200,000 words and that's *with* me having to push some events to the next volume. Turns out these LitRPGs take a *lot* of words, even when you're consciously trying to *avoid* bloat or an endless parade of skill descriptions, character sheets, and more.

And yes, I recognize the irony in saying that after finishing the book with a full character sheet. But it's there for those who want it and separate from the narrative for those who don't!

Book three, *Breaker of Bonds*, will pick up where this one left off, in Mordecai's beloved Crimson Needle, with Wilhemina's fate hanging in the balance.

As for the rest of the series? I know where we're going. I know how we get there. I know at least some of the very many bumps there will be in the road along the way, not just for Brian but for those who dare to call him friend.

And I know that I'm having a blast delving into this world and its characters, even if we've so far only touched upon the poorest duchy of one of the smallest kingdoms on the continent known as the Great Wilds.

There is so, so much to come.

I hope you'll enjoy the journey as much as me.

About the Author

Chris began life as a gleam in someone's eye, but birth and childhood were quick to follow. He's been fortunate enough to live in Spain, Germany, and all over the United States of America, and is planning a tour of the distilleries of Scotland for his 50th birthday.

A graduate of the Johns Hopkins University's Writing Seminars program, he put that degree to ill use for twenty years as a software engineer but has finally circled back around to the idea of writing for a living.

Chris currently lives in Nevada with his angelic wife and ever-expanding whisky collection and occasionally ventures outside to peer upwards, mutter to himself about 'day stars', and then scurry back into the house.

Agent of the Wild is his twelfth novel and the second book in his epic fantasy LitRPG series, *The (Second) Life of Brian*. Chris frequently shares updates on his author website at https://christullbane.com.